for

Courtney Furno

Race Point Light

Race Point Light

by

Dwight Cathcart

Adriana Books
Boston, Massachusetts
2018

Adriana Books
publisher@adrianabooks.com
Boston, Massachusetts

First EPUB edition Edward Wharton
First ebook edition 2010
Revised EPUB 2013 Patricia Rasch

Cover photograph: Commercial Street looking east, Provincetown, Massachusetts, October 22, 2010, 6:15 pm
Photography: Dwight Cathcart

Author photograph
Bill Chisholm

Dialogue involving Joe Dallesandro in two places in part 3, is from *Flesh*, written and directed by Paul Morrissey, produced by Andy Warhol, Score Movies, 1968, renewed by Paul Morrissey, 1996.

Dialogue between Kay and Michael Corleone in part 3, is from *The Godfather*, directed by Francis Ford Coppola, Paramount Pictures, 1972.

Dialogue and description concerning Chi-Chi, in part 4, is from *The City of Night*, by John Rechy, Grove Press, 1994.

In part 5, Fair Shaw's comparison of The Quilt to an epic poem in "There was not, as there is in all epics, an opening sentence—I sing of warfare and a man at war." The reference is to the opening line of *The Aeneid* by Virgil, trans. Robert Fitzgerald. New York: Vintage Books, a Division of Random House. 1983.

"Holy Sonnet XIV," by John Donne, quoted in its entirety by Fair Shaw to Julio in Part 6, is from the edition of Donne's poetry, edited by E. K. Chambers, London: Lawrence & Bullen, 1896, p. 165.

This ebook was printed from 110810.
Revisions from 20160210
This edition printed from:
RPL PDF LULU text 20191001.pdf
RPL PDF LULU cover 20191001.pdf

Race Point Light

1

We got in from Provincetown last night.

While we were there, I went to the beach—it's August and hot—and walked a long stretch of Commercial Street. I like being alone in Provincetown, although being there seems to encourage people to pair off. While I am alone, I carry a piece of paper in my left rear pocket, with a pen, and occasionally pull it out and write something. There is, between Boston and Provincetown, a vast population always on the move from one to the other, people going and coming from the city to the Cape. John Kennedy once said about us, that when we come to the sea, we're coming home.

Provincetown is built on a sandbar at the end of Cape Cod. When you arrive in Provincetown by boat, you see, first, a mere shadow on the horizon, a long thin dark smudge that gradually becomes more substantial until you see the Pilgrim Monument sticking straight up. As you approach town, you become aware that the sand bar the town lies on is less flat than it seems. The Monument is built on a hill. The beaches are like that too. What seems at first to be flat sand actually contains sizeable dunes. These sandy beaches are not nearly as flat as the beaches along the South Carolina coast.

We both went to the beach on Sunday. Even though it is summer, the beaches here are not thickly peopled. We sat on the beach at Long Point, and the nearest person was ten yards away. Great stretches of white crushed shells and small pebbles, almost completely unpopulated. In Provincetown, a man doesn't look out on the beach and see only the bodies that are physically occupying volumes of space here at this moment in August 2002. He looks out on the beach and sees all the bodies that have occupied space here since he first started coming down from Boston to Herring Cove or Race Point twenty or thirty years ago, men who are now dead, married, living in Somerville, San Francisco—or in the South End and the director of a major gay rights organization. And he sees all these bodies with a divided self—the man who is sitting in the sand right now, watching what is happening in the surf, and the man who experienced the beach in 1984, or 1990 when I first met Chris, the man who is my partner, or earlier this summer. A multitude in search of a multitude. As one grows older, I suppose one always is in search of lost time, and the beach, particularly, encourages that. It has something to do with the waves.

Our host's cottage is a monument to memory. Every possible available horizontal and vertical surface is covered with snapshots of fabulously handsome and sexy men in bathing suits or nude, on the beach, whose hairstyles, bathing suit styles, and body styles indicate the date of photographs. But the photographs are in good condition, and you have to study them to see the hairstyles, and first, second, and third impressions are that all of these pictures were taken last weekend. I would guess that half of these men are dead—these are all, like our host, A-list men who would have been in their twenties during the seventies, slightly older than Chris (Chris is 40, and our host is pushing 50), and so the generation that died from AIDS, which is where all the boys on the beach—the prettiest, sexiest, hottest of them—have gone. The men in those pictures are from the generation at Stonewall.

A man Chris knows, a recently-made friend, lives in Truro, and we met after dinner Saturday night for drinks and pool. This new friend of Chris's, named Miguel, brought his new boyfriend, named John. John is in his low twenties (he looks nineteen, maybe), was beautiful, knew it, utterly adorable, and what struck me most was that he has no past—and he doesn't know that. He was like one of those robots you see in movies—*Bladerunner, Artificial Intelligence* —who has just been turned on and who doesn't know he is a robot and therefore thinks he has memories going back to his childhood but which we know were simply implanted there last week by the robot-maker. We know about him that now is when his life begins. There were four of us, three of us over 40 (in ascending order by age —Chris, Miguel, and me), and this kid, and he was different from us in this dramatic way. Some men call men like him—particularly like him, early twenties, late teens, just coming out, just joining up, fresh,

2

new—newbies. I was never a newbie because I wasn't fresh or new, I think, when I came out. I am not sure I ever came out.

At lunch yesterday, in a restaurant by the sea—air-conditioned, because by Sunday none of us were willing to meet for lunch at all if the place was not air conditioned—there were four of us, at least two with AIDS. Our host tells us his doctor says he is going blind and will lose his sight in three years. I had difficulty keeping focused on the conversation going on around me—I was thinking about the beach, how many times I have been here, and the men I have come with who are now dead—and then, finally, our host said, "What are you thinking of?" I didn't want to admit that I was thinking about the dead, here, in this beautiful place, on this beautiful day, so I said something else, which was also true. I said, "I was thinking about how curious it is at the beach. It is as if, when I am here, all the other people I have ever been on any beach with are also here with me, as if time does not exist. But the beach also makes me emphatically aware of how long I have been alive, how long it has been since I was here last, of the effects of time on the beach—erosion—of how we change and the conditions of our lives change. I don't know of any other place that puts such an emphasis on time, both in erasing our awareness of it and in emphasizing how heavily it weighs on us."

Our host started talking about The History Project, which I knew about but had forgotten—an oral history of some kind. I didn't say that I had been talking to John, the twenty-four-year-old newbie, and I wondered what a man like me, who owned all his own memories, could say to a kid like that, who had just arrived on the scene, who hadn't yet discovered what was his and what was implanted in him. Something about how hard it is to sort all that out.

↔

One thousand five hundred miles south of Provincetown, and on the same ocean, 60 years before the luncheon in the air-conditioned restaurant, and 27 years before Stonewall, I sat on the sand under the white glare of the sky, the waves slinging slick sheets of salt water over the flat strand, dribbling a sand castle between my legs. My Aunt Caroline, whose oldest child, Rich, sat nearby in the sand playing with his little brother, taught me to drool the watery sand down the tip of my longest finger. My mother and father were there, along with Uncle Richmond, and my older brother, Cornelius. They had their buckets and shovels, and there were towels on the flat sand. The sand had the quality of being hard—and seemingly dry—when I stepped on it and then of dissolving into mud beneath my foot.

Two men came up and talked to the grownups. They were in bathing suits and had come from next door and said what they were looking for was strong backs. The grownups all laughed. "And weak minds?" and everybody laughed again. All the grownup men went away and took me with them. At the back creek, they had a seine. Some of the men walked along one side of the creek, between the reeds and the water, and the rest walked on the other side, pulling the seine. When they pulled the net out of the water, they dumped all the wiggling things in a basket that somebody was carrying. It was the first time I remembered someone calling a basket a "bushel." Mostly there were crab and shrimp and some fish. That was the first time I had ever seen an eel. It was about as big as my arm—that long and that big around. The mud on the sides of the creek between the reeds and the water became too deep for me to walk—my father was on the other side of the creek—so one of the men picked me up under my arms and lifted me over his head and put me on his shoulders, where I rode, the man's head between my thighs. I could see the man's skin—his hair was short—between the hairs on the top of his head, and when I held on to his head, my hands clamped around his forehead, I felt his sweat on his scalp. When he moved, I rode on the muscle of his shoulders, and the back of his neck rubbed my peepee up and down. I felt a strong feeling at first between my legs from riding on his shoulders, a really nice feeling, and then I felt it all over. My peepee got hard, and I didn't want to get off his shoulders.

↔

There was a game we used to play called "king of the mountain," in which one of the bigger boys on the playground picked one of the smaller boys to ride on his shoulders. Another pair—rider and mount —would attack, one rider attempting to pull the other rider off his horse. His name was Larry. He was taller than me—smooth olive skin, long, straight, black, glossy hair—and stronger, and one day on the playground he discovered I was strong too. I climbed on his shoulders, and Larry maneuvered under me to get us close enough to the other pair for me to grapple with the other rider. The other rider and I gripped hands, and I pulled, and Larry, under me, breathing hard, backed up. The other rider tried to get free, but Larry and I were stronger, and finally I pulled him off his mount. Larry liked carrying me. He told me he liked beating the other guys. I didn't care so much about beating the other guy as I cared about riding Larry, feeling his neck between my thighs. Fighting the other guy was only a way to get to ride the shoulders of this beautiful boy.

↔

I knew Paul Connors only in a mechanical drawing class. He was, maybe, a little bigger than me, pale white skin and long black hair, handsome, with a strong nose and full lips. In the minutes before class began, Paul used to hang out around me. Our desks were really drawing tables with stools, and the boys liked to work standing up. Paul didn't say anything—we were all still pretty shy around each other—but he came over to the space beside my desk next to the window and stood there, looking out the window. Some of us were just developing muscles that showed. Paul's arms were noticeably bigger than those of the rest of the thirty or so boys in the class, and Paul stuck his hands deep in his pockets, pushed so deep that his triceps flexed. I was avid for Paul's triceps and felt my mouth go dry. Then, one day—Paul seemed to invite this—I reached out and stroked Paul's arm. Paul ignored my hand and my fingers, and so, breathless with excitement, I gripped his arm. When Paul still ignored what I was doing, I gripped his triceps with both my hands, gripped it tight, and my dick leapt to erection. Paul gazed out the window as if this weren't happening, pushing his hand deeper into his pocket, pushing hard against the bottom of his pocket so that his triceps bulged even more. My hands, encircling Paul's arm, kneaded the muscles while Paul pushed against the bottom of his pocket to make his triceps bulge, pretending it wasn't happening. After that, I waited, breathless, for Paul to come over to my desk and hang out in front of the window while I felt up his arm and enjoyed a marble-hard erection, unable, almost, to breathe.

Then one day the teacher—bald, gray-haired—saw what we were doing and came over and separated us and said, "Stop that!"

↔

I was walking along a path beside a gravel road in Sewanee on the Cumberland Plateau in Tennessee. Ahead, rising above the trees, was the 1910 rough Gothic tower of the library. Walking along the path with me, some coming toward me and some going in the direction of the library, were other boys, college men in tweed jackets and ties, carrying books. The older boys wore academic gowns, much tattered. One of them was saying, as they went by, apropos Eliot and "Tradition and the Individual Talent," "The past is nothing to rebel against. It is impossible to rebel against it—against tradition. We are part of tradition, every single poet from every period of literature, from Homer to Allen Tate, is a part of the tradition, and this poet can't escape being part of it too. How do you hate it then?" In the late afternoon, early evening, just at dusk, as an autumn mist enveloped everything, the place seemed to compel a swoon of nostalgia for the traditions it embodied—the old South, the old Anglican church, the old country, the old ways, medieval spires above college quadrangles in a great university, a thousand years of learning. And even for things that we didn't then know were old, what they called the life of the mind embodied by the faculty of the college, who served students sherry when we visited on Sunday evenings and wrote books with few footnotes and many repetitions of the phrase It may even be said.

There was a movie shown on Friday nights at the student union building, and frequently this movie was English and a product of the J. Arthur Rank Corporation—they were Anglophile there. When the clip was shown of the bodybuilder, his muscles oiled and deeply tanned, swinging his giant hammer against the brass gong, announcing the movie, there were titters and trills in the audience. I knew that somebody else in the audience beside me was thrilled by the image.

↔

After Sunday school, on Sunday mornings, a gang of us, budding Episcopalians, somewhere between thirteen and seventeen, the boys in coats and ties and the girls in their best dresses, left the Gothic parish house and went across Senate Street to a soda shop in a modern brick apartment building to fill the 45 minutes before church and acolyte—or choir—duty. Beneath the blond wood of the soda fountain counter, there were racks for magazines, and my first memories of the soda shop included many magazines. But something happened, and the magazines were not renewed by the distributor, and whoever was in charge didn't make an effort to make selling magazines one of the sources of income of the shop. The magazines got old and ragged, worn out by the kids who came over after Sunday school, bought a soda, and picked up a magazine to thumb while they chattered. Among the magazines on the rack was a muscle magazine, which had on its cover in the deeply unreal colors of Technicolor a photograph of a bodybuilder on a beach, flexing to show off his pecs. For me, it was the only interesting thing in the shop. And it was so interesting, I couldn't pay attention to anything else. This magazine was never taken from the rack and thumbed by anyone. But it was there, and it became more and more prominent as the other magazines disappeared, as they were thrown away, or kids stole them. Finally, there were only a dozen magazines left, in a rack spacious enough to hold 300, and one of these was the muscle magazine. I noticed that this magazine, curiously, got older and older looking, more and more dog-eared, just as the others did, even though I never saw anyone pick it up. Finally, all the magazines disappeared except the muscle magazine. It was as if it were only my interest that was holding the magazine in the rack. There it was, in all its sexual splendor, on the blond wood rack underneath the counter of the soda fountain. And there it stayed, for months, even, it seemed, for years, giving off, for me, a kind of radioactivity that would rot my bone marrow if anyone ever saw me looking at it. But I couldn't not look. Somebody was looking at it. I was afraid that somebody would see me looking at it, and I developed ways of looking at it without people knowing—by looking at somebody standing almost in front of it, or by looking past it, at the soda jerk, or by going to the soda shop alone before Scouts on Tuesday nights.

↔

Russell, maybe a year older than I, walked down the long polished terrazzo floor toward me, the late sun coming from behind me and lighting him and turning him all golden. He had dark blond hair, slicked back on both sides and a complicated wave of curls in the front over his forehead. His smooth skin was almost the same color as his hair, deeply tanned, unblemished, his t-shirt sleeves rolled up to expose his upper arms, which were not so large as they were shapely, with distinct biceps and triceps and deltoids. It was rumored that he lifted weights. It took my breath away, just to be standing on the same terrazzo floor as he. He walked on past me, going away from me toward another classroom, toward the sun, oblivious to his effect on me. I discovered what hours of the day Russell walked down that hall, and every day, for a whole year, I was there waiting for him, watching him as he went past, feeling the way he made me feel, the sense of glowing, my nerve ends soaked in honey.

↔

Peter McKinnell was a scout master, small, lithe, whose hair shaded from red to gold in the light. He was cool, ironic, humorous, loving, in his late twenties. He had a cabin in the woods in the mountains in North Carolina, and at other times he took us camping in some woods near town. At night, we were in sleeping bags around the fire, and I put my bag down next to his. When the other boys grew quiet, I reached behind me and found Peter's wrist and brought it over me and held it in front of my stomach. His arm was warm and heavy where it lay across my chest and stomach. In a few minutes, Peter pulled his arm away, and I reached behind me and found his wrist and pulled it over me again, like a warm, heavy, hairy blanket that had fallen off my shoulders. I backed up to him, so that I lay on my side in the curve of his body, and there, at some point during the night, in the warm strength of Peter's body, I went to sleep, and Peter would then withdraw his arm.

↔

Connie was a mechanic in the Army at Yakima, a man with white skin and a body like Cellini's Perseus—perfectly globular ass-cheeks —who lay down on a sleeping bag on the grass in a small meadow on the slopes of Mt Rainier and threw back his legs above his head, grinned at me, and said, "Oh, fuck me, Fair!" And Paul was a graduate student in psychology at Vanderbilt whose hard bony body and knobby rough hands suggested he worked with cattle although his doctoral dissertation required that he run rats. Paul would stop in and say, "Put your books down. I have forty minutes before I have to be back at the lab. Wanna fuck?" I would stand up from my desk and turn to Paul, put out my arms wide, and grin. And there was the man named Craig Sexton, six feet four inches, immense and very dark, who came up behind me and spread his basketball-player hand over my shaved head and said, "Christ, you're hot!" I was pleased and felt the hot charge of sex. Just the other day, here in Boston, at work, I turned a corner around a block of cubicles, and saw ahead of me, disappearing through a door into a hallway, the back of a blond closely cropped head, broad shoulders, thickly muscled back, and, a heavily muscled arm pushing open the door. In 1973, in Ann Arbor, Michigan, my wife and I were sitting at a table in a basement dining room of the Village Bell on South University when a waiter came from the kitchen carrying a tray of plates on his palm, holding it high above his head on a beautifully modeled arm.

↔

Chris had wide shoulders and narrow hips, and like some gay men it was easy for him to explore his feminine side. He did drag regularly —he and three or four others had a Mother's Day Brunch that involved a restaurant in the South End, a stretch limo, and a tour of gay bars ending at the Ramrod—and yet he was a big man and had an easy maleness about him.

↔

Like an explosion, like a sufficiently large explosion—like the Big Bang—in which we are still in the midst of exploding fragments, the hum of the explosion still ringing in our ears, and the fragments of the original burst still rushing past, our lives, every single piece, are still rushing away from the center, and you can see it all on a clear day at the beach, where the hum of our birth can be heard in the sound of the waves and provides the continuo for all the music from the boom boxes, just as astronomers say that with a sufficiently large telescope they can see, not to the ends of the universe, but almost to the beginning of time.

Race Point Light

When I was 17, I stood in a crowd on the edge of the dance floor at the pavilion at Myrtle Beach, up the strand from Pawley's, and watched a couple dancing—doing the dirty shag, a dance in which he loosely held her in the traditional way while their pelvises moved in and out against each other, suggesting the movement of coitus. The guy was only a little taller than me, but he had the classic look: he was tanned, blonde, his hair oiled and slicked back on the sides and the front a bunch of curls over his forehead. His sleeves were rolled up to display his upper arms, with the essential components of biceps, triceps, and delts. It thrilled me, and I saw it in beach pavilions all up and down the Atlantic coast for years—muscles, greasy hair, tanned, and showing too much sex. It was an image that didn't last. In 1963 or 1964, men stopped putting oil in their hair and, as the sixties drew to a close, started growing facial hair and longer hair on top. In the early eighties, along with shorter hair again, this time with gel, men began to bulk up. Triceps, biceps, pecs, lats, abs, and delts all got bigger and heavier, but none of this mattered very much. You had to look closely at the photographs to see that things had changed, which meant that nothing had changed very much. Exploding fragments.

↔

On the last Sunday in April, 1950, at 12:30, we were already there at my aunt's, to have a picnic lunch in the garden with all the family— all we had to do was walk next door. Mother called out, "There they are!" She sounded like she was singing. "Caroline! Yoo-hoo! Caroline!" She turned back to us. "Caroline is here!" I was in the swing, on the edge of the grass, and I could see, beyond her, under the trees, their car—it was a beautiful car, big, black, with four doors and a lot of chrome on the front—stopped in the driveway. The front door on the driver's side opened. It was Uncle Richmond Sims. Caroline got out on her side and raised her arm, waving. "We're here!" She was a happy, self-confident woman. They opened the back doors, and my cousins—Richmond, Jonathan, William—all in white shirts and dark ties, long pants, and jackets, tumbled out. They came running across the grass toward me and Cornelius, around the azaleas and jumping over the bulbs in the flowerbeds, running in and out of the shade from the trees. I got off the swing and went toward

10

them. When Caroline passed me, she pinched my cheek and said, "Cutie! You're just like your daddy!" I liked that. I liked her. When Mother had a party, Caroline came over early to do the flower arrangements. She was artistic and friendly, and my favorite aunt.

The garden went from the street in front around both houses all the way to the back where there was a stone wall. There were big oak and hickory trees, two with wisteria vines up the trunks and in the limbs, pale green leaves just coming out, the lacy dogwoods with white blossoms, and azaleas, red and purple and white, big oleander bushes near the houses with their big floppy bunches of white flowers, and around the edge of the garden, ivy and striped grass. In the center was an open space with grass, white iron lawn chairs, and a picnic table. All of us were there, the men standing, smoking cigarettes, and the women sitting in chairs. One of my father's cousins—who was also a cousin of Mother's—was coming with his family, and we were waiting for them before we ate.

Caroline's and Richmond's house was all white, and our house was brick up to the first story and then white above that. The trees hid the tops of the houses, and bushes hid their first floors. It was cooler under the trees. Mother and Caroline, and Caroline's cook, Josina, went back and forth into the house, bringing out food on trays. Mother bought our house when Daddy was away in the Navy during the war so she could be next to her sister.

My grandmother is in a nursing home. There is an oil portrait of her in Caroline's living room that hangs across from a portrait of my grandfather, who is dead. Caroline looked around her at her children and at the platters and covered dishes being collected on the table. She called Mother "darling heart"—"Darling Heart, would you see if Josina has prepared the tray for the sherry?" Eventually the sherry came out—a rectangular mahogany tray with brass handles with a cut glass decanter, and five sherry glasses with small linen cocktail napkins.

All of us cousins played in the sandbox or on the tire swing or the two chain-and-board swings hanging from a pipe near the sandbox. Caroline and Richmond's oldest—Richmond, or Rich— was Cornelius' age, about 13. Rich's brother Jonathan was about my age, 10. The baby, William, was 7. When our family gets together, there are always tiny children toddling around, learning to walk, pushing away the dogs, holding some adult's hands with little fingers. The dogs are mine and Cornelius's—that is, our parents'—cocker spaniels and the neighbors' mongrels, and later there are neighbors who see us in the garden and call and come over. Our family does this most Sundays in warm weather. The sun was directly overhead, so if you weren't under a tree you were out in the sun and it was hot. The women had taken off their hats and were fanning themselves. Ladies don't sweat. They perspire. I noticed that they didn't even do that, and I wondered how they managed not to perspire in the heat.

I wandered around among my relatives. They said that I was a cute kid with big eyes and long lashes. "Hi." I enjoyed being a part of all this, hearing people talking and seeing the familiar faces.

"Why, Fair!" It was Aunt Caroline. "Come here by me and tell me about yourself." Caroline was named after my grandmother, my mother's mother. Before I could answer, she asked another question. "Did you go to church today?"

"I've been playing with my trains." I grinned. "I did go to church, but since church I've been playing with my trains." My father got one of his men to build a big table in a corner of our basement, where I have a great train layout. I spend time there having fun when I am not at Boy Scouts or at music lessons or the orthodontist or at church or somewhere. My trains are Lionel trains. I have a Santa Fe diesel engine and a Pennsylvania RR electric engine and a steam engine from the New York Central Railroad. I have a big crane, too, and four electric switches. I am making a round table and a tunnel. I like learning how to make it work.

"Yes! And do you know who I saw?" It was Mother. "Do you remember Sam Stark? The younger son of Cadwallader Stark?" She was always breaking in on me to say what she wanted to say.

"No—" Aunt Caroline seemed always about to break out laughing. She was older than my mother.

"He was in high school with us, a year ahead of us, ahead of me, so that would make him—about your age—"

"Did he have an older brother?"

"Ah—"

This has been going on forever—these long warm afternoons in the garden. My mother and her sister always did this, except in the middle of the summer, when our family went to the mountains, to Little Switzerland, in North Carolina. My father's family has been going to the mountains for a hundred years to get out of the summer heat. I can remember when my grandfather was still alive and the men had highballs before lunch instead of sherry. It was pretty clear to me that we would be doing this kind of thing all the rest of our lives. On the walls of my grandmother's house, in her front hall and the dining room and going up the stairs were photographs of her family. Most of these photographs are now on the walls of our house next door, and they are in Caroline's house. You keep running into the same faces, over and over. Just who they are is not always clear to me—which ones are ancestors and which ones are aunts and cousins, and which ones are fairly close antecedents and which ones are pretty distant—but it doesn't matter. They are family. All of us have coats of arms in our dining rooms, too, because my grandparents had coats of arms in their dining room, beautiful painted things in matted gold leaf frames. Our house has one for my father's family, the Shaws, my father's mother's family, the Fairs— all silver and gold—and Mother's family, the Jays. It was comfortable and familiar in the houses we went to—the same people seemed to be living in all of them. Some of the people in the pictures are my grandmother's father, who was born in 1854, her paternal grandfather, born in 1815, and in the oil portrait in the dining room, my grandfather's great-grandfather, born in 1766, ten years before the Declaration of Independence was signed. Aunt Caroline and her family go to Trinity Church, the same church my family goes to, an Episcopal church across the street from the State House, built in 1847. It is the biggest one uptown and is a nineteenth-century American Gothic copy on a smaller scale of York Minster in England.

I swung on the chain-and-board swing, then I swung on the tire swing. I pumped hard to make the swing go high. The tire swing was hung after the chain-and-board swing, when we started getting bigger—its rope was longer and the tire at the bottom gave it weight, and two of us could play on it at the same time. Caroline knew all about me, and she was very easy about showing off how close we were. "You are so handsome!" Aunt Caroline said. I grinned. I liked it that we had ways of doing things, like this, the picnic in my aunt's garden on Sunday in warm clear weather. I liked swinging above the heads of the grown-ups, liked it that my family was big, that there were a lot of stories about a lot of people at different times. The women in Mother's family wore their hair in great swooping waves. Mother put her hair up over what she called a "rat," a piece of stuffing that she rolled her hair over. She said everybody used them, but I knew they didn't. It made her hair high in the back.

Uncle Richmond was standing by the swing, pushing the kids. I held on tight and leaned way back. Girls, when they did that, their hair almost dragged the ground. Uncle Richmond wouldn't push me because I was too big. "You're big enough to push the little one." My mother wants me to grow up and be like Uncle Richmond because he is successful and treats Aunt Caroline well. It was hot, so I quit and got in the shade. The sun was directly overhead. When I was little, when Richmond was in the Army in the South Pacific, Caroline and little Rich lived with my grandmother, and then they bought this house.

Cousin Clint came with his family. He is younger than my parents. He and his wife have four children, three under five and a baby. It took them a long time to unpack their things and set up playpens on the lawn. After they came, there were little children running around everywhere. One of the little kids started crying. Caroline took her up and held her in her lap. My mother says she thinks I used to like to sit in Effie's lap because Effie was soft. Effie was my nurse when I was little. Her lap was soft.

The men were standing around behind the chairs, the women were sitting, the little children were everywhere, and Cornelius and Rich were over by the azaleas. Cornelius is 30 months older than me. Jonathan and William were down by the steps into the lower part of the garden talking—and I was in the middle of it all.

Rich organized a game of hide-and-seek. We all started running. It was like white cats running across the lawn, looking for hiding places. The trouble with hide-and-seek around here is that there are not many hiding places, and we've been playing here for so long that there are no new ones to discover. I didn't really like playing with my cousins. Jonathan and William have a code of their own that I don't know. They are tougher than I am in some way, and that confuses me, because Mother says she wants me to be a gentleman. She doesn't want me to be "tough." When she talks about men, being "tough" is a bad thing for a man, a gentleman, to be. Coarse is another bad word. Yet Jonathan and William are tough, and I would have liked to be tough, but I'm not, and there is nothing I can do. It is the same way with the boys at school. I act like it doesn't matter.

I went back to where the adults were. I went over and stood by my dad and watched the people in their light-colored clothes in front of the dark green shrubbery on the green lawn. After a while my dad put his hand down on my neck, his fingers on each side of my neck. I liked that. Then Daddy said, "Go help your mother."

When I came back, they were talking about church.

"The sermon today was very good."

"Who gave it?" In our family, we like to carry on a name, and everybody expects, when I have a son, that I will name him after me. Cornelius is named after my father, who was named after his father. I am named after my father's uncle, Robert Fair. Somebody once told me there were four or five of us in a row, all with the same names— Robert Fair. My mother's father was named William Jay. I have a cousin, the baby, named William after him. There are three Carolines in our immediate family.

"Mr. Bates. Mother loves him so."

"What was the sermon on?"

"Abraham and Isaac. The verse, 'But where is the lamb for the burnt offering?' It was very, very good."

They said that, but what they meant, and they said it all the time, too, was, *Nothing is more important to us than our family.*

My mother and her sister thought it was somehow their duty to be attractive, to laugh and to flirt and to tell funny stories, and so, in their way, they performed their routines for each other and for the men, their husband and brother-in-law, and for cousin Clint. It was one of the qualities of Mother's mother's family, the Laurens, that its members were sweet. But in being sweet, they had an edge, and they were sweet to someone else's disadvantage.

After we had been there a while playing, Aunt Caroline said they had finished bringing out all the food. Uncle Richmond stood at the end of the picnic table. The table had a white cloth on it, and in front of Uncle Richmond was a big silver platter of fried chicken. He had a big silver fork in his right hand, turned so the tines of the fork pointed down, waiting for me to tell him what I wanted. There was a big covered silver dish for rice, a sauce boat for gravy and my grandmother's silver gravy ladle, and silver bowls of lima beans and string beans and creamed asparagus. My aunt had a silver bread tray

with a linen napkin in it, and if I unfolded the napkin, I found
Josina's hot biscuits inside. There was a basket of hot corn bread that
Mother had brought and a stack of white linen napkins near the silver
at the end of the table. There was also a water pitcher—old, silver,
battered, engraved with a big coat of arms of the Jay family, so
highly polished that it seemed made of liquid. There was a big cut
glass bowl of flowers in the middle of the table. We got our food, and
Aunt Caroline gave us iced tea, and then we sat on the bench by the
sandbox or at the picnic table. I went to the sand box. I could see
Uncle Richmond still at the head of the picnic table, using his big
fork to serve the grownups. That is what men do. After it has been
prepared in the kitchen, the man stands at the head of the table in the
dining room and serves the meat to each person. Men don't serve
vegetables.

Mother saw me. "Use your napkin, boys."

"Yes, ma'm," Mother wants me to be a gentleman, use a napkin,
keep my shirt tucked in, tie my tie right, say ma'm and sir when I
speak to adults. I am going to grow up to be a gentleman.

The grownups sat in the white chairs.

"—well, there were 91 of them that they found. Acheson said he
fired them."

"I heard some of them were allowed to resign."

"They should have been charged with treason."

"If there were 91 that they caught, how many do you suppose
there were that weren't caught?"

Richmond shrugged. "The 91 were just in the State Department.
What about Defense and the other Departments?"

"I'll bet they're all over!" Daddy laughed out loud.

"Just when we need loyal, upstanding men working in the
government when we are in this great struggle—" That was Mother.

"I know."

Olin D. Johnston and Burnet Rhett Maybank were the senators
from South Carolina, and my parents didn't like either one because
one of them was lower class and the other, even though he was our
class, was too liberal. The men joked about our church, and a lot
about being married to one of the "Jay girls." Uncle Richmond said,
"I think I spend all my time watering her plants."

"Oh, Rich, you knew what you were getting when you married
me."

16

"But Caroline, don't you know how wonderful he is to put up with us!"

The men always complained about being married to the Jay girls, but they were teasing. The men talked seriously. My father and Uncle Richmond and cousin Clint asked each other about construction projects around town they knew about or were involved in. It was gossip like the women's gossip, but it was about men's things—building, courtrooms, money, death, estates, taxes, the high cost of labor, politics, Negroes. The women in the family talked about food and kids and about how hard it was to get a yard man.

We never had fried chicken when we ate in the dining room. Some of the things were the same whether we ate inside or outside— silver forks and knives and the plates, the rice and gravy, and the vegetables. When we don't have fried chicken, we have a big Virginia smoked ham. Corn is for outdoors, too.

"This is just delicious."

"Do you think so? I had so much to do this morning, I couldn't concentrate. I was almost late for church." Everybody we knew was an Episcopalian.

"Oh, delicious. Just delicious."

Mother didn't believe that. "My things would be much better if I could just use more spices."

Aunt Caroline raised her eyebrows even though she already knew what was going to come.

"You know, Caroline. He won't let me use anything."

Mother said that all the time. My father did not like food that had much seasoning.

"They are such a security risk. They're right. They don't have any loyalty to their own country."

"They have unusual morals."

"I think the Republicans are right."

"What's that?"

"It's evidence of—they call it chronic moral turpitude in the government." Everybody I knew was a Democrat. We have a one-party system in South Carolina.

"Did you read the paper on Friday?" It was Cousin Clint. He was speaking to Uncle Richmond.

"No, I didn't."

"On the testimony of Earl Browder before the committee investigating Senator McCarthy's charges—"

"No."

"McCarthy says he has given the committee the names of two people working for the Voice of America, and if they are not fired, he will have to make a speech on the floor of the Senate, and, he said, he will have to discuss sexual perversion. He said he will have to discuss 'complete and utter degeneracy—'"

"Clint." It was Cousin Anne. The women in our family call the men like that when they think the man is saying something that a gentleman doesn't say in public.

I am in the fourth grade. Mrs. Bateman is my teacher. Miss Schlierkamp was my teacher in the third grade. Miss Henderson said I was the politest boy in the second grade. They also said I was sweet. I will join the Boy Scouts next year. Peter McKinnell is the scout master and has an MG TD. My mother says when I grow up I am going to get married. She also says I am going to have children. That will be weird. She and her sister are both married, and both have children. My father's aunts and uncles didn't get married. They don't come to these things. There are five of them, and only two got married, and only one had children. That's weird, too. In Mother's family, everybody got married, and one had two children and one had three children. I looked at my father's aunts—these were the Fairs—and they didn't have as good a life as my parents and Caroline and Richmond. They get invited to our house for Sunday dinner or for Christmas, but they have little houses and they don't much invite us to their house. It is better to be married and to have children.

"Yoo-hoo!" Everybody turned and looked down the hill. Mrs. Fitzhugh was waving. She was standing in her front yard, across the street from our house, waving at all of us. "Yoo-hoo!"

"Hello!" That was Caroline. She sounded like she was singing.

"Yoo-hoo!" Mrs. Fitzhugh was walking across the street.

"She's waiting to get an invitation to come up," Rich said. Then he mimicked her. "Yoo-hoo!"

Aunt Caroline called to her again. "Come up and have a bite to eat."

"Aw-ah," Mrs. Fitzhugh hesitated. "Oh, just a bite, for a minute." And she came. She sat next to my mother, and Aunt Caroline brought her a plate with food, and a napkin and a fork.

If all of us grew up and got married, nobody would be able to live next door to my mother, because Aunt Caroline already lives there. We wouldn't be able to do this—what my parents and Aunt Caroline are doing, having this picnic—because there wouldn't be a garden between two houses. In the summer the garden looks like a jungle. A person can't even see the street, and a person can't see our house except for the second story, this great white thing rising up out of the green leaves. My aunt's house is bigger than our house. That's another thing that will be different. When I grow up and get married and have children and come back to my parents' house for a picnic, our house will be smaller than my aunt's house. The size house one has depends on the man in the family and how successful he is. My dad and Uncle Richmond are both engineers. Uncle Richmond is the most successful. I have to have something to do, and I have to be successful.

All of us except my father and my uncle are descended from my grandmother. She used to sit in the middle of the lawn in her white chair, smiling and looking around at all of us. My whole family spends a lot of time talking about our ancestors, about a man who signed the Declaration of Independence and the last rice planter in South Carolina, and another man who was supposed to be the richest man in the South in 1860, and my grandmother's ancestor who outfitted 100 men for the Civil War. Everybody says I look just like Cornelius. We have the same coloring, and the same eyes—big eyes that droop at the outer end, and long lashes. And the two of us look like Daddy and his father. Pretty regularly when some really old person sees me, he says, "He looks exactly like old Captain Fair." Captain Fair was a captain in the Confederate Army, and people remember him as a tiny white-haired gentleman with a van Dyke beard. He had big eyes that drooped at the corners. I don't know how it makes me feel to look like so many people. There are three other Rhetts, aside from my mother.

Mrs. Fitzhugh isn't related to any of us. The other thing about Mrs. Fitzhugh is that you don't ever see her anywhere but here, across the street. We only see the people who go to Trinity Church and a few other places although Mother acts as if she knows everybody in town.

I like this. None of my friends have big families, and almost none of them get together with their cousins like we do. Sometimes they come to our house. I love my family. Nothing is more important to me than my family. When I grow up I will get married and have children and we—all of us, Cornelius and whoever he marries and their children, and my wife and I and our children—will all come to Mother's house on Sunday and have picnics in warm weather.

Mother says I am a gentleman. "Dear," Aunt Caroline said, "you look wonderful. A symphony in gray." I am a sweet boy. That's what they all say. Everybody says I am a hugger. My grandmother told me once that someday I will grow up and take my place among the members of the family in our community. I guess I will be like my father. I know how, at ten, to come into a room filled with my grandmother's friends—old ladies in cotton summer dresses with brooches of gold and small pearls at the point of their necklines— and to move from lady to lady around the room until I have spoken to them all. My grandmother said of those to whom much is given, much is required.

My father is the handsomest man in the family—small, compact, with large eyes, dark blond or light brown hair closely cropped in a crew cut that shows off the shape of his skull. He is beautiful. I look at him a lot of times, thinking that if he were not my father, he'd be as handsome as one of the men I have seen on the beach. He spends time outdoors on building projects, so the skin on his hands and neck and face and head is dark brown and sometimes red from the sun. It is his manner, more than his looks, however, that most distinguishes him. He is quiet and intense and doesn't like men who are emotional. He limits showing his feelings to smiles when he first sees you and when he is saying good-bye. He is smart. He feels his engineering training left him only partly educated, so he reads literature and history and philosophy, working his way through the great books— Emerson, Thoreau, and *Moby Dick*—which he got from his membership in the Book of the Month Club (he also got Kinsey's *Sexual Behavior of the Human Male* two years ago, and he read it all). He taught me you want to own the books you read—and keep them—and that you never buy books from the drugstore because they are cheap. At night after supper, he goes to his room—he and

Mother sleep in separate rooms—and sits in an overstuffed chair with a good reading light and reads the works of Voltaire and Milton and all the plays by Shakespeare in chronological order.

My first memory of him is of his getting out of a taxi in front of a bungalow we lived in when he returned home on shore leave during the Second World War, wearing a white Naval officer's uniform, his garrison cap under his arm. I was three or four then, in 1943. I remember other images of him—in bathing suits at the beach, in the mountains at his aunt's, who owned a summer camp for girls, wearing a white, short-sleeved summer shirt that exposed his forearms and hands with large veins that created a sculptural beauty under his skin.

My mother was talking to my aunt. "No, I'll stay and help clean up, Caroline." Mother always said that. She always volunteered. Cousin Clint and his family collected their things and were leaving. Cousin Anne walked toward their car with her three children running around her, and Clint followed them carrying the baby.

"Good-bye everybody!"

"Good-bye!"

"Good-bye!"

"Now," Mother said, "help me carry these things into the kitchen." All of us helped carry in the dishes and platters and glasses and silver and silverware. Josina was there in the kitchen, washing. When everything had been brought in from the garden, and the dishes all washed and put away, Josina went out to the street to catch the bus to go home, and Mother and I went out the back door to walk along the path under the dogwood trees across the garden to our house, where Daddy waited, reading a book in the overstuffed chair in his room. Cornelius had disappeared to play ball. "He is never a help," Mother said. "Never!" She said to me, walking home, "You must always, always, try to be a help, and make me proud of you." The sun was still way above the trees. I spent the rest of the afternoon in the basement working with my trains. My parents had lots of friends. They were all of them people they were friends with in college, but the people they were really friends with were the people they were related to—my mother's sister and her family. These were the people they actually saw all the time. My mother said, "With all the horrible things that we've been through, your father and I would never have made it if we hadn't shared so much.

21

Our families went to the same Episcopal Church. We came from the same kind of people. We knew all the same people. We were the same class. If we hadn't been the same class, we wouldn't have survived. I couldn't ever have gotten through, if it hadn't been for my family." Nothing was more important to any of us than our family.

↔

My mother says we were socially prominent. Her own family, the Jays, had come from upcountry over near Georgia and had been farmers. They were what were called "good country people." They were a large Scotch-Irish family that had come off the farm in the nineteenth century, moved to town and made money and were now spread out over the whole state, had a "family association" that met once a year on a farm in Edgefield, had risen through marriages and industry to the top levels of society, and thought very well of themselves. All the Jay women were members of "The Assembly," an organization that put on a dance once a year where debutantes were presented. To get into The Assembly, your mother had to already be a member. The Jays were never known as thinkers, and the Jays I knew were not very smart—smart enough to make money, some of them, but not to read books or to do what Daddy called *think.* What my mother was talking about when she said we were socially prominent was Daddy's family. Some of this had to do with how long my father's family had been in America. My father had a book that we called The Fair Book but which was really called *The Descendents of Mark Fair.* It was three inches thick and had all the Fairs in it from the first one, Mark Fair, who came to this country in 1633 to Dedham, Massachusetts—it was the Massachusetts Bay Colony then—down to my great, great-grandfather, Robert Fair. Mark Fair's great-grandson, David, was born in 1699 in Dedham and graduated from Yale in 1721. He was something of a rebel, because The Fair Book says he fell in with the wrong crowd at Yale. In 1728, he went to England, attended Oxford, was ordained an Anglican priest in 1729, and was sent to South Carolina as a missionary. In South Carolina, he married Diana Cavendish, a granddaughter of the Royal Governor of the colony of South Carolina. There is a portrait of her in the museum in Charleston by a painter named Jeremiah

Theus. Theus didn't know how to paint eyes—his eyes looked like fish drawn by a grammar school kid. It was one of the family legends that all the Fair men in this country for 320 years had graduated from college. David Fair's being an ordained and educated priest impressed me. The family he left behind in Massachusetts and then in Connecticut produced two presidents of Yale, and one of the hymns in the Episcopal Hymnal was written by another relative in the beginning of the nineteenth century. My first thinking about my future was founded on what I thought of as this tradition of study, of learning, and of books, and, independent of any book I had ever read, this tradition among my Fair ancestors, I thought, distinguished me.

The Fairs went away to school in each generation, studying law, engineering, or chemistry, but came back to their plantations to farm as their fathers had done. My father's Aunt Maury Fair, an elderly lady in her sixties when I was young, lived alone in a house in an older part of town. You reached her door by climbing a long winding path and steps up to a terrace before her door. When I was seven or eight, she and my mother arranged for me to go to her house every Tuesday afternoon for an hour, while she read to me from a book about John Berkeley. Berkeley left his plantation during the Revolution and led a group of guerrilla fighters in sudden nighttime attacks on the British forces, appearing out of the cypress swamps to attack the soldiers in British red coats. Black Mingo was one of the battles they fought, and I dreamed of being John Berkeley, of leading my courageous men against the British in a battle for liberty. John Berkeley's stepson was John Berkeley Fair, my ancestor, and it was through him that my great-aunt Maury and her sisters and brother, when they were children in the late 1870s, came to ride to church on Sundays in a huge coach and four horses that had originally belonged to John Berkeley. "We didn't take it out often, because it required so many horses to pull!" she said, and she would laugh. I was enthralled by the drama of going to church in such a coach, and by the life that Berkeley had led, fighting for freedom at Black Mingo.

We visited Middleton Place once, a plantation on the Ashley River above Charleston, which had lawns descending by terraces down to ornamental pools shaped like butterfly wings, above the rice paddies. There was a famous live oak on the grounds of the house that was said to be the largest live oak in the state. Aunt Maury told me of her father, who also had a plantation on the Ashley River, above Middleton Place, having a discussion with the owner of Middleton Place about who owned the larger tree. They agreed to measure them. Eight plantation workers circled the Fair tree, touching fingertip to fingertip. The same workers were then transported to Middleton Place, going by boat down the river, where it was found that it took eight and a half workers to encircle the Middleton tree. "So," Aunt Maury said, "it turned out the Middleton Place tree was bigger after all—by half a nigger." She burst out laughing. It was Aunt Maury who told me at dinner one Sunday at our house that she would give me a quarter every time she heard me pronounce *pen* with the proper *e* sound.

Aunt Maury and her sister, Beatrice, my father's mother, who married James Shaw, came to Sunday dinner with us every Sunday, when we weren't having a picnic in the garden with Mother's sister. We arrived home from church and went into the living room where the two old ladies inspected themselves in the gilt mirror over the mantle and then reached up and behind their heads to find the hatpins that held their hats. They would lift the hats straight up and then, keeping them level, bring them down in front of them and place them on a side table behind the upholstered chairs. Another of their sisters was Mattie, who lived in Charleston. She was the one who owned the first summer camp for girls in North Carolina. All of us went up there during the summer, and we also went in the fall, to see the leaves change. The three sisters had a brother, the youngest of them, named Robert Fair—I am named after him—who lived on the Ashley River outside Charleston on a plantation called Wespanee.

The Fairs gave the sense that they were better than everybody else—better in a way that was different from the way the Jays thought they were better than everybody else. The Fairs were more refined than others, even than people like the Jays, who had a lot more money. The Fairs had more books in their houses than the other people I was related to. The Jays had almost no books, and what they had were in bookshelves with glass fronts, and it seemed that they were never read. My grandmother Shaw had all the books her husband had bought years before—he died of influenza in 1925— leather-bound editions of Charles Dickens, Ibsen, Bulwer-Lytton, Cooper, Henry James, Melville, Hawthorne, Sir Walter Scott, Robert Louis Stevenson, Thomas Babington Macaulay, Matthew Arnold, Browning, some of which, I knew—it was obvious from the bookplates—had been bought second hand. Sometimes I read some of these books. I read *The Last Days of Pompeii,* and I also read my first Dickens from her library—*David Copperfield.* Once, at dinner, my parents and Aunt Maury were talking about something that had appeared about one of us in the society column in the paper. Mother spoke of the columnist. "She's such a good writer. Her column is so interesting."

Aunt Maury said, "Of course it is. She's the only writer over at the paper who knows who society is."

Aunt Maury occasionally wrote reviews for the morning paper of concerts by local or visiting artists or of plays produced by the community theatre. Those of us in the family were proud that she was asked to review these events. Aunt Maury told us that when she turned in her reviews, the editor of the paper told the copy-editors "not to change a word in Miss Fair's reviews." I was particularly proud of that fact.

Secretly I thought I was more a Fair than any of the others. The Fairs were more aristocratic, more refined, more learned, more driven by the power of language than by action or by politics. The example of my two relatives who had been presidents of Yale during the nineteenth century competed with the example of John Berkeley's heroics at Black Mingo—books competed with shooting people—for my attention, and I vacillated between them. I dreamed of what I would be when I grew up—distinguished, refined, learned, and able to handle a rifle.

Wespanee Plantation, on the Ashley River just above Charleston, was a white frame house with black shutters built on high brick arches, a verandah across the front, a center door with a fan light, and a wide central hallway all the way through to the back. There was an allée of live oak trees leading through the jungle from the road to the lawn surrounding the house, and, directly in front of the steps up to the verandah, an oval pool with brick facing. I heard my father and Uncle Robert discuss, as engineers would, how the oval was drawn. It was, it seems, an ellipse drawn in the ground with chalk held by a string tied in a circle that was looped around two stakes twenty feet apart. Uncle Robert had bought Wespanee and restored it. He had put in the pool, cleaned the allée of undergrowth, and had put in a big pond between the house and the rice paddies along the river. He took me to see the remains of the sluice gates that used the tide to water the rice paddies. It had been fifty years since the sluice gates had been used and at least that long since rice had been grown along the South Carolina coast.

When we visited Uncle Robert, all of us—my father and mother, Cornelius and me, and Uncle Robert and his wife, Sinkler—wandered around the grounds, walking under the great arches of the limbs of the live oak trees hanging with Spanish moss, the broad lawns reaching toward the jungle in the distance and through breaks in the trees to the rice paddies and salt marshes and the wide Ashley River beyond. We were like figures in a Landscape, little humans dressed in elaborate costumes placed in the middle distance in a painting designed to show off the house and the extensive grounds. The landscape invited me to dream of what it must have been like to own such a plantation and to look out from the verandah toward the workers in the fields, holding in one's hand a small quarto volume bound in leather, one's index finger between pages in the middle of the argument Locke was making in *Two Treatises of Government*. John Locke wrote the first South Carolina constitution, when the territory was given by Charles II to the Lords Proprietors. The constitution was called *The Fundamental Constitutions of Carolina* and was written in 1669. The landscape had the curious effect of recalling both a feudal world—lords and vassals, masters and slaves —and the world of the Enlightenment, in which these people left their plantations, went into the swamps with their single-loader rifles, and fought against the British redcoats for the proposition that all men are created equal.

In our house, there were pieces of furniture belonging to all the families I was related to—a secretary and a dining table from the Laurenses, a vase and a dozen silver forks from the Fairs, a huge silver loving cup and a library table and nest of tables from the Shaws, a large silver sugar bowl, the Jay coat of arms engraved in its side, and a Pembroke table from the Jays. Coats of arms were everywhere, representative of roots in England, on silver dishes on the sideboard in the dining room, on cigarette boxes, on rings, in the painted representations on the dining room walls. We had pieces of furniture that were called "slave-made," which meant they had been built on the plantation by my family's slaves. There was something particularly intimate about my connection to the past when I sat in a chair 150 years old made on one of my family's plantations by one of my family's slaves. I floated through my life surrounded by this past, and by the evidence of my father's family's class—the planter aristocracy—and by an awareness of how inextricably twisted together was my own past with the history of this country. It was impossible to be who I was without having a pride of ownership in the American nation. We were there at the beginning, when all of this was forest.

When my mother said, "Make me proud of you," I knew what she wanted.

↔

One Sunday afternoon when I was seven or eight, at the end of a picnic in my aunt's yard, I was sent home mysteriously and, later in the afternoon, I stood at the head of the stairs in our house, not far from the door to our bedroom, and watched as Uncle Richmond backed up the stairs, carrying Daddy's shoulders, while someone else followed, carrying his legs, my father's head lolling back, drunk.

My mother took me into the garden. She sat in one of the white iron chairs, and I hung about her, waiting for her to say something. "Your father is very sick." When she talked about him, or about all the pain he caused her, her eyes always stopped looking at me—or at anything—and looked out into space as if she were looking at the past. "There are some people who can't drink. They are called alcoholics. You are going to hear people talk about how bad they are. But they are not bad. They are sick." There was a perceptible lifting of her head when she said this. Nobody else in our family had been "sick" like this that I knew of. Then she looked directly at me. "You can't inherit alcoholism, but you can inherit the character traits that lead to alcoholism. And that is why I am telling you all this." Then she said, "You are exactly like your father." She was worried, but she was also embarrassed, and so I was worried about him—and embarrassed. We were the Shaws, and there hadn't been anything before that I had to be embarrassed about. How was I like my father? I wanted to please Mother—my father didn't, so I wanted to—but it upset me that she thought I was going to be bad somehow.

My father moved out—Mother said she couldn't handle him—and he lived with my grandmother Shaw for a while, and Cornelius and I went over for supper. My grandmother lived in a dark brown one-story house in the older part of town, up near the university, a house with a heavy roof and wide eaves where everything was dark on the inside. She had big furniture that she got when she got married, and big pieces of silver. She had a silver soup tureen, which stayed on a big dark serving table against the wall behind her place at the table. One time the phone rang while we were there. My father picked up the receiver, and dropped it. Then he screamed, "Goddamn!" He picked up the whole phone and threw it against the wall. It made a huge clattering noise when it hit the wall and fell on the floor. Cornelius and I watched all this, not making any sound, but my grandmother came in. "Cornelius, you're going to break it." He cursed her and cursed the phone.

Things became hard. Mother said she couldn't handle Daddy, and then my grandmother said she couldn't handle him either, so he went to Elmira, New York, where my Uncle James lived, my father's younger brother, and stayed there almost a year. Mother kept saying my father was "sick," but she was embarrassed by it and ashamed— being "sick" with alcoholism was not like being "sick" with other things. I was afraid and didn't know what I could do to help. My mother kept saying we had to all "pull together," but I didn't know what that meant. She said to me, "Your brother is no help at all, so I expect you to be extra helpful."

Cornelius and I went to see our father in Elmira. We took the train to New York. Daddy met us at Pennsylvania Station, and then we went to Grand Central Station and took another train to Elmira. Our father was nervous and irritable and angry the whole time. He took Cornelius and me up to his bedroom in Uncle James's house and started complaining about Mother. "I wrote her and asked her to send me some work clothes, and this is what she sent me." He had a pile of dirty brown work clothes, and he picked up something to show us. "This! She sent me these to work in!" I had never seen my father wear clothes like that. They were what workmen wore. Grease stained. My father always wore suits when he went to work, and these looked like the clothes of a repairman—someone to fix the furnace. I was embarrassed that he had to wear clothes like that. He worked for the same company Uncle James worked for, but not in the offices where Uncle James worked but out back, in the plant somewhere. Uncle James was a chemical engineer, and the company was a big chemical company. He was embarrassed and ashamed and angry, and I wondered what people at home would say if they knew. "Your mother doesn't care. The only thing she cares about is her goddamned family." I wanted to say something to defend Mother, because I thought she was doing the best she could, but he went on and on. It seemed to last forever, there in that bedroom. He was shouting, and I thought my cousins could hear. I was embarrassed that my father was having to live in their house instead of ours and was working at this really bad job and wearing work clothes when my uncle wore suits when he went to work. "And now she doesn't answer my letters. I have written her over and over again about these clothes—" He picked up something, a pair of pants, and held them up in front of us, shaking them. "—about how I can't wear these, but she doesn't answer me." My father was acting like Cornelius and I could do something about it. He was acting as if we could go back to South Carolina and make Mother do what Daddy wanted her to do, and I wanted to say, This is not our fault. We can't do anything. But I didn't say anything, and neither did Cornelius. We just stood there and watched him throwing pants and shirts on the floor and shouting "goddamn" and didn't say anything.

Later, I spoke to Cornelius. "He shouldn't have said those things about Mother."

But Cornelius told me I was not old enough to understand. "Don't pay any attention to it. It's all a crock of shit." My mother said I was exactly like my father, but I didn't know how I was like my father. I only understood that I was not supposed to be like him. I wasn't supposed to be like Cornelius, either.

When we got back to South Carolina, we didn't tell Mother what Daddy had said about her. We told everybody about the train ride to New York by ourselves with no grownups, about visiting the Empire State building, and about the snow in Elmira and making snow angels. Our Aunt Greta, Uncle James's wife, offered coffee to the men and called it "joe," as if she were in the Army. We were poor, Mother said. She said Cornelius and I were going to have to be the men in the family now. I wanted to please her. I wished we weren't poor, and I didn't want my friends to know. Cornelius would not talk to me about it. Cornelius had his friends—he was always out playing ball—and he always acted like our parents were crazy.

Daddy quit drinking after that and came back to South Carolina. He worked for the same company Uncle Richmond worked for, and then he quit working for that company. Then he started his own business, but after a while that didn't work out either, and Mother said he had "lost his business." He had to go to work for a man who used to work for him, who had started up his own business, and both Mother and Daddy were ashamed that he was working for this man. They had to go to dinner at this man's house, and Mother said this man put his arm around her shoulders and said, "Imagine, here I've got my arm around William Jay's daughter's shoulders!" Mother acted as if he had done something awful, but the worst part of it was that my father's drinking had gotten them so they weren't above this man any more. And the Jays had always been above everybody else.

When we had supper, we ate in the dining room, where we had a very old table my father had inherited. It was very valuable, they said. It was in three pieces, two round ends and a middle with gate legs and drop leaves. The round ends were in the living room, and Daddy kept leaning on the drop leaf end of the table supported only by the gate leg, and that made the table top bend. Mother would say, "Cornelius, don't lean on the table." She said it as if it were the first time he had ever done it, but he did it all the time, and every time he did it, she told him not to do it. Then he would get mad and curse her, and she would get hurt. She would tell him not to use such language. They did that every time we had a meal.

Once, Mother called us together—Cornelius and me—in my room, and she sat us down and told us we had to have a talk. She said since our father had lost his business, "I am going to have to go to work." When Mother had to say things like this, she always closed her mouth and lifted her chin a little and looked brave, but ashamed too. After that she got a job teaching school in an Episcopal school in an old mansion out on Millwood—a big house with great Corinthian columns. She also sold *World Book* encyclopedias by going to people's houses and telling them how great the encyclopedia was for children—we had an *Encyclopaedia Britannica* at home—and people paid her to sew lampshades out of silk. She also made her own clothes. She worked very hard, and she told me, "Your father's drinking ruined my life."

My father felt that everybody in the family was comparing him to Uncle Richmond, with Uncle Richmond being a success and Daddy being a failure. When he was with us, my father ran down Uncle Richmond every chance he got, and he said, all the time, "You can't be successful in business and be honest." Being successful in business was a mystery to me. I didn't know what you had to do to be successful—aside from being dishonest—and I didn't know whether I had what it took. It became a big thing for me to be honest.

Often my father said to me, "We love you," but even more often, he would scream at me for something I had done. Usually it was the kind of clumsy things I did—kicking over the wastepaper basket at the head of the stairs when creeping up the stairs at eleven at night after my father had gone to bed. "Goddamn it! What in the hell—!" And then the lights would come on, and my father's door would swing open and there would be my father, in a fury. More often, it was the kind of constant criticism that my father made no effort to hide. "I think your hair is too long. Don't you think?" He wanted me to agree with him. My report cards, which I brought home every six weeks for my parents' signature, always made my father say, "But you didn't make all A's," or "But you could have made all A pluses." There were also the comments, "Is your friend really that much taller than you?" And there were politics, which got worse and worse as I got older and more progressive and my father got older and more conservative. But most of all, there was the sense, encouraged by my mother, that we all needed to be careful around him. Don't disturb him. Don't bother him. Don't upset him. It was, I thought, like living with a dangerous animal in the house that you didn't want to waken.

I came to understand how bad my mother's life was, and I felt responsible. I wanted to make her life better—I knew Cornelius wouldn't help—so I worked at it. She wanted to paint the living room—it hadn't been painted since we moved in—and she taught me how to paint, and then I painted the whole living room and dining room and the front hall. She chose a color she called "a lovely, soft, peach," and she told everybody that I had been "such a help," and that made things better some. But not so much.

We were sitting in the breakfast room, Mother and I at angles to one another at the table, talking after dinner. It was a very small room that connected the kitchen with the dining room, and the table had a pale yellow plaid tablecloth in the center. We had finished cleaning up after dinner, the rest of the family upstairs. All the house was silent except for the sound of her voice.

"I am just worn out. I have to do it all myself, and I am exhausted. He doesn't ever help, you can see, with the meals, with cleaning up afterward, with the yard work, and I can't ever seem to find a yardman. He doesn't pick up after himself. He has these great stacks of magazines lying around, and I ask him and ask him to go through them and pick out the ones he wants to keep and to throw away the rest, and he won't. He says he will, and then he doesn't. He doesn't talk to me. I want him to tell me what is bothering him, and he won't. He goes in his room and reads. I am so lonely. You know how important my family are to me—I couldn't have gotten through without Caroline—but he doesn't want to spend time with them. He doesn't like to go to Caroline and Richmond's house any more, and he used to love going to their house for supper. Now he doesn't want to go anywhere. It is so hard to live with him. He's so difficult. He is so moody. I don't know how we are going to pay the bills this month. And then he went and bought that car, and I feel I can't hold my head up around this town, when we owe as much as we do, and that car is more expensive than we can afford. I feel so humiliated." She put her elbow on the table and rested her forehead on her knuckles, and cried. "I try so hard. My father told me if I'd leave him he'd support me the rest of my life. He said he'd build me a house next door to them, if I'd leave your father. But I swore I would love him forever, in sickness and in health, till death do us part. And I meant that, and I mean to keep my vow." I held her hand while she cried. All of this she had been saying for years.

Cornelius stayed out of all that, mostly, but it made me feel bad about myself because I was exactly like my father. I wanted to please her, and I didn't ever want to cause her pain, but I had no idea how.

↔

I was a boy. I was a boy, and I did all the things boys do—played with model trains, went to Boy Scout meetings, went on overnight camping trips with my troop. I mowed the lawn in the summer and raked the leaves in the fall, and I moved furniture when my mother wanted to rearrange things. I painted the living room and dining room and the hall, and I built things with wood. I built a brick fireplace in the garden. I supposed I was going to be an engineer, like my father and like my great-grandfather, who had built railroad bridges across the Congaree after he came home from Honduras after the Civil War. I was an acolyte in church. Sometimes I followed

32

Cornelius around, but Cornelius didn't like that and told me to go home.

We'd be on the schoolyard—their side and ours—and everybody would be running around. It was hard to see what was happening in the dust and the heat, and then suddenly, there, in front of me, the boys cleared away for a second, and I could see the soft loose gray sand of the schoolyard punched all over with footprints and a boy running in my direction, breathing hard, his eyes darting here and there, chasing a ball that had just hit the ground and bounced, changing directions. The boy changed directions too, following the ball, coming toward me. I was supposed to do something, stop the boy, catch the ball, something, but it was all happening so fast that I didn't know what it was I was supposed to do. I was afraid. This had happened before—it happened every time we played games. Suddenly everything depended on me, and I wouldn't know what was needed, wanted, wouldn't know what I had not done that I should have done or been able to do that would have been right for that moment. Then, before I could figure out what was needed, the ball bounced away, some other boy caught it and threw it, and the one coming toward me glanced at me and then ignored me. The action moved on somewhere else, and I was standing in the middle of the playground ignored by the other boys. The other boys would laugh at me—or, even worse, would look away, embarrassed for me, and the next time at recess when they picked up sides I'd have to hear it again, *You have to take Fair*—with the unstated words—*this time. We took him last time.* There was us, and there was me, and I wasn't one of us, and when my mother went on and on and on about her family, the Jays or the Fairs, about us, I thought, I am not one of us.

My dad bought me a baseball glove and started taking me out in the back yard when he came home from work to "catch." He'd get about as far away from me as the length of our living room and throw the ball to me, and I was supposed to catch it. It came at me really hard and fast, and when I did manage to get my hand in the right place so the ball hit the palm of my hand, it stung something awful, and I'd drop it. Then I'd look at my dad, and he'd look disappointed and with a weary kind of voice say, "Throw it here and let's try it again." But I didn't throw it right, either. I didn't know why I didn't. There was a way to throw it that looked like a girl was

33

throwing it, and there was a way to throw it that boys used. I looked like a girl when I was throwing the ball to Daddy. I didn't want to, but I did. I don't know, since I was a boy, how I learned to throw a ball like a girl and why I didn't just naturally throw like a boy, since I was a boy, but I didn't, and it turned out it was important that I didn't. If everybody had left me alone, how I threw a ball wouldn't have mattered to me. It wasn't something that I woke up in the morning wanting to do, but it mattered to everybody else—the other boys in school, the girls (they didn't want me throwing like them, and I didn't understand that, either), Cornelius, my dad. Everybody somehow knew—Fair doesn't throw like a boy, and that's bad.

The dividing line between the boys who were not good at sports and the boys who were was stronger than the dividing line between boys and girls. There was a lot of stuff back and forth between boys and girls by the time they got to be our age, twelve years old, but there was almost no stuff back and forth between boys who were not good at sports and boys who were. There was nothing back and forth between Cornelius and me. Why didn't my hair just look good, like Cornelius's? Nobody liked boys whose hair didn't look good and who were not good at sports, and when I told my mother—*I don't want to go over there!*—she'd say, "But they're your cousins. Of course you have to go. Don't be silly. You'll have a fine time. Cornelius thinks it's wonderful over there." She didn't want to know what I knew. I got merit badges in Scouts, lots of merit badges, and I became big in Scouts—things that were designed for boys who were brainy and who were not good at sports—and the other stuff I never talked about. There just wasn't anybody else out there to talk about it to. Cornelius was out playing ball. Mother never wanted to hear it. And I thought, I embarrass my dad.

When I was thirteen, my scout leader, George Southwyck, took us on a weekend camping trip to Kiawah Island, a sea island on the coast of South Carolina, south of Charleston. There were five boys. In the middle of a palmetto thicket, we climbed to the second floor of a tall abandoned wooden house with chimneys on both ends, exploring, and could see the ocean beyond. On the first floor, we were still in the middle of the jungle—that is, the palmetto trees were high all around us and obscured the sky—but upstairs we were above the trees and could see all the way beyond the trees to the beach and the sea beyond. We knelt down on the board floor and put our arms on the window sill. Shep Cox, my friend, drew in his breath and said, "Beautiful." There was nothing to see but the ocean beyond the palmetto trees, and the wide strip of white sand separating them.

"This is an old plantation house." This might have been a summer house the plantation owner used because it was nearer the sea and therefore cooler. It had high ceilings, and the windows downstairs that opened onto the porch went almost to the floor. Down here, South Carolina didn't look so much like America as it looked like an island in the Caribbean.

We camped out near the beach, pitched our tents under palmettos and cut fronds to make shelters with, shelters we didn't need but that made us feel like we were in a movie. We ate under the shelters, after we cooked our supper. Then, later, we walked out to the beach and waded in the surf for a long time, until it got dark. Afterward, we built a campfire and told each other terrifying stories until we went to sleep, stories about Negro men gone berserk who went after young white boys with axes and saws and knives.

We talked about George. He was in college, and we thought he was cool. We'd see him carrying the cross on Sundays, the job the most senior acolyte always had.

"He's good looking."

"He's got thin cheeks."

We agreed that we wanted to look like that—have cheeks that sank in and have lines that went from our nose to the corner of our mouth. We agreed that we liked pointed chins. We didn't know anything about him, except that he had a family like Shep's and mine.

"I like his hair."

"Yeah. I wish mine did that."

My hair was somewhere between light brown and dark brown—it got very light in the summer—and was very straight. I wanted my hair to be long and shiny like George's, but I didn't know how to make my hair do what I wanted it to. I wanted it to be long, but my parents wanted me to get crew cuts, so that's what I did. I thought my hair was always a mess, and I had these big teeth.

The next day, we went back to the house to explore some more.

"What do you want to be when you grow up?" This was my friend, Shep.

I didn't know. Something important, like my ancestor from a hundred years ago who was the richest man in the South in 1860. Shep was just like me. Neither one of us was any good at sports. Our parents had known each other when they were in school, and all of us thought we were probably kin somehow, if we ever tried to find out. Shep's family had been in South Carolina as long as mine. Two of his relatives were the Grimké sisters, who were famous before the Civil War for being abolitionists even though they lived in Charleston. That made him a little strange to the rest of us. Nobody in my family was an abolitionist. "I want to be the governor of South Carolina."

"Would you like to be the President?"

"Uh-uh." Neither of us could think of wanting to live somewhere other than South Carolina where our families had always lived.

We sat in the window, our legs hanging outside, not far above the roof of the porch, talking about George. At home, George walked down the hall of the Parish House with a kind of glide, not paying attention to the younger boys. His shoulders were slightly hunched, as if he were continuously shrugging off the importance of what faced him, as if he was always capable of more than was being demanded of him. When somebody spoke to him—"Hi, George"— he turned and noticed you for the first time, and you saw a smile travel out across his face, involving his lips, his chin, his cheeks, his eyes and eyebrows and the lines at the ends of his eyes, and then, finally, his ears and scalp, which moved back in the sheer pleasure of seeing you. "Fair! How are you? Good to see you! How's Scouts?" He slid his hand behind my neck—his fingers touched the lobe of my ear—and for a moment we walked down the hall together, linked by his big hand resting on the back of my neck. Cornelius and George were friends, even though George was a few years older than Cornelius. But they were very different. George seemed to like me, and I didn't think Cornelius was interested at all.

Right then George was down on the beach in his shorts, catching a ball that one of the other scout masters was throwing. The other scout master always seemed to throw high, which meant that George had to jump to catch, and George was the only boy I have ever known who really looked like those drawings of football players they have on the covers of the programs for college games—totally off the sand, legs back behind him, one pulled up and bent at the knee protecting his balls, his whole torso bent back, one arm up and out in back of him, just reaching the ball. He had the trick of being able to stop in the air—or of looking like that was what he was doing.

When I ran down the beach, I knew I didn't look like George. My feet were too big, and my knees were knobby. I knew how I looked because that was the way all of us looked—all the boys my age on the beach at Kiawah—bones and teeth and eyes too big, and not enough meat on us, running awkwardly in the sand, our knees knocking together. Even the ones who were athletic and played sports didn't seem to have any muscle or shape.

George taught us how to do life-saving in the water, and he made a good victim. When he floated in the water, I swam up behind him and put my arm over his shoulder and across his chest, gripping him in his armpit, and then did the side stroke, pulling him behind me. When I did that, I was gripping his chest muscle while George lay back in the water against my whole body. It was something I could feel in my memory afterwards, how it felt to have George's chest muscle in my fist and his warm back lying against my body, alive, strong, and trusting.

George sent us to look for firewood, but there wasn't much available on an island that didn't have many trees, just miles of palmetto thicket. We brought back dead palmetto fronds lying on the sand, and we broke them up into pieces to burn. He wore shorts and Keds, a loose t-shirt, and his black, straight hair hung in his eyes as he bent over the fire. His legs and his forearms were covered with thick, black hair. His hair was like the hair of Larry in grammar school—straight and long and glossy—who played king on the mountain with me. People said George had a girl, that he was going steady.

A year ago I was at Aunt Caroline's when she was giving a cocktail party for a girl making her debut, and I saw George in a tuxedo, his black hair parted on the side and slicked down. He was escorting the girl Aunt Caroline was giving the party for. The girl was my aunt's niece—Uncle Richmond's sister's daughter. She was also my third cousin, through her father.

I was in the music room, fooling around on the piano, when the doorbell rang, and I heard somebody go to the door and invite someone in. Then I heard the voice of a young man in the living room, where my aunt was. "Mrs. Sims! Good evening. I am George

Southwyck." He talked like a grownup. "Yes, ma'm." He was laughing. "I know I've been introduced to you before. But I've grown up since then, and I thought you might not recognize me."

I went in and watched this happening.

George talked to my aunt as if he were her brother. He said to her, a broad smile on his face, "I'm a friend of Cornelius's." He was able to move around the room talking to all the grownups—the men and the ladies—and at the same time pay attention to my cousin, whose name was Sarah. "Thank you for inviting me," he said to Aunt Caroline. "Is there anything I can do for you?"

She smiled. "I don't think so." She really couldn't think of anything George could do at the moment, minutes before everybody else arrived at the party—my mother was there to help, and there were two cooks in the kitchen, two men to pass things, plus two bartenders—but she appreciated it that he had offered. She put her hand on his arm. "You really are the sweetest thing."

He grinned.

So when he took us on the camping trip to Kiawah, lighting the palmetto fronds just at dusk, the light from the fire making the dark, tanned skin on his shins shine, I thought of having seen him through the glass doors standing in Aunt Caroline's living room in his evening clothes, his shoulders against the mantle piece, a drink in one hand, the other in his pocket, his head tilted back and his eyebrows raised slightly, listening almost with an eagerness to another of my cousins telling about hunting deer in the low country. "Ah! Is that what it is like!" He nodded, listening to my cousin, his tanned skin very dark against the very stiff white wing collar of his dress shirt. I thought, when I thought of the future at all, I want to be like that. And now here he was lighting a fire and getting ready to tell us all a ghost story that we all knew would be called The Blue-Lipped Nigger.

↔

When I was 14, I had a paper route, and another boy did also, and every afternoon, we waited on a corner for the papers to be delivered. It was near where we lived. The streets were wide, and the trees almost touched in the middle. When the papers came, we knelt down in the dust and folded them and put them in our bags. We were always giving each other a hard time. Once he said something—he was teasing me about something—and I wanted to tease him back, but he was older and bigger, and I didn't know how, so I said, "Queer! You queer!" The other boy stopped folding and said, "What did you say?"

"I said you were queer."

"You don't know what that means."

I was stopped. Did it mean something that I didn't know? "It means odd." He didn't say anything. "It means strange. Different. It means peculiar." I knew what words meant.

"You shouldn't use words when you don't know what they mean."

Something had happened, and I didn't know what it was. I had heard people use queer before, but now I realized, if it didn't mean odd, then I didn't know what it meant. And now this boy was telling me it meant something that I shouldn't have said.

"You should get Cornelius to tell you what it means."

Life is full of dangers, and when I was walking around the neighborhood that afternoon, in the bright, hot, sun, crossing people's lawns under the high trees, tossing the paper onto their porches, the heavy canvas bag bumping against my knee, I thought, I'm always discovering things I don't know anything about. Queer. The word opened up a whole world, and I didn't know anything about it. Somehow what I had done was either dangerous or stupid, and I didn't know why it was dangerous or stupid. It wasn't that I wasn't good. It was that I wasn't very smart. I couldn't ever remember not knowing what a word meant.

My father had bought us the *Encyclopaedia Britannica*, which had a long article on sculpture with a section of pictures on glossy paper. In the big volumes, which I opened on my lap and looked at page by page, I learned that Greek and Roman sculpture was often of nude men, and I learned what the Renaissance was because I came across a picture of the sculptures on the tomb of Giuliano de' Medici by Michelangelo, which led me to read all I could find about Michelangelo, about Florence, and about the Italian Renaissance. The statues of *Twilight* on Lorenzo de' Medici's tomb, and *Day* on Giuliano's tomb, were overwhelming in themselves, but the statue of Giuliano was powerful enough for me to recall every detail of it when I lay in bed at night after the lights were out, waiting to go to sleep. Proud Giuliano's haughty head was on a strong, muscular, columnar neck, and he had great arms and shoulders, but it was his chest that I dreamed of at night—full, hard, bulging, tight chest muscles with pointed nipples that made my mouth water. Lying in the dark in my bed, I felt sensitive all over. My dick grew hard and big, and it felt like the rubber must feel when someone is blowing up a balloon.

I discovered *David* and *Moses*, and the *Pieta*—the body of the feminine Jesus did nothing for me—and the *Slaves* from the tomb of Julius II, and the huge, relaxed, weary body of the Farnese *Hercules*, a Roman copy of a statue by Lysippus, who lived in Greece in the fourth century BC. I wanted to touch these living men. The idea of touching them was enough to wake me up from my half-somnolent state and place me in a state of breathless physical excitement. I had never felt so before, and when I rebelled against the anxiety of worrying about my parents and about my own inability to do anything about them, or about being a boy, I found that I could drift away on a tide of powerful feelings having to do with the strength of these powerful and beautiful men.

For I did not think of the Farnese *Hercules* as a work of art. Or, I thought of it as a work of art designed to make me feel the way I was feeling, and the more intense the feeling, the greater the work of art. The man leaning on the stump of the tree was a man, fully grown, fully developed, fully used, ready for me. I carried the image of this statue around with me in my head, superimposed on what I was seeing, my teachers, the other boys in the school gym, the boy who sat next to me in class, and saw everywhere a double vision, the world I was born into and the world I was collecting in my head.

I learned what queer meant. I learned, too, not to ask my parents questions like this—not by asking them but by listening to the guys at school and realizing that this was not a question I could ask my parents. My parents made it clear that there were a lot of things a gentleman never spoke of. I didn't ask Cornelius. And I figured out that I was queer. At first it had to do with the feelings I had around certain boys—this was what it meant to have the feelings I had around Paul Connors in mechanical drawing class, Larry on the playing ground in grammar school, Russell Ford in the seventh grade, George Southwyck, and Peter McKinnell's arm over me on camping trips. But about the same time it also had to do with the

Encyclopedia Britannica and with Giuliano de' Medici and his hard, bulbous chest. It had to do with the muscle magazine at the soda shop across from the church on Sunday mornings. The cover of that magazine taught me that there were other magazine covers out there, and I started hanging out at a place my dad took me, the Capitol News Stand on Main Street, just above the State House. My father went there every week to buy all the news magazines—*Time, Newsweek,* and *US News & World Report.* While he was getting his things, I would check out what else was available, and I found the muscle magazines, *Muscle Power, Strength and Health, Muscular Development, and Adonis.* I also found *Physique Pictorial*, a little magazine with pictures and drawings of very muscular, almost naked men in all sorts of poses. The guys looked like Russell—all of them seemed to be blond with slicked-back hair—and their bathing suits were the briefest and tightest I had ever seen. My bathing suits, the kind my mother let me buy, looked like shorts, drawstring, elastic band around the waist, legs that came down to the mid-thigh. I discovered the Tom of Finland books—and Kake. These were like pamphlets, about the size of a sheet of typing paper, on slick paper, with drawings of motorcycle riders who were very muscular and had big—humongous—dicks and wore leather motorcycle jackets and big black leather boots and who fucked each other in the bushes.

The summer I was fourteen, I worked at a swimming club on a lake near Columbia. The life guard, a boy about 17, named Steve, tall, slender, had the hard body of an athlete. He was blond, had short hair, and wore a swimming suit made of stretch fabric that emphasized his butt and crotch. He was friendly, but we didn't become friends. His bathing suit and the scar on his cheekbone—everything about him—suggested he was not from my class, and from a distance I watched his hard muscles sliding under his smooth, tanned skin.

One night, sitting in my bed, my back up against the headboard, I was writing on sheets of paper. I drew the image in my head—Kake's arm—and discovered that drawing pictures could make my dick grow hard. I drew another and another, and the feeling in my dick suffused through my whole body. I found that the feeling could be sustained for an hour or more before I finally went to sleep, exhausted. I could sustain it so long that the feeling began to have a focus again in my cock, something deeper, more pointed, more urgent, more immediately explosive, and that night, when the lights were out, the image of Kake in my mind, I held my cock, and then I stroked it—I discovered what my body was capable of doing, one step at a time—while the feeling became more and more pronounced and explosive, the hard living flesh that was Kake's arm alive in my fingers, until at last, in a paroxysm of contractions in my belly muscles and hard jerking in my hand gripping the skin of my cock, I came.

And no one knew. They paid no attention to what I was discovering I could do with my body—my cock—in the bedroom next to theirs. Cornelius didn't know, my parents didn't know. No one knew. Mother called me into her room one afternoon after work, her face showing the embarrassment she always felt when she had to deal with issues she didn't feel ladies should know anything about, both embarrassed and trying not to laugh from nervousness, and said that she had spoken to Caroline. "Some men," she said, "'dress' themselves on the right, and some men 'dress' themselves on the left." I had no idea what she meant. Then it became clear she was talking about where I hung my dick. "And, if you dress on a side not comfortable for you, your penis will become erect." I was embarrassed. She had talked to my aunt about my penis! She was talking about the fact that I had a hard-on so much so often—I thought I had been hiding it by putting my hand in my pocket and holding my dick down—and, instead of hiding it, it had become so much of a problem she had talked about it with her sister! She wanted me to think about this and to "dress" differently so that I wouldn't "show." She said, "I told Caroline my boys didn't know anything about things like this."

"But I do," I said, although I didn't. "You are the one who doesn't know anything about any of this."

I hated her for doing what she had done, talking about my penis to her sister. Besides, whatever was going on with my dick was caused by something a whole lot more important than which side I dressed on.

None of them knew anything about any of the stuff that was happening to me. I had never heard anyone talk about how you could draw pictures of the arms of strong men and that would make your dick get hard. I also didn't know what, exactly, was the relationship between women's breasts and men, but it was pretty clear—I had figured this out from listening to everybody since grade school—that there was a relationship. But Mother didn't know anything, and neither did anybody else, about the connection between men's arms and my dick. It wasn't in any book we had, it wasn't in any conversation I had ever heard any grownup have, and it wasn't in the movies. You could see in the eyes of the star of the movie that when the beautiful woman came in the room, something was happening. But I knew about men's arms. I thought my mother thought I didn't have any thoughts except the ones she gave me. I was angry with her about this, but I didn't tell her. I thought, this is men's stuff, and she shouldn't have thought that her sister would know anything about it. At the same time, it was not something my father would want to talk about, and I was sure Cornelius would laugh.

After that, I found out what to call it, and every night I drew pictures of men's arms, and, after the lights were out, I masturbated until I came. I discovered that this was sex. I thought that at some point—later—I would have feelings like this about women. Other men did, and I guessed that I was not old enough yet. So I went on, enjoying what I had and waiting to see what would happen.

There was a boy a year older than me, in junior high school, whose name I never knew, but who wore t-shirts every day to school. My own parents required me to wear khaki pants and dress shirts every day. He was much bigger than I was, was well-developed, and his arms had distinct biceps and triceps. I enjoyed looking at him. In my gym class, he wore an old torn sweat shirt that had a ragged hole across the chest, showing his pectoral muscle and one nipple. Another boy mocked him one day. "You only wear that sweat shirt to show off your muscles." He grinned and answered, "You're just jealous because you don't have any." I wasn't jealous of him, but I did want to put my hand on his chest and squeeze the muscle, and I fantasized about his chest at night in the dark.

A long time ago, I read my father's newspaper about the 91 men who were fired from the State Department for being perverts. My father and I had never talked about it, but I had heard adults and had picked up enough to understand what the newspapers were saying. They were saying that perverts couldn't be trusted with the country's secrets, that they were security risks, and that they made it easy for the Communists to infiltrate the government and get our secrets. Ninety-one had been discovered in the State Department, and the

43

newspapers said there must be a lot more that hadn't been discovered. There was a Congressional investigation and for a long time the newspapers were full of it. I knew what being a queer meant. I was a pervert. Therefore I couldn't be trusted. I was a security risk. I was one of the ones they had all been talking about, guilty of what the papers called moral turpitude.

I used to lie awake at night and think about that, being a security risk. When would that happen? After I had gotten my first job, I guessed. I would be in my office, the phone would ring, and I would sell our country's secrets. How we made the hydrogen bombs. I was honest now, and I didn't know what was going to happen to me to make me become a person who would sell out our country's secrets, but I supposed it would happen. I would become a traitor. I didn't think about the details very much, I just knew that it would.

Cornelius was three years older than I was, and he had started dating. By the time I got to high school, Cornelius was already well known and in his last year. He was this cool jock—he knew he was good looking and rude and sexy, and he seemed to expect everyone to look up to him—who had cool friends just like him. They were the same guys I saw at school and fantasized about. Our parents wouldn't allow Cornelius to go steady, but Cornelius did anyway, without letting them know. He made bad grades, was the captain of the football team, and dated the most beautiful girl in school. Cornelius was never around even to be rude to our parents. He left in the morning to go to school and came home late and went directly to his room, and he amazed me with how indifferent he was to them. Mother would say the lawn needed to be raked, and he would say, "Yes, ma'm, I'll do it tomorrow afternoon," and then he wouldn't do it and was unfazed by Mother's complaint. "I was playing ball," he would say, staring at her, daring her to find it an inadequate explanation. She would cry, and he would shrug and walk out. I thought he didn't care at all.

I was 14 or 15, and I had this problem. I wanted to date the kind of boy Cornelius had for friends, yet I didn't know how that could happen. I was supposed to date girls. It seemed so easy for my older brother. Girls seemed to flock around Cornelius. What I wanted was for all the tough boys to flock around me, but they didn't flock around me, because I was a boy too, like them, and boys don't date boys. It was a problem that didn't seem to have a solution. Boys

44

don't date boys. Cornelius dated girls. Everywhere, in all the reading I had done, and in all the movies I had been to see, the boy always dated the girl. David Copperfield got Agnes in the end. So I went home at night, and I jerked off to the black and white images of the Farnese *Hercules* printed on glossy paper in the Sculpture section of the *Encyclopaedia Britannica,* and when I came, the pale, pearl-like liquid shot all over the sheets, and dried on my skin, becoming hard and scab-like, and then mostly flaking off before I woke up in the morning.

We had all reached the age where "being queer" was something we worried about. I was not sure we thought that there were queer people so much as we thought that somebody might act queer. Or we thought that somebody might act straight but really be queer. We were worried that a queer might come on to us, and we were afraid of that. It was a dangerous time, because none of us trusted each other. Not that we were thinking about this all the time—we weren't—but we were alert to danger signs, someone acting effeminate, someone unable to play sports, someone paying too much attention to the other guys, particularly in the johns and in the locker rooms. Cornelius started talking about queers. I heard him say, "He's a fruit."

The goals were to act straight, act as masculine as possible, not to pay any attention to the other guys when they had their dicks out anywhere, and to try not to get in a situation where it was clear you didn't know what to do with a ball. And to try to do all this without seeming fake. It was confusing to me because what seemed to be admired at school were boys who were "tough"—athletes or bullies—and that was just the kind of boy that Mother didn't want me to be. And that was just the kind I liked and wanted to be. I liked Elvis mainly because he seemed so tough—his hair all greasy and shiny—and so sexy. So I bought my jerk-off magazines at the Capitol News Stand—the owner recognized me from my being there with my Dad and stared at me and at the magazines I was buying—and kept my eyes off the guys at school while I thought about tough boys who rolled up their t-shirt sleeves to show off their arms and whose hair was slick and reflected the light and about how sexy they were.

This was something I had to do. I understood that thinking guys were sexy was degenerate—queers were perverts, a security risk—but by the time I discovered this about myself, I had already found out that I was the son of an alcoholic and was probably going to be one of those too. I couldn't do anything about that either—you weren't supposed to talk about either of them—so I just buried them deep in my mind and went on with the business that was in front of me, learning to be a Southern gentleman. What I could talk about was school, why it was important to graduate from high school with a working knowledge of Latin and French, books, classes, Macbeth, what it meant to have separation of church and state, and how Thomas Jefferson got most of his ideas about how men are equal from John Locke, after-school activities, growing up, the importance of my family to the history of South Carolina, politics, why the liberal arts were the best route to a good education, the church and its value as a via media, the atomic bomb and the hydrogen bomb, segregation, States' Rights, Elvis Presley, *Brown v. Board of Education,* Little Richard, Elizabeth Taylor, Katherine Hepburn, Dubose Heyward, Tennessee Williams, William Faulkner, Robert Penn Warren, Montgomery Clift, and Richard Nixon. I just couldn't talk about alcoholism, and I couldn't talk about wanting pegged pants. And I couldn't talk about *Twilight* or *Day* or the Farnese *Hercules,* or Kake or Tom of Finland, or even the waterfront director at Sky Valley—on the day we arrived at camp, another boy, who had also just arrived, was yelling, "Where's Jay Broad? Where is he? Where is that big muscle-bound ape!" and Jay Broad was muscle-bound—or Russell Ford or Paul Connors or the man on the beach who was looking for strong backs. The whole rich life I had going on in my head—which was my sex life—that affected everything about me, was so near to hand that every man I saw on the street, in the garden, at school, in the movies, in the magazines, moved me deeply, jarred my attention away from the world I was in to another world of sex, transformed the world into something else entirely. It wasn't so much that I repressed these feelings—or denied them—it was that there were these feelings and then there were these other feelings, and they didn't have anything to do with one another. They were on separate tracks, like trains going at different speeds across a landscape, and all of us in this train ignored this other train, even though the noise of it was deafening. And I found myself being jerked back and forth between these two roaring trains, one driven by me and huge men and the other by wounded and demanding women. I had thought all the way through high school that eventually I would grow up to be like Cornelius and join the society my parents were members of. But sometimes I was able to admit that whatever my life was going to be like, it was not going to be like Cornelius's. It might be very different, or it might be something like, but it would not be much like Cornelius's. What was hanging between my legs and the way it acted made me know that. There was this other world, which seemed to exist outside of time and which seemed not to require goals or plans or priorities. It was my world alone, and I had to do nothing more than to enter it and feel.

Of course, Mother found my muscle magazines. I had hidden them under my mattress, and she found them when she was making up my bed. I came home from school one day, and she called me into her room, where she was lying on the bed. She asked me to sit down, and I did. She spoke very seriously at first. "When I was straightening up your room this morning, I found some magazines under your mattress." She began to giggle and to struggle to suppress her giggling. She was not comfortable talking about what she was talking about, and it made her giggle. "I know that some men like to look at pictures of women with large breasts. It may be that you are like that." She was being gentle, and she did not seem angry. But I could see that she was very uncomfortable, and it made her giggle. I was tense and anxious about what was to come, and I was angry with her for giggling at something so important. But nothing happened! All she wanted was to let me know that she had found my magazines and she knew that some men were "like that." But they were not women with large breasts. They were men with big chests. She had found the whole idea of these magazines so offensive that she had not looked at them. She knew what she was supposed to say, so she said it—I've seen them—but she had never looked at them. This thing that was so important to me, she found so offensive she couldn't look! I wondered what she would have said if she had been able to see what she was looking at.

I ran for president of the student council and lost and ran for editor of the school newspaper and won. The best thing in high school was to be a jock. But there were three jobs in student government that carried weight—president of the student council, and the editorship of the school newspaper and the editorship of the yearbook. Since I always did well in English classes, I went out for the school newspaper, and I wrote for it the whole time I was in high school. I wasn't an athlete like Cornelius, so that was a strike against me, but I was editor of the paper, and that was a strike in my favor. I don't think I was particularly popular with the most popular girls—I think they sensed some indifference or inability when it came to sex —but I was popular enough, and, more important, I was respected enough. While they never abandoned their admiration for athletes, by the last years of high school the kids had come also to respect students who were really bright. In the endless popularity contest that was high school, I was OK. My parents thought I was doing fine because I never told them anything—or they didn't believe what I did tell them—and they apparently never wondered.

Fairly frequently I told Mother that I didn't have any friends or that I was really unhappy. "I am popular and respected, and I get elected to things, but I have no friends. On Friday night when everybody else is out with their friends, I have no one to go anywhere with."

"You have plenty of friends. You are attractive, you are an eligible young man, you're a gentleman. Don't be silly."

But I knew the truth, and I also knew that my parents did not want to know what I knew.

I knew I was queer. I went to see *Gentlemen Prefer Blondes* when I was 14, and suddenly there on the screen was this whole gym full of musclemen—they were supposed to be Olympic athletes— with Jane Russell singing in the middle of them. I got an instant hard-on—I wanted her to move out of the way so I could see the men —and waited during all the rest of the movie for them to come back and was very disappointed that they didn't. I thought it might be, somehow, my fault that I liked men, but I liked liking men. I knew that I had to keep my feelings hidden, but they were never hidden from me. These were my feelings. They were the only ones I had. And of course I liked them. I began, very slowly, to hate the culture that wanted me to hate myself. But something else was happening. I knew if Mother found out she'd feel that she was in some way responsible. She'd be hurt and humiliated, as she felt about Daddy, and I didn't want to be the cause of that. Whatever I did, I didn't want to humiliate her. I never got to be like Cornelius, who was indifferent to them.

↔

Race Point Light

On May 17, 1954, just after eleven in the morning, when I was in ninth grade mechanical drawing class, a student walked in and called out: "Hey guys, the Supreme Court has just decided that all schools have to be integrated!" Everybody crowded around and started talking all at once. We imagined that tomorrow morning there would be crowds of Negroes out in front of the school trying to get in. We couldn't imagine what it would be like. I tried to think about all of us who were already in the room having to move over to make room for all these Negro children.

The Record that afternoon had a huge, three-line headline. "South Loses in Court. Segregation Must Go. Time to 'Mix' Put Off." The decision was in a case called *Brown v. Board of Education*. It was about a girl in Topeka, Kansas, who wanted to go to a white school. That afternoon the governor of South Carolina said *that the state would resist this assault on our way of life.* The State newspaper headline the next morning read, "SUPREME COURT OUTLAWS SCHOOL SEGREGATION." The Supreme Court did not say when this was supposed to happen, but it was to happen with "all deliberate speed." Everybody was already saying it wasn't going to happen soon.

I knew plenty of Negroes. Everybody I knew, knew Negroes. Everybody I knew had a Negro cook, as we did, and a Negro yard man, and the men who came and trimmed the trees were all Negroes. The cooks in the school were Negroes, and so were the janitors. My grandmother's best friend had two cooks, even though she lived by herself, and most of the construction workers who worked for my father were Negroes. But I didn't know any Negro children, although I think Effie, our cook, had children. She never mentioned them, and none of us ever asked. They had their own schools and playgrounds, churches, and places to go, and their own part of town. Until the guy told us in mechanical drawing class, I don't think any of us had ever thought that there would come a day when somebody would stop us from segregating the races. Already, in the paper that afternoon, people were talking about the mongrelization of the races. We were all going to end up brown, everybody said.

There was talk about constitutional limits and rights and responsibilities, about the growing power of the central government, and my parents talked about what Eisenhower would do.

"What can he do?"

"He has to enforce the Supreme Court decision."

"No he doesn't. Let the Court enforce its own decision. That's what Jackson said to Marshall, isn't it?" My father spoke with the authority of a man who has read history.

My parents talked about a second Reconstruction.

"There'll be federal troops stationed in the schools—"

"—and some soldier with a rifle in every schoolroom."

President Eisenhower said that it was now the law of the land.

When I went into the kitchen and saw Effie, I said, "Hi, Effie," and she responded the way she always did, "Good morning, Mr. Fair." I wondered what she was really thinking. She was friendly and respectful—and distant—and all the adults said you can't ever find out what a Negro is thinking.

Negroes can't be ladies and gentlemen. Just about all of my training at home had to do with learning to be refined and "cultivated," which was Mother's word for knowing who your ancestors are and all your cousins, for knowing different styles of furniture from the period before the Civil War, Sheraton and Hepplewhite and Duncan Phyfe and American Empire, and styles of houses, Greek Revival, Federal, and seventeenth century, and what are the right kinds of sterling silver and how you can tell sterling from plated silver across a crowded room, and after what hour of the day it is all right for a lady to bare her shoulders. Most of this was silly—Mother had a general inability to separate out what was important from what was unimportant—but some of it was useful.

It had seemed appropriate to me that my culture had segregated the races. Our kind of people are separated from the kind of people who were not our kind by the churches we go to, by the clothes we wear, the way we cut our hair, the houses we own, the books we read, the areas of town we live in, the organizations we belong to, by our politics, and most of all, by our language—the soothing, complimentary, blurred language we all use, in which both vowels and consonants are elided, and meaning is obscured. The distinction between Nigras and niggers, everyone says, is one of the class of the speaker. The fact that the very oldest members of my own family said *nigger* was not explained. My mother was always telling me how to compliment the other person over and over again during a conversation without ever repeating myself, and what subjects to avoid in conversation—sex, religion, politics, right and wrong, race, poverty, family squabbles, alcoholism, failure, and anything serious —how to talk so I didn't impinge on the other person and at the same time let the other person know what I was thinking. She would say, "Modulate your voice. Don't speak too loudly, and don't speak too forcefully. You are not supposed to emphasize your words. Everything is meant to flatter your listener. You are supposed to make the sound of your voice, as distinct from what you are saying, pleasant to the person you are speaking to."

Our complaint about what the Supreme Court had done did not have to do with racial hatred, it had to do with constitutional principles and historical movements, with the growing power of the central government, with a concern for the tone and level of culture, with tradition, the past, with carrying things on, with the kind of country we had created, with, even, the way God is worshipped and with God's plan for mankind. It was possible for me to see us as concerned with the large issues of society and them as merely concerned with selfish, thoughtless desires.

On the other hand, Cornelius, while he lived by the rules of the house, clearly didn't believe they applied to him when he was not around Mother. His take on what the Supreme Court had done was *fucking niggers*.

When I was seventeen, in 1956, I went to Europe with a group of students from student councils all around the country. A social studies teacher from my high school went with us, Charles Cook, who was the chaperone for six boys. On the first night, in a bar on ship, I got into a discussion with other students. It was the first time I had spent with people from outside the South, except for my trip to Elmira when my father was still drinking.

We sat in a booth and drank soda and talked. One of the others, a girl from Wisconsin, said, "In the South you are all just racists."

I was shocked. Nobody had ever said that to me before.

I felt myself to be under intense pressure. There were all these kids sitting around this table, and they were all looking at me to see what I was going to do. I said, I hoped with some dignity, "We're trying to protect the structure of our government, trying to protect States' Rights. We're trying to protect our way of life from the oppression of the federal government. I'm proud of my state and of what it is trying to do." It was what I had heard my father say.

But the thing bothered me. I didn't like it that other people saw it in a different way and that they came to the conclusion that I was a racist, that we were racists—Cornelius and I and our parents and my whole family. That implied we hated Negroes, and I didn't think we did, except maybe Cornelius and my mother. Besides, hatred did not have anything to do with the structure of the government or States' Rights or Locke or Jefferson or the image of us on the lawn at Wespanee. But there were parts of the argument I didn't understand. I wrote Mother. "Why is intermarriage between races so bad?"

She wrote back and carefully laid out her answer, even numbering her points. "(1) Do not say that the Negro race is an inferior race. Say that the Negro race, only three generations from slavery, have not reached the educational and cultural level of the white race, and wherever they have been mixed (such as schools in Washington) the level of attainment has dropped. Educationally it sets the white race back about 100 years. (2) Whenever an advanced race marries with a race which is culturally backward, a mongrel race results. And nowhere in the history of the world has a mongrel race of people reached a high state of civilization. (3) We are in favor of giving the Negro every advantage but in the framework of his own race. We feel he is not ready to compete with the white people." She also wrote, "Keep your head and discuss this as little as possible. The people from other sections of the country do not understand because they do not have the thousands that we have—dirty, smelly, uneducated, etc. And all the talking in the world won't change them." I knew where this letter came from. She had gotten my letter with my question and had talked to my father about it. The points that were numbered came from him. The comment at the end about smells came from her. This was bitter.

On that trip, which lasted six weeks, we went to England, Belgium and Holland, Germany, Austria, Switzerland, Italy, and France. Most of the countries had been bombed in the war, and there were great swaths of bombed-out ground and ruins of bombed buildings. Across from the Houses of Parliament in London there was a big hole behind a high wooden fence where there had been a big building before the war. You could drive for blocks through downtown Cologne and see nothing but war ruins. A subject of continuous conversation among us was the Nazis and what they had done to the Jews. I saw the connection between anti-Semitism and

racism—my mother's and my father's racism—and saw the
connection between the Nazis' legal justification for the Holocaust
and my own culture's constitutional arguments in favor of
segregation. No one at home ever talked about lynching, about the
real effects of segregation on children, or about slavery and what it
really was. It was all like *Song of the South*.

One of the boys on the trip—he was in my cabin on the ship
going over and coming back, and we usually shared hotel rooms—
was big and very strong, and played football. He carried huge leather
suitcases that weighed more than I did. I watched him dress and
undress every day, and, like many jocks, he used a heavy after-shave
lotion that gave off a sharp, sweet odor that lingered around him all
during the day. He reminded me of Russell Ford and the odor of his
hair tonic that followed him down the hall in junior high school. I
kept my feelings for him hidden. My letters home from Europe were
like my letters home from summer camp—eager and
accommodating. I wrote about the things I was seeing, the
difficulties we had in traveling, and money, but not about the big guy
with the leather bags, and after I got my mother's letter about
interracial marriage, I never wrote about those things again, either. I
wanted to talk to someone about this stuff, but the only person to talk
to was Mr. Cook, and I didn't know how he felt about it all, so I
didn't mention it.

On the ship coming back, another boy, Bryan Harvey, and I went
up on the deck one night after dinner and took a tour. Bryan was tall
and nice looking and friendly. He was one of the boys that everybody
wanted to be around. He seemed to care about people. At one point,
we stopped and leaned on the railing, the wind blowing in our hair,
the boat making a low rumble underneath us.

"Tell me about the South," Bryan said, as if he were asking me to
tell him about some land on an unexplored coast of South America.

So I told him. "It's warm, and palmetto trees rustle in the wind,
and people are polite to one another. I think people in the South dress
more formally than people elsewhere. We dress up. We care about
the sensibilities of other people, about their comfort." I was speaking
slowly, giving him pictures I had in my mind. "Mother, when she
serves coffee, gets Effie, our cook, to bring out the tray with a big
silver coffee pot and my grandmother's silver cream and sugar that
she got when she got married at the beginning of the twentieth

century, and she serves them. Tell me how you are, she'll say. And then she'll say, Oh, how wonderful. How extremely wonderful. Or she'll say, Dear, how did you stand it? I think people in the South speak slowly because nothing is hurried. People take their time to savor life. The fine texture of it. White linen and mahogany and silver. The weather, the heat, makes people move more slowly. People have lunch in the middle of the day at one p.m., and they have a highball beforehand, and drinks again in the late afternoon, after a long day. People in the South like long meals with big desserts served in cut glass bowls that came from Grandmother, and they like long stories that began in 1873 and didn't end until last week. They love it when the punch line comes 37 years after the start of the joke. They are all great theoretical thinkers—they love to talk about the law and the Constitution—and they like to talk about manners. Manners are a very complicated thing, and we think they are very important, more important, maybe, than the rest of the country thinks they are." I went on, the sounds of the ship and the water making me raise my voice a little, and the lights of the ship creating an island of pale light around us on the water. There was no moon. It was as much the way I wanted it to be as it was the way it was.

At length, Bryan asked, "But what about segregation?"

That. I waited a few moments before saying anything. "We have always gotten along harmoniously, since the beginning. Each of us has our place. We are polite to one another. Can you understand that?" I didn't know if he did.

And after we came home, we didn't stay in touch. I don't know if I really believed we have been polite to one another. The connection between racism, between hatred, and our way of life was still new to me. I was aware, when I was speaking to Bryan, that I was editing what I was saying, emphasizing the gauzy beauty of the South and not talking about the difficult things. I wondered if Bryan knew that I knew what I was doing.

I came home from Europe embarrassed about segregation. I had discovered on the trip that there were many many more people who thought my family and I were racists than who didn't, and it was new to me to feel myself part of a minority. I hadn't even known until then that a minority felt differently. Now I realized that one reason I thought the way I did was that I was white. If I were not white, I

54

would have different ideas. I began to see that my ideas were ideas typical of a Southern white boy with my position in society. I didn't much like discovering that. My blurry vision of the South, even if it were true, was not even a description of the South. It was a description of a class, one class of one race, out of several, in one part of the country, and I was embarrassed at how narrow it must have seemed to Bryan.

It was embarrassing now to go into the kitchen where Effie was to get a glass of milk. It was impossible just to ignore her, get my milk, and say, "Hi, Effie," as I was leaving. The whole system—I realized for the first time that there was a whole system—worked as long as it worked everywhere. There were Negroes around us all the time, everywhere, in the kitchen, in the yard, delivering things to the house, in the kitchen at school. Everybody knew they were there (a friend of Mother's, showing off her new kitchen and its modern appliances, said, "I don't care how many buttons there are to punch, I want a black hand punching them.") and accepted that they were there, and ignored them. But if there was one area where segregation didn't function, as it no longer functioned in the public schools, then we were in the predicament of ignoring the reality of Negroes like Effie most of the time—but then having to accept her reality in that one area. Effie in the kitchen—who had been reduced to a black hand—was a whole person, suddenly, with rights guaranteed by the Supreme Court. And even if the Supreme Court decision didn't apply to anything but public schools, the fact that it applied there meant that, in my mind, it had to be applied to everything else, everywhere else, the bus, the lunch counters downtown, where they lived. Why should they ride in the back of the bus if they could sit next to you in the eighth grade? Why couldn't Negroes move in next door? Why couldn't a Negro man date a white woman if he could go to school with her?

The phrase, over and over again, was *our way of life*. My mother would get a far-away look in her eye when she spoke of it—"our *precious* Southern way of life." The phrase covered everything, from the monument to Confederate women on the grounds of the State House to the cook in the kitchen. It meant the way we do things in South Carolina. The way we talk about race, about miscegenation—or, as our Senator was always saying, *the amalgamation of the races*—about class, and about the disposition of public funds. It meant all the decisions about how the state is governed—and by whom. It meant the whole system whereby there is an us and a them. It was a system that assumed that the past happened a certain way, that there was a past that everyone, the whites and the Negroes, agreed on that defined our respective roles in the settlement of this country. I realized that the past had changed and that my family and I, our race, were not at the center of the past any longer. I knew that what had been going on since the Supreme Court decision was the dispossession of the past of whites like me. I experienced a severe vertigo, for it meant the loss of my future, too, as well as the loss of my past. My life would be different from what I had thought. In the last years of high school, I realized that there was nothing around me that was firm and stable.

I had loved South Carolina, the romance of it, the live oak trees, Wespanee, the image I had in my mind of us in a landscape, the large white house in the distance at the head of a vast lawn, and our family taking our ease under the shade of a mulberry tree, a vast English garden. The images I had in my head were all from the low country, and the plantation was a rice plantation, the plantation workers— who I had to recognize now were enslaved persons—hovering around carrying trays and holding parasols for the white ladies against the sun. The romance of the image had been increased by the fact that it was all gone anyhow. The Civil War had ended all that. I had begun to see that this image—the white house, the vast lawn, the trees, the black slaves—took on different meanings depending on which side of it you looked at. It was one thing when you looked at the side with the white people, sitting under a tree, and another thing when you looked at the slaves carrying the trays of food and cool drinks. Or, looking at the detail produced one picture, and looking at the whole thing produced another. Life became more complex.

There was the little girl. The kid at the heart of the *Brown v. Board of Education* decision was named Linda Brown. Even if her presence upset the beautiful landscape I had in my head, she wasn't a danger in herself. I didn't know anybody who was on her side—not in South Carolina—because all anybody could talk about was the big black bucks and lovely refined Southern white ladies, but she didn't deserve to have to fight for her rights alone. Somebody here in South Carolina should be on her side. I didn't want to be on the side of people who hated other people, and it was inescapable that what I saw in the pictures of people demonstrating against the Supreme Court—they were on the front pages of the newspapers every day— were the faces of people who hated. In church, we never heard anything about it. Trinity was known around the state for the beauty of its ceremonies, its music and choir, the opulence of its building, and I had seen it all my life as a place where, if there were a God, he would be worshipped this way, with the most beautiful poetry and prose the English language had to offer, in its *Book of Common Prayer*. Every Sunday, we recited the General Confession.

> Almighty and most merciful Father; We have erred, and strayed from thy ways like lost sheep. We have followed too much the devices and desires of our own hearts. We have offended against thy holy laws. We have left undone those things which we ought to have done; And we have done those things which we ought not to have done; And there is no health in us.

And yet the subject everybody was talking about was never mentioned there. There were rumors of an attempt to integrate the churches, but this was never mentioned by the rector from the pulpit, and what people whispered was *over my dead body*. Even without leadership from the church, the crisis came home, into the Sunday School, where it came up in classes, and in school, where it came up in Social Studies classes and History classes—What does it mean to be created equal?—and even, sometimes, in English classes where I spent most of my time.

I got in regular arguments with my father, who was always reading something to me out of some magazine and then saying, "Don't you think that's crazy?" I would say "No, sir." And then we'd go at it. Mother said my father was on a dry drunk. He'd be angry and defensive at the same time. "Don't you think they're trying to ruin the country?"

"No, I don't. I think they're trying to get their rights."

"Their rights are for separate schools."

"Their separate schools aren't equal schools."

"You're trying to rewrite the Constitution."

"No." I was absolute. "We have to rewrite the past."

My father became angry and left the table. Mother complained about us fighting. "I just want everybody to be pleasant. And here you've gone and ruined my lovely meal."

"I've ruined it?"

"How could you be so rude to your father! He loves you so."

She wanted us to be friendly and warm to one another. She wanted me to be respectful to her and to Daddy, and she deserved that. When she said, I try so hard, it was clear to me that she did try hard, teaching school and selling World Book and making silk lampshades and cleaning the house and working in her garden and making clothes for herself, but it wasn't enough to make us a happy family, and her bad luck was that somewhere in her mind, she knew we weren't a happy family. She knew Cornelius didn't pay any attention to her or my father. And she didn't know what to do about Cornelius and me to make sure we didn't turn out to be our father. She kept saying, "There's no alcoholism in my family." I thought she saw us becoming more and more like him every day—I didn't know just how that was happening, but I thought she thought it was happening—and it must have driven her crazy. She thought, if we only had more money, but that was impossible. Neither she nor my father knew how to make more money, so she was stuck with the only thing she knew: she could make us more polite. Even I had learned by the last years of high school that there was a pretty limited market for the kind of man she wanted to turn me into. I also knew that when she said, He loves you so, she was manipulating me, using my love for her or for him as a way of preventing me from disagreeing with her about race. I love you so. And to disagree about race was to disagree about what had happened during 300 years of our family's history.

And yet. And yet. When I saw her start to cry—when she said, I try so hard—there was nothing I wanted to do more than to please her. Mother still wore her hair the same way she had always worn it since I was a kid—in that great swooping forties style in which the long hair was pulled up to the back and wrapped over a "rat," a style her sister had abandoned years ago. This irritated me, and even when I felt most tender toward her, I looked at her hair and saw how determined she was to have her own way—how inflexible she was—and it both shocked me and frightened me. She was so tiny and quick, like a squirrel, but incredibly strong—she would wear her hair the way she wanted, even if, by that time, it was 10 years out of date —and I thought, in a contest of wills between us, it would be a miracle if I won. In fact, I didn't ever think I would win in a contest of wills with her. The only way I could get my way would be to leave her and to leave South Carolina. I didn't know, then, exactly what we seemed to be fighting over—that I was somehow not living up to one or the other of the demands she made on me, not writing letters often enough, not being dressed the way she thought was proper, not having spoken to this or that friend of hers somewhere, not agreeing with them that they were not racists—but I knew that I needed more freedom from her, and she resisted. She was unable to say, *You are growing up fine*. She was suspicious of me, afraid that, even in the midst of some triumph, I was going to go bad wrong. She suspected that I was capable of going bad wrong. The doctors had told her that the tendency toward alcoholism could be inherited, and she suspected. I did not have the same respect for her family that I had once had, hers and my father's family. It was also, I thought, because she felt men were somehow doomed to fail her. My father, Cornelius, me. I thought she felt we didn't live up to her father.

And then, of course, I liked boys. I wanted to please her, but I couldn't, ever. And, knowing how my culture wanted me to despise myself, I wasn't sure I wanted to please her. This subject was one that, no matter what the consequences, she was unable even to think of talking about.

We were in her bedroom, a cluttered room with bits and pieces of her sewing everywhere and large pieces of walnut furniture that she had inherited or scrounged from relatives. She sat in a small rocker, and I was on the bed. I did please her, too. I encouraged her to talk about what she could.

"I don't know what to do about my shoes. I have made this wonderful dress out of a beautiful piece of silk—a remnant I found— and now I need shoes to go with it, and I can wear nothing but these —" She gestured to her heeled, lace-up shoes, which she wore because of a foot condition that required that she wear heeled shoes with firm support over the instep. "—these look so awful."

"Oh, I don't think so, Mother. I think—"

"Don't you think so?"

To tell the truth, I didn't know. She had worn heavy, lace-up shoes all my life, and it was difficult to see her shoes and compare them to the shoes other women wore and to see them as other people must have seen them. I supposed they were clunky. But I didn't want to hurt her.

"You have beautiful legs."

"Oh, do you think so?" She put out her leg and turned it from side to side.

"You have beautiful ankles, and beautiful calves."

She lifted her skirt a little. "Do you really think so?"

"Yes, ma'm."

"I have short tendons, the doctor said, and so I have to wear these shoes, and my feet hurt so if I don't wear shoes that give good support, yet they make me look so old, so—"

She didn't finish.

I tried to think of something I could say about her shoes that would make her feel better.

"I don't think, frankly, that people notice them, Mother. You've been wearing them for so long, I think people are accustomed to them and don't notice."

"Do you really think I have pretty legs?"

"Yes, ma'm."

I was aware that she put me in the position of having to flatter her.

↔

I spent the summer reading. Other boys, in the summer before they went away to college, worked to save money, but I read. My father wanted me to read. My father also had refused to allow me to apply for a job at college—one in which I could earn money for the expenses of living away from home—because, he said, "You should spend all your time studying, don't you think?" Having had experience with this, I knew that, in addition to my father's stated reasons for my not working, there was something else: my father's sense of his class. Working during the summer or during the school year meant I needed to work, which meant that my father was not earning enough to provide me with a college education, and people would know. It was silly, and it encouraged me in a class-consciousness I should not have had, but it was there, and no one spoke of it. I had become accustomed to these things that were not spoken of.

We could not speak of what slavery really was, the enslavement of human beings. I came to believe that we couldn't really be Christians—couldn't get into the kingdom of heaven—believing and saying the things we believed, yet I could never bring myself to actually say, You know, I think you and my father are damned to all eternity for the stuff you believe about race. It would have been cruel. It would have been unkind, to so destroy their illusions of their superiority. Unkindness was always a barrier to telling the truth, for the truth is always, it seems, unkind.

For them to be so wrong was unthinkable. And that was another thing I came to understand over the summer before I went to college. In my culture, there were things so awful as to be unthinkable. My parents stayed in their marriage because there was no way out. They gave reasons—I love him, I promised him—but I knew that the real reason was that divorce was unthinkable. My parents and other members of my family could not think that divorce was an option. There was some failure in their brains that made this thought unthinkable. That they were going to hell was unthinkable.

And, of course, homosexuality was unthinkable. Which meant not only that they had never given it a moment's real thought in their whole lives, but that they couldn't. They couldn't conceive of it. They didn't know where it came from, didn't know who did it, didn't know what it meant, had no thoughts, had only fear of the unknown, fear, ignorance, hatred, and a desire to comfort themselves with the assurance that we don't need to know anything about that. Our lives here are so perfect that that will never come to disturb us. That, whatever it is, will never arrive here, among us, here in Columbia, South Carolina. I knew that the way I felt about the arms of men was powerful and clear, and nobody else knew anything about it because they were unable to formulate such thoughts.

As part of this, I began to realize that we tell ourselves stories—not fibs, I don't mean that, but stories, like the ones in novels—which make sense of our lives. In my family, and in a lot of families like mine in the South, we told ourselves that many of the soldiers who had fought for the Stuart kings—these cavaliers—had come to America at the end of the seventeenth century, and, being aristocrats themselves, had established an aristocracy here, a class of refined gentlemen and ladies who peopled the plantation aristocracy, and it was these people who had been the forebears of the people I was descended from. This narrative that we told ourselves—there are actually many versions of this narrative, some more comprehensive than others—explained why we couldn't talk about some things and why we couldn't think about some other things. And it explained to me why my feelings so often seemed so confused. There was no place in the great narrative we told ourselves for a boy who felt as I did.

↔

My mother was sitting at her end of the sofa, sewing, a strong light beside her, to which she held up her work so she could see. "I don't know. I've tried everything I know how to do." She stopped for a moment and put the end of the thread in her mouth so she could thread the needle. "Your brother doesn't seem to care about anything we care about. He goes to school dressed like he lives in the mill village. He wears blue jeans! I've told him I won't have it, that he can't leave the house looking like that, but he just looks at me and walks out, pulling the door behind him. His friends are all toughs. I am embarrassed about him, to be seen with him, his hair is so long. It's hard to hold up my head around this town, with him and the way he acts. His grades are so poor he won't be able to get into any graduate school—law school is out, and medicine, and teaching— and he doesn't care. And your father won't do anything about it. He doesn't even want to talk about it. I think it is too painful for him. All they can talk about is football. But you know your father doesn't really care about football. He likes to read, and that's why he likes to talk to you so much, why he likes to talk about the books you are reading in school. He loves you. He thinks you have the opportunities that he didn't have when he was your age. We came up through the depression, and it scarred us for life. But you! You are smart and you can make something of yourself. You could make him so happy, if you would, just by being kind to him and talking to him. You are very attractive and handsome, and you could make me so proud of you—I'd be so grateful—if you were to do well, grow up and make us proud of you."

She sewed for a few minutes, then she put down her thimble.

She said, "I do so worry about your drinking." She was bringing up a dangerous subject, and she didn't look at me. She looked down at her sewing.

I didn't want to be reproached. They had no reason to complain.

"After all the pain and heartache it has caused us—"

"I'm OK, Mother. I don't drink that much."

"—are you careful?"

"Yes, ma'm."

"But I would just die if anything happened to you, the way it happened to your father. His drinking ruined my life. My father said he would support me the rest of my life if I would leave him, but I promised in sickness and in health—"

"It must have been very hard for you."

Her face crumpled up and tears came to her eyes. "You don't know how it's been for me—"

"He has been difficult—" The word was hers.

"I worry so about you. You never stop being rude to me. You are just like your father. You get so angry, I think you're going to lose your mind."

I had heard this before. She said that, when either of her sons got angry, she was afraid we were losing our sanity.

My closest friend on the faculty was Mr. Cook, who had gone with us to Europe. Mr. Cook was energetic and enthusiastic, and he liked me. He had reddish brown wavy hair that he parted on the side, and a piece of it hung down over one eyebrow. He was smiling and laughing all the time, but his face had the lines across his forehead that made him look tense and in pain, even when he was laughing. He taught social studies and was the faculty sponsor for the student council, so I saw him every day. Once, after a student council meeting—I was a very busy guy, on the student council, a member of the debate team, editor of the school newspaper, an officer of the statewide student newspaper organization—people were standing around talking, some were leaving the room, and I was still sitting in a chair at the table, talking to somebody. Mr. Cook came over and joined the conversation. He stood behind me, talking to both of us, and then he put his hands on my shoulders and gripped them with his fingers. He kneaded the muscle of my shoulders, as if he were giving me a massage. "You're certainly tense!" He smiled in his characteristic way, as if he were in deep pain, and kneaded my shoulders more. "Relax!" I might be tense, but I knew what Mr. Cook was doing. The boy I was talking to watched all this, as if he knew what was going on too. I thought he expected me to do something, but I didn't.

People used to say that homosexuals are a security risk, but they haven't said that for a long time. Homosexuals are sick. I read about it in the magazines my father brought home from the Capitol News Stand. They did not develop properly, and the family dynamic that ought to produce a heterosexual boy instead produced a boy stuck in an earlier, homosexual phase, eternally thirteen, in love with the scout master, whose name was George Southwyck. The failure to develop was the result of a failure of the parents—a father distant and abstracted by work who paid no attention and a mother who paid too much attention, who, missing her husband's attention, turned to her sons for the respect and affection she got no where else, who smothered them with her affection. I read this and recognized it. So. Sometimes I was very angry with my parents for fucking me up so. But, just as often, I knew that my culture really blamed me. They didn't think that anything that had gone wrong with my parents excused me. My culture, which I had loved, hated me. My parents didn't like Jews or Catholics or Negroes. There was no reason to believe that they would like a son who was sick and who wanted to suck cock. Cornelius was very clear about it. Fucking fruits. Perverts. Well, I knew how I had felt when I felt Paul Connors' arms. My feelings might be screwed up. They might actually be sick. But they were mine, and I liked them. I had to hide them, but they were fine. I liked the way my feelings felt.

In 1957, when I graduated from high school, every state in the union considered same-sex sex a crime. In South Carolina, the penalty was five years in prison or a $500 fine.

The last week of school, when the yearbooks were handed out, I discovered that I had been elected Most Likely to Succeed by my senior class.

↔

Sewanee was called "the Mountain," and named the University of the South, in Sewanee, Tennessee. It was an Episcopal men's college founded in 1858, small, with 1300 students on a campus called "the

Domain" that comprised 10,000 acres of mountaintop on the edge of the Cumberland Plateau. Things were patterned on Oxford and Cambridge. It was to have been a collection of colleges, but the Civil War intervened and in the end only one undergraduate college and the Divinity School were founded. The principal architecture was Gothic, the students wore academic gowns over coats and ties, and there was an intimate relationship between faculty and students. The Domain was out in the middle of the mountains, 90 miles from Nashville and 110 miles from Chattanooga.

On the advice of my parents and school counselors, I never considered a school outside the South aside from Princeton, which had always attracted Southerners, or a big state school anywhere, or anything on the West Coast, or any other kind of school. I was accepted into both Sewanee and Princeton, but I couldn't afford Princeton—I think I would like to have gone there—so I found myself going to Sewanee. Its goal, I thought, was to turn out polished, literate, sophisticated gentlemen to staff the universities, churches, court houses, and legislatures of the South. It might be, I thought, that Sewanee had been able to salvage whatever of the South was salvageable, and that the burden of being from the South would not turn out to be so heavy after all.

Many boys from South Carolina went to Sewanee. Shepard Cox, my friend from Columbia. Several cousins from Columbia and Charleston, and Patrick Endicott, my parent's friend who was on the faculty of St Luke's, the Divinity School. It was, I thought, going to be much like home. I didn't have any goals except to grow up and to become polished and in some way learned—and perhaps to write. I still had the image of myself as an Enlightenment gentleman on the lawn at Wespanee. I thought the point in Sewanee's being so far back in the mountains—it had the air of a medieval monastery—was to encourage our study and to intensify our pursuit of wisdom.

Sewanee—the village and the school were indistinguishable— was reached from the valley floor by a two-lane highway that wound up through the coves on the side of the mountain, high rock outcroppings on one side, trees and the valley on the other. On the top of the plateau, I was in the middle of a small medieval village, a couple of Gothic towers, arches, and stone buildings, students and professors everywhere, many wearing tattered black academic gowns. The largest building was the library and tower, at that time the highest building on the Domain. Down University Avenue was St Luke's and a series of smaller stone buildings, the fraternity houses. Off University Avenue were side streets, English country lanes, where faculty members lived.

We unpacked, fraternities rushed, classes started. I took English, French, Political Science, History, and Philosophy. I was greatly excited on my first day of classes, when all the students were out on campus together for the first time. The walkways were crowded with us, and the principal classroom buildings were noisy with our talk. I got into a prestigious fraternity. I was pleased—exhilarated—that the active members treated me kindly and seemed pleased to have me. The older men were good looking, smart, fashionable, and thoughtful. Although there were only a few from South Carolina, compared to the numbers from the other Southern states, I assumed all of us came from the same world I came from: some version of Trinity Church and The Assembly. That is, I assumed we all shared a class.

Since the school was in the mountains, there were two principal weather conditions—brilliant sunshine and fog. Late in the afternoon and early evening were my favorite times of day, and the fog came in all seasons. The place seemed to me to be otherworldly, timeless, aged. The architecture, even though it was not more than one hundred years old, looked back a thousand years and was distinctly different from the neo-classic architecture of principal buildings in Southern cities. Groups of men appeared out of the fog in their ties and tweed jackets, talking to each other and laughing at something. Everything about Sewanee suggested tradition and the ancient customs of England, gentility and learning. Every view spoke of privilege. I felt at home at Sewanee.

I wrote home and told my father about my classes—we began with *The Iliad* and, in Political Science, with the British constitution —because I knew that would please him. I wrote about the other students my parents would know, second and third cousins from Camden and Charleston and Beaufort and Georgetown, or sons of their friends, about paying a call on Patrick Endicott, and about a faculty member they didn't know but who was a relative of people they did know. I didn't join the fraternity my father and his friends wanted me to join, but he understood that Sewanee was a different school and that I should join the best one at Sewanee. Even

Cornelius answered my letter to him—he was at Carolina, and, I think, failing—and proposed that he come up to visit. All of them seemed pleased with me.

At the same time, I discovered that I enjoyed my classes. The professor asked questions—often asked me a question—and I was able to answer him in a way that pleased both of us. I was able to prepare for my classes every day, and I enjoyed my homework. But it was in my written work, from the beginning, that I most often showed what I could do. I liked writing, and when I got the papers back, the professors had written, "Very Fine!" "Excellent!" "Very Fine!" "Superb!" "A Very Interesting Idea!" I got the very highest grades and, of course, wrote my parents about all of them.

The other thing was something I didn't write them about—it was too personal—and it was how pleased I was, beginning with the fact that my fraternity was always said to be among the best on campus, and it was often said to be the best of them all, that I seemed to have found a place at Sewanee. In high school, I felt as if my social life was a series of games, none of it real or meaningful. Now at Sewanee, men seemed to be knocking on my door all the time. We talked about the literature we were studying, about our professors, and our families, about how we felt about what we were doing. Sometimes, in the midst of all this—it was so new to me and so unusual—I thought it was all a false success, that somebody was going to say to me, Oh, no, you thought we were serious! Us? You?! Oh, no. You were never one of us. (Laughter.) We were just pulling your leg. And then other times I thought I was destined for some great success and that the steps I was taking now were just the beginning of some long and glorious road.

Two things intruded.

On the front pages every morning, from my first day at Sewanee, were stories and pictures of the integration of the Little Rock, Arkansas, school system. During the summer before I was to arrive in Sewanee in September, the Capital Citizens Council and the Mother's League of Central High School in Little Rock had been formed and had filed a suit on August 27, 1957, seeking a temporary injunction against the integration of Central High School. The injunction was granted, but just as students arrived at the high school on August 30 a federal judge nullified it. Two days later, Governor Orval Faubus called out the Arkansas National Guard to surround the high school to preserve the peace and avert violence that might be caused, he said, by "extremists" who were coming to Little Rock "in caravans." The next day, the federal judge ordered desegregation to start the next day. On the September 4, nine Negro students attempted to enter Central High School but were turned away by the National Guard. On September 9, the National Council of Church Women issued a statement opposing segregation and called for a prayer service for September 12. On September 20, the day before we were to arrive in Sewanee, the federal judge ruled that Faubus had used the troops to prevent integration, not to quell violence, and the Governor was forced to remove the troops so that integration could proceed.

At Sewanee, we—the white upper-class males who arrived on Saturday, September 21, 1957—were in our tiny hamlet in the mountains of the Cumberland Plateau in the central region of Tennessee and heard, as if by distant rumbling, what was happening in Little Rock, in the foothills of the Quachita Mountains on the other side of the Mississippi. From the safety of our 10,000 acre Domain, we heard of the open danger of the Central High School campus for the kids surrounded by National Guard troops with drawn rifles. I read the papers about Governor Faubus and his belief that if he didn't have the troops there, there would be violence, and then I went to class, where, in the safety of my classroom in our stone Gothic building, we opened our copies of *The Iliad* and studied the tale of the wrath of the epic hero.

We did not think it was bizarre. I went to prayer services myself every day at noon after morning classes, and many of us went to evensong. The services were notable in that they took place in an academic setting, and, often, when the procession started down the center aisle of the Chapel, the crucifer and choir led a line of sumptuously robed academics, each in the academic gown and hood of his university and degree—brilliant scarlets and purples, rich shimmering blacks with stripes of black velvet or gold embroidery on the billowing sleeves. The congregation was composed almost entirely of men, and the hymns, pitched for men's voices, rumbled and swelled with power and majesty.

The Chapel, which had been completed in stone up to the bottom of the clerestory windows and then roofed with wood beams before the Civil War, was finished in stone at the end of my Freshman year, in time for the Centennial. The result was opulent and impressive. Set into the plaster of the walls were marble plaques honoring the memory of various Episcopal bishops and Confederate generals, some of whose granddaughters still reigned at Sewanee as house mothers and presided at table in the Dining Hall. The *Prayer for the University*, written in self-conscious seventeenth-century prose, beseeching God to raise up a "never-failing succession of benefactors" for the university, was read at every service. The services ignored the trauma happening in the next state west of us and to the race next to us. I studied *The Iliad,* read about the race riots in Arkansas, and spent time at the fraternity house drinking. While the Negroes in Little Rock struggled to get a toe-hold in society, we were studying how we were going to get to the top from our present position one rung down.

The other thing that intruded on my evident success came as a surprise. We were required to go to chapel every noon—it was a church school—but we were not required to worship. The Episcopal Church was too worldly to think that it could force salvation on students, consequently there were always, sitting in bunches in the back of the Chapel as the service progressed, students reading the newspaper, ostentatiously disinterested. I discovered that was amusing—and attractive—and I joined them. I was eighteen years old, and I liked the idea of risking damnation and not caring. I knew what the church believed about homosexuality, and I knew the church said I would go to hell.

But whether the church was real or God was real, the sex they condemned was certainly real. At the time, we were reading the *Divine Comedy* and the story of Paolo and Francesca and their torments. The winds that blew Paolo and Francesca about the second circle of Hell also blew at Sewanee, disrupting and even driving the campus intellectual climate.

We were required to take physical education twice a week. I discovered that no one cared what students did in PE after the initial session of organized calisthenics. There were still forty-five minutes to kill, and off the main gym was a weight room where one student worked out on the weights shirtless. He was my height—5'6"— blond, husky, with well-defined and bulging pectorals adorned by pointed nipples of deepest pink. I discovered that other students had found this student working out shirtless, and the weight room was crowded with motionless men sitting on benches, leaning against walls, astride bars of various kinds like crows on a power line, their lidded eyes fixed on the shirtless torso of the one student actually using the weights. It didn't matter, apparently, that when I crossed the room to leave, my erection poked against my gym shorts for everyone to see. I grinned to think of it, being damned because of it.

One pair of roommates—the dark-haired son of a bishop who looked like a basketball player with horned-rimmed glasses and a sharp-nosed, high-browed intellectual poet who sounded like T. S. Eliot and was president of his fraternity—had shared rooms for four years, and, when I visited them down the hall from where I lived, the sharp-nosed poet said, just as the dark-haired basketball player walked in from the bathroom moist and wrapped only in a towel, "Many men here on the Mountain think Bob and I are lovers, but we aren't. We're just really, really close." The dark-haired man stood still for a moment, looking back and forth at me and his roommate, then went to the drawer and got his underwear and went into the bathroom again to dress. I saw that the possibility of sex between men had been raised and then denied. I had never known two young men my age to bring up the possibility of sex between them, even if only to deny it. I thought that at Sewanee I might at last discover what this thing was all about.

At Sewanee, at night, there was always someone asking me to do something with him—drink a beer, go to our favorite tavern, study—and there were always people in my dorm room. I was pleased to be with these guys. They were good-looking, smart, studious, athletic. They wanted to be with me—the call across the campus was, "Hey, Shaw, wait up, and I'll walk with you"—and they were the kind of man I wanted to be with. It felt warm, comfortable, being with men so attractive and so smart. One night I was drinking with these men when somebody, apropos of nothing, said that last year the Dean of the College had expelled several queer men, a purge that was hushed up and that consequently no one knew much about.

Then late one afternoon another first-year student, a member of my fraternity, a relative, and I were walking across the campus toward the Chapel. He was disturbed. "It's my roommate," he said.

I was friends with both of them.

70

"I found him looking at me—in the men's room. I was sitting there, and then I looked up and found him looking at me. He's queer."

"Looking at you? What do you mean?"

"Looking at me! He was hanging over the divider between the stalls. I can't stand that, being in the same room with him looking at me when I am getting dressed."

"How long have you known?"

"I just discovered. I'm going home and tell my dad."

He was telling me, so he didn't think I was one of them.

I asked Patrick about it. Patrick—Frederick Patrick Endicott—whose parents and my parents knew one another, and who himself had been rector of an Episcopal church in Columbia when I was younger, now was at Sewanee teaching at St Luke's. He and his wife lived in the village with their young children. He had the reputation of being a scholar—Patrick was learned, and he should know about these things and wouldn't be shocked by anything—and I wanted to explore what he knew. We were in Patrick's office in St Luke's. I think what I wanted from him was a sophisticated understanding of homosexuality—something beyond queer, and something more nuanced than what the church seemed to put out—that would make it possible for me to think well of myself.

I opened by not being honest. "What do you know about homosexuality?" I was aware that I wanted him to be honest with me, but I wasn't telling him why I wanted to know.

Patrick leaned back in his chair and told me stories of soldiers. "They were out drinking, and they were sitting next to each other in the booth, you know, and one of them put his hand on the thigh of the other one, for a few seconds, and the one whose thigh had been touched realized he liked it. They were far from home, and far from their families, and all around them everything was unfamiliar. They were lonely for what they knew." Patrick was not himself a beautiful man. He had what Aunt Maury had called, after hearing a sermon he gave, "a weak mouth," by which she meant it perpetually drew up on the right side and that it had no lips and not much chin. "So the soldier," Patrick went on, "whose thigh had been touched wondered about it, because he liked it. He wondered why he liked getting touched by the other soldier. He wondered, even, if he were a homosexual." Patrick grimaced. "But that is not what that meant, at all." Patrick's office walls were painted an off white, an ivory color, and the woodwork had been left natural, in the manner of buildings built in the late nineteenth century. On three walls there were bookcases that were as tall as a tall man, all filled with books on church history. His desk, like the desks of many academics, was piled with student papers and blue books and heavy scholarly works. "The soldier was lonely, you see. And the touch of the other soldier's hand was warm—even intimate—and the soldier had missed that warmth and closeness, there far from home in the Army. His liking the touch of the other soldier's hand did not mean that he was a homosexual. It meant, rather, that he was human."

I listened to him as he went on. Patrick was twelve or sixteen years or so older than I—perhaps older than that, it was difficult to tell—and I respected him and admired what he had achieved. In many ways, I wanted to be like him, have an office like his, with the books and the papers about everywhere, and a wife in the village with our children. I liked the off-hand casualness with which he dealt with grave subjects. I didn't interrupt him with questions or comments.

Then Patrick spoke more generally of homosexuals, who didn't want to be considered as good as heterosexuals. "They want to be considered better than heterosexuals." He smiled his wry smile, one side of his mouth pulled up. "And that can never be."

So. I walked back across campus just at dusk from St Luke's, where evensong was sung, to the Chapel and the Dining Hall beyond, soothed—and confused—by my conversation with Patrick. Patrick hadn't asked me why I wanted to know about homosexuality. He had seemed to think it a normal thing for a young man to wonder about. He seemed to be trying to tell me that it was OK if I were out drinking beer and somebody put his hand on my thigh—it was OK to like it—but he seemed also to be saying that it was not OK to do anything about it. And he did say, emphatically, that being a homosexual was not as good as being heterosexual. He agreed with my relative whose roommate was queer. Walking across campus just at the time of day the campus was at its most romantic, I found the whole thing left me feeling disturbed and uneasy. For I knew that if I were a soldier far from home and was in a tavern and another soldier put his hand on my thigh and it was warm and intimate and I liked it, it would be because I was a human who liked the warm touch of men. It might be me who put his hand on the thigh of the soldier next to me. I was disappointed in Patrick. The first time I had had a real conversation on this subject with an adult, I discovered that I knew more than Patrick knew. The campus, at its most romantic, the Gothic tower standing above the trees, was hot with the lust for each other of beautiful young men. I knew that. Yet it was hidden, furtive —*we are just really really close*—and Patrick said it was not as good as the lust of men for women. The university motto, which was reproduced everywhere, was taken from Psalm 133. *Ecce quam bonum et quam iucundum habitare fratres in unum*: Behold how good and joyful a thing it is for brethren to dwell together in unity. What I remembered of my interview with Patrick was that he included himself—and me, I supposed—among that group of soldiers who were far from home and lonely and likely to touch one another because they were human, and when he talked of homosexuals, he spoke of them as they—others, not us, not as good as us—who lived and worked and played somewhere else, not here, on the Mountain.

Bill Bartlett was a year ahead of me, in my fraternity, and it was obvious that he was queer. His father owned orange groves in Florida somewhere, and he drove a small red sports car, an MG, and had a huge Great Dane that rode in the car on the seat next to him. The dog, whose name was Thane, had the biggest nuts of any dog I had ever seen, and since he had very short hair, they were exposed, along with his dick, all the time. I assumed that was the reason Bill had bought him, as a continuous and lively dirty joke.

Bill drank a great deal, and I drank a great deal. We were coming back late one night from Jane's—rumor had it, Jane's had been a whorehouse before it became respectable—where we had been drinking beer since supper. He liked to talk about himself, about growing up on the Gulf Coast of Florida where citrus was the major crop, and what it was like there. He talked about how bad the economy was and how things had "gone." "I've seen things go in my day—" he said, "—the gold lamé drapes—" He spoke of their gold lamé drapes as some of my relatives spoke of their lost plantations. We were driving across the plateau between the Eagle—what we called the hamlet of Monteagle—and Sewanee and had not yet gotten to the gates of the Domain. The terrain was entirely dark, with nothing but the headlights of the sports car to light the way. It was a quiet and intimate moment, and we liked each other, so I asked him.

"What do you do about liking boys?"

There was a long pause.

"Well." Then Bill spoke. "I figure it's just because I am kind of pretty you know, and they like me—" He was speaking very quietly and very carefully. "—so I don't get upset when somebody makes a move on me."

We came around a bend in the road, and the headlights swept over the stone pillars on each side of the road that marked the entrance to the Domain. But that was not what I meant. "No. About your liking boys. What do you do about that?"

"Why do you ask?"

"Because I do."

"Do what?"

"Like boys. Men. I take it you do too. What do you do about that?" I was aware that I had surprised Bill. And that surprised me. I had thought that here, away at college, particularly here, with it all around us, people would exchange views on the subject more openly, more directly.

This time Bill was slower to answer. "I think—" He paused. "—it's a phase I'm going through. I figure I'm going to grow out of it. Someday."

I heard that and thought. I wondered if that would happen. I had never felt anything around a woman like what I felt around men. I wondered how that was going to happen. Would it be that I would meet the right girl—this is what people said, *When you meet the right girl*—and my dick, on its own, would get hard? Or would I have to think about it first, and will it to happen?

"What will make that happen?"

We were in the center of the Domain now, the Chapel up to our left, the student union on our right, the few street lights far between, nothing showing in the blackness.

Bill laughed, a smoky, low laugh, full of alcohol. "God knows. I just hope it does, someday."

Then he stopped the car, and I got out in front of my dorm and went in to bed. The conversation with Bill had not been helpful. The most disturbing thing about it was that there was an element of fear in the way Bill had responded. He was afraid for people to find out.

The next day we did the kind of thing one did with Bill Bartlett. He had found a factory down in the valley below us that made hats for major clothing stores and that sold straw boaters for $5. We got in his red MG and drove down. He bought a boater—I couldn't afford the $5—and, in his blue blazer with brass buttons, khaki pants, blue button-down Oxford cloth shirt and rep-striped tie from Brooks Brothers, and his straw boater, he was the sharpest thing on campus. As it turned out, Bill never brought up the subject again, after I raised it, and I understood that, at Sewanee, it was not to be raised. But I knew that what he said was not true. I liked men. I didn't care about women one way or the other. And this was not a phase I was going through. This was the kind of body I had—or it was the kind of person I was.

On Friday nights, in the crowded student union building, where a movie was about to be shown, the lights went down, the screen lit up with the usual trailers and announcements, and then, there on the screen was the signature image of the J. Arthur Rank Corporation, the English movie studio from which so many of our movies came, the image of an immensely strong man, shirtless, his swollen muscles deeply tanned and oiled, standing beside a gong so big it took up the whole screen. He held in his hands a hammer of some kind, which, with a slow twist of his oiled and muscled torso, he drew back until it was almost behind him, and then, with a slow swing toward the center, he swung the hammer against the gong to produce one low, reverberating gong, announcing the beginning of the movie. During the seconds during which the hammer swung toward the gong, the man's chest muscles bunched up across his rib cage, and I could hear, in the audience, titters and trills from Sewanee students. These were the young men, who, during the daytime, wearing academic gowns and carrying books, went to class to study Corneille or Horace or Pope, who, Patrick said, and he must be speaking for the Church, are not as good as heterosexuals. For the first time, aside from the gym where we watched the shirtless weightlifter, I was sitting in a room where there were other men who liked men. These were the men who bought the muscle magazines and Physique Pictorial. These were the men who were the audience for the scene in the gym on the ship with Jane Russell and for the statue of Guiliano de' Medici. The titter told me that there were others, but I did not want them to titter. I was embarrassed to hear it.

I wanted someone to say something out loud—something direct, honest, coarse, vulgar—as some men did when they saw Marilyn Monroe on the screen. Oh, shit, what tits. That's what men did. Patrick had been wrong to think homosexuals were some place else, but it was the titter in the dark, in front of that powerful image, that made me know Patrick was right about his second point. They certainly didn't act as if they were as good as heterosexuals.

There were questions. Patrick had spoken of they. As in, they don't want to be equal, they want to be better than heterosexuals. Who were these they? Men who were turned on by the chest muscles of the man in the movie from the J. Arthur Rank Corporation. But who was turned on? Was it a defining and consistent characteristic? Was it like a switch? When had this switch been turned on? Could it ever be reversed? Were these they defined by something they sometimes did? Or did they do it because of some defining characteristic I didn't know about yet? Was I, because the arms of men turned me on, different from the student who was turned on by abs? What was it? Was there such a thing as a homosexual? And in the middle of the Mountain, in the middle of the Domain, where all the education took place—the *Odyssey,* The *Iliad*, The *Aenied,* The *Oresteia*, The *Oedipus Cycle,* The *Divine Comedy*, Faust—in Walsh Hall and in the Chapel, where we read from the 1927 *Book of Common Prayer,* which was essentially the version of 1662, who was talking about all this?

Was I a homosexual because of the way I felt around men's arms? Or did I feel about men's arms the way I did because I was a homosexual? What about the way I felt about women and having children and "settling down" as Patrick had done, with an office piled high with books and student papers and community respect? Patrick in his academic gown with the velvet stripes of his PhD from Cambridge? There was no question that I was "a homosexual"—if there was such a thing—but was I always going to be one? Was I a homosexual every hour of the day? Was I totally homosexual all the time? Was I a homosexual to the exclusion of all else? The questions multiplied, like the forces at play in a Donne sonnet, but they didn't cohere.

"Batter my heart," Donne wrote. So. Beat me. The poet reached out for images to explain how he felt and what he needed, and it became clear that the speaker resists the "you" of the poem against his own will: *nor ever chaste except you ravish me.* The critics focused on the strained quality of these images. Donne describes himself as a virtuous woman in a bed fearing—but desiring—the advances of a male intruder. I watched the hard chest of the boy in the weight room and was torn between differing conceptions of chaste.

In any case, after a year when everything had seemed so romantic—every guy walking across campus in his tennis whites showing thighs of death seemed to be waving his racket and calling to me—the romance was now over, and I was back in the situation I had been in, in high school, where I had been alone and lonely, and anxious that somebody would find out. I was back where I had been back then, pretending.

On party weekends, I invited girls to the Mountain and play-acted—as I presumed some of the other boys were play-acting—and considered the extent to which this was virtuous. We all—well, most of us—were looking for girls, for our future wives, and so the effort was necessary. But somewhere, in some place uncommented upon, there was the assumption that we felt something for the girls we were considering as our wives, and I felt nothing. I badly wanted to obey the dictates of my culture. It was inescapable that we were dealing with two men here—ravish, as a verb, was what men do, not women —and the "I" of the poem was, in some way, Donne himself. The image of one man "ravishing" another was disturbing even if I could explain it away with the conventional understanding that this particular male was God himself and with the equally conventional understanding that it was only through this violent act on God's part that Donne could be "chaste." In some way he was married to God. It was confusing and disturbing, and the explanations we got in class did not make these feelings go away. Nothing Patrick had said addressed them, and I did not, in classes or in conversations in the Union or late at night over beer, dare to bring up this question of male rape—despite all, Sewanee did not encourage a free, wide-ranging discussion of ideas. It was inescapable that male rape was what Donne was talking about, *nor ever chaste, except you ravish me.* I should have asked, Why, in seeking to understand his relationship with God, did he resort to this image, of all images, this man who had said, John Donne, Anne Donne, Un-done? And why did chastity come only—*nor ever chaste*—from rape? What had

Michelangelo meant by that chest? I knew that it was inadequate to say, He meant to idealize the male body, which had been made in God's image.

What was I to do if I couldn't escape the image in my mind of being raped by a man when I read the last line of the poem? And couldn't escape the fact that I could only be chaste in the act of being raped by a man? How much of this did Donne intend? Or understand? And why did my professors and the critics go to such lengths to deny what was so obviously there? They were afraid of the way I felt around the boy in the weight room. It didn't scare me, but it terrified these adults. Why? Beyond Deuteronomy and the laws against sodomy, why?

Late in the fall of my sophomore year, at dinner in the Dining Hall, I heard that one of the other major fraternities was experiencing a scandal. The upperclassmen at the table were talking about it. At the time, I didn't ask, but later, in the dorm, I asked an older student, "What were they talking about?"

He was on his way to the men's room, a towel around his shoulders, a tooth brush and tooth paste in his hand, and he looked me over. "They found out one of their pledges was queer, so they de-pledged him. I think he is going to withdraw from the university." He shrugged. Then, before I could say anything, he went on down the hall. I went back to my room and lay on my bed. I couldn't ever tell my parents. Or Cornelius. I thought, I couldn't ever tell my mother.

Later in that winter, a boy, an active member of a fraternity, was expelled from the university for the same reason. There was never an announcement about these things. You just heard about them, so you had to trust that what you heard was the truth. I didn't know either one of these boys, but I knew who they were, and so far as I could tell, they seemed just like me. That is, they didn't have any more distinguishing features than I did. Why were they thrown out and I was still here? What had they done? What had people found out about them? I became circumspect.

The fraternities that had gotten rid of two queer men seemed to encourage a similarity among their members. My own fraternity, on the other hand, seemed to be much looser, more relaxed, and to have less of a type. I could not imagine being asked to leave or being expelled. I knew I was well-liked. But then, who knew who your friends were?

The embarrassed titters in the dark cinema, and Patrick's condescending, rambling discourse about being human, and the rumors that swept campus of expulsions were indicative of how Sewanee—this place that was supposed to be sophisticated and the depository of learning—dealt with it. The hawk-nosed poet had denied it, and even Bill Bartlett had shrugged his shoulders and assumed it would go away.

I became unable to pay attention in classes or to read my books. I was incapable of the kind of steady work that was required, reading each set of poems for the next day's class, having my papers in on time. It was difficult to focus on the work at hand. My grades jumped all over the scale—A's occasionally, B's more often, some C's—and I discovered that my professors couldn't figure me out. Carroll Goodyear—a senior known for being brilliant and for having the prospect of an even more brilliant future—told me one afternoon, walking toward the Chapel, that a professor had asked him if he knew me. The professor said that I was "brilliant—but erratic." Carroll had dark skin and a vocal delivery that poured out a torrent of words. He gave the impression that his words were always trying—and failing—to catch up with his thoughts.

"How did you do that?" Carroll asked. "I've been here three and a half years trying to get that reputation, and you come here for one year and achieve it effortlessly." I was secretly pleased—I didn't want to seem a grind—but "erratic" pointed toward brilliance at the same time it pointed toward something out of control and undependable. I considered dropping out of school. Maybe, I thought, I could join the Army. I told no one on campus, but when I wrote my parents, they were, they said, stunned. "We'll talk about it when you come home at the end of the semester."

Money was also a problem. My parents had not sent me any money all fall, and, to get by, I sold my stereo, one I had made from a kit. I also picked up money by typing term papers for other students. I could make as much as $5 in an afternoon of work. Late in the fall, when a family friend—Mrs. Lincoln, the wife of an Episcopal priest at home—sent me $200, it went to pay for books and pay off debts, and then it was gone, and I was poor again. Mother wrote and asked if I had gambled it all away.

One day, leaving the Dining Hall, I was walking with a cousin, and we heard someone call out behind us. We turned. It was one of the older professors, a single gentleman who affected a walking stick and three piece tweed suits over which he wore his black academic gown.

The professor pointed at us with his stick. "There they go! The Shaw boys!"

We stopped, smiling, and waited.

"I know your kinswoman," the old man said. "Countess Shaw! Who was detained on Ellis Island on charges of moral turpitude!"

He broke out into loud guffaws of laughter and swept on past us.

"What the fuck?!" It was my cousin.

"It was some café society woman in the twenties. She was American, I think, married to an Englishman. She was caught sleeping with someone who wasn't her husband. I've read about it. It was a celebrated scandal in the twenties." But it bothered me. Moral turpitude.

In the late winter of my second year, in the evening, I was in the Union having coffee, when someone ran in and then ran back out into the dark again. Men around me asked what was happening—men stood up and went toward the door—when somebody said, "Somebody's been shot." Men ran out and toward one of the dorms, and somebody who stayed said, "It was an accident. A gun went off." And that was all we knew that night. The next day we heard that a man had been hit, and he was dead by the time they got him to the hospital. Then we began to hear that it had not been an accident at all. Someone had shot the man who died. It had been intentional. We heard these bits of news—or gossip—and put them together into the narrative we were stringing in our minds because nobody seemed to have the whole story, or was willing to tell us the whole story. I had not thought that any of us—any of the students—would have a gun, but I was wrong, and nobody else seemed shocked at the presence of guns among us on campus.

People kept asking, *Why?* and others threw out possibilities. They were having an argument. It was over money. They had been drinking heavily. Then, what went around campus like the winds around the second circle of hell was this sentence: *It was because he was queer.* No one seemed to know—or would say they knew—what this meant. Presumably the dead man—whom no one seemed to know or to know well—was the one who was queer. But I thought a cursory analysis of the story so far would have allowed the guy behind the gun to be the queer. We didn't know. And even if we could have assigned a sexuality to one of the men—or both of them —we didn't know how that had led to one of them dying. No one was asking any questions of anyone who might know. And the matter did not appear in any newspaper and seemed to disappear from the public record. What happened? Afterward, the hawk-nosed poet disappeared into the library, and the people I knew were studying for midterms and there were fewer men in the cinema at the Union. I did know a man who knew a man who knew the man who had carried the dead man down three flights of stairs to his car and driven him to the hospital, where he was taken into the emergency room and pronounced DOA. So something had really happened.

And I guessed that it had involved the queer man coming on to the guy with the gun—he hadn't known he had a gun—and at just the critical moment, the man he wanted to have sex with, instead of breaking into a slow smile and grinning, pulled the gun and killed him. He must have thought he could trust him. I thought I could trust my fraternity brothers, but how did I know that none of them had guns in their rooms? Were they going to kill me instead of breaking into a slow smile and grinning? And what if they didn't wait for me to come on to them? Could I trust those smiles?

I didn't know which was worse, being shot, say, in the heart and feeling the sudden overwhelming pain, and feeling your heart struggle to keep its regular rhythm and finding the struggle to be harder and harder until finally it was too hard, and in a spasm of pain, it quit, or being exposed one day in the student union, coming in, say, one afternoon after classes and heading toward the table where all of us always sat—my fraternity brothers in their tennis whites and their piles of books—and being greeted by some brother saying, "Not here, Shaw, you faggot. Sit somewhere else, you fucking queer." Every time I thought of that, my face flushed hot.

In April, my advisor, Dr. Harrelson, called me in. He was a white-haired gentleman whose tall, stooped posture suggested the elegance of a crane and was sitting behind his desk when I knocked.

Dr. Harrelson had dark eyes which, in combination with his lowered, bushy white eyebrows, seemed to penetrate any defenses I might have had. "I have been quite taken with your performance in class, as well as with your written work, and I look forward to working with you over the next two years." He paused. He looked down, he looked up, then over to the side, out the window. "Have you enjoyed your work this year?"

"Yes sir, very much so." I didn't know what this was all about. He seemed kind. He was a brilliant teacher, but I had been sent for, and there seemed something threatening in this situation.

He smiled. "Of course you have. But—" That but! "I have been watching you, young man, and I have been wondering. Uh—" He glanced out the window. "—uh, I have been wondering if we quite have all of your attention. Can you know what I mean?"

I raised my eyebrows. Then I shook my head.

Dr. Harrelson shook his head. "Of course not. I am being too obscure. I have the sense—something not quite articulated, a feeling perhaps—that you are distracted by something, something that prevents you from focusing sharply on your work. But—" And here he came forward in his chair and laid his arms across his desk. "—but I think it is larger than that, even. I suspect that you are being distracted by something that not only prevents you from the work you have before you but prevents you even from thinking about the larger issues that face you. I speak, of course, of your future, the great work of your life." He considered me carefully, and I wondered if I were responding appropriately to this mystifying approach. "You have a great future, Fair, and I would be very honored if you felt you trusted me enough to talk to me about whatever it is that is bothering you, whatever it is that is distracting you from your course." He smiled. His smile, under his heavy white bushy brows, and his dark, piercing eyes, had the effect almost of a spell being cast. "What is troubling you?"

Patrick Endicott had asked almost the same thing, and so had Dr. Davie, my other English professor, and all of them—and my mother —had implied they thought I was not telling them the whole truth. Cornelius had told our parents that he thought I was "lying."

"I wish," Dr. Harrelson said, with his kindly manner, "that you could see your way clear to tell me what it is, what is going on with you." He paused, and I wondered what to say. "Are you holding something back?" I didn't know what he wanted.

I knew I was not doing as well at Sewanee as I had hoped—as everyone had hoped—and that most of my friends had gotten better grades than I had, and I supposed that what Dr. Harrelson was asking me had to do with why are you not making all A's? But then I also got the idea that Dr. Harrelson thought something worse, deeper, was going on than bad grades. Dr. Harrelson asked me questions: What time did I go to sleep? What did I do last summer? The summer before that? Then he asked me what I was going to do this coming summer.

I had thought of living at home and going to summer school at Carolina.

"Oh, I think that would be very unwise." Dr. Harrelson leaned back in his chair, put his hands behind his head and gazed out the window. "I think you should forget about yourself for a while, forget your schoolwork." This was really what I was concerned about—I seemed to be able to think only of myself. I seemed to obsess on myself. "I think you should do something out of doors that will completely absorb you on the surface. Forget self-analysis for a while. Do something physical—like bricklaying."

When I overcame my astonishment at his suggestion, I mentioned Nantucket—some of us had talked about going to Nantucket for the summer and working in the restaurants there—and Dr. Harrelson pounced on that.

"That's just the thing!" He thought Nantucket a grand idea, since there would be more young people. Dr. Harrelson offered to let me use his office at night if I was having a difficult time finding a place to study, and after that I studied there every night. Dr. Harrelson told me that he thought I had a "brilliant" future ahead of me. But when I left his office that afternoon, he stared at me as if in defeat. I had not answered his question.

Dr. Harrelson told Carroll Goodyear that "that boy has to get it out of his system, whatever has been bothering him. He's erratic, but I have profound expectations for the boy's future." I began a Faulkner phase, writing page after page of high-energy Faulknerian prose until finally my professor asked me to stop. I wrote a few poems—metaphysical conceits drawn from Donne, one an extremely strained image of "tensile wire stretched between two poles, a hemisphere apart"—and then I wrote a short story filled with hidden meaning about a sixteen-year-old American boy spending the weekend with a sixteen-year-old German boy in Cologne, in 1956, based on an experience from my journey to Europe. It mixed cultural clashes with sexual and political undercurrents. Carroll said of it, "Fair, this is superb. This places you among the first rank of Sewanee writers." He asked me to submit my story to the campus literary magazine and told me that this story alone would get me into the literary society. I found I could no more confront my homosexuality directly than the other men on campus. It was all indirection and subterfuge, for there were so many things not to be spoken of.

My father, on the other hand, recommended that I join a book club. I wrote, "I don't see one yet that has a good selection. Most of the clubs select current novels, and I don't want current novels. I want to complete my reading of the classics first. Those are hard to get in the book clubs without getting so much trash first." Mother wrote that I might be becoming a "snob and a bore" and "Cornelius thinks so too."

In the middle of all this, I had to declare a major. I chose English without thinking about it. My father said, "Law and medicine are essentially trade schools. They prepare you to become licensed to practice a skill. That's not what a gentleman does. You want to study history and literature, the monuments of our culture, and place yourself in that tradition." That seemed right to me. "Be a thinker," my father said. Another reason for majoring in English was that it enabled me to put off for several more years the question of what I was to do with my life.

I didn't really know what was wrong and didn't know how to tell anyone—Dr. Harrelson, other students, my parents—I was queer. Once I told them, I was trapped, or exposed, so I couldn't tell them what I wanted to tell them. I had "problems" of some sort. I was "brilliant" but "erratic." I didn't live up to my potential. I drank too much. I didn't think, deep down, that I would ever be the kind of academic my professors at Sewanee were, and I didn't really know if I wanted to. I was a failure. I didn't know what I was to do. I thought that I was undisciplined, that I was unfocussed, that I didn't work hard enough, that I had "problems" that had to do with my parents— my absent father and smothering mother—my childhood, my family, that had to do with my drinking too much. Somehow all these were explanations, or causes, or excuses for the predicament I was in, and when I tried to explain it to someone it seemed right—reasonable— but it never felt right. I didn't want to see a psychiatrist.

I didn't want to be queer. I looked around me and was envious of the men who only had to make good grades and decide which girl they were inviting up for the weekend.

"It's my family." But in the end I didn't know why I was in the predicament I was in, and I didn't know why I was doing what I was about to do. My relationship with almost all my friends had been defined, from our earliest friendship in grade school, by a well-bred reticence that would not allow the kind of open, free-wheeling pouring out of thought and feeling that I needed.

I knew I could not be the kind of man who intentionally caused his mother this much pain. Besides, it was entirely possible that I could tell some man—and then find that he had a gun.

I did, actually, hit on one method of dealing with all this. I told a few people. I had already told Bill Bartlett. I told another fraternity brother. I didn't mean to. It happened, late one night, in his room in the dorm. We were talking about stuff, and I told him. "I'm only attracted to men. All my life, that's all I've ever been attracted to." The guy wanted to know if I was attracted to him. I said, sure, and he seemed pleased and didn't seem upset. I thought, if there are any queer men out there who want to connect with me, they'll hear about me.

But that was not what happened. At some point that spring of my sophomore year, Lee Priest, a guy a year older than I who was a fraternity brother told me that rumor had it that I was worried about being queer. Lee told me, "Everybody wants you to get over it. Stop worrying. You're not queer." Only I was queer. There was no question about that. And that left me thinking none of these guys is any help with this. I knew I was queer, and I liked the way I felt around men, but I didn't know how to put it all together—being queer, being a student, being a son, being a brother. And I couldn't imagine a future as a queer. I didn't know how to think about being queer. Was it really a bad thing to like men? Were there sophisticated, knowledgeable gentlemen who believed it was perfectly all right? Or was everybody telling the truth when they said it was the worst thing there was? The other boys either didn't think about it or they didn't want to talk about their thoughts. Besides, it really wasn't up to the fraternity brothers to decide whether or not I was queer. I felt that what the guys were really saying was, Please don't let it be true that a member of our fraternity that we know and like is queer, because if I was, they'd have to expel me. This was the same thing that was keeping everybody else from dealing directly with being queer. I wanted a safe place, and I was discovering there was no place at Sewanee that was safe. Very very unsafe.

I had never told any of the adults in my life that I was queer, and none of them seemed to see it as a possibility. Of course, Fair is queer. And he doesn't like it. That's his problem. They seemed, all of them, to dare me to be the first to say it. There was an implicit threat here. None of them, including my parents, said, Look, first, we love you. And if you have something to tell us, know that we will love you just as much afterwards as before. Instead, the threat was, You're lying. If we find out about it, whatever it is, we'll cease to love you. The demand was, Don't tell us, and don't let us find out. What I wanted was to be queer and to be respected—I wanted to be respected as I was—and I knew I couldn't get that. I didn't know how to honor myself if I were queer. And nobody else saw that that was the issue. And despite what sometimes seemed to be a flood of queer interest at Sewanee, I knew that most students there dismissed queers as fruits. Even the queer ones thought of themselves as fruits. And none of them were safe. I never met one person on the Mountain who was dealing with this in a sensible, knowledgeable, enlightened way. Why should I trust any of them? I knew that, at Sewanee, it might be that I was surrounded by literate, responsible queers and that I was unable to recognize what was in front of my eyes, or it might be that these literate, responsible queers were living hidden lives so as to prevent me from knowing that they were queer. I didn't know. But what I did know was that the straight ones weren't gentlemen. Either that, or being a gentleman meant committing yourself to a culture where the ordinary means of communication was lying.

Something else happened my last term at Sewanee. My body was filling out. I had gone out for swimming, and apparently that was affecting my musculature.

"We were talking about you—"

"What?"

"How sexy you are—"

I thought, *What the fuck.*

2

Every afternoon, my platoon marched back to the barracks from the rifle range, sweat running down our shaved skulls and soaking our t-shirts, our rifles on our shoulders. We struggled to stay in step and out of the corners of our eyes were aware of the barracks housing other soldiers, men who had already gotten back from the range who were now lounging on the steps and against the railing. There was one soldier on the steps of a barracks we were passing—being in formation, I couldn't turn my head to look at him—whom I saw for at most 20 seconds as I drew up with him and before I went on past him and lost sight of him. This soldier was swarthy—black hair, olive-colored skin, large eyes with black lashes and heavy dark eyebrows, stocky, muscular build barely covered by his white t-shirt, and handsome. He smelled of sex even from the distance of the twenty yards that separated us. My dick leapt to attention, my whole body flushed with sexual excitement, and from then on until the next afternoon when we marched past his barracks and I could see him again, I floated on waves of sex. I never saw him except those times when we marched past, but his image, even among the hundreds of other images of powerfully sexual men, was distinct and memorable.

After basic training, I was trained as a supply clerk—I could type and had two years of college—and was sent to the Yakima Firing Center, outside of Yakima, Washington. I was made supply clerk of a direct automotive support company, a mobile mechanics garage for the heavy equipment of the 4th Infantry Division. I worked alongside Negroes for the first time, and it was the first place I had ever been where my name didn't mean anything. Nobody cared where any of us came from—or who we were or who our parents had been. The only criterion was whether we could do the job. What was asked of me was simple—the ability to type and to obey orders—so I got along well, made a few friends, and spent my off-duty time reading and, like most soldiers, drinking. I wrote letters, but it was a chore because my parents were angry and bewildered and ashamed that I had quit college and had joined the Army and that I had gone in as an enlisted man.

Occasionally the officers of the unit held classes on racial matters—it had only been eleven years since the armed forces of the United States were integrated by President Truman—but it was all presented matter-of-factly. There were racists among us, and racism, but it was personal and not overt or systemic—I don't think—and I got to know some Negroes. All of my sergeants in basic training and advanced training were Negroes, and our supply sergeant, the one I reported to, was a Negro. It was not a big deal, and when I read the papers about the racial disturbances back home, it came from another century. I felt superior to the men I had left behind at Sewanee, which was still segregated. *I* was dealing with it, and they weren't. The racists in the company were men I wanted nothing to do with, even if they hadn't been racists. They were ignorant and without skills, rednecks, which is what they were called in the company.

I met Connie Stephanopolis—Constantine Stephanopolis—my first day in the company. Connie was a little taller than I and a good bit heavier, Greek extraction, very curly wiry black hair, dark skinned, missing his two upper front teeth from an accident he had had with an alligator—he wrestled alligators in South Florida for a living—and he liked to kiss me. He had a wonderful body, and most of the time he wore a plate to cover the gap in his teeth, although, with an insouciance no one else would have been capable of, he took it out whenever it bothered him—or when he forgot it in the morning. We became familiar with it sitting on the table in the bar, among the packs of cigarettes, matches, ashtrays, glasses, and pitchers of beer. Connie was happy, friendly, and totally sexual. Sometimes when he talked to me seriously, he put the back of his hand behind my head and drew my face close to him, whispering to me from so near that from some angles we must have seemed to be kissing. Sometimes, when we were parting, he did kiss me, on the mouth, *like brothers*. His hands were all over me, and he seemed to expect me to touch him, which I did, my arm across his shoulders, sometimes cupping his chest muscles, feeling the hard flesh. On the other hand, he seemed unconscious of what he was doing. He was apparently into girls, had a girl back home in Florida, and wanted to know about the girls I dated before I came into the Army.

Every night he and I and two or three other soldiers went into town with a guy who had a car, and drank beer at a drive-in. There were two main streets in Yakima, which crossed in the middle of town, and we'd get our beer from the drive-in and then drive into town, cross the main intersection, and drive out into the desert on the other side, turn around, come back in to the intersection and turn and drive toward the desert again. When we got back to the drive-in, we'd slow down and drive through the parking lot in a line of other cars all driving slowly through the lot, yelling at people we knew— other soldiers, girls—before we came out on the other side. The carhops wore low white boots with tassels and put trays of draft beer on hooks on the windows. Connie and I usually sat next to each other, my arm across the back of the seat and across his shoulders. Sometimes it was the other way around, and Connie's arm was across my shoulders, a weight I enjoyed feeling. I wondered, at night in the dark in the barracks, after lights out, what it would be like to be in bed with Connie. I knew what he was like naked—we showered together, along with all the other men in the barracks, so I knew what his uncut cock looked like, and his balls, and I knew what his arms and chest felt like, but I didn't know anything else—and as I drifted off to sleep, most nights I had an erection in my hand from the thought of being in bed with Connie. I wanted to kiss him— really kiss him, our mouths open, our tongues entwined. I wanted to kiss his *eyelids*.

Taking a three-day pass and hitchhiking up into the Cascade Mountains to Rainier National Park was Connie's idea—"Do you like to hike? Wouldn't it be great to go up into the mountains?"—and I said, *sure*. I don't think Connie had planned it—he probably had not thought about it until the moment, over beer, when he asked me —and I don't think, for Connie, that there was a goal. After I agreed to the hike, Connie nodded and said, "Great. That's going to be great," and then he ordered another pitcher, and he didn't mention it again until he said, one day, "I've got next weekend off. See if you can get off too. For our hike."

So in May 1960 we hitchhiked up, packing only K-rations, toothbrushes, beer, two bottles of bourbon, and sleeping bags. We got a ride to the entrance of the park and then another ride up to the lodge, and from there we got a map of the trails and chose one and set off up the side of Mt. Rainier, through the forest of dark green evergreens. In an hour, we found a clearing up on the side of the mountain from which we could see, through the trees, the valley below. The mountain at this height was so steep that it was like camping halfway up a cliff—the mountain loomed over us, and the valley seemed to open up beneath our feet. It gave me vertigo, as if I were about to fall. Connie spread out his sleeping bag and opened a beer, lay back, and stretched. "This is paradise, ain't it?"

I spread out my sleeping bag next to Connie's and lay down.

"No sergeants. No officers."

"Just us." Connie rolled over to lie next to me and grinned.

We sipped our beers and talked about Army things for a while, about two officers from Texas Tech who had just arrived in the company. We ate something and drank more beer.

"What do you read all the time? What are those books you read all the time?"

I laughed. I was intensely aware of Connie, lying on his stomach next to me, and of our being alone miles from anywhere and anyone. The park was not fully open yet, and there were very few staff members at the lodge down below and no one on the trails. Under all the hemlocks were great mounds of snow for use later with the bourbon.

"I'm reading *Crime and Punishment*. It's by Fyodor Dostoyevsky."

"Who's he?" Connie grinned.

"A Russian. It's about a man who kills an old woman and how he finally gives himself up."

"They catch him?"

"No, they don't have any proof that he did it. He just gives up, stops hiding."

Connie leaned over me. He put his head on my chest and lay there. "That seems stupid, if he had gotten away with it."

"He feels guilty."

"Guilt is for shit."

Connie snuggled down onto my chest. Neither of us said anything for a long while. The late afternoon sun had gone down below the mountains on the other side of the valley, and we were in deep blue shadow. The deep blue of the sky, the blue shadow, and the dark green of the trees, with the piles of white snow. Connie and I were both wearing t-shirts, but Connie's body was warm across my chest and belly. I brought my hand down and stroked Connie's back. Connie was lying directly across my erection. Then I ran my fingers through his hair—it was strong curly hair—searching slowly with the tips of my fingers for his scalp underneath his hair.

Eventually, Connie raised himself on his elbows, one on each side of my torso, and reached forward and kissed me, at first just his lips against my lips, then he pulled back and came down again with his lips apart. We kissed again, my arms around Connie's body. Connie pulled back and grinned. "This is fine, huh?"

I smiled. "Fine. *Fine.*"

"I've wanted to do this ever since I first saw you in the company."

"You knew?"

"I could see the way you looked at me." He grinned. "I knew you wanted me as much as I wanted you." He paused. "You gonna let me suck your cock?"

I laughed. "Of course."

But first we fixed drinks—the bourbon and the snow—then we both tried to get into one sleeping bag, but it was too small. "We'll have to buy us a two-man sleeping bag before we come back up here next time," Connie said, so we lay naked on one with the other on top, and first Connie sucked me off and then I sucked Connie off, and then we fucked each other. I kissed his eyelids.

"Is this your first time?"

I nodded.

"You should have told me. I would have tried not to hurt you."

"It didn't hurt. You were wonderful."

The sun went down, and we drank some more, put back on our t-shirts and long johns against the cold.

We spent the weekend hiking up the mountain and then down into the valley and having sex in our own private glen.

"Why is it that you haven't had sex before?"

"I never found the right person." Or the right place or the right time. And it was never out in the open.

"You had sex with women then?" He was lying on his back, nude, and I lay with my head across his stomach, facing his bush. My left arm lay across his thigh, and I toyed with his cock, stroking it.

"No. I haven't found the right person."

"Am I the right person?"

"You're the right person." He was physically right, he was kind, thoughtful of me, he admired me and was interested in me, and, of course, we were lying on sleeping bags in a small corner of the most beautiful meadow on earth.

"Women are fine, too."

"Yeah. I guess." I had already started grieving for Connie. This was an interlude for Connie between women. I knew Connie liked me, found me sexy, liked having sex with me, would have sex with me again—there would be more hikes up into the mountains, next time with a double sleeping bag—but eventually we would go our separate ways.

We did go camping twice more before I got out of the Army. We had sex and drank, and Connie sometimes talked about the women he was seeing and asked about women in my life. He also talked about men, one he had in Florida when he was wrestling alligators. He seemed to assume there was somebody—or would be some body —and the sex between the two of us seemed to meld seamlessly into the rest of his sex life, without wounds.

"Have you ever fallen in love with a guy?" It was my question.

"I'm in love with you." Connie grinned.

"Would you like to spend your life with me?" I imagined it. Would I give up back home for this?

He was serious. "You?"

"Me."

"I don't know." Connie laughed. "And a woman?"

"Just us." It was possible.

"Are you in love with me?"

"Maybe. Yes. I think so."

"Holy shit." Connie laughed. "*You're in love with me!*" He shook his head. "I just like to fuck. And you're so hot. You don't even know how hot you are. Do you know I have heard other guys talk about you? About how they'd like to get you into bed?"

We had a lovers' quarrel over something trivial. We had had sex and enjoyed each other, but we couldn't talk except about girls and beer and the Army—we couldn't really talk about loving each other or about the hurt that had happened—and from then on we treated each other like spurned lovers, passing each other in the barrack's aisle ostentatiously ignoring the other's presence, and I stopped joining the others on their nightly passes into town. I was reading— *The Idiot, Anna Karenina, War and Peace,* books by Albert Camus, *The Myth of Sisyphus,* and *The Rebel*—and I went by myself up to Mt Rainier and camped for three or four days at a time. It was the first time in my life that I was alone. I went to the movies alone, went up into the mountains alone, hitchhiked to Vancouver alone, went to Fort Lewis alone—with my thoughts. I was thinking about the country, and about the race problems back home—the politicians were still fighting it—and about life, about how narrow my parents were and about the great world of learning, and about sex and how hard it was. I had never lost anyone before, and I grieved over the loss of Connie, the loss of his body and his sex—his beautiful cock —the loss of his kisses in the aisle in the barracks in front of everybody, the loss of his affection and of his admiration. It was hard to go about my business, carrying the weight of such a loss. I had been at Ft Lewis on January 5, 1960 when I found in the day room a copy of the paper and read that Albert Camus had died in an automobile accident outside of Paris the day before. I went out onto the base that night, walking the wet gravel paths between the barracks buildings, feeling that I had lost the one person who knew what it was all about, who knew how alienated it was possible to be. He had written that, if life was this way, *why not commit suicide?* Why not indeed? I was in the company day room that fall, watching TV the night John Kennedy was elected President, and I watched him and his wife and his family walk out onto the stage of the high school in Hyannisport and receive the cheers of the crowd. I felt that things were going to be different, now. Both Kennedy and Camus were enormously sexy and good-looking men and both promised something that I thought must be wise and profound. They had courage. It was a tragedy that Camus was dead, and dead in such a meaningless way. One weekend I sat under a hemlock tree on the slope of Mt Rainier, after breaking up with Connie, reading the *Myth of Sisyphus*, and thinking of what I had to do—push my rock—and, as Camus said, *I had to know exactly what I was doing.*

I was selected Soldier of the Month for the 4th Infantry Division at one point, and, at another, the wife of one of the other soldiers— we were at a bar in town getting drunk—told me I was an alcoholic. "I know who you are. You are just one of those alcoholics from the South. I've met your type before." I was a type. Another girl, whom I had rebuffed after she came on to me, told me, "You're nothing but a fucking queer."

The week I joined the Army, the first sergeant stood in front of the whole company and laid down the law to all of us about passes and theft and barracks life generally. "And don't think, in the middle of the night, when I hear some little pitter-patter of bare feet in the barracks, that I don't know what it is. If some of you are queer, and if you think you can go sneaking off into bed with some other troop in the middle of the night and you think that nobody will know, just remember that I know everything that goes on in my barracks. The thing we do with you guys is put you out on a Section 5." After Connie left, I became very careful, and when a soldier came on to me, I told him to go fuck himself.

I went to see an Episcopal priest in Yakima—I had to talk to someone, and there was no one else—and said, "What am I supposed to do?"

He paused for a moment before answering. "As long as you're in the Army, don't tell anybody."

I had another question. "Is there a way to be queer and to have people respect you?"

He thought. At length, he said, "Probably not. Not in our culture. Maybe if you went somewhere. Maybe Europe."

I went home for a cousin's wedding. It was a big social event. All of our extended family were there, and, since my cousin had graduated from the university, many faculty members were there. I was moved by the symbolism of the ceremony, the father giving the bride away and the groom taking his place in front of the assembled guests in an entirely full church. I was one of the groomsmen— Cornelius, who was going to work for Uncle Robert Fair, was another—and watched the service from the front of the church, this big public ceremony that amounted to an imprimatur from the culture on my cousin and his new wife. Cornelius attended all the festivities with a beautiful woman, an Italian-American girl whose father was a colonel in the Army at Fort Jackson.

The last morning home, the day I was supposed to catch the plane back to Washington, Mother came in my bedroom. She sat on my bed and patted my thigh until I woke up. "I wanted to catch you now while it is still possible to talk."

I was trying to wake up. I felt her hand on my thigh, and I resented it. "What time is it?"

"Six-thirty. Uh, Six-forty-five." She continued to pat my thigh.

"Don't *do* that." I pulled away from her. "Don't ever do that. What do you want?"

"I need to talk to you before you leave today, and if I wait until later in the day, it will be impossible to have a—a private— conversation."

"What do you want to talk about?" I couldn't think what she needed to talk to me about that could justify her coming into my bedroom at this hour unasked.

"I need to talk to you about your father. I know you are thinking about going back to Sewanee when you get out of the Army, but I want to ask you not to do that. I want you to come back to South Carolina and matriculate in the university here. I can't handle your father, and I need for you to come home and live here when you get out of the Army and help me with him. Will you do that?"

She was asking me to transfer from Sewanee to South Carolina, with all the difference in degrees that would mean. I wanted to write, and the Sewanee degree was worth more than a South Carolina degree. I could get a better education at Sewanee than at USC. I didn't want to go to South Carolina. She said she wanted me to help her with Daddy, but there was nothing I could do for him, and what she was really asking me was to come home and be supportive of *her*. Besides, Cornelius was already there. This was all about alcohol. But in the end I gave in. When I got out, I did what she asked me to do.

Since adolescence, since high school, one of the ways I had developed of dealing with Mother was to give her what she wanted while taking pride in giving her what she wanted. Now, I was prepared to spend the next two years giving her what she wanted but secretly enjoying my sacrifice. That is, I was prepared to have it both ways.

Just before I got out, a new group of troops arrived in the company and started making remarks about me. "Shaw's queer." One of them was this big good-looking guy, a mechanic like most of the men in the company, who had to come to the orderly room occasionally to get some paper signed, who made snide remarks in a loud whisper. "Fucking queer," he'd say as he took the paper from me. This got to be a big thing, and I began to think I had to do something about it—it had something to do with being a dog, Faulkner would have said—so one day I went down to the barracks of this big guy and told him I had heard what he was saying about me.

"So?"

"So I've come to tell you to stop."

He grinned. He shrugged. "Ya gotta make me, it seems to me."

Suddenly, I found myself fighting this guy. The guys in the barracks gathered round to watch. I jumped him, and the other guy threw me around—against a metal locker—and I got up from the floor and rushed him again. He threw me off him again, up against a bunk bed. I was breathing hard, and it hurt getting thrown against the locker and the bed, but I thought I had to stand and fight, even if I lost. I wanted to hurt him, but that was probably not going to happen. He was hurting *me*. But that mattered less than my standing up and saying, *I'm brave enough, even if I am not strong enough, to call you.* He threw me onto a footlocker—he wasn't trying very hard— and then people pulled me off him. They were people I knew who had come down to the barracks when they heard I was fighting the big mechanic. I was aware, when I had my hands on him, right in the middle of the fight, that what I really wanted to do was to feel his muscles. I wanted to *fuck* him. But they pulled me off him and separated us—made him go to his bunk and made me get out of the barracks, which was not my barracks—and so it was over. I had wanted to *kiss* him. Afterward, my first sergeant said to me, "It seems to me, if you're going to get in a fight, you need to be sure you're going to win." But he missed the point. Afterward, I found no one called me *queer* anymore, even though the big mechanic had clearly won. I had stood up for myself, and that mattered.

Because this is what had happened. The fight had not been over whether I was queer. The big mechanic probably still thought that I was queer. The fight had been over whether I was a coward. Whether it was OK to treat a queer any way one wanted to. I had shown him that I was not a coward and that it wasn't OK to treat a queer like shit. I won that one.

I wondered if being in the Army was an equivalent to *bricklaying*. I told the Episcopal priest, "I'm a queer. And that is my problem." It was the first time I had ever defined the issue. I had had something for a little bit with Connie, and we respected each other even if we hadn't told anyone, and I had stood up for myself in the fight with the big mechanic. In a place where no one knew who I was, I had found a way to live. That was something. I had also learned something about class. But it wasn't very much. For a time there, I had tried to imagine a life with Connie, and I could almost do it. And then I tried to imagine a life *like* Connie's—marriage, and a man on the side, or men. But there was the grief. I would have a man on the side for sex, and I would fall in love with him, and when it was over, I'd have the grief. I was not like Connie, though I was like Connie in many ways. I would fall in love and I would grieve at the loss when it was over, and I would wish that I were dead.

↔

Every day I came home from the university and, at one, my father and I had dinner, a full meal served on good china with silver utensils and serving dishes, and the cook, Effie, passing trays of vegetables, clearing things away, and bringing in dessert. My mother was teaching school, but she insisted on having Effie there to serve my father and me. Coming back from the Army, I knew how all this looked, the two of us sitting at a table with decent china and silver and a woman in the kitchen cooking lunch for us that she then served, coming to me with the tray, "String beans, Mr. Fair?"

My father came home from work carrying the weekly news magazines, which he read during dinner, and about which he made comments—usually how the Kennedys were ruining the country. My father hated them, hated their liberalism, but most of all he hated the fact that they were rich. "The old man bought the presidency for him. *Bought it!*" And he hated Jackie—she was "vulgar" he said. "The

White House has always been furnished with antiques. Look at the pictures from the Eisenhower administration. Why do they say *she* did it?" Then he would say, "Don't you agree?"

I adored them. I cut a picture out of *The New York Times Magazine* that showed them in an intimate moment in the great hall of the White House, apparently waiting for guests to arrive, she in a long white gown and he in white tie and tails. They were beautiful and glamorous, they invited Pablo Casals to the White House, and in his press conferences he spoke a rich, sophisticated, complex language that suggested a man who thought deeply. During one crisis, when the National Guard was called up and a reporter asked a question about the fairness of some being called up and others not, the President accepted the accusation with the comment, "Life is unfair." It was undeniably true, and Ike had never been able to reach that level of simple profundity. That two such rich, beautiful people could be so aware that *life is unfair* struck me as wonderful and reason enough to rejoice in the possibilities that, even if the basic unfairness of life could not be eliminated, *it was possible to make it less unfair.* But first one had to recognize what it was and tell the truth.

My Shakespeare professor, lecturing on Shakespeare's sonnets, spoke for 10 or 15 minutes on platonic love between men. It was a little set piece, this lecture on platonic love between men, inserted into her lectures on the poems to answer the question no one in the class had raised. My American literature professor gave his version of the same lecture when he came to Whitman's Calamus Poems. It was as if they were aware that, out there somewhere, someone was wondering, Why is he writing to a *man*? and they wanted to cut off debate before it got started.

I fought with my father over the Kennedys and over Nixon, over the Bay of Pigs, over integration, and laughed at my mother's pretensions to landed aristocracy. She came home one afternoon with a copy of a privately printed book of genealogy, the work of a Jay cousin, a profoundly silly book by a man educated in the nineteenth century that read like the marble plaques on the walls of the chapel at Sewanee—flowery, overdone, unbelievable. Mother said, "These were *fine* men!"

"Maybe so, but you can't tell it from this book."

Mother, at dinner, was sorting out the weekend obligations. "Caroline and Richmond's party is tomorrow, and I want both of you to go." She looked sweetly at us, as if it were a natural and normal request for her to make. Cornelius was no longer living at home.

"Can't. There's a ball game tomorrow, so we're all going to be tail-gating." Cornelius raised his eyebrows. *What do you make of that?* "Why don't you ask Fair, here. He doesn't have anything to do."

I shrugged. "I don't have a date, and I am not going to the game tomorrow, but I do have things to do, and I am not going to the party."

"Why don't you have a date, Fair? Big party."

"My business. And Mother, let me repeat, I am not going to pick up Cornelius' slack around here."

She started crying. "I need you, and Cornelius can't."

"Sorry, Mother. Cornelius won't."

Cornelius was laughing.

I slipped back into the world of Trinity Church, debutante parties, family gatherings, school, studies, but it was all so much bullshit. I had no sex, and I didn't date, except to debutante parties, which were arranged. I never saw Cornelius, who, I was told, was still dating the Italian-American whose father was a colonel. Mother sniffed when she said it, but she also sighed, indicating there was nothing she could do. I knew that I was the one she thought she could control.

The phone rang one day. It was a cousin a couple of generations older than me who lived in Camden, known as "horse country" but also the center of a large cotton-planting area. His name was Terrill Laurens, and he was having a party for a debutante. "We need stags. Why don't you fill your car with five or six eligible young men and come over for the party?" Terrill lived on a place out in the country called Five Oaks. There was a band in the front drawing room, the furniture had been taken out in both this and the back drawing room, and the dancing was going on in both. There was champagne and food. I was taken into another, smaller room at the back where ten or fifteen adults were drinking whiskey and was introduced all around. "You know Fair Shaw, Caroline Laurens Jay's grandson, Rhett Jay Shaw's son. Lives in Columbia. He was nice enough to come over for the party with a car full of young men." Terrill wore patent leather pumps with brown socks.

Terrill Laurens was notorious in the family for having written a book, which, in itself was surprising, but the subject of the book had caused dismay. The book was titled *Dusky Romance* and the plot centered on the sexual relationship before the Civil War between one of the Laurens men and a female slave. It was said that when it was published my grandmother—my mother's mother and Terrill's first cousin—had organized a committee of women in the family and had gone around the state buying up copies. I asked my grandmother once about Terrill's book, and she said, "Book? Terrill never wrote a book."

I asked him about it, and Terrill seemed delighted. "So you've heard about it? Let me show it to you." He pulled down a book from the bookcase, obviously proud. It was a cheaply printed but expensively bound volume, with *Dusky Romance* on the cover in large gold script and under it, smaller and in serif type, *Terrill Laurens*. So Terrill had written a book. That meant my grandmother had bought up the copies as the family legend said she had, and, I thought, these two facts meant that what he had written was the truth. People in the family knew that men in the family, before the Civil War, had had sex with slave women, and these people in the family were trying to hide that fact now.

Much of my social training and that of my peers culminated, and had its point, in the debutante season. I knew where all this came from—my parents' generation was the fag end of the plantation aristocracy of a hundred years ago—and it had nothing to do with my life or with my education, although I had vague notions of someday writing a novel about it all in the manner of Edith Wharton. I held myself aloof from it while participating in all of it. While the life I led was a great distance from the struggles of Negroes— although these struggles were going on all around us—I thought I understood to some degree what they were after, which was what I had been told I already had, and what I myself also sought, *a place*. I was able to read in the papers the stories on the attempts of young Negro men and women to gain their place in the world, at lunch counters, in the voting booth, in the schools, and on public streets. The conflict between their struggles on the street and our levity in this or that debutante party gave rise to a certain amount of disquiet that almost none of us ever talked about.

As I listened to my cousins and my aunt and uncle and my parents, I could see that, although they varied in the degree to which they were sympathetic to the struggles of Negroes, they didn't vary in the degree to which they felt there was a line which was not to be crossed. *Our* life *here* is not to be disturbed. A friend of my parents had married a Jew, which still caused comment twenty-five years later. Without ever using the word *nigger*, my family consistently gave the message that Negroes were Negroes, and we are *us*. In fact, *Methodists* are not *us*, either. The line was stronger, even, than race.

It was easy to tell at the debutante parties who was not really there. The single, older men, always escorting some widow, some divorced woman, or some youngish woman older than the debutantes but still of marriageable age. I knew that these men were probably homosexual, and I knew that this was the part that was arranged for them to play in our culture, and it was never spoken of. Homosexual men of our class were allowed to present themselves as members of society only as ersatz heterosexual men. *Oh, yes! He's bringing Bonny Nelson!* These men lived on the margins. Whether they had another life behind closed doors—or in another city—I didn't know, but it was clear to me that if I continued to live in South Carolina and didn't get married, that is the life I would have.

I am not, by nature, an outlaw. I think, under most circumstances, I will take the easier way, if it is possible, and, given the circumstances of my life, it is usually possible. I know men who have said to their parents, *fuck no*, and left—that is sometimes what I think Cornelius has done—and I read of people who have run away, men who disappear into the dark of some big city street and are never heard of again. But I like who I am. I think I would accept being who I am in South Carolina—and would take up my place here when I get out of school—if I saw a place for me. I like the formality of manners with which my family conduct their lives. I like the way they try to take the long view and have a sense of themselves as meaning something—even though I feel they are fairly disastrously wrong about what they mean.

I don't know which of several reasons is the preeminent one for leaving South Carolina for good—the local racism, my inability to find a place for myself as a homosexual, the closed nature of society, its conservatism, or my own family's severely screwed-up emotional relationships, which restrict or corrupt the image I have of a civilized life open to the great literature and high culture of the past. In a society where *place* fought with *the past* for preeminence, I couldn't see that I had either a place or a future.

My medieval history professor, a man just at the beginning of his career, maybe 30 years old, was giving back papers in class one day. When he came to me, he said he had forgotten to bring my paper to class. "Would you mind dropping by my apartment this afternoon to pick it up?" When I arrived, he answered the door, invited me in, asked me to "wait a minute," disappeared into the back part of the apartment, and then reappeared, *naked*, and said, "I don't think I can find your paper!"

"Perhaps it would be well—it would give you time to find it—if I came back at some other time?" My eyes never left *his eyes*.

Jesus, what an asshole. I picked up a small circle of friends, none of whom went to debutante parties or had names that appeared on monuments or in history books, and none of whom were Episcopalians. All were English majors, but I was not willing, or not able, to drop out of the world I had been born into. I carried on parallel lives—debutantes, my family, and Trinity Church, on the one hand, and school, my small circle of friends, and drinking, on the other—while scorning everything. One of my friends was the son of a newspaperman in Columbia, a skeptical guy with a satiric approach to things. He was straight, husky in the manner of a bear, and called me "Shaw." "Hey! Shaw! Let's go drink a beer!" And we would. His name was "Stockman." He had other names before that, but he identified himself on the phone as "Stockman." "Shaw," he'd say, "Stockman here." He found the local mores absurd.

"Can you believe this bullshit? While the rest of the country is talking about what's *right*, South Carolina is talking about who their mothers were." There was a game played at parties called *muthawuzza.* It went like this: *And who, dear, was your mother? Mother was a Jay, you know, of the Eutaw Jays?*

"But you know Shaw, South Carolina has been isolated from the beginning. We weren't in sync with the eighteenth century, why should we be in sync with the twentieth?"

We talked about girls—he introduced me to some of the girls he knew—and about dating, and we talked about the absurdity of the debutante season, but we didn't talk about sex between men.

Stockman liked to drink, and we met at debutante parties and found our way out onto the terrace to talk.

"Have you seen how drunk your cousin is? Christ, I wish I were like that. I've been trying to get drunk all night. I'm losing my drinking skills. I can't make it happen any more."

"You've stopped giving it your full attention."

He looked at me over his glass. "I think you must be right. I keep getting distracted by all the beauty here."

"Right."

"I'm joking, Shaw. Christ what a bunch. There's not a soul here who's had an original thought since the Carolina Cup. I think it's the heat. All they can do in weather like this is get angry as hell, go off, muskets firing in all directions, and attack some fort—or lynch some poor nigger bastard. They don't know how to have a reasonable conversation because the weather hasn't cooled down during the lifetimes of most of the people in the state alive today."

He finished off his drink.

"Tell me about your family. That's always good for a gasp."

Stockman was going to be a newspaperman, he said, but I thought he was going into politics. He was big enough to be a football player, but he had the manner of a politician—friendly, overpowering, cynical, lacking subtlety. He was constantly amazed by what passed for reasonable conduct around him. "In what other civilized society in the whole fucking world—aside from the USSR —do you find a major candidate running for the *Senate* in the general election *unopposed*? Holy shit. You'd think that having somebody run against him would have good entertainment value, at the least. It indicates what a lock the political structure has on this state. They don't *have* any opposition. It's not that people don't have ideas, it's that whatever opposition there is gets smothered months, years, before the election, and by the time the—I was about to say 'children'—the *voters* have a chance to make their wishes known, there's only one person to vote for. Pure Eastern Europe. We might as well be Bulgaria. The range of public opinion under the umbrella of the Democratic Party runs the gamut from A to C. People down here never heard of the separation of Church and State—look where

Trinity Church is, 200 yards across the street from the State House!
You Episcopalians seem to think you are the fourth branch of
government—and while they're talking about the feds taking over
everything, the churches, unopposed, have already gotten a lock on it
all. The reason there's so much drinking down here is that everyone
is trying to handle the stress of being polite. They hate each other.
They hate Negroes. They hate the North, the Kennedys, anyone who
is more successful than they are, but they have to be polite. And the
stress of being polite while they are in the midst of hating people just
makes them crazy. Have you noticed how really crazy people are
down here? And how many alcoholics? In what other culture do
adults spend major amounts of money giving parties at which vast
quantities of alcohol are served to underage guests? AA is thinking of
moving its national headquarters to West Columbia. Tell me about
Cornelius. I saw him last night at Elinor Barnstable's party. He's
cool. He doesn't give a shit, does he?" We smoked cigarettes. "And
how many minutes, Shaw, are you going to hang around this state
after you graduate?" After a time, Stockman's tone seemed like all
the others—an avoidance of the issue.

Cornelius was like us. His way of avoiding the issue was *he
played ball*. It was a way of doing something he enjoyed doing and
was good at, but it was also what reading was to me, a way of escape
from my confinement. I had come to think that my brother was
merely marking time, waiting for things to sort themselves out before
he revealed himself. I also thought that since he played ball,
Cornelius was forgiven his clothes and his manners and his
toughness. Mother stayed angry at Cornelius—she told me again and
again how Cornelius failed her—but Cornelius was growing into
what they all expected him to grow into, *a man*. Playing ball was
within the parameters of the acceptable. He could play ball until he
found a way out, or he could play ball until he found a way in, and
everybody, despite Mother, was having to give Cornelius time.

Anger was always, with the two of us, Cornelius and me, just
below the surface, ready to erupt at any moment—which was usually
when we were drinking—when our Southern manner failed us. I ran
into him late one night at a party.

He usually didn't speak first.

"Hi Cornelius. Have you tried the punch?"

"I did my drinking before I came." He didn't look at me.

106

"It's good."

Then he saw me. "What's up, Fair, still dateless?"

"You shit."

"Really pisses you off not to have a date?"

"You should try reading a book, Cornelius."

During the eighteen months when I was getting my degree from the University of South Carolina, I tried not to have direct confrontations with my father and my mother or my brother, but I erupted into shouting matches with all of them when they pressed too hard. The problem was that none of us wanted, or were able, to deal with the accumulated pain around our house.

Mother, when we were alone, said, "It is so *difficult* living with your father." This was no secret. She told everybody how difficult it was living with him. But she also said, "I love him so," which may have been true. To my father's face, she was more indirect. "I went by to see Helen Seabrook this afternoon. I wanted to take some cuttings from the alba plena in Mother's garden. She was so sweet. We had tea and caught up on our families. George is doing so well, you know. He is now senior partner of his law firm. They have such a lovely home. Their garden is so lovely—she had two men out there working while I was there, putting in dogwoods along the property edge. They have just come back from the Caribbean. She says it was such a rest for both of them. She complimented me on my sewing. She asked where I had gotten this dress, and I said I made it. She said I was so smart, what with teaching and all the other things I do." As she talked, I watched him wilt and finally leave the table. She put her head in her hand, her elbow resting on the table, and started to cry. "I try *so* hard."

Daddy was unable to please her, and she was unable to quit telling him that he didn't please her, and there was nothing for me to do about any of that. Her *I try so hard* was a trump card she played on the last trick, which turned the whole game around and put everybody else down. Her *I try so hard* left the complainer feeling like shit, feeling selfish and thoughtless and as if he didn't really understand. I ended up wanting to comfort her—and apologize for my bad behavior—when I had started out feeling an overpowering urge to strangle her. Her life was hard and a disappointment to her, and there was something primal in my desire to please her and in my frustrated anger against her.

Mother was very small, and when she hugged me, she took my shoulders in both hands and pulled me toward her until our upper bodies touched, and then she allowed her cheek to graze mine. When I did put both my arms around her, there wasn't a lot there to hug, and she was unable to put both her arms around me to hug me back.

"You and Daddy are more willing to accept Cornelius on his terms than you are to accept me."

She acted surprised. "Why do you feel that?"

"I have always felt that. You always find fault with me. I can't seem to please you."

"Well, we do the best we can." And that was the end of it. To argue with that was to argue with the best they could do, which was pointless.

I insisted. "It is hard to feel good about myself."

"Why is that hard? You are an eligible young man in Columbia, you're attractive, and everybody says so." She didn't want to know.

She complained about Cornelius to me and about me to Cornelius, as if to make certain that only one was in favor at a time. I didn't know whether it was the South, or my parents' class, or my parents themselves that made them so unable to speak directly.

Cornelius and I took our father on a hike through Linville Gorge in North Carolina, a hike my father had taken often when he was a boy. He was 50 now, and he said he wanted to do it one last time. We took a friend of ours, a guy with a slightly too-small mouth and small eyes, and black hair.

The hike was a mistake. The five day trek was longer than any of us had remembered, harder than it had seemed the last time, and bitter. I could do nothing right. I hiked too fast or too slow. I didn't pack Daddy's backpack correctly. I said what my father thought were stupid things. At one point our friend asked me, "Does your father always criticize you like that?" I was so busy keeping myself together and trying to keep Daddy together that I hadn't noticed what Daddy was doing to me. Cornelius walked on ahead. You could almost hear him grinding his teeth.

Daddy had inexplicably brought along a bath towel. In the rain, and deep in the mountains in the damp terrain, in mountain laurel thickets that had to be climbed through, the towel became soaked, and I discovered my father laboring over giant boulders, a soaking towel tied to his backpack. He was exhausted, weak, desperate, and I stopped him and told him we had to lighten his load. I untied the towel. "This can be thrown away."

"That's your mother's towel."

"I know. But you are about to have a heart attack, and she's not going to care about the towel if you come back dead."

"I don't want to throw it away."

"Dad, we have to. It is too heavy for you to carry. We only have one more day, and we don't need a towel. I don't want to carry it. It's gotten wet, and it is very heavy. Cornelius doesn't want to carry it. Let's throw it away. It's cotton. It'll rot quickly here in the woods and leave no trace."

He was suddenly enraged. "I brought that towel up to Linville, and I am going to take it back down again—" It was a hand monogrammed towel. "—Goddamn it, don't you touch that towel!"

I threw it away, and Daddy came back down from Linville defeated, when the hike had been meant to provide him with a final triumph. We were driven, all of us, by fear and anger that erupted frequently and sporadically and by an unhappiness so deep it seemed Paleolithic. And it never seemed to end.

"Put a happy face on!" It was Mother. "Be cheerful!"

My mother watched me as if she were certain I carried a virus that, unattended, was going to infect us all. She knew that, somehow, I had lost faith in her world, and she didn't know how to cope with the dangers I presented. She didn't so much treat me with a new-found respect—I was now 23—as treat me with a deepening wariness. I was dangerous. I had taken Cornelius' place in the family.

She sat in the rocking chair in her room sewing, and I sat on the bed, my back up against the large carved walnut headboard, listening to her. "I wanted to talk to you because you are going to leave soon, and we might not have another chance. Things are so hectic nowadays that I hardly have time to think. I don't know how much you know of what is going on. Cornelius and his new girl are getting serious. They are thinking of marriage. There is all that. And then your father is very unhappy in his job and is thinking of looking around." A small inlaid mahogany sewing table did double duty for a bedside table and so had thimbles and pincushions next to a telephone and a stack of magazines. The pictures on the walls were of us—snapshots of Cornelius and me and Daddy—in frames arranged without regard for artistic effect. "And I am *very* worried about you. You don't seem to have a firm grip on your future. You are so like your father. You are a dreamer. You have these grand plans, and nothing ever seems to come of them. You left Sewanee before you were through, without really knowing why you were going into the Army, but that might have been OK if you had come home with a clear notion of what you wanted to do, but you didn't. Now you are going to New York without a plan. *Why* are you going to New York?"

I was startled. I looked at her. I was so accustomed to listening to Mother ramble on with her complaints that I had allowed my mind to wander. Now, suddenly, she wanted to know about New York. "I don't know. I need to get away from South Carolina." I made that do for an answer.

"Why do you need to get away from South Carolina? What is it that is not good enough about South Carolina for you?"

"It's too conservative." I didn't want to talk to her about what it really was. She would never leave me alone if I lived in South Carolina. I had no freedom to work out the details of my life here. It was *her* I was leaving—and it was also South Carolina.

"I don't understand your wanting to abandon what you have here. You have always been dissatisfied here, and I don't know why that is. It has been good enough for us, and good enough for Cornelius. You are always dissatisfied, and that is just like your father. You never just accept things the way they are. Accept the place you have here—"

I wondered what place that was.

"—accept your family and the people who love you."

Fleetingly I considered telling Mother I was queer. But to tell her was to let her tell me that she tried so hard and that I made it so much harder for her. I didn't want to give her one more reason for being a martyr. She bore all her burdens while she pointed out to everyone the burdens she had to bear, and I did not want to hear, again, how I —how we all—had added to the burdens she bore. This one, I had to deal with myself. Only, it was worse than that. She would find my homosexuality unbelievable—*you're intelligent, you're attractive, you're Fair Shaw*—and she would no more be able to believe I was queer than she could believe I was a Negro. She had been able to look at my bodybuilding magazines, which she had found under my mattress when I was 14, and think that they were pictures of *women with big breasts*. I could say, *I'm queer,* and she would say, "Oh no. You were born in the summer. You have gray eyes, just like your brother."

"You drink too much. You are going to ruin your life. I think it was because you were drinking too much at Sewanee that you left. You go out drinking almost every night. And you don't seem to be interested in finding a lovely girl. Somebody like Henrietta. Cornelius is settling down. You are going to end up just like your father, with all these dreams, none of them realized, unhappy, unfulfilled, unable to admit to yourself what went wrong, how you had wasted your life."

I lifted my chin slightly. She had asked me to change schools for her, for no good reason. This was hard, and I didn't know what I was able to say. What if what she said were true? But how could this woman say—formulate the words which would express—the truth about *anything*?

"Get a job—get a profession—find a lovely girl, settle down, get married, do what you have to do. Make us proud of you. As it is, it is hard for me to hold my head up around this town, you seem so feckless."

Well. I left after a time and went downstairs. Then I went out with Stockman and got beer. We sat in the car and drank until almost midnight and got very drunk. Only Stockman was real clear about his future. It would all be *fine*. He didn't have any more idea about his future than I had, but it would work out. "I don't know what the fuck I'm going to be doing in five years. But I do know it's going to be *fun*. I am not going to do anything with my life that is not going to be fun. Jesus, what they talk about around here is duty! Who the fuck needs that?"

I wondered. If you do *these things* you get *those things*. It was a social contract. You pay your bills and your taxes, and you get certain things in return. I believed that. If I did what my mother said —the profession, the lovely girl, the marriage, the life—then I would get in return *the place in the community*. I was cynical when Stockman and I were together, but way underneath my cynicism was a faith that a man got what he paid for. The social contract was clear, and I believed it was real. If I did my part, my culture would do its part. Even queer sex was part of this contract. You didn't do it, and you got respect. Except that it was more, *If you don't do queer sex, then we will have a social contract with you.* This was hard, because the contract asked more of me than it asked of Cornelius, who didn't want to feel men's arms and therefore didn't have to give up any fucking thing.

Much of what I learned at Carolina was *data.* That is, what I learned there were dates, the names of movements, the principal characteristics of schools, membership lists, the names of plays, and the like. I did not learn how to read, more than I already knew, and I didn't learn why read. But I did well there and came away with the best wishes and recommendation letters of the best professors—and with the same kind of applause that I had gotten at Sewanee. "Your son is going to be a great critic someday," my Shakespeare professor, whose child was taught by Mother at the Episcopal school with giant Corinthian columns, told Mother. I had done nothing to resolve the great crisis I faced except to run away, but I had gotten entry—in the form of the piece of paper called a *diploma*—into the celebration of high culture that I had first been introduced to at Sewanee.

Despite all the parties and the family gatherings and the daily lunches with my father and other family members, I had spent the time in South Carolina alone, ministering to my sexual needs with my hand. There was no other possibility. Except, except, of course, my medieval history professor, who stood in the doorway naked and said he couldn't find my paper. I might have said, "Oh, fuck the paper. Come here and suck my dick." Maybe then I would have connected with the homosexual community.

At a party that winter, I was on the terrace of a house on Forest Lake, looking out across the lake in the early evening, the pine trees across the water black and tall and spiky against the darkening blue sky. I had a bourbon and water in my hand—my drink of choice—and I wore a tuxedo. Behind me, in the house, was the party. There was a five-piece band at one end of the living room, and a bar in the library with bartenders in white coats. Young men in tuxedos and young women in floor length evening gowns slowly danced the shag, being careful not to spill their drinks. I considered the South and its murky, bloody history. If I stayed, I would suffer the paralyzing conflict of fear and anger that all of them suffered. I had dreamt of being able to save them all, somehow, through learning, through style, through grace. Well, I would restore my *self*, even if I could not save my family, to some version of the lawn at Wespanee. I would do it for myself alone. When I left South Carolina, I would not come back.

"Fair?"

I heard my name.

"Is that you?"

I turned and saw a tall young man coming toward me from the house. It was full dark now, and the lights from the house shone in my eyes and cast this figure in shadow, and I didn't, at first, recognize him.

"I didn't know you were coming tonight."

It was Cornelius. Cornelius. What was this all about?

Cornelius joined me, leaning on his arms against the balustrade next to me. "I hear you are graduating."

"At the end of January." We had not seen each other all fall, and only once or twice at large family gatherings. Christmas eve. Debutante parties like this one, occasionally.

"That means you're graduating early."

"Yes. I did it in a year and a half."

"What was the rush?"

"I want to be done with it."

"What are you going to do?"

"New York. I want to go to New York."

My brother laughed quietly. I was astonished at Cornelius. He was in a tuxedo also, and looked very good in it, his athletic build, his handsome face with the large gray eyes of the Shaws, their long eyelashes, the same eyes and lashes that I knew I myself had. I thought, had things been different, we could have been friends. *We could have been lovers.*

"I don't understand wanting to leave." Cornelius gestured toward the lake and the final pale sliver of blue above the trees on the other side. "It's such a beautiful place, Fair." The word in the family was that Cornelius had "found himself." He was doing well working for Uncle Robert, and he was dating now the daughter of the best-known defense attorney in the state. It was said now that he was going to be a great success. "I love it here." I don't think we had ever had a real conversation, man-to-man, between adults. "I don't understand why you're leaving." He looked over at me. "But then there's a good chance you'll come back. Maybe you can teach at the University of South Carolina." He put his arm around my shoulders.

"This is where you belong." He squeezed my shoulder muscle, the place where the trap leads into the delt. "It's such an easy place to love. All our family is here. They've always been here. Forever, since the beginning. The weather, the soft breeze, the women. My God, have you ever seen such women as there are here? The most beautiful women in the world." He smiled as if he has discovered something amazing. "And they'll forgive you anything." Then he said, "Look at me. All I had to do was get a job, and even Mother forgave me!" He laughed harshly out loud. "Look. Go to New York. Get it out of your system. Then come home. And when you do, let's be friends, hear? I think you did the right thing, you got a good education. Mine sucks. I fucked that up real good. I admire you, I really do, you're cool, and when you come back home, we can be real good friends, maybe go to a football game or two, or hunting down on the Santee—"

I listened to Cornelius talking. *He* would be a success here. Like all of them here, he would say he loved you right up to the moment it become clear he had no idea who you were. He acted like I had never known him before, like we had no past.

"Did Mother ask you to talk to me?"

"Now—" Cornelius got this good ole boy grin on his face—it was called a shit-eatin' grin—and shook his head. "Now what gave you that idea!"

"Knowing Mother and knowing the way she handles us. That's what gave me that idea." Then I asked again. "Did she?"

"Well, uh, yes."

The problem was that Cornelius and I did not, in our whole lives, have a history of mature, serious conversations. I wondered if it were possible to seize this moment and to make something of it. He was embarrassed at being caught in his deception, at being manipulated by Mother. He wanted something that would get him out of his discomfort. Maybe.

"Cornelius, I'd like to talk to you. Something about me." Then, "Do you have a minute?"

He was not worried. He had been drinking and was relaxed, and he smiled at me. "Sure. What do you want to talk about?"

"It's not bad. It's about me, something you don't know."

I was taking too long with this, and he was getting worried. "Shoot."

"Look, Cornelius, the reason I am not going to stay in South Carolina—" I was right now right up against the hard edge of it. "—is that I'm a homosexual, and I'm going to find a place that's—" I wasn't, now, looking out at the lake. I was looking at him.

He glanced at me. "Oh—" For a second, Cornelius looked like he was in real pain. He shook his head. "Oh, Fair, is that *true?*" He had his hands on the balustrade and stiffened his arms, looking down at his drink.

"Yes, it is true."

"Oh—"

"It's true. I've always known, since I was a kid."

"Ah, man, I *love* you, don't you know that?"

"What are you telling me, Cornelius?"

"No, it's that—" He couldn't find words. "—it's that I love you and I don't want to see you do something awful like this to yourself."

"And to you. You have a queer brother."

"Oh, man, don't say that. That's not true. Ah, Fair, what a mess! This is horrible."

"I've always been queer—"

"Ah, no! You were just—" He still couldn't find the words. "—a little—"

"Effeminate is the word you're looking for. I've always been queer. When I was in the Army I had something for a good many months with a very beautiful man."

"Oh!" He caught his hands together—wove his fingers together—and straightened his arms and pushed down, pivoting back and forth. "Oh, Fair. You're going to ruin your life."

I waited that one out. It would take a few minutes for him to come around.

"Fair. Oh, why are you telling me this, now? Oh, Fair—"

"I guess because we are not going to see each other for a long time, and you don't really understand why I am going to New York, and I thought you deserved to know." I was watching him, trying to gauge his response while I talked. "I thought, a minute ago, that it might be possible for us, like adults, to become friends. You know we never have been. I thought your knowing that I am queer might bring us closer together. There's nothing wrong with it."

He didn't say anything. *We* didn't say anything. I waited. He looked at me, then at his watch. "I have to go." Then he picked up his drink—

"See ya, Cornelius."

—and turned and walked away, across the terrace and into the house.

I picked up my pack of cigarettes from the balustrade. I gripped my drink tightly.

↔

Our apartment was on the upper West Side, off-Broadway, on West 91st Street. Edward was a big friendly man, something like Connie in that he was very sexual, but unlike Connie in that he never brushed up against the line that separated friendliness between men from sexual activity between men. Like many very sexy straight men, he seemed unaware of the effect he might be having on men who liked men. The whole idea seemed not to occur to him, but he was very stimulating to be around, to have around in the apartment, and he and I got along well and did a lot of drinking together— *Double bourbon on the rocks, please*—in bars all over the city. It may have been his size that made people look to him as a problem-solver, and while he was having sex widely around the city, he was also taking on people's difficulties, helping this woman with this, moving furniture for that one.

In New York I wrote. I spent every moment writing when I was not out drinking, but what I was writing about—a Southern boy growing up on a plantation in the nineteen-fifties—didn't go anywhere, and a friend who actually had grown up on a plantation, in Mississippi, told me my main problem was I didn't know anything about farming. When I wasn't writing, I was exploring the museums in the city—the Metropolitan, the Frick, the Guggenheim, the Modern, the Whitney—but I spent most of my time in the first two, which had the old masters. In the Metropolitan, I saw for the first time the bronze bust of Cosimo de' Medici by Benvenuto Cellini, with its magnificent breastplate displaying Cosimo's enlarged nipples being bitten by eagles. This led me to read *The Autobiography of Benvenuto Cellini* and to discover that Cellini had been charged with the crime of sodomy in Renaissance Florence and had spent time in jail. Cellini carried on affairs with his male assistants and with other men that lasted for years—at the same time having affairs with women and even getting married and fathering children. I also found pictures of Cellini's bronze *Perseus* in the Loggia dei Lanzi in the Piazza della Signoria, a statue whose high, rounded buttocks suggested the quality of Cellini's interest in his model.

Also in the Metropolitan, I found the engraving of the Farnese *Hercules* by Hendrick Goltzius, the Dutch artist who had spent time in Rome in 1590 and 1591 and was impressed by classical sculpture he found there. Oddly, Goltzius drew the statue of *Hercules* from the rear. The effect is to throw Hercules' muscular back and his rounded, hard buttocks into high relief and to make them, inescapably, into sexual objects. The lines, a complex of hatch marks and curved parallels, are intensely engraved across the buttocks and the backs of the legs, the lower spinal erectors, and the enormous trapezius muscles, some close together and some spaced wide apart, so as to give the back of Hercules' body a hard and bulging musculature. The back itself, an expanse of latissimus dorsi divided by the deep crevasse between the spinal erectors, is vast and seems to pulse with power. The smooth leg biceps and calves, because of the lighter handling of the lines, seem to glow as if they have been oiled.

Caroline Rowland, a cousin my age, had left South Carolina four or five years before and had established herself in the television industry in the city as an actress on one of the soap operas. She lived with another woman, and I suspected they were lovers, but they never discussed it, so I didn't know. The three of us spent a lot of time drinking—Virginia Gentleman and Maker's Mark—in their apartment, talking about the South.

Cornelius did not write, and I did not write. Mother's letters and phone calls didn't indicate that he had said anything to her, but she did write, once, "Did something happen between you and Cornelius before you went to New York? He is upset about something, and I think it is with you. Mainly all he can think about is Henrietta, but he does sometimes seem upset with you about something. Do you know what it could be? I hate so for you two to quarrel. You love each other so. I think he may be upset that you went to New York."

I formed the habit of reading *The New York Times* every morning. Alone, I explored New York—all over the various neighborhoods on the upper West Side where we lived and Fifth Avenue as far uptown as the Guggenheim. I hung out in Times Square watching the chaotic, sexually-driven scene, and I went down to Trinity Church and to Wall Street and took the Staten Island Ferry. I went to the top of the Empire State Building, and I went to the Village.

I went to a party on Bank Street at the home of a young woman whose father taught at NYU. The house was packed high with bookcases filled with books—brilliant book jackets giving the titles of academic and recent political and historical texts—and the tables were piled with art books and stacks of what seemed like all the books I was reading about in *The New York Review of Books,* which had just begun to be published. The guests were all academics or the college-aged children of academics.

A young woman introduced herself, a student in political science at NYU. Very pretty. Very serious.

"What are you doing in New York?"

"Working."

"At what?"

"I am writing a novel. And I am supporting myself by working for a captive advertising agency for the Prudential Insurance Company."

"What does that mean?"

"That we write copy for internal advertising, the kind of thing they give to customers or to agents who are selling to customers. I do it for the money." I gripped my bourbon and water tightly.

"Tell me about the South." It was the question on everyone's lips.

"It's hot. Everything, as Faulkner says, hangs on too long, including the summer. It's filled with family and relatives and ancestors, and it's small, so I left."

"Don't you ever plan to go back?"

"No."

I was very drunk.

She asked me what my novel was about.

"A young man who can't cope with his family. It's a tragedy."

"Do you hate them very much?"

"No. I was wrong. It's a *problem* play." I laughed harshly.

"Why are you so sardonic?"

I didn't take her home and have sex, although I knew I could have. But during the spring, I got to know a woman who lived in our apartment building, and sometimes I went to her apartment to talk. I would bring a bottle of bourbon, and she would provide ice and glasses. Eventually this led to her coming on to me.

"You're very attractive yourself." We were talking about men she dated—she was maybe five years older than I, had long brown hair, and worked in Wall Street—and what she liked in men. "You have beautiful eyes—" They all said that. "—and I like the way you are very thoughtful. What I mean is the way you think all the time about what it all means. I like that in a man. Somebody who is smarter than I am. It makes me feel safe." She laughed. "I think brains are very sexy."

I could see where this was going, and, thinking of the end of it, I wondered if I could do it. I felt no physical attraction to her.

We were sitting on the sofa, divided by the center cushion, on which sat an ashtray. It was an efficiency apartment, in which everything but the bathroom was in one room, and the sofa folded out to make her bed. She reached across the space dividing us and touched my hand. "I think *you* are very sexy."

I put my hand on top of hers and squeezed it. I leaned over and kissed her. I wondered if something were going to happen now— when would my dick get hard—but nothing happened. I considered quickly whether I should stop this now, or whether I should explore some more, and I decided that there was nothing to be lost by continuing, except the possibility of some embarrassment at the end.

I kissed her again, and she put her hands on my shoulders, kneading my shoulder muscles. Then she slid her hands behind my back and pulled me closer. I noticed the difference between her body and a man's. I missed the hardness of a man's body, of Connie's body. I also missed the mass of a man's body. She was small. We positioned ourselves so that my arm, around her shoulders, allowed my hand to rest on her breast, and I cupped it, thinking about Connie's pectoral muscles. She unbuttoned her blouse and unsnapped her bra, and my hand now cupped her bare breast. I felt her nipple in the palm of my hand, and I pulled my hand back enough to tug slightly on it while I kissed her. She groaned and arched her back, and I tugged lightly on both her nipples.

We got up and got undressed and pulled out the sofa bed and got in. I had never seen a vagina up close and didn't know exactly what I was to do with it, and my instincts didn't lead me to know, as they had with Connie's body. My cock was now erect, and I knew I would be OK. I *was* OK. Slightly clumsy—I had been clumsy with Connie, too, the first time—but OK. Everything worked as it was supposed to. She seemed pleased, and afterward I was elated. Later, in my own apartment, I fixed a drink and walked around the apartment—I was too excited to sit down for long—from the living room to the kitchen to the bedroom upstairs and back downstairs to the living room, where I dropped myself down on the sofa, sipped my drink, and then leapt up again to walk around the apartment, elated, excited, full of myself. *I did it!*

I was drawn, sometimes, to try to find homosexual hangouts. I knew they ought not to be hard to find. Bars in New York would lose their license to sell liquor if they were found selling to homosexuals, and some bars had signs in the windows telling homosexuals not to enter. Life already seemed complicated enough without chancing an arrest for indecent exposure or public lewdness or for being a public nuisance. I was afraid of the danger of homosexual bars—from the police, violence from the other men—but I was also repelled by what I saw of the culture, which seemed profoundly in rebellion against the professional middle class that I thought I was headed toward. I was also afraid of doing it alone, going down to the Village and going into one of the bars alone.

Even so, I liked New York. I liked the men. I liked the men of all shades of brown—from very dark bitter chocolate to a shade so light it was almost white. I liked men with dark very curly hair—they reminded me of Connie—and I liked men who knew how sexy they were. New York was full of such men, with dark eyes and long lashes—and deep shadows around their eyes. I liked the chaos of New York, the abutment of forces almost out of control, the violence of feelings, the dirt and the smells. The city seemed driven by sex. I would have liked to have sex with one of these men—I imagined the kind of sex we could have!—but I had no desire to join the homosexual culture that I knew was there, which seemed dirty, rebellious, chaotic, and furtive.

Once, Edward and I were on the East Side at the apartment of some girls we knew when someone came in breathlessly. "Kennedy's here, at the Pierre, and if we go back now, we'll be able to see him."

So we went running back down to the Pierre, where there were many policemen and motorcycles and the street was blocked off. There, in the middle of all this controlled confusion—it reminded me of Army maneuvers, many vehicles, many uniformed men, whistles, shouts, a controlled and ordered mayhem—was the Presidential limousine, a very long, very dark blue car. We waited. Then the hotel door burst open, and a crowd of Secret Service men came out onto the sidewalk, and, in their midst, were President and Mrs. Kennedy. Before we could see them really—I could tell he was in white tie and she was in an evening gown—they disappeared into the car. Then something completely unexpected happened.

There appeared to be a light inside the car, for it came on as they entered the car, and it bathed them in a soft distinct glow. It made them seem holy. They seemed to have a glow like the glow around saints, or it made them seem like a pair of the Olympian gods bathed in their own aura. I saw this for only a second, then the sirens started and the motorcycles moved. And the car, in their midst, moved off smoothly toward Fifth Avenue.

I burst out laughing. "What the fuck!"

"They have their own special light inside their car so people can see them better."

"I think it was focused especially on their faces!"

It was Glamour. I had never seen anything like that. I was aware that it was manufactured, this glamour. My father, I knew, would have hated it, but I was entranced.

Last fall, while still thrashing around for some sense of direction, and as a way of getting my parents off my back, I had applied to several Southern universities, Vanderbilt University, in Nashville, Tennessee, among them. Now, in the spring, Vanderbilt wrote and offered me the largest scholarship they had in their possession. It would be a free year, so I accepted, and I made plans to leave at the end of the summer.

In the middle of the day, June 11, 1963, George Wallace, the governor of Alabama, stood in the school house door, as he had said he would, at the University of Alabama, attempting to block the enrollment of two Negro students who had legally enrolled at the university.

President Kennedy nationalized the Alabama National Guard and ordered them to enforce the orders of the federal courts. My phone rang about six in the evening. It was my father. "The Kennedys are going to have the federal government take over the whole of the United States." My father personalized the issue—it was "the Kennedys," not "the President" or "the Democrats" or "the Administration" or "the government." "Don't you agree?"

"Well, no, sir."

"How can you not agree? The federal government has never had anything to do with education before. Wallace is right about that. Now the Kennedys are moving the federal government into the area of state-supported college education, against the Constitution—"

"No, sir, I don't agree. The Constitution says that all citizens shall have the equal protection of the laws—"

"Well your brother agrees with me!"

My father handed the phone to Mother, who asked me *what* had I done to Cornelius, who was *very* upset with me. I didn't agree with my father, but I didn't want to fight him either, and I respected him, too, in some areas. He was smart, he read a great deal. In fact, we both read many of the same books—my father read *my* books— although we didn't agree on what they meant, and I recognized that he had had a hard life. I knew he felt very threatened by the civil rights movement. If he wasn't special because he was white, what was he doing where he was on the social pyramid? He had not been a success in anything, anywhere in his life, and he was a recovering alcoholic whose drinking had ruined his wife's life. The phone call was the beginning of something, too. It was the first time I could remember my father saying that *Cornelius* was on his side.

That night, June 11, 1963, at nine, President Kennedy gave his first major civil rights speech. "We are confronted primarily with a moral issue. It is as old as the Scriptures and is as clear as the American Constitution." It was moving and eloquent, and it was decisive and unequivocal, and it was unmistakably *right,* and it was extremely powerful. I was proud. Our country was not irredeemably corrupted. But the next day, Medgar Evers was assassinated in his driveway, and the country had blood all over it again.

One night late in the summer, Edward came home and came into the kitchen and fixed a drink and joined me at the table. "Something is wrong between us, and I think it's because of me, somehow, and I want to talk about that." I was listening to him intently. He spoke very slowly, in a low tone, and very deliberately, and when he was speaking to me, I was forced to hang on every word he said, waiting for enough of it to come out for me to tell what he was talking about. "I think that you are pissed off at me for something. Am I right?"

Edward, during the months we had shared an apartment in the city, had regularly brought girls home with him, and I waked up in the middle of the night hearing him fucking her in the next bed over.

"Is it that I bring girls home?"

That had not been very comfortable for me, but that wasn't it. "No, you haven't done anything wrong."

"Then what is it?"

I knew what it was. There was a whole range of pressures I was under that made me vulnerable—Cornelius' silence, my parents' regular harping on graduate school, my not having connected with a guy, the general pressures of New York itself, my worry over whether it was right to go south again for graduate school, whether I was learning what I needed to learn to be a writer. And there was Edward in the bed next to mine, often enough with a woman. Part of it was envy, I suppose. I wanted to be able to bring someone home with me as he did. I could have brought the girl from Bank Street home—and plenty of others—if I had cared about bringing a female home. It could have been as easy for me as it was for Edward. And then I was envious of him because he brought women home, and I wished I wanted to do that. But then, I wanted him to want me, just as I had wanted Cornelius' friends to want me, when I was in high school. As spring had rolled over into summer, I had thought my life would have been easier if Edward and I had not lived together. It was hard to be in the same room with him. Many times, I wished he would simply disappear. And when he appeared again, the same Edward—happy, cheerful, capable, sexy, and strong—I found him irritating and intrusive. *Oh, shit, just get out.*

And yet here he was trying to talk. I was struck by how good he was being about all this. He was trying to do what I had seen him do at parties and bars around the city—find out what was bothering people and *fix it.* He was right, *something* was wrong, but it wasn't his fault and he couldn't fix it. I was weary, and I was disappointed with where I was, with New York, with myself. I had no defenses, and at that moment I didn't take the effort to hide.

"I'm a homosexual. And this has been a hard time for me—this whole year—and that has made it difficult to live with you. I am strongly attracted to you." I waited for him to say something. Finally he did.

"Then you're sick."

He could have called me a degenerate or pervert, the words the culture used. He could have called me any of the words the church people used, *sinful, evil, damned, bad,* or that the criminal justice system used, *criminal,* or he could have said, "You're a fruit." But he didn't use any of those words either. I knew that, at that moment, the most progressive thing that most people could say was *you're sick.* And then he did what Edward always tried to do, *he tried to fix it.*

"You need help. You need to see a psychiatrist. If I can find you one, will you go?"

I was glad he was still talking to me—I had been right, there had been little possibility that when I told him I was attracted to him he would leap up out of his chair screaming at me—so I nodded.

"Emily's roommate sees a psychiatrist, and I think I can get his name for you. Will you go if I get his name?"

The psychiatrist had an office on the Upper East Side, and I went, agreed to pay him $70 an hour, which I couldn't afford but which I thought would be worth it if it worked, and I began. "I am a homosexual, and I have always been a homosexual as long as I can remember—" He was in his fifties, I guessed, and his room was all brown and the blinds were pulled down and turned so you could only see bars of bright light between the slats, and he never said anything, not even when I first came into the room the first day. He listened.

I had known people in therapy—I knew the same girl Edward knew who went to this doctor—but what actually went on in a therapy session was a mystery to me, and I thought, once I tell him I am a homosexual, he will ask me questions to help me go in the right direction, but he didn't. There was a pause, and he did not say anything, and then, since I was uncomfortable with the silence, I went on and said something else.

I told him about the muscle magazines and about bodybuilders, about the man pulling the seine with me on his shoulders, his neck between my legs. I told him about Russell Ford and his shiny hair and muscular arms, and about Paul Connors. I told him I had had sex with a man, but that was several years ago, and I masturbated every night, that girls seemed to like me—I had had sex with a woman, but I had never felt anything around girls that I felt around men. I told him about the naked Medieval English History professor, and I told him about Bill Bartlett. I told him about Edward Markman and how difficult it was to share an apartment with him, pretending all the time that I wasn't sexually aware of him. I told him I liked the feelings, looked forward most of the day to the time when I was alone at night in my bed and could take my cock in my hand, and stroke it. I told him I didn't think I was bad or wrong or sick— Edward was wrong about that—to have these feelings, but I told him I would like not to have these feelings because they complicated everything and made it impossible for me to think clearly about what I wanted to do with my life. I didn't want to live as an outlaw. I *really* hated the homosexual bars in the Village with the peephole in the door. What I didn't say was that I didn't know whether I really wanted to lose these feelings. I didn't know what I would be like without them—I had had them all my life—and to ask that they be removed was like asking that my whole personality be removed and replaced with—someone else—which was unthinkable.

Then it was over. It was good. I had never been able to talk about it all—most of it—before, and it was a release to be able to let it all come out, but walking down Fifth Avenue afterward I couldn't think what I would say to him the next time. But the next time I told him more of the same kind of thing—I told him about the Episcopal priest in Yakima, Washington, and about the soldier who had come on to me, and about Connie Stephanopolis and the weekends up in the Cascades walking up the side of the mountain among the hemlocks and then coming back to our clearing and having sex. How wonderful that was. But he still didn't say anything.

I went once more, and this time I told him about how my culture seemed not to want to know about my sex, about the people who had in effect told me I was not telling the truth but didn't want to know the truth. I told him about my family, how my father went to his room and read, and my mother was always disappointed in me and could never be satisfied, and about Cornelius who was never there and didn't give a shit—he had said, *Oh! No!*—and he seemed interested in this last. But then my father came to NY to get me and to drive me home to South Carolina so I could go to graduate school, and it never went anywhere. In the car, I was driving down the New Jersey Turnpike—feeling partly defeated by New York and partly excited by the prospect of graduate school—and my father was in the shotgun next to me, sitting forward and turned a little toward me, his left arm along the back of the seat between us, leaning over and talking very intensely and urgently to me.

"—it is impossible to make money in business if you're honest. Mr. Cutler didn't make any money until the war came and he started getting government contracts, and you know what government contracts are like—there's no control—and he started making money hand over fist. I don't mean to say he was the only one, but he was the one I knew about. I watched it happen. And then Richmond came into the business. Everybody said I was better than he was. Nobody had any respect for Richmond except Mr. Cutler, and yet Richmond was promoted and promoted until he was over me, and then when Mr. Cutler died, Richmond was able to buy out the business. People all over town say he doesn't know a thing about running that business. Did you know he almost flunked out of Furman? *Flunked out!* And now he is running one of the biggest businesses in the state, and he doesn't know a thing about it. He has to hire people who know what they're doing. I was talking to Carlton Fitzwood the other day, and Carlton says he doesn't even know how to read a set of plans—"

At the end of August 1963, and just days before I went to Vanderbilt, Martin Luther King, Jr., spoke at the Civil Rights March in Washington, saying, "I have a dream that one day this nation will rise up and live out the true meaning of its creed. We hold these truths to be self-evident: that all men are created equal." My father didn't ever really want to know what was going on with me. I believed, since I was 24 and since my father was an intelligent man, that he *must* know or suspect that his son was a homosexual. And I believed that the reason it never came up—that sex never came up as a subject between us—was that my father did not want me to confirm what he must have known. The alternative, the *only* alternative to this, was that my father was unable to see what was plainly in front of his eyes, unable to conceive of the conclusion to the syllogism whose major and minor premises were self-evidently true. I needed to know the answer to this question, which had eaten at me since I was thirteen: *Will you still love me?*

I thought about my relationship to the words they used for queers—*pervert, degenerate, deviate, invert, faggot.* I had heard Cornelius call queers *fruits.* The odd thing was that I didn't *feel* sick. I was who I was. I got up in the morning and I went through my day, and I felt OK. I did well, usually, at what I attempted, except ball and things like that. When I actually was sick, I felt sick. I had a fever, and I felt weak, breathless. But I never felt sick. I knew all of them— including Edward—said I was sick, and if they had the chance, they'd tell me to my face that I was sick. And it was something I had to think about all the time because you had to hide it if you were going to get anywhere in this world. I *knew* people thought what I thought about was degenerate. And that limited my options if I let them know what was in my mind. Having people think that I was sick may have meant that I *was* sick—I didn't know about that—but it certainly meant that I didn't have the same freedom other people had.

↔

One day going to the Grill, a little one-story concrete box with a neon sign that stayed open 24 hours a day serving Vanderbilt students who wanted a coffee or fried eggs at two in the morning, I found a student out front handing out sheets of paper. The flyer said, "Join Us," and asked for my support of a boycott of the Grill because it refused to serve Negro students at Vanderbilt University, Scarritt, and Peabody College. None of the three colleges had any Negro students, but they differed in whether they were officially segregated. The movement had come home to me. The flyer asked me to stop spending my money here, where I regularly did spend my money. The request was direct. It was not asking me to argue with my father but to change my ways. I called the number on the flyer and signed up to give out flyers every day at noon for an hour.

I got to know people in the English department. The boycott of the Grill became a notorious cause on campus, and the "Southerners" on the faculty and among the students had strong feelings about it. Some in the department organized a counter-protest in which they determined to eat all their meals at the Grill to counteract the effects of the boycott. Some of these were the kind of would-be patrician Southerners who, under normal circumstances, would never have gone to a place like the Grill—it was no more than a steak-and-eggs and sausage-and-eggs kind of greasy spoon—but they arrived in front of the Grill, took flyers from me and with a great show of haughty disdain tore them up into tiny little pieces and threw the pieces onto the sidewalk, then went inside. I scorned this ostentatious display. I did this for an hour every day, and, like workers on a shift, those of us on the picket line phoned back and forth among ourselves. *Can you take my Tuesday shift? I have a seminar I have to attend.*

I became known on campus as a liberal or an activist. There was little danger in this. There were others on the faculty and among the students who supported the boycott and who were active in civil rights activities around town. Nashville itself was segregated, like most Southern cities, and was in the middle of redneck countryside, deeply conservative, deeply Christian. The public discourse differed in tone from elsewhere in the South: there was no talk of constitutional issues here—the talk was of *commies* and *sin*.

Most of the other students who took part—I didn't know any of them—balanced their obligations to the movement with their obligations to school, working their volunteer hours around their class time. I was walking in a picket line one day on the main road into downtown. The buildings on both sides of the road were seedy two- and three-story brick buildings. It was a slightly cool, windy fall day, brilliant blue sky. Most of the people in the circle were Negroes from the Negro schools in town. We had dropped our book bags in a pile near a lamppost, and we moved, carrying signs the organizers had made for us, in a circle in front of some business establishment —a dime store, a drug store, nothing I had ever been to before— when the police arrived with a van. The police stood in a small group between us and the van, and I was watching all this with some apprehension, since this was my first demonstration, and I didn't know what to expect. I had found out about the demonstration from flyers taped to trees around campus. Finally, as we walked in our circle, a policeman stepped forward and put out his billy club across the chest of one of us, stopping him. He gestured toward the van, and the picketer quietly walked over and got into the back of the van, without protest. He had expected to be arrested. Then, when five or six had gotten into the van, the police closed the door, and the van took off toward the jail where they would be held until court the next

morning, charged with disorderly conduct. The rest of us were
allowed to resume our circling under the eyes of the police. I had
known that an arrest was a possibility—it was in the papers every
day, the arrest of students in picket lines—but I had not thought very
seriously about it when I decided to take part in the demonstration.
Now the reality was before me. When the van came back, the
procedure started again. The policeman put out his billy club, the
person peeled away from the circle, leading five or six others behind
him into the police van, which drove away again. They went with a
remarkable dignity and composure. I was still in the circle. I was
thinking that, if the policeman put out his billy club across the chest
of any of the people four or five ahead of me in line, I would go to
jail. It was possible to count off ahead in the line and estimate when
the policeman would send my group to the van. I started thinking
about a seminar I was scheduled for in about an hour at school—a
seminar in Victorian literature with the department head—and began
to calculate the importance of the seminar against the importance of
going to jail. I didn't mind being arrested, but I minded missing the
seminar—that is, I minded offending the department head. It was
possible for me, given the logistics of the thing, to step out of the
picket line before the policeman got to me, hand the sign to someone
else, and simply walk away. What was my duty? What did my
integrity require? What good would be done for anybody by my
going to jail overnight? I was there, in the middle of a demonstration
—demonstrations like these were going on all over town, every day,
and most of the participants, both police and pickets, were very
practiced at the procedures—but it seemed clear to me that the
demonstration was still for *them,* and I was still a long way from
feeling the obligations of brotherhood, so I decided the immediate
need was not to skip the seminar. I stepped out of line, handed my
sign to somebody else, grabbed my book bag, and walked away. The
troubling aspect of this was that I knew while I was doing it that the
Negro kids in the picket line with me didn't have the same freedom
that I had to choose not to go to jail. If you were a Negro, you
couldn't just walk away. And it would cost them something if they
went to jail. There was no point in going if it didn't cost something. I
made the Victorian literature seminar at two o'clock. I didn't go to
jail, but I did demonstrate.

It was an exhilarating time. The issues were large and clear. There were a right and a wrong, and it was easy to tell the difference. Those who were against the full integration of Negro citizens into American life were wrong. I knew that. John Kennedy had said, "We are confronted primarily with a moral issue." And the Negroes on the picket lines and at the lunch counters had their heads up, their eyes on the far distance. I had never seen an ennobling taking place. It was like watching a Transfiguration right in front of me on the city sidewalk. The cops didn't understand. They thought it was all about their exercise of police authority, but it was really about these Negro kids undergoing a Transfiguration on the sidewalk, and the cops were just painted into the lower corners of the picture by a member of the artist's workshop. The Transfiguration took place precisely between the picket circle and the cops van, so I missed it, but I saw what was happening and knew what to call it.

There was a homosexual community on campus. Jack Dexter, a graduate student in English from New Orleans, lived off campus with his lover, and at least some of the graduate English student community seemed to accept this. Jack was my height, slender, blond, pretty, witty, funny, and very preppy. He wore coats and ties every day to class. I never met his boyfriend, but I knew he was older than we were—perhaps 35—and the two of them lived in a modern apartment complex, a U-shaped building around a swimming pool, apartments with sliding glass doors and modern appliances. I had to get some papers or books from Jack one afternoon, and I knocked on his door. Jack opened it, and behind him, I saw into the apartment. The room seemed full of men. They appeared to be naked, but it must have been that they all had on tiny nylon swimming suits, their skin darkly tanned and glowing with suntan oil. They all seemed blond—they couldn't have *all* been blond—but they all seemed beautiful. Gorgeous. The curtains had been pulled across the full-length glass doors onto the terrace and the swimming pool, and the room was in semi-darkness, this mass of beautiful men seen in the shadows sitting motionless, draped over one another. Jack gave me what I wanted—some book, perhaps notes—and made some small, tense, inconsequential talk, and then closed the door again, and I was left in the hallway, next to the concrete stairs, this briefly revealed erotic vision of men without women.

I never saw that kind of thing again, although I did connect with a different kind of queer. I was in an American Literature seminar one afternoon—the subject was Hawthorne and the secret room—and the seminar room had a very high ceiling with a fake hammer-beam roof. I was scribbling away while the seminar leader was reading his paper when I looked up and suddenly realized that this man slightly older than I, sitting directly across the table from me, was staring at me. He caught my eye, and for a second I could not look away. Then *I blushed.* The man saw that, without smiling, and I looked back down on the paper and began to write again, feeling my face hot.

I made no effort to follow up on his advance. He was not very attractive, and I didn't like the way he had come on to me, in a seminar. There were enough men around whom I knew to be homosexual to know that, with some courage and guts, I could get away with it as Jack had done and as this guy across the table was now doing, coming on to me right in the middle of an American Literature seminar. But it would have to be, to some extent, in secret.

Later, days later, I woke up late one morning in my dorm room, a big room I shared with another student, our single beds at right angles to each other against the walls, to find the man from the seminar, whose name was Dan Chester, leaning over me, about to kiss me. He did kiss me. He was maybe ten years older than I, the kind of slightly plump 35-year old who would lose all his looks at 40, a local high school teacher who was trying to get a doctorate.

"I've always wondered whether you were queer. When I saw you blush, I knew. "

We had sex, and afterward I went into the bathroom to shower. When I came out, he took the towel I had tied around my stomach and untied it, and ran his fingers over my belly, marveling at my flat stomach. "You're so young." I felt pretty flat about the whole thing. I knew he was exploiting me—I hadn't done anything to encourage him—but I was curious and willing to be exploited. *What is this going to be like?* One weekend, Dan's wife was to be out of town. He persuaded me to come over and spend the night with him. I did, but I didn't enjoy it. I kept thinking of Scarlett O'Hara in her red dress standing in the doorway, looking defiant. I didn't like the tone of the thing—doing something underhanded and slimy while his wife was out of town. He was the first married man I knew who was attracted to boys. The biggest problem with it was that the sex was all for him. I wondered if Dan could get it off with anybody. Maybe I wasn't *anybody*. I had no idea whether I was especially attractive. I knew that I was certainly not as beautiful as the men in Jack's room or the men in New York.

Paul Huntley was something different entirely. He was from Texas, working on a doctorate in psychology, and kept odd hours—he'd have to leave the bar at times like 11:30 at night to go back to the lab where he was running rats. We saw each other in the dorm and then saw each other in the bar, and, in the way of people whose lives throw them together, we started joining each other for beer. I told him that I was a homosexual, thinking I was being courageous, and Paul laughed at me. "I'm as queer as you, don't you know that?" Paul was tall, blond, not pretty, but sexy enough. He looked tough and rangy, as if he spent summers herding cattle—he had very rough hands, knobby and veiny—and apparently he was able to pick up tricks around campus all the time. He would tell me about getting picked up by older men—since we were both 24, many men on campus were older than we were, most graduate students, most law students, most medical students, all the faculty—and would provide me with all the sexual details. We began to come back to the dorm from drinking beer and have sex—I instigated this—which was usually rough and quick. I was aware that Paul had something that I didn't have, and I worried about that. Men came on to me too, and I was unsure why I was turning them down when neither Paul nor Jack did. Paul had sex as a necessary release. It was something he did with the same urgency that he took a dump, and the same thoughtlessness. Of *course* he had sex, but he got up from the bed and pulled on his pants. "Now I have to go to the lab and run rats."

This was the way my sex with Paul was conducted—between Paul's trips to the lab, his classes, his urgent meetings with his thesis advisor. Paul's attractiveness depended partly on his commitment to his work. He seemed never to be wholly there when we were together, his mind always on the experiment he was conducting in the lab, which made our time together seem important—minutes stolen from something of greater moment. *A man's gotta do what a man's gotta do.*

"I can't help it, I'm here at Vanderbilt to do this work, and it has to come first for me. I can't put it off or put it aside or ignore it. The data have to be taken at certain specified intervals. It's there, it has to be done." Then he was out the door. Our sex was conducted with the intensity—the fury—of a man milking a cow before the barn finished burning down.

I was in rehearsals for a play, and one night I was out back behind the theatre, hanging on a railing along a kind of loading dock, smoking a cigarette, waiting for my next scene, when a man who played a soldier came out, nodded to me, and walked down the steps below the railing into the parking lot and started smoking a cigarette too. This man was dark-skinned, black hair, handsome like Michelangelo's Brutus, and tough. He wasn't into acting. He had been recruited by somebody who thought the way he looked would satisfy the demands of the part. He was, maybe, a football player. Another actor came out and hung on the railing with me. He lit his cigarette, and we hung over the railing for a while. The only thing to look at was Brutus, down below. "I've done him," the other actor said, gesturing down into the dark below.

"Is he queer?"

"No, don't think so. Maybe though. Who knows." He took a drag off his cigarette. "I just offered to do him, and he said OK, so we did it last night, after the show." He gestured. "Down there, in the parking lot, in the dark. It was *fine.*"

I thought of doing the dark-skinned, black-haired football player who was acting a soldier in the play. I wondered if he had a big dick. I imagined how it was, my friend kneeling in the parking lot in the dark in front of this Brutus, Brutus throwing his head back as my friend's mouth slid over his dick, feeling the warm wet sleeve of my friend's throat as it closed over his cock.

"You ought to try him. I bet you could get him to let you do him too."

The idea was disturbing. I would have liked to have him in bed, but the idea of doing him there in the dark in the parking lot—kneeling in front of him—put me off. I imagined what it would be like to have *him* kneeling in front of *me*. If I could have had him in a mountain meadow—

"Maybe. I'll see." We flicked our cigarettes off into the dark, and when the soldier came back up the steps, we three all went in together into the backstage area of the theatre. I accepted that I was a homosexual, and I could imagine my life in 10 years, in which I had sex with men, but I could not imagine being a homosexual, living the kind of life homosexuals lived, on the margins and in the shadows, in an ambiguous place in society, *in the parking lot in the dark*. I was already committed to a life lived in some way in public, as a fully-qualified member of society. When I thought of my future, I thought in heterosexual terms because my culture thought in those terms, even though I enjoyed sex with Paul when we had time for it, and I enjoyed my masturbatory fantasy life and had no sex with women.

That fall I made a name for myself in classes, in demonstrations around town, and on the sidewalk in front of the Campus Grill where I was from noon to one every day handing out flyers asking people to support the boycott. Then, in late November, on a brilliant cold Friday afternoon, I was there, almost through with my shift, when the woman who owned the place stuck her head out the door and yelled at me. "They shot the President!"

"What did you say?"

"They shot President Kennedy! In Dallas!" She was a redneck, and she hated the picketers.

"Is he OK?" I had never heard of anything like that before. I tried to remember when a President had been shot at before.

"No! He's not. They don't know yet how bad it is."

I didn't know what to do, and for a few more minutes, I stood there, handing out flyers. I started asking people what they knew, but most of them hadn't heard.

The woman stuck her head out the door again. "They've taken him to the hospital."

"Who did it?"

Her face contorted. "People like you. Fucking commies. Why don't you leave well enough alone? People like you killed him."

"He was *for* integration, lady." I was at first unable to comprehend what the woman was saying. *Killed him.* I thought she had said, *shot at him.* Something terrible had happened, and it was difficult to tell what it was. Then, it came on me in waves—*the President has been shot, he might die*—which took my breath away. I was already thinking, *He was young, beautiful.* Then, around one, I began to feel foolish handing out my flyers trying to integrate the Campus Grill when the country was experiencing this catastrophe. A little after one, I took my flyers and went into my dorm next door. Upstairs people were hanging around the TV in the common room, and just as I walked in, the reporter on the screen was saying, "He announced that President John Fitzgerald Kennedy died today at one in the afternoon in Parkland Memorial Hospital in Dallas, Texas." I couldn't breathe, and I went into my room and sat on my bed for a minute and stared at the floor. But I wanted to know more so I got up and went back into the common room where the TV was and watched. After a bit somebody said classes had been cancelled for the rest of the day. There was some talk, but mainly guys—it was an all-male dorm—sat around staring at the TV screen.

The grief I felt was personal. There was something that President Kennedy had meant to me that had to do with my being queer—it had to do with Kennedy's being beautiful and good and with his wanting things to be different. It had to do with his being different from other politicians, from Nixon, because he spoke more directly and more truthfully. He had come to the presidency in November 1960 just after I had turned 21 in June 1960—and it seemed, just as I was coming out into a new world of my own, that he was offering me a new world, release from the agonies of the last six years of the civil rights struggles. That is, he offered the country a way to resolve the conflict when no one else had been able to offer anything but the same old tired constitutional arguments about States' Rights. He knew the new language that had to be used.

President Kennedy gave the impression that he lived all his life in public, that there were no secrets, nothing hidden, that his life was seamless, that he moved with ease from the most private moments to the most public, without the jarring grinding of gears which was so characteristic of my own life. For the Kennedys the light in the car seemed always to be on, and everything, whether it was in front of the camera or not, seemed to be lived the same way. I admired the integrity about that. I liked it too that he spoke so often about the value of public service. I didn't ever intend to be a politician, but writing is a kind of public service, in the sense that one is serving the community. I wanted to make a contribution to the culture, and President Kennedy was the first public leader in my life who had defined a context for that or who seemed to have an idea of the value of such a contribution. I had imagined myself in some undefined public way saying, *We are confronted primarily with a moral issue.*

And now it was over. As the long afternoon wore on, more information came from the television set, and different ones of us got up to go out to the telephone booth in the hall to make phone calls or to get them, talking to people we cared about. They said it was a man named Lee Harvey Oswald, who had been in Russia, and everyone around the room nodded. The casket was taken from the hospital to the airport and loaded onto Air Force One and then the plane took off. We didn't stop watching even then. We watched as different people were interviewed, and we became familiar with the grassy knoll and the Texas School Book Depository and Parkland Memorial. At 10:30 or so that night, the plane arrived in Washington, and we watched the honor guard take the casket off the elevated platform and slide it into the hearse. After that, it was the funeral. I talked to my parents, and my father found it necessary to say that he had never been an admirer of the Kennedys.

I went out with friends to drink beer—the TV was on at the bar —and we talked about what it would be like now. People talked about Lyndon Johnson and how he would be—I thought he certainly wasn't as articulate as John Kennedy—and about the picture in the airplane of Johnson being sworn in as President with Jackie Kennedy standing right beside him, blood-stained. It did feel as if the things we had been working for—integration of the Campus Grill and of the city of Nashville and public accommodations across the South— wouldn't happen now. Nothing that I wanted would happen now. We needed clarity, and we weren't going to get that now. The rest of the weekend was spent in front of the television, with occasional forays down the street to Irelands', the bar at the foot of 21st Avenue South, and to my room for long stretches of time alone feeling numb. On Monday, my father said the whole thing—the state funeral—was being overdone. There was the coffin, there were the military bands, there were Jacqueline Kennedy and the two children, and then, at the end, there was the grave and the flame and the dark, and the cameras couldn't stop filming and broadcasting the image of that flame on the grave in the dark.

The next month, December 17, *The New York Times* published an article on the front page whose headline was "Growth of Overt Homosexuality In City Provokes Wide Concern."

> The problem of homosexuality in New York became
> the focus yesterday of increased attention by the
> State Liquor Authority and the Police Department.

The liquor authority announced the revocation
of the liquor licenses of two more homosexual
haunts that had been repeatedly raided by the police.
The places were the Fawn, at 795 Washington Street
near Jane Street, and the Heights Supper Club at 80
Montague Street, Brooklyn.

The city's most sensitive open secret—the
presence of what is the greatest homosexual
population in the world and its increasing openness
—has become the subject of growing concern of
psychiatrists, religious leaders and the police.

The Police Commissioner said, "Homosexuality is another one
of the many problems confronting law enforcement in this city.
However, the underlying factors in homosexuality are not criminal
but rather medical and sociological in nature."

The paper called the two closed bars "congregating points for
homosexuals and degenerates" and "fag joints." The article said as
many as 80 "deviates" were found dancing together at the Fawn, and
in the length of the article homosexuals were referred to as "the
invert world," "the dregs of the invert world," "the painted, grossly
effeminate 'queens.'" It said homosexuals suffer from "basic
emotional instability." The article noted that "policemen used
specialists known in the department as 'actors' to get evidence." And
the article introduced me to the word *gay*. "The word 'gay' has been
appropriated as the adjective for homosexual."

The Times quoted a Roman Catholic priest saying, "'The
increase in homosexuality is only one aspect of the general
atmosphere of moral breakdown that has been going on around us,'
says Monsignor Robert Gallaher of the Youth Counseling Service of
the Roman Catholic Archdiocese of New York." But psychiatrists
were given major space in the article. "In almost every homosexual
case, they found some combination of what they termed a 'close-
binding, intimate' mother and/or a hostile, detached or unrespected
father, or other parental aberrations.'" A Dr. Socarides was quoted
saying, "The homosexual is ill."

I was shamed. I thought they were right about the sleazy joints
in New York, but I hated having it in *The Times* that I was, myself,
evidence of the *general atmosphere of moral breakdown that has*

been going on around us and hated the words they used about me—
invert, deviate, fag. What I wanted to be was a respected member of
the community, and I was tormented because I didn't know if I was
—or could be. I hated the article and the way it talked about me. I
hated it that it was *The Times* that published the article. I was
shamed, even though no one around me knew. I felt humiliated, and I
carried that around with me.

Courage. The word people I knew used was *guts,* as in, *Paul has
guts.* I thought I was gutsy enough, and I wondered if the word was
the right one. I felt it had something more to do with something else
—the trade-offs that were necessary. One professor, in a seminar that
met once a week, assigned reports on Wednesday that were due the
following Wednesday. The conflict was between the need to
complete the report in six days and the need to write a good report. I
—and everyone else—was aware of the shortcuts we all took in
those reports, the minor and sometimes major sleights-of-hand I took
to make a seven-day report sound like a report on which I had spent
a month. One traded off a comprehensive and profound knowledge
of the subject for a knowledge that could be achieved in seven days.
Some of us said we traded off substance for flash. The overriding
requirement in Paul's life was his work. Sex was limited to a
physiological need. Paul couldn't have it all, so he took what was
necessary and possible. He didn't have time for an affair. Connie
Stephanopolis' single-mindedness had lasted just as long as our
weekends in the Cascades.

It seemed to me that there were a number of different goals I
faced—writing a novel, finding someone to connect with in some
serious way, finding a release for my desires for men, retaining the
respect of my family, gaining the respect of my peers. And I was
aware that not all of these goals could be achieved in one lifetime. I
didn't know if it was possible to have at the same time the respect of
both my mother and, say, Paul, especially if they knew each other.
Also, I didn't know yet which of my goals was the most profound—
to know required a clarity I didn't have—so I couldn't set priorities.
Paul was clear—his degree was more important than a relationship. I
was not sure that my degree took precedence over anything since I
had only come to Vanderbilt because it was a free year. The whole
analogy worked as long as the two pieces being compared were
roughly equal. If the comparison was between, say, going to jail and

going to a seminar, and one were a Negro, there was no question about a trade-off. One went to jail. And I realized pretty quickly that I should have gone to jail.

I wrote a short story, and then I saw, on a tree on campus, a flyer announcing a one-act play contest, so I wrote a play based on something that had happened to me in the Army. It had two principal characters—one in handcuffs and the one who had put him there—and the question the play attempted to deal with was, *Who is guilty?* The short story was published, and the play was produced, and people seemed to like what I had written. I did well in school, but I did best in the poets who were most conflicted about themselves. I had a talent for analyzing poets who said, black *and* white. I am innocent *and* I am guilty. I read Whitman and I liked him, but it was easiest for me to understand his conflicts. I read Faulkner again and walked around campus repeating over and over to myself the final lines of *Absalom, Absalom!*

"Now I want you to tell me just one thing more. Why do you hate the South?"

"I dont hate it," Quentin said, quickly, at once, immediately; "I dont hate it," he said. *I dont hate it* he thought, panting in the cold air, the iron New England dark: *I dont. I dont! I dont hate it! I dont hate it!*

I wrote my Master's thesis on Djuna Barnes, a novelist from the 1930s, who was determinedly obscure—she was writing about lesbian women in the 30s so obscurity was a virtue—she was writing about lesbian women in the 30s so obscurity was a virtue— and whose novel was put together like a poem by Eliot, all bits and pieces and *no story.* I was considering writing my doctoral dissertation on John Donne, the most conflicted poet in the language.

↔

It is important to be clear about what was happening at Vanderbilt. The work was demanding, and I found that with some attention I could make A's. That is, with a little attention, I could be the best student in the class, and that "little attention" left me with time for drinking. But even with the demands of class and the demands of drinking, I still had time for the most important thing in my life—my writing. I wrote every day, usually for several hours at the end of the day, which were my best hours. I wrote about the Army, and I wrote about New York. I wrote about South Carolina. I wrote about parties and drinking. But I didn't write about anything queer. I had in my mind the list of places I could publish my short stories and none of them took queer stories. I thought about a story that I'd like to write, about me and Paul, for example, and then accepted the fact that I had never read a story like that. The story I could imagine writing, and getting published, was some story about a man and his parents, or a man and his friends, or about his work. But not about a man in love. So I didn't write that kind of story. If I had tried to write about me and Paul, I'd have to change the story, because I had never read anywhere a story like what was happening to me and Paul. And that was pretty terrible, because I knew that half of literature is about a man in love.

↔

The Civil Rights Act of 1964 was passed finally on June 2, 1964. It declared that the civil rights of citizens of the United States could not be abridged by the state or by public accommodations involved in interstate commerce on account of race, color, religion, or national origin, and was the Act President Kennedy had fought for before he was killed. At the end of June or the beginning of July, papers began to carry news that three civil rights workers, members of CORE, had disappeared in Philadelphia. Mississippi, the night of June 21. We assumed they were murdered, but the FBI mounted a huge search. Their car was found two days after they disappeared, and on August 4, their bodies were found under a dam outside of Philadelphia, Mississippi. All this was while I was writing my MA thesis on Djuna Barnes. That summer was Freedom Summer in Mississippi.

↔

In the fall of 1964, a white woman about my age showed up on a picket line downtown. I had seen her on campus. She was small, had short black hair, and a very pale skin. She was across the circle from me, walking as if she was aware she was being photographed. We were in front of a dime store that had a segregated lunch counter, and

140

the group of us walked in our circle, waiting for the other side to do something. The picketers were not trying to get inside—that had not been the plan—and as long as we stayed outside, we were not arrested. The police hung around listlessly for an hour and when they accepted that the group was not going to try to get inside, they left. The group began to break up. The white woman from Vanderbilt carried her book bag over her shoulder instead of dropping it in the pile with the others, and when I decided to leave, she left the circle too and followed me.

She caught up with me, and while we waited for the light to change, she spoke.

"I saw you last year in front of the Campus Grill."

I looked over.

"My name is Naomi Schumann."

"I'm Fair Shaw."

She smiled. "That's a beautiful name."

"It is my great-uncle's."

"Is he as good looking as you?"

"He's much better looking than I am."

"Good genes."

"May be."

We walked back toward campus.

"I see you everywhere in town at these things."

"That must be someone else. I have only done the Campus Grill on a regular basis and then that kind of thing—" I nodded back toward the dime store. "—three or four times. I should do more."

"I feel I see you all the time."

She was an undergraduate at Vanderbilt and lived back in the area where I lived, between 21st Avenue South and 16th Avenue South, where the students and the musicians lived. Her hair was so black and her skin so pale, she might have been Irish—or French. She struggled a little under the weight of her book bag, but when I asked if I could help, she said she could handle it, and she did.

"You're in English."

"Yes."

"I thought everybody in English was a right-wing professional Southerner. How do you survive over there?"

"I don't know. I do very well. I am sure there are some teachers who dislike what people are doing, but they don't ever say anything.

Some of them were rude last year over the Campus Grill boycott, but when they are back in their classrooms, they don't bring it up."

"Takes courage."

"Want a beer?"

"Sure."

And we did and talked about civil rights demonstrations around Nashville.

This new girl began to show up at Ireland's. Naomi Schumann— her family was Franco-American—sat in the corner of the booth, her hair cut very short, her eyes outlined by heavy eyeliner, and wearing long silver earrings. She was quiet and tended to lift her chin slightly. She also was careful about the way her lips covered her teeth, and she closed her lips—but not her jaw—decisively over her teeth when she had finished expressing a thought. She smoked, had lived on the West Coast for several years working in the film industry, and was cool.

We both liked country music—Nashville was the home of the Grand Ole Opry, the home of country music in the US of A—and took our patronage from Ireland's, a typical campus tavern, all subdued lighting and bright lights on the juke box consoles in each booth, to Pat's, around the corner, where the lights were bright everywhere and there was a *lot* of formica and chrome—and better music. There we listened to records of Kris Kristofferson singing "Help Me Make It Through the Night." On Friday and Saturday nights Pat's had live entertainment, singers and groups with banjos and guitars singing old, *old*, standards—some of them were so old they were in Child Ballads, which I was studying at the time. They also sang some new ones. Our favorite singers were Violet and Mac, an old couple who sang long love songs to each other. We liked arriving at Pat's at midnight in our shades, with smokes, listening to the original versions of songs Loretta Lynn and Tammy Wynette made hits of.

The phone rang. "Close your books. I have tickets for the Opry. Waylon is on." So we went to the Opry, and Waylon Jennings sang "Love of the Common People"—*Living on dreams ain't easy*—and later, when I proposed that we go over to the Parthenon and explore, she said, "I hear it's made of concrete. Is that so?"

"Sure is."

"Kind of takes the sting off it, doesn't it?" Then she laughed hard.

We went and walked around the building, which was suggestive of the exuberance of 1897 centennial celebrations and of the aspirations of the state.

"They wanted to be an Athens, then. What would they build today in the same circumstances?"

"I don't think they look anywhere else for inspiration now. I think between the Opry and the local churches, they think they have all the inspiration they need." The Greek ideal, the demos and the *Symposium,* had long ago been abandoned.

Naomi liked talking about literature, about politics, about sex, about the Kennedys—Bobby and Teddy—and Lyndon Johnson, the discovery of the bodies of Chaney, Goodman, and Schwerner, and *the war.* And toward the end of September, we talked about what was happening at Berkeley.

"Can you understand that at all?"

She shrugged. "I guess. The students don't want to be controlled by the administration."

"But what is this about free speech?"

"The administration is trying to tell the students what they can talk about and tell them where they can talk. The kids understand that speech is a stand-in for political action. The administration is trying to control the political action of the students."

On October 2, she said, "Did you see the paper this morning? The guy on top of the cop's car?"

"What was that about?"

"They sent a cop car on campus to arrest this student for breaking the rules about what can be advocated for, and they got him in the car, but hundreds of other students sat down around the car, so the cops couldn't move. The kid is in the car and the car is in the middle of the Berkeley Campus, surrounded by hundreds of students, all immobile."

We were both from the South—Naomi was from Tennessee—so we had Faulkner in common, as well as experience with the usual redneck attitudes. Naomi wore dressy clothes every day—heels and real dresses, as if she were going to work downtown—and when she wasn't looking through them, she had her shades pushed up and back across the top of her head.

I saw her a couple of times a week on campus in the student union, but she was working very hard, and there were the demonstrations that she went to more often than I did, so when we did get together it was because one or the other had made a special effort. She would leave me a note: *Two thousand students around the cop car. Berkeley Admin. at a loss. Let's talk. Coffee after your class? N* Or there would be a phone call: "Meet me at Pat's in 30 minutes." Naomi joined the loose group of graduate students I saw regularly. It was no big deal—usually there were a number of them around—and only a few times were we alone together. But she occupied a larger place than others in our crowd because she had her own apartment— she and I were the only ones with apartments—so often, when we were together, it was at her place and no one else was there. Instead of getting together in the dining hall or for beer later at Pat's, we were having supper at Naomi's or drinking beer at Naomi's. She also occupied a larger place for me in our crowd because she was more political than the others. *Berkeley Admin. at a loss.*

It was about the same thing Freedom Summer was about, using many of the same people. Conservatives in power, young people determined to change things. And it came down to political advocacy. Speech. Words. What it was about was all these beat-up veterans of Freedom Summer coming back from Mississippi where they had faced truly dangerous—murderous—racists and finding in California that they were facing a conservative governor and university administration who were linked with the industrial and commercial power structure of the state who did not want these fearless kids just back from staring down the devil disrupting the tranquil peace of the West Coast. The kids wanted nothing more than to explode all the cozy relationships between the politicians and the corporations, right there, right then, in the middle of the 1964 Presidential election campaign. The Berkeley administration was livid at the students around the police car, and every move they made brought another thousand students out into the campus.

One night she found me several blocks up 21st Avenue South from Vanderbilt, walking home.

"Do you want a ride?"

She was laughing in a way that suggested she knew she had pulled something off. I got in, and we drove to my place. We had a drink—she liked vodka drinks so I started buying vodka after that—and talked about Freedom Summer.

"No, I didn't go. I stayed in Nashville and wrote my MA thesis. I think that was the wrong thing to have done."

She shrugged. "I went. But then both my parents went too—I mean they were in Jackson, and I was in Greenwood—so I felt that if they felt they had to do it, I couldn't not go."

That surprised me, to find someone who had parents activist enough to take part in Freedom Summer. "That's fine."

"They're not liberals, honey, they're leftist radicals."

"I can't imagine what that would be like."

"Going to Mississippi?"

"No, having radical parents."

I told her about my own.

"I can't imagine that, either."

It thrilled me that her family was so different from mine and that their beliefs were in such violent conflict with the conservative segregationist beliefs of most Southerners. This news of Naomi's leftist parents connected them to the great world beyond the South and gave them a sheen of worldliness that my own family didn't have.

White people like Naomi's parents were sometimes called *nigger-lovers* by racists around us. Being a nigger-lover—the phrase itself was coarse beyond belief—was as far beyond the limits of acceptable behavior as it was possible to be. The Schumanns and their daughter Naomi, way beyond what they themselves could have imagined, represented an opposition to the life I had led and therefore represented freedom to me to leave South Carolina, to live my life as I chose, to mount a critique of the political system in America.

One night I let her into my apartment and then went back to my bedroom to get my coat. When I returned, I found her standing in the middle of the living room, dressed for outdoors, in blue, her hair brushed up and back, showing off the long silver earrings, waiting for me to go with her out to dinner, waiting for me to accept and to admire her. My mother used to talk about how important it was that a woman "present" herself—be aware of her presence among other people. That meant that, before she went out, she made sure her hair was done, that she wore appropriate jewelry and carried a handbag.

The goal was, I knew, for the woman to present herself as a *lady.* Now, staring at this woman, whose image—the shades pushed back on top of her head, the handmade earrings—suggested the Village, I saw that with the few changes she had made, she was suggesting something else entirely, a woman from my parents' own class, which caused me to think of her in a new way. The night ahead would be fun, stimulating, a little crazy, and—I also knew—I could take this woman home. She and my mother might not enjoy each other's company, but they wouldn't be at each other's throats.

Another night, a warm night in early October, I said to her, "Let's go to the Parthenon again."

"Oh, Christ, that place haunts me." It was what it looked like, but it was also what it was made of—a fourth-level debasement of an ideal. We liked to go there just because it was so fake. "It should never have been done."

"It wasn't meant to be permanent. It wasn't, and then it was."

"But it is, it so is," she said. She told me I was too much East Coast. "You're such a WASP gentleman."

"Too much so?"

"Oh, God, yes. You need to be less formal, less polite. Don't think so much about other people. I wish you would try to be more crude." She laughed. "Relax."

I laughed. "Oh, shit."

"That's a start." Then, "I know it will be difficult for you."

"Oh, fuck."

She laughed. "I try to get my dad to be more like a gentleman. He thinks being crude is being *honest.* "

"I'm honest."

"I think you are. You just need to relax a little. Loosen up. In California they'd say you were uptight."

She was teasing, but she was right. I had never been as loose as, say, Stockman, or Cornelius. Or Connie.

We walked around the giant building in the dark park, lit only by occasional street lamps. Even as it was, made of concrete and situated in a city park in a low depression instead of high up on the Acropolis, a bad copy of an ideal, it still was impressive, looking back to Athenian democracy. The things it called to mind were inexpressibly grand. Knowledge, the free exchange of ideas, democracy, the celebration of art, philosophy, the beginning of western culture. We held hands, walking around the building, and then we climbed the big steps of the crepidoma onto the stylobate, the topmost step and the floor of the temple. We stood between the columns, surveying the park before us, and then stepped into the dark of the peristyle, behind the columns. We strolled down the aisle, in and out of the light from the park, which formed a striped pattern of shadows against the wall of the naos.

"How do you know the names?"

"I read about it. I took an Art History course and had to memorize the parts. And I've been in Nashville a year."

I was thrilled to be there, walking behind the colonnade with Naomi. "Socrates says that when the men of Athens met in the Assembly to vote on policy, and the discussion was not about technical matters but about the governing of the city, the man who was allowed to speak could be anyone—a rich man, a poor man, a shoe-maker or a blacksmith. Anyone."

"It does rather make it holy ground, doesn't it. If it were just not concrete!"

"I know. They built it for the Centennial of Tennessee statehood. Then they rebuilt it in concrete, because people liked it and wanted to keep it here."

"Forever."

It actually had tiny pebbles embedded in the concrete. The builders went to some trouble to match the rose color of the marble.

"I like this."

"So do I."

"Despite what it's made of, it suggests permanence. The idea of it. Democracy—"

"The Parthenon suggests Athens, and *Athens* suggests democracy."

"—right. Have you read Tocqueville? His opening pages are wonderful."

"—about unstoppable democracy."

"He has a lot to say later about what all that means. But he is rather awed by the movement toward democracy, how every single action through history has resulted in *more* democracy, *more* participation by *more* people."

"Someday we may finally arrive at the place the Greeks were 2500 years ago."

"Only with women participating too, and no slaves."

She turned to me, and we put our arms around each other and kissed. It was the natural thing to do—the right person, the right time and place. We held on to each other for a long while.

I kissed her neck, first on one side and then on the other. Then I bent over her a little and caught her behind her back and lifted her up and kissed her, and she kissed me back.

We sat down on the cool concrete, our backs against the wall, deep in the shadows of the peristyle, and held hands. Then she lay down, and I lay down beside her. She fumbled at my pants as I pulled down her skirt and pushed up her blouse. There was no hurry, and we took our time, and gradually, playing with her nipples, I rose, and she lubricated, and I entered her.

Afterward, she kissed me and smiled.

"An homage to Aphrodite in the temple to Athena."

She laughed. "You would. If it just weren't concrete! And what are all these little pebbles! What is that all about!" She laughed again, "Jesus! Ain't life somethin'?"

I was elated. I could trust my body. I was still queer. I knew that. But I wasn't trapped by it. Being queer wasn't the only thing I was. It was different with her than it had been with Connie, whose big, hard body remained in my permanent memory. I would never forget how that felt. But it felt good with her, too. I could get accustomed to her size and her softness, her breasts and her vagina. I understood, now, more about Cellini. My elation, I knew, arose at least partly from my having achieved what they said couldn't be achieved.

"It is all about how to understand the past," I said to her one night at Pat's, where we were drinking beer. We were talking about Faulkner. She sat across the booth from me, her legs up on the bench beside her, her head tilted back slightly. "He takes the same material I've been hearing about all my life—the settlement of the wilderness, whites, Negro slaves, plantations, cotton—"

"—women, the Indians—"

I laughed. "—sure, the women and the Indians, and puts them together in a way that is totally different from the story they tell in South Carolina. And yet you know *he must be right*."

"Actions have consequences."

"Because the men who settled the South, most of them, must have been like Sutpen. There must have been many, many, more men like Sutpen than like Sartoris."

"—who *tore*—" She smiled. "Miss Rosa."

Our favorite book was *Absalom, Absalom.*

"Very different from what they like around here—" By which she meant, around *Vanderbilt.* "—Southern books all about gentlemen and their *honor.*"

"Faulkner is very modern. His men are all entrepreneurs, capitalists on the make. They are like late 19th century robber barons, except they deal in cotton and slaves instead of gold and the railroads."

"Sutpen, who destroyed his own dream!"

"His end was implicit in his beginning."

Naomi's father was an academic at the University of Tennessee in Knoxville, an economist. There was a certain ruthlessness about what she said about him that suggested Sutpen. Naomi thought her parents would understand the comparison. My own family would not have been able to see themselves in Sutpen. They would have seen themselves as Compsons or Sartorises. "Any myth of the past that skips over the taming of the wilderness—and what that did to the men who did it, and to the Indians and Negroes and poor whites—"

"The taming of the American wilderness had built into it the foundation of what was going to ruin it all."

"—is a lie. In America, oddly, southern literature is about the question, How do you deal with the past? What is the past? *What is past?*"

Naomi said, "It doesn't ever seem to go away. It's about secrets that stay in the attic."

"—in the memories of old women."

"It's not really about the past. It's about time. Some things never slide away into the past. They aren't subject to that process by which things recede and fade away. They stay with us, present, acting on us, forever. Slavery is one. As long as there is a United States of America, we will be dealing with slavery. It will never go away. The people who were slaves are dead, and their children are dead, and maybe their children's children are dead. And there aren't any slaves in America any more. But slavery is still here, with us, in the present, acting on us, warping our moral sense, bending our light, confusing us, making us unable to understand ourselves and our place in the universe. It is now in our genes—we are all, before it is over, going to be the children of slaves—Jim Bonds from coast to coast, which would be fine as long as we didn't carry the blood of *slave-holders* too. There is nothing we can do to make it *be* past."

In fantasies of my life, I imagined myself leaning against the mantelpiece, drink in hand, other hand in pocket, listening to my guest with a half-smile on my face, just at the moment my wife walked into the room, and just before I said, "Oh, *Helen*, come over and join us. Dr. Kajolian has a theory about British Honduras and Reconstruction." Then as she moved to my side and my arm encircled her shoulders, I said to her, "Haven't you been reading in that period in the South Carolina archives?" And she would say, smiling up at me, "Fair, dinner is about to be served." Then, to Dr. Kojolian, "I *have* been reading in that period, and I would love to talk to you about it. I read your last book. Perhaps later?" The house would be large, the ceilings high, the silver glowing, the china white and gold, and the guests all colors and ethnic groups. I imagined Naomi in ten years. The interesting thing about her was that you could *see* her in Los Angeles, her short hair, her silver earrings, strolling into some movie studio, carrying a briefcase and the half-completed manuscript of some very art-house movie. *And* I could see her in my mother's garden, drinking sherry. I found myself adjusting my fantasy to fit Naomi.

One night, I was telling her about the Southerners on the faculty. "I sat in the Southern Literature lecture for the first ten days, and then I couldn't take it any more and walked out. Later, when I went to drop it, I found I had let the deadline pass, so I had either to go back to the course, make up the lost work, stomach the professor's sentimental racist views, or *take an F*. I chose to take an F."

She laughed. "That's good. That's real good. I like that. Something extravagant about that, something over-the-top."

We bragged about each other to friends and colleagues, over beer and cigarettes, late at night at Pat's, when it was time to brag about feats of strength. "Only," she said, "won't you join me at the demonstration tomorrow?"

"I have a report to finish on Milton."

She smiled. I had the report to finish and a demonstration to go to and I couldn't do both, so I did both partly. The report was not as good as it might have been—I got an A—and I didn't stay at the demonstration as long as I might have, although I stayed until the press left. And I got by.

"What must it be like to be Mario Savio?"

She smiled at me and took my arm, and we walked across campus together. I felt she liked me just because I did put school first.

"He's so clear, so driven. You watch him—listen to him speaking—and he seems like a very wise man, and the voices he wants to free are essential voices speaking some profound truth about the country."

So we drifted toward something important. Gary Grimes, who was from Carmel, thought that sucked. "Next thing you'll be buying a washer and a dryer, and it will all be over for you two. You used to be interesting, and now you're going to get married, and you're going to buy a washer and a dryer, and someday, if you are still conscious, you're going to say, 'Remember the fall of 1964? Back when we were still able to think? Feel? Back when we were still interesting?' Don't do this thing, guys!" We couldn't even acknowledge to ourselves what it was Gary was talking about.

Everybody liked Naomi—was even in awe of her—and almost nobody liked the idea that we were getting close. While everybody seemed to like both of us, people seemed fearful of what was to come. Gary's fear of the washer and dryer was typical. The idea seemed to be, *You're great, each one of you; you're great together; but don't, please don't, get married.* Some of this was in the air—that is, in 1964 people on campuses around the country were beginning to attack the whole idea of marriage. *Stay free.* Some of it may have come from a person's antipathy to either Naomi or me—*Fair, you can do better than that.* Or, *Naomi, you can do better than that.* Or some of it suggested the choice was wrong—*Fair, she's not for you.* But some of it came from a place that was unexpected and new. *Fair, you're queer. Don't marry Naomi.* Or, *Naomi, he's queer.* Sometimes the response—a double-whammy—came from a friend, like Paul. "Well, I'm surprised. If it's going to work, it'll work because Naomi is determined to make it work."

Three weeks before the elections, Presidential aide Walter Jenkins was arrested in the men's room of a Washington, DC, YMCA and charged with indecent conduct with another man, a story on the front pages of the papers for a couple of weeks. He resigned from the White House staff, and there was comment in the media that this would affect the election, in which President Johnson was running against Senator Barry Goldwater. Goldwater declined to comment on the scandal, and Mrs. Johnson, to everyone's surprise, seemed to defend Jenkins. "He's *sick*," she was reported to have said, "and he needs help." Her entire statement, issued the day after his arrest, said, "My heart is aching today for someone who has reached the point of exhaustion in dedicated service to his country. Walter Jenkins has been carrying incredible hours and burdens since President Kennedy's assassination. He is now receiving the medical attention that he needs." This was a softer response than the response others were making—that he was a degenerate, a corrupting influence on the youth of the nation, evidence of the decadence that was the Democratic party, a *criminal,* and that he should go to jail. But by the day of the election, the story had faded. Johnson won in the largest landslide in the history of the republic. The FBI arrested 19 men on December 4, 1964, for the murders of Chaney, Goodman, and Schwerner.

"It's a story about a woman who has everything. She has money, looks, intelligence, position—" We were talking about *Portrait of a Lady,* about which she was writing a paper. We were sitting in our booth again. Gary Grimes had just left. He liked what he saw in us. He liked the sense we gave of having everything. That is, we had looks, intelligence, position, achievement, and freedom. He liked it that we had both gone so far in escaping the South, which was all around us. Of course he didn't like it that we were a couple. "—and she screws it. She picks *exactly* the wrong man to marry. She could have married anyone. With her money, she could have married a very poor man. But she picks the man who is going to ruin her life, who is going to kill her, inch by inch, paralyze her with his banal and trivial life. Is that what it is about? Is this *it?* " She lit a cigarette. Actually, she got it out of her bag, and I reached across the table with the lighter and lit her cigarette. "So the bitter reader laughs? Of course, it would not have been a novel. It would have been a fairy tale if she had used her freedom and her intelligence to marry the perfect man *and live happily ever after.* Nobody but children wants to read such a book. It hasn't been done since Jane Austen. And of course her books are about how impossible it is to find the right man. What a miracle it is when you find him. But, to get back to the book James wrote, is the book about her wrong choice? Or is it about something else?" She was looking through the haze of smoke beyond me, behind my head, at people coming in the door, at someone standing at the cash register. "Is it inevitable that people make wrong choices? And is it that the book is about the inevitability of wrong choices—even with perfect freedom we make wrong choices and who, after all, has perfect freedom?—and the book is about how, at the end of our lives, we have to live with our wrong choices, and *that* is what is interesting about us, *how* we learn to live with our wrong choices?"

"Othello makes a wrong choice and then is allowed to die, straight off."

"Ah! But James is after something more modern. How do you look in the doorway, entering your drawing room in your small Roman palazzo, living with your disastrous choice?"

I laughed. "Naomi, she looks fabulous. A black velvet dress with a bustle, I believe." She grinned back at me. "Besides, you have it all wrong."

"What, *all* wrong?"

"*Portrait of a Lady*. It isn't about making a choice at all."

"No? What is it about, then?"

"Isabel, in her social class, in her world, must marry. She doesn't really have the liberty to go to London, say, and establish herself as a free spirit. Or Paris, or Rome."

"But—"

"Uh-uh. Her world is very conventional. Nobody in that world thinks in the kind of terms that you are thinking of—*what kind of choice is this perfectly free girl going to make?*—they think in a different way entirely. *What kind of husband is this woman—who must choose a husband—going to choose?* It is a very different kind of question. There is an iron necessity behind everything she does, and she is not free."

"Where did you read that?"

"Everybody says that."

Paul scorned the whole thing. "What are you doing with a woman! You're queer, Fair. Accept that." Paul liked Naomi, thought she was interesting to be with when they were drinking beer, liked to hear her talk, although he himself was not much interested in politics or literature. But he said, "You don't belong with a woman, you belong with a man. I mean *sex*. Get your degree, get a job teaching, fuck men. That's what you should do with your life. Marriage is a whole different ball of wax. It introduces things you aren't meant for." We went back to the dorm, and I fucked him—and then Paul fucked me—and the issue was unresolved.

"Teaching is not enough for me. Fucking is not enough for me. I want something more than either of them."

"*What? What* is more important to a man than his profession and sex?"

"Another person, Paul. A whole person. Culture. A whole society. I have to be connected to a whole society. You fuck and you go to the lab to run rats—"

"That's what I have to do *now*. I don't know what I will have to do in the future."

"But this is *now* for me. Naomi is *now*."

We were in the student union having hamburgers. Naomi read from the newspaper. "Listen to this. This is from last night, December 2. It's Mario Savio. Listen.: 'There is a time when the operation of the machine becomes so odious, makes you so sick at heart, that you can't take part; you can't even passively take part, and you've got to put your bodies upon the gears and upon the wheels, upon the levers, upon all the apparatus, and you've got to make it stop. And you've got to indicate to the people who run it, to the people who own it, that unless you're free, the machine will be prevented from working at all!'" She put down the paper and lit a cigarette. "I wish I had been there."

"Read it again,"

She did.

"Holy shit. It would have been like being there when—when—"

"—when something stupendous was said. I don't think anybody has said anything stupendous during my lifetime."

"Oh, yes. Oh, yes. John Kennedy. *We are confronted primarily with a moral issue.* That had never been said before, and it so needed to be said. It made it inescapable. It became a moral issue that we could not turn away from."

She became cynical. "That the nation immediately turned away from."

"Oh, don't. Please, don't." I was aware that I was showing her something about myself that wasn't also true of her.

154

"OK."

"I am only 24, and twice now men have said things that I suspect will be remembered as long as this republic stands."

She watched me.

"The administration at Berkeley—the California political establishment—is afraid of what all those students at all those tables are advocating. To be free, people have to speak and then to advocate for their causes—" My hands were on the table in front of me, taking the book of matches and turning it over and over, my eyes staring beyond the matches deep into the table. I looked at Naomi. "And if there are all these voices speaking their truth, then the one voice speaking *official* truth can be defeated." I went back to twirling the book of matches, my thumb and forefinger in the spaces where the cover folded over, while the fingers of my other hand pushed the book over and over. "The reason authority wants to silence the people is that it is speaking lies."

Naomi studied me. "You should be more active."

On December eighth, after the sit-in, the arrests, the jail, the mass meeting, and the attempt of the cops to prevent him from speaking—after Mario Savio had won—we were talking again. "The reason Mario Savio has now won the battle is that it only takes one man, saying *this is so important that I will lie down and die defending my truth* for truth, tricked out with power, to fade away." He also knew what he believed, and I don't think the administration of Berkeley did.

"No, no. It took thousands of students to commit themselves. Mario Savio couldn't do it by himself—" Then "Well, yes. Mario—"

Just before the holidays, I went to student health and told them I needed to see a psychiatrist—there was really nowhere else to go. I knew it had not worked before, but I thought this time, on a university campus, with a new doctor, it had a chance. I was assigned to a resident at Vanderbilt Hospital, young, maybe early thirties, big, soft, and doughy with short black hair. I went to Dr. Coleman once or twice a week for two or three weeks before Christmas, and we agreed that I should come to see him after the holidays. I did this because I felt stressed. I was overworked, I seemed constantly behind and unable to catch up, and the trade-offs that I had to make seemed to get larger and larger. Instead of having to trade off a solid knowledge of a subject for a paper which could be turned in on time,

I found myself faking a whole course so I could turn my attention to another course with a professor who might be more important to me. What was important. I told the psychiatrist I was queer. Coleman didn't say much. Occasionally, he asked a question, but he never told me that I ought to do this or that or should stop doing this or that. I thought he would tell me to stop drinking so much, but he didn't. "I'm queer, and I'm dating this girl." And I thought we were both assuming that this meant he was going to do something for me, help me not to be queer any more *so I could do this other thing*. Or not to want girls anymore so I could concentrate on fucking men. He *must* be there, I thought, to help me clarify things, make me more content, *happier*. I told him most of the same things I had told the psychiatrist in New York—I thought it was important to tell him what kind of guy turned me on, so I told him about slicked back blond hair and muscular arms—but he didn't seem to care. I didn't like guys who were girlish, I liked guys who were rough looking, like Brutus, the guy who played the soldier, and I thought that made a difference. I told him about Paul Connors in the seventh grade, about Connie Stephanopolis wrestling alligators, and about Edward—and about Paul Huntley with the rough hands and the rats. I told him about wanting to get my PhD and wanting to write a novel—and about wanting to be a "success." I talked and talked, and I didn't know where I was supposed to be going with it all, and I didn't know what Dr. Coleman was supposed to be doing in all this, aside from what he was doing, which was nodding and asking occasional questions. I told him about my distant father and my smothering mother. I told him my mother felt that I was holding something back from her. She felt I was somehow lying. It seemed to be what he was expecting. He accepted what I was saying in the terms I was using, but he didn't seem interested.

I said, "I think I am in love with Mario Savio. I love him standing on top of the police car, preaching to the masses. He is so intense. He's so clear. He is like Christ. There is nothing ambivalent about him. I think I could put my coat down in the mud for him, follow him to the battle *for him*. Sometimes I think I could die for him. He's like Kennedy, you know? Only younger and even more idealistic, even clearer. I admired Kennedy's wisdom—*life is unfair* —and it sometimes seems to me that he was an older Savio, one who had suffered." I didn't know what I was talking about, and I didn't know where this was leading. "Or maybe it's that he was just a Savio with more experience. *We're going to have to suffer,* you know what I mean? Maybe? This fall, I was so acutely aware of Freedom Summer and of the guys who went down, and I didn't, and I could have. I *knew* why it was important to go. I hid in the library instead, writing my MA thesis, pretending that *this* was what I was supposed to do with my life right now when I knew it wasn't true. The boys were murdered, and it could have been me. Should have been me. Two of them weren't even from the South, and I am, and I should have done something. They *acted.* I slide through. I don't know what I believe." The doctor listened to all this. I noticed that he didn't do what most people do when they are listening to someone—what Naomi did when I ran on—*nod, murmer little encouragements, make little exclamations.* He sat there stump-like. "I have these choices to make—"

Coleman gave me prescriptions for tranquilizers. I filled the first one, but then I didn't take any more. I didn't like the way they made me feel. Every time I saw him, he gave me another prescription— he'd say, "Do you need another prescription?" and I would say, *sure,* and then I'd file it away in my wallet along with all the others.

I went home for the holidays that year—the year of Freedom Summer—and the talk was of the debutante season and of the arrest of the nineteen men for the murders of Chaney, Goodman, and Schwerner, shot and killed for trying to register Negroes to vote, and about Mario Savio on top of the car at Berkeley. "Outside agitators," my father called them. "I read that most of them are communist." I felt an anxiety all during the holidays, dressed up in my tuxedo or tail coat, drink in my hand, dancing with some girl. Having sex with another man, people said, was "degenerate." A "degenerate" or a "pervert" was somebody who had sex with other men. To have sex with another man was a sin. It was an abomination. It was something a man could do—or not do. He could choose. A homosexual—a queer—was somebody who had sex only with his own sex, for whom it was not a choice. These meanings were slippery and conflicted with one another, but they all had to do with what you did with your dick and your mouth and your ass and with what you thought about what you did. Some of them had to do with whole people, with men, with *me*—that is, with my conception of myself— and some didn't. And even if the difference between a man who was

homosexual and a man who had sex sometimes—or most of the time
—with men could be sorted out, I knew that in everyday language,
people lumped all that together, didn't make any distinctions, and
called us all *faggots*. What was new about Paul's response was that
he said I was a different *kind of person* from what I thought I was—
that this kind of person does this kind of thing, and consequently
there are situations where this kind of person does not belong. A
"queer" does not belong in a "marriage." Or maybe it was that a
"homosexual" does not belong in a marriage. I didn't like that. It
limited my freedom. I thought of Cellini. When I had thought about
it before, I said to myself that all I had to do to make myself ready
for marriage was to refrain from sucking men's cocks and to quit
wanting to suck men's cocks—or to accustom myself to the idea of
the life of Constantine Stephanopolis. Paul was saying I needed to be
a different kind of person. I needed to stop being the kind of man
who always wanted only men. Or else I needed to be the kind of man
who had a different life from the life that I had imagined.

    Want. I couldn't figure out the place of my desires in all this. I
desired alcohol. But I could stop drinking if I had to—my father had
—and then, I thought, I could go on with my life. In what way did
my desires make me a different kind of person? I had spoken to
Patrick at Sewanee and to the priest in Yakima and to Edward and
the psychiatrist in New York, and now to the psychiatrist at
Vanderbilt. Priests had one language, *repent,* and psychiatrists
another, *talk,* and sex researchers still another, *tell me what you do,*
and Paul had still another, *Get your degree, get a job, fuck men.* What
was I to do to be *chaste*?

    There had always been trade-offs. You can't *ever* have it all. A
profession, a relationship, satisfying sex, the respect of your
community. There are always things you have to sleight to get other
things more important. I couldn't see that any of these was so central
that it had to take precedence over every other thing. Men give up
their professions for their wives—or their wives for their professions.
They give up having children for their wives or their professions.
They give up their professions for their children. They give up *sex*
for every reason under the sun. And then give up every possible
personal satisfaction for the respect of mankind. Men even give up
their *lives* for abstractions, for *honor*. It is unclear to me that any of
this is preordained, that my freedom to act is limited by what I am.

Men are free. And even if they aren't free of every constraint, they learn to live with their accommodations. Sleight this for that, fudge this for that, *hedge* their bets.

My mother was worried about my father. "He makes it so difficult to love him. He is angry all the time. The littlest thing sets him off. He is so self-pitying, and he has temper tantrums all the time —that's what worries me so about you, you have temper tantrums— he is on a dry drunk, his friends say. He hates to be around my family —he can't stand your Uncle Richmond, and the other day he was rude to Caroline. After supper he goes into his bedroom and closes the door and reads his books all evening. The only time he enjoys himself is when you boys come home." She was in the kitchen cleaning up after supper, and I was sitting on the back stairs down into the kitchen listening to her and watching what she was doing. Her facial muscles were knotted up, and one eyebrow was higher than the other with tension. "He drinks too much coffee and smokes too many cigarettes. And you are so *rude* to him! He does nothing but look forward to your coming home and being able to talk to you about the books you are reading, and you do nothing but fight with him. And *what* did you do to Cornelius!"

"I didn't do anything to Cornelius. I don't know what you are talking about."

"Well, he is furious at you over something. Did you insult Henrietta?"

"Of course not."

"Well, you did something."

We talked on. The house was quiet, and my father was upstairs in his room, the door shut. Mother moved quickly around the kitchen, doing the chores, wiping her hands on the dish towel thoughtlessly and hanging it up again on the rod above the sink. She wandered over her own family, giving me news of various members, and then over people I knew in town.

"Charles Cook died."

"Oh, no. He was young, wasn't he?" Cook was the teacher I had had in high school who had led the group of us who had gone to Europe when I was sixteen, eight years ago.

"Yes." She shrugged.

"What did he die of?"

When my mother had something to say unpleasant or perhaps that shouldn't be spoken of, she had the habit of lowering her voice, as if speaking so no one could hear.

"He killed himself."

"*Suicide?*"

She nodded.

"*Why?*"

"He was charged with something—"

"*Charged!* With what?"

Here her voice became *very* low. "It had something to do with a student, I believe."

"A boy?"

"He did something with a boy. Or proposed to do something with a boy." She wrung out the dish cloth and hung it on the rack. "I don't know anything else about it."

Cook. Mr. Cook. I could feel his hands on my shoulders, kneading the muscles there while the student looked on. *There had been others.* Good God.

"I always liked him."

"I know you did." She looked at me. "Did he ever try anything —improper—with you?"

I shrugged. "No. Not that I was aware of." He hadn't "tried" anything with me. He hadn't proposed anything to me. But he had done what he wanted to do—he had put his hands on my shoulders and had felt me, and I guess that was what he wanted—and I had let him do it.

We talked on about other things and didn't come back to Charles Cook, him with the pained, strained look on his face.

"Maybe it would be good if Dad went back to AA meetings."

"He's not going back to AA meetings, he's done with that." Mother said. "It's a tragedy that he has to do the work he does—he's so much better qualified than that—and he feels so humiliated."

There was a dance that night at nine. I was to pick up friends to go, and after a while I left the kitchen to get into my tux. I called the guys to let them know I was picking them up—the younger brother of a friend of Cornelius's and a boy I had known since Mrs. Chelsea's dancing school—and after a while I left. I would not kill myself. I would not do anything *improper*. I was Robert Fair Shaw. I would do what had to be done. I picked up the guys, and we had a great deal to drink—we got drunk—and then afterward, we went to a drive-in and drank more and talked about girls and whose parents had given the best parties and which ones served spiked punch and which ones served mixed drinks and how spiked punch was terrible. And none of us talked about having sex with boys or about Charles Cook, who had killed himself.

Cornelius was at the dance with his fiancée Henrietta. We ran into each other at the bar, and Cornelius took me back to meet Henrietta. "We're going to be married some time in the late spring, early summer. We want you to come."

Henrietta kissed me on the cheek and said, "We do so hope you can come and be in the wedding. We love you so."

Cornelius made no reference to anything. He smiled and was gracious, and whatever had passed between us on the terrace of the house on Forest Lake while the partygoers inside danced the slow shag was buried deep behind his beautiful gray eyes with long lashes. I suspected that it would always remain there until I myself dug it up. Things got buried in this family—the way we were abused as children, the way Cornelius abused me when we were growing up —and were expected never to be remembered. I don't know how they did that, forgot things.

Charles Cook had been kind to me, and seemed to be understanding, when I had needed kindness. He had been good at what he did—he taught civics classes and was the faculty advisor for the student council—and he encouraged students, all of us. All of the students liked him and respected him. He paid attention to us and listened. He was the only teacher in high school that I imagined going back to and having a conversation with, talking about what there was to do with one's life and why it mattered to do something that mattered. I had not kept up with him after graduating, had not kept him informed of where I was and what I was doing and why. I had not been kind to him. I knew, even if Mother didn't, that Cook had an interest in boys. I could have given him more—even without sex—than I gave him, which was just a feel, which was nothing. I felt grief for him, because it must have been hard, and I despised myself for not having cared.

↔

A half dozen of us were at Pat's having drinks. We had all come back two days early from the holidays and, by prior arrangement, had met for supper at Pat's. Paul Huntley was there, some others, and Naomi and me. People were talking about how terrible the holidays had been with our parents and all the jerks at home and how glad we were to be back at school—but how shitty it was to have to come back to school and face exams. After supper, there was desultory talk about what to do next. Somebody suggested a movie. The others left, and Naomi and Paul were on the other side of the booth, next to one another, looking at the paper to see what was on. I was across from them, seeing them together. Nothing seemed to be happening, except that I was aware I was being left out. They were *together*, and I was alone across from them. I didn't want to go to the movies. I didn't want to be with them.

I told them so and got my coat and left. I started walking up 21st Avenue South toward my apartment, and when I got to a drug store, I filled a prescription for tranquilizers. Then I bought a six-pack of beer and popped one open and started drinking. I swallowed a handful of the pills—small oval blue ones—and drank the beer to wash them down. I did this for half a mile or so, until I got to another drug store, where I got another prescription filled. I popped open another can of beer and drank that too, washing down another handful of pills. I did this over and over, until I had taken all the pills and drunk a six-pack of beer—which was on top of all that I had had to drink earlier in the evening at Pat's.

I knew what I was doing. I wondered if I would pass out before I got home, and I walked carefully along the side of the road so I would not be in traffic. I didn't want to fall and get run over. When I had seen Naomi and Paul in the booth together, I was very tired of my life. Nothing was clear except that I was lonely, and I didn't see any way out of all this. The streets were empty, and it was cold, and after a while I left 21st Avenue South and turned into the small streets in the district near my apartment. It was less built-up than around Vanderbilt. Here the houses had broad lawns in front and sat far back from the street, the lights inside shining out on the lawns and making me feel they could see me. I kept the beer in the paper bag and the prescription bottles in my pocket, and I only took another handful of the pills when I was sure there were no cars coming that could see me.

It wasn't that I was like Charles Cook, who had been charged with something. It was that I suffered fatigue. I couldn't get up to handle any of it any more. I would go home, get in bed, drink the last of the beer and take the last of the pills, and go to sleep. And that would be the end of all of it—my parents, my family, Cornelius, Paul, Naomi, Chester, Dr. Coleman, Edward, Connie, Charles Cook, Russell Ford, the boys with slicked back blond hair and big arms, Linville Gorge, Kiawah, Pawleys, Myrtle, Trinity Church, and all the lovely girls in their gowns and corsages. Everything in graduate school was leading toward teaching, which I wasn't interested in doing. I didn't know why I was doing it. When I thought I couldn't get up to handle it anymore, I didn't know what *it* was. The sex thing I had handled all of my life. I know what I want—a decent, respectable job teaching good students and the opportunity to write respected criticism, the chance to lean against the mantle with a drink in my hand and listen to my guests talking of the New Criticism and some poem by T. S. Eliot—and that doesn't seem hard to get. But the effort it requires—and that handling *sex* requires, and somehow that thinking well of myself requires, and that all the rest of it requires—is too much. I did it because I no longer cared about the struggle. Things changed so much so fast. Every time I felt I had a grip on it, I discovered that things had changed again, the stakes gotten higher, the basic rules altered beyond recognition, the goal just over the *next* hill. At home, I took off my clothes and put on pajamas—I had this odd sense that I didn't want to be discovered naked—and turned out the light and went to bed. *Why not commit suicide?*

I was almost asleep—I was very tired—when the phone rang. It was Naomi. "I was worried about you." Her voice, always low and soft, seemed even softer. "After you left, we decided we didn't want to go to the movies either. I came home. Are you all right?"

"I'm fine."

I agreed to see her the next day. I didn't know what I was saying.

I stood by the desk near the phone, thinking, *I have to decide what to do.* It was hard to think. I called Dr. Coleman and told him what I had done. He asked how many pills I had taken—and how many beers. He asked if I could get back into town by myself "—or should I send an ambulance?" I thought I could get there on my own, and he said to meet him at the hospital in 10 minutes. I took off my pajamas and pulled on my clothes and got a taxi back into town to the hospital, where they were waiting for me. Dr. Coleman arrived in a few minutes, talked to me about what I had done and why I had done it—I didn't really know. "It was something about Naomi and Paul and the movies"—and they pumped my stomach and had a woman sit with me all night keeping me awake. "Please go away. I want to sleep."

She was an old woman who didn't seem like a nurse. "No. I am not going away, and you are not going to sleep. They have paid me to sit here with you and keep you awake, and I am going to do that."

I came to hate her, that night.

After a couple of days, they moved me out of intensive care into the psychiatric ward, and Dr. Coleman told me I would be there for several weeks. So I didn't start school with the rest of the gang, I didn't finish that semester, and I didn't start the new semester at the end of January. Instead, I stayed in the locked psychiatric ward in the middle of the Vanderbilt campus for six weeks, and the only person who had anything to do with me during that time was Naomi.

The ward was OK. I saw Dr. Coleman every day and quickly ran out of things to talk to him about, and I made friends among the other patients. We couldn't go anywhere—there was only one door in or out of the ward, and that was locked all the time—but I didn't have anywhere to go anyway. They ran some tests on me. After that, I got the reputation on the ward of being a "genius," which was pleasurable. Apparently one of the nurses had seen the results of some test and had told some of the other patients. There was also a series of pictures about which I was supposed to talk. Several of these were pictures—they were pen-and-ink drawings with careful shading—of men. One was a picture of men, apparently soldiers on bivouac, lying around on the ground outside a small cottage, their legs and arms entangled. They were in uniform and had rifles and backpacks scattered around them. One had his leg lying across the thigh of the man lying next to him. They were close enough to each other, and entangled enough in each other, to give the viewer the idea that they might, in another moment, start hugging and kissing one another. I pointed this out to Dr. Coleman. He asked me what I thought of that. That seemed odd, because I had already told him I was queer, and I wondered if he were trying to find out if I were *really* queer.

"I guess I don't think they ought to be lying that close to one another. When I was in the Army, we went on hikes, and we never lay sprawled on top of each other like that." But I didn't want to give him the impression that I was afraid of what I was seeing. "I think it's a sexy picture."

That seemed to satisfy him. I tried, in these sessions with Dr. Coleman, to sort out what I felt about homosexuality, but it was a muddle. I tried to stick to one kind of language when I talked about these things—I tried to talk in terms that a guy uses with psychiatrists—but that was hard. *Sick. Ill.* Dr. Coleman did the same thing the psychiatrist in New York had done—he kept whatever he knew to himself and didn't let me in on it. The problem with sticking to *sick, ill* was that there were all these other words that floated around, unattached to any body of thought. And while a guy might say *sick* or *ill,* he might be thinking *fruit. Fruit,* Cornelius had used it. That was the worst of those words. I winced whenever I heard it, even when someone was referring to things that grew on trees. Or attached to a completely different body of thought. *Criminal.* Sodomy was a crime in Tennessee, and Paul and I could have been charged with a crime for what we did with one another. When I grew desperate with anxiety over the point of all this, I returned to telling him about my family. It seemed right—homosexuals always returned to talking about their families when they couldn't find anything else to say—but it never got us anywhere. "—My mother was too close. She never left me alone. She even talked to her sister about my *penis.* And she wanted me to tell her all the time how pretty she was—"

Aside from seeing Coleman every day, I had nothing to do. We had a crafts room, and I made things out of leather. We played cards. There was always a nurse on duty in the common room, and sometimes she joined us to make a fourth at bridge. There was a young woman about my age who was pregnant, from Georgia somewhere. She had what people called "bedroom eyes," which meant that she always looked like she had just waked up, and she talked in a soft voice, like Naomi.

"I'm not here, honey," she said. "I'm on an extended trip to Europe. That's what my parents have told everybody. I got pregnant, and I am not married, so my parents sent me here to stay until the baby is born, and then I'll go to Europe for a quickie so I'll have something to talk about—and pictures to show—when I go home."

"What about the baby?"

She shrugged. "Put it up for adoption."

We became friends.

One day I asked Dr. Coleman a question. "What exactly am I doing here? I mean, aside from the fact that I tried to kill myself. What is this we're doing together in these sessions? Is this therapy? Is this psychoanalysis? What do I call what I am doing with you?"

Coleman said, "I can answer that. You are engaged in psychoanalytically-oriented psychotherapy." And that seemed to please him and shut me up. But it didn't answer the main question. I didn't understand the goal. What were we trying to do here? It was a mystery to me. I *thought* maybe what we were trying to do was to put me back together—ease me over whatever crisis I had had—so I could go back to dazzling people in seminars. Like being exhausted and being unable to read any longer, and taking a nap and getting up afterward and finding that it was now, once again, possible to continue to read? Or was it somehow an attempt at a fundamental alteration of my personality? If that was it—did I really want such a thing?—when was it going to happen? What was the process?

Beginning a week after I entered the hospital, I fell apart. At first, I had just gone on with it—*I'm queer, and I took 90 pills, had my stomach pumped, and now I am getting over it*—and felt largely unscathed by events. Then one day I woke up and felt like I couldn't get out of bed, my hands shook, and my knees felt like they would not hold me up. I couldn't talk. I started crying at the littlest thing. I thought, *I am having a nervous breakdown*—occasionally I wondered what the clinical meaning of that term was—and it felt odd to be having one *after* the big crisis. I felt different, weak, when I had never felt weak before. I had always been strong, able to do whatever it was that had to be done, and now everything defeated me. I sat on the john and was unable to finish the process I had begun, and I started to cry. I put my hand on the plaster wall next to me and then put my forehead on my hand and wept. The crying lasted for weeks.

After six weeks, when I got out, everything was pretty much the same as it had been when I went in. The crying stopped. My parents had wanted to come to Nashville to visit me while I was in the hospital, but I didn't let them, and after I got out my father came alone.

We were at Ireland's, having lunch.

"What happened?"

"I tried to kill myself."

"That was a damn-fool thing to do, don't you think?"

He went back to South Carolina after three tense days, and I went back to studying and trying to make up all the incompletes I had to take when I went into the hospital. I was aware that, when I went into the hospital, none of my friends called or came to see me except Naomi. I saw Naomi every day—we were a public couple now—and I also saw Paul sometimes, usually at night, when we'd sleep together but no longer had sex. What seemed to have happened was that I realized that I was flawed, and my life would be more difficult because I was, but it would not be impossible. I was eighteen-sided peg trying to fit into an sixteen-sided hole. Or something. I would find a way—had already found a way—around the problem. I was strong, bright, hard-working, focused, capable, and the people who mattered were behind me. Naomi was for me. And my body was on my side. I would be able to do it, even if it was hard.

A lecturer in the department—a woman around 40—invited me to Sunday dinner one week. Her husband picked me up at my apartment to take me to their house. He was a psychologist at Vanderbilt, and he let me know he didn't approve of psychiatrists.

"Do you know I have been in the psychiatric ward at the hospital?"

"Sure."

"Why don't you like psychiatrists?"

"They have theories, but they don't do research. Psychology is founded on research."

I thought of Paul running his rats.

I asked him about the difference between directive and non-directive therapy. Caroline, my cousin in New York, used to talk about her therapist, who was non-directive, and she wouldn't have it any other way. This psychologist, Dr. Carlton, said he was "directive. I know more. So of course I try to direct the patient." I wondered whether I would like that. I got the sense that Carlton didn't like what had happened to me, but he never came right out and said it, and while I thought he probably knew why I was in the hospital and that I was queer, he never directly said anything about that either. Everybody was being very polite and not intruding on anybody else's privacy, but Carlton was angry, I could tell, and he *hated* Naomi.

We—Naomi and I—were talking about the civil rights movement, and I raised the issue of the little girl at the center of the 1954 decision.

"No," Naomi said. "It's not about a little girl. This is not about being kind to a little girl. This is about finding the places where the system as it currently works denies basic rights to a whole class of people. Negroes. Students. Women. Our system works for many people, but if you're a Negro, it doesn't work. So we need to change the system so that this whole class of people can be brought into the system and have the same rights as everybody else. Do you see? This is what Mario Savio meant when he talked about throwing his body into the machine. The machine is the problem, not whether or not you have sympathy for a little girl, and the victims are not *a* little girl, they are a whole class of people who have been systematically excluded. You have to, first, be able to see Negroes as a class of people who are being treated differently *for no legitimate reason*."

In 1964, there were no national figures known to be homosexual. There were only those whom people suspected. If I had thought about it, I could name them—Tennessee Williams I could think of— no sports figures, no politicians, a few ballet dancers but I didn't know their names, a playwright or two (aside from Tennessee Williams I couldn't think of any), no actors, no writers aside from Gore Vidal, who had just published *Julian*, Truman Capote, who had just published *In Cold Blood,* and Andrew Gide and *The Immoralist*, which I had never read, and Allen Ginsberg, whom I had never read either. Shakespeare's love for the Young Man, Whitman—I knew what I was reading (they were writing about sex with men), but did that mean they were homosexual? I didn't know. The Greeks. Of course, but that was in another country. In my world, which included all of the United States, the number of homosexual persons who were publicly acknowledged homosexuals I could count on the fingers of *one* hand. I knew what my family would say. I was not willing to give up my family, or the respect of my family, for sex. Or the respect of my culture. It would be a lifetime of sex in the dark, my saying, "Can I *do* you?" kneeling in some parking lot behind some theatre, it would be a lifetime of lying. *He's bringing Bonny Nelson. Painted grossly effeminate queens.*

Gradually I completed the incompletes I had accumulated, and Naomi and I dated, and we spent time at Pat's. One night late in the spring, we were there, drinking beer. There had been other people there with us earlier in the evening, but they had gone, and Naomi and I were still there, drinking draft pitchers, and talking.

"It was because, you see, you and Paul were sitting in the booth together talking about what movie to see, and something in me snapped. I wasn't jealous. It was that, I have this, this *sexual* issue that I have to deal with. And I am dealing with it. I am a homosexual. And the doctors—" What I was about to say wasn't *quite* true, but it was true enough. "—say they can cure me. If I go long enough, stay in therapy long enough, I will stop being attracted to men." The doctors had never said anything about what their goal was, but I had understood what they were after, even if no one said anything. A *cure.* I didn't have to explain this very deeply to her, because queers going to a psychiatrist to be cured was what everybody assumed queers ought to be doing—it was what Edward had said I should do. Lady Bird Johnson had said that Walter Jenkins was *sick,* and afterwards he had gone to the hospital to be cured, and everybody had praised her for being so understanding. Naomi would be understanding too. I was sick—the word had taken on an unreality, had lost its ability to communicate meaning—and I was going to a doctor to be cured. I told her, "I've been a homosexual all my life. I've always been attracted to men. And now I am doing something about it."

I told her about my family. I knew how to present it so it exactly replicated what the books said. "My father paid almost no attention to us growing up. He never hugged us, never gave us baths, never dressed us. And Mother hovered around, never leaving us alone, never giving us space—" I didn't tell her, but I thought of the time my mother had found my muscle magazines under the mattress and had pulled them out and looked at them. I also didn't tell her how my mother thought they were all of women.

Naomi asked questions. "How long have you been seeing a psychiatrist?"

I told her *about a year*, which, I knew implied 12 months of therapy, which was not true. It was more like 4 or 5 months. You could say, truthfully, that I had been in therapy, off and on, for two years.

She asked if it seemed to be helping. "Some of my friends are in therapy, and they don't think it is helping."

"I don't know. I go, I do what I am supposed to do. I think it must be helping." *It may have been* helping. I had seen two psychiatrists and then I had sex with Naomi, and now I wanted— something.

It was what I had to say to her, and she had to take it. *I* had to take it. It was all I had. It seemed to me that the alternative was Brutus in the parking lot in the dark.

"Are you seeing any men now?"

"No. Not since last fall." That was true. Paul and I had had sex the last time in October.

"Thanks for telling me." She didn't seem to be worried. I thought she was feeling that I was doing what I was supposed to be doing. She seemed to feel that everything was going to be OK. I also thought it was going to be OK, but sometimes, late at night, in bed before I went to sleep, I wondered *how* is it going to be OK? How is it going to happen? I had never read anything about exactly how it was supposed to come about. She had asked the minimal questions— *Are you seeing someone now?*—and then seemed relieved to let me handle it.

Because it *did* have to do with Naomi and Paul sitting in the booth together, both of whom I had slept with, and it had to do with the paralyzing effect of seeing these two people, both of whom I had loved, talking together; Naomi and the future she promised that was so familiar and Paul and the future he pointed to—Paul had certainly not promised anything—that was so unclear and unknown. The past, I knew, never goes away, but neither does the future. I had come right to the edge of the precipice and had been incapable of living with the vertigo.

That night, I told Naomi about reading a book when I was in the Army. "I read this passage at the very end of *Crime and Punishment* in which Roskolnikov, in Siberia, looks across the river and sees the herdsmen, who are like black dots, in a place where time itself seemed to have stopped. Over there 'in the boundless steppe, awash with sunlight' the people are not like the ones on this side. Over there is freedom, not just the freedom from the prison—it's a freedom from the torment he feels, freedom from the people like himself, who are tormented. It's a book about freedom. About becoming free."

I admitted to Naomi how ambitious I was, ambitious for much more than leaning against a mantelpiece, my fingers wrapped around a silver julep cup with bourbon and water. "He gave us Miss Rosa Coldfield, who couldn't stop talking, who *had* to tell the truth about what had happened to her sister and to Henry and Charles and Judith. *When nobody wanted to hear.* Faulkner gave all of us a way to think —not just about the South—but about slavery, about the timelessness of human failure. He understood what there was to be understood, and then he sat down and wrote it all out. *This is what happened. This is what went wrong. These are the consequences.*" I described for her what I thought Faulkner had wanted to achieve, and what he had actually achieved. "I want to write, and to discover in my words a way to freedom from the chaos that seems to be around us." I was aware while I was talking that I had never talked to anyone before like this, used language like this, committed myself so completely and openly. I had never really wanted to teach. I wanted to write. And laying my arm along a mantle was only one of the fantasies I had for my life, and not the most compelling one.

On the way out, she held my hand, and when we were in the street, she stepped in front of me and leaned up and kissed me, and smiled. "I like it that you are so ambitious."

As it became more publicly known that Naomi and I were a couple, the people we knew at school—some of them—became more and more brutal toward us. Once, in the student union where we were having coffee, a woman I knew at the next table over—she was a woman who had gone to New Orleans with a gang of us the year before—said loudly in Naomi's hearing, "Fair Shaw is queer." I thought, *yes*.

No doctor or priest has ever said to me, *What we are working on here is getting you to accept your homosexuality.* Only Paul said, *fuck men.* And I have never found a description of a life for a man who fucked men that was a public life and that earned the respect of the community. It was unthinkable. I thought of Connie. I felt grief. *You are always on my mind.*

For I wanted to be a man. Men are strong, like the man on the banks of the back creek who had picked me up and settled me on his shoulders and then had gone about the labor of pulling the seine.

Men are strong, able to hold their families together in difficult times, capable of earning money to provide for their families' needs, of loving their wives and children, of being reassuring and supportive of those they loved. Men don't need reassurance and support themselves. They *provide* and are not provided for. Men don't ask for things back. Men make a place for their families in the community, and they are a model for their children. They live open, honest lives, and their motives are transparent, to do good for others. They are like Uncle Richmond, who is a leader in Columbia, being photographed for the newspaper making speeches in favor of things that will better the community. Men go out into the world, as John Kennedy did, because they believe that *we can do better,* so that the lives of their children can be richer, happier, more filled with a deeper experience of life. And they do all these things without hope of being repaid in any material way, but by doing them, they earn the respect of their community, which is the contract. *Men do good and earn respect.*

Several weeks later, we were at Pat's again, drinking beer, this time just ourselves. She sat across from me in the bright room, her long silver earrings glinting in the reflected light, looking beautiful. We played the juke box and talked about our friends. Naomi had a heart-shaped, serene face, in the manner of the faces of women in French court painting. It was intelligent, willful, and passionate. It was a kind, serious face. It had nothing in common with the large-eyed caressing faces of Southern women I knew, who were continuously responding with raised eyebrows and widened eyes, pursed lips, and sucked-in cheeks to what was being said to them. Naomi radiated an inner curiosity, contentment, and calm that I found irresistible.

"Where would you like to live?"

"Oh, that's easy. New Orleans."

I grinned. "So would I. Why? What do you like about it?"

"The French influence everywhere. I love getting away from the Anglo world, from the Protestant world around us here—this strong sense of sin—and into the worldliness of a Roman Catholic world. Around here they pretend to be shocked if you commit a sin. In the Roman Catholic world, particularly in southern European countries, they just say *say twelve hail Marys and go and sin no more. See you next week.* I like that. They have a better sense of people."

I liked that too. "People will fail, won't they. I like the French Quarter."

"Ah, me too. And if you can't get a house in the French Quarter, there's the Garden District."

"This big white Greek Revival house built in 1820—"

"*Yeah.* Something with a porch on the front and one-story columns—"

"And windows that go to the floor."

"Ah, yes."

We rambled on, dreaming, passing a fantasy back and forth between us.

"Very urban, very close to the street, even on the street, what yard there is would be behind—I'm not much interested in grass— and the walkway from the sidewalk to the steps would be black and white marble."

"Cracked from use and age."

She smiled. "There'd be children running in and out, and students—" She had a sleepy smile on her face. "—and, of course, people coming for political meetings of all kinds, all the time. The phone would ring constantly. '*Hello? I'm calling about flyers for the demonstration this evening, and do we have enough candles?*' Children's toys would be everywhere—blocks and dolls. I see the whole thing as kind of hip and ratty."

"Inside, everything would be painted white. Antiques and oriental rugs and some really good modern furniture—glass and steel —and abstract expressionist prints on the walls."

"Yes. Posters of exhibitions at the Modern. There's a wonderful one by Pollock. Do you like Op Art?"

"Yes, who?"

"Vasarely. Do you know him?"

I grinned. "Of course."

"I love his stuff."

"I do too. Things bulging out of the plane of the picture, breaking through two dimensions into three dimensions, entering *time.*"

I could see my whole future: the two of us joined lightly together, sharing our lives, our books, our children, our house, our goals, our attitudes, our politics, our friends (who would be of all colors and races), capable of ranging over the whole spectrum of our culture from low to high and knowledgeable about everything. My life would be honest, respectable, and transparent. I felt immensely strong, powerful, capable. I felt an immense tenderness toward her. I loved her.

3

During the four years between August 1965, when Naomi and I were married, and June 29, 1969, the country—the one I thought I was entering as I started my marriage and my career—experienced a structural collapse. Under President Johnson, the nature of the Vietnam War changed from a communist insurgency in the south that the US was helping to combat to a civil war in which the US had intervened. National focus shifted from civil rights to the war. Majorities began to believe that the United States was an aggressor against the independence of nations, an aggression that was *failing*, as was apparent after the Tet Offensive on January 30, 1968. Everybody now saw the war was being lost and the government had lied to the people. Everywhere I looked, received truths gave way to revolutionary calls for justice. Students at universities across the country, led by the Students for a Democratic Society, mounted street demonstrations to call the nation to a higher, better, understanding of itself, and political structures caved in. People were paranoid about the spying by government agencies, the police, the FBI, the CIA, about wiretapping and the infiltration of leftist and antiwar groups to which I and my friends belonged.

These years presented a spectacle that none of us had ever seen before—gangs of kids in the street facing down the police, demonstrators screaming obscenities at the President, police with dogs and fire hoses attacking crowds of unarmed *white* students. On February 8, 1968, before we left Nashville, black students in Orangeburg, South Carolina, on the campus of South Carolina State University, historically the state black college, demonstrated to integrate a bowling alley that was still segregated, four years after the passage of the Civil Rights Act of 1964. They lit a bonfire, the police arrived on campus in force, one was hurt, and one policeman fired a gun. Other cops fired. Three unarmed black students were murdered by the police. On April 4, 1968, Martin Luther King, Jr., was assassinated on the balcony of the Lorraine Motel in Memphis. *The Times* headline read, "WHITE IS SUSPECTED." The next day *The Times* headline, three lines deep across the entire page, read, "ARMY TROOPS IN CAPITAL AS NEGROES RIOT; GUARD SENT INTO CHICAGO, DETROIT, BOSTON; JOHNSON ASKS A JOINT SESSION OF CONGRESS." And another article on the front page carried the headline, "7 Die as Fires and Looting Spread in Chicago Rioting."

The explosive, revolutionary energy also found outlet in France, which was paralyzed by student revolts. On May 19, 1968, under the headline, "The Students Sow Seeds of a Revolution," *The Times* stated, "What started modestly as little more than a student 'happening' three weeks ago has become a country-wide tide of discontent and revolutionary fever that threatens the basic institutions of France and may yet bring the downfall of the Government." On May 21, the headline in *The Times* was "FRANCE IS NEAR PARALYSIS AS MILLIONS JOIN STRIKE." On May 30, the headline over the leading article on the front page was "DE GAULLE GOES TO RURAL HOME AMID SPECULATION HE WILL QUIT."

Andy Warhol was shot—but not killed—on June 3, 1968 at his factory in Union Square in New York, and then, just after midnight, early in the morning of June 5, 1968, Bobby Kennedy was shot and wounded critically in the kitchen of the Ambassador Hotel in Los Angeles. He had just given a victory speech after winning the California Democratic primary. The picture on the front page of *The Times* was of Bobby lying on the floor, the camera peering over the shoulders of staff and medical persons, his eyes open and staring fixedly straight up, the picture obscene in its violence. He died the next day, on June 6, and for the next three days the nation was transfixed. In Nashville, on TV, I watched the funeral in New York and the mourners traveling to Grand Central Station—cameras everywhere catching the lines of them even as they moved across the concourse and down the stairs to the tracks and the funeral train— and then the slow traverse of the train down the tracks from New York through New Jersey and Delaware and Maryland to Washington. Millions of people lined the tracks, what *The Times* on June 9, 1968 called "an almost unbroken succession of station

178

throngs, urban street crowds and clusters of small-town mourners." *The Times* said, "The train's route took it through the greatest concentrations of population on the continent, and in many places it seemed as if whole towns had turned out." Two were killed in Elizabeth, New Jersey, while they stood on nearby tracks, run over by an express train going in the opposite direction, after which the train slowed to little more than a walk, the agony prolonged into the night. *The Times* said, "The train cortege has been part of the American legend since Walt Whitman immortalized Abraham Lincoln's funeral train back to Illinois in 'When Lilacs Last in the Dooryard Bloomed.'"

Students took over deans' offices at Harvard and at universities across the country. Russian tanks rolled into Prague on August 20, 1968, ending the brief moment of liberalization, and, at the end of the summer, August twenty-fifth to thirtieth, 1968, the Democratic Convention in Chicago attracted anti-war demonstrators into the street, who, like every other American under 30, after the murders of King and then Kennedy, seemed to have lost all hope. The National Guard was called out on Mayor Daley's request, and for three nights it beat the demonstrators with clubs and gassed them with teargas. The scenes were broadcast from cameras in the windows of the Chicago Hilton, across the street from Grant Park, and it was as if all of America was in the middle of a riot of police. Along with the rest of the country, I watched all this in stunned amazement. It seemed that the life of the nation was being marked by one very large public funeral after another and by waves of rioting—and the whole world I had grown up with was self-destructing.

When Naomi and I arrived in Ann Arbor, Michigan in the fall of 1968, we found that a new Administration Building was being completed, built, according to a widely-believed rumor on campus, to make it an impregnable fortress against students, a giant eight-story almost windowless cube on a windowless plinth, capable of being entered by only two doors, which gave into a corridor entirely lined with brick. The only way to the second floor offices was by elevator, which could be disabled by the flick of a switch inside. It was as ugly as a jail. By the fall of 1968, the lines of battle were clear: It was *us* against the establishment, us against the *pigs,* us against capitalism, us against the honkies, us against the *system*. Like everyone else on campus (and Mario Savio five years earlier), I

179

found myself using language like *the dispossessed*. The crisis that the country faced, and had been facing since the beginning of the civil rights movement, was resolving itself into a conflict for the meaning of America between those in power in their impregnable fortresses and the powerless in the streets.

There were other political struggles going on—sex, drugs, and rock and roll. People just a little younger than I looked different—long bushy uncombed hair, jeans, beards—and they smoked grass and seemed to have sex whenever they felt like it. The music was the Beatles, the Rolling Stones, Janis Joplin, Aretha Franklin, the Supremes, Bob Dylan, Simon and Garfunkel's *Bridge Over Troubled Waters. Hair* opened off-Broadway in 1967—everybody knew the line *SODOMY, FELLATIO, CUNNILINGUS, PEDERASTY!*—and Arthur was the hottest discotheque in New York. Sexual liberation exploded on the country by 1968 because of the pill and the women's movement, with Betty Freidan's *The Feminine Mystique* and Simone de Beauvoir's *The Second Sex,* and because kids no longer had respect for the way older people did anything.

I had been on the front line four years before—the coolest guys were out picketing—and I suddenly found now that I was out of date. I was an *older folk.* On June 27, 1969, I was *thirty.* My life had taken on a measure of stability in the last four years. I completed my course work for my doctorate in December 1967, chose a subject for my dissertation based on a seminar report on John Donne that had been well-received, chose a dissertation committee and got professors to agree to serve, studied for and passed my comprehensive oral examinations, went with Naomi to Boston for two months of reading in the Houghton Library at Harvard, and returned to Nashville on March 1, 1968—after the Orangeburg Massacre and before the assassination of Martin Luther King—with the commitment to myself to write a chapter of my dissertation each month while all of us watched, amazed and shocked, the murders of Martin Luther King, Bobby Kennedy, the Chicago riots, and the fall of the French government. I finished my dissertation on the first of August. The night I completed my degree, I drove up in front of our house exhilarated with triumph to find Naomi coming down the steps carrying a gift for me—an enormous brandy snifter filled with bourbon on the rocks. I accepted a tenure-track position in the Department of English at the University of Michigan, and as soon as

Race Point Light

I received the appointment letter, Naomi went off the pill and got pregnant, and Judith was born in February 1969.

While other young men between twenty and thirty were shucking off responsibilities and allegiances to middle-class respectability and joining the counterculture or the anti-war movement, I was permanently right in the middle of it—the respectable middle class—saving to buy a house and a washer and dryer. My leftist credentials at that point consisted of my commitment to the civil rights movement in Nashville and the anti-war movement in Ann Arbor. My conflict was between my need to stand with those against the system on the one hand and my obligations to Naomi and Judith to achieve success in my profession on the other. It was not a new dilemma. I said, as I had said in Nashville, *I can't go to jail, I have to go to class.* I was already *in* my profession, and while the anti-war movement had burgeoned—exploded—since 1965, I couldn't abandon the life I was already committed to. I stayed where I was, but the conflict between my need to join the movement—to be against the war and for a transformation of the whole American contract—and my need to fill my obligations to Naomi and Judith remained sharp and painful. I was aware of my hypocrisy. I *liked* the life I had, even if it was not as clean as I wanted, but I was torn. I went to work every day while Naomi stayed home and looked after the baby, I did what I was told by the administration, and I unwillingly paid my taxes to support the war.

On Sunday morning, June 29, 1969, in Ann Arbor, Michigan, I sat in the kitchen of a small brown, rented bungalow—two bedrooms downstairs, one upstairs under the eaves, one bathroom—and read *The Ann Arbor News,* which I glanced at before reading *The New York Times*. The big news was the investiture of the Prince of Wales, which was to take place in Caernarvon on Tuesday, July 1, a big royal story that produced articles and pictures every day. It was a warm, early summer day, brilliant sunshine outside, and bright sunlight from the window lit the room. Naomi stood at the stove, barefoot, frying bacon. She wore a housecoat, her hair bedraggled from last night. On the wall above my head was a large unframed Caravaggio poster Naomi had found and stuck to the wall with pushpins. I wore jeans and a t-shirt. I had my elbows on the table, my forearms along the wood, and leaned over the pages I was reading. I had long, thick, brown hair, also bedraggled, that hung over my forehead and covered my ears and reached, in back, just to my shoulders. I moved, settled my elbow on the table and my head in my palm, which also served to push away my hair. I liked the little cottage, which was much like a Cape, though it was made of brick, and I liked the way we fit into it, guests upstairs under the eaves, our own bedroom at the front, and our Judith in the bedroom behind ours. We had found two prints of Modigliani paintings that we hung in the living room, matted with black velvet and framed in plain dark wood. Naomi had found a salvage wood coffee table, a rectangle the length of the sofa with legs in each corner whose top she had covered with grass cloth. On it we had put a dark mottled brown pottery ashtray big enough to be a salver in a church. There was a large silver coffee and tea service on a silver tray on a chest, a wedding present from my parents.

I stretched and looked around the kitchen. My home. I picked up Judith from her playpen and held her in my lap, talking to her. "Do you know you are beautiful?" I put my face to her stomach and blew, and she giggled. Around town I was known as *Dr. Shaw*, or *Professor Shaw*, but at home with my little girl, I was *Pa*. I crossed my legs and settled her on my instep, holding her hands, and she began to laugh. I bounced my foot gently under her—*ride a cock horse to Banbury* Cross—while she giggled. I put her down on her back and went over to Naomi and kissed her. She smiled before going back to the bacon. We did that all day long, passing one another as we went about our separate chores and stopping for a moment to kiss or hug and say, *I love you,* pleased with ourselves, our child, our little cottage, and our lives. "I'm on my way," I said to Naomi. I was an assistant professor at the University of Michigan, I had escaped the South, and I found myself in a place where it seemed even the politicians were on the right side of the things that mattered. I had to stop sometimes to remind myself that all this was really happening, that I really was here among people who thought and were doing something important, for I believed that teaching was important, that the academy did have a major role to play in the life of the nation, and that I had a chance to play a major role in the life of the academy. Today there would be a book on *Measure for Measure* to read for this fall's classes.

182

We had breakfast, and I washed up afterwards. Naomi and I entertained frequently—we had people over for drinks two or three times a week and usually had people for dinner once during the weekend. I liked that, making our home a center of social life in our crowd, and I thought that what we were doing was also part of the academy, an extension of the life of reading, research, criticism, teaching, and writing. At our last dinner party, people's conversation moved easily among their teaching and their research and their writing and their personal lives. I liked the idea of working toward something where all the different parts seemed to have a place. Our house was like that—some eighteenth-century silver, Op Art pictures, pottery, an antique chest, which all seemed to go together. Our friends were like that too. In their differing sensibilities, they each illuminated what they shared with the others, which was a certain seriousness, a thoughtfulness, about their lives. The constituent parts of my life were coming together.

I sat down again at the kitchen table to *The Times*, turning the pages, scanning for something interesting. On page 33 of the first section, there was an article in the left column with this headline: "4 POLICEMEN HURT IN 'VILLAGE' RAID: Melee Near Sheridan Square Follows Action at Bar." The article was about a police raid on a bar in Greenwich Village called the Stonewall Inn. I knew Sheridan Square and knew the neighborhood. Because I did, I read the article.

Shortly after three on Saturday morning, the day before, the police had raided the Stonewall, "known for its homosexual clientele," and "hundreds of young men went on a rampage." I read casually at first and then my interest intensified, focusing on the astonishing story being developed in successive paragraphs. The article said "the young men threw bricks, bottles, garbage, pennies, and a parking meter at the policemen." Later, "a large crowd formed in the square after being evicted from the bar." The crowd "grew to close to 400 during the melee, which lasted about 45 minutes." The story also described events early Saturday night, when "throngs of young men congregated outside the inn…reading aloud condemnations of the police."

I laid the paper down on the table. Today was the second day after my thirtieth birthday. I recognized the parts of the scene—the police, the angry men on the street condemning them, the reporter unable to see why the men were angry, the headline, *4 POLICEMEN*

HURT. It was not the police who were hurt. Without knowing any more, I knew that much. The young men were standing up for themselves, and I could read through the lines of the article to see what they, like the kids on the street in Nashville, must have looked like—outraged by the sense of their own mistreatment. It came on me like a sudden chill. I had not foreseen this. There had been another possibility aside from kneeling in the parking lot in front of Brutus. Even after years of street demonstrations by blacks and by students against the war, I had not been prepared to see this. *Of course.*

During the years between my marriage in 1965 and the Stonewall Rebellion, I had made a conscious effort to marginalize my homosexual feelings. I had waited, curious, to see what would happen. When it didn't happen—that is, when I continued to want men—I waited longer, in the meantime getting on with what had to be done, finishing my doctorate, getting a job, finding a place to live in Ann Arbor, teaching my classes, marching in demonstrations against the war and against racism. Occasionally, I would think, *I am still having homosexual feelings.* It was manageable, if bothersome, and I felt I had the support of Naomi and of my culture. I was doing the right thing, the *responsible* thing. Even my parents and Cornelius seemed to approve of my new respectability. My mother wrote, "We are so proud of what you have accomplished, getting your doctorate so expeditiously and earning the respect of your professors. I told Caroline about your dissertation on John Donne, and she says you are a genius! You and Naomi should be very proud of yourselves. You are going to make fine parents for your precious little girl." Paul had said, *Get your degree, get a job, fuck men.* Now, the newspaper on the table in front of me was evidence of a population of homosexuals who were *not* marginalizing their feelings, they were parading them in the street. Homosexuals no longer felt *being responsible* was a goal to drive toward.

On Monday, the next day, June 30, 1969—the *Detroit Free Press* headlined an article, "Gay Wales Waits for New Prince"—*The Times* had a second article, this time on page 22 of the first section, entitled "POLICE AGAIN ROUT 'VILLAGE' YOUTHS, Outbreak by 400 Follows a Near-Riot Over Raid." "Heavy police reinforcements cleared the Sheridan Square area of Greenwich Village again yesterday morning when large crowds of young men, angered by a police raid on an inn frequented by homosexuals, swept through the area." The article said the police were "unable" to control the crowd, "some of whom were throwing bottles and lighting small fires." "At least two men were clubbed to the ground," and "three persons were arrested on charges of harassment and disorderly conduct." "The police were denounced by last night's crowd for allegedly harassing homosexuals. Graffiti on the boarded-up windows of the inn included: 'Support gay power' and 'Legalize gay bars.'" *Gay*. There it was again.

The question of whether homosexuality was a sin or an illness, or a crime, had now been superseded by the question raised by the men in the Village. *When are we going to get our place in the American republic?* There was a strong black fist on the posters for the Black Panthers, and the text of the poster on the door of the Stonewall Inn said *Gay Power*. I saw a strong *gay* fist. It was a new way of seeing homosexual—gay—people, as strong, powerful, healthy forces taking their place among the peoples of the earth.

Allen Ginsberg said after the Stonewall riots, "The guys were so beautiful. They've lost that wounded look that fags all had ten years ago." It was obvious to me from that moment on Monday morning that the place to be was on the street with other gay people—I belonged with them—but I was in my kitchen with my wife at the stove and our child in the playpen, unable to move and unable to abandon them. They were mine, and I was theirs, and there was no way to walk out. She was only 4 months old. Her arrival had made my situation, it seemed to me, permanent and irremediable. Men have wives and children, and they support them. They make commitments and take on burdens. They are strong, and they protect their loved ones.

All young people, coming out of school, are tested. The testing of an academic takes specific forms: *Is he a successful teacher? Has he proven real achievement as a scholar and writer? Can he show that he is capable of a lifetime of scholarly achievement?* I had five years to demonstrate my abilities—until the fall of 1973—but for me there was another test. I had made a bet that I could marry and make my marriage a success, that I could be a good father and a good husband, that I could play my part in giving Judith the chance to be a happy productive loving person. I had made a bet that I was a good person, that I was a man who could do all the things men do.

Another, even more amorphous test, was the question of whether I could prove, as an adult, that I was a serious, mature member of my community.

Now, suddenly, the hordes of young gay men in public presented an image that none of us had ever seen before—gay men who were not only gay but had a whole life behind them. They were like Effie in our kitchen at home after the 1954 Supreme Court decision—they had jobs, friends, apartments, *lives*. This was in direct contradiction to the life I led, which was suddenly *the closet*. I had not even known the word before. What had I called myself before Stonewall? The only thing to be said about me now was that I was a closeted gay man.

I was in exactly the wrong place to be, and there was no way to get out. While the world around me was shucking off coats and ties and slipping into farmers' overalls, floating on a haze of marijuana and hash, crowding the streets in demonstrations in favor of black power, gay power, women's power, drugs, for free love, and against the war, I was dressed conservatively, leaving my wife and child at home and walking across the campus to teach a class in Renaissance literature. I saw now that 1965 was almost the last possible moment in which I could have gotten married and still believed that marriage was the answer to anything. Four years later, almost nobody thought marriage was the answer to any serious question. I had been transformed into an Uncle Tom.

One week after the riots, on July 6, 1969, the *Detroit Free Press* printed a letter to the editor written by a couple in suburban Detroit.

> We originally felt that the violent youth groups were very wrong in their actions against the so-called establishment. However, after being rebuffed on practically all sides as we expressed our opinions to our government leaders in a polite fashion, we wonder if the young people are not correct in assuming revolution is the only way to change things.
>
> We feel that the path our government is following is morally wrong. Unless we are able to put the needs of the poor and the deprived, the problems of the urban areas, and the control of pollution of air, water, and countryside ahead of our

desires for a continual bloodbath against
communism, we shall fall like a house of cards. The
proper way to defeat communism is to offer
something better. If we cannot do this, we deserve to
fail.

↔

After a lecture on *Absalom! Absalom!* to a large class, I faced six or
eight students, all male, standing in a semi-circle. It was a
sophomore class in the novel, and I had gotten the reputation of
being good on Faulkner, I presumed because I was Southern, but I
hoped because I was good on Faulkner. I found that a dozen students
who were not signed up for this particular section of the course
showed up to hear me lecture. These students facing me after class
were all unfamiliar to me, and I started on the left.

"Yes?"

The student raised an issue about the novel—it had to do with
the weight of the past on Yoknapatawpha County—and all of them
listened while I answered. I moved from him to the next student, and
then the next. I was focusing intensely on each student as he talked—
I was under pressure to speak well and knowledgeably about the
novel—and I was only aware of the student to whom I was speaking.
By this time there may have been as many as fifteen students in a
semi-circle around me.

Then I turned and saw the next one, long blond hair turned
golden by the light coming in from behind him, deeply tanned,
wearing glasses with gold frames and lenses tinted gold. I was jerked
from an intense concentration on Faulkner's conversation between
Quentin and Shreve in the iron-cold New England winter of
Cambridge, Massachusetts, to the warm pink and golden glow of this
beautiful man. This man in the gold framed glasses had just appeared
and struck me dumb with wonder. I could barely think. He had come
from nowhere, had not come from anything inside me, had attacked
me, and had *won*.

↔

My classes were held in a big room almost filled with about 100 students. I was at the front corner of the room, talking about the closet scene in *Hamlet*.

"OK. What are you smiling at?"

The student's name was Dick. He had a great mop of frizzy light-brown hair, and he was smiling. "He's just killed Polonius, and now everything is changed. Up to the moment he killed Polonius, he might have been able to get away with killing Claudius. Now he's got blood on his hands, and he's not going to be able to mount a clean revenge. Now the playgoer can see the end of the play."

"Why?"

"He's no longer a virtuous avenger. He's set things in motion that are going to lead to his own death. He kills Polonius, Laertes kills him. But the suspense we talked about is now immeasurably larger than it used to be. The question now is, *How bad is this going to be?*"

"Hey, great. Thanks. That's exactly right. What would the play have been like had Gertrude actually known about the murder and had Hamlet found out about it in this scene?"

"It would have been a less compelling play—"

"Why is that?"

"Hamlet's situation would have been clearer—there're *us* and there are *them*, and he could do what he had to do against *them*, and, since they are murderers, he would not have been so conflicted about it. As it is, he has to act, but he knows that a lot of people are going to get ground up in his war against Claudius, people who are not guilty of murder, but who are on the side of those who are—but who, in some way, are also on *his* side."

"Like who?"

"Gertrude is the one we are talking about, but there is Polonius, who is not guilty of murder, just stupidity. Ophelia, who is not guilty of anything but is fated to die. Rosencrantz and Guildenstern, of course—"

"—*whom I will trust as I will adders fanged*—"

"Right. And Hamlet himself, who is both guilty and innocent."

"What is this play about?"

"One thing it is about is the impossibility—or the difficulty—of a clean revenge."

"Great. So what is the play about?"

"All the other revenge tragedies written before this one. The ones you talked about last week. People die in this one—all those except Claudius—because they are stupid and wrong, not because they are guilty of a crime."

"But that doesn't make his predicament any less overwhelming."

"It makes it worse."

"Why?"

"Because it is impossible to sort things out. Everybody is in some way the cause of what happens."

"Wait, there is something else. Who is responsible for all these people getting ground up?"

"Fate."

"Yes, of course. 'There's a special providence in the fall of a sparrow.' There was already rottenness in Denmark before the ghost appears. What else?"

They shrug.

"Hamlet is acting in the real world. In the real world, sometimes you have to act and you can't let the confusion and contradictions— the *rottenness*—of the real world stop you. You have to be able to cut through all the bullshit, the conflicting currents and conflicting ideas and perceptions and all the ignorant and stupid and malevolent forces and *find the right step to take.* Hamlet can't do that. He waits until fate—in the form of the bet with Laertes—operates to force the issue. It is not until he discovers the wine is poisoned that he acts. And when he does, when he acts, finally, in a kind of spasm of fury, all the structure of Denmark falls apart. Who is responsible for the debacle at the end?"

"Hamlet?" He didn't want to say it.

"Well maybe. Probably, at least in part." I closed my text. "Now, let's look at the entrance of the ghost. Line one hundred and one."

I had never taught before. I had gotten scholarships at Vanderbilt, enough money to cover my expenses, and so had never had to apply for a teaching assistantship. When I arrived at the University of Michigan, I had never stood in front of a classroom of students. I became convinced that it was a talent one was born with that couldn't be learned. Other men who had been hired with me got in the classroom for the first time and discovered they hated it. One man told me, "It's stressful. I find that as soon as I am out of one class, I am already stressing about the next one. I have to prepare.

Can I prepare? Can I prepare enough? *How* do I prepare? I used to like being a student. Now I find that I hate them. No, I am *afraid* of them. What are they going to do to me? I feel like I am constantly in danger of being seen as stupid. The classroom is a minefield. I don't ever know when things are going to explode." On the other hand, I felt it was like arriving in England after traveling on the continent. *They speak my language here.* It was inspiriting, and it allowed a vast expansion of my ability to communicate, all the barriers to an exchange removed. I asked one day in class, "What are the courtiers feeling during Claudius's first speech, the one that begins, *Though yet of Hamlet our dear brother's death, the memory be green—?"* They laughed. *Like listening to Nixon,* and the class erupted with laughter. I had been anxious before my first classes, the first week or two, and then I discovered that it had happened that my students and I were at home together, working on the same thing, able to trust one another, and to talk.

↔

At a large picnic organized by the department at the beginning of the term, a woman spoke to me. We were near the table with the food and the washtubs with the beer.

"So what do you do?" she asked.

"I teach—"

"No, I meant, what do you *do?"*

I didn't know what she meant, except she somehow wanted me to justify myself. "I want to overthrow the whole fucking government, for one thing."

"That's a start," she said, unimpressed.

The truth was, I had come to Ann Arbor to live the life I was living. It was the life Patrick Endicott had lived at Sewanee and a version of the lawn at Wespanee. It was, I hoped, a "considered life."

She was a lecturer in English, putting her husband through medical school. "Have you read *The Teachings of Don Juan?"* It was a book that had just come out and that people were reading that fall about using drugs as a way of breaking through to new ways of knowing.

"No. I haven't. I think I am already finding new ways of knowing."

"And what are they?"

"Every time another national leader is assassinated, I have to find a whole new way of knowing. The Orangeburg Massacre. Most of the recent riots—the ones in Chicago—require that we rethink everything again, all the way from the beginning. I wonder if any of us are going to have the kind of life we planned. And then of course there is bourbon—"

She laughed.

"Do you drink tequila?"

Her husband asked, "Do you ever do hash?"

Drugs were their drug of choice. Aside from pot occasionally, Naomi and I had not done drugs. We had not even experimented much with alcoholic drinks beyond bourbon and vodka. This woman, it seems, was into the sexual concerns of D. H. Lawrence, and she also wrote. They shared the same politics everyone else had, new left radicalism, although they, like Naomi and me, lived as middle-class professionals.

She looked around her at the hillside leading down to the lake, covered right now with academics of all ages drinking beer and playing ball, and said, "I wonder if the minds of the younger generation are in good hands."

When we left the picnic, they came home with us—they went by their house first to check on the babysitter and their children—and the four of us drank the rest of the evening.

"What made you come here," she asked.

"Here?"

"Ann Arbor."

"It was the best job I could get. I wanted to get out of the South." I fixed her a scotch and water.

"You'll enjoy some of it. The politics are horrendous. It's an insane place—"

"It's an insane time."

"—and some of it you won't enjoy at all. It's surprising that you came here. It's the Midwest—we're only 40 miles from Detroit. I hate the traffic, the smog. I would have thought you would have chosen a smaller school, one less democratic. What Kissinger said about the academy is true here." *University politics are vicious precisely because the stakes are so small.* "You'd be amazed at what these men are willing to do to each other. They fight over *status*. I find it so tiresome among supposedly enlightened people." She asked again, "Why did you come here?"

I shrugged. "Neither of us wanted to stay in the South. There are the politicians like Strom Thurmond. The schools are bad. They were still fighting integration as recently as this past spring, and we—both of us—have professional goals that can't be realized if most of our energies are going into forcing the system to provide basic American rights to black students. Besides, our families are in the South, and we wanted to get away from them." I didn't say that this last one was the real one.

"Why didn't you stay and fight?"

"Neither of us thought the South was worth fighting for. We just left. I did visit Tuskegee Institute, once. I thought it might be a place I could make a contribution. But I felt so patronizing being there that I changed my mind." After a moment, I said, "It had to do with escaping the South. Escaping the past."

"Ah, but honey, you can't do that, I didn't think. You can't avoid dealing with it. No, your conflict is not about the South and the North. It has to do with something else. You don't explain yourself very clearly, the conflict between your political ideas and your class. It makes it hard to know you."

↔

There were perhaps five or six gay men in the department. "Welcome to Ann Arbor," my officemate, a gay man, said with a broad smile when I first arrived. Then, "I hear you're married!" with an even broader grin. My officemate made use of this by engaging in *double-entendres* with me. "I don't think I was *up* for marriage, actually." He laughed. He was, to a point, friendly. While I was not attracted to any of the gay men I worked with, my relationships with them were easier than with straight men. They never asked the question straight men always asked when they found out I was gay, *Why did you get married?*

"I *know* why, honey." My officemate grinned.

What I found most difficult were unattached straight men. In late 1969, we were at a cocktail party—sixty people in a large living room—and somebody turned to me and introduced the man she was talking to.

The man was tall and had angular features, almost, but not quite, handsome, slender, wearing a suit, unaffected by the current sixties styles.

"Hello. I'm Amos Reid." He had a steady gaze and looked me directly in the eye, and we shook hands.

"I'm Fair Shaw."

"Did you go to the demonstration yesterday?"

"I was in class until late."

"There were 20,000 people there."

"In Ann Arbor you can get 20,000 just by putting up a sign calling for a demonstration—"

We talked about the university and about Ann Arbor. "I've never seen so many people wearing bib overalls."

"I don't suppose I notice." But I had noticed. I liked the style. Blue jeans, work shirts, macramé belts, high-topped brown boots. "It seems romantic. I came here from Vanderbilt."

"Ah, the Fugitives."

There was some sexual tension in the exchange, something, I thought, in his eyes, but I was not clear and didn't know what to make of it. Reid was from the South too—Louisiana—and we talked about LSUNO and New Orleans.

I called Naomi over and introduced them.

"Tell me about your politics down there. I'm told you have the most corrupt politics in the nation." She laughed. "I've read *All the King's Men.*"

"God, it's wonderful. It's better than football. Would you like a drink? Then I'll tell you all about it." Reid went to get us drinks.

Perhaps the sexual tension was all on my side. I sometimes wondered if my own attraction for certain men made them respond to me, even if they weren't gay. Perhaps unconsciously they responded to my attraction. Reid entertained us with stories, this sheriff of that county, that governor, all of whom had ended up in jail, the ones who didn't die first.

"You've got nothing on Strom. He just keeps on talking segregation while everybody in the state knows he's got a daughter by his family's maid." They laughed.

Half a dozen came by our house after the party, and I stood leaning against the counter in the kitchen, while Reid leaned over me —he was much taller—and talked on and on, tossing off drink after drink. "There's not going to be a revolution in this country. The whole working class has been bought off by the system. There is no revolutionary class in America, except the students, who are not suff 194iciently numerous to be effective."

I wondered, *Is he gay? Is he coming on to me? Am I coming on to him? What?*

Bob Curry and his wife were also there. Bob was about my height but stocky as opposed to my build, and when he stood near the mantel against which I was leaning, he put his hand on the mantel behind my shoulder and leaned on it and talked seriously about the state of the world. His wife sat on the sofa with other wives, talking about children and child-rearing.

"It's the basic bestial nature of mankind. You put 300,000 kids together in an open field and no controls, and that is what you have happen. Eight people dead." The Rolling Stones concert at Altamont Speedway had happened the weekend before.

"Four people dead. One stabbing, one drowning, and two men killed when a car ran over them."

Bob shrugged. "None of that would have happened if they hadn't been doing drugs."

I raised my glass. "And what are we doing?"

"It's hard, isn't it. It's a terrible time to be a man. What is it about women? Have you read *The Feminine Mystique?* I understand all that, she's right, but I think it sucks to be a man right now. This wasn't the way it was supposed to be when I was growing up, where you knew pretty much what it was going to be like." He was almost whispering in my ear—he didn't want to say inflammatory things too loudly in front of the women—but he was so close to me, it was the way Connie used to talk to me. He was almost *kissing* me.

Others were there, including Greg Stiefel and his wife, Anne. Greg was from Illinois, a large man with long hair that curled around his neck, knowing watchful eyes, and a considered way of speaking. He called me *Fair*, as if he were using a title, and he said, on first coming into our house, "I suppose it is that you are from the South that makes you care about such things," letting his gaze move from object to object to picture to picture. When he said something witty, he would grimace and then smile. "You care more about how you do things than what you are doing. For you, style is a moral question. I like that. It was a moral question for the eighteenth century, too."

I had several close friends who were married, with whom Naomi and I developed close friendships. It worked best if I could have as a friend a guy whose wife was also a friend of Naomi's. I found the sexual tension was less when there were four of us and the friendship was fairly equally distributed among all four. On the other hand, the male half of these couples added a level of comfort, or a *frisson* of sexual interest, that I would otherwise have missed.

"Did you read that there were two babies born at the Stones concert?" Greg laughed. "Imagine. Twenty years from now, *Where were you born? Uh, the Altamont Speedway, December 6, 1969.* My mom was on a bad trip and woke up and found she had had me!"

Bob Curry and I were leaving campus together one afternoon, walking toward the Burns Park district where we lived. We stopped in at a tavern to have a drink and talked about politics—the first year of the Nixon administration—and about our teaching and what we were writing, about our children, and then about our wives. Curry was concerned about his wife's orgasms. "You know they say women can have multiple orgasms. *Multiple!* I don't know if I can make her have one, much less *multiple.* Shit. Life has gotten so hard." He rambled on until I broke in.

"I'm not straight."

Curry looked at me as if I had started speaking Urdu—it was not so much the new language as it was the need to shift from the language we both knew—and bunched his eyebrows.

"I'm gay. I'm happy to be having an erection. The idea of worrying about how many orgasms she is having is a fairly baroque worry."

"How long have you known?"

"Always."

"Why are you married?"

"It was 1965, that's what they said homosexuals ought to do. I wanted the kind of life I've got now—I didn't want to live a furtive life, I wanted something coherent—and Naomi and I fell in love and got married. Besides, I am free. I can do what I want."

During my time in Ann Arbor, I ended up telling all these men that I was gay, making explicit what may have been only a rumor or a surmise. I told them because the moment was warm and intimate, and I was feeling close to the man I was talking to. I told them because I was in need of intimacy, solace, warmth. *There is something about me that you don't know, and if we are to be friends, I want you to know.* I also told them because I felt I needed to explain myself, to justify my life. *What you don't know, though, is that I am gay.* I told them because the coolest people in our lives were out on the streets, in the movement, the counter-culture, those in rebellion against the system, and gay people were the newest, most rebellious people—and rebellious in the most dangerous ways—any of us knew. The consequences were nil. I occasionally wondered what the consequences would have been in Yakima, Washington, if I had told my first sergeant that I was gay. Had things changed in ten years? And what about Sewanee?

One night late at a party, I told Tony Parada, a guy who had come to Michigan a couple of years after I did. "I'm gay."

"Shit. I know that." Tony grinned. "Cutie."

I laughed.

"But thanks for telling me."

When I wondered why I told them, I thought it was a way of being closer to them, but it also had to do with my integrity. Before the riots at the Stonewall, a line had divided those who participated in homosexual sex from those who didn't. Now the line is drawn between straight men and gay men, on the one hand, all of whom are *out*, and a second group—*closeted* gay men, who decline or are unable or refuse to acknowledge their gayness. Since Stonewall, any gay man who is not *out* is lying. I ended up in the position I had tried to avoid when I asked Naomi to marry me, with my integrity in shreds. Making sure that a substantial number of men knew I was gay was a way of limiting the damage.

Telling men that I was gay had a downside, however. If the man was easy with it, if it made no difference to him, or, even worse, if the man seemed to *like* it that I was queer, it opened up possibilities —specifically the possibility of sex—without which my life would have been calmer. Standing in the semi-dark hallway of a large, barn-like house belonging to one of the senior professors in our crowd, talking to Tony Parada, I said, "I'm fucked up."

"You want me to drive you home?"

"No, man. That's not what I mean. I'm fucked."

"What can I do?"

"Kiss me."

And Tony did, laughed first, and then did, something that complicated our relationship from that moment on because I could never get it out of my mind that *kissing Tony* was a possibility within the confines of my marriage. It was usually easiest to handle among our own crowd of young academics where physical closeness, alcohol, and a certain worldliness enabled me to relax in a safe environment whose boundaries were usually observed. But when alcohol and a worldliness combined with a late hour, sometimes boundaries were crossed, and things became difficult.

The worst moments were when I was not in such an environment, and the thing came on me unawares, as with the student who had appeared all golden in front of me after a class. It was worst with students, since the interactions with students were so frequently spontaneous and sudden and the environment was so unsafe. One of my students in a sophomore poetry class was this big, good-looking guy. He started coming around to my office to "talk," as he said, and he would lower himself into the chair, spread his thighs, and talk about his life and his studies, his parents, his girlfriend, and of course his problems. I was only just out of graduate school myself, was only about 10 years older than this student, but that appeared to be enough to have turned me into a father-figure for the kid. He towered over me, was a kind of sensitive jock, and told me that he taught weightlifting to earn extra money.

Once he came by, upset because his girl had left him, and he and I went out onto the grass and sat cross-legged facing each other while this big boy cried in anguish over his girl's leaving him. The relationship with this student was disturbing because I found him so sexually compelling, because he was so young, and because he was impossible to avoid. This last was one of the difficult parts of teaching, being unavoidably thrown with young men who were at or near the height of their urgent sexual needs, with huge unmet sexual needs of my own, and in a situation where it was clearly impossible for me to reach out to them.

My largest class had about 90 students, and while I got to know them all during the course of the term, for much of the term I didn't know them except by sight. Once, halfway through a term, when the weather had first turned warm and the students were all suddenly out in t-shirts, a student appeared in front of my desk, and I realized I had been looking at him in heavy sweaters since January and now

197

here he was half-naked with a body of death—big pecs, huge arms, trapezius muscles—and he wanted to *talk*. "Can I come back with you to your office and talk for a little bit?"

It wasn't about Shakespeare. It was about what he wanted to do with his life. His parents wanted him to go into the Army, and he didn't want to go, and he didn't know what to do. "I want to please them." He sat in the chair opposite me, gripping his fists together and moving them up and down in front of him, "but I don't know how and still be true to myself. I don't want to go to Vietnam." He looked at me with anguish all over his face. "What am I to do?"

These contemporary, 20-year-old versions of Giuliano de' Medici appeared in my office and wanted to talk about *life*. It drove me crazy, but not crazy enough to say what some professors said, "I'll talk to you about the class I am teaching and nothing else, and I will talk to you only during my regularly scheduled office hours." *And put a shirt on.* One of the difficulties was that I was still very young too, and the stress of living the way I did, in the profession I had found myself in, was made more intense by the fact that sex was not restricted to one side of the desk. I wondered, looking back on it, how many professors *I* had driven crazy—thoughtlessly, insouciantly, carelessly—when I was 19. *My Medieval History Professor.*

Once, in the middle of the winter, late in the afternoon, long after it had already turned dark, I was crossing South State Street in front of Angell Hall going to the Union. There was snow piled high everywhere, and the walks were deep ruts. The snow was coming down in heavy wet flakes, and suddenly I heard someone cry out, "Dr Shaw! Dr Shaw! Wait up!"

I turned, and three young men came running up. They were all bundled against the snow—knitted caps pulled down below their eyebrows, long scarves wrapped around their necks and faces, gloves, big winter coats. I had never seen any of them before. They all had full beards and very long hair. But their eyes—they were almost the only part of them that showed—were bright enough to twinkle. They looked like peasants out of *Dr Zhivago*, going off to topple the Tsar. They were, all of them, beautiful men. Where had they come from? Why did they want *me?* If they had proposed to me at that moment that we all go away to Siberia—since I had no defense against this beauty—I would have gone. As it turned out,

198

they had heard of me from somewhere. They were all honors students. One of them said, "We'd like to ask you if you would run an honors seminar in Absurdist Literature—Sartre and Beckett and those guys—this winter term." I hadn't planned this encounter, hadn't longed for it, didn't intend to act on my feelings, but there it was. It had reached up out of the snow bank, had grabbed me by the throat, and had choked me almost until I couldn't breathe.

This was the first period in my life when the beauty of men was celebrated. Long hair, beards, mustaches, earrings, beads, scarves tied over the head, knee-high boots, jewelry. Once a student, tall, slender, wearing bib overalls, with shoulder-length hair, leaned over my desk to point out something to me in the text of *Twelfth Night*, and his hair fell forward and exposed gold hoop earrings the size of quarters. I had never seen big earrings on a man before, and the romance of it stopped me with the hot blast of lust. The student was talking about Viola, and I found it hard to think. It was this quality, this celebration of beauty rather than the more conventional handsomeness of men, that I found so unnerving. Men came to class in *skirts*. One student came every day wrapped in a sheet. I found that my life was tolerable to the extent that I had male companionship, even if that companionship was not sexual. With Naomi, the children, my work at the university, and male companionship, I was OK. But, underneath this, there was a level of disease, of stress and tension, and it came from the constant and inescapable presence of beautiful men. It was not something I could do anything about. Always, my release from this tension was in Naomi's body, which was inevitably disappointing. It wasn't merely that I was a gay man in a marriage that troubled me, it was that I had promised—and she expected, and everybody assumed—monogamy.

On June 28, 1970, in New York, between 5,000 and 15,000 men and women marched in the first commemoration of the Stonewall riots, the Christopher Street Liberation Day March, from Sheridan Square up Sixth Avenue to the Sheep Meadow in Central Park. *15,000 gay men and women in the daylight on the streets of New York! The Times* headline the next day said, "Thousands of Homosexuals Hold a Protest Rally in Central Park." *The Times* article was direct straightforward news reporting and lacked the obtuse point of view of the articles about Stonewall a year ago. It quoted one leader saying, "It serves notice on every politician in the state and nation that homosexuals are not going to hide any more. We're becoming militant, and we won't be harassed and degraded any more." Afterward, I saw in newspapers and magazines a picture that appeared on a poster about this time in New York—a New York street scene with fifteen young men and women looking much like my students, long hair, jeans, beads, arms over each other's shoulders, striding or skipping down the middle of the street, grinning, laughing, apprehensive, determined. The heading said, *COME OUT! Join the sisters & brothers of the Gay Liberation Front!* They seemed to be having such fun, there in the middle of the street, *gay.* Later that year, *Boys in the Band* was released, a revelation to me, who, despite what the critics were saying about the movie, saw decent gay men—friends in the city—caring for each other. I hated the married man, who was so clearly a coward. It was the first time I had ever seen gay men portrayed center screen, and what they showed, above all else, was their bravery in the midst of profound danger—and their wit. I was exhilarated by the style in which they faced down dragons. They never stopped being funny. The line that became so famous in the reviews of the movie, *Show me a happy homosexual, and I'll show you a gay corpse,* contained the paradox of all truly great, and black, drama—the fact of *King Lear*'s existence shows a way of transcending the point of the play— for the wit of the line demonstrated that *wit is still possible* despite everything, and they never stopped caring for one another. *I'll call you tomorrow.*

Maurice was published in 1970. By E. M. Forster, it was the first gay novel in English by a major author, and it seemed everybody had known it was there. They were just waiting for Forster to die before it was published. Written in 1913-1914, it was a romance in which Maurice Hall discovers his homosexuality, comes to terms with it, and gives up everything, his job, his position in society, and his family for Alec Scudder. Maurice and Scudder share everything, "All I have. Which includes my body." It ends with their going away together into the "greenwood." But I finished reading it (I read it at school) knowing that it was a story about the great narrative of my life, that you can't have everything, and some things are more important than other things, and some things have to be given up. It was about loss—and gain—and about the possibility that what was given up was less valuable than what was gained.

Race Point Light

After that, in 1971, we went to see *Sunday, Bloody Sunday.* The next year we saw *Cabaret*, with Liza Minelli, Michael York, and Joel Grey, based on Christopher Isherwood's *Goodbye to Berlin*, in which Michael York says, "Screw Maximilian!" And Liza Minelli says, "I do!" And Michael answers quietly, "So do I." She says, "You two bastards."

It was a hugely comic disaster, what had happened to me. I meant to do what my culture meant for me to do, find the girl and marry her and settle down into a professional life—that was the social contract, and it is what Michael York's character in *Cabaret* proposes to do—and then the culture, gay and straight alike, changed all the rules on me. Now, the same qualities I had tried to suppress in myself had been resurrected and were the qualities that my own generation, the hippest of them anyway, were celebrating. Sometimes I could not stop laughing. It was an incredible joke. The people I was most drawn to—the ones who looked like they were assaulting the Winter Palace and who had in fact brought down Lyndon Johnson's presidency two years before—were the ones *now* celebrating the style of free love that I had abandoned four years before. With beads and in communes in which everybody was sleeping with anyone. By 1969, everyone—rock stars, students, hippies, surfers, the Weathermen—was having sex with everyone, and Mick Jagger was wearing lipstick. It ate at my soul. Everything I did seemed dishonest to me. If I wasn't living as a gay man, I was lying, and every time I opened my mouth, I tasted the lies dribbling out.

It was the way I lived. It was not that I was lying about this one thing, my homosexuality—when, for example, the other man asked, *Are you gay?,* and I answered, *No,* for that never happened—it was that everything about my life was a lie, the way I dressed, the work I did, the house I owned, the way I presented myself as married, the books I read, the movies I went to, the way I arrayed myself with the other married, straight men in the living room while our wives were in the kitchen. Even my relationship with my children—because when I walked down the street with them, one on each side of me, holding their hands and laughing and talking with them, because when I did all this, I *seemed* straight—was part of a lie. My colleague, a man from the Romance Languages department who wore very brief suede leather shorts, who said, "I thought you were straight," proved how successful I was in my lies. No matter how many men I told *I am gay,* when I showed myself I had all the attributes of a straight man, and the men who saw me walk into a room had the right, even the cause, to think me straight, and *I had caused them to think I was straight,* until I chose to tell them, *I'm gay.* I had maintained control of my image, I knew, while other men, I thought, said, *This is the way I am, I can do no other.*

So, it didn't matter any longer whether I had been sinful or sick. The culture, the part of it I admired and wanted to be a part of, had moved on, and whatever had driven me when I was an adolescent and young man no longer figured—chimeras that had long vanished. These things—and my conception of my class, and my ambition—that had vanished had been real and present when they had driven me into my marriage. And now that they were gone, I had difficulty explaining how it was that I had gotten where I was and difficulty explaining to myself how it was that I had not caused this catastrophe.

I read John Rechy's novel, *City of Night,* published in 1963. It was a first-person account of a male hustler from El Paso who had moved to New York, then to Los Angeles and San Francisco, ending up in New Orleans during Mardi Gras. It had an underground reputation of a sort as a lurid account of a certain kind of life, so I picked it up for the sex. The sex was disappointing—Rechy seemed ashamed of it—but it was a revelation of what New York had been during the year I had lived there. So *that's* what had gone on! Rechy calls them *youngmen*, handsome, tough, disinterested, and aggressively heterosexual, and their "scores," the men who paid for sex with them, were familiar enough for me to be able to place myself in that scene. I would not have been one of the *youngmen*. I would have been one of those who purchased them. The narrator referred to the "franticness of their search" for sex. The book was disturbing because it showed a world—a seedy, squalid world—I had come close to and then avoided and because that world seemed more compelling than my own. Rechy may have been ashamed of the sex, but he liked his characters, and he knew how to make them seem more alive than I felt.

↔

Race Point Light

Our son, Ames, was born in late 1970. He was blond, like his sister, although his hair was curly. I got up when the baby cried and sat in a rocking chair and read *Romeo and Juliet* to him, having a romantic notion that hearing iambic pentameter at 3 months would make his ear sensitive to the beauty of language, just as hearing the seventeenth century rhythms of the General Confession had, I thought, affected my whole life. Both Naomi and I held them for hours, believing it was the best way to let them know they were loved.

While they had much of the same coloring, and therefore looked alike, their personalities were distinctly different. Judith was volatile, while Ames was reserved. I paid attention and wondered how much their differences were due to gender. Our culture seemed to accept that there were no biological differences between males and females. All apparent differences were said to be the result of social conditioning. But Judith and Ames seemed so different that I could not believe that their genders had nothing to do with it.

Their names, Judith and Ames, were drawn from far back in Naomi's family. I had known years before I met Naomi that I would not name a son after myself—if I had, my son would have been Robert Fair Shaw, Jr., and I wanted any son of mine to have a clean start with a fresh name. I was just superstitious enough to fear that naming a son after me would not only carry on the name but also prolong into a new generation the unhappiness my father and I had both felt as children. This caused anger among my own family, who had expected me to "carry on" my name. Mother wrote. "We are distressed at your choice of names for your son. We had all assumed you would naturally want to name him after yourself—and after your great uncle. Your name means so much because a person before you carried it, and when you were born we wanted to honor that tradition and carry on the name. Names are terribly important. They tell others who you are, who you come from, and you have chosen to abandon that tradition and to give your son a meaningless name that will prevent people from knowing who he is. You have made a terrible mistake—you have let your anger at us blind you to what you are doing—and you have not only deprived your son of a heritage that is rightfully his, you have also deprived us of the comfort of knowing that the names we bear will be carried on into the next generations after we are dead." I no longer believed any of this.

We liked old houses painted white everywhere, giant paper flowers from Mexico, Plexiglas cubes for coffee tables, antiques of mahogany, oriental rugs, and abstract expressionist paintings. We liked framed posters, and Design Research, cats and dogs, Creative Playthings, the Narnia series, *Lord of the Rings*, Waylon Jennings and "Living in the Love of the Common People" and anything by June Carter, the Black Panthers, Bobby Kennedy, and the Upper Peninsula, where we went one summer for a week, renting a cabin on the shores of Lake Michigan. We never forgot the fantasy of the house in the Garden District of New Orleans, and we discovered that each of our houses, as we moved from an apartment into a small bungalow into a substantial house near the university, was more and more closely an approximation of the large white Greek Revival house with one-story columns on the street that we had first discussed at Pat's in Nashville in 1965.

One night in the kitchen while we were doing dishes, Naomi said, "I think I'm going to go back to school. You may not be here forever, but we know we are going to be here at least until 1975, and if I start something now, this summer maybe, I can get most of the work on a doctorate done before you come up for tenure. Or maybe law school."

It was what was expected. Naomi was unusual in that she stayed home with the children. Among our crowd, it was expected that a woman would want to work at a job of her own, and it was expected that the job would be—or lead to—a career. One woman, whose husband came to Ann Arbor with me, was in the UM Law School. Another, Anne Stiefel, Greg's wife, was getting a PhD in Social Work, and several others were just waiting until their children were three or four before they went back to school full time. What Naomi had proposed was an element in the life of all of us. Now that our children were entering pre-school, it was to be expected that she would think of her future.

Feminism—the kind of feminism our crowd was familiar with in Ann Arbor—resulted in an alteration of the fundamental agreement that was our marriage. I wrote Cornelius, still in South Carolina and married to Henrietta and the father of three children. "We are in the midst of the women's movement here in Ann Arbor. I think it happened in the last three or four years, sometime after 1966 or so. We have several friends who were married just before that, and they are incredibly stressed by the shift in how people understand the relations between the sexes. On the other hand, the people who got married more recently—just two or three years later—seem to have different kinds of marriages altogether. You can feel it, sitting at the dinner table with them. I don't think Naomi ever thought of these things before we were married. Now we are all in the front lines of a revolution. A friend of ours says she would never have married her husband if she had 'known.'" Cornelius did not answer.

↔

Once a student called and asked if he could come over to talk about a paper, and he did. I took him into the living room. We sat on the sofa, the paper first on the student's lap and then on mine, as we passed it back and forth, talking about different passages, raising questions and floating ideas. The image I presented—my house, Naomi, the children upstairs—pleased me. I was aware that I enjoyed showing off for the young man. But he was the kind most dangerous for me. He was a big athlete, or rather he was a very good, very smart student who was a big athlete, the big tight muscles of his body straining against his clothes, the odor of some aftershave, cologne, or hair tonic, his size—he took up twice as much space on the sofa as I did. When we finished, I walked him to the door, said *good-bye*, and closed the door after him. The encounter had left me feeling blown away, and I needed to talk it through, bring myself back to where I lived, in my house with Naomi and my children. I went into the kitchen, where Naomi was washing dishes.

"That was very difficult."

She looked at me. "What's the matter?"

"He's the kind of man I am most turned on by. I didn't do anything to get him to come over here. He did that on his own. I said *yes*, come on over and we can talk, and we did. But I find it very difficult to work that closely with some male students. It isn't that it was here. It would have been the same at school. The paper would be on my desk, and we'd be sitting next to each other—"

Naomi was crying.

"—and I am blown away by the power of this body sitting next to me. It *unmoors* me."

There had been other times since our marriage that Naomi cried. Once the subject of her parents came up—we were at a restaurant—and I said, "I wonder if they love you at all. They seem to treat you as a kind of afterthought, something beside the point, other than their politics, which seem to consume all of their interests and energies —." I realized, just as I was getting started on her parents, who, it turned out, really were interested in nothing but their politics and really didn't care about her, that she was crying. I was so upset with myself for making her cry, for going so deeply—invading her privacy—by saying her parents didn't love her, that, and this was instinctive for me, I backed off, dropped the subject, and then said, "I'll never mention that again." I thought later that my idea must have been to spare her further pain. It was also to spare myself the pain of seeing Naomi do what my mother had done all my life, weep at the pain a man had caused her.

Now, watching her standing in front of the sink, crying at my having brought up my sexual response to the male student, I responded instinctively again. "I'm sorry. I didn't know it caused you so much pain. I'll never mention it again." I knew what I had done. I had rung down a metal shutter on an area of my life that I couldn't possibly deal with alone. Now suddenly I was able to think very clearly. I saw the error as mine. I had agreed, at least twice in our married life, that it was OK for her to respond with tears to a difficult subject, and, by crying, to close it off as a subject of discussion. When she cried, I was powerless against her and took her part against myself.

Since Stonewall she must have known that it was possible for me to come out—not to go into the shadows, which in Nashville we had thought was the only option, but to go out onto the street, *out and proud,* an entirely different and attractive possibility. The tension between us was raised noticeably, and she became less flexible, less accepting, and markedly more brittle.

So I found that Naomi and I—the couple who could talk about anything—became like my parents, who had many things that were not to be spoken of. The only difference was that I never forgot. We continued on, talking freely about politics, about our children, about our house, Naomi's new career at the law school, my teaching, our friends, but the thing that was never to be spoken of was my sudden lust for a man, which I could do nothing about. I was surprised to have discovered that this very strong woman, who seemed to be more liberated—and more concerned with *being* liberated—than any woman I knew in Ann Arbor, had such reserves of *tears*. It wasn't because I had discovered lust for a student. It was because I had acknowledged that, despite the therapy in Nashville, I was still queer. And worse, I had spoken of it to her. She wanted, apparently, to be able to feel that her marriage, at its base, was stable. To be reminded that her husband was queer was to be reminded how fragile what we had was, subject to the power of every passing male to draw her husband's attention from her. Now, on the streets, proud gay men were adding to her burden with the chant in demonstrations, *Come out! Come out!* She wouldn't want to be reminded that our marriage was a closet for her husband. I did not want to hurt her, but by accepting her tears as a reason not to talk I was hurting her, and myself, and enabling her to base our marriage on a lie. I realized, almost as soon as I said, *I'll never mention this again,* that almost the only way we could stay married was to build emotional ties that were stronger than whatever sexual forces separated us. I had no idea how to do that. That, or become comfortable telling lies to one another.

Despite being queer, I learned what I had to know to satisfy Naomi. I was naturally slow to come with her—I would have been much much faster with a man—but this pace seemed to please her, and she complimented me. Half the time I really wanted to have sex with her. The other half, I was willing to do it for her, described with a series of double negatives—*it was something I was not unwilling to do, something that was not infrequently satisfying.* I was able to have sex with her, during those times when I had no particular desire, because I loved her, because what she represented to me was immensely more to me than her vagina—or my cock. She was kind. She was funny. She was thoughtful, generous, had a brain with which she thought deeply about the events of the day, read widely and kept up with developments in the great movements of our time, she looked good when we had guests over or when we went out, she had thoughts—she had *views*—on current controversies, she was a very good mother, and the people in the department whom I most admired, admired Naomi. She had style. And she loved me.

↔

Naomi and I visited our parents in the South twice a year, and on one of these visits, at my parents' house, Cornelius and Henrietta were there for lunch with their children. We were in the garden—everyone was there, Aunt Caroline, Uncle Richmond, their sons Jonathan, William, and Rich, with their wives and their children, about thirty people in all—the children playing in the same sandbox Cornelius and I had played in when we were children, or on the swings, and the adults sitting around in the same white iron chairs my parents had sat in 25 years before. Cornelius followed me to a corner of the yard— beyond the dogwood trees, which made a dark green wall and created a little glade—where I was checking on Ames and Judith and put his arm around my shoulder.

"How *are* you?" While I wrote fairly often, Cornelius never wrote. Henrietta carried on the correspondence from them. Her letters were invariably polite, warm in the way some Southern people are—*We have missed you so all spring!*—and totally non-communicative, a little social note on flowered notepaper that I found trivializing and banal.

"I'm OK, I suppose. I'm working very hard, and we like our house."

"Do you like Ann Arbor?"

"It's a great university. It's an exciting place to be." I didn't like Cornelius' hand on my shoulder.

We talked about drugs that were available in Ann Arbor.

"It's mostly grass and hash, but there is a lot of it. Students offer me pot all the time. A student invited me over a week ago, and we smoked. It was fine." I laughed. "Who would have thought it?"

Since that time on the terrace of that house on the lake, Cornelius had never mentioned my being gay. When I had seen him during the intervening years, I wondered occasionally how he did that, know something important about someone, and manage never to refer to it.

He grinned. "Sounds like you've got a great life."

"I do. Things are good. Naomi and I, and the two children, and my job." Then I said something more private. "Being gay causes problems sometimes—"

Cornelius looked pained.

"—but everything really is OK, but it's also something of a mess, too—"

"You're still gay?"

"Oh, yes, man, I'm still gay."

The younger women went back and forth from the house to the garden with trays while Mother and the older women looked after the children. Everything was as it had been when I was a child, and I wondered if my children would remember this one Sunday in May in the garden at Aunt Caroline's.

Cornelius and Henrietta left soon after they ate. I wondered if Cornelius had ever told Henrietta that I was queer. Later that day Naomi and I and our two children left for Knoxville to visit her parents, who didn't love her. Naomi insisted we stay in Knoxville for five days, and her parents barely interrupted their routine of university meetings, board meetings, political organizations of various kinds for various causes, and their work among the black community, where they were both teaching classes in alternative education schools. "Dear, you two go ahead and feed the children and put them to bed. And fix yourself something to eat. I am sure you can find something in the pantry. There's sausage in the freezer, I think. We'll be late. Probably very late, because after the meeting we'll be going to the Kokoloff's for drinks, and it's such a long way over there."

That night I told Naomi about my conversation with Cornelius and about Cornelius' response. "I told him the therapy thing did not work and that I am still queer. I have to say that to you even if it causes you pain."

The children were in bed asleep, the Schumanns were out, and we were in the guest bedroom, preparing for bed.

"I know you are gay." She was crying again. "I know you've told people you are gay. I just want us to be OK. I don't want anything to happen that is going to hurt us."

It was difficult to talk to her when she was crying, but I forced myself forward. "What are we to do?"

"I don't know." She was sobbing.

There were, first, the children. They were not to have the same childhood I had had, the constant bickering between their parents, thinking their parents' unhappiness was their fault, feeling that there was something they were supposed to do to make their parents happy and not knowing what that was. They were not to have a life where things were not spoken of. They were to have a life in which their lives today were the same as their lives yesterday, in which stability and coherence governed, and in which they were told the truth not distorted by prejudice and a sense of class. I was where I was, I was the principal male care-giver to these children who had not asked to be brought into the world, who were the result of my own and Naomi's desires and needs, and there was no way that I could, now, alter the promise I had implicitly made to them the day they were conceived: *I will love you. I will care for you and nurture you, I will protect you, and I will give you whatever it is you need to equip yourself for your life. I will never abandon you.* What I had for the children was not a contract in the usual sense—like a marriage contract—in which each contractor promises certain things in exchange for things promised by the other contractor. The children were brought into the world without having been asked, and there was nothing they could promise me in exchange for what I owed them just for having decided to father them. Mother used to speak of what we owed her. Respect, obedience, *et cetera, et cetera.* But my children didn't owe me anything. The obligations were entirely on my side. I could not lie to them.

And there was Naomi. I loved her. My obligations to her— implicit in my question, *Will you marry me?*—were to *honor* her, which meant, at the least, not to betray her. That meant monogamy. And while I felt that my culture had screwed me through vast carelessness and indifference and ignorance—sometimes I thought it was through profound malevolence—the commitments Naomi and I had made in that booth in that tavern in Nashville in the spring of 1965 were not the commitments of two representatives of a culture but the assumptions of two individual people, and they were binding.

"Is it possible to talk about what has happened?" I sat in an upholstered chair, a small table by my side, while she stood in front of the mirror, brushing her hair, tears down her cheeks. What I meant was, *we know more now*, and *we know now what went wrong.* But Naomi continued to brush her hair, even to *angrily* brush her hair, and I understood that what she was saying was *We will continue on as if there have been no changes.*

"No?" I presumed not. I sighed. "OK." There had to be something admirable, I thought—it was something left over from my mother—about finding a partner and sticking with her. How I was to deal with my lies was unclear to me.

210

The safest place for me to deal with my homosexual feelings was in my conversations with Naomi. I needed to be able to say to her, "I feel this way, and it causes me pain." And then I needed to have her say, "Tell me about it." If she didn't say that, if she made it so I went to somebody else for sympathy, or understanding, then someday that somebody else was going to be a male who offered, along with the sympathy and understanding, sex. I could not understand why Naomi thought that crying was the best way to protect our marriage.

↔

There was another aspect of all this that began to occur to me after our trip South. During most of the last ten years, Cornelius had been clear that he did not want me to be queer, and when I lived a heterosexual life, as he implied that he wanted, he never acknowledged that my giving him what he wanted might actually have cost me something. He did not want the responsibility of telling me not to be queer, but he also did not want the responsibility of asking me how much pain was involved for me in not being queer.

Once I realized that people might make large demands on me, but never acknowledge what those demands might cost, I began to see it everywhere. Mother had asked me to change schools to help her with my father, and once I did it, she never mentioned it again. Naomi was willing to ask me to live as a heterosexual, but she was unwilling to acknowledge that living like that might cost me something. And, of course, I had decided myself to live as a heterosexual, and I was on a minute-by-minute basis unwilling to count the costs of my own decision.

↔

The Students for a Democratic Society had been on the periphery of my vision since New York. Founded in 1959, it became the largest student organization on the left during the time I was in Nashville and Ann Arbor, focusing its protests against American society on economic injustice and then on stopping the war. By 1969, however, the SDS had begun to break up into factions, of which the most famous was the Weathermen, a Marxist-Leninist group who were similar to the Black Panthers in that they seemed to have the same take on America, were incredibly sexy, threatened violence, seemed out of control, and presented themselves as outlaws. Coffee houses in Ann Arbor always had three posters—the silk screen in blood red of Che Guevara, who had been killed on October 9, 1967, long black hair blowing around his face, Huey Newton of the Black Panthers sitting in a fan-backed wicker chair holding a spear and a rifle and wearing a black beret, and the boyish, beautiful Jim Morrison of The Doors. While the Weathermen never produced a similar star, I was drawn to the Weathermen, as I was drawn to the Black Panthers, by their endgame arguments. *Nothing had worked.* No matter how large the demonstration, Nixon and his war machine continued to prosecute the war. Corporations still seemed to own and control everything. Driven mad by their own impotence in the struggle, the Weathermen had called for four Days of Rage starting October 8, 1969. The *Detroit Free Press* said, "Illinois national guardsmen, 2,500 strong, were ordered into Chicago Thursday to help the city cope with violent young purveyors of a new and destructive brand of radical protest." Then, when it came, the *Free Press* said, "Thursday's free-for-all was as bizarre as the wild destruction Wednesday night that introduced Chicago and the nation to the first genuinely violent street offensive to be staged since mass war protests began." The reporter wrote, "Though decimated by arrests, the militants threatened to create even more disruption in what they call 'Pig City' as they drive toward a Saturday parade in protest of the Vietnam war, racism, poverty, capitalism and the trial of eight men charged with conspiracy to riot" during the Democratic convention last year.

That struck me as being appropriate. When faced with an unassailable foe, I was beginning to think it right to express rage. Several hundred Weathermen converged on Lincoln Park in Chicago in an attempt to "bring the war home," in four days of rioting and burning cars, breaking windows, and skirmishing with police. They meant to mount a terrorist campaign against the American war machine on American soil. On Sunday, the *Free Press* lead headline said, "March Explodes in Violence." This was a long way from ten years ago, when Martin Luther King had led his people in prayer on the Pettus bridge outside of Selma—it was an equally long way from the lawn at Wespanee—but I understood what they were doing. They were demonstrating that they knew how violent the system was in its pursuit of the war. They were not witnessing to the violence, they were fighting back, answering violence with violence. It was immensely satisfying.

We talked after the children were in bed.

"You agree to give up some small portion of your freedom for the greater good, a good not merely for the greater number, but for yourself." This was Naomi. "You agree to obey the laws in the assumption that everyone else will also obey the laws and you will therefore be free to assume that you won't be robbed or murdered in your bed. It is a social contract we all have with one another. One manifestation of this social contract is the Constitution. We give up anarchic freedom—the freedom to do *anything*—in order to get a kind of civil freedom, the freedom to do anything within the law. The Weathermen are not merely attacking Daley or the government, they are attacking all of us, they are shredding the social contract. It is a terrible thing these men and women are doing in Chicago. Besides, it is ineffective."

This caused me pain. "That's true only when the structures of government actually do work for the betterment of men. When they don't, when they actively work against the material happiness of the people, then the contract is broken. If people—men and women— live within the laws, if they are law-abiding, and they discover that the government is committing violence on them, then there is no social contract. If the people have no effect on the government, if the government is no longer responsive, if the government is composed of law-*breakers*, if it is no longer a representative democracy, if there is no longer any way to reach the government through the ballot box, if the people are treated inequitably, if the people are no longer given a choice, then the social contract has been broken. If you have people —law-abiding citizens—who are consistently treated as second-class citizens, citizens who are discriminated against by their own government, to which they have given their allegiance—if there is no equal protection of the laws—then there is no social contract. Men and women against whom the government commits violence have no reason to be law-abiding. Instead, they have a duty to bring down the government, to say with their bodies, *I will not let you touch me without fighting.*" We began to have political arguments.

↔

In early February 1970, black students on the Michigan campus called a meeting to make a list of demands to be presented to the university administration. The demands, according to the student newspaper, *The Michigan Daily*, on February 3, 1970, concerned the "black studies program, financial aids, admissions, recruitment of black students and faculty, and counseling." They organized under the name Black Action Movement, and a spokesman for the group was quoted in *The Daily* saying, "Because we represent the black tax-paying citizens of this state and this nation, we can demand that this tax-supported university cease its practice of racial elitism. This is not a private school for whites only." They demanded principally that the university take action to ensure that the percentage of students at the university who were black would match the percentage of black people in the general population.

But over the next two weeks, the Regents temporized, and BAM started disrupting life on campus, starting with sit-ins in the college of Literature, Science, and the Arts, and then with actions in the UGLI, the Undergraduate Library. *The Daily* said, "Thousands of books in the Undergraduate Library were rearranged for the second day in a row by a group of over 100 black students yesterday afternoon after they walked out of a meeting with the Regents on increasing minority enrollment." The President of the university, Robben Fleming, announced that he was going to send the names of students "convicted of creating a contention during the LSA building sit-in, and who are receiving financial aid from the state, to the agencies administering the scholarship programs." The campus discussed what "trashing" meant and whether it was a legitimate tactic for BAM to use against the Regents, and if it had not been legitimate *at first,* then at what point did it become legitimate? Finally, on Thursday, March 19, 1970, after the Regents had taken no action, BAM called for a strike with the goal of shutting down the university until their demands were met. The strike began at 10 AM on Friday, March 20, 1970. By Tuesday, March 24, 1970, *The Daily* had an editorial entitled, "Open it up or shut it down." I did not have to discuss with myself what I was going to do. I honored the picket line and called off my classes for the duration of the strike.

BAM needed classroom space off campus for classes, and Naomi and another woman set themselves up as "classroom central," and our phone number was distributed to teachers looking for space.

214

Naomi was on the phone constantly, calling local churches and progressive groups in town, determining what space was available. When the phone rang, she assigned teachers to the available space. I met with my classes to tell them I would not hold class on campus during the duration of the strike and that my classes would be held in the basement of a church nearby. Some students complained.

I said to my class, "If we teach here, and if we go to school here, we participate in a system which is, at this moment, unfair to black students. We cannot be part of a system which doles out its benefits unfairly. If we are a part of such a system, then we are corrupted by that system. So we must refuse to be a part of such a system until it changes. That is what this strike is about, and that is what my participation is about. Join us in the basement of the Huron Valley Methodist Church on Monday at 9 AM. I will meet my classes there for the duration of the strike."

So we went off-campus. At the end of the first week of the strike, class attendance in the College of Literature, Science, and the Arts was down 75%, according to *The Daily*, and television news teams in Detroit were rolling dollies with TV cameras down the main hall of the main classroom building for the College of Literature, Science, and the Arts, showing all their viewers that there were, in fact, no classes being held and that the strike had effectively shut down the university. The Regents caved in, and BAM ended the strike on April 1, 1970.

The chairman of my department was pissed at me. I was walking down a corridor in a classroom building when I saw him coming toward me, agitated and angry. The man accosted me. "What kind of an operation do you think I am running, here!" I knew that he was part of the system, and he was one of those BAM was trying to demonstrate their power to, and when the chairman exhibited his anger to me, he was also exhibiting just how successful the strike had been. I grinned. "We're just trying to get a little equality on the Michigan campus. That's all. And apparently we are getting it." Black students had found a way to make the system respond. Trashing the UGLI was one of the tactics used to support their cause. *Shutting it down* was another.

There were others. In the summer of 1970, in the daylight, two people having sex in the middle of the intersection of South University and Church Street drew a huge crowd, which drew police and riot squads. The bank at the corner of South University and East University thereafter replaced its glass windows with opaque material.

↔

After our first year, we moved from our apartment into a small bungalow where we stayed a year and began seriously looking for a house. We found one near campus, on a corner. All along the sidewalk were very large lilac bushes that bloomed in the spring. One of the porches was screened, and the former owner had left porch furniture that we began to make use of as soon as we bought the house. Even before we moved in, people started coming by, and the porch seemed filled with people having drinks during the whole time the house was being painted. I kept liquor stocked, and Naomi kept food there for guests, ready, should someone drop in.

We wanted everything inside white, and a friend knew of some young guys who were doing painting jobs around town, former students of hers. I called, and for the first weeks after we got the house, one of them—Robbie Knott—was there all the time, pulling down wallpaper and painting while Naomi and I and the children had guests on the porch. Robbie was tall, broad-shouldered, narrow-hipped, blond, with a beautiful blond mustache, and wore a white t-shirt that showed off his body. He was professional, friendly, helpful, and respectful.

"You have a lot of friends," he said after a crowd had left one day.

I laughed. "They come for drinks and to see our new house."

"You're very popular."

"We're lucky."

"Are they people from the university?"

"All of them."

One afternoon I went by the new house to check on the work before going home. I found Robbie still there. We walked through the empty rooms together, first upstairs and then downstairs, and then out onto the porch, checking out what had been done. Robbie complimented me.

"It's a beautiful house, Fair. You're bringing all that out by what you are doing to it." While all the rooms were white, there was a very small entryway with an outer front door and an inner glass door

into the front hall that was painted an intense jungle green. "I *really*
like that," Robbie said. He put his arm around my shoulders and
squeezed my shoulder muscle. I felt that, but I didn't respond. Was
Robbie coming on to me? He was five, six, seven years younger than
me. I didn't know. But whatever Robbie was doing, and whatever I
wanted to do—I wanted to turn and put my arms around Robbie and
hug him—I didn't respond. My obligations were to Naomi and the
children, and I couldn't respond.

Men came on to me in different ways. Occasionally gay men on
the faculty started with a meaningful comment—"I think Warren
Beatty is extraordinary *looking.*"—which established a shared
interest. I would agree, and the conversation would proceed by
innuendo until some kind of declaration was made by the other man.
If an invitation was to be made, usually I saw it coming and was able
to deflect it before it arrived. But others were less indirect. Robbie
Knott's innocent, almost unconscious, openness to me left me
unaware that what might come was a proposition and left him
vulnerable to being hurt when I ignored him.

The problem for Naomi and me was that at any moment I might,
without warning, slip over the line between straight and gay. It might
be Robbie, or it might be a student, or it might be some colleague—
the guy in Romance Languages who liked to wear very short suede
shorts that invited attention. Or it might be some irresistible force on
the street, some hot stud who would turn the corner and suddenly be
there in front of me—and destroy our lives. The possibilities for
disaster were as numerous as the number of men who carried cocks
between their legs. How could a man say, "I will *never* give in"? We
both knew this. At any moment, I might step over the line, which
seemed always to be 3 centimeters in front of me, into *gay.* Our
marriage was defined by fears.

Straight men have been dealing with the possibility of adultery
ever since marriage was invented, but while heterosexual adultery
might lead to the discovery that the man could not keep his vows, it
would not lead to the discovery that he had a different kind of sexual
orientation or that he was a different kind of person. While
forgiveness seems possible for a man who has committed adultery
with a woman, forgiveness does not seem to be an adequate or
appropriate response to a man who has committed adultery with a
man. What is required is a readjustment of the whole marriage

construction. *I am not like other men, you can't pretend I am like other men, our marriage is not like other marriages.* Or it might be —if we agree that *marriage* may include a partner whose natural inclination is to be continually attracted sexually to his own sex, a desire which is never to be satisfied. This was where I found myself. We had agreed to go into a marriage where one of the partners was to make a sacrifice defined by a continuous and absolute denial of sex, a sacrifice not matched by a similar sacrifice by the other partner, and a sacrifice which was not to be acknowledged.

There were no gay men in our crowd, aside from me, although there were gay men in the department. People seemed to accept the fact that these men were gay. Some of them were quite senior men. But these men, if they had partners, didn't bring them to departmental functions, and they never brought them to private parties either. I made a point several times of inviting a gay man to bring someone if he'd like, but no gay man ever did. I didn't know any couples, and so far as I knew no one in the department came out while I was there. The only explanation for this was that, despite Stonewall, old beliefs were still operating at some level in the culture in Ann Arbor.

I did discover cruising areas, by accident, while I was in Ann Arbor. Late one afternoon, I was on the second floor of one of the classroom buildings when I needed to take a leak. I stopped into a men's room I had never used before. When the door closed behind me, I realized the room was crowded for that time of day. It was clear what was going on, and it was also clear from the response of the others what could happen if I decided to stay and take part, but I didn't stay. I also discovered a bar in town that catered to gay men.

I was aware from the constant reporting in the newspapers of what was going on in New York and San Francisco. The Gay Liberation Front, named after Algerian freedom fighters and the Viet Cong, was formed in New York in July 1969, immediately after Stonewall. The name itself was a revelation—militant and out and absolutely clear about what it wanted. From August 24 to August 30, 1969, the North American Conference of Homophile Organizations met in Kansas City and produced a radical manifesto that began:

> We see the persecution of homosexuality as part of a
> general attempt to oppress all minorities and keep them

powerless. Our fate is linked with these minorities; if the detention camps are filled tomorrow with blacks, hippies and other radicals, we will not escape that fate, all our attempts to dissociate ourselves from them notwithstanding. A common struggle, however, will bring common triumph ... Our enemies, an implacable, repressive governmental system; much of organized religion, business and medicine, will not be moved by appeasement or appeals to reason and justice, but only by power and force.

The cry of the Gay Liberation Front was *No revolution without us!,* and it focused on the same broad goals as the rest of the liberation movement—freedom for all people from oppressive social controls of all kinds but especially from the culture's definitions of gender, from heterosexual hegemony, and from narrowly circumscribed sexuality.

The GLF, like many liberationist groups, had no officers, no members but those who showed up, no majority rule. The GLF was joined almost immediately by the Gay Activists Alliance, founded on December 21, 1969. For the GAA, gay liberation seemed to mean the liberation of gay people from the oppression of straight bigotry in the laws and in the attitudes of straight culture. It demanded basic rights, the first of which was "The right to our own feelings. This is the right to feel attracted to the beauty of members of our own sex and to embrace those feelings as truly our own, free from any question or challenge whatsoever by any other person, institution, or moral authority." While this news was daily before me in the pages of the newspapers, it still presented only a distant prospect to a man at a school near Detroit in the heart of the Midwest.

Late in 1969, people began to talk about a new book, *Everything You Ever Wanted to Know About Sex*,* by David Reuben. That is, the newspapers wrote about it, it was a bestseller, and it was everywhere in the media. It was hard to avoid references to it, although none of my friends spoke of it. They wouldn't have, since it was a popular book and therefore didn't attract academics. But the book got press because it was in tune with the times. It told people what they wanted to hear, that sex is good, that masturbation is good, that orgasms are good, but it also had a chapter on homosexuality, in which, probably, it also told people what they want to hear. Dr. Reuben says, "The usual homosexual experience is mutual masturbation. It is fast, easy, and requires a minimum amount of equipment. The chaps simply undress, get into bed, and manipulate each other's penises to the point of orgasm. Three to five minutes should be enough for the entire operation." There was more, a lot more, on clothes and homosexuals, on women and homosexuals, on S&M and homosexuals. Reuben's style was off-hand and snide, casual and jokey. I remembered masturbating Connie in the meadow under Mt Rainier, above Paradise Lodge, and I found Reuben's book repellant.

City of Night is an analysis of sex, too, of what men are driven to, and what they will do, or not do, to get what they want. It is more comprehensive than Reuben's book, even though Reuben's book is called *Everything* about sex. *City of Night* is an analysis of what men can and can't do in their drive to escape loneliness, an encyclopedia of men and of situations in their *franticsearch.* It was easy, reading the book, to concentrate on the *scores*, but it was necessary in the end to listen to what the narrator says about sex and its uses for the *youngman* himself. It was possible that *I* had traded sex—sex with Naomi—for the life I had and that I was no more than a hustler, like the *youngman,* who got $20 each time, and it was as difficult for me to accept myself and what I was doing as it was for the narrator of Rechy's book.

↔

We were liked the way we were. There was a crowd we were drawn into of junior members of the department like me and senior members, including the department chair, all of whom had wives and children and were active scholars in their fields. Greg and Anne Steifel were in this crowd, as was a senior member whose field was the seventeenth century like mine, and his wife, a tiny beautiful white-haired lady with marvelous cheekbones who wore black, and a man who had just brought out a major, authorized biography of F. Scott Fitzgerald, and his wife. There was also a couple who were invited everywhere because, in addition to being smart, they were young and beautiful and had money. At 32, I was becoming aware of the attractions of youth. It was "our crowd."

Naomi and I invited our guests for eight, and they arrived shortly after and had drinks for an hour. The lady who wore black had a favorite outfit, a cocktail suit with a short cape trimmed in what she called "monkey fur," something with long black hair. She spoke in a low hoarse whisper, and once, early in our friendship, she took my forearm and pulled me down so she could whisper in my ear.

"Do you believe in original sin?"

I burst out laughing. She didn't, and her husband did, and she wanted to know about me. "No, I don't think I do." In the seventeenth century, beliefs like that were not uncommon, and it was not uncommon for a man who spent his life studying a period to gradually adopt its beliefs.

I certainly drank as if I were fallen. In the South, drinking heavily was a part of the social scene. My drinking, which had been somewhat camouflaged by Southern culture, now became seriously heavy and exposed. I started leaving campus after my morning classes and walking down South University Avenue to the Village Bell, a restaurant patronized by university people, and drinking through what should have been my lunch time, coming back to campus just before my afternoon class at two. I would sit at a table by myself, my books around me, and drink bourbon on the rocks, one after the other, for two hours. I found, walking in another direction, toward town, a more working-class bar, less frequented by academics, where I could drink without being observed by anyone who knew anyone who knew me. When I arrived home to have my first drink of the afternoon, I was already lit. I handled it well, very rarely got out of control, and rarely embarrassed myself, but it was always there, and it became true that if there were no alcohol at a particular place, I didn't go.

"I always like to come to your house, because you always have enough liquor," the wife of the Fitzgerald biographer said. "I do so hate it when the host runs out." She was wearing a long silver lamé dress and matching shoes, and she lay in the hammock on our porch while the rest of our guests were inside. She smoked, and flicked her butts into the lilac bushes. "Most academics have no style."

Greg, particularly, had a sense of the way Naomi and I worked together. "I like your manner, Shaw." He smiled. He liked our *Southern* manner, the way we entertained, and the way we played off each other as host and hostess. "You're seeing to drinks, and Naomi is seeing to food, and you're both making people feel easy. In my view there are two kinds of Southerners—the tight ones who are worried about committing a sin (they're all Baptists) and then there are ones who are easy. Shaw, you're easy." We did have a way of doing things that people seemed to respond to—political, social, literate, and, as Greg said, *easy*.

I laughed. I told him about my conversation about original sin. "I do believe we are all fallen, though from what is unclear. Hamlet had something to say about this. What is required is a certain degree of forgiveness. A certain degree of *ease*, of *laissez-faire,* of, perhaps, *forgetfulness.*" Having lost respect for my culture—having even gained a hatred for the aspects of it that denied basic human rights to blacks and women and certain small countries around the world whose citizens had yellow skin, and for those aspects of the military-industrial complex that had been exposed—I came not only to accept but to admire all those who rose up in rebellion. In my own world, that meant the people who broke the rules, who drank too much, had the wrong kind of sex, scorned the standards of academia, broke the rules of decorum. I hated only those who were racists or class-ridden or who *liked the way things were.*

Greg and I, like all very new professors, had been assigned the job of being faculty advisors to students. In addition to advising our own students, we kept regular hours in the counseling center where we advised freshmen and sophomores on choice of major, on fulfilling English major and degree requirements. After doing this for a couple of years, we proposed major changes in the way faculty and departmental approval was given, a new method giving students more freedom and more responsibility for their own course of study. One afternoon we found ourselves in a departmental meeting, sitting by chance in the middle of the room, fielding questions on the new proposals from colleagues in the department. It became clear we were facing a hostile audience who felt anarchy would result from giving students so much power over themselves, but as we faced our hostile colleagues, we gradually came to have our backs to each other as we faced our colleagues all around us. I would take the darts from one side of the room and Greg would take the darts from the other. And we helped each other, adding points to the other's answer, or elaborating on the other's comment.

When it was over, a man who had been around several years longer than either Greg or I spoke to me. He was smiling. "I liked that."

"What's that?"

"Seeing the two of you fending off all these old toads in the department. You were in control of the meeting. You clearly knew what you were talking about, and you were articulate in supporting your position. You ended up occupying the progressive, enlightened positions at the same time you were making anyone who opposed you look like troglodytes." He smiled again. "Congratulations!" The proposals were adopted, and Greg and Anne, who was as proud of Greg as he was of her, came to our house for drinks, where we celebrated.

At our party, the men were talking about the war. "Almost all of our troops have come home now."

"Senator Aiken was right all along." I wiped the sweat off my glass. "Even Nixon acknowledged it, only he calls it *Vietnamization.*"

"Terrible word."

"I've been meaning, Fair, to ask you why you used *stymie* in that piece I read of yours. You're writing about seventeenth century lyric poetry, and you used *stymie!* Why?"

"Because it meant what I wanted it to mean." I laughed. The chairman was a contentious sort, and I saw that I was being challenged just as a way of passing the time.

"But the word comes from golf! You should be more careful when you write."

Greg, who had joined us, said, "Victor writes for the *very* select few."

Greg was devoted to learning. He wrote well in a witty style that was at the same time clear and easy. He also had courage to express not only what he thought but what he felt. He said very easily, *I love you, Shaw.* I suspected that he was far more willing to go all the way in understanding what I had to say than I was in telling him. He was ironic, saw the world clearly, and was open to what was around him. He was also devoted to Anne. They supported one another, and seemed to allow each other to have separate lives. They trusted each other. I knew that I cared less about my career than Greg did about his. My job was too much associated with my commitment to Naomi and the children, seemed to be too much for others, for me to give it the devotion that Greg did to his.

Occasionally I wandered back in my mind to the months I spent in New York, when I had been determined to write fiction, and I wondered how I had ended up here, doing this. I made the tour, checking on people's drinks and suggesting the *hors d'oeurvres* on trays placed around the rooms. Then I went into the kitchen, where five or six people stood around with drinks in their hands, talking and nibbling at the food Naomi was organizing. The scene was the fulfillment of a dream I had had for years and had its roots in similar evenings in similar houses in South Carolina—elegant, casual, intelligent, *easy.* But it remained true that when I lived in New York, I had planned to do something else with my life.

When my parents came to visit, however, I couldn't get them to be as pleased as I tried to be about my life. They stopped on the top step at the front door and turned to look at the lawn—the large lilac bushes enclosing the yard from the street and the enormous elms giving shade—and Mother said, "I *see.*" She was somehow suspicious of the house and garden, as if they had been stolen, and inside the house the abstract expressionist posters made her turn her attention to a mahogany Pembroke table given us by a relative as a wedding present. The giant Marimekko prints we used for the curtains in the children's rooms also made her avert her eyes. She was pleased that I had finished my doctorate and always addressed her letters to me as "Dr R. Fair Shaw," but I taught at the University of Michigan, where no one she knew taught, and she hinted that she would like it very much if we moved back to South Carolina and I got a position at the university there. When I introduced my friends, she was condescending to them, as if she thought they would know, as she certainly knew, why there could be no intimate friendship between them, for she didn't know any of their families. She received my friends as if she were a duchess—a slightly seedy and worn-out duchess—and she treated them to charming story after charming story about her family in South Carolina, which was her way of keeping them at bay. She thought I wanted news of South Carolina. "I suppose you will want to know about Caroline and her family," and before I could answer, she would start in and chatter on. Mother talked obsessively about Cornelius and his new house, and about Henrietta and how much good work she was doing with the

Junior League, and about their children. I had a beautiful home in a beautiful town and a position at a fine university, and she hardly noticed. In the early seventies, she still wore her hair in the forties style, a sweep of hair pulled up from the back and rolled over a "rat" at the crown of her head. It was flamboyantly artificial in a period when many young woman Naomi's age didn't own combs. My father still wanted to sit down in the living room while the women were in the kitchen and talk "books." He wasn't interested in my children or in my job. He wanted, I knew, for me to pay attention to him. *Talk to me about Candide.* What I was or did didn't really matter to them as long as they were paid attention to, and when they left I was deflated. The whole life that Naomi and I had built together, including our children, was merely an intricate hindrance to my parents' getting the attention they wanted. I felt sometimes that, when they were with me in Nashville or here in Ann Arbor, the attention they demanded was a way of their being reassured that they still possessed the position that they had in South Carolina, even in this strange and foreign place. My *whole life* had not pleased them because it was not a whole life in South Carolina.

I mentioned her having asked me not to go back to Sewanee. Mother seemed surprised. "I don't think I ever asked you to do that!" When I told her she did, she said, "How odd! If I asked you, why don't I remember?" They exhibited a vast carelessness about their demands on me, and I had given in for decades.

In the September 1970 *Harper's*, I read a poisonous article by a man named Joseph Epstein, called *Homo/Hetero: The Struggle for Sexual Identity.* I ordinarily didn't read *Harper's*—it was too establishment for me—but I picked this issue up off the stand because it had on the cover a magnificently built bodybuilder holding one arm behind his back so as to flex his triceps muscle, and, like the student in gold, it stopped me. I bought it and walked down the Diag—the major walkway crossing the central campus from one corner to the other—reading it, holding it wide open with both hands as I navigated past the students and over cracks in the concrete and along walks. Epstein wrote, "I do think homosexuality an anathema, and hence homosexuals cursed." Epstein wrote in a slangy, casual, urban prose, and his pose was sophisticated and off-hand. He seemed widely read, and I was aware that he came close to an ideal that I had carried with me ever since I had lived in New York—the agnostic writer who couldn't be roused to passion by anything but whose attitude toward all that passed him was irony and well-bred contempt. But I was amazed at what this sophisticated man allowed to show in the bare skin beneath his cuffs—the fur of an animal. The whole thing was so wrong, and yet, since it wasn't argued in a point-by-point manner, it was hard to point to the root of his error. I walked past the library and past the UGLI toward the arch out onto South University street, reading the long article—eleven full pages—through the crowds of students, until I got to Epstein's final lines, in which, speaking of his sons, he said "nothing they could ever do would make me sadder than if any of them were to become homosexual. For then I should know them condemned to a state of permanent niggerdom among men, their lives, whatever adjustment they might make to their condition, to be lived out as part of the pain of the earth." I turned onto South University and walked toward South Forest and my home and my wife.

Our guests talked about the bombing of Cambodia, supply routes, sanctuaries, the imperial presidency, the decline of student activism, and the Watergate hearings. The tone was leftist academic —fairly continuous reference to books and articles people had read, to the Democratic Party and the Socialist Worker's Party, and to the decline in power of unions, to the art scene in New York and London and Paris and Rome. Many of these people got on the first plane out of Detroit as soon as they had turned in their grades and were gone from the first of May to the end of August. I was aware of the privilege these people—including Naomi and I—exercised in their lives, their money and position insulating them from the grinding reality of most people's lives. Victor announced that he and his wife would be at a villa on Lake Constance after the middle of May, and Bob Curry was going on a walking tour of the Lake District. Everybody, it seemed, was going to stop by the British Museum at some point during the summer. Naomi and I were ourselves going to Rome for two months. "We will be on the Terme di Tito, just above the Colosseum." People told me what *trattoria* to patronize and what season tickets got you into the most museums.

We also talked about the tenure decisions the younger guests had to undergo.

"I figure you either have to write articles for the journals or you have to write a book. You can't do both. There is not enough time," said one man, a serious, dedicated intellectual from the Midwest who was writing serious scholarship, article by article.

"But how many articles is enough?" Matthew Cullinane, everyone knew, was turning out an article every six months and was very sure of himself. "I figure you have to have at least six in major journals like PMLA or JEGP or *Renaissance Quarterly.* Anything published anywhere else is worthless."

"There is no point in turning out a book and then publishing it at Kentucky."

"What're you doing Shaw?"

I had decided to turn my doctoral dissertation into a book. I was the only one turning a dissertation into a book, and the others went silent when I told them. It was not likely that they went silent because they were impressed. More likely they went silent because mine was a higher-risk strategy and therefore more dangerous, even foolish. Better a collection of well-thought-out articles.

They drifted away. The anxiety all of us felt had surfaced for a moment and shown its desperate head and had then subsided. People went back into the kitchen for something to drink.

As dinner proceeded slowly from course to course and through a variety of wines to dessert and coffee and brandy—and more hard liquor for those who wanted it—I was pleased with what we had done, and disappointed with it. It was, I realized, a familiar feeling, something of emptiness, something ungrounded. The lawn at Wespanee looked back to the founding of the colony—it was situated on the river on which the colony had been built—but more than a place situated on the land, it was a place situated for me in the history of my culture, in a time when learning and political activity —John Berkeley at Black Mingo—formed a coherent whole. And yet, while these were learned people, they were not politically active people, despite what they said in these rooms. I thought, *I've changed.* Surveying my own living room, I thought, *this is an elite* gathered together for dinner, talking about politics but in no way personally involved. These are the people against whom the people in the street demonstrate. These people in my rooms are the establishment, and what I saw around me—including my own house, its furnishings, the art on the walls, the silver and china on which we had eaten—was representative of the class to which we all belonged.

↔

I was obsessed with what had happened to me or with what I had done. I went back over in my mind the times when I could have gotten it right—when Connie and I had lain on the sleeping bag in the meadow on the side of Mt Rainier. I could have said then, my arm around Connie's shoulders, "I like to suck cock, and I am OK, and I am never going to have anything to do with women." I would have come home from Yakima and spent those last 18 months in South Carolina finding cock. Instead of seeing the time with Connie as Connie himself saw it—as an interlude—I could have seen it as the main attraction and reorganized my life around it. And in New York, I could have followed one of the dark-skinned beauties into a bar in the Village and settled then what I was about. *Get your degree, get a job, fuck men.* I had not been able to hear Paul Huntley. My culture told me that I had not come out, that I had gotten married because I was afraid. I had always seen myself as a man with courage. It was like having to admit that I was a racist, admitting to a character flaw from which there was no recovery. *Fair is just a coward.* I hadn't known, when they said the kid was shot in the dorm at Sewanee, that their demands would be endless and never satisfied and that I might as well refuse *now*.

I tried to explain it away. I had been a young man on the make. I had had my career in the forefront of my mind, and I wanted to be a success. I had wanted to live my life in public, with no secrets, no private part that was hidden. I had wanted to please my parents. I had resisted the image of doing Brutus in the dark, on my knees. I had been very proud. My pride had had its roots in my family, but I had carried it on, developed it, nurtured it, seeing myself with my integrity intact, seamless, flawless. *He was too proud to be queer.* So I had been dishonest with myself and gotten myself into a predicament from which there was no escape. The closet: I was hiding my real nature in the dark, while living a lie in public. There was no way to be proud and be closeted. I had changed from being a man struggling to do the right thing and avoiding living a life of lies and disguises—to being a man living a life of lies and disguises without the courage to do the right thing, which was to divorce my wife, quit my job, and come out. And I had not pleased my parents. My proposal of marriage to Naomi had been stupid and gutless. That night at Mac's, I had been swept by good feelings for Naomi and had spoken before I thought. Later, between the moment of the proposal and the wedding, I had wondered if it was the right thing to do—I had moments of panic—but I had done it, and I had stood by my word.

But sometimes I was aware of another wind blowing. Joe Dallesandro sometimes looked like a fifteen year old kid, and sometimes he looked like a 25 year old hustler and junkie, which rumor had it that he was. He was the star of several movies made by Paul Morrissey in the late sixties and early seventies, long brown hair, a beard along the edge of his chin, a tattoo saying "Joe" on his arm, and, in some of the movies, a body that looked like Michelangelo's *David*. In *Flesh*, in 1968, he was a hustler. He was sitting naked on the couch, and his trick asked him about Joe's girlfriend.

> *I married her,* Joe said.
> *You didn't marry her, you can't lie to me.*
> *I did marry her.*
> *Gay as you are?*
> *Gay as I am. Maybe. Whatever.*
> *You're not really going to marry her, right?*
> *I married her. I'm sorry. It's just what I had to do. At the*
>   *time. One of those things. But uh, you know.*
> Then the trick climbed on top of Joe and said, *Well I'm*
>   *going to blow ya.*

I married her. I'm sorry. It's just what I had to do. At the time. One of those things. But uh, you know. OK, so it happened. But why had he done it?

I talked to Greg about being queer. We were in a car going home, just the two of us, coming home from the university, and I told him.

Greg hesitated for a moment and then said, "It makes me feel closer to you. I always knew you were self-created." He smiled. "I've always liked that about you. I suspect you are very different from what you were as an adolescent. I've always thought you must have decided at some point what kind of person you wanted to be— some fierce moral avatar—and then you set about becoming the person in your mind. There's something hugely admirable about that, the effort, the determination, the sheer skill it must take to create yourself."

Greg admired me for reasons that I didn't understand, but the exchange left me cold. I was closeted, and I was lying, and there was nothing admirable about any of that.

Once I was helping some friends unload a big truck full of someone's furniture—all of these young faculty members seemed to be moving every year to bigger, better houses, and we were accustomed to acting as a moving crew—and one of the others was a big, cuddly Irish guy with piercing eyes and a constant smile who stopped in the middle of some maneuver with a sofa and said to me, "It's difficult to like you, Fair, when you don't like yourself."

The people I liked were the ones in the middle of the cultural turmoil—who were deeply into the thrilling chaos of it—and I knew that I wasn't. I had not known that I was supposed to stand up for myself as the black students had stood up for themselves on the sidewalk in front of the police in Nashville. I tried to remember others who had done it, and I couldn't. Fear—ignorance—had kept all of us from acknowledging that we were queer. Paul Huntley had never said in public, in a mixed crowd, *I'm gay.* None of them had. Not even the other gay men in the department at Michigan.

Tony Parada had told me one afternoon, over beer at a tavern near the Law School, "Sometimes it is difficult being around you, Fair. I have the sense, when I am around you, that you are incredibly stressed all the time, that you are tormented, and that you are almost —*almost*—unable to bear it. Being around you sometimes is like being around a disaster about to happen or being around somebody who is about to find out he has failed at—not just a course or a paper or something trivial but at—*the whole thing.*" He shrugged and raised his eyebrows. "Of course, on the other hand—" He grinned. "—the sense of danger people have around you is one of the things that makes you attractive. It's what makes some of us like to climb mountains. You can get killed—fall 3,000 feet on the rocks—but if you don't die, my God, what an adrenalin rush!"

↔

My friend the man who taught in Romance Languages, before dinner one night at his house, while the women were in the kitchen, talked about a professor in his department, a gay man, "who is ashamed of being gay, I think." I didn't know whether he knew I was gay, but the comment suggested an attitude that was not limited to my world in Ann Arbor. In the whole culture people seemed to feel that queers who were not out were *ashamed. I* was ashamed, and maybe I was ashamed of being gay, of all of the things you did associated with kneeling in front of Brutus in the parking lot. But I was certainly ashamed of having misread the future, misread what I was, misread my choices, ashamed of living the way I lived. My shame now was like the shame I had felt in Nashville after leaving the demonstration. *I should have stayed.* But it didn't matter whether I was really ashamed of being gay. What hurt was that I knew my friends thought I was ashamed of being gay, because that was the way my life looked.

↔

In the summer we rented a house at Pawley's and invited my parents and Cornelius and his family to come down to the beach and visit us —Cornelius and Henrietta never came to Michigan. The visits were brief, and everybody was on his best behavior, but Cornelius was not interested in Ann Arbor or our life there, and Henrietta played the perfect Southern woman by arriving with already baked hams and roasts and never allowed a personal remark to pass her lips. We had landed on the moon, the country was in the middle of the largest political scandal of its history, half a dozen of its most important political leaders had been assassinated, the United States was headed for the most catastrophic military defeat in its history, their brother and brother-in-law was queer, and *none* of this ever crossed their lips. Cornelius spent his energies attacking our father, who had had a heart attack and was now an invalid. He imitated Daddy's slow shuffle around the room, mocking his helplessness and inviting Naomi and me to laugh with him. He said, "My father is ruining my mother's life."

"I think they pretty much share the responsibility for whatever has happened to them, Cornelius."

"That's bullshit."

We moved on to less charged subjects, on to the subject all young people our age talked about—our children.

Henrietta had much to say about raising children, but she summed it up at the end: "I was gently reared, and I intend to rear my children the same way."

During these stays on the South Carolina coast, I spent long hours sitting on the beach playing with the children, dribbling sandcastles and wading in the surf, and taking long walks in which I led them, dancing backwards down the beach, while they followed me, copying my dancing movements and shrieking with laughter. I also spent time on the beach doing the kind of nothing that people do on beaches, watching the surf come in one wave after another, watching the walkers on the beach—first they'd be going south and then about an hour later you'd see them coming back north again—and occasionally watching the man running hard down the beach in a tight bathing suit that showed off his nuts, his arms clenched so that his shoulders were in a tight hunch, wet hair flopping from one side to the other as his body's weight fell on the right foot and then the left foot then the right. I was bemused by the fact that on the beach changes don't happen quickly—except when there is a storm and half the beach washes away, like Stonewall—but that you can't ever stop paying attention to how the beach is changing, even though it doesn't seem to be changing. When I was a little boy, the distance from the porch to the high-water mark was not nearly as far as it was now. Then on other stretches of the beach, houses that used to be so far back from the water you couldn't see the surf from the front porch were now way out over the high-water mark. Those people ought to get movers to pick up those houses and move them back 500 feet. Nothing seems to be changing, right up to the day your house washes away.

I found, when I returned to South Carolina for visits, that life there had gone on—or not gone on—at a different pace from my own life in NYC, Nashville, and Ann Arbor. These people seemed unaffected by later events. It was as if these events had not happened for them. They were still obsessed with their old concerns of family, class, religion, and race. Their sense of superiority had apparently not been challenged by all the years since 1954. My mother said of Henrietta, "She is so wonderful. She puts up with all of us," with its mock self-deprecating humor, its continued concern for self, its self-referential language, its measurement of others on the basis of whether or not they fit in with her family. Mother had been saying that about one or another person who was somehow allied to the family and who was a favorite of hers, for at least twenty-five years.

Naomi and I and the children arrived home from one of these visits to find the undergraduate whom we had left looking after the house with a story to tell. He was embarrassed, he said, to tell us he had had a party in the house while we were gone—neither Naomi nor I cared about that—but during the party, while the guests, all students, were tripping on acid, someone had knocked on the front door, insistently, loudly, shouting through the door, "Open up!" and when the door stuck and they couldn't get it open, whoever was on the other side threw himself against the door, splintering the doorjamb around the lock. It was the police who charged into my house. They wanted to know who owned the house, and where Fair Shaw was. They asked for identification all around from all the young people. It seems, while Naomi and I were on the South Carolina coast, on Pawley's Island, someone had made a death threat against the Governor of South Carolina, who was also on the island that week. The state cops had found that there was a "strange" car on the island, bearing out-of-state license plates. The car was mine. The state cops requested assistance from the Michigan cops, who tracked down the owner of the plates and my address. It seemed I was suspected of having made death threats against the governor, based on the fact that I was from out of state.

In *City of Night*, the exchange of money was a way of denying feeling—or of acknowledging that it didn't exist or couldn't be assuaged. It was a book about a hunger so great it couldn't be fed. *I'll give you money instead.* "'Oh, yes, my dear,' Miss Destiny said, 'there *is* a God, and He is one hell of a joker. Just—look—' and she indicates her lovely green satin dress and then waves her hand over the entire room. '*Trapped!*'…But one day, in the most lavish drag youve evuh seen—heels! and gown! and beads! and spangled earrings!—Im going to storm heaven and protest! *Here I am!!!!!* I'll yell—and I'll shake my beads at Him….And God will cringe!'"

↔

On March 6, 1970, a townhouse on West Eleventh Street, just off Fifth Avenue, exploded, killing three people who were members of the Weather Underground and who had been building bombs with which to "bring the war home." On April 30, 1970, Nixon announced an "incursion" into Cambodia, a non-combatant in the Vietnamese War that, it was already widely known, the United States, guided by Nixon and Kissinger, had been bombing since 1969. On May 4, 1970, at Kent State University in Ohio, four students among several hundred demonstrating against the Cambodian incursion were shot and killed on campus by members of the Ohio National Guard, resulting in demonstrations on university campuses all across the country by students furious at their own impotence at stopping the bombing and enraged that the National Guard had pulled weapons on one of their own. On May 9, 1970, a hundred thousand people demonstrated in Washington at a demonstration called "the Mobilization." On May 14, 1970, at Jackson State, in Jackson, Mississippi, police fired at a student dormitory, killing two men and wounding nine. The students had been protesting the Kent State killings. On August 24, 1970, a Weather Underground bomb exploded in a laboratory at the University of Wisconsin in Madison. On June 13, 1971, *The New York Times* began to publish the Pentagon Papers. Thousands of pages from the government's own files showed that presidents of the United States had lied *for thirty years* about American involvement in Indo-China. And Nixon went to China in February, 1972, grinning as if he didn't have to tell the American people the truth about anything. At the end of March 1972, the North Vietnamese mounted an offensive against the South, and the next day Nixon ordered the bombing of North Vietnam. In early May, B-52s began to bomb Hanoi and Haiphong and to mine Haiphong harbor. This was followed by what seemed to me to be the endless nitpicking of the diplomats in Paris attempting to negotiate a truce among the opposing parties—and by the 1972 election. George Wallace, running for President, was shot five times on May 15, 1972 and paralyzed apparently permanently. On June 17, 1972, it was revealed that "plumbers" had been arrested after breaking into the headquarters of the Democratic Party in the Watergate. The news caused a sensation. Within a few weeks, it was clear that the burglars had been hired by the Nixon White House. Then, on December 18, 1972, in Operation Linebacker II, Nixon ordered a new bombing campaign against Hanoi and Haiphong, which went on for 11 days and came to be known as the "Christmas Bombing," and which many commentators called the heaviest bombardment of any city anywhere in the world since the bombing of Dresden during World War II, and which the North Vietnamese called "insane." In the times we lived in, it was impossible to get the government to tell the truth about the war, about Cambodia, about the bombing, about the plumbers and the Watergate Office Building, about race. Even when the evidence was out there on the front pages of the newspapers, and confirmed in court, the government of Richard Nixon still lied. But the larger truth was that all governments lied. On July 25, 1972, *The Washington Times* reported on the Tuskegee Experiment, which had begun in 1932 and was *still ongoing*. The US Public Health Service was conducting experiments on 399 black men in the late stages of syphilis. The men were not ever told what disease they were suffering from or its seriousness and were never offered medications which could have cured them. *The New York Times* said, "The Tuskegee Study began 10 years before penicillin was found to be a cure for syphilis and 15 years before the drug became widely available, yet even after penicillin became common, and while its use probably could have helped or saved a number of the experiment subjects, the drug was denied them." Harry Reasoner, the news anchor, said the experiment "used human beings as laboratory animals in a long and inefficient study of how long it takes syphilis to kill someone." It was like the Nazi medical experiments on Jews, and it was the *United States government* that had done it, to its own citizens.

↔

The principal focus of the Gay Liberation Front and the Gay Activist Alliance was the determination among psychiatrists and psychologists that gay people were "sick" and could be "cured." Since the 1950s, this determination was used throughout the culture as the basis for preventing gay people from serving in the Army, getting security clearances, getting visas to come to America, serving in the diplomatic corps, and as the basis for sodomy laws and laws against gay bars and gathering places. With the loss of the authority of the churches, psychiatry and psychology had taken over the function of guardian of morals. Newspapers covered the annual meetings of these organizations and the demonstrations by gay people demanding that they retract their diagnosis. The gay activists argued that the place of homosexuals in America was the result, not of the innate qualities of homosexuals, but of a system that had, for a thousand years, excluded them.

On May 11, 1970, one week after the Kent State killings, the annual meeting of the American Psychiatric Association in San Francisco was the focus of a Gay Liberation Front zap. Irving Bieber, a psychiatrist and the author of a homophobic 1962 book on homosexuality, was infamous among homosexuals for his view that homosexuality was a mental illness. Gary Alinder, in an essay "Gay Liberation Meets the Shrinks," quotes Bieber saying at the meeting, "I never said homosexuals were sick—what I said was that they had displaced sexual adjustment."

A GLF member screamed, "That's the same thing, motherfucker!"

Alinder describes a session on reparative therapy—shock treatment and drugs designed to induce nausea in the patient at the sight of homoerotic photographs—when a demonstrator shouted, "Torture!"

The GLF activists stopped the meeting, and when the psychiatrists asked them to wait until the end of the session to make comments, the GLF yelled, "We've waited long enough!"

On May 3, 1971, the Gay Liberation Front pulled off demonstrations at the American Psychiatric Association convention in Washington. *The Advocate* quoted Frank Kameny, a leader of the New York Mattachine Society, denouncing the right of psychiatrists to discuss the question of homosexuality. "Psychiatry is the enemy incarnate. Psychiatry has waged relentless war of extermination against us. You may take this as a declaration of war against you!'"

On October 2, 1972, the New York Gay Activist Alliance attacked the Association for the Advancement of Behavior Therapy, passing out leaflets outside the meeting which denounced the use of aversion techniques to make gay men straight,

On February 9, 1973, *The New York Times,* under the headline "Psychiatrists Review Stand on Homosexuals," reported that the APA "began deliberating" the question of removing homosexuality from the list of pathological conditions. *The Times* article was structured around a summary of the presentation made by the Gay Activist Alliance to the Committee on Nomenclature and around representative responses made by the leader of the committee. While the article summarized studies that favored removal, it presented summaries of no studies opposed to removal. It didn't seem as if the psychiatrists themselves had any deeply held beliefs on or knowledge about the subject. The article—18 inches of type—made them seem stupid and unscientific. Not one of these men who had presided over a profession that had done incalculable damage to millions of homosexuals in my lifetime was quoted giving a scientific rationale for the psychiatric diagnosis of illness. And Freud was quoted in support of the gay position.

Finally, on December 15, 1973, the Nomenclature Committee of the American Psychiatric Association removed homosexuality from the list of mental disorders. *The Times* article for the next day read, "Psychiatrists, in a Shift, Declare Homosexuality no Mental Illness." I noted the word *shift*, which seemed an odd word to describe such a momentous event. The article said the APA was "altering a position it had held for nearly a century." *Altering!* In a *shift!* "The association leaders insisted they had not given in to pressure from homosexual groups." What had they given in to? They had had no reason for their diagnosis, no scientific reason, no studies, no research, *nothing.* And when the gay men were rude, they caved in. Gay leaders were quoted saying, "The diagnosis of homosexuality as an illness has been the cornerstone of oppression for a tenth of our population." And, it "has forced many gay women and men to think of themselves as freaks." And, "It has been used as a tool of discrimination in the private sector, and in the civil service, military, Immigration and Naturalization Service, health services, adoption and child custody courts." And at the moment of crisis, psychiatrists had nothing to say to *The Times* in support of their damnable policy.

But the psychiatrists who still believed homosexuality a pathology maneuvered the APA into submitting the changes to the membership. Finally, in April, 1974, the results showed that of the 10,000 psychiatrists who voted, sixty percent were in favor of the removal from the diagnostic manual. Forty percent still believed homosexuality was an illness. Robert Spitzer, a psychiatrist and a member of the nomenclature committee that had originally addressed the issue, was asked by *The Advocate* whether times had changed or had the psychiatrists been wrong all along. "I would have to say we were wrong." I felt the APA—and every individual psychiatrist—should be forced to pay reparations for their crimes.

Naomi and I saw *The Godfather* when it came out, with its dark brown velvet colors and assumption of the nearness of death and Kay's final question, "Is it true?"

And Michael's answer, *Don't ask me about my business, Kay.*

Is it true?

Don't ask me about my business.

No, and—

And then Michael's long pause. *Just this one time, this one time, I will let you ask me about my affairs.*

And so she asked again, *Is it true?*

He answered, although the audience had seen him do it, *No.* Many critics pointed out that the mafia, as presented in the movie, acted like a corporation and much of the language of the mafia was the language of business. At the end of Part I, the Corleone family were about to move to Las Vegas and become legitimate. But it was also a movie about power and the corrupting effects of power. The corrupting effects of power were not limited merely to Michael Corleone and the mafia overlords in New York. Power also corrupted politicians, men who had power over women, *white* men who had power over black men, straight men who had power over gay men, doctors who had power over patients. It had corrupted Nixon, and it had corrupted every single psychiatrist, professionals who, because they belonged to a discipline that had done such damage, had been, themselves, collectively and individually, corrupted by it, whatever their individual beliefs on the diagnosis of homosexuals. *Did you do it? No.*

The times we lived in were a great pivotal point in history—when sex, gender, race were all being rethought and redefined, and their relation to what was called American democracy being fought over. The whole American contract was being rewritten. That's what *radical* meant. I remembered the great debates over segregation in the fifties and my realization that my parents were on the wrong side of the debate, that the debate was eventually going to come to a resolution, and my parents, I could already tell, were going to be on the wrong end of the argument. I knew the argument had not ended with the passage of the Civil Rights Act of 1964 and that the argument over race was part of the larger, immensely larger, argument over democracy in America—whether there was such a thing—which had already engulfed the races of America and the

genders of America and had now engulfed the sexualities of
America. The great question was: *Is there actually a Democracy in
America?*

↔

Spiro Agnew, the Vice-President of the United States, resigned on
October 10, 1973. I heard it from someone in the elevator in Haven
Hall, going upstairs to my office. The man said, "Hey, did you hear?
Spiro Agnew has *resigned!* He's admitted taking *bribes!*" The next
day *The Times* headline, three lines deep, said, "AGNEW QUITS
VICE PRESIDENCY AND ADMITS TAX EVASION IN '67;
NIXON CONSULTS ON SUCCESSOR." He had evaded paying
taxes on payments he had received from state contractors who were
"favored by Mr. Agnew in the award of state contracts." *The Times*
quoted Elliott Richardson, the Attorney General, saying that

> evidence available to the Government 'establishes a
> pattern of substantial cash payments to the defendant
> during the period when he served as Governor of
> Maryland, in return for engineering contracts with
> the State of Maryland. Payments by the principal
> large engineering firms began while the defendant
> was County Executive of Baltimore County in the
> early nineteen sixties and continued into 1971. The
> evidence also discloses payments by another
> engineer up to and including December 1972.' The
> time period covered thus extended well into Mr.
> Agnew's first term as Vice-President, beginning
> January 20, 1969, and Mr. Richardson said that the
> Government's witness 'would testify to having made
> direct payments to the Vice President.'

The Saturday Night Massacre occurred on October 20, 1973.
Nixon had ordered the Attorney General, Elliott Richardson, to fire
the Independent Counsel, Archibald Cox, and the Attorney General
had refused the order and then resigned. Immediately, the same order
was given his assistant, William Ruckelshaus, who also refused and
then resigned. Finally, a man named Robert Bork, the Solicitor
General of the United States, was found to be willing to comply with

the President's order to fire Archibald Cox. The government was ceasing to function because of its own internal rot.

Someone at a dinner party—another faculty dinner party, with too many opinions and too much alcohol—had taken the line that the original break-in was a "third rate burglary," and that it was being used by the Democrats as a way of overturning the election of 1972 by extra-democratic means. I was furious. "The robbery goes to the heart of our corrupted democracy. If democracy means anything, it means that we have a government *of the people*, which means that the will of the people must be determined at regular intervals by holding elections, and that the central, inescapable duty of the government is to make certain that those elections are fairly held and the will of the people is accurately determined. The political parties must act toward each other not only within the bounds of the law but within the bounds of decency so that when the election results are announced all citizens can look on them and say, *This has been fair.* What the Republicans tried to do when they broke into the offices of the Democratic National Committee in the Watergate Office Building was to subvert the democratic process at its heart. This was no simple third-rate robbery, this was an assault on the government of the United States. These robbers were trying to steal the government from the people. They were trying to rob me. They were trying to rob all of us, Democrats and Republicans alike, because they were saying, your vote doesn't matter. You don't matter."

By the end of 1973, the US had announced a near-total withdrawal of its troops from Vietnam. Richard Nixon himself resigned on August 8, 1974, to escape certain conviction on three impeachment articles, after the "smoking gun" they'd been looking for, for two years, was finally found in his tapes. His own words, caught on his own tapes, were *prima facie* evidence of his having committed high crimes and misdemeanors. His own words, clumsy, inarticulate as they were, proved that he had abused the power of his office.

> When you get in these people when you … get these
> people in, say: "Look, the problem is that this will
> open the whole, the whole Bay of Pigs thing, and the
> President just feels that" ah, without going into the
> details … don't, don't lie to them to the extent to say
> there is no involvement, but just say there is sort of a

comedy of errors, bizarre, without getting into it,
"the President believes that it is going to open the
whole Bay of Pigs thing up again. And, ah because
these people are plugging for, for keeps and that they
should call the FBI in and say that we wish for the
country, don't go any further into this case," period.

Since I had watched the election returns in 1960 in Yakima,
Washington, I had been drawn to the left by the glamour of John
Kennedy and then by the very different kind of glamour of those in
the street, which I had first seen in Nashville in 1963, and today, the
glamour of the SDS and the Black Panthers and the Weathermen who
were as sexy as they were radical in their analysis of a government
captured by corporations and run for the white straight rich, a
government not only deaf to the people but contemptuous of them.
The proper response to such a government was a raised fist. I had
first seen this symbol in the pictures of the Summer Olympics in
Mexico City in 1968, pictures of Tommie Smith and John Carlos, the
track and field medal winners, raising gloved fists above their heads
during the playing of the American national anthem. It was the
insolence of the thing that moved me, the flagrant abuse of decorum,
the dramatic demonstration that they no longer cared about a white
America that no longer cared about them. The raised fist had become
a symbol of the Black Panther party and appeared on posters, a silk-
screened, almost abstract clenched fist. The image had been adopted
by gay men in New York. I *liked* being in the street, my fist raised,
yelling, *Hell, no!*

The system responded only to a raised fist—or to empty
classroom buildings. The system was never aware of anyone outside
the system. It was deaf and blind. I said to Greg, "I am at home with
the political climate in the country—with the Weathermen and their
Days of Rage. I *like it* that they are reckless and heedless and
dangerous. They shift the whole political debate to the left, open up
possibilities nobody had dared think of before. If we are not to have
justice, then we won't have decorum. We will have chaos. If
something isn't done, we will have revolution."

↔

The issue posed by homosexuality in the culture was no longer that homosexual men wanted to suck cock, it was that this culture refused to acknowledge that gay people are Americans. This was an incomparable revolution in cultural understanding, a change so great as to be almost incomprehensible. A man on one side of that great divide would find it impossible to understand the language of a man on the other. The truth was that there was to be no revolution. It was like the end of *The Damned*, in which the future held only the distant past, the most barbarous reaction. After 1968 and after the election of Richard Nixon, in fact, I saw now that the country—even while it was experiencing the Weathermen and their Days of Rage—had been swept by a drowning tide pulling us backward.

↔

Naomi had settled with ease into her house and her motherhood, her marriage, her studies at the law school, and her political activities. She was in her third year, and the language that we had used between us—the language used by people who had gone to Mississippi for Freedom Summer, the language of Mario Savio, standing on the roof of the police car at a rally of the Free Speech Movement, the language of Naomi's own parents—was less and less the language she used, which was the language of lawyers and had to do with legal precedent and the sense of the Congress and the plain meaning of laws. We had spoken as if the revolution were already here, and the question before us was the steps to be taken to dismantle the *ancien regime*. The change was as much in emotional tone as it was in the choice of words. "First," she now said, "they have to consider the makeup of the legislature. Only 36% can be considered to be truly liberal. People don't understand how conservative the Upper Peninsula is, and the union-dominated cities of East Lansing and Kalamazoo." Naomi was leaving me. She had started this process when the children arrived. She was as intensely focused on them as I was, but she was also focused on her work, and under the pressure of her marriage and of her parenting, she had become very active—that is, a very busy career woman—and more establishment than her parents were and than she and I had been. So we came apart, driven by our separate political movements—the women's movement and the gay movement were out of sync with one another—and fueled by the fear both of us had of what I, as a closeted gay man, was capable of doing in the Age of Stonewall.

We could have loved each other and stayed married if we hadn't demanded monogamy of each other, if I had understood that a man need not choose between gay and straight, if I had been able to accept that Stonewall was wrong—it was not necessarily lying for a man to like men and also be in a marriage—if we had understood that the contract we had made with each other in August 1965 could be renegotiated, if we had been kinder to one another, if we had not been so afraid. Most of all, we might have been able to work it out if we could have talked about it. But we were both afraid of our marriage breaking up. *Fear* was not so much of my being gay as of losing what we had—our children, our house, and most of all, our place—so we didn't talk. While the culture in the times we were living through played around with images of maleness—Mick Jagger and his lipstick—it wasn't serious about renegotiating what marriage or even maleness was all about, nothing like the renegotiation that was going on around femaleness. We didn't ever acknowledge that in the history of mankind there were many millions of men who had sex with men while procreating with women. Benvenuto Cellini was one of these, and I never thought to say, *What he can do, I can do,* and so I never thought to ask, *What is necessary for that to happen?* What kept us together were our own failures as people—and our children. *Here* was the failure of courage.

↔

All the testing of young assistant professors like me took place, by contract, at the beginning of the sixth year of a young teacher's career and resulted in an examination of the young teacher's record by a specially appointed committee, which made a recommendation to the Executive Committee of the Department of English, which then voted the candidate up or down. If the candidate was voted down, he or she was given one more one-year contract, with the stipulation that this would be the last contract the teacher would get and that he or she must use this last contract to find another job. If the candidate was voted up, he or she was recommended for promotion to Associate Professor with tenure, this recommendation going forward to the Dean and then to President, after which, at the end of the school year, he or she was promoted and given tenure. These procedures were governed by the rules of the American Association of University Professors and were followed by all accredited colleges and universities in the United States.

I had to provide evidence of my work as a teacher and evidence of my scholarship. The first was easy. The second required, in my case, that I turn my dissertation into a publishable book. Many young men had been given tenure on the strength of one good book. A second book was insurance. A series of articles—people said it would take six or more—in major journals was a gamble. It was clear to me that I needed a book, and perhaps two. My doctoral dissertation, while good enough in its way, needed to be rethought and rewritten. After a couple of years at Michigan, and when I had gotten my feet on the ground in my teaching, I set about rereading all the basic research I had done for the dissertation and all the basic scholarship and criticism of John Donne. Then I had to begin again and write a new book.

This was hard because I was drinking heavily and because my teaching load was already demanding. I came in from the university and found Naomi waiting to have a drink, so I fixed both of us drinks while I played with the children, watched the news on TV, and got the children ready for bed. By the time I was ready to work, I was unable to work, so I didn't work. And Naomi didn't mention my not working. My drinking became the third big issue—after Naomi's parents' indifference to her and after my desire for men—that was not to be spoken of.

Everyone was under stress, and it showed in predictable places. The marriages of our friends began to come unglued.

One of my colleagues made a point of inviting me home after work. His wife spoke directly to me.

"We are experiencing difficulties in our marriage, and we wanted to talk to you. There is, now, another person in our marriage."

"What she means is that—" He hesitated. "—I am having an affair."

I had told him that I was gay, and that may have made me seem to them a sympathetic person for this revelation.

"How long has this been going on?"

"Six months, since last fall—" It was now late spring.

"Who is it?"

"A student."

"She's my graduate student, a teaching assistant. She grades papers."

"And I have been taken up entirely with the girls—" They had two little girls. "—and he has felt I have not been supportive."

"So I turned to this graduate student."

"Let's see. You're stressed from overwork and loneliness so you have an affair with a graduate student. A sexual solution to a non-sexual problem."

We talked on until late at night, drinking and talking about sex and its power to solve—or not solve—every issue. I thought that his "sexual solution to a non-sexual problem" was a stupid thing to have done, and I didn't have much sympathy for this straight man who couldn't keep his dick in his pants. I had been monogamous since I had first asked Naomi to marry me.

Another colleague had been suffering stress from overwork. He had published two small non-scholarly books since arriving at Michigan, neither of which would help him get tenure, and was not happy. His real problem, I thought, was that he was in over his head. He had been successful all his life, had degrees from two major universities on the West Coast, had gotten this job at Michigan, a third major university, and was now up against a tenure decision, and for the first time in his life, he wasn't smart enough to get what he wanted. He worked very hard, but the books he turned out were laughably lightweight. Publishers of textbooks were always coming around the offices looking for young professors like me who could be persuaded to write a textbook that could be marketed to smaller schools in the rest of the country as by *Professor X, from the University of Michigan!* The publishers would make money, and the young professor at Michigan, perhaps, would get something—but not much—out of it. He had gotten caught up in this scheme and had allowed his name to be put on collections which he had edited. I assumed he knew they were worthless books, even while he was working very hard putting them out.

There were others. There was a rumor that one young teacher was screwing a graduate student, and then an announcement that another young couple were getting a divorce because the husband had had an affair with his wife's female colleague. One wife tried to commit suicide. One of our colleagues, one of the group who had been hired with me in 1968, quit teaching and went to medical school with the parting comment, "I have never hated doing anything so much in my whole miserable life as I have hated teaching English at the University of Michigan." Another one quit and turned to religion.

The politics in the department were vicious as well. In the late sixties and early seventies, many English departments around the country changed the way they were governed. In the past, a man would be hired as chairman of the department on an open contract, and many of these men ran their departments like little dukedoms, staying on until they reached an advanced age, sometimes for 20 or 25 years. Now there was political pressure from all professorial ranks to limit the contracts of chairmen to one or two terms of three years each, to turn the chairmanship into a rotating position filled by people from the department. This movement increased the opportunity for political activity on the part of various factions of professors. There were, naturally, the old-guard conservatives and the young Turks of all ages, and the tenure decisions were caught up in this political infighting. In my own department, governance had moved from an old "Duke" who had held the position for years, to a man who held it for one term of five years, and then to another. There was a faction of the faculty who had been passed over and who felt ignored and devalued and who therefore opposed everything the current chairman offered. The department divided in its politics, its governance, and even in its social life. It was ugly and unnecessary, the ugliness of it replicated the ugliness of the politics of the nation, and it caused me, who felt myself a victim in a number of different ways, to agree sometimes with the colleague who was going to be a doctor.

Because, while I was trying to stay sober long enough to turn my dissertation into a book, I was accepting another fact about myself that I had avoided acknowledging before: I was not a scholar. I knew many men who were. Shep Cox, my friend from Columbia, who had attended the University of Wisconsin and gotten a PhD in history, was. Shep arranged things so that he could go to London to the British Museum every summer and had completed a doctoral dissertation on the British banking system, which, he acknowledged, was *dull as dishwater*, but which, he said shyly, *I like*. He was fascinated by the process by which the British banking system—the first truly modern banking system in the world—had developed. He *liked* spending time in the British Museum.

Greg Steifel was another. *He* said, one night late, "My idea of going to heaven is to be allowed to go to the British Museum reading room and spend the rest of eternity there." His field was the visionary poetry of William Blake. He was working on a massive, comprehensive, definitive critical edition, and when the rest of us came up for tenure, in 1973, he arranged to take a year off and go to London to the British Museum to read. Greg's project was clearly bigger than any of ours, and he seemed wise to take the time to complete it.

On the other hand, while I enjoyed writing the occasional critical analysis of a poem or a novel or play, I had no talent for anything else or for any real scholarship. The whole process by which one became a scholar seemed foreign to my nature. I loved books, even books of scholarship and criticism. What I did not feel drawn toward was that kind of writing myself. So I did not go into the tenure decision thinking it was going to be obviously easy. If they gave me tenure, it would be a fluke or because in some way they had misread me.

↔

The central campus is a large square bounded by South University, South State, North University, and East University. Running from the corner of South University and East University to South State and North University is a broad concrete walk called "the Diag," which runs past the library in the middle of the square. Angell Hall with its annexes, Mason Hall and Haven Hall, is a large neo-classical building on South State. The Diag, running through the middle of the campus, connects a small business district along South University with a larger business district on South State, anchored by the Nickels Arcade, an elegant galleria of small jewelry shops and clothing stores. There are book stores in both areas. The university has no central bookstore, and textbook orders are handled by the professors' choice of stores. In the middle of the square bounded by these streets, and in front of the library, is a large plaza, which seems always crowded with students and teachers coming from and going to the library and the large classroom buildings around the periphery of the campus and also with crowds assembled to hear people haranguing the crowd on political issues, their voices amplified by portable loudspeakers. The whole campus is shaded by large elms and maple trees.

Around this central campus, the university has spread out into adjoining neighborhoods. The law school is along South State Street next to the central campus, and the school of social work is across South University at the corner of East University. Other schools have spilled across the boundaries. Fraternities and sororities, large Georgian mansions, are strung out along Washtenaw Avenue, which comes in under the trees on a diagonal to the central campus. Interspersed among these university buildings are medical buildings and other buildings for professions of various kinds—and consultants who do research, drawn to the area by the community of scholars at the university.

The students thrilled me, the crowds of them moving down the Diag from building to building between classes, stopping on the plaza in front of the library to listen for a moment to speakers on the subject of the war, women in the culture, the oppression of blacks, but particularly the war, the war, the war. The students were the best there were from Michigan. But they were also from everywhere in the country and from abroad and were sophisticated, cosmopolitan, eager to learn, serious about what they were doing, and politically engaged. Politically, they were very liberal, but they were also very volatile, and, at the same time, fun-loving. The students lived in the neighborhoods near campus, which was also where Naomi and I lived our first two years in Ann Arbor, and they all gave the sense that they were not going to do it the way their parents had done it. They were into experimentation of all kinds—but particularly sex, drugs, and rock and roll, and, of course, the way they looked. The place gave off an air of excitement even when the Diag was empty. The students wanted to do well, and when they went on to graduate school, they wanted to do even better. For me, the excitement of being at Michigan, after being at South Carolina and Vanderbilt, was almost continuous, a rush induced by the place itself, represented by the Diag, cutting across the campus. Once, during the BAM strike, I was in my office on the second floor of Haven Hall overlooking the central campus and the Diag and heard shouting down below, and I put down my papers and turned in my chair to look out through the bare trees at whatever was causing the commotion. It was a crowd of students shouting, perhaps 100 of them—they were moving like a hurricane across the campus, a wild circular, violent, centrifuge of them—and in their midst, as in the quiet eye, were President and Mrs. Robben Fleming, walking quickly, her hand in the crook of his arm, down the Diag, across the campus, toward the Michigan Union on the other side of State Street, looking frightened and defiant. It was emblematic of life in Ann Arbor during the years I was there, these very bright, very accomplished students, reduced to screaming at power, which was afraid of them.

I suffered from a general paralysis. Emotional, intellectual, physical. I was a good father, and we gave parties, and I taught what many students seemed to think were very good classes, and, in the end, I turned my doctoral dissertation into a good book, an analysis of the love poems of John Donne as arguments of a special kind—a kind very popular in the early seventeenth century for people who wanted to be good but who were trapped by a system of laws into feeling that they were very bad. This was published by a good press. But I couldn't think.

And when the tenure decision was made in the fall of 1973, at the beginning of my sixth year in Ann Arbor, I was caught in a political struggle between the two groups in the department who disagreed on the future and their place in the system—and on me— and I was denied tenure. As a result, the chairman of the department, having been defeated, resigned and went to another university. There were recriminations back and forth among the various cliques—all six who had come up with me were also denied tenure, although I was the only one who had a book accepted for publication—and Naomi and I packed up to leave.

The young faculty members who had come up with me—and had been, like me, denied tenure—retreated into themselves, and the social life that had been so much a part of our lives in Ann Arbor suddenly died. One senior man who had been a member of our crowd came down to my office shortly afterward. He was hesitant and asked, "Can I come in?" I shrugged and gestured toward the chair. "I don't know whether you would like to talk at all about what has happened, but I wanted to tell you how sorry I am about the decision. You must not take this as any personal or professional judgment on you. It was merely departmental politics. That crowd —" He was referring to the clique that voted against me. "—was using you as a way of getting back at the chair. They don't care about you. They cared only about damaging the chairman." I heard that, and, like Horatio, did *in part* believe it, but I was aware of the issues that this man was not addressing, my waiting too long to get my book into print, our purchase of our house—we had bought the home of the retiring chairman, which meant that we had stepped out of our place in the order of things—my drinking. I felt much more responsible for what had happened, apparently, than the men around me believed me to be. At the same time, I would not be defeated by it.

I wrote Mother. "The decision was on a tie vote, I was told, in a clean division between two factions in the department. I was told that it had less to do with me than with an on-going fight in the department over governance. I am very sorry to have to tell you this —I know you will be disappointed—but there is nothing I can do. It might have been better if my book were already in print instead of being merely 'in press,' but I couldn't hurry that along either. Naomi is well and holding up under all this, although of course she is disappointed—we both like Ann Arbor—and the children seem excited about the possibility of a move and new friends and a new house. I love you, and I will write again in the next several days when things settle down."

I also wrote Shep, my friend from childhood who had the PhD from Wisconsin and taught in the South. "I have no talent for this kind of work, Shep, unlike you, and I made a mistake getting into it. I love teaching, but given *publish or perish*, I perished. My book was accepted for publication but not soon enough to get it out before the decisions were made so the committee had to read it in manuscript, which is always less impressive than a bound copy. I should have started turning the dissertation into a book a year earlier than I did. It feels terrible. I feel like a failure."

Shep wrote back, "Don't. Too many people get ground up in these decisions, and too many of these decisions are made for reasons they ought not to be made."

And I wrote my brother. "Mother will have told you my news. I don't want you to believe everything she says. She makes everything into such a tragedy. This is not a tragedy. I am OK, and Naomi is OK, and the children of course are OK, excited about the move. I am to go first and find us a place to live, and then I will come back to

Ann Arbor and get Naomi and the children and we will all go back together."

What I did not write any of them was that I thought the real reason for my not getting tenure was my drinking.

On September 9, 1974, *The Times* reported that the day before, Gerald Ford had given Richard Nixon an unconditional pardon of any crimes he may have committed against the United States during his term of office. *The Times* said Nixon issued a statement saying he was "wrong in not acting more decisively and more forthrightly in dealing with Watergate." Everyone noted that he did not say he was wrong to have sent the burglars into the Democratic National Committee or that he was wrong to have subverted the CIA and the FBI, or that he was wrong to have abused the powers of his office, or that he was wrong to have bombed Cambodia. He did not say he was wrong to have lied to the American people—*I am not a crook*—and, God knows, he did not say he was wrong to have invented and then pursued his Southern strategy in which he had sent covert racist messages to racists by which messages he had originally gotten elected. *Did you do it? No.*

On April 30, 1975, the Vietnam war ended with the fall of Saigon. I watched the TV images of American and South Vietnamese troops abandoning their equipment in the road, the hundreds of screaming Vietnamese outside the gates of the US Embassy in Saigon trying to get out of the country, and the final, appalling images of the helicopter taking off from the roof of the embassy, people on the roof trying to jump up and grab the runners. It was an image that spoke of failure, fear, desperation, panic. It was an image that appeared the next morning on the front pages of *The New York Times* and the *Detroit Free Press*, and then at the beginning of the next week on the covers of the newsmagazines, and then later in monthly magazines, and then in books. The failure of the American experiment in imperial power, it seemed, would never go away. Whenever I saw it, my heart beat rapidly, and I went cold. Why had we been there in the first place? How could we have failed so? Why weren't we able to declare surrender, admit what we had done, and, with dignity, quit the field? It was an undignified, squalid rout after 14 years of war. *Did I believe in original sin?* Remembering the image, I felt shame.

251

On January 14, 1975, *The Times* printed an article by Michael Valente, "On Homosexuality," which looked at the inability of Americans to discuss, dispassionately, the issue. "It is disconcerting, to find critics of homosexuality discoursing heatedly from a plateau of ignorance and bewilderment." Valente was concerned about why it was that so many social critics had difficulty dealing the issue of homosexuality. He made comparisons between homosexuality—the desire for members of the same sex—and snail eating, which most people, he believed, could discuss with equanimity. He concluded that most people understand that anybody, given the right conditioning, or the right sense of freedom of action, could eat a snail, but most people don't have the right conditioning or the right sense of freedom of action to enable them to have sex with their own gender. Desiring Russell Ford was not the same thing as desiring a snail, and to say it was, was to debase and corrupt the whole discourse on sexuality. And it was *The Times* that had done it.

And a week later, *The Times* reported that *Let My People Come*, a musical at the Village Gate on Bleeker Street, had been charged by the State Liquor Authority with being a "lewd, and indecent performance." One of the songs, "Come in My Mouth," had the singers sing,

> I can feel all your strength… what would you like
> me to do?
> I'll take you inch by inch, just let me worship you…
> You taste so good… give me some…
> My mouth is a hole… fuck me… fuck me…

Let My People Come was closer to the emotional and physical reality of my life than *The Times* and Michael Valente and than the whole critical dialogue.

In January 1975, the American Psychological Association removed homosexuality from its list of mental disorders after years of demonstrations by queers in the streets. While this action might help future generations of gay people, I thought it was inadequate and too late. There were, now, generations of gay men and women living in America who had been crippled by the bigotry of these mental health professionals, who had told them they were "sick" and should change. The psychologists had committed what should have

252

been a prosecutable crime against gay people, and the culture's response was amnesia.

↔

Just before we moved to Maine, where I had gotten a job at the University of Maine, we were with friends and the tenure decisions came up—no others who had been denied tenure were there—and some senior professor said, "Oh, well. Don't worry. Everybody gets denied tenure his first time around."

I had never told anyone that the job at Michigan was interwoven with my marriage to Naomi and that both were payoffs for my giving up what I had given up—my writing, and *men*—and if I ended up in some second rate school far from the center of things with a wife and children and the need to write academic books, and *no men,* the exchange would no longer be worth it.

↔

We saw a movie, *Nashville,* by Robert Altman. The opening sequence ended with an astonishing, gigantic pile-up of cars on the freeway into Nashville. The movie followed over one weekend a large cast of characters associated in some way with the country music industry and with politics and ended with an assassination attempt on the steps of the Parthenon, where Naomi and I had had sex the first time. The movie was not about Nashville or even about the country music scene but was, instead, about the cultural crisis that America had faced during the last decade—the Vietnam war, the assassinations, Watergate, the abject failure of politics, and, in the greater distance, the long anguish over civil rights and the long conflict over the nature of democracy. It had beautiful, sexy, arrogant Keith Carradine in knee-high boots, tight jeans, loose white shirt and dark leather vest with long, straight dark blond hair and dark sexual drives. The whole long last scene of the movie was set in this place intimately familiar to me, the concrete Parthenon, suggestive of both fifth century BC Athens and twentieth century America— assassinations in both—and the need to pick up the pieces and *to get on with it.* It had the lushness of character, the violence, the vulgarity —was there any Southern politician more vulgar than Richard

Nixon?—of the Nashville that I had remembered, but also of the America that I knew. It had the unknown soldier, who had the whole history of the sixties and early seventies as motive, and a young man with the Weathermen as a model, who pulled the trigger in a moment, I thought, of unbelievable rage.

And it also had something else. Just after the bullet was fired and the star struck and fallen on the stage, blood everywhere, Henry Gibson handed off the microphone in his left hand, to—somebody— while saying, "Sing! Sing, somebody!" and the moviegoer saw his hand with the microphone thrust beyond the right edge of the screen and then pull back without the microphone and, as the camera swung right, it revealed the microphone again, this time in a hand that was there, just happened to be there, and when the camera panned slightly again to the right, the screen showed Barbara Harris, who had taken the microphone being given away and, after a moment's confusion and indecision, who had begun to sing, *You may say, I ain't free, but it don't worry me.* Her voice, at first hesitant and wavering, gathered strength as it went along, gathered to her the attention of the crowd, gathered to her their need to be a part of America too, took on a sure rhythm. She picked up the bouquet of dropped flowers—picked up the reins of government, *I have some rights of memory in this kingdom*—and became the nearest thing America has to royalty, a *star.*

4

But first I had to die.

In a fog, with no idea where we were going, one Sunday morning, Naomi and I found a white, Greek Revival mansion with one-story columns on Main Street—Maine, like the Garden District, is full of them—that had stood empty for two years, and bought it because it fit the image we had had of ourselves thirteen years before.

Elvis Presley, fat and ugly, died on August 16, 1977, on the floor of his bedroom at Graceland in Memphis, Tennessee. He was 42. The next day *The Times* said, "the image was of a working-class rebel, pushing sex into the nation's consciousness long before the 'sexual revolution.' With his ominous, greasy, swirling locks, his leather jacket and his aggressive undulations, Elvis was a performer whom parents abhorred, young women adored and young men instantly imitated." Young *men* adored him too. Despite what had happened to him as he grew older, he was a beautiful man—his eyes, his eyelashes, his full lips, and, of course, his long, dark, glossy hair— and he had merged in my memory with the boy on whose shoulders I had ridden on the playground in the fifth grade, and all the other men from my adolescence. The same glossy hair. What made him different, of course, was his voice, that warm driving baritone that carried me back to the time when I first discovered sex.

The power in our relationship had shifted from me to Naomi. It may have seemed at one point that ours was a traditional marriage composed of a talented, ambitious young academic and his wife and children, but this conventional view gradually altered over the years to its opposite, a young, talented, accomplished lawyer and her children with a husband who was a failed academic pretending to be straight. It was Naomi's money, largely, that we lived on now—my own money went into the joint account and went to pay monthly bills, while she kept hers in a separate account which she controlled.

I didn't even know how much she had, and when we came to the point of buying something, I had to ask, "Can we afford it?"

↔

My father had a heart attack several years after we moved to Maine. His need for attention was so great—and my own predicament required so much of my own attention—that we had never been close. He had the heart attack the day before the four of us were to go to Tennessee to visit Naomi's family. I went to South Carolina, and Naomi and the children went to Knoxville.

The waiting room of the hospital—a square box of a room painted institutional green with brown leatherette chairs and sofas—was filled with family members, Cornelius and Henrietta, Mother, Aunt Caroline, Uncle Richmond, and various cousins. Just after I walked in, I heard the full, tremulous voice of the bishop of South Carolina, who walked in right after me, entering the room of distraught family members with the polished and professionally-caring manner of Episcopal clerics. I went in to my father and left the bishop to attend to Mother.

Daddy lay in the bed with his eyes closed. Apparently he was dying, although the doctors said that he might survive as long as six months. They didn't know. I stood by the bed. I slid my fingers into my father's hand and held it for a few moments.

He spoke. "Oh you've come. I am sorry. I know this is spring break. I didn't mean for them to interrupt your vacation."

"I am very sorry, Daddy." My father didn't respond. I could hear the bishop in the outer room. *How do priests make their voices sound like that? Imposing.* "I love you."

My father waited a moment before speaking. "I know you do."

I know you do. I did love him. I hadn't expected him to say that he knew that I did, and it seemed like a gift. He could have punished me by saying that he had not known I loved him—I would have remembered that forever—so it had never been as bad as I had thought it was. I had wanted to be able to dislike his beliefs without telling him that I disliked *him.* That was what I had wanted from them, too.

Naomi wanted me to join them in Knoxville, so I left Columbia, left my father, who knew I loved him, and went to Naomi and the children. On the plane I thought of the number of times in the last forty-eight hours I had heard people say Daddy was a "gentleman." I don't often hear that word in my present life in Maine, and it was odd to hear it in South Carolina. The idea of a gentleman was classist and sexist and racist. We returned to Maine Sunday night.

Three days later, when Cornelius called to say my father had died, we went back to the airport and got on a plane and went to South Carolina. The plane kept putting down at one little airport after another, from Maine to South Carolina, and each time we took off again, the stewardess brought me two little bottles of bourbon with two plastic cups of ice, and when we finally got off the plane in South Carolina for my father's funeral, I was drunk.

I knew my father was an angry man, that he was intelligent, demanding, funny, "cute" my Aunt Caroline said, but I didn't *know* him. His father had died when my father was about twelve. What sense of loss had he experienced all his life? I knew that my father had defended me when I was a kid and unable to throw the ball and had run into the house from the garden, screaming, "Goddamn you! Goddamn you!" while Cornelius had laughed at me and Mother wanted to punish me. He had told her to wait. "It's OK," he said. He had *known* something that day. In the limousine on the way to the church, at Trinity, and then later at the cemetery, I wondered what my father's life had been like with Mother. Bounded by her family, Trinity, debutantes, she had never seen the larger picture that my father had seen. It must have been paralyzing for him to be married to her, without the option of divorce. He had been driven to the right, to hate the Kennedys, blacks, Jews. I wondered what he had thought of queers—he would have accepted me before Mother did—and was glad he was dead.

After the service, my mother, in her absurd, forties hair-do, swooping up and over the back of her head, refused to leave the seats under the tent. She wanted to stay while the gravediggers lowered the casket and shoveled in the dirt. The etiquette of the ceremony required that all the mourners, everyone who had come to the cemetery, had to stay too, for they could not leave until the principal mourner left. So we all stayed and listened while the gravediggers' shovels filled in the hole with soft dirt, which fell with muffled *thumps* into the pit. On the way home, my mother was in the first car with Cornelius and Henrietta, and Naomi and I were in the second car with Aunt Caroline and Uncle Richmond. Others were in cars that followed. Aunt Caroline asked the driver to take us past the graves of my grandmother Shaw and of the Fairs, Aunt Maury Fair and her sisters and their brother, Robert Fair, whose name I bear. Everything was carefully maintained.

↔

"The news has been so depressing this week, it has been hard to read the newspapers. Did you read *Time?*" The Jonestown suicides had happened two weeks before. "Appalling." We were having people for dinner.

"What makes people join cults?"

Naomi had prepared a huge roast, and people fixed small plates with salad and slices of roast beef and balanced them on their laps.

Everyone there was married—all our friends were married, and all had children.

The doctor from next door came into the living room, where I was standing next to the piano. He raised his glass to me. "You have a great life. Summers off. Long vacations at Christmas—when do you go back to teaching, the middle of January?—Spring Break, a long weekend at Thanksgiving." He grinned. "I should have gone into teaching." He was a good-looking guy and had a good body—I had seen his weights at their house—but he was shy, and, I thought, probably dominated by his wife. I thought it was probably his wife who had talked him into buying the house next door. He was leaving out that at the hospital he earned four or five times what I earned at the university. "God, I have to put in the hours. Now that I'm finished with my residency, I'd like to ease up a little."

We talked about his house. "We're in a cash crunch right now. There is all this stuff our house needs—" It was forty years older than our house. "—and then," he laughed, "there's furniture! I had no idea a house like that would take so much furniture! Do you know we don't have *any*thing in the living room? And we've been in for two years?"

Young doctors had a bad reputation in the local real estate market. They came to town to stay for a while, with no cash and with enormous earning power and bottomless credit, and they were able to buy the biggest, grandest houses in the area—and found themselves so loaded up with debt they were unable to maintain and furnish the houses they had bought. In four or five years, they moved out of the area, leaving a battered house in worse shape than they had found it. Often these houses were distinguished by architecture and by history, and the doctors who bought them but didn't have money to maintain them were considered vandals by the real estate people. On the other hand, everybody was making money on them.

I talked to a man who used big work horses, bigger than I had ever seen before.

"I get them in Ohio. You have to go down for auctions. I go down and spend a week when the auctions are scheduled and check out what's available. I take my truck, and then I bring them back up here."

"But the thing I don't understand is why do you do it? You're a teacher."

"Teaching doesn't occupy enough of my energies."

There were two questions, the farming itself, and then the farming with animals instead of with tractors.

He grinned. "I hate machines."

While he farmed, his real source of income was the university— he was an employee of the State of Maine—and the farming was merely an expensive and bizarre hobby. There was another teacher at the university who had left Berkeley and moved to Maine to farm while getting most of his money from the taxpayers. He died when his tractor turned over on him. The back-to-the-land movement in the sixties had produced peculiar configurations in people's lives.

By this time, the house was crowded with people.

Naomi came into the living room. "Hello." She smiled. "How is the farming going?" She didn't bother to ask about his teaching. "I'd like to see your horses."

People talked about what a disappointment Jimmy Carter was, and about the effect of the recession on the state economy, which had never been strong, and the reductions in state appropriations for the university.

"I don't know how you and Naomi can do this kind of thing." It was the wife of a colleague. "I guess if you have a house this big, you need to invite a lot of people to fill it up, don't you?" We were standing in front of the fireplace where there was a small fire going in the coal grate, warming the seat of my pants. "I'd rather spend my money some other way, and my time too. If you didn't have this kind of party, we wouldn't have to come, and I could stay home and read a book. Is there one interesting person—aside from me and you—in this whole large house?" Then she said, "Why don't you leave Maine?"

"I can't. I haven't written a second book, and you know that is the only way to get out of a place like this."

"Then get to it, my man. Get out of here. You are going to die if you stay."

I was irritated. "Why don't you leave?"

She shrugged. "I am different from you. I can make accommodations you can't make. It won't kill me the way it will you. I don't know quite why that is, but it is. It's not that I am stronger than you, just different. Besides, I have the children, and I have Bobby," her husband, "and I can't leave them. Go on now, get out of here. You need a city."

"I think I need another drink." I was leaning back against the mantle, surveying the beautiful scene in front of us, my house, my guests, my town.

"You need to stop that, too. I saw you last week having lunch by yourself in the Cracker Box, and I noticed that you never got around to ordering *food*."

The living room was actually two adjoining parlors on the right side of the house, one behind the other, with matching black marble fireplaces with coal grates and ornate cast iron fronts. The windows in the two parlors went all the way to the floor and had wooden interior shutters, called Indian shutters in the area. There was a grand piano in the front parlor, and occasional chairs, and in the back parlor a large 1810 secretary, a glass and steel coffee table by a master of modern design, a sofa and chairs. Next to the two parlors, running from front to back, was a hallway with stairs. There were two doors in each parlor connecting to this hallway.

Our guests were reasonably dressed—coats, ties—but they looked like Mainers, like they came from a rural-to-forest environment. None of them were alcoholics, that I knew of. What craziness they had was tied to things like horses or obsessive-compulsive behavior around the faculty union. Most of them planned to stay here forever. One couple expected to retire here and then move back to New York City. Others liked the small town life, but not necessarily the university life. There were no out gay people at the university, and no out gay people at the party. There were single women in my house who could only have been termed "old maids." They were my age and had let Naomi and me know from the beginning that they wanted to get married but couldn't find a man.

"Would you kill yourself if I ordered you to drink Kool-Aid?" It was my older colleague, whose wife was also a lawyer.

I laughed. "I'd do anything you asked me to."

I leaned back against the mantle and talked with him. "Do you suppose they felt happy, dying for Jim Jones?"

"I think they thought they were dying for the Lord."

"I wonder what they were feeling. Were they afraid? Fearful that Jones wasn't right but afraid not to do what he wanted? Or do you suppose they were happy, dying with their teacher?" My eyes wandered around the room—these large handsome rooms—and rested on my guests, one after another, golden in the candlelight. "Maybe, on the other hand, they didn't know they were going to *die*. Maybe they thought it was just Kool-Aid. Just a cool drink in the heat. Maybe they knew they were going to die but were happy to be dying in the company of the teacher. Happy to do anything with him."

He listened, swirling his drink.

"Maybe it was that they were happy to be with each other, whatever that meant. Happy that they had friends and that they were in a community of friendly people. And they didn't care if that meant dying." My father had not seemed afraid of dying. He seemed merely uncomfortable, and death would be an end to that discomfort. My father had let his sense of class separate him from AA, which might have been a comfort in the last 30 years of his life.

It was a bad time. Carter wasn't right, and there was not anyone else on the horizon. The country had turned right with the turn into the new decade—there had been Watergate and the end of the Vietnam war—and now people seemed to want to hunker down in a place where it was warm, hunker down with old comfortable beliefs about God and the countryside. People I know—these people at my party—don't like cities. In 1975, President Ford had said to New York: *Drop Dead.* People who hate machines seem also to hate the cities. The only people who come to Maine as a way station on the way to something else are doctors. Vandals. Sexy vandals. Most of my guests saw it as the end of the road.

The men who peopled the bars and taverns of *City of Night* were a bizarre collection—far more bizarre than my own guests—and they knew it. There was Miss Destiny, who wanted to come down a winding staircase at her wedding, and who had a vision of hell: "'*Oh, God!*...Sometimes when Im very high and sitting maybe at the 1-2-3, I imagine that an angel suddenly appears and stands on the balcony where the band is going—or maybe Im on Main Street or in Pershing Square—and the angel says, "All right, boys and girls, this is it, the world is ending, and Heaven or Hell will be to spend eternity just as you are now, in the same place among the same people—*Forever!*" And hearing this, Im terrified and I know suddenly what that means —and I start to run but I cant run fast enough for the evil angel, he sees me and stops me and Im Caught....'" Or Chi-Chi, in New Orleans at Mardi Gras, about whom the narrator says, "And you'll notice, beyond the lace drag, the idealized body of a powerful man. Her arms, beneath the delicate lace ruffles which dance up and down in curves, are bulgingly muscled, deeply vein-rooted. Her legs, supported precariously on the wobbly high-heeled witchshoes when she stands, reveal themselves strong and firm, molded solidly, massively, as if by years of physical labor or exercise which necessitates sustained straining." And Kathy. "'Kathy, … Kathy.' 'Yes, baby?' 'Why are you smiling?' 'Because,' she said easily, 'Im going to die.'"

I talked to my guests, and to Naomi, and drank until very late in the evening when finally everyone went home. There hadn't been a man at the party I had wanted, aside from my next door neighbor the doctor maybe, and I knew I was going to die.

↔

I didn't decide to quit drinking so much as I did it, in the same way I was doing everything, in a trance or somnolent state of semi-consciousness. It didn't even seem hard for me to do, because I couldn't think that it would be hard. I couldn't think enough about tomorrow to know that tomorrow would be hell. *I am going to do this,* and I dove off the cliff into the cold, deep water.

I picked up the phone and called a man I knew at the university and asked, "Who would you call around here if your problem was alcohol?"

"Rosenthal, Eastern Maine Medical Center."

I looked up the number for the Eastern Maine Medical Center, called Dr. Rosenthal, and on Friday, March 23, 1979, when I was 39 years old—my father's age when he quit drinking—I entered the hospital for 28 days for alcohol treatment.

Naomi was in Tennessee with her parents, and I told her, and she cried, but I said there was nothing else to do. I told Judith and Ames one night after they had taken their baths and were dressed for bed. "I want you to remember that I love you, and I will love you all the days of your life."

I went through the same wrenching experience everybody else went through—that my father had gone through 32 years earlier— who was an alcoholic and who must quit drinking. The first week, I was medicated on Valium, and after that I felt disoriented and drugged like the day I woke up in the Vanderbilt Hospital and thought my consciousness was caving in.

Each patient was assigned a counselor, and mine was a white-haired English woman, perhaps 50 or so, the wife of a retired American diplomat. She said, "So, what do you want to do with the rest of your life?"

I sat bent over with my head on my hands.

"Get rid of the life I have."

She laughed. "What do you mean by that?"

"Divorce my wife and leave the university."

"They all say that."

She told me to go to meetings.

Naomi came to the hospital almost every day. One day, sitting in a small room for visitors, she opened her bag and put on the table the mail I had received.

"The bookstore at the university called and said the book you ordered came in. I picked it up for you." She pulled it out of her bag. It was *Dancer from the Dance* by Andrew Holleran. It had been reviewed in *The New York Times Book Review* several weeks before. The reviewer had said it was the finest gay novel to come out since Stonewall.

265

"I read it." She looked at me, distressed. "I have to tell you that I don't think homosexuality is as good as heterosexuality."

I was suddenly on the Mountain in Patrick Endicott's office. "OK. But I am still gay." I was angry with her for reading my book before I had read it. I was angry with her for reading a book *of mine*. It was an invasion of my privacy. I don't think I had ever before cared whether someone read one of my books, but now I cared that she had put a judgment on a book I wanted to read, before I had had a chance to read it myself. In my present state in rehab I was too drugged-up to actually read *Dancer from the Dance*.

I settled in to being sober. Sometimes it takes several years to clear up, and during that time Naomi and I substituted friends who didn't drink for friends who did. It became too awkward, too uncomfortable, to have friends over who were drinking when I wasn't, and it was too difficult to go places where they were serving alcohol. Also, I found pretty quickly that the only thing I found interesting was recovery from alcoholism, and the only people interested in that were people who had gone through that process themselves. So I gradually found my friends in AA. Naomi and I parented our children, and we worked on our house, went to AA and Al-Anon meetings, but we had our separate jobs and separate lives and shared nothing else.

Our house was on the edge of a plateau that fell away to low ground that ran to the river and was regularly flooded in the spring runoffs. Ames and I crossed the railroad tracks and went down into the lowland, and then on to the Penobscot River. Ames was excited. "A kid who has this in his backyard doesn't need to go to summer camp!" I painted a nine-foot square on the driveway, divided into quarters, and when I got home from the university in the afternoon, Ames and his friends were playing there with a ball.

I started reading *The Lord of the Rings* to them, me sitting in the middle of a full-sized bed and Ames and Judith on either side. I read using distinct voices for each character, and, of course, they liked the low rumble of the Ents best of all. Ames stuck with me through the whole three volumes. Judith, in the middle of *The Return of the King*, grew impatient and read the rest of it to herself, which was faster.

I went to a support group for gay men recovering from alcoholism. At the kitchen table, Naomi looked at me. "I didn't know you were going to that group. Why are you going to that group?"

"I am a gay alcoholic."

She started crying. Her face was contorted, tears ran down her cheeks, her chin quivered. Her hands were shaking. "How can you do this to me? Look what you are doing to me!" She was sobbing. "Look at me!"

I saw her very clearly at that moment.

"I can see that you are crying. I can't help that. You are crying to make me get back in line—which is to deny I am gay. You can cry or not cry, but I am a gay alcoholic going to a support group for gay alcoholics. You can think what you'd like, one way or the other, about homosexuality, but I have to tell you that I am not going to stay married to a woman who dislikes being married to a gay man. That's what I am. I am gay, and that is not going to change, and I am not going to apologize for it, to you or to anybody."

I went further. "I think if we are creative about this, we can come through it. But it has to be something we share. It can't be my problem only. If we do this now, while I still want to be married to you—"

I suggested she go to therapy—a licensed social worker—to see if she could get help, and we both did, briefly, but she quit going after two sessions. She said there was nothing wrong with *her*. I told her then that I took back all my marriage vows. "I don't know how long we will be married, but I no longer promise to be married to you *till death do us part.* And I no longer promise to be monogamous. I will stay married to you only so long as it is good for me."

She stared at me, this time not crying.

Our house was being painted. The painters were in the yard, chipping away at old paint, the shutters from the house on saw-horses. One of the painters was an effeminate young man in his early twenties. When Naomi walked in from the garden, I was at the kitchen table where I saw them through the window. She looked out the window at the painters, the effeminate young man queening it in their midst, and said, "I couldn't bear for you to be like that." She was pushing me very hard to get back in line, and I was aware of it. I shrugged.

Her legal work threw her in contact with women's groups around the state, and I hardly recognized her. She had become what we had disliked. She was plugged into the power structure of the state, and she seemed to have forgotten what we had believed together—that power corrupted. She had become a woman concerned with her business, and at the same time she played the victim, acting as if I had chosen purposefully to do this to her. For Naomi, I became the villain, and I didn't know how she had gotten there from where we had started together.

The rule, which was laid down for each new AA member, was *Go to ninety meetings in ninety days.* In the Bangor area, the meeting held at the hospital was quite large—two hundred people—but most were small neighborhood meetings. There was a range of people, lumbermen, paper mill workers and management, university students, professors, staff of all kinds, townspeople. I reoriented my life around Alcoholics Anonymous and learned what it meant to stay sober. *The most important thing is not to drink.*

I wrote Mother and told her I was an alcoholic.

"How could you have deliberately become an alcoholic, after all the pain that alcohol has caused us in our lives?"

One wondered. I wrote this: "After Cornelius settled down and got a job and married Henrietta, he could do no wrong, I became the black sheep of our family. I couldn't do anything right. I had a PhD, a published book, a wife and children, and taught in a university, and you never could find it in yourself to approve."

She wrote that I was wrong.

I wrote her that I was gay.

"I am stunned. How long have you known you were a hommo? (sp?)" She wrote, "I know nothing about it." She asked me if Cornelius knew, and I told her Cornelius had known for fifteen years. "How odd. Why didn't I know?"

"Because you didn't like Jews and blacks. You didn't like anybody except people like yourself, and I knew that from my childhood. I *knew* you would turn on me if I told you when I first found out—when I was eleven."

She didn't mention it again. She wrote me, "All you ever do is criticize me."

Gradually, it happened that my best friends were in AA, some who had been around for years, some who were as new as I. One, who was even newer than I by several weeks, was a man, early thirties, a painter, who took to me, asked me to pick him up on my way to the meeting, suggested we have coffee afterward, and began to call. His name was Andy Darwell—actually Anderson Darwell—

but he signed his pictures *A. Darwell*, in a tall, thin, waving script that he put on his paintings, apparently with a fountain pen. He was tall, had long brown hair that curled around his throat, and always had paint under his fingernails. He lived in a loft in the center of town, and one night he showed me his paintings there, in which half-asleep figures with thin, flowing garments floated and tumbled through bubbling royal blue waters, suggesting a reverie, a dream, as if all of life were a prolonged gestation.

"How does it feel to be gay around here?"

"I'm lonely."

"But you live well."

"But I live well." I always had to acknowledge that.

He wasn't gay, but he seemed to like to talk, and for the first time in a long time, I was having coffee with someone who wanted to know about the South. Andy was unselfconscious about his beauty, but I think he was aware of the energy between us. It was a pleasure, working through the problems of the Big Book with him.

I read *Dancer from the Dance*. It is about Malone, who is a little slow coming out—he doesn't do it until his middle twenties—and when he does, he goes to New York. He is middle-class, beautiful, well-educated, restrained, well-mannered, and he does the things I didn't do, even to picking up a man, Frankie Oliveiri, an Italian-American subway worker, and falling in love with him. Malone seems to be from the same kind of middle-class family as I am, so I read the book, looking for myself in the Everard Baths, on Fire Island, on the Lower East Side, amidst all the sex. The book ends mysteriously. Malone may have run away from his world in New York and Fire Island, or he may have committed suicide, and it doesn't provide the kind of happily-ever-after ending that I had hoped for. The timing is unclear, but it appears Malone was my age. He seems to have walked into the waters of Long Island Sound when he was just my age, late thirties.

For the first time since my freshman year at Sewanee, I took up swimming. I bought a Speedo and goggles, a gym bag, and started going to the swimming pool at the university during my lunch hour. At first it was rough—I hadn't done laps since I was eighteen—but I liked the way I felt after a swim, and I began to like the way my body felt to my touch. I hardened up, and my muscles got bigger, particularly my shoulders and chest and back. Being an academic

269

and thinking that one started with a book in any endeavor, I bought a book on swimming that had a chapter on weight training, so I bought a set of weights and a weight bench. I bought a book on that, too, and started buying the muscle magazines—the same ones I had bought when I was 13 and jerked off to—to read about the training programs, in addition to looking at the pictures. This time I didn't hide them. I swam every day and lifted every other day and was amazed when I looked at myself in the mirror. I looked younger, stronger, athletic, and began to feel energetic, and not as if I were going to die.

In the summer of 1982 Naomi and I and the children prepared to go to London for a sabbatical year. I was supposed to do research in the British Museum for a new book—I still had no idea what to do research on—but my real reason was to get away from Maine. I had made friends in AA—Andy, an ironworker, a carpenter, a teacher— and I wanted to spend a day at the lake with these guys before I went away for a year. Naomi was opposed—I think she thought there might be sex if four guys went to the lake together—and I gave in to her, as I gave in to her in most things. I wanted to go on a bike trip to the coast alone, and she was also opposed to that.

On returning to London from Scotland in September, I was walking along South Eaton Place in Belgravia one morning, thinking about my life, when the thought that I had not been able to conceive reached full expression in my head. *Get a divorce.* It had no conscious antecedent in my mind. The thing was true and right, beyond all argument.

For several months, I carried the thought around in my head. *Get a divorce.* It would be hard, but Naomi and the children would be OK. Judith was 13 and Ames was 11, and they would be OK, at least in part because *I* would be OK, and I would be able to love them. I went to Southwark every day to a gym, and to an AA meeting in Bloomsbury and to the British Museum in the afternoon to read, searching for something to write a book on. At the gym, I made friends, a white man who was the star of the morning crowd at the gym and a black man with a deep South London accent that I found very confusing.

I came home from an AA meeting in the basement of St Martin's-in-the-Fields, and found Naomi on the sofa in the living room, reading a book. The house was quiet, and the children asleep. It began with her posing a question to me.

"We don't talk enough." She was concerned. "I feel as if we haven't talked in days. How are you? Are you OK?" It was at this point, in the past, when I would reassure her that all was well.

"I think so. I have been—" I couldn't think of a word. "—disordered, I suppose I could call it, recently, since last spring. Nothing seems to help." I was answering in a different way, and she was tensing up. I sat down on the sofa. "The reason is us. I am not able to get beyond *us*." I listened to the sound of the traffic outside. "I knew that I couldn't do anything about myself until I quit drinking, but quitting drinking exposed other problems." Naomi sat at the other end of the sofa, her ankles crossed, looking at me. I had thought all this through beforehand, and what I was saying was rehearsed. I began to hear my voice, as if from a distance, echoing down a hall. "We got married at a time when people thought that was what gay men should do, and then we discovered that it didn't work. We should not have gotten married. The Stonewall Rebellion occurred, and out there now are gay men living happy, productive, fulfilled lives as gay men. You seem to feel that you will be happiest married to a gay man, but you don't seem happy to me. And while you want to be married to a gay man, you don't want him to be gay. You have never found a way to be comfortable married to a gay man. We were married, Naomi, before the world was divided into gay and straight. Now it is, and we ended up on opposing sides. Our marriage can't lead to happiness for me. I wanted to be here with you and Ames and Judith when they were growing up, but that's impossible. When I get back to the US, I am going to sue for divorce." She heard me out. There was a long silence after I finished. We both knew this was momentous.

Finally she spoke. "I don't know how long I have been afraid you would say this."

"I'm sorry."

"Is there something we can do?" She started to cry.

I spoke slowly. "No. It's over, now, Naomi. Our marriage is over." I had no idea if leaving her was the solution to everything, but I knew that it was a step.

"*Over?*"

"*Over.*"

The next night, when the children were in bed and we could speak again, she raised the issue again of what we could do.

"There's nothing we can do." I was afraid of her tears. I was afraid if I allowed any kind of discussion of this that I would not be able to hold onto what I needed to do. "I am very sorry, Naomi, but our marriage is over, as of yesterday."

"How can you say that—" She seemed truly bewildered. "—when we've had all this time together, how can you just end it like this?"

I waited for a moment. "If we had worked it out ten years ago, or fifteen, or five, *sometime* before now, we might have been able to do it. But we didn't. Now it is too late."

"How can *you* be the one to say it is too late?"

"I didn't decide one day it was too late, I *discovered* one day it was too late. It came to me. It was when I realized I didn't want to be married to you any more. I can't go back now to the time when I wanted to be married to you. If we had been able to work things out, somehow, while I still wanted to be married to you, we might have saved our marriage. But we didn't, and now I don't, and it is too late."

She cried. "Christ, I'm angry at you."

"I am gay, Naomi. Marriage to a woman—in our culture—is for straight men. What do you want me to do?"

"Do what you have done since 1965."

"I can't stay married to you and feel good about myself. I can't stay married to you and stay sober at the same time. The only way I was able to stay married to you was to stay drunk all the time." We had, years ago, fallen into the rut where sex was about pleasing her.

She didn't say anything for a time. "What is so important that you are willing to cause me and the children so much pain?"

"I am." What that meant was that somehow, in some way, a marriage had to be based on the respect the two parties had for each other, yet Naomi had no real respect for me as a gay man. I needed to be in a relationship where what I was, was honored. Naomi could not do that.

"We need to talk about the children." I was forcing this on her. "The first thing the children will want to be assured of is that they are going to be taken care of. They will want to stay where they are, in their house, and I suppose you will want to stay there also. So I believe that when we tell them, we should say that their lives will be disturbed as little as possible, that you and they will continue to live where you now live, and that I will live nearby. We will work out some division of what we own to care for the children and their education."

She seemed to assent.

"I think we need to be explicit that our divorce is not their fault, that we both love them, and that we will continue to love them."

We didn't plan to tell them right away, but Naomi cried at unexpected moments during the day, and the children would soon know, if they didn't already, that something was going on. I told them after supper one night. I had been right, their first need was to know what was going to happen to them. Judith was angry, and Ames was desolate. "Please remember what I say. This is not your fault, and we both still love both of you. And we will both still be in your lives from now on, just in a different way. I am getting a divorce because I am a gay man." They knew what that meant. "I can't feel good about myself in this marriage."

I rented a bed-sit and moved out.

↔

I saw the children every day, at first going over to the house for the evening meal and then later picking them up and going out for fish and chips or pizza. In the afternoons, I went by Judith's or Ames's school and walked home with them. When they had friends from America visiting, I took them all to the Tower.

Once I had told Naomi and the children, I did what I had to do, and I said the things that had to be said. I had difficulty breathing, and difficulty sleeping, but I didn't waver. Once I told her that I was going to seek a divorce when we got back to the States, I refused to be drawn into a discussion of our marriage, which was now over.

Naomi now wanted to talk all the time, and she called me at my bed-sit to talk.

"We're the two most intimately involved, and we should be able to comfort one another."

But I was afraid I would not be able to hold out against her and the powerful weapons she had at her disposal—both our families were lining up on her side—and I would not give in to her. I steeled myself against her.

Within a few days of moving out of the house in London. I picked up a young dude in Knightsbridge and took him back to my apartment and had sex. I went to gay AA and met gay men there, and took them home and had sex, and went to Suffolk to spend a weekend with two gay Brits at a 300-year-old cottage on a village green across from an even older church. These two had been together for fifteen years, and they had guests other than me for the weekend. I was fascinated by the fact that these were gay men who had been together almost as long as Naomi and I had been together, and I began to know that I had much to learn. At an AA meeting, I met a tremendously sexy man who arranged a weekend for the two of us at Oxford, where we had sex in an old inn. The next morning, after breakfast, we had the innkeeper make us a couple of picnic boxes and rented a punt for several hours. I was told by my gay friends in London not to go back to America before I had gone to Amsterdam. I stayed in a small gay hotel called The New Yorker in a seventeenth century house on a canal, where I had sex with both the owner and his lover, and went out twice a day and had sex at the Day Baths and at the Night Baths. I went to Denmark and had sex with a tall blond Dane who looked like a Viking, and then I came back to London and picked up men in the parks and brought them back to my bed-sit and had long, hot, intense sex.

Judith and Ames joined me for the movies—I took them to the second *Star Wars* movie, and I took them one weekend to the south coast, to Cornwall, to St Michael's Mount, and to Salisbury Cathedral—but their trauma was written across their faces and was impossible not to see. They had a right to a life they were at the center of, and right now they were terribly off balance. They were afraid of me, afraid of what I might do—or not do—and they didn't know whether I still loved them. I tried to soothe their fears, but it was difficult.

The Royal Academy held an exhibition on the English landscape with particular attention to Richard Wilson. The pictures were all paintings similar to the image of Wespanee that I had carried around in my head since I was ten. There was such a thing as an "English country house painting," which had predictable elements—a large house, the owner of the house and his family at their ease on a lawn or under a shade tree, several farm workers from the estate demonstrating their own leisure and pleasure, and, surrounding all, the grounds of the estate. The catalogue said that these paintings emphasized the natural order of things—God in his heaven, the king on his throne, the lord on his lawn in front of his house, and the workers, happy in the fields—and minimized the equation that the magnificence of the lord's estate depended on the relative poverty of the estate workers. It was a myth that people adopted to minimize the trauma of living in a chaotic and economically rapacious world.

Our separation and divorce were ugly, long, and difficult. Frankie, in *Dancer from the Dance*, had simply left his wife and child, but that was only in a novel. I wrote Mother. "I have tried for 16 years to make a success of my marriage, but I am a gay man, and I can no longer pretend that I am not." For the next several weeks, I got one or two letters from her every day, her anger scrawled across the page, five or six lines to the page. She was traumatized by what I proposed to do, and she didn't know how to talk about it, what words to use, or what thoughts she was supposed to have. She wrote me not to tell my brother "because Cornelius has so much on him right now. His oldest son is graduating from college, and they are having a big party—."

She went to her doctor and asked him about homosexuality. He told her that he didn't know anything about it either, "except that they're all going to die of this new disease everyone is talking about." She seemed to make an effort to be understanding—"If you can't be a husband to Naomi, then it is best for you to get a divorce."—but she wrote Naomi. I found the letter on the dining room table when I went over to pick up the children. "He says he's talking to gay alcoholics. What do gay alcoholics know about anything?" She also wrote me, "Now that you have come out, you won't be able to teach any more." She meant that homosexuals shouldn't be allowed to work with children. She had forgotten that I had told her I was gay two years before. Cornelius did not write or call, and Henrietta waited to write until I had come back to Maine from London seven months later, after her party for the graduate. She spoke of hearing about my "troubles" and said, "We love you both." Then she never mentioned it again. Her letters were all about her children, little social notes on flowered paper, often on Christmas cards during all seasons of the year, and she never answered my letters. Neither she nor Cornelius ever used the word "gay." I had hoped that once I decided to leave Naomi my family would accept it as a fact and accept me as a gay man, but it didn't happen, and I was bitter. My mother told me that Cornelius thought I had been "selfish" to leave Naomi and the children. Henrietta told Mother that I had embarrassed the whole family. My sister-in-law had said to Mother, "I have plenty of gay friends who are married. They have Tuesday nights off." But to me directly they maintained silence.

What a waste. When a person asks that kind of sacrifice from you, it is always stupid to give them what they want, because just asking that much shows they have no lively idea about your reality. They will ask for the sacrifice—"Do it for me, dear, please."—and when you have made the sacrifice, they will forget that it was a sacrifice and that it was they who asked you for it.

I wrote Andy.

> I left Naomi at the end of last month (that is, two weeks ago) and moved to a bedsit in South London. I would not imagine that you are surprised about this. This didn't come about because of a crisis (although it caused a crisis, certainly). Rather, it seemed to have happened because one day I was able to conceive of a divorce. Once I could conceive of it, the idea was suddenly fully-grown in my brain. I have never been surer of anything in my life.
>
> I did not write you earlier because it was important to go through the initial steps (telling Naomi, telling the children, telling my family) before I broke into that chain and told anyone who also mattered to me. I have thought of you every day, even though I have not been writing you. You are with me, and I appreciate your comforting presence.
>
> I see the children every day, except when Naomi has taken them off somewhere. I also see Naomi every day. Naomi does not forgive me and cannot believe I am destroying our marriage in this way. She cries seemingly all the time, and she is *very* angry. I have told her I will not change my mind. I am *way* ahead of Naomi and my mother and other

straight people I have corresponded with. I assume
you will be with me.

This is all going to work out. The kids are trying
hard to keep a relationship with me in the face of
some pretty horrendous opposition, and as long as
they still want to have a connection, we'll manage,
and we'll come out OK in the end. Their maternal
grandparents are urging them to abandon me.

Right now life sucks. But there are some good
things. We saw the Royal Shakespeare Company
Twelfth Night in Stratford, directed by Trevor Nunn.
It opens with a set taken directly out of a Piranesi
print—piles of trash almost sinking the lopsided gate
posts of Olivia's house. In short, the play opens just
after the end of the Roman Empire and you feel the
presence of death, rot, decay, and the ends of things.
On the other hand, with such a setting, one knows
there are treasures buried under all that debris—the
Belvedere torso, for one thing—and love, once
discovered, will triumph over the devastation of
Empire. It is a magnificent production. We saw it on
April 24, 1983. Happy Birthday.

Two days ago I saw Helen Mirren playing
Cleopatra at a small theatre in the Barbican—she
played it barefoot—and I also spend a lot of time in
museums and galleries. I will write you soon about
the Wallace Collection.

I go to meetings everyday at noon in
Bloomsbury, and I still go to the gym every day in
South London.

After I returned to America, I was myself—for whom a "social
life" had been as important as breathing—dropped from the social
life of the Department and very quickly lost contact with the people I
worked with and with what friends Naomi and I had had in town.
Naomi stopped talking to me. We communicated now only about
money—child support and about arrangements for the children but
not about the children.

I found, however, that there were people in Maine. For three years, I had been discovering the recovering alcoholics at meetings all around the Bangor area and found among them the intimacy that I had lost when I left Ann Arbor. Now, among a smaller group, I found the gay recovering alcoholics, who were mostly kids, just out of high school, college age, and early twenties. To them, I think, I was the father they were still searching for. For me, they were *me*, young and gay, slightly battered, but with a chance and with hope. My phone rang all the time.

I could hardly talk to my family about anything that mattered, and yet, still, underneath it all, I felt a powerful need for us to remain connected. I understood more deeply than they did what was happening to us as I moved from the straight world into the gay world. It was possible for all of us to remain connected *if* we— Cornelius and I—remained in communication, if we talked to each other constantly. If we didn't, I would drift on into the gay world, and they would drift deeper into whatever world they were in, and the distance between us would increase and increase until we could no longer reach out and touch one another, no longer imagine each other's worlds, and we would lose each other.

It was always there in my head, a sense that I was losing everything—the *root* of everything—that mattered to me. My mother and my brother didn't seem to know that *right now* was the time they needed to get off their asses and *talk* seriously.

I lay on my bed at night and felt it—the grief—and it gradually went away. I thought about my name *Fair*, which carried with it the images of, even the odors of, Aunt Maury Fair and my grandmother, and my memory of their father's graveside monument in Columbia, and of Uncle Robert's long entanglement with us—I had been named after him—and the three hundred years stretching back past the whole of the history of the United States, to the deeper, more brilliant colonial period, back to Mark Fair and 1633 and Dedham, none of which now had anything to do with my life as a gay man in Orono, Maine. I thought about my cousins and my aunts and uncles, and I thought those people were welcome to come along with me on the journey I was beginning, but it would be OK if they chose not to, and I was going on my journey whether they came or not.

Why are people not delighted when a guy comes out? The first instinctive response of people here in Maine—and in South Carolina

—to my ending my marriage to Naomi was to condemn me. And that from just about everybody. You would have thought that, on almost any social issue, there would be some people who disagreed, who did not go along with the dominant view. But in this case, almost every single person that I was aware of thought it was a despicable thing that I was doing. That's amazing. If you proposed the end of the income tax, people would have differing views on that proposal, but apparently all of my former friends, all of the people I worked with, all of the members of my family—*all* these people thought I was doing a terrible thing. That is astonishing. Some people must think that the state of marriage is so inviolate that there are no reasons for breaking it. If there is a reason, I have it, but I have not encountered one person—except gay people—who finds that being gay is a legitimate reason to leave a marriage. I suspect, however, that some of these heterosexuals have something else going on. It may be that what is happening is the expression of a personal animosity toward me—people think that I am a shit—but it is unlikely that every single straight person in town thinks I am a shit. So I think something else, something bigger, is going on. What I did, when I left Naomi, reminded them of how important and irrepressible sex is. It is *so* important that even marriages have to bow down before it, and people don't like to hear that, because for generations straight people have told queers to just *suck it up*. Give up sex, and live according to our rules. And I think that the furor caused by my leaving Naomi—I have been told that my leaving Naomi was the biggest scandal in this town in years—reminds them of just how homophobic our culture is, and they don't want to know these things.

I had never been close to people in the department, but in the year after I returned to Maine from London, I was isolated by their design. I was invited nowhere, and in the faculty lounge where members went to pick up mail, I have been ignored, and when I speak to colleagues, they make excuses and leave. I never liked it in Maine—many people who moved to Maine had in mind a certain kind of rural life that held no interest for me—so one morning, I went in to the department chair and told him I was resigning at the end of the school year, in August 1984. I didn't know what I would do for a living, but whatever it was, I would not be doing it here, in Maine.

There was another reason for leaving Maine. Naomi had taken steps to treat me like a battering husband. She required that I call before I came by the house to get the children "even if all of us know beforehand you are coming," and she didn't want to allow me to come into her house when I came to get the children. We were headed toward an angry divorce.

There were few gay people included among the people I knew, a high school teacher and a few others. I found out I was the only out gay man on a university faculty of 500. Once, a woman I knew who worked with Naomi on the board of a local feminist organization—she seemed to feel she had to explain herself—said to me, "I am sure you will understand in this difficult time, now that you and Naomi are separated, that my loyalties are to Naomi, and I intend to be supportive of her, now that you have come out."

I heard her, and said, "Oh, sure," not caring about this particular woman. This woman was herself a lesbian and had worked with Naomi in various organizations around town for a number of years, and the way she was sorting out her priorities interested me.

She went on, "I only have one thing to say to you. And that is this: 'What took you so long?'" She raised her eyebrow.

It had something to do with the timing of my leaving Naomi, which did not please her. When I did what she seemed to have thought that I should do, she decided to give emotional support to the person I had to act against, and she was clear in her refusal to give me emotional support while I did what she thought I should do. I had supported the goals of the women's movement since at least 1968—for fifteen years—and now I found that women active in the women's movement in the area had turned on me. A colleague joined me in the dining hall at lunch one day—he was curious about what was happening to me—and had hardly sat down to the table when he said, laughing, "Shaw, you have infuriated every single feminist we know."

I shrugged. "I am a gay man, Branch. My marriage didn't work. I left. Now what do you want me to say?"

At a small meeting of four professors, a male colleague turned to me when the meeting was over, as the other members were gathering their books and papers together, and said, "You have done two horrible things to your wife."

It seemed to be the way I lived my life.

"I know what you're talking about. I am an alcoholic. Alcoholism is to some degree inherited. No one becomes an alcoholic on purpose. I don't owe anyone an apology for being an alcoholic. As for being gay, I was born gay. I got married in a time when every major institution in our culture said that *getting married* was the right thing to do for gay men. Every psychiatrist I ever saw recommended that. They also said they could 'cure' me. They were wrong. They were ignorant of what they were doing. Naomi has known since before we were married that I was gay. I know that because I told her. We were both victims of our ignorant culture. And you, my friend, are as ignorant and judgmental as our ignorant and judgmental culture. I have done nothing wrong to anybody, and I owe no apologies. And you can tell people I said that."

↔

On the way from the straight world into what passed for a gay world in Maine, that is, on the way toward coming out into the gay world— as is the way with all traveling—I passed people on the road who were on their own journeys.

The phone rang in the early evening, and this indecipherable south London accent came on the phone. It was the big blond man about ten years younger than I who was friendly when we introduced ourselves in the gym in Southwark. He had long, thick, unkempt hair and was about six feet and 225 pounds. He had the kind of big, well-shaped muscles that some bodybuilders had—broad shoulders, thick chest muscles, and narrow hips. That fall, he and his girl friend had invited me and Naomi to the theatre, but when I called him and suggested we get together—just us two—he had said he was busy.

"Are you sorry you went back to the States without getting to know me better?"

I laughed. "Of course." This time, since I had officially left Naomi and was living alone, I wanted to be sure that my situation and I both were clear. "Were *you* sorry?"

The voice on the other end hesitated, then said tentatively, "Uh, yeah, I think so."

"Well, you could have, if you had wanted to. I called you and invited you."

"Uh, I couldn't, then."

281

"And now you want to."

"Uh, yeah."

"Let's be clear what we're talking about. I'm gay, and you're a big sexy guy, and I wanted you when I was in London, but you didn't want anything to do with me, and now that I am back in the States you want—what? What is it you want now?"

"You like my body?" He was the star of the gym during the hours I was there.

"I think everybody does."

He grunted. He was talking just above a whisper.

"Why are you whispering?"

He didn't answer at first. "I'm not alone."

I saw what it was. "You have your girlfriend in your flat with you and its—" I checked my watch and saw it must be one a.m. in London. "—one a.m. and she's asleep, and you're outside in the hall talking, whispering, to me about sex."

"Uh-huh," he said. "That's pretty much it."

I told him I couldn't come back to London anytime soon—my divorce was going to be expensive—and invited him to come to the States. But he said he couldn't come, and he didn't write letters, but he would call again, *sometime.*

"Why didn't you ask me when you were here?"

"I did, big guy. Only I didn't know you were gay—"

"I'm not gay."

I laughed. "Then what are you proposing?"

He paused. "Maybe—let you do something."

Down there, in the parking lot, in the dark.

He called again several months later, and the call, like the first one, had the atmosphere of phone sex.

"Yeah, I'm sitting on the floor in the hall. I can't talk too loud."

"What do you have on?"

"A t-shirt."

"Pants?"

"No. Nothing. I'm holding my cock."

What was he? He had said he was not gay, but he wanted sex with me. Eventually, I ceased to think about him—as often as he had occupied me when I was going to the gym every morning in South London.

That kind of thing happened again. One afternoon in July, one month before I was to leave the university, a friend from AA called. He was a member of the large Franco-American population in the area, and we had become friends, going out for coffee after meetings and talking about working the program. He was older than I— perhaps 50—and was in the early years of his second marriage, and had grown children. He had a crewcut, large, sad eyes, and a compact, hard body, the result, I think, of spending a lot of time outdoors camping and hiking. He was a solid, interesting, stable man. He had seen me drinking at noontime at local dives before I quit, and we talked about that. We talked about divorce—"It took me seven years to get over my divorce," he said—and we talked about our children.

Now he was saying something different. "I'd like to talk to you about something."

"What's up?"

"It's about being gay." He spoke in a matter-of-fact way, as if he were talking about the conditions of the roads after snow.

"What about it?"

"Everybody I know seems to be doing it—"

I laughed. "You want to know what the attraction is?"

"I want to know more about it."

"Have you ever been attracted to a man?"

"Uh—no. In my mind."

"What do you mean?"

"I think about men sometimes when I am having sex with my wife."

"Sometimes?"

"All the time."

I suspected that this was getting close to home.

"Any particular person?"

He paused. "Uh—you."

"Me. Oh."

He wanted to get together. "I just want to talk."

Well, I said that would be OK.

But when he came over, he said, "Oh, sure, I've fantasized about you since I first learned who you were, when you first moved here from Michigan. I always think about you when I'm having sex."

"You fantasize about having sex with *me*?"

"Uh-uh. More like just seeing you—fantasizing about your body, about seeing you naked."

We were sitting on the sofa, a sofa small enough to put us fairly close to one another, but he made it clear that he didn't really want to have sex with me. After having a cup of coffee and talking for a few minutes, he left.

What was the connection between what he was doing with his body when he was having sex with his wife and what was going on in his mind?

In a movie Naomi and I had seen in Ann Arbor in our first year there, *Flesh,* by Paul Morrissey, Joe Dallesandro was on the street with a group of hustlers.

Joe spoke to one of the other hustlers.

> *You straight? (unintelligible answer) Nobody's straight. What's straight. (unintelligible answer) Being straight or being not straight. You just do whatever you have to do. (unintelligible answer) It's hard. It's hard to learn how to do that. But once you got that down pat, don't even worry about it no more—.*

Now, when I spoke in AA meetings, which was every night, I identified myself, "I'm Fair, and I'm an alcoholic—," and then I said, "—and I'm gay." That is, I came out in each meeting. I had written Andy from London that I was now officially out.

Back in Maine, at the pizza parlor after a meeting, Andy said, "Ah, man, you've been out forever. I knew you were gay from the first time I laid eyes on you." He pushed himself away from the table, back against the Naugahyde of the seat, grinning. "You never have been able to be closeted around me."

"Well, a lot of people never had a clue."

"Ah, man, the thing about you is how tense you are, as if you're working at some big thing that you don't know you're big enough to handle—or can get done in time—and it keeps you on edge. That's what gives you away. That, and how you look at me." He grinned.

I laughed. "You noticed that, did you?" Then, "Well, you *are* beautiful."

"Come on now. I'm an artist. *Beautiful* is not enough. Tell me something specific."

"OK. If that's what you want." I looked him over. He posed a little. "I think I'd begin with your hair, which—"

"I was pulling your leg, Fair."

"I know. Do you know there's a scene where—it's in *Twelfth Night*—where Olivia asks Viola to inventory her beauty? And Viola says, *item,* something or other, and then goes on to the next item? I'd be willing to inventory your beauty, Andy."

"I know. I know you would, and I love you for that, and *Jesus*, sometimes, the way things are going, it would be great to just sit here quietly while somebody else—while *you*—tell me I'm OK, because most of the time I don't think I'm OK—"

"I know. *I know.* You're OK, Andy. If we do this in a more organized fashion, it's called a Step Four."

"Will you be my sponsor?"

"Yes."

"Instead of itemizing my beauty, will you tell me whether you think I have any talent as a painter?"

"Yes, and it's nice to think that you think I've always been out. That's nice."

However, this was not the end of it. Beginning in London, at the *Gay's The Word* bookshop, after I left Naomi, and then at *Glad Day* in Boston, I had been reading about the condition of gay people in America, about the concepts of *gay* and *straight*. I had been reading British and Australian sociologists and French theorists, most of them books written in the last ten or fifteen years, since Stonewall. I had also been reading the gay weekly newspapers both in London and here in America—*Bay Windows, Gay Community News,* the *Washington Blade, New York Native.* And I re-read Kinsey's *Sexual Behavior in the Human Male* which I had first read when I was in the Army. Some of these books and newspapers assumed that the world was divided between gay people and straight people, and others followed Kinsey's continuum. There was no consensus.

While I was sorting these things out, I was getting phone calls from the bodybuilder in South London and from the Franco-American in Orono, who reminded me how little my culture understood these matters—or even had the language to describe them. Both of these men were straight—I had no reason to believe that either man was hiding something from himself—and yet one had proposed to have sex with me and the other thought of me while having sex with his wife. I knew how that was—I had thought of a host of men while having sex with my wife—but these men didn't seem to see that their actions and their language and their self-awareness were not synchronous. They were straight, but it was straight with a twist.

Where, in all this confusion of theory, were the boys at Sewanee and in the Army who seemed to feel they could have sex with anyone? Where was Connie Stephanopolis in all this? And the men who were so famous, whose celebrity was so brilliant, that they could call themselves one thing and yet everyone knew they were the other—so that there was no question of their being closeted?

This very complicated set of physical and emotional states and drives, this concept pushed at and shoved and kneaded by every force in the culture, this *thing* seen differently by almost everyone who experienced it, formed the defining characteristic of everyone in the population.

I had had the notion, when I had thought of it, that if I ever left Naomi everyone would understand my leaving her, including Naomi. It seemed self-evidently true in the current culture that a gay man should get out of a marriage, and yet people had hated it when I left her, hated me. People did not think being gay was a legitimate reason to leave a marriage. A gay man should not get married, but a gay man in a marriage should not get out. I tried to understand their thinking, these people who were condemning me for leaving Naomi. It was as if the culture had not decided what were the actions proper to a gay man and what were the actions proper to a straight man. It was like it was before God had separated the light from the dark and the ocean from the dry land.

And it was no wonder. There is no way to find out what is true about sexuality. We don't know, because we haven't lived with it long enough, how accurately *gay/straight* maps the biology of our sexuality. Is our sexuality—the sexuality of all of humankind—divided into two kinds? The concept of homosexuality was only introduced in 1869, and people had no freedom to choose between them after 1869 and only a theoretical freedom to choose between them after 1969. That theoretical freedom didn't begin to be actual until very recently. That is, only in the very recent past, and only in a few large cities and places like Provincetown, has it been almost as easy to be a gay person as to be a straight person, and it has never been equally as easy. As a consequence, almost everything we know about homosexuality that depends on self-reporting is underreported or skewed. Everywhere else—smaller cities, suburbia, conservative America—homophobia skews the answers to all questions, so we don't have enough of an accurate database to tell much of anything about ourselves, how many of us there are, whether we are really divided up this way between two opposites, gay and straight, or whether we spread out along a continuum as Kinsey would have it. Until we have more data, Kinsey, Freud, Cellini—our own eyes if we would believe them—all suggest that our basic theoretical structures are wrong. Even in a place like Provincetown, where a person can feel reasonably safe saying anything he wants in answer to the question, *What do you like?*, usually the person asking the question doesn't ask it right. He says, *Are you gay or are you straight?*, limiting answers to two possibilities. The questioner should, of course, ask this: *Please list all the things that turn you on. (Check off as many boxes as apply. Ask the questioner for extra sheets of paper if necessary. You may take as much time as you need.)*

The reality, beyond all theory, is that the concepts of *gay* and *straight* are only two of the concepts—along with Kinsey's continuum—floating around in our culture, knocking into things and hurting people, and when people need some word like *gay*, they reach up and grab it and apply it. People helplessly follow their drives wherever they lead, and they make up theory, both gay and straight, to impose order on this chaos. If the confusion did not cause me such pain, it would make me laugh. The confusion—this chaos—is freedom. Mardi Gras, in Rechy's book, is "the crowd's day of complete freedom, if anarchy is complete freedom." It is cultural anarchy, and it is the only truth. "'Man, you gotta admire those dam queens like Darlin Dolly an them....They sure have got guts. They live the way they gotta live.'"

The oddest thing was my discovery that straight people don't even think they have a sexuality. They don't seem to think they *need* a theory of themselves. I was invited places, once or twice, during my last months in Maine, and I was confronted by the kind of derisive anti-gay bigotry that I had not faced since the Army. At a dinner party, a woman accused me of flaunting my sexuality, a woman who herself had nine children and who arrived at every dinner party with one in her arms. "My God, woman, *Flaunt!*" I said.

"You come in here like a Spanish Galleon, all sails flying, *flaunting* the fact that you fuck men! Are you blind to your own behavior?"

Gay: It is the category that the culture offers me that most closely matches my biology and psychology. But I have no idea if *gay* is exactly what I am, and it is absolutely clear to me that I don't match the category at all points. And there are many men who are not gay and are not straight either.

Chi-Chi, the character in John Rechy's book, is being photographed by tourists at a bar during Mardi Gras. It is a volatile situation. Everybody is drinking, and many different kinds of people are thrown with other kinds of people whom they don't know or understand. There also seems to be a difference in power. The tourists think they have a power over the native residents of the bar they don't in fact have.

Looking into the camera as he inches closer to her, the man addresses Chi-Chi:

> "Come on, sweetheart, you go ahead and give us a real big fairy pose!"
>
> "And don't forget to say 'cheethe,'" his wife lisped poisonously.
>
> Instantly!—as if a wire had been uncoiled— Chi-Chi sprang away from the supporting wall toward the man with the camera. She didn't even bother to adjust the lace dress; it clung carelessly to one leg, over the knee, revealing the powerful leg. She glared at the man for long seconds, with a hatred greater than she could possibly have felt toward one individual; and she gnashes suddenly at him: "*You* come on, father-fucker!"

There is no agreement about what concepts to apply to the reality all around us, and no agreement about the language to use to describe the concepts. But what does seem clear is that, given a particular issue, people will pick and choose among the various conflicting and disconnected conceptions of human sexuality and of the social order to the end that they can justify a condemnation of the gay person—or protect the structures of the straight world.

Because what is much more obviously true—and supported by all the data—is that for all of the last two thousand years, whatever freedom men and women into same sex sex have been able to find for themselves, all men and women have been subjected to a continuous homophobic assault led by the churches. Ever since the concept of *homosexuality* was invented in 1869, and later, since the Stonewall rebellion in 1969, we have been subjected to a continuous and pointed assault from the government, from the churches, and from the healing professions, so much as to make it necessary to say that no one knows what any of us would be like in a world without homophobia, a world in which we actually are free to know our feelings and to pursue them. We are still decades, centuries, from a world without homophobia, so how is it possible to say what any of us are? How is it possible to characterize us? Or, for that matter, to define what any of us know?

↔

Naomi committed more time to her legal work, she said because she needed the money. She was concerned about the children's college education. I felt she was using her larger income to keep the children from me. She was using her money as a weapon. Ours was a traditional divorce between two persons who had unequal financial resources, only in traditional divorces in the past it was the woman who got screwed.

↔

In the middle of my last summer in Maine, on a Thursday morning, my phone rang. It was a social worker at a medical center in Millinocket, Maine.

"Am I speaking to Professor Fair Shaw?"

Then she asked, "Do you teach at the University of Maine?"

And finally, she said, "I do apologize, sir, but I need to verify that I am speaking to the correct person before I pass on my message to you. Do you know Anderson Darwell?"

"Yes." Andy with the curly, flowing hair.

"Oh, sir, I have some news that is not good. Can you speak to me for a moment?"

Then, finally, she told her story. "Mr. Darwell is here in the medical center at Millinocket. He is in intensive care at the hospital. He is in very, very serious condition. His condition has gotten worse. Professor Shaw, Mr. Darwell has no family and no friends here in Millinocket, and it appears that no one will be able to come very soon to be with him. I thought, since I found that you knew him, and that you lived in Maine, that you might be willing—and able—to come up to Millinocket very soon."

"Certainly I can come. Is he seriously sick? What—?"

"Oh, sir, Professor Shaw, he's not sick. He was beaten. He was attacked in the woods west of here. He was hiking, they think, with a friend. They can't—the Forest Service men and the state police— can't find the friend, but they found Mr. Darwell, someone just happened to be on a road, an access road nobody ever much uses, and found him lying in the middle of the—"

I was trying to think what I needed to know. "He's not going to die—"

"Oh, sir. We hope not, but it would be best if you could come right away. The doctors feel at this point that it is very encouraging that he is still alive. It would mean so much to him if there were somebody here that he knew, anybody at all—"

It was an hour-and-a-half drive, and I got my backpack and ran through my apartment picking up things—shirts, socks, toothbrush, razor—and stopped only to call the university to tell them what had happened and that I would call again tomorrow, before closing the door behind me and jumping in the car. I had forgotten things. I ran back in and got a map of Maine—I had never been to Millinocket before—and my checkbook and dark glasses and was on my way again. I couldn't call Ames and Judith because they were in Europe for the summer with Naomi.

Why was he beaten? I had forgotten to ask. Andy was with a friend. They were hiking, or camping, west of here. When had I last seen him? At a meeting a few weeks ago. It had been comforting being with Andy. He was warm, sympathetic, open physically to me, and when he smiled his eyes sparkled. It was painful to think of him, this man who seemed to thrive so on human contact, alone in the medical center in Millinocket. The road up I-95 is a beautiful drive, and I have not ever driven it when I was in a hurry.

In Millinocket, a question at a service station got me directions to the medical center, and a question at the information desk at the main entrance brought out a young woman who appeared distressed and relieved at the same time. "I am *so* glad you are here! It would have been so awful if—something had happened and he had not had *any*body here with him that he knew."

"What has happened?"

"I'm Serena Levesque. I am the one who spoke with you earlier on the phone."

"I'm Fair Shaw. What happened?"

"Well, he—" She paused. "How well do you know him?"

"We are friends. I haven't seen him for a number of weeks."

"—he's dying. He's in a coma—" It was difficult hearing the words, and I swayed on my feet. "—and the medical staff don't think he will come out of it." She looked at me, concerned for me. We were walking rapidly back toward a bank of elevators. On the way up, she continued to talk. "He was barely conscious when they found him, and I don't think he regained consciousness but once, briefly, after he arrived here. The way we found you was there was a diary, an address book of some kind, in his jacket pocket, and your name was in it. I spent part of last night trying to find his family. Until I finally got your number. I was so relieved. I hated it that this man would die on me, and I would be the only human being there for him. I mean, aside from the usual staff." She put her hand on my arm. "I am so glad you are here to take that responsibility off me."

We walked quickly down the long corridor. "I am going to take you in and let you get yourself settled, and then I am going to go find the doctor, who will come up and talk to you." She smiled grimly. "Until we find a family member, you are it, I am afraid." She was at the door. "Wait." She put her hand on the door, which stopped me from opening it. "Before you go in, I should warn you about what you are about to see. He has been *very* badly beaten—" Beautiful Anderson Darwell. "—It may be a shock. If you feel faint, please sit down and put your head between your knees. I don't want—" She smiled her tight, grim smile. "—to have *two* of you unconscious in there!"

Then she pushed open the door and went in, allowing me to follow. The room—pale green, asphalt tile floor, large window covered with blinds, much equipment around, one bed, the head slightly raised—was the conventional hospital room that I knew from every hospital visit and every movie in my life, and the body lying in the bed was almost as indistinguishable. Motionless, Andy's torso was covered by a spotless, smooth, unwrinkled sheet, IV drips attached to needles inserted in his exposed arms. The top of his skull and one eye were covered in bandages. The eye and cheek that were exposed were bruised and swollen. There was a tube inserted into his mouth, bubbling, the skin on his lips broken. There were machines monitoring his heart and his brain activity and his breathing.

"Are you all right?" She put her hand on my upper arm. "You're not going to faint on me, are you?"

"No." I was whispering.

Noticing that, she said, "I don't think he can hear you."

He had always been able to hear me, no matter what it was I had said to him.

"I am going to find a doctor, now. You make yourself comfortable. There's a nurses' station down the hall. I'll be back in a few minutes—maybe half an hour, I don't know." She glanced at Andy. "Can you believe someone could hate that much?"

"What do you mean, *hate that much?*"

She stepped back, looking at me as if seeing me for the first time. "Oh—" She seemed surprised, even upset. "—you don't *know.*"

"Know what?"

"I forgot, I didn't realize how long it's been since you and I talked this morning. I didn't know then—"

"Know *what?*"

"He was beaten because he was gay." She checked her watch. "I really do have to go now. I'll be right back with the doctor." And then she walked briskly out of the room.

It was an old fear. Andy was unconscious, hardly breathing, the machines making more noise than he did. It was as old as the playground in grammar school, when I was six or seven, far too young to know what *queer* was, not too young to have made the connection between my erection and the other boys on the playground, and not too young to know already that something was wrong, that I was different—not one of *us*—not too young to have been threatened because of my difference, or too young to be afraid. I had been afraid of this, of being hurt. The machine pumped in and out. I wondered if Andy were beyond hurt, now. I did not sit on the bed—it might disturb him—and the chair was too far away, so, steadying myself against the mattress, my legs bending slowly at the knees, I came to kneel beside the bed, my forearms up on the surface of the bed and the side of my head lowered onto the sheet, feeling all the terror of being seven.

I talked to the doctor. The social worker had it wrong; last night the state police had arrested two men in a bar bragging about having jumped two faggots in the woods up near Screw Augur Falls and had been able to get enough information out of the other people at the bar to find the victims in the morning. Andy was by the side of the trail, barely alive. His friend was found later in the woods, dead.

"But he isn't gay," I told the doctor.

"The men thought he was. That's why they killed him."

I looked at the doctor. He was impenetrable. "I knew him fairly well for four or five years, and I don't think he is gay, and he knew *I* am gay and would have told me if he was."

I sat with Andy for the rest of the evening. The social worker arranged for me to be allowed to spend the night sleeping sitting up in the chair beside Andy's bed. Occasionally during the night, I was wakened by nurses coming in to check on Andy's vital signs.

The "address book" that the social worker had referred to—the one with my address in it—was actually a book of metaphysical poetry which I had given Andy when he got his one year chip, Donne's *Songs and Sonnets*. It had a short note to Andy in the front, with my name—*Fair Shaw, Orono, Maine, 1980*—and it was from that, that they had been able to find me. Andy had carried no other identification that connected him to anybody. The police had called contact numbers listed with his credit card companies, but there had been no answer and no responses to the messages they left.

I thought that, as open as Andy was about himself, it was possible that he might have ended up in the same sleeping bag with his hiking companion. I thought, if Andy and I had ever gone hiking together, we would probably have ended up in the same sleeping bag. But Andy wasn't gay. Whatever Andy did out in the woods, he'd go back to town to his girl, as Connie had probably gone back to his girl after our weekends above Paradise Lodge in the Cascades. I didn't know, and neither did anyone else, what had happened in the woods before Andy and his friend were attacked.

In the half-light of the hospital room, sitting by the side of the bed, watching Andy's hurt body lying still under the sheets, I was struck by the cause and effect. He was gay—or seemed to be gay—so he was beaten. I rested my elbows on the arms of the chair and then made a tent of my forearms. I remembered the fear of being beaten up. When I was a child, I had seen it happen on the school ground, the bigger boys showing off their strength by beating up the smaller ones. They had said, *sissy*, and when they were older, they said, *queer*. For a long time, I had been afraid to look squarely at a boy for fear he would say, *What are you looking at, faggot?*, and then hit me. I had been afraid of this, the physical hurt. The pain in my body. I had been most afraid of being hurt around my face, around my eyes, and in my groin, the most delicate parts of myself. I had never been injured physically because I was gay, but I was aware of the extent of my psychic injuries, the fear that seemed never to leave me and which I was unable to quite escape, no matter how strong and indestructible I had become. The fear had been an indication of my own weakness, which seemed indistinguishable from my being gay. Seeing Andy on the bed, all but dead, I felt I myself had been attacked and defeated. I felt weak and defeated. I lowered my head onto my hands, resting my chin on my thumbs. I couldn't find a way of saying to myself, *But it happened to Andy, not to me,* because somewhere deep in me it seemed to have happened to me, and it had happened because I was seven years old, on the playground, not one of *us,* and I was weak and couldn't play ball and because I was gay.

The nurse came in again and found me. "Are you all right?"

"No." How could I be all right, with Andy there on the bed dying? I shook my head. "No, I am not all right."

She watched me for a few minutes. "You must love him."

I pulled back and looked for something to wipe my eyes. My sleeve. "No. Well, yes. Of course I do. I didn't know him well. He is a friend of mine. A beautiful friend. He is an artist."

She did what she had come into the room to do—fiddled with the IV drips, flicked the bags with her middle finger, punched some buttons, smoothed the sheets. "It won't be long now."

"He's dying?"

"I would think so."

"He won't wake up again."

"No, I wouldn't think so. Pretty soon now."

This was coming from somewhere in me way deeper than where my memories of Andy lay.

"I could bring you some tea—or coffee. Would you like that?" Then, before I could focus on what she had said, "Or you could go down to the snack bar. The machines there work all night. Ice cream? Or peanuts?"

Somewhere, down deep in me, where I lived, beyond all pretense, I hurt and felt weak and defeated. I crossed my arms and rested my elbows on the arms of the chair again, and then I lowered my head down onto my arms.

Eventually, beautiful Andy did die, about five in the morning as the sky outside was becoming light, of what the doctors called "massive head injuries." I had the odd experience of feeling that I had died too—as if it were all over now—but also the even odder realization that I had escaped this time, like the feeling I had when I was seven and realized that it was the *other* boy who had gotten called *queer* and was pushed and shoved and kicked, while I was able to walk away.

The nursing staff came in to do its business. There was some bustle among them, and then I saw them with the sheet.

"Oh, wait, please." I wouldn't have another chance. I stood by the bed and took him in, itemizing what I saw.

When I walked out of the room and down the hall toward the light, I passed a man in an anorak with tousled brown hair, sharp features, who stopped me. "Did you know the kid in there?"

"What kid?" I was having trouble focusing.

"The guy who got beat up. The young man."

I was aware of how tired I was. The guy was very insistent. Intrusive. He was a beautiful man, and this man had no right.

"Yes."

"Were you a friend of his?"

"I knew him pretty well."

"Were you on the camping trip?"

"Who are you?"

"I'm Arnie Babcock. I'm from the newspaper. I just found out about the murders."

I pulled back as if I had touched something hot.

Babcock noticed. "I'm sorry about your friends."

I eased up. "Thanks."

The man was gentler this time. "We're going to run an article about it. A murder up here is pretty unusual, and two is unheard of. We're pretty impressed by what the cops say about the reason, too. Can I talk to you?"

It was hard for me to be open with this man. We sat down on the brown vinyl couches by the elevators.

"I was hoping I could get over here before he died." He opened his bag and pulled out a tape recorder and a pad and pencil and wrote. "Can I quote you?"

"Yes."

"Your name?"

"Fair Shaw."

"Where do you live?"

"Orono, Maine."

"What do you do?"

"I teach. University of Maine. Department of English."

"You don't look like a professor—" He paused. "—the jeans, t-shirt, earring." He smiled uncertainly. "I bet you are the only professor there with an earring."

"Maybe." This hurt. "I don't know."

"Can I include that in the article that you teach at the university?"

"Yes."

"Are you gay?"

"Yes. I'm gay—"

"Can I say you're gay?"

"Yes. But the dead men were not gay. At least one of them wasn't, the one in there, Andy Darwell. I've been told what the police say. That may have been why the guys attacked them, but at least one of them wasn't gay."

"Why would they have attacked them then?"

"I don't know. Because they hated gay men." The elevator arrived and the door opened and a nurse, very busy, walked out and down the hall. "Maybe they thought they were gay."

"How did you know them?"

"I didn't know them. I only knew Andy Darwell. The one who died this morning. He was a friend." I watched the spindle of the recorder turn. "He was quiet. He never raised his voice. And he smiled often. I think he found me amusing—I am older, and I have come from a very different world than his—and I think he loved me. I think he found everything amusing, the quirks we all have, and yet he had such sympathy, too. Such sweet caring for people. People were drawn to him, drawn to open up to him. He was a sweet guy." I spoke of what a good friend he was, and how close we were. I did not speak of AA or of any aspect of his life that he had told me about when we were talking about Program.

"I don't know how to ask this. But would you have known if he was gay?"

"I think I would. But maybe not. Maybe he was exploring. I don't know."

"What do you mean, 'exploring'?"

"You know. Maybe he went with women and then later decided to explore going with men. I don't know."

The reporter didn't seem to understand that. "How is Maine for gay people?"

I looked at him for a moment. "No worse than everywhere else."

Later, I got in my car and drove back to Orono. It was an hour-and-a-half drive back south, and I had time to think. The fear I had felt as a child had been about real things that caused real damage to real bodies. Andy didn't care much about the division between gay and straight, and yet there he was. I was so angry, it was difficult to drive.

The next morning, Saturday, the *Bangor Daily News* carried a small article on the first page of the second section about the murders. It quoted me saying I didn't think Andy and his friend were gay. Then, on Sunday morning, *The New York Times* had a small article in the national section on the murders. It said the police said they were murdered because they were gay. It quoted the Associated Press, which said, "According to Professor Fair Shaw, a well-known gay man on the faculty of the University of Maine, who knew both murdered men, the men were not gay."

5

On my first night in Boston, there were 200 men in curving rows of folding chairs in the basement of a Back Bay church listening to George, the night's speaker.

"I had lost my job, I was staying in an apartment that belonged to another man, and now here I was, waking up in bed with some man I had never seen before, and *I didn't know where my clothes were.*"

He was interrupted. There was noise on my left. I saw a man rising from his seat. This man, who was very thin, stood upright and moved to his left in the space between his row and the row ahead of him, stumbling over other men's feet, and mumbling.

George tried to go on, "I didn't know where my clothes were," but the noise was so great, he stopped and watched what was happening.

By now the thin man was in the aisle on the left side of the room, going toward the speaker. His mumbling was louder, now. Then he said, in a clear voice, "I need to speak!"

George, surprised, shrugged. "Sure."

"I need to say something right now." The thin man looked crazed. "I need to talk right now!"

George stepped back so the thin man could take the microphone.

There was confusion in the thin man's face. He wore a loose t-shirt and jeans and flip-flops and had a silver ring on each finger. He started talking into the microphone, but it didn't come out as intelligible language. It sounded to me like mumbling. The men in the room stiffened and craned their necks to see.

A heavyset man half rose in his chair and stood, stooped over, watching all this and waiting to see what was going to happen.

"I need to make this clear." Then the man at the microphone mumbled again. But it was worse than mumbling. It wasn't language. There was a disconnect between his brain and his mouth. "I—"

The heavyset man who half-stood at his place now rose up straight and walked up to the front. He was a heavyset butch number with short, blond hair spiked up, and a tight t-shirt. He put his hand on the stricken man's shoulder, who looked confused. Two other men joined him. Then the stricken man recognized them—and smiled. He was about to say something—it was clear he had in his mind some particular thing he wanted to say—but what came out was a kind of burble. "*Bree-goo.*" He seemed surprised to hear himself say *bree-goo*.

"It's OK. You were great." The heavyset man with spiked hair slid his hand along the stricken man's shoulder until it reached his neck, and then he put his whole palm and his fingers on the back of the man's neck and pulled him gently toward him, pulling his head toward his shoulder, where it came to rest, and the stricken man started very quietly to cry, making unintelligible sounds.

"Oh, *Arnold.*"

All of us watched all of this.

"It's OK, you were great. I learned a lot from you." Then the heavyset man began a low, soft running patter for Arnold's ears only. "Come with me. I'll take care of you. We'll take care of you. Nothing will happen to you. Everything is going to be *all right.*" He held Arnold tightly, encircled him with his arms, and said, quietly, to no one in particular, almost a whisper, "Someone call an ambulance."

Two men near the door jumped up and ran out.

The heavyset man led Arnold across the front of the room to the side, whispering gently to him without stopping—the room of 200 men frozen still, watching all this—and then down the long aisle along the wall to the back past me, his arm around him, Arnold's head tilted sideways onto the heavyset man's shoulder, tears running down his face, fretful, not comprehending what was happening to him, followed by the other two men. Someone opened the back door for the little group, and they disappeared into the dark. None of them came back.

302

Arnold had a cancer of the brain and was suffering from dementia. Only his close friends had known this, before he lost it at the meeting in front of me and all Boston gay AA.

It had been called, first, *Gay Cancer*, and then it was called *Gay-Related Immune Disease,* or *GRID*, then it was called AIDS, and the community I joined when I got off Interstate 95 after driving down from Maine was one of the places where the disease had taken root. I rented an apartment in the Fenway and went to meetings at Mass General Hospital, walking between the two—my idea of hell was having a car in Boston—down Charles Street through the Public Garden and out Commonwealth Avenue, passing all the churches in the Back Bay in whose basements AA meetings were held when they weren't being held at Mass General.

This gay community was not like Andrew Holleran's descriptions of the Lower East Side. One night, I was walking through the Garden after a meeting—I was thinking about Ames and Judith and about finding a job—when I heard my name. I stopped and turned. It was a young man from the meeting whose first name I knew—John—but about whom I knew nothing else. We were not close. He was out of breath from running.

"Can we talk? I'll walk with you."

"What's up?"

"Well—" He stopped. "Well—"

"It's OK. Take your time."

We turned and walked out of the Garden and crossed Arlington Street into the median strip down the middle of Commonwealth.

The young man finally spoke. "I just found out today—" His chest heaved, like a sob. "—that I have KS." He looked at me with horror.

"Oh, *no.*" I stopped and looked up at him. He was a pretty, ordinary-looking young man. Sweet. Nice.

His face was crumpling up into tears. "And I don't know what to *do.*"

"Have you told anyone? Do you have a friend?"

"No. *No.* I can't tell *anyone* this. I have been frantic all afternoon, so I stayed in my room with the door closed for fear that my roommate would guess and throw me out. I don't know what to *do.* I don't know where to *go.*" Then he said to me, "T*ell me what to do.* What am I supposed to do! I'm going to *die!*"

I held him for a few moments, wrapped his thin body in my arms and held him. Then I led him over to one of the marble benches along the walkway, where we sat down.

"I am so afraid—" He sat up straight with his knees together, his fingers entwined in his lap, very primly. "—and I didn't know anyone to tell but you." He blew his nose and wiped his tears with the back of his hand. "I am so *afraid*." He looked over at me sitting beside him. "Do you know what I am to do?"

I didn't know what he was to do. It was a death sentence. I had heard of men who found out they were sick—and they died before the month was out. Men disappeared from the bars, and you heard later they'd been in the hospital for a week, and then you heard they were dead. It seemed to happen in days. They died of *pneumocystis carinii* pneumonia, and Kaposi's sarcoma, and a long list of other bizarre invasions—*toxoplasmosis*, *cytomegalovirus*, and wasting disease. They ceased to be able to walk, they lost weight until they seemed to starve to death, they lost their minds. And the doctors were unable to stop it. They had nothing, no thing to halt it, or even to slow it down. It had happened so suddenly, first in New York and San Francisco, then in other major cities like Boston, that men didn't know anything was wrong with them—*they didn't know what to look for*—until they were near death. I had first heard about it in 1982 when I was in London, and it had simmered like a pot on the periphery of my mind during the year in Maine. And when I arrived in Boston, on Labor Day in 1984, the *Morbidity and Mortality Weekly Report*—called MMWR—said there had been 2,643 AIDS cases across the country so far in 1984 and 50 in Massachusetts, and it seemed true that no one was doing anything about it. Now, it moved to the center of my vision. *Right here.* For me, the scene on the marble bench on Commonwealth Avenue was repeated over and over, although many more times men I heard of simply disappeared and died, too ashamed or afraid or hopeless—or too sick—to tell anyone.

"Walk with me." John, it turned out, was John Levine. I had planned to write, but changed my mind. "Come walk home with me, and we can talk." We did, stopping off to get coffee and then going to my apartment.

John sat on the other end of the sofa. "I've never thought about dying. About death. I'm twenty-seven. I never thought it was something I had to think about. I am not even used to being out of school, and I thought the next thing I had to think about was having a career. Now I can't think about a career. Have you ever thought about dying?"

Before I could answer, John asked another question. "Are you infected?"

I was about to answer when John spoke again. "I don't know how I am going to tell my mother. Or my roommate."

The AIDS Action Committee, a group from the Fenway Community Health Center, which catered to the gay and lesbian communities, was founded the year before I arrived in Boston. Called *AIDS Action* or *The Committee* by people I knew, it was a group of gay men who had grown angry waiting for the medical establishment to respond to the crisis and furious at the government of Ronald Reagan for ignoring it and who saw that if the crisis was to be confronted, they'd have to do it themselves. By the time I arrived in Boston, the best coverage of the news was not in *The New York Times*, it was in the gay papers in Boston and New York—*Gay Community News* in Boston and *The Advocate* and *The New York Native* in New York, papers reporting from the gay street about the disease that was spreading among us all. These papers were not new to me. I had been reading them sporadically since I got back from England, which is to say, since I came out.

Because I was 45, had six years of sobriety behind me, and because most of the people in AA rooms were younger—up to 25 years younger—than me, young, fresh, trying to learn to stay sober, and afraid of getting sick, I became an "old-timer," someone to be called even before I felt I knew enough. John had thought of me as a person to talk to because he had seen me in meetings and thought I knew what I was doing, and he could count on my not saying anything to anybody.

Having survived Ann Arbor and Maine, having divorced Naomi, having left the university, and having stayed sober, I did know what I was doing, to a degree. Soon my phone rang constantly, men sick or men afraid of getting sick, men out on a slip, men trying to come back, men seeking some kind of assurance. Even though I myself had not had the sexual experience of these men—I was only a little more than a year and a half from the day in London when I had moved out of the house I shared with Naomi and Judith and Ames—I had the experience with staying sober that these men wanted. I found a place for myself in the large, volatile, warm gay community of AA in Boston. The phone rang with calls from men in AA, and it rang every night—late, at their bed time—with calls from Judith and Ames, who had just gotten their first phones. They were connecting. All of us, my children and I and my friends in AA, I think, were learning how to be close while in another part of the city or in another state. Most of us didn't know how to do that. Judith and Ames didn't know—I didn't either—whether the two hundred miles between Maine and Boston was important or whether it was a distance that could easily be gotten around by a car and a telephone. And, in like manner, many men I came to know in AA were in a state of continuous anxiety since they felt so alone, and the question was, *How can we break down this alone-ness?* There was always the telephone, but I don't think we knew how to use the telephone. *How do you talk so that when you stop talking you feel less alone?* It gradually came to me. The idea, I thought, was to give the other person the quotidian detail of my life and so allow him or her to experience me as I experienced myself. And I learned to listen during long *long* monologues as guys from the meetings and my own two children—Judith calling at one in the morning after her dates—gave me bit by bit the detail from which their lives were created.

To bring in money, I painted houses at the invitation of a woman I had met in a meeting, and I waited tables at a Mexican restaurant in Cambridge. For something more permanent, I needed to find a way to support myself—and I had child support to pay for Ames and Judith—so I could put my energy into writing. At coffee after a meeting, I was telling John, who was around me all the time now, and the other guys about it. "I've only had two jobs in my life—real jobs—and I've only looked for jobs, gone on the job market, twice, and I have *no idea* how to find something I'd like to do."

That night, leaving the coffee shop, someone said, "I've got something for you, man. I have a job that I love—"

I was interested. It was a guy named Kirk. We stopped. "What's that?"

The kid shrugged. "Doing temp work." He lit a cigarette and leaned back against the wall of the building. "It's different every day. Sometimes it's great, and sometimes not so great, but even when it isn't great, I know it is going to change tomorrow." He gestured.

"Look, I know it's nothing great, but it is a paycheck coming in, and it's going to hold me until I find something else. It gives me time, you know, Fair? And that's what I need. Time."

Fascinating. "What's the name of your agency?"

By the end of the week, I was working, typing for some company downtown. It brought in money, and it answered the question *How am I to live?* while I wrote. As the kid had said, it gave me time for things to sort themselves out, and every Friday afternoon after work, I was able to leave Boston with the rush hour traffic and drive up to Maine to see Judith and Ames, coming back on Sunday evening. They needed reassurance that I was still in their lives, that they were still in my life, and that we constituted a family, and I needed reassurance that we still could love one another.

On October 27, 1984, the MMWR said there were 60 cases of AIDS in Massachusetts, almost all of them in Boston. The problem with this number was that while the gay community in Boston was big—one of the largest in the country—many of those who were sick seemed to come from the same crowd. When I arrived in Boston, I found that many people knew half a dozen or more men who were sick. For some people in Boston, it seemed as if all their friends were being taken sick. It felt as if the whole community was dying.

No one knew what caused AIDS.

"We know it's HTLV-III, and it's spread by sex and by blood-to-blood contact."

"But that doesn't help much. If I get my blood in contact with your blood, OK, I know I'll get it—if you have it—but they also say it is in all the body fluids. The paper the other day said it is in men's *tears*. Does that mean if you cry on me, *I'll get it?*"

"The New York Native says that Gallo—" Robert Gallo, the scientist with the National Institutes of Health who discovered the virus. "—said it is in our saliva."

"What about kissing?"

"If it's in our saliva, then we're all dead. If it passes that easily. All of us." This was Tim, who was very young, very slender, very redheaded, very boyish, and very angry.

We were having this conversation in the Harvard Gardens, a restaurant in a fifties-style low building at the foot of Cambridge Street. The Harvard Gardens had, at some point in the past, let it be known that they would be hospitable to queer alcoholics drinking coffee for an hour after their meetings, and so that is where we went. It was downscale, the waitresses were older women, and the clientele seemed to be drawn from the working people in the establishments in the neighborhood. It was a very ordinary place for our extraordinary conversations. Sometimes there were only three or four of us, sometimes ten or fifteen, and we sat at tables pushed together.

"I've just given up sex." It was a tall young man about thirty, who looked as if he were in deep pain. "I've started painting my apartment. I've been meaning to do it for years."

The rest of us stared.

"Nobody knows about kissing. *The Gay Community News* says that having HTLV-III in saliva does not mean that it is transmissible by saliva."

"They say that, but do they know that?"

This was hysteria. If the infection were easily spread, there would be many more men with AIDS than there were. We were four years into the epidemic, but nobody knew. Nobody even knew how many had been infected. The numbers *The Native* published came from the Centers for Disease Control, but everyone said the numbers were vastly underreported. So the numbers I read in the *MMWR*— which also came from the CDC—in the Boston Public Library were also underreported.

"And what about the others? Blowjobs. What about that? Rimming?"

"They are all unsafe. Practice safe sex. Use a condom. Don't rim." I read this.

"I am just so afraid," The tall man's name was Jake. "Nobody has proven that condoms prevent infection."

"No, but they prevent all the other sexually transmittable diseases, and they presume—"

"What about *sweat?*"

"It's kissing that bothers me."

"I can't tell you how angry I am."

I observed the red-headed young man at the other end of the table, Tim Byrne. *The Native*, in August, had had a column by a man entitled, "Young and Angry in New York." The writer was 25, and he had waited all his life for the freedom he would find in New York, and now that he was out, what he found was something different. "Welcome to New York—Death City USA."

Tim looked around at all of them, some of them men my age. "It's men your age that I resent most. You had all those years of freedom." He lit a cigarette. It was said that Jerry Falwell had been invited to the White House to discuss the "AIDS problem."

Leaving the Harvard Gardens and walking out Boylston, Tim Byrne and I crossed Mass Avenue and walked on outer Boylston past the O'Reilly monument with its bronze depictions of Eire and her two beautiful sons, honoring John Boyle O'Reilly. At the intersection with The Fenway, Tim spoke. "Would you like to go to the Ramrod?" It was a gay leather bar, a storefront with painted windows, a bar on the left when you first came in, and, up five or six steps, another longer bar on the left, and then, at the back, a pool table. The space between the bars on the left and the wall on the right was never more than ten feet, which was one of the things I liked about it, the sense of it being crowded with men wearing motorcycle boots with the straps over the instep and the rings on the side, jeans, and leather. Leather vests, leather motorcycle jackets, leather harnesses across their chests and backs. It was also full of gay men from the AA meetings, talking program, oblivious to the drinking going on around them. I had not expected that. Tim and I talked about disease—the two diseases with which we were confronted— our eyes on each other, and beyond us, the milling crowd of men looking for men.

Some gave up sex completely and declined to touch any other man. Others thought it was OK to be the recipient of a blowjob but not to give one, or to be the active partner in anal intercourse but not the passive partner. It was said that the virus was hard to catch, that you had to have thousands of partners before you caught it. Since I had had only thirty or forty men in my life, I wondered if that meant I was safe. The papers also reported that men who had contracted the disease had been hard users of poppers, and people thought they might be a cause—or a contributing factor. A study quoted in *The Native* said poppers might affect whether you get PCP or KS.

One night after a meeting, a man whose name was Leo Andrelli joined our crowd when we went out for coffee. Leo asked me what I was doing. It was a regular question when men came together.

"I use a condom. I don't rim. I don't let anyone come in my mouth. I make him use a condom." It was inadequate. Leo wanted me to say more. I remembered a man I had picked up who had rimmed me, and I wondered if I should have stopped him. I had rimmed a man in London, a year and a half ago, but the incidence of the disease was not as high then, in London, as it was in America, now. And nobody really trusted condoms. I was negotiating my life moment by moment. What I found actually happening, when I brought someone home from the bar, was we masturbated each other. We were not accustomed to using condoms, so we went with something we knew. When I brought a man home, I felt his body, I hugged, I kissed, deep kisses, as if I thought I could *taste* every different part of him, while I fumbled with his clothes, his leather harness and his studded belt, and then I took his cock gently, pulling on it and stroking it. We fell on the bed and continued playing with each other's cocks until he began to explore my body with his hands, feeling my shoulders and my arms. I was feeling *his* shoulders and his arms, and then I began to lick his chest and to tug lightly on his tits with my teeth. He arched his back and tensed all over. I licked him between his legs, on his balls, and in the space behind his scrotum. He began to play with his own cock, to breathe heavily and rapidly, and in a few minutes he came. Then he turned his attention to me, and I came. We held one another, and then we gradually relaxed in one another's arms.

It was very different from what Dr. Reuben had described in *Everything You Ever Wanted to Know About Sex.*

"What about *pre-come?*"

"I don't know. I don't think they know. What I pay attention to is *no exchange of body fluids.* I am not sure they are convinced there is such a thing as pre-come."

"People talk about it."

"It may just be the beginning of ejaculation—"

"Will a condom really protect me?"

"They say it will."

"It makes it a little difficult to plan, doesn't it? *The Native* has this feature where they give the latest number on AIDS cases. The most recent numbers are 6,330 cases around the country, 102 here in Massachusetts." I lit a cigarette. "They estimate that 60% or so of gay men in San Francisco are infected. Then they think that must be impossible. Why is that impossible? Fairly small city. I have sex with you and you and you, you have sex with him and him and him, and each one of them has sex with three others. Pretty soon, in about the tenth generation—or in a few months—the virus, which started with me, has infected everybody in the city or everybody who is having sex. I don't understand why they don't understand that."

It was a catastrophe for everybody, but it was different for me than it was for many of these men. They were accustomed to having sex one way, and then they had been told to change. On the other hand, I had had so little male-male sex that everything I did with another man was wonderful. It all felt like a huge, and unexpected, gift. This put me in the same group of men as very young guys just coming out because, essentially, I was just coming out. On the other hand, it was odd to sense, in the midst of all this beauty, that what I was doing was fatally dangerous.

Tim Byrne said we were all going to be dead in five years. He looked around the table and said, "We are all going to be gone. These are our last years, guys. We are expendable. They talk about populations at risk, us and the IV drug users and the Haitians, and in the view of our culture, we are expendable. They don't think they need to spend tax money—real money, the billions it is going to cost to stop this thing, find a cure and a vaccine—on us because we are not important. Jerry Falwell and Pat Robertson, the Christian right, are driving national health policy." The other men heard Tim and then went on talking about safe sex, how to keep themselves safe. They didn't want to have to think about what Tim was telling them they *had* to think about, but Tim was right, this very young, very slender, very angry kid.

It was something we all talked about all the time, what you could do together, and it was something that was almost never talked about, the disease itself. Who had it, where they were with it, what their difficulties were with it, how sick they were, why there was no cure. Even though the medical establishment had settled on HTLV-III as the virus that caused AIDS, there was uncertainty, and *The Native* kept pointing out that if the medical establishment had settled too soon on the cause *and had gotten it wrong,* then the pursuit of a cure and of a vaccine would fail. Every week, *The Native* carried major stories, beginning before I arrived in Boston, by Ann Giudici Fettner that pointed out the consequences of pursuing a cure for a virus that was not causing the disease. We had to take on faith what the medical establishment was saying—what the AIDS Action Committee was saying—about the virus that caused AIDS, on what constituted safe sex, on what condoms could do, on how to save our lives.

The Native considered HTLV-III to be an hypothesis adopted as proven fact by the medical establishment. *The Native* proposed, as a counter hypothesis, the African Swine Fever Virus. I and my friends read about these controversies but didn't know how to resolve the conflict in the medical establishment. There was no test for the virus, when I arrived in Boston. There was a new blood test for the antibodies, but James W. Curran, Director of the AIDS Program of the Centers for Disease Control, said, according to *The Native,* that "the meaning of the blood test for antibody to LAV/HTLV-III, beyond indicating exposure to the virus, remains unknown." The same article suggested that medicine did not know whether a person who tested positive for antibodies was infected, nor did medicine know whether that person was infectious. Dr. Curran advised that until the meaning of the results of the test was known gay men should not take the test.

"I want to know about the test." Leo was asking, over coffee, after a meeting. "They imply that a positive result does not necessarily mean I have AIDS."

"I don't know. I don't think they know. I read everything I can get my hands on, and I don't think anybody knows what a test result is going to mean. The tests don't test anything but antibodies to the virus. *The Native* says don't take the test. There are going to be huge percentages of people coming up positive when nobody knows what that means. Then they are all concerned about confidentiality. If you get a positive result, and the word gets out, you could be fired, you could lose your insurance, you could be quarantined. I don't know all the horrible things that could happen. Your landlord could throw you out on the street. Gallo is not even sure how the disease is transmitted. He said, 'I'd be very careful how I dealt with my mother.' My *mother!*"

"Holy shit."

The cover of *The Native* that week, October 8, 1984, in huge block letters that took up the whole of the front page, read, DON'T

TAKE THE TEST! A writer said, "This test is extremely dangerous and at present should be avoided at all costs."

The gang—Tim Byrne, John Levine, Kirk, Lee—was at the coffee shop after a meeting talking about it when Tim spoke of having seen his doctor that day. "I have fewer T cells than I have fingernails," which was the way he told us he had AIDS.

On the way home, I asked Tim, "How long have you known?"

"Six months, I guess."

"I'm sorry."

He shrugged, and at the next corner, he turned and went to his house and left me to go on to the Garden and to my thoughts about Ames and Judith, who, at 13 and 15, were entering the world that Tim and the rest of us had been talking about.

The ones who were afraid were the ones who had been sexually active. Many men my age were no longer sexually very active, so they listened to all this with some serenity. The problem was that none of us knew when the epidemic had started, so we didn't know who was safe and who was not. It was the younger ones who were frantic because they had had the most sex the most recently. These men sitting around me at the table were afraid because they were young and had their whole lives at risk. There was the possibility that they would die before they had lived. Since I was as sexually active as the young men, I thought I'd die, too, before I had lived.

But fear was only one of the dangers facing us. The other was confusion—about the virus, the antibodies to the virus, the test, how the virus was passed (my *mother!*), who had it, how one could best protect oneself. I think I must have been more accustomed to ambiguities, to a sense that the authorities *don't have it right* than the young men were. I had accepted the immutable truths of my culture for years—the narrative we are all told—and had almost destroyed my life because of it. Now, I read in *The Native* that "we should not expect scientific technology to rescue us from AIDS for the next few years." Dr. Curran had also been worried about the results of the test being used to discriminate against persons with AIDS.

On weekends, I usually went to Maine to be with the kids. I'd take them out to supper, and AIDS was often what we talked about. My sense was that Judith and Ames were growing up into a world in which AIDS was a fact, and they were not shocked by it, the way older people were. I was almost certain they were both having sex. It was probable they were not using condoms. If they were to survive the epidemic, it would be because Maine was far away and in the great lottery we were all playing, the odds were tremendously against their getting the virus. They were in Maine, they were kids, and they were both straight—these would save them. Beyond that, I counted on Naomi's and my having presented on an almost daily basis since they were small a progressive fact-based acceptance of sex in one's life to get them through. They could read, and they were not ignorant.

In Boston in the winter of 1984, no one could find the freedom from all constraints suggested by *City of Night* and by *Dancer From The Dance*. I found fear among some men—and courage and selflessness among others. The man who had risen to his feet at the AA meeting and helped Arnold out to the ambulance was a type, a strong thoughtful man willing to do what was necessary. These men were gentle with each other. They didn't seem afraid of getting the virus themselves—many of them had the virus—and they seemed to demonstrate the courage and compassion, that, I imagined, courageous men demonstrate in battle.

I was having coffee with David Sepe after a meeting. David was in his early thirties, my size, dark brown hair, a slender lithe body, who had been sober half as long as I and lived across the river in Cambridge. He and I had met at the first meeting I attended in Boston, the time when Arnold had lost it, and now we had coffee and talked on the phone. Like some alcoholics, he was very controlled, and it may have been that one of the reasons he liked me was that I was easy.

"My last boyfriend died a year ago, before people knew it was a virus. We knew something sexual was up because of all the guys getting it—it wasn't going to be something in the air or the water— and we knew it wasn't something in our so-called 'lifestyle' because the guys getting it had such different styles. Not all of them were in the fast lane, and not all of them took drugs, so I started being careful several years ago. There was enough talk, you know, for us to get the message. Besides, I'm thirty-two now, and I am too old for this shit. But how do you feel? It must be a shock coming out into this."

"I had thought there would be sex available everywhere."

"Oh, that's still going on. You see, everybody in the gay community knew what was really happening, but we like to present ourselves as just a bunch of guys, fucking like rabbits, and having the time of our lives. Do you feel you're the victim of a bait and switch?"

The Native said there were almost 8,000 cumulative AIDS cases at the end of 1984.

↔

I signed up with the AIDS Action Committee AIDS Hotline and volunteered one evening a week on the phones.

"Uh—" The caller was never prepared. "Uh—I was out last night. With another man. And we, uh—" Then he got it together. "We had been doing poppers, and we just, we didn't, ah, we didn't use a condom, and I wondered if I did anything wrong."

"Wrong? No. But you placed yourself at risk of picking up the virus. You fucked?"

"Yes."

"When you have anal intercourse without a condom, you are engaging in high risk behavior—"

"Oh, shit." There was a long pause. "What should I do?"

"Go to one of the anonymous testing sites. The Commonwealth maintains them so we can find out if we are positive without giving our name. If you are positive, see a doctor and take his advice. Consider not doing poppers when you are about to have sex."

"Am I going to die?"

"We're all going to die." In the darkened room, whispering into the phone, hearing the whispers of the men in the booths around me, and listening to the quiet voice on the other end, I felt very close to whoever it was, this man who had done poppers and then had fucked without a rubber and was now afraid he was going to die. "But if you picked up something last night, you aren't going to die *soon*, and you may have years left ahead of you. In the meantime, think about the poppers."

"Thanks."

"Have a good life." I gave him the number to call for the anonymous testing sites.

"Thanks."

"Good-bye."

The red light was flashing again.

Sometimes the men tried to keep it impersonal, even though they were talking about intimate matters, as if they were asking the best way to use a hammer. They seemed to like not having to give their names and that there was no way to trace them. They could say anything. But what they said to me was not anything criminal—*Last night I stole $200,000*—or even morally reprehensible. It was just the usual stuff about men not being perfect. *I know I shouldn't have, but I fucked this guy last night without a condom, and I don't know if I have it, and I don't want anyone to die because of what I did. I think I love him.* It was the usual pain of the world. Only here, in the darkened room, with these whispered voices, the pain of the world seemed very close and very intimate. These men were—they seemed to me to be—very ordinary, regular guys, and they were placed in a situation where death was very close, and one could be either a giver or a receiver without meaning it, without knowing it, until it was too late, through mere carelessness. Mere carelessness could result so easily in the transmission of the virus that it could easily be confused with malicious intent, and I wanted to say, *Hey, guy, you didn't intend this.* Yet I didn't want to encourage carelessness, and I didn't want to absolve men of responsibility for their—and their brothers'—lives.

"What I want," I said to David one night, "is to tell them that they are responsible for what they do and at the same time to forgive them when they don't do what they should. Somewhere in all this has to be forgiveness."

"You're like the Catholic Church."

"No." I was clear on that. "I forgive them even if they don't repent. And I am not God."

Once David said, *You forgive everyone but yourself.* But I didn't forgive Ronald Reagan, who has never uttered the word *AIDS* in the first five years of the epidemic, and I didn't forgive the health officials who keep saying, even now, "We have plenty of money to fight this disease, and we don't need Congress to appropriate more," and I didn't forgive Cornelius and Henrietta, who have never answered my letters when I have written to them about AIDS, and I didn't forgive my mother, who said, "What I feel sorriest for are the *innocent* victims," by which she meant, she said, the wives and children who were hurt by the men who had gone out and gotten this disease by having sex with men.

Race Point Light

The sex was there at the Ramrod when I wanted it, and I knew where to go if I wanted it outdoors or at the baths. It was even there if I wanted it at AA meetings. It was there on the streets. But I had not been prepared for the fact that that did not characterize the gay community. When I came to Boston, what I found was freedom in the time of plague. It was freedom restrained by the moral requirements of a communal disaster, by the great commandments, *Do no harm,* and *Help.*

I settled in, into a world that was free, anxious, self-enclosed, comfortable, desperate, besieged, and defined by both fear and sympathy. It was not Malone's Lower East Side. I lifted weights at home every other day and swam a mile at the Y every day. I wrote two or three hours every night. At meetings, men hugged, then pulled away and looked hard at each other and said, "How *are* you?" to which they were not expected to say, *fine.* My apartment in the Fenway was a ten-minute walk from the Ramrod—down to the left for a block to Jersey, turn left for a block to Peterborough, then right for a block to Kilmarnock, left for a block to Queensbury, then right for a long block to the intersection of Park Drive. My apartment was on the left, on Park. *Come by and get me for the meeting,* and they would, calling from the payphone in front of the laundromat behind my building—*I'm here*—to which I answered, *I'll be right out.* The last time I had been called from the street was at Vanderbilt when my friends had called and I had grabbed my shades and check book and had run for the door. Later that night, after the meeting, after the long walk home, after an hour at the Ramrod, I'd say to the man I was talking to, *I'm just around the corner. Would you like to come?*

I told the men in AA all there was to tell. Lee, about 30, a carpenter, a gentle man with a kind smile and curly hair, and I had left a meeting and were walking toward the Fenway, out Commonwealth Avenue, past the monuments. We walked on until we got to Charlesgate, at the statue of Lief Eriksson gazing, as if into the distance, at the street ramp 100 yards away, and I said good-bye to Lee and went to the Ramrod. Two young men joined me to talk, acting like it was an obvious thing that they would want to hang around me. I enjoyed that, but I left them to take a leak, and later in the evening, I passed them again, and they laughed. I was grinning. "What's up with you two?" They were just kids—maybe twenty-two years old.

"Oh." One of them looked at me. "We've just been standing here watching you, as you walk around the room, oblivious to everybody, getting hit on every few minutes—"

During the years leading up to my marriage and the years of my marriage, I had not allowed myself to notice that men responded sexually to me, and now when it happened, I didn't know men were hitting on me. I was pleased that men liked me, but I was flummoxed, too, not knowing what I was doing to make it happen, not knowing how to recognize it when it happened, and not knowing how to respond. What I knew was that I liked being there.

I picked up a man and brought him home and had sex. I began to wear, as was the style, a heavy black leather belt and black leather vest, and boots, and the men I picked up wore leather also. I liked the toughness of it, and I looked good in it. It was also the look of an outlaw, which is the way I felt, in rebellion. I felt true, all the way through. In my leather with my spiked up hair, I picked up men and had sex, and wondered about the dangers and comforts of the gay community.

As weather grew colder, I needed a jacket. I went through the clothes I brought down with me from Maine and took most of them, tweed jackets with leather patches I used to teach in, to the Goodwill. I threw away all my pants and shoes and bought black jeans, black t-shirts, and black boots, leather motorcycle boots, and now I needed a jacket. I saw one that I liked on a guy at an AA meeting, a classic motorcycle jacket with the zippers and pockets and studs and epaulets, that came down just to his belt. At a leather store on Charles Street I put it on. I looked like the guys in the Tom of Finland pictures. Then I wore it outside into the fall afternoon and walked home across the Public Garden and out Newbury Street through the crowds on the sidewalk and the crowded cafés, aware as I strode along that men were watching me. It was a good moment. I had bought the jacket to attract the attention of men, and now I was able to feel myself admired, which I had never allowed myself before. Now, for the first time in my life, it was happening, and I heard it, remembered it later and savored it, felt the compliment and knew what had caused it.

At the Ramrod, the search was less for beauty, what Malone was looking for, than for the promise of a certain kind of sex that involved a level of pain and a certain extent of trust between the two men. I was surprised that everyone in AA was not into S&M—both involved surrender to something greater than themselves. The only difference was that in AA, you could never be the Higher Power.

↔

I was alone much of the time. I wandered through the Museum of Fine Arts, looking at the pictures and sculpture, the painting *The Wrestlers*, by George Luks, in the nineteenth century gallery, with its strong men struggling, their backs tensed and arched, their legs interlocked, and *Fray Hortensio Felix Paravicino*, by El Greco, an intensely knowing man with a small smile, and eyes that seemed to be both experiencing tragedy and meditating upon it. In the Greek and Roman galleries, I came upon the small Roman reproduction of the Farnese *Hercules,* and the *Hanging Marsyas*, with its delicately carved testicles against the thigh. I enjoyed the freedom I had to look at pictures and statues of nude men and to appreciate their shoulders and arms, their backs and buttocks. I was able to stand in front of a statue of a nude man and to appreciate what the artist had seen in the model, the crease under the back of the buttock, the delicate curve down and in of the abdomen, the way the balls hung against the thigh, the fit of the deltoids into the trapezius. It was what Warhol had seen in the body of Joe Dallesandro—a beautiful thing. I found one of the most wonderful sculptures in the museum, the *Assyrian Winged Diety*, a large low-relief stone slab carved with a winged god striding forward. The point of Greek sculpture from the period was to approximate some ideal of beauty. On the other hand, the Assyrians were abstracting some ideal of power. The god is powerfully built, his arms and legs showing developed muscles that are beyond athleticism. His arms are bound by metal bands, and he has powerful shoulders. He wears very heavy gold earrings and a necklace, and the tight curls of his hair are carefully arranged. It is a vision of male power that no subsequent western civilization possessed. At the Fogg at Harvard, it was possible to see the Sargent watercolors of the dark-skinned boys swimming and to marvel at his admiration for the beauty of a naked boy. The Cellini bust of Bindo Altoviti in the Gardner is a powerful portrait of a man in middle age, and I learned the man whose autobiography I had read when I was in New York in 1963, twenty years ago, appreciated the power, as opposed to the

319

beauty, of men, one locus of which is in their eyes. Altoviti has eyes that rest on the viewer with benign interest. The bust changed my idea of what Cellini's workshop assistants may have been like.

Tim and I went to Cambridge to the Fogg, Harvard's art museum. I told him I was taking him over there to see what Alexander looked like, who had also had his battles to fight, and fought all of them when he was very young.

We stood in front of a head of Alexander.

"Is that him?"

"Yes. Once you get one of these heads fixed in your mind, you can recognize him in museums everywhere, and you don't need to read the card. They are all of the same person."

"Jesus. That's Alexander the Great."

He walked around it. It was only a head, not quite life-size, mounted on a small bronze rod drilled up into the neck, on a pedestal perhaps four-and-a-half feet high.

"That is what he really looked like?"

"Apparently. The ancient world agreed that this was what he looked like, and there are hundreds of statues of him in museums all over the world, all having the same features."

"He looks desperate."

"He's got large eyes. He's beautiful."

"I know, but he looks like he's faced with more than he can handle." Then, "He's got beautiful hair."

"Some statues have a body too, there's one here somewhere, but I have never seen one that had arms or legs."

Tim was circling the sculpture. "He looks like he is pleading."

"That may be a result of the current state of the head—the nose is almost gone, and you can't see what the eyes were meant to look like."

"I know, but the mouth is open, as if he is exhausted, and the head is thrown back a little as if he has just run a marathon—do you see?—and he is too exhausted to care what people think of him."

We looked at the other one of Alexander, this one with a torso.

Tim grinned. "He's got a nice ass."

When Ames and Judith came to town, we toured the same museums. We also visited the Giust Gallery on Washington Street which had plaster casts of classical sculpture made from the nineteenth century Caproni molds. Ames and I examined busts of

Brutus and Athena, and of Hermes from the statue at Olympia of Hermes with the Infant Dionysus. The owner of the gallery entertained them by asking them to stand in front of various busts and then to answer the question, "Does Athena like you?"

But most of the time I was alone. In the *Shaw Memorial* across Beacon Street from the State House, I studied the faces of the men and their arrangement in ranks. It was a monument to the Massachusetts 54th Volunteer Regiment during the Civil War made up of Black men who had enlisted to fight for the union even though they ran a particular danger of being captured on Southern battlefields and then enslaved. Many of the men and most of the officers were killed in a battle for Fort Wagner, outside of Charleston, South Carolina.

Augustus Saint Gaudens created the bronze high relief sculpture, and Charles McKim designed the white marble frame, terrace, and staircase holding the bronze relief. The sculpture is extraordinarily moving, these heroic men marching off to war—for many of them to their deaths—for the cause of freedom and for racial equality.

It should have raised a very clear response in the viewer, but it didn't. It was difficult to tell who was being honored here. It is called *The Shaw Memorial*. "Shaw" is the name of the white colonel, Robert Gould Shaw, age 25 when he marched off to war, who was the son of a prominent Boston abolitionist family. It is not "The 54th Regiment Memorial." It is Shaw on his horse, sword drawn, who occupies the largest place in the center of the sculpture. In the original quotations, incised in the marble, is the phrase "guard of dusky hue," and Shaw and the other white officers are praised for having "cast in their lot with men of a despised race." The "men," beautifully and individually realized, all black, march off to war beside, in front of, and behind the colonel. Originally, only the names of the white officers were included on the memorial. Someone must have realized that the focus of the monument was wrong—or ambiguous, and the monument that I walked around and took pictures of, one of the great works of public art in America, was also a monument to the history of changing taste. It was only during a major renovation of the sculpture and the marble casing that the names of the individual black enlisted men were added, in 1982, only two years before I arrived in Boston. On the back of the monument, under the words, "The Memory of the Just is Blessed," are the men's names.

I did all this while walking around the city, and a friend at a meeting said, "I see you everywhere." I was exploring what I hoped was to become my city, putting down my roots in it. It was important to me that Boston had great museums—truly great museums—greater than anything else in the country outside of New York or Washington.

I went to a dance Saturday of Thanksgiving weekend. I wore a tuxedo and black patent leather pumps that I used to wear out with Naomi. My friend Vincent, who was a stylist on Newbury Street, had cut my hair and spiked it up, and I wore long dangling rhinestone earrings. I arrived at the dance alone—the dance was in City Hall—and walked up the ceremonial staircase outside, entered the building, and stood alone for a moment at the head of the large staircase. I was excited and expectant, wondering what would happen. Suddenly, someone spoke from behind my shoulder.

"Fair, you're finally having your prom, aren't you?"

I laughed.

"Fair, you're gorgeous. Will you spend the rest of your life with me? Or at least dance every single dance with me, tonight, now?"

I turned around to find the man from AA, Lee. We walked together down the long ceremonial staircase to the dance floor, and danced, and danced, Lee's head on my shoulder. At the end of the evening Lee said, "You lead beautifully." I had had practice.

Since I arrived in Boston in September, 1984, I had been writing short stories and novellas—nothing I had shown anyone. Some of these were sexy, almost pornographic, and others were more ruminations on a point. All of them were gay stories. That is, they had gay characters in gay situations—men with men, men with their families, men at work. One of them, which I came to call the Royal Academy Story, was about two men attending the exhibition, *Painting in Naples 1606-1705 from Caravaggio to Giordano*, October 2, 1982-December 12, 1982, at the Royal Academy in London. Walking through the rooms of the Royal Academy, looking at the pictures of saints in agony, these two men struggled with each other to resolve the imbalance of power between them and to understand the pain they felt.

Race Point Light

I was also writing on a new subject, something longer. I brooded over the events that had happened in Maine. When I returned home from Millinocket after Anderson Darwell and his friend were murdered, the local Unitarian-Universalist church held a memorial service for the two men. Then, in the two months before I was to leave the university and move to Boston, a gay organization was formed to address questions of homophobia in Bangor. Many gay people who lived in Maine, but who had been closeted, came out, and the murders and the organizing afterward attracted national attention. I was writing about these events—what it meant to have a friend murdered—thinking about them as I walked around the city or stood in front of statues in the museums or on the streets, beneath the heroic statues of fighters for freedom along Boylston street at the edge of the Public Garden, about the conceptions of maleness and the conceptions of gender that prompted such passion, carrying with me a sheet of paper folded in my hip pocket and a pen with which to write. It was clear that I was writing about those events in Maine, but I was also writing about myself here, now.

I was affected by the obvious way I was changing—the leather, the earring, the fact that all my friends were now homosexuals, the main things I looked at in the Museum of Fine Arts were representations of men, the only places I went in town were gay places, aside from *The Boston Globe* the only things I read were gay newspapers—and thought, perhaps this was what they mean by *coming out*. It is deeper, broader, more comprehensive, more obvious, than merely acknowledging one's same-sex desire or than telling another person or even all other people. My picture, identified as a gay man, along with my name and work address, had appeared on the front page of *The Sunday New York Times* when Andy was murdered, so telling all other people had been taken care of before I came to Boston. What was happening to me was more than the sum of all that. It had to do with finding my place in a distinct community, defined, like all communities, by a sense of place and time, by papers and shops and a look and gathering places and sexual attitudes, by a sense of *us*—and by a sense of history. I had not had a sense of us since I had been a kid on the playground in Columbia, South Carolina. This sense of us was most intense for me at three locations in the city—gay AA meetings, at the bookstore called Glad Day on Winter Street in the Downtown Crossing, and at the Ramrod.

Books, sex, AA. I had to go to work every day and work with straight people, but I passed through them untouched. A scrim dropped down all around me, and the only people who passed through it were other gay men, who appeared around me suddenly, out of the crowd and fully present for me. The sense of *us* in the gay world in Boston was so natural, so right for me that for the first time I needed no translator, needed no armor, felt at home. It hadn't taken me any time to learn to be gay.

A friend had a theory—any man could have any other man, which was near to Malone's theory that, "Over a long enough period of time, everyone goes to bed with everyone else"—and it seemed to be coming true for me. I was in the bar and had to make a phone call, which meant that I had to walk toward the front door and turn right at the end of the bar to the telephone. As I rounded the bar, I saw a man who was strikingly good looking. I made the phone call, then turned and came back past the man, who was sitting at the bar alone. He had the beauty—and magnetism—of some movie stars and an assurance with it, as if it were easy to be the very type of beauty that the whole culture admired. He had short, loosely curly dark hair, large eyes with long eyelashes, a dark tan, and a smile that seemed to me to say, *This is going to be fine.*

I moved up to the bar next to him, breathless with his beauty, and said—just as the man looked over at me and smiled—"I think you are the most beautiful man I have ever seen."

The guy laughed. "Thanks." He seemed genuinely pleased. We talked for a few minutes, and then we prepared to leave. When we were standing at the coat check window to get our coats, the man behind the counter looked at us and said, "This is just what I would have thought would happen. You're gorgeous, and *you're* gorgeous, and so naturally you two are going home together." He grinned.

I loved the city, the range of possibilities it presented, the energy created by a million people in too small a space, the sexual and intellectual and social potential on the small peninsula thrusting north into Boston Harbor. I enjoyed too the demands made on me by my move to Boston, the need to find a place to live and to work and have friends and buy books and to have sex. When I received a letter from my mother or even one of Henrietta's odd missives—letters written on Christmas cards and mailed from the Caribbean in

February—I wondered how difficult it must be to stay alive when your whole life had been lived in one town.

One aspect of this sense of us was the sense we all had of being besieged by the virus and of having the health crisis ignored by the government. We were being eaten alive, and the immense powers of the federal health establishment were being withheld from us. Tim said to me, "You're thinking about some beautiful man you're seen or some book you want to write and you suddenly see in front of you the front page of the *Gay Community News* with a headline saying *the president has cut funding for AIDS research* and instead of thinking about the future—the man or the book—you're thinking about all the dangers around you, about wills and do you have enough health insurance or, in my case, any health insurance—" Worse, there seemed to be a scandal submerged under the inaction. Ever since arriving in Boston and having access to gay news on a regular basis, I became aware of something corrupt going on which had to do with Robert Gallo, who everybody called the discoverer of HTLV-III, the AIDS virus, Luc Montagnier, the French medical researcher at the Pasteur Institute who, it was widely agreed, had discovered LAV, the AIDS virus, Gallo's rise to power in the CDC, and federal funding for research and who got it. It was constantly pointed out in the gay press that there could not be two AIDS viruses. In the stench arising from all this, what seemed to be discernible was that power struggles in the CDC, the competition for the Nobel Prize, and political considerations by the Republican Party, all were playing a larger role than the desire to save the lives of gay men, IV drug users, and Haitians. The Health and Human Services people said, even when Congress asked them directly, that they didn't need any more money, but the gay papers said that what the HHS people were doing was shifting AIDS dollars from one budget into another, and that privately these same HHS people acknowledged that they were in desperate need.

It wasn't that there were merely two different kinds of people, there were two distinct worlds, and the straight world didn't know anything about the gay world—and what it knew, it condemned. (Gay people, most of whom had grown up in straight families, already knew all they needed to know about that world.) Straight men didn't know what was going on in the gay community, and not only about sex. They had their fantasies about gay bars, but they didn't know what communal centers these bars were, groups of men talking program in various parts of the room—or what neighborhood business got transacted there, what organizations there were in the gay community, and for what purposes. I knew this because I myself hadn't known. I realized that it was not a community so much as it was a world that I had not known about. I was driving a bunch of young straight men home after a waitering job, when I drove past the Ramrod. One of the young men said, "That's where the toughest gay men in Boston hang out." The young man didn't know anything about gay people, and he was running off at the mouth. My mother spoke of innocent victims of the epidemic, not knowing any of the men with whom I sat on marble benches who talked about terror.

While I was affected by what was happening to me, my sudden and rapid transformation into what people called a gay man, it was really the things I was doing when I had sex and the gender of the people with whom I had sex that had changed. I accepted that I was in something called the gay community and its ways were congenial to me, and I accepted that I now identified myself as a gay man, but I had lived too long before I came to this community to think that I had changed in any fundamental way. Nor did I believe that these things were stable. The world of sex and sexuality had profoundly changed too regularly for me to believe that this too, wouldn't change.

I was writing about a man who, because of the murder of a friend, came out into the gay world that I was now a part of. And because the murdered friend, who was not gay, was murdered because the murderers thought he was gay, I pondered, on my walks around the city, a plot that would somehow arise out of the conflict among the kinds of things I had expected to find when I arrived in Boston and the things I found, between what the men in Maine thought they were murdering—they were murdering some idea in their heads, not something in Andy—and what they murdered, between what had appeared to happen to me and what had happened to me. It was between my mother's sense of innocent victims and my memories of my conversations on the marble benches, between the straight guy's toughest gay men in town and my own long, intimate conversations with gay alcoholics, shouted above the loudest music in Boston. I walked across the plaza before City Hall and down the broad staircase to Congress Street. I wanted my novel to be big and complex, to have many characters and a many-sided take on its subject. I wanted to investigate an idea, and the idea was far too complex to be contained by one man's perception of the world. In December, 1985, I began to write seriously on a novel, and I threw away earlier efforts. That afternoon, when I got home, I opened a new file on my computer and began to write. The first words were *This is what happened on Saturday.*

In February 1985, *The Native* printed the story of the Reagan administration's plan to cut funding for AIDS research by 15 million dollars. *The Native* said, "It is ironic that the Reagan administration plans to cut the budget for AIDS research by as much as 15 million dollars, yet the US holds the patent rights on the test kit. This means that the US government is making money from the dead and dying."

↔

In March, I took Judith and Ames to South Carolina to visit my family. I asked Mother to arrange an evening when the young people and I could be with Cornelius and Henrietta and their children. Late in the afternoon on the day we arrived, Mother had a picnic in the yard. The dogwoods were just beginning to come out, the azaleas had been out for a week or ten days, and the gardens had the lush quality that gardens in New England almost never reach. Aunt Caroline was the first to arrive, bringing a large silver bowl of azalea blossoms for the center of one of the tables. She called to me, "Oh! It's just wonderful that you're here!" Then she said, "I'll be right back." She went back to her house next door and reappeared in a moment with a large bowl of potato salad. Ames and Judith and I were sitting in the swings—the same swings I had played on when I was a child—while my mother was puttering around the table, arranging a roast, loaves of bread to be sliced, chilled marinated green beans. Cornelius, when he arrived, was going to set up a bar in the kitchen for those who wanted drinks.

I strolled around the garden with Ames and Judith, telling them stories about my childhood, some they had heard before, when they were very young, and had forgotten. I told them good things—how beautiful the garden was in spring when I was a little boy, how my grandmother always looked like her portrait, sitting at the head of her table, regal in her arm chair, how kind she had always been to me—

while we walked behind the garage on the lush thick grass among the oleanders and dogwood trees and around the giant camellia bushes. I walked in the middle, between them, and we held hands. I nodded toward the garage. "That was where I used to hide when we'd play hide-and-seek."

Aunt Caroline called out to us. "Yoo-hoo!" in the way the sisters had. "Come over here! Here we are! We thought we'd lost you!" It seemed warm and friendly, and it seemed as it had when I had been a child, but I was not a little boy any more. I was 46, my children were 16 and 14, and my aunt was in her seventies.

"Come over here—" My aunt was speaking to my children. "—I want to introduce you to some of your cousins." She took them away.

This wasn't working. I wanted them not to hate my family, to accept them as an important part of their lives, but they already knew that I had been fighting these people for years over racism, conservative politics, and homophobia, and there was no going back. The damage had already been done, and I could not prevent them from knowing. By this time, there were many people in the garden, my cousins and their children, and others, second cousins, and their children, Caroline and Richmond and, of course, my mother, whom I saw for the first time in this setting without my father. The whole thing was very sad. I had hoped that my children would not experience the loss that I had experienced. And they didn't. They lived too far away and had never felt possessed by these people.

"They were so cute together," Mother was saying, describing some couple at a party. Then, "I must bring out the asparagus," and she was off to the house to get a tray.

I wandered among the crowd. Aunt Caroline had both my children in tow, taking them from cousin to cousin. "And this is your cousin Halcott! His mother and your father are second cousins. His grandmother and your grandmother were first cousins."

I thought of rescuing Ames and Judith but thought I would let it happen for a while longer. There was a chance that they would get on better in this place if I were not around and in the way. I thought that Aunt Caroline had it wrong. I was surprised that she didn't know how to connect with my children. Instead of taking them from cousin to cousin, she should have sat down with them and talked to them about themselves. *Tell me about yourself.* And then she should have listened while they talked. They would never forget her, if she did that. Now what they would remember about my aunt was that she was that lady who introduced them to all those people. Then I heard someone behind me, a woman.

"Fair! It's me, Caroline!"

And I turned and faced a cousin, Caroline Howell. There were half a dozen women and girls named Caroline in the family.

"Oh, Fair, it's so good you've finally come back to South Carolina." She was a tall, handsome woman whose blond hair hung in a loose pageboy around her face. "Give me a hug."

"Caroline, I've missed you." Actually, it was the world of which she was a part that I missed.

When she pulled away, she looked at me and smiled. "Can we talk?"

I pulled back and looked at her. In her mid-forties, she was a beautiful woman. This was what she had been maturing into since our childhood. I held her hand. "How are you?"

"I'm wonderful. But what I want to know about is you. Tell me about your divorce. What happened?"

"I'm gay. I was no longer able to live in the heterosexual institution called marriage." I said all this with a slight smile. "And Naomi and I separated, that is, I left her and sued for divorce, and now I live in Boston, writing a book. I've brought the children down to see their relatives because we haven't been here in several years."

She watched me, closely, not smiling. "That's what the earring is all about, is that it?"

"Well, Caroline, there are straight men who wear earrings. But, yes—" I laughed. "—that's what it's all about."

She narrowed her eyelids. "That must have taken courage."

I shook my head. "Actually, not much."

"Well, I think it must take courage. Do they—" She nodded over her shoulder at the sedate crowd behind her. "—know?"

"I don't know about all of them, but everybody knows." I put my hand on Caroline's arm. "Caroline, I was on the front page of *The Times,* identified as a gay man." I laughed. "Everybody ought to know."

"No!" She seemed aghast and didn't ask how I had gotten on the front page of *The Times*, what I had done to get myself there.

"Did Cornelius see it?"

I laughed. "Apparently so. Mother says they were ripshit."

Caroline laughed. "I can imagine. Cornelius is such a toad. But they didn't talk to you?"

I shook my head. "No. Nothing."

"Amazing." Then she backtracked. "No, actually it is not amazing at all. It is typical of them."

I was watching my children back beyond Caroline as they were shepherded around the garden. They had found some cousins their own age—Richmond Jr.'s children—and were seeming to be having a better time than at first.

"I always knew you wouldn't stay around here and be ordinary." We watched the children for a few minutes. "What is it like, living in Boston?"

I watched my children carefully for the moment they needed to be rescued. "We are in the middle of AIDS, Caroline."

"Oh, it's terrible. We read about it every day in the paper. Do you know anyone?"

"I know men. There are almost 9,000 cases in the country now."

"Lord."

She looked at my face for a moment, and then she turned from me to the garden, toward the others. "Where are your children?"

I nodded toward them. "Over there, talking to Rich Sims' children. They're standing by Uncle Richmond. Do you see them? I have a boy 14 and a girl 16."

She searched the crowd. "Oh, yes. I see them. They're beautiful. Fair, they look like all the Shaws." She watched them for a few moments. "Do you think we are just a lot of straight WASPs, this crowd on the lawn?"

I laughed. "Well, you are, aren't you?"

"Oh, look, there's Cornelius—" Cornelius and Henrietta had come into the garden.

I excused myself. "Let's talk again later, OK?" And I left her and went over to speak to Cornelius.

Uncle Robert Fair had died, and since he had no direct heirs, Cornelius had inherited his company, a real estate development firm with offices in Charleston and Columbia. Cornelius entered the garden with the authority of a man who had made money, but, I felt, he also entered with the authority of a man assured of his own beauty. None of the other men in the family had inherited beauty

330

from anybody, even though some of the women were themselves beautiful. Cornelius had gone from strength to strength. His boyhood good looks, the straight, glossy, black hair, white skin, large expressive eyes with long black lashes, had matured into a handsomeness that was peculiarly American—physical, external, open, athletic. And he was clearly angry. He spoke shortly to the people who greeted him and seemed to be barely civil to the women. The sun was coming from behind the trees now, and most of the garden was in shadow.

Cornelius must have set up the bar because he carried a drink in his hand, and now I noticed other men and women carrying drinks. Cornelius and Henrietta were now surrounded by a group of men and women of their age—that is, in their late forties. I joined the group, which parted slightly to give me entrance. I was aware that some of them seemed vaguely familiar. They may have been my cousins who had moved from their twenties to their forties—lost their youth and become middle-aged—while I wasn't paying attention. I was face-to-face with Henrietta and Cornelius.

"Hello, Henrietta." I smiled.

"Hello, Fair." Henrietta did not smile.

Cornelius watched this.

A pause was beginning. "It is good to see you." This was really what I had come south for, to express good will toward my family.

"Oh, it's good to see you." She looked around, as if for a break in the small crowd which watched us, silently. "Where are those young people?" She stretched, slightly, as if to see over the heads of our audience.

I turned to my brother. "Hello, Cornelius." I smiled. "It is good to see you again."

Cornelius tilted his head back, as if to stretch his neck above his collar, then lowered it. "Hello." He was angry at me, and he didn't mind showing it. He looked down at his drink, swirled the ice, then turned away and moved through the crowd toward other people I couldn't see.

Henrietta suddenly said, "Oh, there they are!" And she moved away also, leaving me among this small group of people who were vaguely familiar but unknown to me.

"I am Fair Shaw."

A woman introduced herself. She was a cousin whom I had last seen when she was a child. I looked at the other people surrounding me, smiled at them all, then turned toward the lawn that was behind me, crossed my arms over my chest, spread my legs slightly, and observed the scene. The people around me gradually drifted away.

The casual assumption of superiority among these people was partly from ideas and feelings having to do with race and partly from ideas and feelings having to do with class. I wondered if I had passed that on to Ames and Judith. It was astonishing, coming from my life in Boston to this group, where the settled ways of doing things seemed a protection against all dangers.

The men were all in coats and ties, and the women in heels. In Boston, in my crowd, men took some care with their appearance, and some of them spent a great deal of money on clothes, but they didn't wear ties. The way my relatives in the South dressed had not changed since I lived here, attending debutante parties with Stockman during the Kennedy Administration. Their style gave the same sense of admiration that they felt for each other, unchanged in twenty years. No one talked politics, I presumed because they all agreed or because it was impolite to bring up potentially divisive subjects. I was pretty sure of what they really thought, under their manners. It had been eight years since I had last been here—I was still married to Naomi then, and I had come for Daddy's funeral— and they had gotten very little news of me in the intervening years. My mother's way was to tell her relatives only what she thought was good news and to conceal bad or difficult news, so these people would have heard the minimum: that Naomi and I were divorcing, that I had left the university and moved to Boston. When the picture of me, identified as a gay man, had appeared in *The Times,* my mother had explained it privately to Aunt Caroline, who, I presumed, had then told everyone "privately." So it had been whispered about among them all. Looking around the garden at these lovely people, I wondered how I was to enter into a dialogue with any of them on the subject of my being gay, or even if I should try. Then I remembered my earring. I pulled on it gently, and smiled. Caroline Howell had seen the point. While Mother and Aunt Caroline might whisper, *The Times* and my earring showed that I myself was speaking in a normal voice, and it was up to these people, if they wanted to, to respond.

Later, Rich Sims, my first cousin, walked past, headed toward the tables. He nodded, "Hello," but didn't slow down in his traverse toward the food. His wife, a woman I had always liked, was following her husband, and she smiled, "Hello, Fair," as she walked by. She didn't stop to speak.

There were men—Jonathan Sims, his father, and a man I didn't know—standing by the dogwood in the dusk. They all had drinks. They were talking.

"—he bid it, and then he came in over contract by three percent, and he whined and complained until I took him to court—"

"I know what he told you. I've had to deal with that bastard. He said, 'The rise in the price of steel, plus the rise in the price of oil—' Isn't that what he told you?"

"Ah—"

"Hello, Jonathan, Uncle Richmond. Hello." I turned to the other man. "My name is Fair Shaw."

"Yes. I know." He turned to the others. "Excuse me, gentlemen." He turned away.

"He is my father-in-law," Jonathan said. "How are you?"

"I'm fine." I wondered how far this was going to go. "It was a long flight down, but we got in about four, a couple of hours ago, I guess."

The other men didn't say anything.

"The weather in Massachusetts right now is still late winter, and here it feels like late spring."

"Uh-huh."

"You got a divorce."

"Yes. In December."

"That was really necessary." It was said as a question.

"Yes."

There was silence. I considered, for a moment, what to do, and then I turned slightly to face the gathering, spread my legs slightly, and folded my arms across my chest.

The other two men drifted away, and I was left in front of the dogwoods on the edge of the lawn. The sun had gone down, was behind the houses, and now twilight gathered itself in the garden. It was what we all keep telling ourselves, a beautiful place, in the spring with the flowers in bloom and the grass already a deep green, and between the trees the glimpse of the white houses, the men in coats and ties and the women in summer dresses and heels, small children playing around the tables and on the swings, and on the tables white linen and the glint of large pieces of silver. This was a scene that, for me, was at least forty years old. These people—these beautiful people—had been raised to take their places on this lawn, or on a lawn like this one, the sun filtered through the green leaves of the trees, the old garden shrubs in full bloom, to talk in subdued voices of the events of the day, the state of the church and its activities, the rise and fall—and rise and fall and rise—of the family fortunes.

Henrietta and Cornelius were standing among a group of young people that included Ames and Judith. Cornelius spoke gravely to each of them, drink in his hand, his highly polished shoes leaving a light imprint in the grass. I watched as Cornelius paid special attention to Ames, drawing him to him, putting his hand behind the boy's neck, and talking to him in the low, slow, voice for which he was known.

"We have missed you so," a low voice said at my shoulder.

I turned. It was the friend of my mother's, Cynthia Pope.

"It's been so long since we've seen you. You stay away too long!" She had very large eyes and high cheekbones and always spoke softly and always had a bright, expectant smile. She smiled now and seemed to wait for my response. Her brown hair was streaked with gray.

"I know, Cynthia. It's good to see you too, and I have stayed away a very long time." I put my hands on her shoulders and brought her toward me and hugged her lightly.

"You must have been very busy."

"I've had a lot to contend with in the last several years, the last three years, and—"

"Tell me about it." Then she was quiet, waiting for me to speak. She had always been like this, since I was a child. Now she must be 65.

"I divorced Naomi."

"That must have been painful."

I shrugged. "It was."

"Can you talk about it?"

"I couldn't take it anymore. I am gay, Cynthia, and I was married almost 19 years." There were pauses between my sentences. "I

334

almost drank myself to death, and I finally realized I had to get out of my marriage. I didn't feel that I had much choice. I told Naomi, then I left her, and later I divorced her." I shrugged. "She didn't like it, but there wasn't really a choice. We were killing each other. I came out. And I moved to Boston last fall."

She seemed very concerned. "Are you all right?"

"I think!" I laughed. "I think I am. I have a job, I am writing a book. My children love me. They let me love them. Guys love me." She smiled briefly at that. "I'm sober." I shrugged. "What else is there?"

She was very serious. "That must have been very hard."

"It has been."

"I want you to be happy."

"I want to be happy."

"Your mother loves you very much."

"I know." I paused. "I know. I love her."

"I think she thinks you are angry with her for something."

So. Mother asked her to speak to me. "Cynthia, this has been a hard time." I could see, beyond her shoulder, the soft twilight of the southern evening in the garden, the spots of white which were the blossoms of the dogwood against the darkening green of the trees, the light-colored clothing of the women and the children against the green shadows. It was a beautiful moment. "When I changed the way I was living, I knew it was going to put a—" I thought, wondering what word to use. "—distance between me and many of the people I loved. I knew they were going to find it inexplicable, strange, and I wanted to try to reduce the amount of distance between us by talking, by writing letters about what had happened. I wrote Mother a good many letters, and I wrote Cornelius and Henrietta." There were the shrill cries of children in the dark. "But it was much more difficult than I had imagined. I think they didn't understand what was happening. We could have kept that distance to a minimum, or even eliminated it, but I think they were affronted by my letters. Cornelius never answered any of them. Mother argued with me." I laughed, softly. "Mother told me I'd have to quit teaching now because a gay man can't work with children. She kept telling me horrible things that Cornelius and Henrietta said. I embarrassed the whole family, I was being selfish. Apparently Henrietta said she knew plenty of gay men in marriages—they take Tuesday nights off. It was one of those times when everybody has enormous needs, needs so great that they can't see how much everybody else is in pain too, and so all of us got angry and have stayed that way for two years." I lit a cigarette and looked at Cynthia, her large eyes and her concern. "I am, to some degree, getting over it. I think I know what happened. I have some sympathy for them. But the problem, Cynthia, is that the distance is still there, is now worse, greater, than it was before. They hate what I did, and—you know, I don't know whether they are homophobic or not, or just against people getting divorced, or maybe just against my divorcing this particular woman, but they act like they are homophobic. Mother has these weird ideas, truly hurtful ideas about homosexuality, just when I need her to be accepting and loving, and if what she says is true about Cornelius then I think he is homophobic too. I am convinced Henrietta is a bigot."

"Oh—" She put her hand on my chest. "—but Fair, you don't know. They need time, you must give them time—"

"They've all known I was gay—Mother for more than five years, and Cornelius and Henrietta for longer than twenty years. You'd have thought they would be accustomed to the idea by now. I don't know. I think we are now in a place where, if they don't get over it, the distance between us is going to become so great that the separation between us will become permanent. Cynthia—" I slid my hand across her shoulders and moved so I was standing next to her. I gripped her shoulder and pulled her close to me. "The reason I am here this weekend is to see if this split can be healed."

She looked at me.

"In any case, let's try, you and me, to remain friends, can we?"

She smiled as if she had come through a period of deep pain herself. "I hope so." She loosened herself from my grip and turned toward me. "Fair." She paused, as if looking for a way to express herself. "You are being careful, aren't you?"

"I am being careful."

Be careful. The disease mode. It is possible to come out into a variety of modes. In the eighties—now—we most often come out into the disease mode, where the assumption is that the gay community means disease. And coming out into that means working your way past that into a mode where all is healthy.

By now, many of the people at the party had left. Cynthia herself left, after saying good-bye to Mother. Ames and Judith came over and grasped my arms and hung on me.

"I'm tired, Dad." It was Ames. "Can we go home?"

"Me too." It was Judith. "Can we go into the house?"

"Yes, you may."

And they did. I looked around me and saw Caroline Howell.

"So. How are you holding up?" She moved her head slightly to indicate that she meant, under all this around behind me.

"The cousins. Yes."

"I also mean the sibling."

"I'm doing OK, Caroline. This is what I expected it to be." The tone set by my family was of a gentle interest in each other, and the kinds of responses people made were within the narrow range between *I am very well* and *Oh, it's not been a very good week.*

She looked intently at me, trying to discover my meaning. "Has this afternoon been all right for you?"

She wanted to know more than I was willing to give, right now. What would she do with what I could tell her? I raised my eyebrows. "Of course." On the other hand, was there any point in not telling the truth?

"What are you doing in Boston?"

"Work? Money?"

That was what she meant.

"Odd jobs. What I am really doing is beginning to write a novel."

"On what?"

"It's about the place where gay people and straight people rub up against each other." I laughed. "It's about us."

She was perplexed.

Cornelius and Henrietta and their sons, young Cornelius and Joseph and Fair, were still by the tables, talking to a few stragglers. I wandered around what was left of the party, speaking to people I knew and introducing myself to people I didn't. I didn't have to introduce myself, actually, because I looked so much like Cornelius that people knew before I could speak. Finally, I went toward the tables and joined Cornelius and Henrietta.

"—I think we are going to Pawley's the first couple of weeks in August, but Henrietta is going to be in the mountains for most of the

summer, and so I don't know when we could do it." He smiled. "I
hope you will forgive us for not being able to come." Then, "Do you
think you could come to Pawley's for our party?" He had seen me
join them.

"Oh, do." It was Henrietta. "It would be such fun, and we would
appreciate it so." She had seen me join them also, and had smiled.

The other man said, "I don't know. We'll have to see. We're not
going to be at Pawley's then, but maybe we could go for the weekend—or something. I'll have to see what the children are doing."

It was left at that. The other couple made their good-byes, and
Henrietta walked with them as they made their way into the house.

Cornelius and I were left facing one another. Cornelius was
tense, his face flushed.

"Who is the mayor of Boston?"

For a moment, I could not think. Then, "I don't know. Ray
Flynn. I think."

"What kind of mayor is he?"

He had, at one point, been supportive of some issue a gay group
was pushing, so I said, "I think he is a very good mayor." But I could
not remember what the issue was and whether it was actually a good
thing that Flynn had done.

"Well." Cornelius turned and walked toward the house. I
followed.

All our children were in the house, Ames and Judith were on the
side porch, and Cornelius' children were in the living room.
Cornelius fixed himself and Henrietta drinks, and they went into the
kitchen, where Mother was, cleaning up after the picnic. Aunt
Caroline had just left. I went onto the porch.

"How are you guys?"

"Dad!" Ames spoke softly. "You have a fucked-up family."

I laughed. "What do you mean?" It was full dark now.

"I'll tell you later."

I stood behind him and ran my fingers through Ames's hair. "You
two were wonderful this afternoon. I appreciate it that you were
willing to come and spend time here. I love you."

Judith got up and came over and put her arms around me. "I love
you too. Can we go for a walk later, maybe?"

"That'd be great. Just the three of us."

Later, Cornelius and Henrietta came onto the porch. Cornelius seemed angry again, his jaw clenched and his forehead furrowed, his brows pulled together. His face was flushed deep red. Henrietta said, "We're going to have to go now. It is so late." Cornelius went into the living room, and I heard him talking to his children. I could tell from the noises that they were getting up to go.

"I do so miss your mother," Henrietta said, speaking to Ames and Judith. "We love her so. I hope, when you get back to Maine that you will tell her we miss her so, and that we hope to see her soon. Will you do that?"

Ames and Judith looked at her, and then, realizing she wanted some kind of response, both of them nodded.

"I do hope she is well."

Judith spoke. "I think she is very well."

"Oh, that's so good." Henrietta smiled at both of them. "It has been perfectly wonderful seeing you this visit."

The children grinned.

"Well!" She looked up, and saw me. She smiled. And then she turned and was gone through the door into the living room, and we heard them talking briefly before they went to the front door. I heard Mother talking to them, and then the sounds they made in leaving no longer came from the living room, they came from the front porch and the front steps. I could hear them calling, "Bye."

"Good-bye."

"Good-bye, Grandmother."

"Have a safe trip home."

"We will. Thanks for everything."

"Thank you for everything."

"Good-bye."

We heard the car doors opening and closing and the car starting, its lights coming on and illuminating the street, and then moving out into our full view as it picked up speed and drove away, up toward Devine.

We did take a walk. But first Mother came onto the porch and offered everyone ice cream, which nobody wanted. "These young folks would like to take a walk, so I thought we'd do that for a little bit. We'll be back in half an hour."

We left through the porch door and walked out through the garden to the street. I was very tired. It was a long flight down from

Boston—there were several stops, and the stewardess kept asking me if I wanted a drink—and the picnic had been tiring. I had enjoyed the conversation with Caroline and the one with Cynthia. There had been no men there I knew or had ever been friends with. I had never cared much for young Richmond and Jonathan and William, Caroline's sons. We never spoke the same language. The little party had been beautiful to look at—everyone in South Carolina seemed to dress for everything—but what was missing was fatal if it were missing. I was in the third or fourth grade when I realized I was not one of us. I left South Carolina because I was not. There was no reason for me to have supposed that I would be one of them now.

"How much longer are we going to be here, Dad?" It was Ames. We were crossing the street into the park, where I had played as a child. I held their hands, and when Ames spoke, I squeezed his hand.

I laughed quietly. "Today is Wednesday, and we go home on Sunday. So we are going to be here three more days."

"Oh, Dad."

"I know. It wasn't much fun. I am sorry about that." I spoke to Judith. "How was it with the young people?"

"It was OK." Judith was being brave for me. What, I supposed, she meant, but wasn't saying, was *It was shitty*.

We walked down into the park, by the small building where I had gone to kindergarten, and then down to the basketball court and the merry-go-round and the jungle gym. These were lit, and Ames ran ahead and climbed on the jungle gym. They had hated it, and I could tell it depressed them. It depressed me, too. It was a long, expensive, wasted trip.

↔

On May 8, 1985, I read in the inside pages of the Metro section of *The Boston Globe* that neighbors of a gay male couple in Roxbury were upset that two weeks ago two foster children, a twenty-two-month old boy and his three-and-a-half year old brother, had been placed with the gay couple. The article featured the concerns of persons in the neighborhood who were against the placement of the two boys. The reporter didn't ask the opinion of any gay people. I went to an AA meeting that evening and said, "*The Globe* seems homophobic—" The gang laughed. I had had an idea that it was only in small towns—in the South, in Maine—that homophobia existed.

The next day, the story moved from the inside pages to the front page of the Metro section. The headline read, "Placement of Foster Children with Gay Couple Is Revoked." I felt nauseated. I was in the middle of fixing myself something to eat for breakfast, and I put everything back into the refrigerator and lit a cigarette instead and drank coffee, sitting in my living room and staring at the paper. This would play into the hands of the Schumanns and my own mother, if they knew about it. It was what Naomi had hinted at when she threatened me with a fight in court over the children. Someone in the Governor's office had called the head of the Department of Social Services and ordered the removal of the children. The two gay men had had them for only two weeks, and now the Governor, his staff, the head of the Department of Social Services, and the newspaper were carelessly branding the two men and doing it on the second front page of the paper. Without using the words, they implied of the two men, *They're unfit parents.* There was the first article, then the second announcing the revocation of the placement, then two days later another announcing the two men's legal challenge, on the next day, two articles, and a week after the first, a long interview with the two men, who expressed their anger at the DSS and *The Globe* for exploiting their predicament, and the next day an article on the gay community's response to the choice of judge who was to review the case, and three days later, on May 20, 1985, an article examining the likelihood of gays committing child abuse. Reporter David Farrell wrote, "No power on earth will ever change the immutable natural law involving conception of babies and the optimum environment in which this law dictates they be raised." There was a week's worth of articles after that, concluding with an opinion column in which Ellen Goodman wrote, "I have never understood the need of gay couples to define their relationships as 'family.'"

↔

In the June 3, 1985, issue of *The Native*, whose front page was entirely taken up with the question, "SHOULD GALLO AND ESSEX BE IN JAIL?", the major thrust of the cover article was worry that the federal health establishment had too quickly adopted

Robert Gallo's retrovirus as the cause of AIDS and therefore had entirely bought into Gallo's leadership. I read, "Only papers on which Gallo is a co-author may be published from work done on 'his' virus. This means that any evidence contrary to the HTLV-III theory would remain unpublished."

In the summer of 1985, Tim and I went to Crane's beach for the day. We took the train up to Ipswich and then walked. The water was cold, and there were no crowds.

We got to the beach around noon on a day without clouds—intense sun and low wind—and spread out a blanket and opened our cooler. Tim pulled off his t-shirt and shorts, leaving only a brief nylon suit that barely covered his genitals and didn't cover his buttocks. It was an act of defiance. Tim had gone from being slender to being skinny. Before, when I had seen him in the Y, his muscles had not been developed, but they were there, noticeable under his white skin, smooth, elastic, flexible, perhaps even strong. Now it seemed as if he didn't eat enough. His bones showed at his shoulders, his elbows, his hips, and his knees. He appeared to have grown arteries in his temple.

"I know." He looked down and inspected his front. "It shows now, doesn't it?"

"You look skinnier. Otherwise OK."

"I don't care who sees it. This is what I am."

"Right. It's OK." I lay down on the blanket. And in a few moments he did also, and his hand found mine, and while we lay there, we held hands. I don't know what mine felt like, but his was bony and sweaty.

The sun was harsh and relentless, and the wind weak and ineffectual. I thought that this would be a short day at the beach. I turned over, and my hand found Tim's hand again.

"Would you put something on my back?"

I found the bottle and spread it across his shoulders and down his spine and then everywhere.

"I pay attention to you, to what you say in meetings and afterwards, and when we are together. You are driven by your writing —that, and your children. Sometimes I think you have your whole book in your head and are just writing it all down, then I hear you talk about making changes—cutting a chapter, throwing a whole chapter away, cutting it by ten percent." He was lying face down on the blanket, his face turned toward me, his eyes closed. He spoke one sentence, paused, closed his mouth, and then spoke another sentence. "When I hear that you are making adjustments to the book, I know the thing is still being made. I like that. You're not just writing it down, you are creating it word by word, from day to day. Not many of our friends are doing big things right now. In the last year, I don't think any of our friends have chosen to go to graduate school—get a PhD or go to law school—or have embarked on any big projects. The times are against that." He opened his eyes. "Have you thought of that? The times are against big projects? People like me get out of school, come out, come to Boston, get sick, and die before we have had a chance to do anything big. I've hardly had time to find out who I am, much less write something big." He closed his eyes and lay there next to me, our hands connecting us.

I didn't say anything. I let him talk, and occasionally I grunted assent—or said uh-huh—which was enough to let him know he was being heard and that he could go on.

"You're lucky. You've had time. You could do all those things you've done in your life—your achievements and your mistakes—and now, when you are 46, you can write about it all. And even at 46 you don't have to worry about dying next year. Having time makes you incredibly lucky."

Later, when we were in the water, I held him for a long time. I was not writing about it all, but I knew what he was talking about. He was being robbed.

He spoke, his thin voice in my ear. "I used to have dreams." He pulled away, his hands on my shoulders and looked at me, and then he grinned. "My dreams now are that I will get through what I have to get through without blowing it. I don't want to act badly, you know?"

We went back, and I dropped myself down, and Tim eased himself down onto our blanket.

"I haven't decided what I want to be." He laughed again. "I used to think the big question was, 'Am I going to be a doctor or a lawyer?' Now I think the big question—that I haven't begun to answer yet—is, 'Am I going to die accepting my death with serenity?' or 'Am I going to curse God and die?'" Then he turned onto his side and put his hands under his cheek and stared at me. "Do I have enough time to make that decision?"

"Oh, do both, Tim, do both. Acceptance does not mean losing your balls."

"Sometimes it feels that way. Give in to horrific injustice."

"Anyway, it is a waste of energy to curse God. Curse Ronald Reagan instead. Curse the people who are not funding AIDS research. Curse Robert Gallo."

"Ah yes, Gallo."

The New York Native reported in its issue of 2 September 1985/16 September 1985 that AIDS cases had doubled in a year, to 12,932.

↔

One night before the winter holidays I found that Naomi had arranged things so that Judith and Ames would spend only one night with me. It had been part of my divorce settlement that holidays were to be shared equally. But what had happened was that she always found reason to shorten the children's time with me. This kept me perpetually confused as to what I was supposed to do. It was snowing, and I left the meeting and walked down Charles Street, through the Public Garden, and out Commonwealth, passing statues. The message of the meeting, as always, was the Serenity Prayer, but the conundrum for recovering alcoholics was the meaning of "acceptance." Always one had to accept, but what was one to accept? The need to surrender in some way? Or was it the need to fight on? It was the subject of our conversation at Crane's Beach. Surrender sometimes meant surrendering to the need to fight on. Here in the middle of the AIDS epidemic, there was nothing left to do but to fight the federal government, the disease itself, the inertia of health organizations, the triumph of despair. One couldn't escape. Surrender could also mean leaving the battlefield. If I were committed to accept what had to be accepted—those things I cannot change—did that mean I had to accept an adversarial relationship with Naomi? Or did it mean something else? The snow was everywhere. It was not cold, but the snow was thick, and that night, weaving my way around the monuments, which were covered with snow, through the snow, I was impaled on the idea of surrender and its meanings.

In the Harvard Gardens, I observed the men around me confronting this issue of acceptance around AIDS. Men were intensely angry that the virus had entered their community, preventing them from living the life they wanted and felt they deserved. These men had so recently given up alcohol that they still felt deprived of a huge part of their lives and were not yet capable of fully comprehending the deprivations associated with HTLV-III. The anger I saw around the table was a problem, and not just for recovering alcoholics. It was also a problem for men who had to fight against the prevalence of the belief in the culture that they had brought it on themselves. They were not just losing freedom, they were also losing self-respect. This virus put them in danger of losing the two greatest gifts granted them by Stonewall.

I talked to Tim.

"Do your children love you?"

"Yes, of course."

He turned his attention to the meeting that was about to begin, and I considered his question.

I suspected that, at least at the beginning, and perhaps for years, the meaning of acceptance had to be determined all over again each time.

Did I have balls? Was it required that I fight? Is that what a man must do? The protector of his family, the authority, law-giver, provider—what must a man be? She had challenged me repeatedly since I had left her, and here in front of me was the dilemma, if I gave in to her did that make me less of a man?

I trudged through the snow, feeling the stress of her demands and the stress of the demands put upon me by what I felt myself to be—a man and a father—and felt how tired I was of all that. I thought, how comfortable it would be to walk away from these battles and to let Naomi have whatever it was she wanted. The children and I did love one another. Would that be enough? That might be enough. I could give up everything else and make that be enough. I could make loving each other be enough.

I considered that. *Loving each other is enough.* I considered all the times when it was only winning that was enough. This was simpler and clearer. Loving one another would be enough.

I would say to Judith and Ames: I love you. Everything I said to them would be an elaboration or a variation on that theme. I would accept everything they did and everything they were, and if they could only come for one night during the holidays, I would accept

345

that, I would be glad, and it would be wonderful. I would not fight Naomi any more on any issue. I was free. I was gay. My children loved me. I loved them. Everything else was detail.

↔

On December 19, 1985, President Ronald Reagan received his most extensive briefing to date on the government's efforts to fight AIDS. The briefing lasted thirty minutes.

↔

On Wednesday nights, I was always at the AIDS Action Hotline, in the darkened room, in a booth, talking in a low voice into the phone above the whispers in the other booths. "You're going to make mistakes. We all do."

The voice on the other end broke in. "Have you ever made a mistake?"

I laughed.

"I mean about sex."

"Of course. I fell in love with the wrong person. I wanted the wrong things, stuck with it longer than I should have, long after it was clear I had gotten it wrong, was bull-headed about it all, couldn't accept the fact that I had made such a huge mistake, was embarrassed that I had gotten it so wrong. I don't know. Sometimes I think everything I did up to the time I was 46 was a mistake." Except my children.

"How old are you?"

"47."

"You don't sound that old."

"Well I am."

"Did you ever have unsafe sex?"

"Yes. I did even though I knew it was unsafe. People are going to do things that are unsafe. They smoke. They screw without condoms. They fall in love with the wrong person. Now, if you can accept that, then you are ready to move on to reducing the likelihood of your picking up the virus. If you can stop beating up on yourself for the times you fail, you can move on to the problem of increasing the number of times you succeed. You don't have to believe that because you failed this time you will fail every time—or that you are a failure. You're not a failure as a person, as a human being, just because you had sex last night without a condom."

"I feel like the worst person in the world."

"Well, you're not. The point is, look at your behavior last night. What made it likely you were going to have unsafe sex. What can you change?"

"I don't know."

"Were you drinking?"

"Yes."

"A lot?"

"I was drinking a lot."

"Can you go one day without drinking?"

"I don't know." The voice was anguished.

"Do it. One day. Then call us again."

"I think I can do that." He sounded doubtful.

"You know there's always AA."

"Have you ever been?"

"I go all the time."

"Do you drink now?"

"No."

"Do you do drugs?"

"No."

"For how long?"

"Years."

"Oh, God."

"You know, it's possible to change your whole way of life, if you take it one step at a time." Or, I thought, it's possible to change your whole life overnight, or between lunch and dinner, too, if you want to, or have to bad enough.

There was, on the Hotline, none of the jockeying around, attempting to find out where the other person was, judging—and misjudging—how the other person was receiving what you were saying that characterized person-to-person contact. There were just two voices, and neither knew who the other was, so it was a conversation cut off from consequences. He couldn't like me less because of what I said—and he couldn't come to admire me because of what I said, either. His connection was only with my voice. And what he would like—or not like—would be my voice. The

347

conversation was cut off from circumstance. I knew nothing of the other person—age, race, economic status, sexuality—and the Committee had drilled into the volunteers that we were to give out no important information about ourselves. The other person wanted only one thing—*love me*—and it was easy for me to give them that, for the length of the call.

"I see this guy, this hot guy, and I want him. I have this need for him right at that moment, to grapple with him in some hard way, struggle, you know?, till we determine who's going to win. That's what I like best about sex, dominating this other guy, spreading his legs. It's so basic, so elemental, proving that I am stronger than he is, even if I know and he knows from the beginning that this is what we're going to do—I'm going to fuck him—still there's the struggle, and I can't live without that. I'm showing who I am, what I am, and I'm doing it in a place much more profound than in an office or anywhere else. It's in my bed, where we don't have any of the things that define us—you know, money and clothes and houses and jobs and the other ways men have of defining themselves—Jesus! I don't even know who he is! He could be some hotshit something or other somewhere important, and I've got my cock up his ass and am driving him home—he's got his hands above his head bracing himself against the bed, and he's groaning—and I'm the biggest cock on the block at that moment, and how can I give that up? Huh? Say something!"

"Man, you got me going there!"

The guy laughed. "You liked that, huh?"

"At what point do you put on the condom?"

"Ah, man, that's the point. Here I am in the midst of this hot fantasy, and you guys want me to stop and act like a wuss."

"Why did you call?"

"Why, uh—" He stammered. "Have you ever felt the way I do?"

"I like 'em big and strong, bigger than I am." I was whispering into the phone. "And the bigger he is, the better I like it when I am on top of him, his legs spread and up on my shoulders, and I'm pushing into him, and he's groaning, and I know I'm hurting him, and I like that, too—"

"Yeah, that's what I'm talking about."

"—but before I lose myself in all that, I put on a condom because one of us may have the virus, and I don't want to give it to him or get it from him, you know? The virus is not a part of the sex I have in my mind. I have to remember that I am a man even if I stop and put on a condom, that being a man is more than just the size of my cock and what I can do with it in bed with another man. 'Cause I care about the other guy even while I'm fucking him. I care about myself, too, and all of that makes me need to put on a condom. It has to do with being a man. Can you see that?"

"I don't know." The voice spoke softly and slowly. "Being a man has so much to do with what I can do with my cock, man. I don't want to think about him. It's just what I can do with him, you know? Fuck him?"

I didn't know where to go. "There's something exciting, though, about my cock, when I have an erection and I pull on the condom and it grips it, pulls tight around it, and it's even more exciting when I think I'm doing what men do—take care of things, do what is necessary. It makes me feel hot, not just the thing around my cock but the knowledge that I am taking care of myself and of him. I love that—the sense I have sometimes that I am taking care of myself and of the man I am with. I am not just fucking him, I am taking care of him. I'm plunging into him and hurting him and taking care of him all at the same time."

The voice spoke slowly. "Go on."

"It's part of sex, isn't it, to take care of his needs too. Isn't that what a man does? Takes care of his man. Don't you want to take care of your man?"

There was a long pause. "Yes." Then, "This is hot, talking to you. Talking about fucking. This is as good as sex."

"I've enjoyed this."

"You make it seem very different from the way I saw it."

"Do you think you'll try a condom next time?"

There was a pause. "OK."

"Good."

"I'll try it your way. Take care of my man. I like that."

"Good."

"Can I see you sometime?"

"No. That's against the rules. The Committee won't allow that."

"What do you look like?"

I laughed quietly. "I can't tell you."

"You hot?"

The other guy had developed a lust for my voice.

It had to do with how they thought of themselves as men. Conceiving of ourselves as men, because of the culture we live in, confines us to thinking about ourselves in a certain way, restricts our range of options in our relations with other people. All this is complicated by the culture's particular condemnation of homosexuality—gay men are not really men. I hear it every Wednesday night, the need to prove, despite the culture's condemnation, that we are men after all.

In *The Native*, I read that Reagan "slashed" AIDS funding.

↔

In the spring of 1986, my life took on an order I couldn't remember it ever having before. After work, and before whatever I was going to do later, on Monday, Wednesday, and Friday, I went home and lifted weights for an hour. After I quit drinking, I had bought a decent steel weight bench and had been adding to the iron weight plates ever since, until I now had 700 pounds. All of this was crammed into a corner of my bedroom, where I had just enough space to lift. Every day after work, on days when I didn't lift, I went to the Y on Huntington Avenue and swam a mile. I prepared a pasta dish for dinner, and usually I completed my workout and my meal by 7:30, leaving me the next four hours or so for writing—or for the Hotline or the AA meeting. At 11:30 or midnight on most nights, I walked to the Ramrod and hung out for half an hour or forty-five minutes, talking to people I knew or even picking up someone and bringing him home for sex. Sometimes this man stayed the night. After the first two or three months in Boston, I cut back my AA meetings to one night a week—usually Monday. I had the AIDS Hotline on Wednesdays. On both of these nights I was often able to get in some writing time. I found that the walk through the city from the Back Bay to the Fens stimulated me, gave me time to think, and made me want to sit down to the computer before the bar or bed. This routine continued through the weekend, with the difference that I ran errands, wrote more during the day, and started my workouts earlier.

The Y was as absorbing sexually as the Ramrod. From the first, I noticed that the other men in the locker room were very open about their interest in each other, boldly checking each other out. The man came over—he was naked—and stood by my bench where I was tying my shoes. "What are you doing after?"

"Nothing." I sat up and checked him out.

"Wanna do something with me?"

"Sure."

So we would. The Y was less stressful than the Ramrod, since the point of being there was less frankly sexual, and this made it easier to connect. I picked up at least as many men in the Y as I did at the Ramrod. The shower at the Y is one of the sexiest places in Boston, and also one of the safest. The showers are two rooms the same size that open to one another through a door in the middle of their long sides. At this end are the lockers, at the far end the pool. Each of these two rooms has sixteen shower heads, eight on each side, and men take a long time getting clean. I saw a man under the head across from me, soaping himself. A man is never sexier than when his body glistens with soap. The Y was so free that it was possible to stare at the man opposite me for as long as I would stare at a painting in the Museum of Fine Arts, minutely examining his body parts and the way they moved together. The other man knew he was being examined and either enjoyed it or ignored it. Apparently it is one of the unofficial rules of this establishment that you allow yourself to be examined by whoever wants to examine you. Some men, it is clear, are displaying themselves. They invite the other men to enjoy them displaying their own bodies. Sometimes, I would turn from facing the wall to face the room and find the man opposite me stroking his erect cock while examining me. I knew that I could respond any way I wanted—there were no rules on that—but the decent thing was either to continue whatever I was doing and ignore the other man, while letting the other man complete what he was doing, or to get into the spirit of the thing and display myself while the other man masturbated. I caught the man's eye—and grinned— but I knew that even a grin was an intrusion into the other man's fantasy, so I ended my grin and prolonged my soaping myself until the other man had finished. Sometimes, it was me whose cock rose at the sight of another man, and who stroked himself until he was hard. There are "stars"—and men who know they are "stars"—whom men wait for, the swimmers and the bodybuilders, who become erect at all the erections they are causing. All this sexual activity is watched by the other men in the showers, some of whom must be straight, or not.

Some men just come into the showers, shower, wash off, and are gone. But my sense of things was that at least half the men in the shower at any moment are there because they want to see naked men, want to see men's cocks, without being hassled by the virtue police. They provide for each other a kind of continuously-running porno movie, where the shower scene, in which the star enjoys his own body, never ends.

The sauna was another center of sexual activity, but here it was more hands-on. Usually the lights are turned off, and the small room is illuminated only by light shining in through the window. While there, I became aware that I was being observed, and the man moved his seat to be closer to me, letting his towel fall away to reveal his erect cock, which, standing there next to me, he invited me to stroke. The sexual activity usually did not proceed beyond this mutual masturbation, but it was available there, all the time.

The staff at the Y made sporadic attempts to stop all this—it was as if they felt they had to—but their hearts didn't seem to be in it, and when they stuck their heads inside the sauna or walked through the shower, all the activity stopped for a moment and then resumed when they were gone. They seemed to be enforcing rules they didn't believe in, or no longer believed in. For the truth was that we were doing what the Y was intended to enable us to do, swimming, lifting weights, running, playing squash, even while we were adding to the list of exercises in our workouts the exercise the Y had not been designed for, safe sexual stimulation and release.

Sometimes these men became friends—I got to know two men who had been together for ten years who both taught at Boston University, Ken Mecklinburg and Carl Coker, and I met a tall, beautifully-built man, Bruce Nadler, who used the weight room and displayed himself in the shower, and these friendships extended beyond the confines of the Y. We had dinner together, and, in some cases, our encounters in the Y led to sex in my apartment. Bruce met my children, and we went to the movies. But more usually, when I saw these men on the street, we acknowledged each other with a nod or a smile and then went on, content for the sexual encounters in the Y to remain there.

I don't know what class the men were in the showers in the Y. They were naked, and they were beautiful, and I didn't know, or care about, the class of the man I brought home. Some spoke educated

English, some didn't. There was a range of classes for a man to express in his speech, and I found that I fellated men who expressed them all.

Talking to David Sepe one night after leaving the Y, I said, "It is not that I am moving into the working class, although my life now has some aspects of that. It is that I am moving out of the class system. I became aware of class issues, beginning in the late sixties, and I suppose I thought I was moving in that direction a long time before I actually started doing it. We had this big house, and we had too much money. Now, I seem to be moving out of any class."

David was skeptical. "Yes, with your PhD and that educated upper class way you have of speaking, and the whole way you hold yourself—as if you have just left a lecture hall, as if you are waiting a moment before looking over your shoulder to see if the students are following you—you are as middle-class as you have ever been. My own parents are working class—" David had gone to a junior college. "—and I think I'll always be working class, all my life, no matter how far up the ladder I climb. I think the difference between me and you is that you see working class people as more free because we are not chained by the things you are chained by—all those expectations of your middle-class family—and I see you as more free because you are more free. You have all that education, which means you can move back and forth between the working class and the middle-class and the upper class. Besides, you can't ever really be working class."

I laughed. "OK. You're right. I carry the detritus of all kinds of former lives, I guess."

David said kindly, "Yes."

It was not that I was now leaving the class system. It was that I was now recognizing a process that had been going on for years. David and I were friends.

Perhaps it was just that I was, myself, becoming coarse, but it was hard for a gay man who picked up men at the Ramrod or masturbated naked in a shower with other men, or who talked about safer sex one night a week at the Committee in the middle of an epidemic that was taking out everybody, not to feel that the whole idea was irrelevant. Henrietta had said, "I was gently reared, and I am going to rear my children the same way." Walking home through

353

the Fenway, I turned that thought over in my mind and found her formula astonishing.

Of course, class issues permeated our lives. They were inescapable. They determined the ways that both Naomi and I dealt with my being gay, and they determined how we had gone through our divorce. Both of us were middle-class WASPs, which meant that we grew up being fairly rigid about sexual matters. You got married once in your life, you did not commit adultery, but when you did it was with a woman, and the man was considered to be the head of the household. When Henrietta had said that she had known plenty of men in marriages who were gay, "They had Tuesday nights off," she was lying because that was not what one ran in to in the class and ethnicity that we all—Henrietta and Cornelius and Naomi and I— shared. In other classes and ethnicities, it really did seem to be sometimes true that a married man might have a relationship with another man on the side. Benvenuto Cellini had certainly that kind of marriage, and it is probable that Shakespeare did also, his wife in Stratford and he in London. Various kings of England had had that kind of marriage, and sexy men who fought alligators for a living in Florida did, but it was not common among the white Anglo-Saxon protestant middle-class in Columbia, South Carolina, in the last half of the twentieth century.

In the world of our class and ethnicity, it was demeaning for a man to have to submit to any level of secrecy for the sex which he desired, so Henrietta's formula meant that in our class it could only be demeaning for me to have "Tuesday nights off." Oddly, the whole gay world that had grown up since Stonewall shared many of these same protestant middle-class values. If I was going to be gay, or into same-sex sex, it could not be within the institution of marriage to a woman. The gay world was even more rigid than my ex-wife on that matter. A truly accepting, sophisticated and benign indifference to the private arrangements men and women made for their lives, such as one sometimes read could be found among the highest reaches of the aristocracy and the nobility—if such classes still existed—seemed to be beyond the gay community.

Naomi did not try to punish me financially in our divorce. She might have tried to force a high level of child support on me or even to obtain alimony, but she knew that our marriage was the reverse of one of those where the man is the principal breadwinner. While I earned what university professors at my level earned, she earned several times that. She accepted a smaller-than-usual child support, but she obtained a larger-than-usual share of our house and its furnishings, with the agreement that if I accepted these arrangements, she would educate the children. Had I been the principal breadwinner of the family, I might have used my money to assert a sexual independence outside my relationship to Naomi that I didn't have when I wasn't the principal breadwinner. But it would have been costly both to stay in the marriage when having sex outside it and to leave the marriage.

↔

One afternoon I was sitting in the sauna at the Y with a friend, a balding man in his early thirties with good pecs and gold-to-red hair at his crotch, when another man came in, younger, taller, a swimmer, a man with the broad shoulders and long arms and big hands, and those rangy muscles that come from hours at laps in the pool.

"You know who I met in the pool?" I spoke to my friend with the gold-to-red hair at his crotch.

We were all three naked—sweat making our faces and chests shine—and had allowed our towels to fall off, down around our feet.

"Who?"

"D'Artagnan. In the pool. Just now. He was coming up behind me when I stopped for a minute, and he stopped too. He said *Hi*, so I introduced myself, and that's when he told me."

Gold-to-red-hair was leaning back against the wall, his eyes closed. He smiled. "D'Artagnan." There was a long pause. "That's fine." Then he opened his eyes and looked at me. "I met a man last week named Achilles."

The swimmer and I laughed. "Achilles!"

"Yep. Achilles." He put his hands on the bench and pushed himself up, turned around and grabbed his towel, turned and smiled, raising his chin way up. "Achilles." Then he pushed open the door, said "Bye," and left.

I closed my eyes and smiled. I wondered if it were true. Achilles. I heard movement in the sauna and opened my eyes.

The swimmer had gotten his towel from the bench and had moved over toward me and sat down next to me. He was smiling at me as he let his towel fall open across his hips, revealing his erection. Then he spoke. "My name is Patroclus."

I had longish brown hair when I arrived in Boston from Maine, and Vincent saw to it that it was cut off quickly to a crewcut. But as I settled into life as a gay man in Boston, I experimented, letting it grow shoulder length, then bleaching it to a brassy blond, then, in the late eighties, cutting it off again, first to a crewcut, then—on the advice of a friend, I bought an electric trimmer—cutting it myself, back to 1/4" all over, then to 1/8" all over. It was a popular style in the bar, buzzed head and steel earrings. One night getting dressed to go to the bar, at about midnight, I used the trimmer and trimmed my hair back to the scalp. I arrived at the Ramrod and, as usual, a group of men were hanging out on the pavement out front. As I went past them, one said, "Shit. That's hot." I smiled and went into the bar, past the milling, shirtless men whose torsos gleamed with sweat, into the back room, where the lights were out. I was letting my eyes grow accustomed to the dark when I felt a man's hand slide over my scalp, an immense hand that seemed large enough to hold my whole head like a basketball. I turned. It was Craig Sexton, a giant, extraordinarily good looking man who was said to act in porn films. The big man whispered, "You have no idea how hot you are."

I laughed.

One day, when I was leaving the Y, I was walking down a long corridor from the reception area out to Huntington Avenue, when I heard a man behind me calling, "Hey! Hey!"

I turned and there was a man a few inches taller than I, attractive, short hair slicked back, around forty, worn in some indefinable way, very sexy.

"Hey, wait up."

I waited for him. I did not know the man.

When the man with the slicked back hair drew up with me, I turned and the two of us walked toward the light on Huntington. As we moved toward the light, the man put his arm around my shoulders and leaned over slightly to speak, in a whisper, in my ear.

"Was you—" he whispered, "—was you ever in Leavenworth?"

Crossing Tremont one night around eleven, I waited in the middle of the block for the traffic to clear. I was dressed for the bar, wearing full leather, boots, and a t-shirt. Suddenly one of the cars in the traffic lane threw on its brakes and pulled over 40 feet past me. A man who looked to be in his middle-forties—my age—jumped out of the car, a conservatively dressed middle-class man, and came running back toward me. I was transfixed by what was happening.

He came running up to me, and, out of breath, whispered, "Can I blow ya?"

One evening, I had come in from work, had worked out, and then had sat down to the computer for an hour's writing before going to an AA meeting. I had a character in the American Rockies, on a motorcycle, at night, careering around curves far above valleys several thousand feet deep, his hair flying, feeling free. I felt, sitting at the keyboard, the exhilaration a man might feel going around curves up into the Rockies, and I was typing with a kind of breathless hope that whatever I felt would last long enough to get my character through to the end of the paragraph. Then I hit the key hard on that last letter, said, *Goddamn,* saved my material, got up, went to the meeting, still glowing from the energy I had put into the page, and when I arrived, blowing into the building, a man asked, "How are you?"

"I'm fine, man."

The man grinned back at me. "And you look it, too."

When I came down to Boston, I was 44 years old, and I thought I was too old to connect with any man, but I found very soon that gay men—like straight men—have many tastes. While some men like partners who are very young, and others like partners who are their own age, there are many gay men who like partners who are my age. So I found myself being pursued by men who were a range of ages. For myself, size mattered more than age, and the men who shared my bed were the whole range of possibilities. But none stayed long. I was not ready for a partnership.

Just as I learned where the bookstores were, I learned what bars to go to and where I would find men. It was a case of having it all together. For a time I seemed to rise above the earth, the earth mortals walked on, as I moved on into my novel, the first third of it, as it began to come together, one strand after another falling like live electrical cables into my hands ready to be woven into the pattern I was making. Amelia, my friend in Maine, felt it too. Even without knowing how much more there was to the novel, she felt it gathering power. All the narrative threads were coming together and gathering speed. Only I knew how it was going to proceed.

Nobody in any of my former lives seemed interested in any of these changes in me, except my children. I wrote Mother, and I wrote Cornelius and Henrietta. Cornelius and Henrietta didn't respond, and Mother ignored what I had written in favor of a letter giving me all the "news" of my family in South Carolina. I tempered what I wrote Mother, shaped it for her ears, but much of what I was living through was there, if she wanted to know it:

I have been going to the Y to swim, and I lift weights at home. I have met interesting people at the Y and at AA meetings and I've dated a good many. There is a large community of gay AA people in Boston, and we call each other frequently, so I am rarely alone. All these places—AA and the Y and the others—are interesting because of all the different kinds of people whom one meets. I volunteer at the AIDS Hotline, one advantage of which is that we have very up-to-date information on HTLV-III and transmission. Men who are concerned about safe sex practices call in.

It is harsh that my relationship with Cornelius and Henrietta is so bad. What drives them? The message they give me—unspoken but there nevertheless—is that they never liked my divorcing Naomi, nor did they like my coming out. That's a shame, because that means we'll probably never be close. I understand that we were never very close.

Ames was here last weekend. He has been down twice since Labor Day and seems to like Boston. We go to the movies—we went to see *Silverado* when he was here—and sometimes out for meals, and I have taken them all over the city to see the sights. Of course, they've been coming to Boston since they were small so they know the city well. They have brought their friends, and we have long talks. I have introduced them to my friends, gay men from AA and a few other places I've enjoyed. I date often, but no one special. I introduce them all to the kids, so they'll know what they're getting in to. The wounds from the divorce gradually heal, and I am able to be more forward-looking.

↔

Leo Andrelli called late one night.

"So we had sex, and I found out only later that he has KS, and I am really bummed out about that. He should have told me. What do you think of somebody having sex with somebody and not telling them that he has KS?"

"Wait a minute. Why should you depend on him to save your life? He is as into the sex as you are, and you count on him to be more responsible than you are? It is your responsibility to save your own life. You make sure you use a condom. And if he is the active partner, you make sure he uses a condom. Otherwise, you don't have sex. He has no responsibility that you can count on to save your life."

"But don't you think—"

"No. You have the responsibility to look after your own health. We are not talking about him, here. What if a man offers you a drink? Whose responsibility is it to see that you don't take it? Yours or his?"

Leo was quiet. Finally, he said, "Mine."

My training classes with AIDS Action and my work with AA fed back and forth into each other.

Tim Byrne called. I had finished working out and had made a pot of coffee. I had been preparing to sit down to the computer. He started talking, very fast. "I'm not drinking, but I stay so angry all the time it is hard to get anything done. I get angry at my roommate for all the little things—his mother calls all the time and he stays on the phone with her for hours. I don't think he tips enough when he handles the check when we go out to dinner. I'm angry that I can't drink. I am really pissed that I can't do poppers. I'm angry about having AIDS, about my friends getting sick, about the government not giving enough funding, about Reagan. I get up in the morning with a knot in my stomach, and I can't go to sleep at night. I lie there grinding my teeth, and I think, if I could just get a drink—just one—I'd be OK, just one to relax me, to help me feel comfortable again somehow inside my skin, to help me stop hating so much. I am not like these other guys, I enjoyed drinking. I really liked it. I only quit because I thought it was ruining my life, but you know it was my life, and I ought to be able to do anything I want with it. The way I was, was better than the way I am. That's the hardest part of all. I hate myself. I feel so angry at myself all the time. I listen to the men in the meetings, and I wonder why I can't feel serene the way the others do, all calm and peaceful—you can see it in their faces, you know? *Your* face?—and I think, what am I doing wrong? Why am I failing so at this? I think I have failed all my life."

I listened. "I'm hearing everything you're saying. Go on."

"I can't go on. That's the point. I've reached the end of my rope."

"Not so far. Not so far. You can still talk about it. Tell me more." The young man didn't say anything. "Come on, talk to me."

Finally, Tim spoke again, this time very slowly. "I do think I have failed at everything all my life. I knew I was better than this. I didn't do as well as I should have in school. I just didn't pay much attention. I didn't care. I didn't care what they thought. I thought they'd think bad of me. I knew they'd think that I wasn't any good, you know? Just a wasted guy." His sentences came out one at a time, with long pauses between them. "Just a wasted guy. I had talent. I had ability. The guys tell me I am OK looking. But I couldn't get focused, you know? I would try it for a little bit, and then give up. I never graduated from college. It just didn't seem worth the effort. Really it was that I knew I'd fail before it was over. I knew I would never get through, so I quit. And when I came to Boston, I thought I fit right in, drinking as much as the other guys. But it went bad somehow, and after a while I could never make the bad feelings go away. I could never forget them. They were just with me all the time, like now. Like this anger I have. I am depressed and angry."

I am depressed and angry. I took a breath. "Tim, I want you to hear something real clear. And know it. I love you. You're beautiful. I love the way you are. What you look like. The way you struggle so to get sober and to deal with having AIDS. I love it how angry you are. Tim, there's nothing about you that I don't love. Do you know that?"

He was silent.

"Do you know that?"

"I guess. Yes. I know that." He was resentful.

"OK. I love you. I am not ever going to stop loving you. Do you know that?"

"Yes." He was reluctant, but he said it.

"Now. You have to also hear this. Guy, you can kill yourself now and short-circuit the process, bring it to an end, or you can stick with it and watch to see what happens. You don't know what the future is going to bring. You really don't know what the future is going to bring. The future, if you stay off alcohol and drugs, will bring some kind of change. You are not going to stay depressed and angry forever. And keep calling me. Call regularly, and we can keep talking. Maybe this is your time to be depressed and angry. You have to learn to accept that. This is your time to feel the feelings you are feeling. So feel them. Roll with it. And then later, it will be your time to feel content."

"I don't believe that. I don't want to feel the way I am feeling."

"Has that made you feel better?"

Tim laughed. "No."

"You may not want to feel this way—nobody wants to feel bad —but this is the way you are right now. So accept that. Accept the things you cannot change. Tomorrow, some tomorrow—if you stay off alcohol and drugs—will be different."

"Is that really true?"

"It is really true."

"What happened with you?"

"Just what I am telling you. I spent years being depressed and angry. Then one day—in London, I was walking down South Eaton Place—what I was supposed to do came to me, and it was absolutely clear. So I did it, and now I am here talking to you. And sober."

"This doesn't piss you off, me calling you all the time?"

"No."

But he wouldn't let me go. "Do you ever get depressed and angry?"

I laughed. "Oh, honey, of course. Not all the time, but regularly. I'm an alcoholic. But it doesn't last forever. And I can handle it. I've been doing this long enough to know it's not going to make me drink, or kill myself, so I just wait it out. And I have friends, like you, who will listen to me."

We said good-bye—I told him again that I loved him—and hung up, and I turned to my computer and to writing about people up in Maine who had been very depressed and angry in the summer of 1984 after two of theirs were murdered. I felt that what I was doing on the phone was just passing on what I had been told by René, and David, and by that counselor in rehab who had passed on the folk wisdom of all the people who had gone before her. I was doing this even while I was educating myself in ways to be gay. I didn't, of course, actually know if things would be different. Are things getting better? Are things going to be better? But it was the only thing to say, and Tim didn't know that yet. It was the only thing to say to someone like him on the phone, who was pissed and angry. You had to hope they keep on fighting. The problem of course was that Tim was dying. This was where the program broke down. He did not have the time to give it. He might be dead before he got it together and it was his time to be content. But then, maybe not.

↔

My principal source of books was Glad Day Bookshop—to give it its proper title, *The Glad Day Gay and Lesbian Liberation Bookstore*. Before I moved to Boston, I came down on weekends. I told a straight woman who asked that I had gone to a gay bookstore.

She looked at me and grinned in a conspiratorial way. "Porno!" She had no idea.

Winter Street is a one-block street that connects Downtown Crossing with Boston Common and about ten years ago was made a pedestrian walkway. It is narrow and short and lined with six or eight story buildings, and is usually dark, with light at both ends, on the Common and in the Crossing. Winter Street becomes Summer Street on the other side of the Crossing. Flags and banners hang from the second story all along the street. The shops are for athletic shoes, cheap jewelry, three branches of various banks, a coffee shop, a shop for socks. Upstairs over these small shops, up near the Common, is Glad Day, which announces itself with a rainbow flag hanging from the window and a large graphic of the Blake painting.

The staircase upstairs is narrow and dark, made of white marble, a contrast that marks much of Glad Day. Inside the small space, I was surprised the first time I went at how many men were there. There is porno there. It is hard for a small independent book store like Glad Day to make it financially without income from video rentals, but the only porno I am aware of when I walk in is video, more than I have ever seen before. I go in and stand in front of the racks, looking at the tiny pictures on the cardboard video cases of men having sex with each other, trying to decide whether I want to rent one that night.

Near the videos is a rack of magazines. These are magazines that come out once a month and contain pornographic fiction, graphic spreads of naked models, personal ads, and advertisements for sex toys. The names of the most popular magazines are *Honcho, Bound & Gagged, Master,* and *Drummer*. There are also one-of-a-kind magazines devoted to pictures of a particular model or of a particular sexual taste. Above these are magazines with fewer pictures and more text—*Christopher Street*, fiction, politics, and social commentary, *The Advocate*, which has politics and social commentary, and gay travel guides from abroad, *GaiPied* from Paris, and *TimeOut* from London. I buy any of these magazines when they have something serious to say about the place of gay people in western culture. The nice thing about the magazine rack is that the man looking for something to jerk off to has to stand next to the man looking for political theory, and that forms a bond, even if it lasts only a minute. There is always the possibility, and it has happened to me occasionally, that what the man next to me is holding in his hand —porno or political theory—draws my attention away from what I am holding in my hand, or vice versa, and we end up buying the same thing, or better yet—*Hi, I'm Fair Shaw*—leaving together.

That kind of interchange among the varied interests of the gay community is what makes the close confines of the Glad Day so stimulating. At the Ramrod, I can see that the men are all trying to be the same thing—Tom of Finland's boyfriends—but at Glad Day, the body types range across the whole of human possibility, or at least the whole of human possibility that interests homosexuals. There are women there too, and whole sections of the store are devoted to their concerns—women's fiction, women's erotica, women's porno, feminist theory—but there is so much going on among the men I do not pay much attention to anyone else.

One of the things going on with me that requires my visits to Glad Day is that, since I left Naomi, I have been trying to read all the basic texts on homosexuality while at the same time keeping up with current work. That means that I read John Addington Symonds' *A Problem in Greek Ethics*, published originally in 1873, and *A Problem in Modern Ethics*, published originally in 1891. I was pleased that Glad Day had these books in stock when I asked for them. Few university book stores would have stocked them. I also read *Iolaus*, by Edward Carpenter, first published in 1902 and republished in 1982. And I went back and re-read all of *Leaves of Grass*, in the 1891 edition.

Glad Day is a community center. At the head of the staircase leading up from the street, there is a large bulletin board to which people are free to tack their notices—apartments for rent, meetings of various kinds, groups forming, speakers coming to Boston, people looking for roommates. The shop is also a place to buy gay paraphernalia—pink triangle pins, rainbow flags, beads, stuff you might decorate yourself with on Gay Pride—and it is a kind of neighborhood gay bookstore for the city. Underlying all this, almost hidden among the other books and magazines, is what I recognized from my experience with university bookstores. It is a classy, intellectually-oriented university bookstore for the gay community. It carries first editions of current good gay literature, it regularly carries books from university presses that have a gay angle, it carries all current translations of Proust, and current biographies of gay figures. Almost every time I go into Glad Day looking for a book, they have it. And on the rare times when they don't have it in stock, they know about it, apologize for not having it, then offer to get it for me.

I read John D'Emilio's book, *Sexual Politics, Sexual Communities*, Perry Deane's *God's Bullies*, Dennis Altman's *The Homosexualization of America* and Altman's *Homosexual: Oppression and Liberation*, Harvey Fierstein's *Torch Song Trilogy*, Andrew Holleran's *Nights in Aruba*, Edmund White's *A Boy's Own Story*, and Phil Andros' *$tud*. I bought all these books at Glad Day. The manager told me that the goal of the owners has been to build a comprehensive bookstore for the gay community. The bookstore really is comprehensive—there are very few English-language publications that have some gay concern that Glad Day does not handle. But the other aspect of Glad Day that I notice is the way videos and books and magazines that have a purely sexual interest are integrated among the rest of the offerings. I think, in that way, Glad Day is ahead of the major bookstores in the city, just as the gay community is ahead of the straight community. Sex is integrated more completely into our lives.

I was told by a former friend from Maine, "You have become very narrow," because I dress for gay men, am surrounded by gay men whenever I am not at work, read gay newspapers, read only books by gay men about gay issues, see principally movies which have some gay angle, and, in short, am exactly like straight men, who confine their connections to the rest of humanity to those people and endeavors that share their sexuality. I laughed at my former friend from Maine.

I had been in Boston two years, and the AIDS cases had doubled again, according to *The Native,* to 24,576 cases as of September 8, 1986. Of those, approximately 55% are dead, 508 in Massachusetts by this date. When I had first arrived in Boston, people said it was not certain that all who were infected went on to get AIDS and then to die, but it has been a long time since anyone had said that.

In May 1986, as a result of negotiations between Robert Gallo, the American scientist who had discovered HTLV-III and Luc Montagnier, the French scientist who had discovered LAV, it was agreed that HTLV-III and LAV were the same virus and would henceforth be called human immunodeficiency virus or HIV.

↔

Judith called to share the details of her life. She called very late at night, after she had been out on a date, telling me what they had done and where they had gone. She talked about boy troubles, an issue we shared. Ames called less frequently, but his calls were more pointed. "Dad, life sucks." Then he asked some question that had been bothering him. He didn't have time for details, and I thought that he thought it would invade his privacy to start sharing the details of his life with his dad.

After the holidays, they came for three days. I bought a tree and ornaments and put it up. I bought presents for them and wrapped them. My apartment looked good, and I had food, and I was ready. The doorbell rang, and they were there, hugging me.

They were utterly beautiful. They were both blond, Judith's hair straight and Ames's slightly curly. They were bright, eager, intelligent, thoughtful. I asked them what they wanted to do during their visit.

"Hang out, Dad." It was Judith.

"Yeah, hang out with Dad." Ames was excited to be in Boston with his dad.

"Well, we'll hang out then." I hugged them both.

"How are your friends?" I named Judith's friends in Maine.

"They're OK. Marcia is acting strange right now, and Sarah's parents are getting a divorce, so she's acting weird all the time too, but aside from that, things are good." Then she grinned. "I've got a new boyfriend."

"Tell me about him."

"He's tall, and he has blond hair, and he's cool." All her boyfriends were tall and blond and cool.

They opened presents. I gave Ames aluminum Dungeons and Dragons figures of Gothic monsters with wings and Judith a few CDs of music she liked. I had other things they could open later.

"Dad, you have cool hair." Ames was always checking me out on the cool scale. "You cut it all off."

"Yup. And I expect I am going to cut more off before I am done with it."

Ames came over to my chair and put out his hand tentatively and touched, lightly, the top of my head. "It's prickly!" He grinned.

We had supper, eating from plates on our laps in the living room, looking occasionally at the unopened gifts under the tree.

It was good that all three of us were together. When they came separately, they each had a chance to tell their stories to me and to ask me about mine. They were interested in different aspects of my life and wanted to do different things in Boston. But it was fine, now. Later, the two of them would share the pullout bed in the living room.

There were clothes for them, and music tapes for both of them, and, for my big present for Judith, I had some earrings that I had found, made by an Israeli jeweler of silver and bits and pieces of Roman glass, and, for Ames, a pocket tape player with headphones with more tapes. They had shirts for me and two books. They seemed pleased, and it was all OK, after the meal in the warm apartment lit by the tree.

There were paper and wrappings everywhere, the bright colors and shiny wrappings and ribbons from the gifts decorating the apartment.

I had picked up a new job recently. "It's essentially a typing job, and the pay is not good, but I can live on it, and it is good because it doesn't use my mind. I come home in the afternoon fairly rested and able to write all evening. I might be tired, but I am not mentally tired. I don't have to think at work. I can do all that stuff without thinking."

They grinned.

"I couldn't write if I had a job that was demanding. The whole point in living the way I am living is that I am writing, and I have to put that first."

They were impressed by the weight of the stack of pages. They talked about computers—I had bought one the year before, and Ames was getting his grandfather Schumann to give him one—and about the various possibilities. Judith was more interested in her car—she had been given one by her mother, and she wanted to take me for a ride tomorrow—and in her choices for college. She wanted a college that was not structured in the traditional way and that would allow her to create her own course of study. She had been clear about that for a year or two. There were only half a dozen schools in the Northeast that provided this kind of education.

Ames was a musician. He and his friends gathered most afternoons in the barn attached to Ames' house and jammed. He was into The Police and Led Zeppelin. When he arrived in Boston to visit me, he always had a guitar with him, and, as he grew older, sometimes two. He liked to visit the guitar shops along Mass Avenue near Berklee. He bought an amplifier and an equalizer to take home with him, and at my place he picked out tunes constantly, making his music an accompaniment to whatever we were doing in the apartment. Judith was a political activist. She read books on the civil rights era and on the sixties and was sensitive to racial and gender questions. She told me about different teachers she had at school—a male professor who favored the boys, and a principal who didn't like what she was doing with her hair, which was spiked up like her dad's. She had gotten a nose piercing in London when she was fourteen, and she got grief for that at school from some of the other students. The three of us shared something we didn't often talk about but was there nonetheless: We were out of the mainstream, into hard rock, the rights of minorities and women, and of course, the rights of gay people. I watched them grow up and blossom. Ames was still three or four inches shorter than I was, and Judith was my height, and both of them liked to hold hands or sit next to me on the sofa. Ames was very physical in his affection for me and touched me all the time.

Ames played his guitar, his beautiful blond curls falling over his forehead. Judith and I stopped talking to listen. When he saw that he had an audience, Ames' playing became more organized, and he went from playing chords to more melodic parts of tunes. Judith and I listened in the dim room, lit only by the tree, the tangle of bright shiny paper wrappings around our feet.

↔

My book was turning into an investigation into loss—loss at Andy's death, but also the loss of my youth and young adulthood, the years when I was still searching for a way to be in my culture and, somehow, to accommodate my same-sex feelings, the loss of Connie on the slopes of Mt Rainier, and even though Naomi and I were still tense and suspicious over everything that had to do with the children, her loss, too, and the loss of the life we had built together. And with the others, there was my family. I had fought losing them for years, and now I was preparing for the break. I had found, in Maine that summer after Andy's death, that I was not unique, that the gay people around me had also experienced the death of Andy Darwell by being forced to revisit the memories of other losses, family, friends, positions, communities, and cultures.

When Andy died, I had been reading John D'Emilio's book, *Sexual Politics, Sexual Communities*, an investigation into the development of a gay community in the United States. How did a shared sexuality come to mean a shared community? I saw, in what we were doing in Bangor in the summer of 1984, that my friends and I were creating a community, and I kept a box of clippings and letters, everything that passed through my fingers that summer. I had known, almost from the beginning, that I would write a book addressing the political questions we faced. Others moved naturally in the direction of minority politics, toward the goal of having an effect on the legislative process by way of the ballot box. Still others turned toward creating a separate community of our own, independent of the larger world. And some, in the aftermath of Andy's violent death, found sex, or love.

In investigating these things, I had to deal with other questions— What did it mean for these people to be gay? Where did the concept come from? And how many different answers did the question have? In the instance of Andy, who the media had decided was gay, the determination of a person's sexuality didn't even mean that a person

368

had to be in to same-sex sex. The only thing that was necessary, apparently, was that the culture, gay and straight alike, had to perceive the victim as gay, as other, or queer.

There was no single answer to any of the questions Andy's death raised, which meant that the reader had to hear the whole cacophonous conversation among the people who were affected by Andy's death to begin to understand what it meant to be gay in Maine in 1984.

↔

I corresponded with a woman, a relative, in South Carolina, and she asked to see what I was writing. I sent her the first several chapters, and she told Mother that she had seen the beginning of the manuscript. Mother asked to see it, and the relative turned it over to her. And that was how my mother came to read the first chapters of my book. When we spoke the next time, Mother complimented me on my handling of the dialogue at a certain point, and then, before she went on to another topic, she said, "Next time, write something cheerful."

↔

Amelia was fifteen or so years older than I, brilliant dyed blond hair, eyes the blue of enameled gold, wonderful cheekbones. She was a gossip of the highest order, although she was deeply discreet herself, a translator of French poetry, a publisher of a small Maine literary quarterly, and a poet of demanding and intellectual poems, mostly longish—twenty or thirty lines.

I had invited her to tea during the summer that Anderson Darwell was murdered, and when she arrived, I held open the door and said, "You're the first woman I have seen all week who is not either a lesbian or an alcoholic."

She smiled her brilliant smile. "But I don't know that the jury has decided on either of those!"

When I left Maine and moved to Boston, we started a correspondence that centered around my fiction and her poetry.

19 October 1987

Dear Amelia,

Part II is difficult to cope with. I have made these changes: the section that takes place at night following the Memorial Service, I have moved to the very end of Part I. A kind of astringent to clear the pallet before Part II. Now I work on shaping Part II, focussing on the main point.

I went by to see a friend yesterday who has suddenly been diagnosed with AIDS. He speaks of death and the ends of things and whether he has made a "contribution" and of what that could be. He says he feels in limbo, not knowing whether he has six days or six weeks or—-what. What should he be planning for? We sat there calmly discussing these things, and I was aware, in some part of my mind, that this was bizarre in the extreme, us sitting in his beautifully designed home, talking of death. My eyes wandered around the room, everything a pearl gray, with black leather and chrome furniture, large vividly colored abstracts on the wall, and bowls of cut flowers.

Another friend is in Brigham and Women's Hospital waiting for transfer to Shattuck Hospital. He can't get out of bed now, is incontinent, tubes in his arms. They take them to Shattuck when there is no other place for them, and they die there.

Re: the above. Sometimes I think my life is bizarre—that is all life—is bizarre in the extreme.

25 Oct 87: Today is Wednesday of my last week at this job. My last day is next Tuesday. I do not have another job yet, and I get anxious about that occasionally. A number of possibilities—that is, avenues of investigation—but no jobs yet. I want a Medici prince.

Love, Fair

David, in responding to something I said, said, "Well, you know, you have only been out about five years."

I contemplated the subtext of David's remarks. "I remember how betrayed I felt by everybody after Stonewall. I had worked out a way to live, and then everybody changed how they thought about things —people who were not out were closeted—and I started thinking that way too, and my life became untenable. I had been put in the position where I was lying, and I couldn't live that way. Stonewall meant that eventually I would have to divorce my wife. Well, first I had to drink myself near death, and eventually I did that. In any case, I have become suspicious of the way we think about these things. At least once in my adult life, the whole culture has changed, radically, the way it thinks about these things, and when it did that, it left a whole range of people without a rationale for the way they were living. Now, as long as I will accept the definition of "coming out" that everybody agrees on—which is that I was closeted before—then I can sink, happily, back into my ocean. And I am almost willing to do that. Just for a little peace." I lit a cigarette. "But peace comes at the price of acknowledging that I lived almost twenty years of my life illegitimately—not having come to terms, not having accepted, not having been honest with myself."

"Jesus, Fair, you're hard on yourself. I didn't mean—that's not what we mean about coming out."

"Isn't it?"

I proposed to Judith and Ames that we move beyond straight and gay. For a time—for six months or so—I said, half with a smile, "I was straight, and then I was gay, and now I am me." I played around with the possibility of not being either one, of never having been either one, and I found that appealing, but it was hard, and I didn't really feel like taking on great issues now, in my third year in Boston. I just wanted to write my book, go to the Ramrod and have sex, go to the Y and swim and take showers, and love my children. Also, there was AIDS. The tendency of the members of the gay community to see themselves as a distinct people, as blacks had seen themselves as a distinct people, was mirrored by the Reagan Administration and the conservatives who saw those getting the disease as a distinct people whose needs need not be acknowledged by the federal government. Everything about me, my own needs, pressure from my culture, pushed me into a definition of self in which I only half believed and from which I maintained a very private distance.

My straight friend in the Belgrade Lakes District wrote the other day about "coming out." He says the process it describes sounds furtive—sneaking out, as if it were the backdoor, and you were sneaking past your parents—which is one of the problems with the term. Only gay people who have already done it, come through it, know that there is nothing furtive about it. But the implication of the term also suggests the same qualities—you're inside and you come out into the outside, with all that inside and outside suggest in our language—and yet not everyone feels the same way about what happened before coming out. The variety of reasons not to come out —prior commitment, cowardice, honoring one's parents—and the variety of reasons to come out—sex, respect for oneself, indifference to the feelings of others—illustrate how limited all our language is around these issues.

On one of his trips to Boston, Ames asked, "Why do gay people have to come out? That's terrible that they have to come out. Straight people don't have to come out."

↔

Call me Shaw. I didn't often use my first two names. I told men I met, Call me Shaw. Swimming up the lane, in which I was the only occupant, my head turned rhythmically up to the right for breath at the appropriate moment during the cycling of my arms, my legs kicking. Robert Fair Shaw. Fair Shaw. Shaw. Fair. Man. Boy. Boy Scout. Acolyte. Freshman. Sophomore. Junior. Senior. College Man. Husband. Doctor. Professor. Stud. Gay man. Queer. Faggot. Call me Shaw. On the Hotline, I never gave my name, but sometimes I said, Call me 'guy.'

The other man would say, "Guy?"

"That'll do," and then I'd laugh. "What can I do for you?"

"Well, guy—" He'd laugh. "I have a need—, I want to, to talk to somebody. Can you listen for a minute?"

Guy seemed to be intimate, and it gave them something to call me, a handle they could use that wasn't my real name, and I found myself using it sometimes on the street with friends—"Hey, guy, when am I going to see you again?"—just because, oddly, it seemed more affectionate than the use of the man's name. Man worked the same way.

"I guess—" The man on the phone was talking. "—you must hear all this over and over."

"No—" It was a long, drawn-out vowel. "—you'd be surprised. Everybody is different." I was talking in that low, slow voice, mouth-close-to-the-mike that I used. "On the other hand, we're all alike, you know? Anyway, don't worry about whether I've heard all this before. Tell me what's bothering you."

"Uh—" He couldn't get his act together. "Uh—I'm a, you know, a truck driver. And I go on these long runs, and every so often—all the guys feel this way—it gets really hard and you need to get serviced." He paused. "Do you know what that is?"

I thought I did.

"Uh—" The voice on the other end hesitated. "I'm straight. Do you guys help straight guys?"

I laughed, a little. "Anybody can pick up HIV, man. We don't discriminate. And I do know what 'service' means. You need to stop off and get a blowjob."

"Yes, that's it. On these long runs, you need to stop every so often and get it off, and I did, about a week ago. And, well, I've got a regular girl, and when I got home the next afternoon, I did what I always do when I get home, we had sex—she expected me to, you know—but I have been thinking since that morning when this woman serviced me, that maybe I shouldn't have done that. I have been reading some things in the paper about what you ought to do and what you ought not to do, and then I started to go crazy about maybe giving my girl this thing—"

I was drawn to the man's sincerity—that's what always drew me in—and to the difficulty he had speaking about it.

"—so finally tonight I thought I'd call somebody—you guys are listed in the phone book—and see what I can find out. Did I do something wrong?" He was in pain. "Did I give her AIDS?" Then, before I could say anything, he said, "Can I get AIDS from a hooker when she gives me head?" Then, as if the railing on the porch had broken and everyone lined up behind it started falling too, helplessly, one by one, he said, Should I tell my girl friend? Can I forget about it? Do I have to tell my woman? Have I got it?

I suggested we start back at the beginning. "Let's start first with the thing that happened last week, you know, the woman at the truck stop—is that where it happened?—and your girl at home and you." I asked whether he used a condom with either woman, and then I sketched out for him what people seemed to know at this point. "I think what you did was pretty low risk. The virus passes more easily from the man to the woman in these circumstances." Then, "Do you have genital sores?"

He didn't have them. "That's a relief."

"How do you know you don't already have it?" Most of these men called frantic with fear that they had picked up something and they wanted to be reassured. They hardly ever thought they might already be infected and passing it on to other people.

"Ah, I don't think so—"

"But you don't know—" Having reassured him, I came on strong. "—if you're going to have unprotected sex, you're going to pick up something eventually, guy. Even if the risk of picking up something with this particular woman that morning was pretty low, if you've been doing this regularly over a period of time, then it's likely you're going to get something eventually. And it may be that your number came up that morning." I paused. "Do you hear me?"

The other man didn't say anything.

"Do you hear me, guy? If you've been doing this for a long time, on a regular basis, even if what you're doing is low risk, the chances of your picking up something are increased. Do you hear that?"

Finally the truck driver spoke, very quietly, softly. "Yes. I hear you."

"You got her life in your hands. You got your life in your hands. You've got the life of the woman at the truck stop in your hands. You got to think about your need to get serviced."

"What should I do?"

"Since 1985, there has been a test available. You should go to one of the anonymous testing sites available in Massachusetts and get a test. Then have it done again in six months. You need to consider the kind of risk you're putting yourself in by getting serviced regularly when you're on the road."

"Are you telling me to quit getting blowjobs?"

"No. To reduce your risk, use a condom. And if you are going to continue to have sex outside of your relationship, you should consider having a test on a regular basis—every six months—and also consider using a condom every time you have sex with anyone. You need to do these things if you are going to start taking care of yourself and of the people around you."

"You're tough, you know?"

I laughed. "I try to pass on what I am told."

"They teach you guys?"

"Yes. We want to pass on to you enough information so you can start taking care of yourself."

"I guess you don't have many straight guys calling you, do you?"

"Actually, I don't know. A lot of people let us know who they're having sex with, but sometimes people don't tell us. And then it's easy to present yourself as gay or straight by changing pronouns. Say, I was fucking him when you're really fucking her."

He laughed this time. "I guess so. I didn't think of that." He paused. "Have you ever put yourself at risk?"

"Sure, I am a gay man."

"What'd you do?"

"I stopped behaving that way. I got a test. I started using a condom."

"Am I crazy?'

"No."

"Anybody ever ask these questions before?"

"All the time, every night."

"Anybody ever afraid to get the test?"

"Everybody is."

"You mean other people have these thoughts?"

"Everybody does, now, all the time."

"I didn't think you were gay. Sometimes I did, and sometimes I didn't."

I laughed. "We're not supposed to tell anything about ourselves. It should be that the only thing you have to deal with is a voice."

"I like you."

"Thanks." Then, "Will you start taking care of yourself?"

"Yes. I will." Then, "I really like you. You're a good man. You're good, you know? It's good talking to you. I like you."

"I like you too."

"Thanks."

"You're welcome."

"You helped me a lot."

One night after a stint at the Hotline, I was waiting for the elevator when the doors opened. The only man in the elevator was a man I knew. I stepped in. "Hello, Tim. How are you?"

"Hello, Fair." His face was clean-shaven and had a cluster of lesions across his upper lip and his lower lip, around his mouth, as if a new-fangled Van Dyke beard had been tattooed into his skin. He saw me glance at his lips and chin.

"Oh, Tim, I am sorry."

Tim shrugged and smiled. There is nothing to be done.

According to *The Native,* there were now 33,482 cases in the country and 680 cases in Massachusetts, 499 in Boston, of whom 58% were dead.

↔

Law of Desire, by Pedro Almodovar, opens like *The Stuntman*, with a series of camera-pullbacks that each time reveal a new reality. Who is this movie about? About the nude boy on the bed masturbating himself in an ecstasy of sexual excitement? About the director and his assistant, lascivious old men who are making a movie about the nude boy on the bed, who are themselves boiling with sexual excitement? Or about the beautiful Carmen Maura, who is caught by the camera just as she comes out of the darkened cinema, exhilarated, coming into the lobby, toward the camera, stimulated by what she has just seen—the nude boy on the bed being directed by the two old men—searching for someone with whom to share her excitement. I was so exhilarated by *Law of Desire* on walking out of the cinema I felt like Carmen Maura, and when I found it would run four more nights I went back every night, five times in all, before it left town. It made me want to run home and write.

Law of Desire is Spanish Baroque in the late twentieth century. I realized as the movie unfolds that it is inescapably about the grandest themes—memory, desire, love, death, faith, the nature of final things, the power of art. The movie has three gay men—and one transsexual woman. It has a simple plot: A man named Pablo, a movie writer and director, is in love with one young man, who doesn't love him back, and is accosted by a second young man who tries to break them up and who eventually murders the first young man. The second young man, because he cannot now have the man he murdered for, spends one hour with him and then kills himself. The man at the center of the narrative—the director—throws his typewriter out the window at the end of the movie, as the cause of it all, and it ignites an explosion in the trash bin below. It is about the importance of desire, and it is about hope—Carmen Maura sees the handsome cop just before the credits begin to roll—and it is about the critical importance of art. The movie is operatic, limited to its very simple plot and to elemental human emotions—lust, love, jealousy, fear—and directed at the primal questions: What is love? What is the place of memory in our lives? Pablo, the director, writes and directs a movie called *Sex Life of a Clam,* does serious drugs, and is, as he himself says, "very self-centered." He loves the young man who cannot return his love, as if it were another kind of affectation, like the cineastes who love his movies. The second young man, Antonio, who can be called a stalker, proves the power of Pablo's movies, even if Pablo has no respect for them, and proves to him that love is not merely an affectation. And in the stunning conclusion, showing him that sometimes desire means death, Antonio gives Pablo back to himself. I was proud to be gay, proud of Almodovar for having made such a great gay movie, made it so tightly—every screen, every word, contributes to the power of the final image that is so unexpected as to be astonishing, but then, I realized, absolutely fitting and right. Pablo the writer and director, in bed after having had sex with Antonio, hears a gun and runs into the next room where he finds Antonio a suicide. Pablo kneels on the floor, a home-made altar to the Virgin above and behind him, and cradles the limp, lifeless body of Antonio across his lap, rocking it and crooning with grief, a gay pieta. Pablo the director says of a love letter he had written, "That was just a joke." But the young man who pursues him all the way through the movie says, "Love is never a joke." In our time, when sex between men is under continuous attack—the pope calls it a "severe moral failing"—the movie and Antonio proclaim that sex between men really is worth dying for.

↔

I went to the big march in Washington in the late summer of 1987 and while there went down to the Ellipse and viewed the Quilt. Friends of a person who has died of AIDS gather, like the women in a neighborhood gathered a hundred years ago, to sew a quilt to memorialize the man who has died. These quilts, of uniform size, are sewn together into panels that are brought out and displayed on occasions like this big march in Washington.

I had never seen the Quilt before, and I wandered around among the panels lying out on the grass. They were like clothes lying on the ground. I was afraid it would rain. They didn't belong under the harsh sunlight, either, which would bleach the colors, and I wanted the organizers to take the quilt inside. Walking away, toward the Washington Monument, I realized the Quilt raised feelings in me that were too private for outdoors. I saw men crying, and I wanted to shelter them from this enormous monumental federal space.

I was 48 years old in June. About ten years ago, when I first read *Dancer from the Dance*, I was 39, just a year older than Malone, who turned to the boy who had fallen in love with him and dismissed him with the line, "I'm thirty-eight." Malone and I were born about the same time, sometime in 1939, and we reached the end of things sometime in the late seventies—1977 for Malone, 1979 for me. Malone left the party at the end of the book saying he was 38 and went into the bay and was never heard from again, although various people offered various hypotheses about what had happened to him. For myself, I quit drinking at 39 in 1979, ending my old life as decisively as Malone had ended his when he went into the bay. Our generation was, many of us, one of the generations being memorialized back there on the Mall. The generation ten years younger than I—those born around 1950—was the youngest of those hardest hit. Since the beginning, it has been men 30 to 39 in 1980 who provided the largest percentages of those with AIDS. Some of us died of AIDS, some walked into the bay, some quit drinking. If Malone had not gone into the bay and disappeared—if he had lived another five years—he would probably now be memorialized in the Quilt.

At the end of his book, Malone is bitter about the people who surround him. He says to the boy, "Make no mistake, these are visual people," who experience on the surface of the eye and have no deeper thought or knowledge. He says he was looking for "love." And his not finding it was the result of his making the same mistake all men make who look for love. I think that is what I thought ten years ago when I first read the book.

But Malone looked for love, as I believe all the men memorialized back there in the Quilt looked for it, in the places that were available to him. In those places, Malone gave himself over completely to the search. One of the two men who exchange letters in the framing story says, "No, darling, mourn no longer for Malone. He knew very well how gorgeous life is—that was the light in him that you, and I, and all the queens fell in love with." It was easy to read *Dancer from the Dance* as a cautionary tale or as a tragedy. Harder to read it for what it was.

What then had happened to Malone? It was a story of the dance —*O body swayed to music, O brightening glance,/How can we know the dancer from the dance?*—and the dance was over, the discaire had quit, the musicians had gone home. And Malone, more prescient than most, had vanished. More even than Holleran could have known, the dance was over by the late seventies, and epidemiologists in the future would date the epidemic from the period marked by the Pink and Green Party, the fire at the Everard Baths, and the disappearance of Anthony Malone.

↔

I met a man, Reed Powers, while walking on the Mall. Reed had AIDS but was still able to work. He was a travel writer and now, from California, wrote me long letters about his travels and his plans, letters enclosing pictures of his house and expressing a desire to come to Boston to see me. Reed wrote from California, from the East Coast, from the South of France, the Lake District, Sweden, St Petersburg. His letters came on pale yellow hotel stationery with the curiously enlarged hotel logo and always stood out, with their scrawled handwriting and exotic return address, among my mail from my other friends.

His letters, from places which had only a literary reality for me, carried with them an increasing sense of fairy tale. He wrote first of the possibility of visiting me. "Perhaps on my next trip, I could swing by Boston." Then he wrote, "Perhaps I could come for Christmas." Later, he switched the invitation: "Would you like to come to California for Christmas?" Thinking that none of these things was going to happen, I agreed to everything—or ignored the hints and invitations. After all, in the same letters that carried the invitations, Reed was telling me about his KS, his recent bout with PCP, his peripheral neuropathy. We hardly knew each other. Then there was a letter with the startling line, "I will be arriving in Boston in ten days, at 4 o'clock, on American." There were many men I corresponded with, but, I realized, very few of them actually had the money to say, "I'll be on American at 4:00 on Thursday."

I didn't feel I could say no, didn't feel I should say no. On Thursday, he walked through the security gates into the luggage retrieval area, this tall, gaunt man, maybe 35, with closely cropped reddish-gold hair, whose name was Reed Powers, and who greeted me, grinning. "We have a lot of catching up to do!"

We caught a cab into town to the Fenway, Reed telling me on the way in about his travels in the Iberian peninsula. And then, just before we arrived home, Reed said, "But there is something we need to do first, right away, as soon as we get to your place."

"What's that?"

"Oh, I'll show you."

So we went in and dumped Reed's bags, and when I came back to the bedroom from getting Reed a drink, I found Reed taking off his shirt. He hung it over the back of a chair. Now he was pulling up his t-shirt. He was very thin. What was merely an attractively lined face—a young man who had aged early from life in the fast lane, maybe—was, in his torso and limbs, the ravages of disease. Reed struggled with the t-shirt to get it up over his shoulders and his head. I reached out to help him. It needed to be stretched to pull over his shoulders, to be pulled up and then over his head. He was revealing a landscape of white skin mottled with the dark maroon marks of Kaposi's sarcoma. Each of the marks was about an inch long and about half an inch wide. These cancers seemed to float just under the surface of the skin all over Reed's back. Reed was standing in front of the mirror to show me the front of his torso. I could see his whole chest in the mirror, covered over with the same cancers. They would not have shown so vividly if Reed's skin had not been so pale. This was what "we have to do," to show Reed to me as he was. I put out my hands on both sides of Reed's torso and ran my fingers up Reed's back, over the dark maroon lesions, touching most of them, up to his shoulders, where I gripped lightly Reed's traps and then patted him in the corner of his neck.

"You have a lot of these little buggers, don't you?" Reed turned to me, and I ran my hands over his chest and down his sides over the lesions. "I've never seen so many." Then, "Kiss me."

380

He did. I presumed that it was for this that Reed had come from wherever he had come, to present himself and to be accepted—to be touched and accepted—and I touched him and accepted him. Soon we were in bed and had sex, and then, because Reed was exhausted from the long plane ride, he asked if I would mind if he went on to sleep. Actually, that night he showed symptoms of some intestinal viral infection, and the next morning he said he should be at home in his bed rather than in mine, so he called and in a couple of hours we were in a taxi, Reed next to me, holding my hand—Reed lifted it up and clasped it between his right and his left—and thanking me all the way to the airport for a wonderful time, having gotten what he came to Boston to get. Then Reed was back on the plane, this time for Los Angeles.

↔

October 21, 1987
Dear Amelia,

Our letters crossed. I don't know when I will be in Orono again. I've told the children I have to stay home for a while with no company, to recuperate. Judith has been here every weekend since the first of August, or I have been in Maine, and I begin to get desperate about my own things— the book, letters, etc. I feel the way you do, however. I would like an afternoon around a teapot—couldn't we arrange that at my place?—with you.

I was coming home from a meeting this afternoon and ran into a young man I've known from AA: young Irish kid (somewhere in his twenties), beautiful, graceful in the way the Irish kids can be, slender, beautiful blue eyes, who tells me about his brother who has just quit drinking and who is driving him crazy. We talk, we walk down across the Common and the Public Garden to Commonwealth Ave. The end of a beautiful fall day. We cross Arlington, Berkeley— and he says, I don't know if you know what's been happening with me. I see him in AA, he came once and I showed him about word processing—that's about the extent of our relationship. He has been diagnosed with AIDS. I was mad with rage. Then, within minutes—he's going on telling me about when he was diagnosed and what medications he is taking and how he has doctors all over town—I still have the rage, but I'm feeling I want to take this kid in my arms and hold him and make it all all right. I want to fight his battles for him. I don't even want him to walk any more down the middle of Commonwealth Avenue, past all the statues: I want to carry him. He's going on about Louise Hay (remember me writing you about her?) and acupuncture and some drug they make from thistles that they use in Europe, and then I feel utterly helpless, and I begin to see I've got no part in all of this, that it's his life and I have to just stand by. He was serene—he's made his will and written powers of attorney and decided on a Catholic service in New Hampshire for his family's sake and cremation and a memorial service in Boston for his own. "I don't really have anything to leave," he says, grinning. "A book, some clothes." We go to Montillio's for sandwiches and he tells me about his rage: He tells me about the stigma of AIDS, how even in AA there are people who simply turn away if he tries to talk about it.

Anyway, I love you. Please, let's not let the rest of the winter and spring go by before we see each other again.

Love,
Fair

This seemed to happen once a week.

↔

I became accustomed to phone calls which began, "Do you remember Don O'Hara?" or "I've just come from the hospital. It's Angelo Mastroiantonio—" Or there were the moments when the person sitting across from me said, "Fair, I don't think this can last much longer—" Most of these men were in their twenties or early thirties. This must be what the trenches on the Western Front were like—or some regiments in the Civil War—where half the men who went out died. I got letters from my mother—she was in her early seventies—filled with news of the latest funerals among the next generation ahead of hers. What can be learned from a woman who dies, after a full life, at 87 or 94? And what can be learned from a young man of 27 dying before he has a chance? I found my mother is uninterested in these deaths among the very young, as if they didn't signify.

It was easy to calculate who is being struck down. It is those who were twenty to thirty years old in 1969 and so those who had the whole of the seventies to participate in the sexual freedom described in *The Dancer from the Dance*. The leading edge of the generation that is now beginning to survive are those who reached their early twenties in about 1980 and so learned before they came out fully into the gay world that they had to be careful. The generation that is dying are those who, in 1980, were between the ages of 30 and about 40. Five years later, in 1985, this dying generation was between 35 and 45. I myself came out after the discovery of AIDS and so escaped becoming infected, and therefore was in the same "generation" with those who were 20 in 1980.

I wrote Amelia:

> So: I think of you often, but if I don't write, how are you to know that? Last night, at the AIDS Action Committee, I was in a room of recovering alcoholics —eight of us— and four of them were under 30, and all had been tested positive for HIV except me. Under 30. I discovered a friend there—38 years old, Vincent, who cuts Judith's hair when she comes to Boston and has cut mine since I first arrived in Boston, sober 2 years, a sponsee of mine, once—who, it seems, has been seropositive for 18 months and hasn't told anyone. Aside from the youth of most of them, the other note that was struck over and over as the meeting progressed: "Of course, I can't tell my parents now. Mother would cry and Dad would just get angry—at me. He'd say I brought it on myself! I'll tell them later, when I get sick, when I have to—" I think of all these kids trying to handle this—this!—and all those parents, sitting in some suburb somewhere and how cheated all of them—parents and kids alike—are.
> Afterward Vincent and I went to dinner and he talked of the "healing services" he goes to. The guru of the movement, Amelia, is a woman from California named Louise Hay. (I think I have told you something of this before.) There are

books and tapes which circulate. These services are
something like AA meetings: a person collects the tapes and
books and then designates a night and invites people, then
the whole thing takes on a life of its own, although,
apparently, dependent on one strong personality to keep it
going (in that way, unlike AA). The idea is that cancer (or
whatever) is a consequence of bad thoughts and that by
correcting bad thoughts you can heal yourself. She says she
had cervical cancer, caused by her having learned to hate her
genitals as a consequence of childhood experiences. She
learned to love herself, she says, and the cancer went into
remission. Vince, last night, said she said the gay
community's self-absorption with itself, its obsession with
youth, "caused" AIDS. So, all these gay men are sitting
around on the floor of different apartments all over Boston
(the country, for all I know) trying to heal their bodies by
learning to "love" themselves. I asked Vince what a gay man
with AIDS was to feel if he went through all this and then
found himself dying anyway. It looks to me like just another
way to express the ancient metaphor of illness-as-
punishment: If you don't learn to love yourself, I'll kill you.
I hate it that gay people are doing this to themselves, they
already carry such a burden. I appear to be in a minority
about all this. I don't want to come on strong to people who
are finding solace in Louise Hay, but I won't take part in it. I
was asked to go to one the other day and declined.
So many gay people, with AIDS and without, are seized with
guilt, Amelia, over their behavior in the 70s and 80s, when
everything went crazy, sexually. It crops up all the time in
their conversation: They make little wry jokes about
promiscuity and roll their eyes in a self-deprecating way. I
want people to be tough—you know?—, to say, I had sex
with anything that moved after I came out and it was right
for me and right for all of us, then, in the then-current state
of things. That it's not OK now is a consequence of a virus
that came from nowhere and not, repeat, not the consequence
of my having rethought my sexual activity in the seventies
and eighties. Here's an irony: Straight men lose all
composure when a gay man mentions "queer" in some

provocative way. They have no defenses against it. On the other hand, gay men lose all composure when straight people whisper "promiscuous." They don't know how to handle it. I wish gay men would learn to keep their eyes steady and their breath under control and say, strongly, "sure." And by their manner sever the connection between the word and the disease and the moral judgment.

When did I last see you? The night you and I and Ames waited for the plane! What a weird experience! The announcer kept saying, "This is the last call for the flight to Iceland!" And you were talking about your friend in London, and Ames was going to sleep on my shoulder.

I finished a little chapter ("Willie") to be inserted at the beginning of Part II, and have been working on a second ("Deborah") section to follow ("Ben") and to take place the same afternoon (Sunday) as the basketball. I am about to finish that one, too. I see clearly all the way to the end of Part II and think I will hold off sending you anything until I am finished with Part II. The chapters from here on out will follow one another very quickly and depend in part for their effect on their strong connections with one another so a good bit of their effect will be lost if they are taken one at a time. It will be late in the spring before I send you anything, if I stick to this schedule.

I am doing well. I haven't smoked in a month and am exercising regularly and my "head" is OK. I am pursuing (very gently, very tentatively) a young man (actually, [should I admit this to you?] two young men) and that provides a little excitement to my life, but it is not an excitement I depend on. I write, and that's what makes my life OK. I do need money, however. I am not making it on my salary, really, and late this spring or this summer I will be flat broke and something will have to give: I'll have to sell the car and something else, I suppose. That presents no real terrors, just a hassle. Do you have any serious thoughts on sending this whole MS to a publisher/agent and trying to sell it for some cash?

Write me and let me know you are thinking of me.

And then, a month later, I wrote a woman I had originally known in Ann Arbor but who had moved to Maine.

> It was good to talk to you. Stabilizing. I am so much in the middle of this book that I can't tell what's up, sometimes. The fears: I have the vocabulary of a twelve-year old, and the imagination of an accountant. What I am trying to say is either banal or untrue. No one will want to publish this book, or if they do, no one will buy it, etc. A friend called it "compelling," and while I am in the middle of some chapter, I have no sense of the power of what I am doing, whether or not it has any power at all.
>
> Wednesday of this week: A man I know from AA comes upstairs in the building where we both work and talks. He has been diagnosed with ARC the day before. He has one of those things in the intestines that won't let him keep any food in him, and he looks gaunt. A month ago, he looked like he has purposefully lost his excess weight. Now he looks gaunt. He's Irish Catholic, ruddy, red hair, used to be hunky, 35 years old. He is going into a trial program for an experimental drug—the only way to get the drug—but he won't know for six months whether he's getting the drug or the placebo. His biggest problem: I've got to tell my parents I'm gay. Then I got to tell them I'm dying.
>
> Yesterday: The guy who cuts my hair has been seropositive for several years. We talk about the summer. Him: Are you going anywhere? Me: No. I just need to stay home and write. Are you? Him: I go to Provincetown every weekend. New York, sometimes. I'm going to San Francisco for the Fourth. I'm running all the time. I'm exhausted. I don't know why I'm running all the time. I can't seem to stop running all the time. He's clipping the split ends off my hair.
>
> The man generally known in the press as "America's major gay writer" recently published an essay telling what he thinks should be the parameters within which a novelist should handle the AIDS crisis: There should be no humor in an AIDS novel. I seriously doubt that.

In many ways, the city seems untouched. The talk here is all of Dukakis and the presidency, although *The Boston Globe* has an editorial every two or three weeks saying "Nothing is being done about AIDS." Summer is upon us and people have gotten tans, and life goes on, such as it is. The problem is not just that the disease has hit two groups that the rest of the population doesn't like, but that it has hit those two groups very hard and left the rest of the population largely untouched (except for the odd panicked truck driver). And so we experience a time warp: We feel like it is the summer of London, 1665, and for everyone else it is 1955 and Eisenhower. Reagan got the Commission's report and tabled it.

Ames is hanging out in Orono, and Judith is in Provincetown. They seem well.

ADDED July 6: Life is a last ditch effort, and when I let myself, I can feel desperation.

On the other hand: I was at the Y last night, swimming, and a friend suggested dinner. It turned into a long utterly enchanting evening. First dinner at a place in Jamaica Plain, a tavern/saloon with tin ceilings and beautifully carved columns with acanthus leaves and sawdust floor, and a marvelous mix of people. We've always liked one another, but the conversation went on and on all evening, the way it should, from one thing to another, foliating. We went for ice cream later and then for a walk around Jamaica Pond as dusk turned to dark. We explored the Parkman memorial: wonderful monument—a stele topped by a half-length classical male nude topped by late nineteenth century head. The whole evening was as if it had been spun out of the flax of our separate lives. It was very fine. At the end it was dark and from a high point above the pond, you could look across the water, beyond the forest on the other side, to the towers of Boston.

I was telling my friend—his name is Lee, a carpenter— last night that most of the things I do, I have been doing long enough now so that I know they work, and I don't have the kind of anxiety I used to have: AA works. I go to meetings for Adult Children of Alcoholics. That works. I can work for

Blue Shield and support myself. That works. I have been
writing long enough to know I can do that. The other
question—Whether I can sell it—is something else entirely. I
know now that Ames and Judith and I can love one another
and maintain our relationship using the telephone and the
bus lines—did I tell you Judith has a car?—and so we don't
need to be afraid. There aren't any big areas in my life right
now that are black holes. It is all pretty much explored
territory. All this is one of the comforting aspects, I suspect,
of growing older. It is also wonderfully liberating. I'm not
trapped by anyone or anything. I'm free. And I don't think
any of this contradicts what I was writing several days ago,
when I began this letter.

Anyway, life is good and bad at the same time. We fulfill
the Chinese curse: We live in interesting times.

Write, dear heart. Now you know all there is to know
about me. You owe me.

Lee had asked me what my book was about. I said that it was
about the consequences of the deaths of two men in the wilderness,
but it was also about how we conceive homosexuality, how we make
it what we want it to be. Lee didn't understand that, and I continued.
"You are a deeply spiritual person, and you find in your sexuality a
source of spiritual growth. I am not, so I don't. Other people find it a
source of horror, or of evil. Ronald Reagan and George Bush are
very disturbed by it. People find it reason enough to kill people. I
think the expression of my sexuality makes me feel whole. The pope
says it is evidence of a deep moral disorder. My mother, because she
sees everything through the prism of class, thinks it is déclassé and
not to be spoken of, and you and I think it is the only thing to be
spoken of." I put my arm around Lee's shoulder. "We haven't spoken
of anything else for the last two hours. Some people think
homosexuality is the cause of AIDS, and many people around me
think it is the only thing that is going to get us through the epidemic.
And it is not just a division between us and them. The pope, and
fundamentalist preachers generally, think they understand it exactly,
and yet other religious people think homosexuality is a mystery—not
to be understood. And we are not in agreement. You go to an AA
meeting and listen carefully, and you hear people describe

homosexuality in one way, and I hear it described in another way. It is a wonder we are not shouting at one another. Nobody much wonders where it came from, but they all seem to have different ideas about what to do about it, now that it is here."

"People used to wonder where it came from."

"Right. But no more. Is it a question of the hormones—the hormones only?—or is it something that involves a whole social being, that affects even our sense of humor? Does it affect, for example, our taste? Is it the genes? Is it learned? Some people think it is more inherited than learned, others think the opposite. And of course, there is the young man I talked to the other night—"

"Don't tell me—"

"He has started dreaming of women's breasts."

"I did that too, for a while."

"Confusing, isn't it."

We didn't try to come to a conclusion, and when it got dark enough, we left the path and walked back to Lee's truck.

"Are you going to tell us what it is, in your book?"

"No. I'm just going to explore options, explore the ramifications of options."

Lee smiled, and we hugged, in the small confines of the cab of his truck, and then Lee drove me back to my apartment.

Several weeks later, I wrote Amelia:

> Leaving the Y, I ran into a young man (29) who used to be the lover of David Sepe, about whom I have written occasionally. I met the young man, Dennis, when I first moved to Boston, when he was 23. He was wild, tall, willowy, feminine, huge eyes on which he used makeup, slender. Then he and David broke up, and I didn't see Dennis until recently, in the Y. Dennis is now swimming regularly, lifting weights, and his whole body has changed. He is stocky, hard, hunky, no makeup now. We are walking down the steps from the Y. Me: How're things? Dennis: OK. But I'm sick of being gay. Me: What does that mean? Dennis: I've done it all. Every bit of it. Then Dennis tells me about visiting his folks that morning (this was yesterday, Sunday) and his brother and sister were there with their spouses and the children, and he was "Uncle Dennis" to everybody.

Dennis: I want to have children, but they say it takes a woman. Then, we see a couple walking toward us—young, Hispanic, he is much more beautiful than she is in that Latin way—and Dennis nods at them as they pass. He says to me, "I still notice only the man."

For me, being gay—living on Park Drive in the Fenway, as a gay man among tens of thousands of other gay men, in a city of interlocking circles of men with differing but related interests, what Ken Mecklenburg had called "a large and volatile gay community"— unlocked my energies and my abilities and enabled me to fill up page after page with words. My sexuality touched everything I was. It may be true that all novels in this century that are seriously gay novels are coming-out stories.

The man upstairs on the sixth floor, Mark, stopped by one night. He dropped onto the sofa, threw a leg over the arm, leaned back, and said, "Oh, shit." He is Irish, probably, is in his twenties, working-class, probably grew up in South Boston, had curly blond hair and smoked continuously. He leaned his head back against the wall. "He left me."

"What's going on?"

He shrugged. "I told him I was positive. He said he didn't want to be with me anymore. Then he walked out." He raised his eyebrows and pushed his mouth down on his teeth. "So. That's done with."

I was sitting in a chair across from Mark, but I got up and went across to the sofa. I reached out for Mark's hand. "How're you doing with that?"

Mark suddenly turned to me, and we embraced, and he began to cry. I held him for a long time. It wasn't that this was common, but it wasn't rare either, for two men to split up when one of them was diagnosed with HIV infection. Some men's boyfriends wanted nothing to do with them after they tested positive for HIV. Men brought it up in AA. I wondered how a man could think that an illness—no matter what kind—was sufficient reason to break up a relationship.

↔

World AIDS Day—the first in the world—was marked in Boston by an editorial in The Boston Globe and by symposia and panel discussions around the city. The Museum of Fine Arts greeted me, when I arrived, with a small sheet of paper on which were listed fifteen or twenty works in various parts of the museum, chosen by the curators. These works, according to the introductory paragraph at the head of the sheet, were the personal choices of the various curators and had for these curators a personal meaning somehow associated with World AIDS Day. There was no map to tell where these works of art were in the museum, no signs, and the only mark was a small paper sticker of bright green placed on the label for the work.

Two were very ferocious stone dragons in the Japanese galleries which, in Japan, were set up on either side of a door to keep the inhabitants safe from all harm.

Another was a small clear quartz and gold amulet, about 700 BC, in the Nubian collection designed to be worn on a cord around the neck. I had to stoop, almost kneel, to be able to see it. The clear quartz was round and hollowed out, and on top was a gold head of Hathor, wearing her crown of cow's horns and the sun disk between them. The thing itself was beautiful, something you might like to pick up and hold in your hand, rub with the heel of your thumb, warm slightly from your own body heat, but it would hang on your chest with the weight of quartz and gold and announce its value. Its associations with the goddess—fertility, renewal, health—all added to the value of the object, and its new associations with World AIDS Day, with all the sick men I knew, made me want to give it to some one man so that he could carry it and warm it with his palm and be protected by it, this very, very, valuable, very beautiful object.

Another item was in the Greek sculpture collection, a small statuette made of clay about ten inches tall of a mourning woman, from about 600 BC. The woman was fully robed, only her face and hands showing out from under the dark fabric, which fell straight from her shoulders and even gathered slightly on the ground. She was facing dead on, and her arms were lifted so that her hands almost rested—seemed to be about to rest—on the sides of her skull in a gesture of grief and mourning.

There were others around the museum. Part of the experience that day was trying to discover why the curator had chosen the piece, what it was in this piece that made the curator associate it with the universal catastrophe being marked by World AIDS Day, for no piece was marked with more than a small green sticker on the label.

↔

Maurice, played out against the backdrop of the Oscar Wilde trials of 17 years earlier, is a fantasy, a fairy tale grounded in reality, a wonderful romance, for in this book, the boy gets the boy and they live happily ever after. I read it over and over. I never got tired of reading the last half of the book, where Maurice goes down to Southampton to see Alec's boat off for the Argentine, and then discovers that Alec is not on the boat. The afternoon had broken in to glory. He races back to Penge to find Alec in the boathouse and to hear him say, "And now we shan't be parted no more, and that's finished." It was a hugely satisfying, exhilarating finish that I savored, and when the movie came out, I went to see Hugh Grant and Rupert Graves and James Wilby play out their parts. It didn't have the power of the book—movies don't—but at the end, when Rupert Graves gave James Wilby his great open-mouthed kiss and then ravenous hug, it seemed more believable, and they seemed younger than in the book, and more capable of doing what they had to do now to live together, which would not be the fairytale ending ever after in a kingdom of French castles but would instead be a life of hard labor. The point of the book, and of the movie, was that they dealt with their subject directly and didn't flinch. You saw Wilby's ass when he got out of bed from having sex with Graves, and you saw Graves's ass when he got out of bed from having sex with Wilby. For a subject which had never been dealt with directly before, this was, even in a fairy tale, revolutionary.

But there was something deeper going on in *Maurice*, something familiar. The three men at the heart of the novel differed in various ways—by class, by intellectual capacity, by capacity to feel, by ability to understand what was important. It became apparent early on that the man with the most secure place in society—Clive Durham—would be unable to give up that place for Maurice. The novel seems to exist to explore the question, *How much are you willing to give up, to have everything,* that is, *to have the one you love?* For Durham, very little. As the novel progresses, it becomes clear that you can't have it all, that life is a series of trade-offs and surrenders—decisions as to what you will give up in order to hang on to something greater. When Alec enters the novel on the end of a stepladder, he shows Maurice what it looks like when a man gives up everything—with no promise of anything in return. Maurice learns from that. At the end Maurice and Alec give up their families, their jobs, their places in society, their homes, the respect of their peers, everything, for each other. And what made all this so satisfying was that I knew this was the way life was. You only learn the value of things when you have learned what you have had to give up to get them.

↔

I was thinking about Stonewall, about the roving gangs of young gay men, moving through the West Village, confronting the organized platoons of riot police with their heavy equipment and armor and arms. I could see the scene as if from above—the grid of streets, the riot police blocking one or another narrow street, and the fluid gangs dissolving and disappearing into the darkness and then regrouping behind the riot police lines.

It was a metaphor for gay life. The young gay men were the guerilla forces, operating as Mao had it *in the population,* grouping to form forces to attack and then dissolving and regrouping elsewhere. The enemy was the police and the riot squads who, with their big equipment, could be one day here, another day there, but who lacked flexibility. It was a kind of guerilla warfare in which the invading forces—the police—had an infinite number of men and an infinite amount of money to throw at the local population, and an infinite amount of imagination, and the uprising, which was us, had therefore to react against napalm attacks one day, heavy bombers the next, broad sweeps of artillery and armed cavalry, and invasions by whole divisions of infantry. There would never be an end to the ways the invading forces would find to oppress gay people, and never be an end to the ways gay people would have to find to fight and escape and destroy the invaders.

↔

Mark, from upstairs, left me a note and invited me to watch a movie. It was one from several years ago, with Aiden Quinn and Ben Gazzara. Mark said it was the first TV movie about AIDS. Somebody had given him a copy. Aiden was beautiful, his eyes almost as big as his face and so sad, and Ben Gazzara, who apparently owned a lumber yard, was angry and hurt, too, that his only son was gay. Mark liked it—he was right, there had been nothing else like it on the tube—but I didn't. It had the tone of an elegy—things lost never to be found again—and that was not the tone of things around Boston. People that I knew were angry as hell even in the midst of their grief. When Aiden Quinn's character got sick, he broke up with his partner and went home to his family, and all through the movie his family were there to take care of him. That had not been my experience since 1984. The whole point of organizations like the AIDS Action Committee was that the families of these men were usually not there to care for them.

↔

Judith was in Amherst, at Hampshire College, a small, progressive college founded during the sixties. She came to see me regularly. It was a joke between us, that I would arrive home from work, and one of my messages would be from her. "Dad, by the time you get this, I will be almost to Boston to spend the night. I look forward to it." But this time, I was on the bus—I had sold my car and was using public transportation everywhere—to visit her. I was sitting in the window seat, and a man in a suit with a briefcase was sitting next to me.

"What takes you to the Valley?"

"My daughter is there at school."

"Does she like the school?" He wanted to know how long she had been there, and whether she got around to the other schools in the Valley—Smith, Mt Holyoke, Amherst, U Mass. He asked what I did for a living.

"I am writing a gay political novel. I work in the financial district during the day to support myself."

He was maybe eight or ten years younger than I. I was 49. He worked for Michael Dukakis, the Democratic governor of the state, who was currently running for President. This man was on his campaign staff.

He started feeling me out about my support for Michael Dukakis.

"I usually vote Democratic on the local level."

He wanted to know if I would support Dukakis for President.

"No." I told him. "I am a gay man going to visit my daughter. Several years ago, the Commonwealth was put through a trauma by the Governor over the foster care of the two boys adopted by the gay couple. I assume, as everyone else assumes, that the Governor called the shots in the removal of the two boys from the gay couple's home and the reversal of the Department of Social Services' judgment on the fitness of the two gay men. This debacle was entirely the responsibility of the Governor, and during the whole ugly mess, nobody proved otherwise or even suggested otherwise."

While I spoke, the man nodded, listening quietly.

"I divorced my wife four years ago. Various members of my family and my ex-wife's family have tried to maintain that I am not a fit father for my children, and I have worked hard to maintain a good loving relationship with my children. In the midst of all this, the Governor removed two children from the home of a gay couple, making clear to everyone who reads The Boston Globe that he does not think this couple can be fit parents for the children. The Governor reached deeply into my personal life when he did that, and he did it carelessly, indifferent to the health and well-being of all the gay families in the Commonwealth of Massachusetts. He was indifferent to the health and well-being of my family, and I could never support him for President. I intend to vote for the Socialist Worker's Party candidate, whoever that is."

↔

Most people I knew were volunteering in some way at the Committee, and in late 1988 I switched programs, leaving the Hotline and moving into the Buddy Program.

I wrote Amelia.

> I have been assigned a buddy. I'll be writing about that. His name is Alex, and he is currently in the hospital. He is a long-term survivor (four or five years) and is very sick, retinitis in one eye, which is almost gone now, and pneumocystis pneumonia three times. Do you remember

when the second bout of PCP killed people? So, we are
making medical progress. I have talked to him a good bit,
but our schedules have prevented us from seeing one
another. (He doesn't want to see me on days he sees his
doctors, and he sees his doctors most days.) I hope that will
happen this Wednesday. He is from Worcester. He is weak,
but still mobile, and gets about. He lives alone. He is seeing
the doctors today, so he doesn't want to see me tonight.

On Wednesday I went onto the AIDS ward and down to
Alex's room. He was asleep, and while the nurse said it was
OK to wake him, I didn't. I saw him—that is, I came into the
room and watched this sleeping form—but I never found
him awake and able to talk.

Finally things fell into place. Alex, after two weeks in
the hospital, came home. He was tall and had big bones and
closely cropped dark hair. He lay in his bed when I walked
in.

"I'm Fair Shaw. Are you Alex?'

"Fair! You won't believe what it has been like. I was
supposed to have come home yesterday afternoon right after
lunch, and I had lined up my friend Diarmuid to take me
home and get me settled, when the nurse suddenly came in
and said they weren't going to release me until four or five
because they were going to run more tests on my legs. They
think I have peripheral neuropathy. Did I tell you this? I
certainly have dementia, Diarmuid says. But my doctors
have not said that. And how would they know anyway?
Diarmuid says I've acted like I had dementia for years. And
then they are concerned about peripheral neuropathy. It has
been a ghastly day."

I went over to the bed and picked up Alex's hand and
held it for a few moments. Alex watched me make these
movements. He had never seen me before, although we had
talked on the phone, and he seemed to be watching me from
a great distance. Then I laid his hand back down on the bed,
carefully, so as not to hurt him. I thought I would not stay
but a few minutes—fifteen at the most—because the energy
Alex had would not last, and I thought it best to come
frequently for short visits than to come for long visits.

"How are you?" I sat down in the chair. "Are you OK?"

"Oh—" Alex gazed at the ceiling. "—it is hard to tell. My legs hurt so—." He looked over at me. "Who are you?"

I smiled. "I'm Fair Shaw. I am from the AIDS Action Committee. I am your buddy. This is the first time we've met."

"Have we met before?"

I shook my head. "No. We haven't. I wanted to, but you were in the hospital, and we couldn't. Now that you are home from the hospital, I've come to see you."

Alex seemed to think about that for a long time. "I thought I knew you, and now I don't think I do." Then. "Yes, I think I do remember you. And I don't like you. I wish you'd leave."

I smiled and didn't move. "I'll leave if you want me to, Alex. But maybe before I go you'd like to tell me how it has been for you today. Would you like just to talk? Then, maybe you'd like to tell me if there is anything I can do for you? How is your laundry? Your food? Is there a nurse coming by to look after you? Is there anything I can do for you that will make your life better?"

Alex was confused. He looked again at the ceiling, then back at me. "I don't know. I don't know what I need." He clearly didn't know me, but the fight had gone out of him. He was on the edge of tears. "I don't know."

"Is there a nurse coming by?"

Alex looked panicked.

"May I use your telephone?"

Actually, there was a nurse assigned to Alex, and she would come every morning and every afternoon and had already been by once today.

I told Alex that a nurse would come by, and got back Alex's stupefying anxiety. "May I come to visit you again?"

I was supposed to have spent Saturday evening with Alex, but unexpectedly Alex's family from Worcester came down and took him home for the weekend. When he got back, Alex told me the trip home had not been good: He developed a low grade fever and spent the weekend sleeping on his mother's sofa. He was disappointed and sad—he had

wanted to visit relatives and friends—and angry. But Alex
was apparently a compulsively happy person. He put a good
face on things. He was too sick to work now, but fortunately,
he had good insurance and disability. He was to have laser
surgery on his retina on Wednesday. Alex: "Doctor, what are
my choices?" Doctor: "You'll go blind if you don't have this
operation." Alex: "And what if I have the surgery?" Doctor:
"You'll probably go blind." Alex seemed to survive on black
humor, that and talking endlessly, as if he could maintain his
life by an insistent constant voice, and through it all, he
slipped in and out of dementia.

I wrote Ames.

My life is crazy. There is too much going on at one time. My
buddy, Alex, is now in the hospice—which is where people
go when the hospitals cannot do anything else for them.
They go there, essentially, to die. I visit him every day.
Sometimes he knows me, and sometimes not, but he seems
to like having visitors. I have never watched someone die
before. You usually do this when you get to Mother's age
and the people a little older than you start dying, and, since
they are your friends, you go to visit them and then go to
their funerals. And, they die of old age, and that seems to be
a fairly quiet way to die. This is all very different. We are
looking after men, men frequently we don't even know very
well, and they are dying of a raft of strange diseases. And
their biological families are not central to this process.
Sometimes they are not there at all.

The hospice was a large home in Roxbury that had been
renovated by contractors and interior decorators in the gay
community. Alex's room was attractive, soothing, rather
stylish—the decorators had done their work well and for
nothing—and I found Alex staring hard at a large
impressionist print on the opposite wall.

"I don't like that picture," he said. If you didn't look
closely, it could have been by Monet on an off week.

398

Impressionist, pastels, trees and a field, the whole drenched in sunlight.

It was not by one of the masters. "Why not, Alex?"

"It is an ugly, mean, picture."

At one point Alex had to go to the bathroom, and I helped him. He wore a hospital johnny that tied behind the neck and fell open down the back. I allowed Alex to put his arm around my shoulders and to lean on me as I helped him to the bathroom. Alex's body was beginning to be bone only, the flesh having wasted all away. His hips seemed abnormally wide, and the joints in his legs were larger than his thighs. I understood that Alex had once been this big hunky guy, but now he was nearly nothing but a skeleton—and hot to the touch. At one point, traversing the room toward the bath, Alex lost his footing and almost fell, and I realized that as thin as Alex was, he still weighed too much for me to handle. Even his skeleton alone weighed so much that I staggered under Alex's falling weight before I could get him righted again. I got him seated on the toilet, the johnny pulled out of the way. "Would you like me to stay?" I wanted to give him privacy if that was what he wanted, but Alex was going about his business, and seemed to have forgotten me. Alex no longer cared about his privacy. Here, in the face of the extreme suffering in the tastefully renovated room, privacy was irrelevant. Alex wanted to go back to bed, but first I cleaned him up and got him a new johnny—the other had become soiled—before supporting him back to the bed in the corner of the room.

I wrote Mother.

My buddy died last Thursday (today is Sunday). I don't know what he died of—general failure would be a way of putting it—but it seems it was peaceful. It happened in the morning, and I had visited him the afternoon before, which I am glad of. Judith was here, which helped, although I have felt grief and anger at hard moments since then. He suffered terribly until fairly recently, when he seemed to take off into a world of his own—eyes closed, mumbling of fantasies.

Shakespeare says Falstaff died "babbling of green fields," which is what Alex did.

Alex's funeral was this weekend and was held in a church here. Beautiful service, beautiful building. There were Bach and hymns "from the Church in Japan" and testimonials from his sister-in-law and a man from the motorcycle club. At the end, the family donated his "colors"—a black leather vest with the motor cycle club emblem on it—to the club, which is now going to sew a quilt for him. His sister-in-law wrote me, but the letter lies unopened on my shelf. I don't know why I can't seem to bring myself to open it.

Alex's death and funeral were unusual because his family was involved. In most of the deaths that I knew, the family stayed completely away from the dying man. Usually, a funeral is held by the family in the man's hometown, and none of the gay community are told about it. Then, several weeks later, a memorial service is held in Boston, and public notices are inserted in the *Gay Community News* or *Bay Windows*, and a hundred or so of the dead man's friends come to honor him. There are two completely separate grieving processes going on at the same time.

In my own life, there are at least two grieving processes going on. One is the continuous grieving process arising out of the deaths and mortal illnesses around me, the sense of loss that everyone we know is experiencing as they go through their lives seven years into the epidemic. This is a kind of communal grieving. Then there are the people I know personally.

When Vincent was dying over several weeks, his lover called and I went over to see him. He lay on the sofa, sweat running off his forehead, his eyes half opened, breathing shallowly. He didn't want to talk to me. I held his hand, and sometimes I could feel him increasing the pressure on my fingers. I stayed with him for an hour or more. He didn't want to talk, he just wanted me to stay with him, which I did.

↔

One night there was a message from Tim Byrne. "Call me. Can I come over?"

It was after nine o'clock. I called.

"I've just come back from New York. I was there all week. You know *The Normal Heart*, Larry Kramer? He organized this sit-in in Wall Street this week, on Tuesday—"

"Were you there?"

"Did you hear about it?"

"Of course I did! I read about it in *The Native* last week, about their plans to do it. Men have been talking about it at the Ramrod every night."

"I was there, honey—" He grinned, proudly.

"You were there! It is all anybody in Boston has been able to talk about!"

"Oh, I was there!"

"Tell me."

"Well, I was in a bar on Bleecker Street and I heard about it— this was on Sunday night—and the goal was to call attention to the fact that the Federal Drug Administration was not approving experimental drugs fast enough." He pulled his feet up on the sofa and reached for the ash tray and lit a cigarette. "So I went down. Oh, Jesus, this is what I've been looking for."

"How many people were there?"

He shrugged. "Who knows. A lot. Two hundred maybe."

"Was that enough?"

"They trained us the night before. They told us how to deal with the cops. We stopped traffic on Wall Street. We completely stopped traffic! And we made *The Native*—"

"I know, I saw it, it was a great!"

"—and every tabloid in the city. It was so fine. Every one of them carried our message that the FDA has been slow in approving experimental drugs. There is only one drug that has been approved, and that one is toxic and not very helpful. We made them listen to us, and Jesus, they heard us! Now everybody can hear us."

Tim was no longer a skinny kid. When a man loses fat in his face, it ages him, and I had watched dozens of men go from looking like they were in their late twenties to looking like they were in their late forties. Tim looked like a sick man—with KS around his mouth

—who was forty-five years old. I think he was about 26 when I first met him, and now he is twenty-nine.

"We were fighting back! We were screaming at the cops! They were trying to clear the road, and we refused! We blocked the street!"

He was having difficulty expressing to me how satisfying that was, fighting back. I could see the scene, Stonewall again.

"We made them use rubber gloves and face masks. They looked horrible."

Kramer, the author of *Faggots* and *The Normal Heart*, took the sit-in and made of it a new organization—ACT UP. AIDS Coalition to Unleash Power. From that week on, ACT UP was everywhere in the gay press, *Bay Windows, Gay Community News, The Native*, the *Advocate*, and also fairly regularly in the mainstream press, *The Globe* and *The Times*.

"The idea is to capture the media, to organize an event so as to draw media attention to the single, specific point we want to make. The FDA approval of experimental medications. The number of experimental drugs in the pipeline waiting for approval. Most people do not pay attention to these things, so they don't know that the FDA has a chokehold on the medications that are out there, and most people don't know that at this point, there is only one medication approved for us to take."

An ACT UP chapter was formed in Boston, and the logo began to appear everywhere—small black poster with large pink triangle in the center and underneath, SILENCE=DEATH. Tim arrived at my place with a bookbag filled with ACT UP materials.

"It's something I can do, you know? Sharpening the distinction between us on the one hand and the government on the other is a worthwhile thing to do. That way people won't think that everything is OK. We have to get the message out that everything is not OK. I like ACT UP because the message is political. At meetings, they say, AIDS is a political crisis. It is not merely a medical crisis. It is a political crisis. We have to speak up. Don't we? We have to tell what's happening."

The interesting thing was that *The New York Times* didn't carry that initial demonstration in Wall Street. They didn't pay any attention. The newspaper of record.

The other interesting thing is that I wrote friends in various places about these demonstrations and ACT UP, and some men wrote back and said, "'bout time," while several of my friends wrote back and said, "I can't imagine what demonstrations have to do with any of this." There seemed to be a generational gap, and it seemed that men who came out in the late fifties or early sixties were so accustomed to living quiet lives—I suppose this was the reason—in which they didn't call attention to themselves, even if they didn't feel they were closeted, that they couldn't conceive of getting out in the street and screaming at Power. And yet it had become evident that was the only way it was going to work.

↔

I wrote Amelia.

> Yesterday I took off the day from work to finish reworking the three chapters I sent to St Martins, and, at the end of the day, after everything was in the mail, I went swimming. Afterwards, the shower was crowded with men—people who had come off the squash courts, from the weight room, the track upstairs, swimmers: all ages and conditions. In the corner of the shower room, sharing a head, were two boys, eighteen or nineteen, turned to the wall or to the corner, but explicitly turned toward each other, washing each other's bodies, oblivious to everything and everybody else in this crowded room. I only have eyes for you. Some of the men stared, fascinated, other men turned away and spoke loudly to each other, determined to ignore the boys. The boys were oblivious, soaping and stroking each other's bodies. It was a pastoral.

Henrietta wrote me:

> September 20, 1988
> Dear Fair,
> Fall is upon us and the children have returned to school. Autumn is a lovely time of year, as Nature gathers itself and prepares for Winter.

Our children are doing very well. Cornelius, Jr., has graduated from Princeton and is settling down to serious work as we expected him to. He has prepared for a career in law, but is going to take a year off before law school at Carolina. We are very proud of him, especially of the wonderful record he has made.

Joseph is doing very well at UVa. He was elected president of his class and also editor of the student newspaper.

I spend a great deal of time preparing the garden for the winter, and Cornelius helps me any time he has a moment away from his work. He almost never has a moment!

We miss you so at these important times in our lives, and we will be thinking of you among our nearest family when the cold weather comes and we all withdraw into the warmth of the fireside.

Love,
Henrietta

And I wrote Henrietta:

September 27, 1988
Dear Henrietta and Cornelius,

I divorced Naomi and came out gay. I wrote you about all that. I wrote you about the AIDS epidemic and the lack of response by the Administration in Washington, even about their stumbling, bumbling steps which seem to have made things worse than if they did nothing at all. I wrote you about homophobia in the government at all levels, in the churches (including your own, the Protestant Episcopal Church in the United States) and in the press. I have written you about my volunteer work for the AIDS Action Committee, and I have written you about ACT UP and about the countless demonstrations I have attended or been witness to, I wrote you about the murder of my friend by some boys who thought he was gay, and I have written you about writing a book about the events in Maine after his murder. I have written you about my anger and my grief at the place of gay people in America during this decade.

You have not ever responded to any of these things about which I have written you. And then I get a letter from you, a little social note with one paragraph on the season and then another paragraph on each of your sons and a closing paragraph in which you say you miss me so.

I have told you this before: your unwillingness to acknowledge the substance of my letters—your inability to answer my letters—is unmistakable evidence of your bigotry.

Fair

↔

When we arrived at the Matthews Arena on the Northeastern University campus, we found that all the doors along one side— usually open to the street only to allow people to leave after a hockey game—were wide open, and instead of having to enter through the main door of the arena, we were able to walk directly from the street into the arena. When we got inside, we were on the level with the highest row of bleachers, and we got to the floor of the arena by climbing down. People on the floor—the arena was crowded—were not speaking to one another. Spread out across the floor, covering almost the entire arena, was the Quilt, and between sections, the organizers had left pathways, for people who moved slowly from panel to panel.

We moved onto the floor, uncertain, not knowing where or how to begin to visit the Quilt. It didn't have a beginning or a start or a place from which it was best viewed. There was not, as there is in all epics, an opening sentence—*I sing of warfare and a man at war*— that carries you into the narrative, focuses your attention and tells you what you are about to see or read or hear, and lifts you from the plane of ordinary life to the realm of epic action. Here, to us standing in a clump of people in the space between the edge of the floor of Matthews Arena and the Quilt, there was nothing but the edge of it, not the first quilt but one of the nearer quilts of many with which to start. It was to be a random experience. We broke away from the people at the edge and moved toward it.

There were the short ends of four quilts along the edge that we approached, quilts showing brilliant colors, which was, perhaps, the dominant impression of the whole vast floor of quilts, seen here in front of us and between the people walking among them. Brilliant reds and greens and yellows and blues and blacks and whites. We moved to the left, toward a path between two panels, to walk along the long side of quilts, the better to be able to see what we looked at. On our right was a brilliant parrot green, sewn of shimmering satin, a field of parrot green satin. Up close, it was possible to see there was a name hand stitched across the top in silk-like golden thread. Oliver Hayden Martin. Underneath, in the same golden thread, were dates 1958-1985. And that was all. I contemplated this, thinking how young he was—born in 1958 and dead three years ago—before I saw, across the bottom, in small letters and even smaller, more delicate stitches, *We ache that you are gone.* A group of men around a table, in a kitchen perhaps, the quilt spread out, carefully doing the needlework that created the words in the parrot-green satin. I examined the stitching at the top of the panel and then the stitching at the bottom, comparing. Had the same man done both? Had each word been done by a different man? It was impossible to tell. And why parrot-green satin? It was not very beautiful. I realized—it had been impossible really to see it in Washington last year—that I didn't know what issues to raise, what questions to ask.

I understood the way these things were done, because I had gotten calls myself to come "next Thursday night at eight" to sew a quilt for some friend of ours. One person had taken the initiative and had bought the materials. Sometimes I got printed invitations from someone announcing that there would be a bee on a certain date for someone I had known, addressed to Mr. Fair Shaw, 211 Park Drive, Boston, MA 02117.

We moved up along the side of a panel. Each quilt was three feet by six feet, and each panel was twelve feet on a side. There are a number of ways eight quilts can be sewn into one panel, and we had to move around the bottom left corner to see the next quilt, a playful one, employing baby blue printed cotton, and, toward one end, a much beat-up teddy bear. Letters, formed by quilted cotton of a different pattern of a slightly darker blue, made a wave from upper left to lower right. WE REMEMBER TOMMY MANNING. 1952-1986.

This arena was a better place for the quilt than the Ellipse, which was too big, too exposed to the sun and wind and to the possibility of damp ground, and more suitable for the feelings the quilt aroused. I felt I could actually see some significant portion of what was on the floor. I pointed to Tommy Manning's quilt. "It looks like a quilted bedspread. Like a bed, with a pillow, with his teddy bear." This raised the question of what Tommy Manning had been like. Soft, cuddly, boyish, babyish? I turned to Tim, walking beside me. "If you were to make a quilt for me, what would you make it of?"

"Black leather, honey." Tim laughed. "Very, very black. With chains."

I laughed. "Jesus. Exposed."

I wondered how many of these quilts contained hidden jokes.

We walked on around the panel, reading the quilts. Most of the quilts were made of cotton, or of a cotton-like material, some solid color, sometimes with a contrasting color for a border. They had names—ARNOLD COOK—and dates—1948-1985—and sometimes something else, a line of poetry, some reference to some activity of the dead man—FIRST BASEMAN FOR THE ASBURY PARK SLUGGERS, SOUTHERN CALIFORNIA GAY LEAGUE— and sometimes something that came from somewhere else entirely. "He was always a model for the rest of us, even when he was sickest."

Tim pointed at the line, using his cane. "There it is, the impossible standard, to suffer stoically and to be a model to men."

"You don't have to do it any particular way."

"And one of you will put on my quilt, 'He was never really a model for any kind of behavior to anybody who knew him.'"

"Tim, man, it's going to be OK."

"You're going to put on my quilt, 'Jesus, he pissed off everybody who knew him!'"

"Tim."

We walked on, and then he wanted to sit down, so we returned to the steps.

"This is hard. The emotion is so raw."

"I imagine a bunch of guys sitting around a kitchen table making those things, most of them men who've never picked up a needle before in their lives. Trying to sew and crying at the same time. Telling stories about their friend and crying—and laughing—and arguing about what to put on the quilt. Somebody says, 'I think he was the biggest user of cocaine in Eastern Massachusetts!'

Somebody else says, 'Nah, there were plenty of guys who used more than him.'"

"Uh-uh. Usually in cases like that, there's some control queen who has already decided everything." I could think of several.

"You going to do it for me?"

"Do you want one?" I tried to read his face.

"I don't know." Tim thought for a moment. "Let's go outside and smoke a cigarette." So we made the laborious journey back up the bleacher steps to the doors and to the outside where Tim sat on the steps and smoked. "If you organized it, it wouldn't be so bad. I think I could trust you—"

"I guess—"

"—not to be too kitschy."

We both laughed. "Do you have a teddy bear?"

"I hate this."

"What?"

"Giving up control of things like this. I've always cared so much about how I presented myself."

"Hmmm."

"Did you see the one in there with the guy in drag?"

"With the cigarette holder?"

"Yeah. Do you suppose he wanted that?"

"That may have been the way he presented himself. The Quilt is for the living. It's the guys who are survivors who want to do this. Do you care after you are dead?"

"I care a lot about me and my name and how I am seen. The guys who have made those quilts in there have used the ones who are dead—"

"I hope they do it with respect."

"I already feel like I am dead."

I held his hand.

"I look almost as old as you."

His face was mainly skin pulled tight across bone.

"I am too sick to do what I'd really like to do—"

"What is that?"

"—ACT UP. Take part in their next demonstrations." He looked at me. "We're not through with Reagan."

We sat in the sun for a while, leaning on our elbows on the step behind. Tim smoked. He looked at his leg, which quivered, and we talked. Occasionally he reached over and, without looking at what he was doing, held my hand.

Back inside, as we approached the Quilt, a woman moved toward us. She held a Kleenex in her hand, which was up near her face, and she was looking into the Kleenex with tears in her eyes. There was more noise than I had thought at first, although it was not noticeable when you first come in from outside. The arena was so big and the ceiling so high, it swallowed up the voices of people and turned them into something coming out of the ceiling, a kind of high-pitched clatter.

Tim, maneuvering with his cane, slid his hand into the crook of my arm and held onto me.

"Hi, guys." It was two men from AA. "You just arriving?"

"We've been here for a while." I smiled.

"Have you seen the quilts of anybody you know?"

"No. Not yet."

"How are you?"

"I'm OK. I'm feeling OK." Tim's hand gripped my arm tightly. When he shifted his weight on his feet, he pulled hard on my arm. He seemed sometimes to sway.

One of them hugged me and was about to hug Tim, when Tim said, "No, uh-uh," and shook his head.

"Don't. It hurts him."

"Oh, sorry."

Then they were gone. Tim used to be the kind of boy men called "willowy," by which, I think, they meant tall, slender, flexible, stooped as a willow tree seems to lean over and droop. Now, leaning on his cane, he had a certain stiffness about him.

We were standing next to a quilt in a checked pattern in gray— slate gray—and white. Superimposed on the check pattern were large block letters in black. RANDALL FORTNEY PERRY. 1951-1986. Then in smaller block letters, WRITER, EDITOR, ACTIVIST, FRIEND, LOVER. It began to be clear to me that the Quilt had to be read, not merely seen. I saw people standing on the edge of a panel, twisting their heads to read the words on a quilt placed at right angles to them. It may be that there were not enough words on the quilts, that it would have been better if there had been more—more of a narrative, more of a life story of the men who had died, so we could see them more clearly. The Shaw and the 54th Regiment Memorial was mainly to be seen, taken in at a glance, the heroism of the men on the face of the memorial, absorbed instantly, but there were actually plenty of words incised in the marble. What I found around me had to be read one word at a time. Since this was so, the "story" I experienced on the floor of the arena at Northeastern University was different from the story the next man experienced, with a different opening line, climax, and conclusion, even if the broad outlines were the same.

Coming toward us as the crowds opened up was a small procession—two uniformed medical attendants and Leo Andrelli, whose face was contorting in an effort to control his emotions. The attendants were at the head and the foot of a stretcher on wheels, on which lay Leo's boyfriend, Garey. Tim and I stood aside for a moment, allowing them to come up to us through the crowd. "Hello."

"Hello." It was Leo. Garey stared straight ahead. It may have been that he was unable to speak, or that he couldn't see, or both, or something else. Leo looked at him and then at us. "Garey wanted to come, so I fixed it so he could come. And now here we are. Are you all right?" He took us both in with his glance.

"Yes. I am fine. Tim?"

"I have a little difficulty walking, but I am fine too." He spoke directly to Garey. "It is good to see you, Garey. I am Tim Byrne." Tim and Garey had sat at the table drinking coffee many hours in my presence.

Garey didn't move or acknowledge Tim.

In a moment they moved on, an attendant at the foot and one at the head, moving the stretcher through the crowds, directed by Leo, who continued to make an effort to control the muscles of his face.

We turned again to the quilts. But in a moment we began to hear a male voice over the public address system, and in a few moments it became clear that this voice was reading names. This was done in a slow, measured way, very formal, almost stylized. "Victor Abreu." A very long pause. "Andrew John Abromovitch." A very long pause.

"They are reading the names of all the people who have died of AIDS in Massachusetts since the epidemic began." That was Tim. "I read about it."

The quilt on our left was one in which the size of the lettering had been expanded to take up the entire quilt. KENNETH

RANDOLPH, the two names stacked on top of each other. The background in black canvas and the letters in white. Very bold.

Tim leaned over and spoke. "It's called The Names Project. They are afraid that the individual people—their names—will be lost in the current emphasis on numbers, percentages, rates, all the epidemiology of this disease. So they are reading out the names of the people who have died."

"I don't think I wanted to come, but you asked me, so I came with you. And I'm surprised, actually. I didn't expect to find this. It has a political aspect. There is, underneath all this, something subversive." I looked around the giant arena. "People who die of AIDS seem to disappear. The newspapers say in obituaries that a man died of a 'long illness,' and that he has been survived by his brother and his sister-in-law and his nieces and nephews, but never by the man with whom he lived for 14 years and with whom he shared his life. In death, the man's whole identity is suddenly bleached of anything gay. I think that must be one of the points of all this, that The Names Project do what it is doing at this moment, say, 'These are the names of gay men, and they died of AIDS. Many of them certainly are dead because of inaction by the American government during the eight years of the epidemic.' It's an indictment. People don't tell you that about the Quilt."

"We don't know that all of them are gay."

I shrugged. "The vast majority of them, according to The Native's numbers."

So we went on, bearing witness to the names of those who have died, and, at the same time, saying that what this government has to say about AIDS is not all there is to be said. As we moved, we heard the voice of the man reading names. *Walter Allen. Charles Allendorf. Steven Allensworth.* On our right was a quilt with the single word, MATTHEW in the middle against a flowered pink and pale blue chintz background, and on our left was a quilt with the name GARY MARSDEN in large emphatic black letters down the middle of a field of elegant gray satin.

Sometimes Tim leaned on me like women at the turn of the last century leaned on men. I would not have come to the display of the Quilt if it hadn't been for him. It has something of a bad reputation. People say that, in a time when manpower is so short in the gay community, moving the Quilt around the country is labor-intensive.

There must be at least a hundred people here volunteering to help with the crowds, to do the manual labor of unpacking and packing the Quilt, and to read the names. It is here for three days, so times three. It is visiting twenty cities, so times twenty. Then there is the money. It costs money to truck the Quilt from one city to another. We need this money to provide services for ourselves—for the ones who are sick in our cities. Tim called and asked if I was going. He said, "I know all that. I've heard it all. But I want to go. Will you go with me?" His feelings got the better of his politics, and since his legs were giving him trouble and making it difficult for him to go alone, I said, "I'll go."

He said, coming over, "It's nothing but kitsch, and it wastes our resources—," as if I were going to criticize him.

What he didn't say was that it was ours.

We passed quilts made of canvas and of cotton, of silk and of satin, linen, rayon, nylon, wool, corduroy, denim. They tended to be of sturdier fabrics because the organizers had suggested that the sturdier fabrics would last longer, but some of the quilts displayed even so delicate a fabric as lace.

Next to us was a very striking quilt whose white block letters were laid out in two lines against a coral background. It drew attention to itself from yards away: MICHAEL WILLIAM SCOTT, 1959-1985. It left a sense of him: simple, direct, rich.

Tim stared at it for a moment. "I like that. I like the color—and the white."

We could see up beyond the people around us to the open doors to the brilliant sunshine outside and to the people going in and out.

"I like it that they are different—."

"Unique, Fair, unique. Like the men."

"Each is unique. Yet all part of the same enterprise. All of them, now, finally, out."

"Only the ones with last names and dates. There are plenty with only first names and without any dates."

"Ah, yes." MATTHEW. There was still a difference.

"They've died, still closeted. They didn't have courage to face their families."

"Oh, Tim, there are plenty of reasons for not coming out aside from fear of families."

"Fear of society. Fear of being hurt. Fear—"

"Do you miss your family?"

"Of course."

"Yes. I do too." I missed what I always missed in them—respect, caring—whether we were in touch or not.

In addition to the variety of colors and materials, and conception, there was also a range of skill employed in these quilts, both in design and in execution. We were beside a silver one, with black satin letters. Here, the stitching was clumsy throughout. BO TURTORRO, MY BEST BABE. 1946-1986. It gave a strong sense of the stitcher's affection for Bo and of the obligation the stitcher felt toward Bo as he sewed. I wondered where they had played out their love for each other—a leather bar? a drag bar? motorcycle club? "Look, Tim. Where did they meet?"

He stared at the silver lamé for a moment and then broke out into a grin. "Oh, honey, look at the silver lamé. It could be anywhere!" He gripped my arm, and we went on.

The democratic universe of the Quilt. It was like the Y. Each person was free to pursue whatever private interests he might have—seventeenth century English lyric poetry, unknown and unimagined procedures with obscure body parts—but here in this place he was gay.

"Hi, guys." It was David Sepe. David always looked clean cut—short, neatly trimmed hair, freshly pressed shirts and pants. "Have you been here long?"

"Not long," Tim said. "It only feels like a lifetime."

"I know how you feel."

"How could you possibly know how I feel?"

There was a sudden chill. David was here with his boyfriend.

"Hi. I am Fair Shaw."

"I'm John McConaghey." The boyfriend smiled, uncertainly. He didn't know what to do with Tim's question. "They are beautiful."

"Yes."

"And moving."

"Yes, they are." The feeling in the gay community. The many feelings in the gay community. The feelings in the many parts of the gay community. The many feelings in the many gay communities. "It is hard, isn't it?"

They both nodded.

"Are you going to read?" David was solicitous.

"No. I didn't know I was coming. I didn't volunteer. Are you?"

"Yes, in about twenty minutes. Maybe we could talk afterward?"

"That'd be good. We're going to go on. OK?"

David and I and John hugged, and then we moved on down the path among the crowd of men and women moving with us and against us. We passed another woman, maybe 45, this time with a man, whose free hand held a handkerchief that she held up to her face, where tears streamed from her cheeks. She looked at it before she blotted her eyes. I wanted to take Tim to a place where we could talk. "Would you like to sit on the bleachers?"

He mumbled yes.

When we were seated—we had come all the way across the floor since the last time we had rested—he drew a breath and spoke. "I hate this."

"We can leave if you want to. Anytime you want to. Would you like to go now?"

"No. It's that—the whole thing makes me so angry. This is all so well-bred and polite, these quilts on the floor treated with such respect—these pieces of cloth—by all these very polite people walking around with hankies to their eyes. It's all so sad, and yet it makes me so angry that this many men have died who didn't have to. If the government had cared, they could have put some effort into prevention. They lie when they say they have sufficiently funded the research laboratories. They don't care at all about a cure. We are all so sad, and the visitors here today say, *It's so hard, it's so tragic,* I get so tired of hearing that. I want to mount a revolution. I want to go outside and stick my cane in the ground and declare my own Days of Rage that all these wonderful people are dying, and our government doesn't give a shit. I wonder how many gay men give a shit. It's easy to be polite. If you make a quilt for me, put on it, *He wanted a revolution!* I am speechless with anger that this should have happened now, during the administration of this man, who has no idea what is happening. What suffering, what loss. What his responsibilities are."

Tears were running down his face. We sat at the edge of the Arena floor, causing no notice at all because half the men there, it seemed, had wet cheeks.

After a while, I touched him on his shoulder—I had to be very careful with that nowadays—and said, "I love you, Tim." Then, "Would you like to go?"

"Oh, Fair, no place is good for me now. I hurt wherever I am. And please don't patronize me." He stood up. "No. I've changed my mind. Put on my quilt, *He worked to bring down the government.*" He grinned at me.

"OK."

"No, let's see some more, some more of the horrors. And I love you too."

So we went out onto the floor and were immediately swept up in the sound of the man's voice intoning the names of the dead.

He was reading the names in alphabetical order. He had not gotten through the "b's," and I thought, they have a long afternoon ahead of them. They should have done it in random order, as it had happened. Alphabetizing it tidied it up.

We got to the edge of the panels. We abandoned our effort to take the quilts in an orderly fashion—beginning on the right and working our way across the huge floor—and plunged into the display somewhere directly in front of us. We would never be able to see it all in any case.

There were, in the panel on our right, four quilts alike, each with a different name. The background was a brilliant yellow-green and turquoise and blue done in a pattern that looked like flamestitch, like the aurora borealis. The names stretched, in light blue script, from one end of each quilt to the other, across the top, and, at the bottom of each quilt, in small script matching the one above, were the words, *member of the cast, Chorus Line, Broadway production, 1979-1985.* People said that there was a quilt for Michael Bennett somewhere, and one for Rock Hudson. The man's voice had stopped, and after a few moments, a woman's voice came on, reading names.

"Do you still think it is kitsch?"

"Oh, sure. It has all the elements. It is handmade, and not very well done at that, it looks back to a rural past, it is manufactured sentiment. It is designed to make us cry. It operates by making public what should be private. It is in pretty bad taste, most of it." Tim grimaced. "And I can't get enough of it."

I think what happened was that the deaths, once they started, came so rapidly that men did not have time to grieve. And many of the organs of our culture—the government, the medical profession initially, public health, the churches, the media—were often saying in one way or another that we brought it on ourselves. Many of these men's own families abandoned them. And in such an atmosphere, the balance of unspent grief accumulated and accumulated, so that at a memorial service for a man, it would seem as if the attendees were grieving for the death of a whole culture.

We walked on, moving slowly to accommodate Tim's cane.

"What does the doctor say about your legs?"

"He says it's not caused by the drugs I am taking, which sucks, because if it were, I could just switch drugs. As it is, he's given me medication and is looking at my diet. It seems I have a severe case of it, and I may have to just live with it. Or maybe not. They don't know. I am not supposed to stand for long periods."

"Tim."

He shrugged and grinned. "I love it when you worry about me."

"Do you want to sit down?"

"No. I'll tell you."

We moved on. There was one on the left, of magenta, with lettering in a pale violet. HOWARD WILMORE and his dates 1961-1983 and *A Beautiful Man.*

"I like the color in that one." Tim pointed with his cane.

"I could have brought one of those little folding stools."

"Oh, don't, Fair."

"I like worrying over you."

"If this goes on much longer I may not be able to do anything about it."

"Whether they were out or not when they died, they still died of AIDS. The vast majority of them got it from anal intercourse. And they have all of them suffered because of government malevolence toward persons with AIDS."

"Or indifference."

"The same thing."

"The government and society at large. Jerry Falwell is driving national health policy. Indifference to persons with AIDS is the same thing as malevolence toward gay people. Where does this come from, Fair? Do you think about that?"

"Where does what come from?"

"Society's malevolence toward gay people."

But he didn't wait for an answer. Tim saw a quilt, and he walked over to it and stood before it, head bowed. It was black with a giant pink triangle in the middle whose topmost point almost touched the top edge of the quilt and whose bottom edge hovered about an inch from the bottom of the quilt. Across the bottom, from one side to the other, in white block letters, it read, AIDS ACTIVIST, WILLING FIGHTER, LEADER. Across the top was his name, ANDREW TEMPLE SIMS and his dates 1945-1984.

Tim turned to me. "I like that. Put that on my quilt."

"So you want a quilt."

Tim shrugged. "You decide."

"So this is, in itself, subversive. In itself it's an indictment of the government. Every time we join together and do something like this —do what the government should be doing, in this case, acknowledging the dead in a great national catastrophe—"

"—taking on the medical establishment—"

"—is an indictment of the government for not doing it. OK, I'll decide." I whispered in his ear. "And you'll like it."

He walked away, and I followed. We strolled down the pathways between the panels, stopping occasionally over this or that quilt—the construction of one, the language on another—and sometimes exchanged comments. He moved ahead of me with the energy that has characterized all his actions during the four years I have known him. Then he stopped and waited for me to catch up.

"I have something to tell you."

"What's that?"

"I think I have a boyfriend."

"Congratulations! Who is he?"

"A guy at the Living Center—" The Living Center was the community center for persons with AIDS. "—I'll tell you later, when —if—it develops into something."

"That's fine. That's wonderful."

And a little later, he spoke again.

"Fair, will you look after things?"

I waited a moment to answer. "Sure."

Tim grinned.

"We need to sit down with a piece of paper and a pencil and talk about what you want. I think we should see a lawyer." So that was settled.

"Was it fear of your family that made you stay closeted—stay in your marriage—so long?"

"I think it was fear of losing them. I don't think I was afraid of them. They couldn't do anything to me—I didn't even live in their town—but I was afraid of losing them. It was something primitive, I guess. Fear of finding myself alone in the world. It was unimaginable. It was unthinkable, that I would lose them. In the end, I did lose them—I am in the process right now of losing them—no matter what I did. But maybe another question is, 'Was it fear of my family that made me get married?'"

"Well?"

"I don't know. I certainly found it difficult to stand up to my mother and my brother. I wish that we had had a better relationship. I think that, given my little slice of Western Culture—middle class White Anglo-Saxon Protestant in South Carolina in the forties and fifties—it would have been an unimaginable miracle if I had not done the expected thing. Gotten married."

"I guess so."

"Are you hearing anything from your family?"

"Not for a year or two. It's been, ah, actually—" He calculated. "—32 months."

"That's tough. You handling that?"

He shrugged. "What else?" Then he took my arm and leaned down to whisper in my ear. "I have it. Put on my quilt, *He worked to bring about the collapse of Western Culture.*"

"Anything you say, beautiful. I like that one. Two people I know are worried that Western Culture is going to collapse. You and I are worried that it won't collapse. Or won't collapse fast enough." For most people the social contract still operates. But for others, for us, it is long gone. I don't understand why more people don't know that. It all cracked up and floated away in little pieces. "Are you in pain?"

"Oh, sure. But I can stand this." He took my arm again, leaning in to me like Odette at the end of *In the Shadow of Young Girls in Flower*. "Lead on."

6

I was walking from the Back Bay into the South End—tall narrow brick houses, narrow streets, leafy trees blocking a view of anything more than fifteen feet tall—and heard rhythmic male shouting coming from somewhere a good distance away, beyond the houses and softened by the trees, and then as I moved on toward the end of the block, I heard more clearly rhythmic shouting composed of many male voices in unison, until finally, when I turned a corner, I was faced with a memory from thirty years ago. I was in basic training in 1959, at Ft Jackson, South Carolina, and I heard and saw for the first time a platoon of recruits trotting in step down the roadway between the barracks shouting in musical, rhythmic answer to a drill sergeant. There, on the streets of the South End in Boston, was a platoon of men running toward me in step, all wearing black jeans and black shirts—as in a uniform—with highly polished black combat boots and black berets pulled to the side, shouting in time with the scraping sounds their boots made on the city pavement, raised fists punching the air, "We're here! We're queer! Get used to it!" This was enough to bring me to a halt, to make me stop and absorb this whole new concept of ourselves. This was not like anything that had ever gone before. This demonstration was not part of any established gay celebration. It was a bunch of gay men—queers—seizing the middle of the street and occupying it with panache and bravado—*We're queer*—saying, *Get used to it*. There was nothing polite about it, nothing of the usual give-and-take of social discourse. It was brash, muscular, defiant, and it asked for no response. These men assumed ownership of their space in the city, asked no permission, and that was entirely new. They were called *Queer Nation*. Within a month, I no longer stopped to watch them pass, and stopped listening to their chants. They had become familiar, and their chant had taken root deep in my brain.

One day, with Chris, I was walking from the Back Bay Station out Dartmouth to the Metropolitan for breakfast—he worked at night and didn't start his day until two in the afternoon—and we heard them as we crossed Columbus and saw, down Appleton, a platoon of men jogging toward us. Queer Nation seemed to me, even if it was not, a near relation of ACT UP. It used queer shock tactics to gather the media's attention and to force queer men to a higher level of self-love and pride and to a higher understanding of their relation to the political order. It was talking to *us*. We watched them come closer.

"Everything is different now. It's on everybody's mind." Chris had wonder in his voice. "It's changed the way people walk down the street, the way we hold our shoulders, in just a few months. Is it the chant? The image of those guys? Jesus, that's powerful." He looked at them and squinted and smiled, his characteristic way of showing approval.

We waited for the platoon. They punctuated their chant with raised fists—Tommy Smith and John Carlos in Mexico City in 1968 —and came toward us, sliding their boots into the city pavement, making the harsh rhythmic *shsh shsh shsh* sound. The men—their black boots and black denim, heavy belts, black berets—had the sexual power of a platoon of soldiers, undifferentiated, physical, strong, trained to be brave, and they made clear why a kid seeing a military parade would think, "I want to be like that." They jogged down the city street as if they were there to quell an uprising. They had power, and they had *glamour*.

"I love it." He turned to me, shook his head, and said, "Oh, lordy."

They were not all big men, but they seemed like they were. Big handsome guys.

He was laughing. "God, let's go home and screw."

I smiled and gripped his hand.

He looked at me. "Of course the point is not to go home and have sex so much as it is to stay on the street and *be queer*, to claim our space, here, now, without permission. There wouldn't be a Queer Nation if there weren't a hostility to queers."

Men came by we knew.

"Hi, guys." The man smiled and didn't stop. "Beautiful day, isn't it?" Then, "Did you see them?" He grinned, then he was gone.

"Chris, Fair." Another one waved as he went by. "You look great together." Then after about ten feet, he turned again and looked at us. "Hot." He grinned. Chris squinted and grinned. "Makes you want to go somewhere and start a fight with somebody without a shirt on, don't it?" And, shaking his head, he went on his way.

Another came around the corner, saw us, and punched his fist into the air. "I'm queer!" Then he broke out into a broad grin. "I think I'll go find a Republican." He laughed. "God damn!"

I gripped Chris's hand. When we had sex the first time, the next morning Chris sent me flowers. He took me out to dinner two nights later. Chris's eyes crinkled when he smiled, and he pulled up his lip, showing teeth. His hair was long enough to touch his shoulders. He was a big man himself, one hundred and ninety pounds or more. On the day we were prevented from crossing Columbus Avenue because of the platoon of hot guys from Queer Nation, I was fifty-one, and we marked the first week of knowing one another.

When we were sitting at a table in the restaurant, the clatter of gay Boston around us, he said, "I think the effect of all of these people—the guys in Queer Nation, ACT UP—is that we have more space in the city. It seems like we are not so confined as we were. I like that." Then he pushed back against the table. "What would you like to do this afternoon? What would make you happy?"

↔

It was after one-thirty in the morning. We were at the Ramrod, and Chris was working. I was on a stool on the customer's side of the bar, hanging out near Chris. Another bartender asked him a question. "Did you see Alexios?"

"Yeah, he stopped by. We talked for a few minutes." Everybody, it seemed, stopped by to talk to Chris.

"He looks good."

"He's been spending time at the gym."

"I haven't seen him for a long time."

"Months."

"Where has he been?"

"He was in Paris. He thought there'd be somebody there who could help him—"

"And?"

"—but there wasn't."

Chris and the other bartender worked a bar with two registers, one at each end, and at slow times toward the end of the night they stood next to each other, leaning against the ice boxes, their arms across their chests, engaged in low level conversation while they waited for closing so they could restock and cash out. They smiled at customers—friends—who were leaving, and nodded good-bye.

Last call was at one-forty-five. This call—usually made by the manager on duty—began a fairly complicated procedure that lasted about an hour and involved all the customers and all the staff and resulted in the closing down of the bar for the night.

"He must be bummed," the other bartender was saying.

"He was. When he came back, he went to bed and didn't get up for a week. He'd borrowed all this money from his parents, and now he is still infected and he's spent all the money. He's pretty desperate." I had been at the bar for the last hour, waiting until Chris was ready to go home. Later, at about three or so, we'd leave together and walk over into the South End where he lived—or we might walk to my apartment in the Fenway. "AZT is the only thing available."

The other bartender said, "There's plenty of things available, but you can only get them in Mexico—or South America."

"There are many men who are desperate."

The lights flickered—it was two o'clock, closing time—the music was turned off, and Chris and the other bartender began the process of restocking their bar, making lists of what was needed.

The lights started coming up at 2:05, and the bar started the process of losing its drama and its sexiness.

I began to hear the voices more distinctly that only a few minutes before had been smothered by the music. The background of noise in a room with that many people was gradually more audible. Customers slowly moved toward the doors and out onto the street. I knew, because I had been one of them, that men gathered on the sidewalk just outside to watch other men coming out and maybe to find a likely one they had missed inside in the dark. Men on the inside couldn't see the men on the street because the windows were painted black.

At the same time the lights started coming up, security began to urge customers toward the door onto the street, beginning at the back of the bar behind the pool table. Many of them had to walk by me.

"'Bye Phil, 'bye Chris, 'bye Fair!" A man walked by us calling out on his way down the stairs toward the door. When he got by the lower bar, he did it again. "'Bye George, 'bye Bill, 'bye Conrad."

People shouted back at him.

"'Bye Al!" We could hear all this because the music was lower and the shouts echoed on the concrete.

There were six bartenders on duty at the end of the night on Saturday, and two barbacks, and four or five men who provided security, a coat check man, and a man who sold leather items in a small booth at the back, approximately fourteen in all. In addition to these, there was a manager on duty all throughout the night. Chris was the assistant manager as well as a bartender. During the course of the night, there were maybe as many as 600 customers.

"You OK?" Chris was looking out for me.

"I'm fine. Waiting for you."

"Is this boring for you?"

"I like this." I did. He worried about my being bored, since I didn't drink, but I had always liked the Ramrod, the grit and the sex. "I like watching the men." After I moved to Boston six years ago, I had been one of them. It would have been more accurate to have said, *I like watching them do what I have spent a lot of time doing and what I don't do now because I have you.*

Chris, going about his business, was satisfying to watch. He moved with the grace of a dancer. He had wide shoulders and a small waist and an ass shown off in his tight jeans. He had a close-trimmed dark moustache and beard, and the rest of his hair was dark and long and wispy and loosely curly. His blue eyes changed depending on whether he was concentrating on you, or was lost in thought. Often I wondered what he was thinking, or feeling, and sometimes it was impossible to tell. Tonight, a man about Chris's age hung on the bar and talked to him when he wasn't busy.

When I turned around and leaned my back against the bar, resting my weight on my elbows, I could see the long narrow space from the front door on my right to the men's room behind the pool table on my left, all the way at the back of the building. Across from me, against the wall, and under large charcoal drawings of muscular men in leather harnesses, there were still men standing two and three deep facing the narrow space between me and them. The stools on either side of me were still occupied, and there were men standing between the stools. All these men were talking among themselves—they could be heard distinctly now—but almost all of them were also checking out the action, who was leaving alone and so might be still available.

All night, in this narrow space, a long procession of men had moved from the front door to the pool table at the back and then back again, moving so close to one another that at the end of the night a man's sweat was mixed with the sweat of dozens of other men. Most of the men had bare chests, and many wore studded harnesses, wristbands, and bands around their biceps. Leather was the prevalent style—boots, chaps, leather pants, belts, harnesses, and garrison caps. Men wanted a pumped body—their own or the other man's—to fill out the leather. The men who were the most pumped got the most attention.

Two men came by that I knew from program and stopped in front of me. "Hi guys."

The younger one took my hand and held it while the older one slid in next to me and put his arm around my neck. We hugged, then we kissed. He pulled away and put his hands on both sides of my head, holding me while he looked at me. "Jesus, I've missed you. Are you OK?"

"I'm OK." I kissed him again.

"Really?"

"Yeah. I'm spending a lot of time with Chris." The unspoken questions were always, *Are you drinking? Are you sick?*

He checked Chris out behind the bar, counting out his money. "*He* looks good."

The young one checked him out too. "You both do."

"Thanks." I laughed. "You do too. I like your leather."

"Let's get together for dinner. A good restaurant somewhere." Then, "I mean this."

The younger one said, "We've been going to meetings with Louise Hay, and I'd like to tell you about that."

"Yeah. Let's do." Louise Hay was less popular now.

We kissed, and they were gone.

The men at the Ramrod seemed only superficially to be alike. The dress code, both the one imposed by the bar and the much stricter one imposed by the men on themselves, was rigid enough that it was difficult to tell anything about their lives outside. In most places, men announce their class by their clothes, but the dress code at the Ramrod was about sex, not class. Many times, you might have sex with a man before you found out what he did for a living—class either got in the way of the sex or became another fetish like leather. The night I took Chris home with me, I knew he was a bartender because I had seen him working, but I also knew about his music because he told me about it walking home—that was unusual—and after we had sex and were lying in bed talking about ourselves and about the possibilities that were opening up before us, I discovered that he was principally a musician, had graduated from the New England Conservatory of Music, and that he worked at the bar to support himself between gigs. I don't know which of the two was the more attractive to me. His sex, that is, his leather and his body, was compelling to me, but his way of life—he lived like me, working at one thing so he could do another—was attractive to me in an entirely different way.

The lights had come up enough to see the men. There was a wider range of ages than could be seen at first. Some of them were barely of legal age, but, in the light, it was possible to see that a good many were in their forties or older.

The flow of men down the aisle toward the door picked up a little. They knew they didn't have to be on the street until two-thirty, and they were taking their time.

Craig Sexton, a sexy, very good-looking, very kind, gentle man who was maybe a foot taller than I was, came up in front of me. He slid his enormous fingers behind my neck and leaned down and kissed me. "How are you two?" He nodded toward Chris behind the bar. "Are you guys OK?"

I looked over my shoulder. Chris looked up from his money and smiled.

"Hey, man. When are we going to go to Provincetown?"

"Next week." Then, in a lower register, to me, Chris said, "Next week?" It was a question.

"You OK?"

Chris grinned. "I'm fine."

Craig turned back to me. "How's your writing? When are we going to see some of it?"

"Soon. I have one book going the rounds of publishers in New York, and I am half through another one."

"That's fine. Remember. I want to see it, now." He squeezed the back of my neck, then he was on his way to the door.

This went on for twenty minutes or so. Men saw me there with Chris and knew I didn't have to leave with them, so they needed to come by and speak. They stopped off and kissed and said good-bye. I have done that too, on leaving a bar, said good-bye to the bartender who was looking after me and then to a series of bartenders I was passing as I headed out, to the security guys and the coat-check man, and the manager if I passed him. This seemed to bring an end to this part of the evening better than merely walking out—acknowledging that we were friends.

Sometimes the man saying good-bye seemed to be coming on to me. There was plenty of sex in the room, but mixed in with that was the touching of friends.

"I've been trying to talk to you all night." He was in his late twenties. He was slender and had floppy blond hair that almost covered one eye. He was wearing a black t-shirt and jeans. "Give me a hug."

I did, we did, and then he stood in front of me, between my legs, and let his arms stay around my shoulders. I linked my arms behind his waist.

"What's up?"

"Oh, Fair, I've fallen in love, and I want to come to see you and talk about it. Can I?"

I laughed. "Call me tomorrow. Call me anytime. You can come over one night this week, and we'll get something to eat at Sorrento's." We hugged again. "Is he here tonight?"

"Uh-uh. No." He looked around behind him. "Here? I don't think he likes the Ramrod." He looked back at me again, this time with his face lighted up. "He's beautiful. I want you to meet him. You'll love him. I'll bring him over. My life is going to change now." Then he hugged me again, he kissed me, and was gone.

"Who was that?" Chris was behind me.

I turned around.

He smiled. "He's in love with you."

"He's not in love with me. He's just found a new boyfriend that he wants to introduce to me. His name is Cal, Calvin—I don't know his last name—and I know him from meetings."

"He's in love with you."

"You're in love with me. I'm in love with you. Cal is in love with somebody whose name we don't know and have never met and —" I shrugged. "—may never meet."

"You love me?"

"Of course."

"Good." He grinned, then he went back to his work. Maybe Cal was in love with me. I was old enough to be his father, and I think it was easy for them to find fathers among this crowd and to fall in love. But who knew. I think, if he was, Cal didn't know it and was moving on already to whoever the new one was he thought he was in love with.

Behind me, the barback was bringing the beer, and Chris was restocking the coolers. He looked up at me but his mind was somewhere else, and I knew that even though he liked having me there, my presence distracted him. Being in love with Chris didn't affect my writing, but it did give everything else a focus it had lacked. Sexually, I was more at ease than I had ever been, and I felt more relaxed and contented than before. I didn't have to go to the bar except to see Chris, and I could do that as well at home. I didn't see many of the men I used to see, and I didn't go to so many AA meetings. I went to the Y and did my thing and left. My life had gotten simpler. There were my writing, Chris, my kids. Everything else was subordinate. I think the same thing was true for Chris.

I turned around again. There weren't many men left in the bar. The lights were fully on. Without the music and the dark, the bar had lost its magic—concrete floors, concrete block walls painted black, ceiling a jumble of pipes and cables painted black. Without music, the bare concrete gave off echoes.

I left Chris's bar and walked into the back area. Two men standing beside the pool table were arguing.

"There're a whole lot of medicines that we could be taking if the government would let us, but the FDA won't release them to be used."

"I just don't believe that."

"What part of that don't you believe? That there are a lot of medicines out there? Or that the government won't release them?"

"First, I don't believe that there are a lot of medicines. There's only AZT."

"Well there've been articles about what you can buy in Tijuana —"

"I just don't believe there's anything out there that will work that our own doctors don't know about—"

"You are so fucking ignorant, man—"

This was an old argument. I leaned against the wall and listened. Chris passed on his way to the basement and listened for a moment. We stood next to one another, our shoulders and arms touching, and listened.

I met Chris on a Tuesday night, and Ames and Judith came to town on Saturday to spend the night. I invited Chris to dinner with them. Judith was twenty then, and Ames was nineteen. Chris had to leave at ten o'clock that night to go to work. They talked about what he did—they both knew about the Ramrod—and that he was a musician. Ames and Chris talked about their different kinds of music, and everything went well. If there was anyone stressed by the evening, it was Chris, who told me later that he thought I had invited him so the young people, who were only about ten years younger than he, could pass on him.

"Did I pass?"

"It was not about that. I wanted you to see me as I am. I am a father with children who are permanently a part of my life, and there is no point in us proceeding if you can't handle that."

Chris seemed to like it that I had children, *so I passed.* We straightened all that out, and everybody seemed to be OK about everybody.

"This virus has been around for a long time, man, it just hasn't been around for a long time in America. It's been in third world countries—Africa, South America, Central America—and those people have been dealing with it for centuries the way they have been dealing with every other medical problem, using herbs and local remedies, and there are remedies that are available to us, too, if we go there to get them. Tijuana. Africa. And then there's Paris, man. French medicine is not hung up on queers the way our medical establishment is. They don't *care*—"

We walked back toward Chris's bar. "I won't be but a moment. I'm about through here." He was wiping down his bar.

I talked to other staff members—a security guard and the manager—while I watched Chris. He was finishing up a few last things having to do with restocking. He was watching me, too, and sometimes we would connect and notice the other one watching. We didn't have to smile or make any sort of acknowledgment of what was happening, because we could see it happening. We knew each other.

After all customers were out of the bar at 2:30, the bartenders would then start to count money in the registers.

"Chris is lucky to have you." It was the coat check man.

He had the ability to love. Though he was not talkative, and he didn't give up intimacies easily, once he was persuaded to give them up, he exposed a complex, loving character. I never knew a person like him before. When I tried to get under the love, to the dislike, because that is what had always been under the love before, the need to control, I found there were deeper levels of love. I didn't know what to make of this, since I had no experience with it. I no longer doubted that Naomi had loved me, but underneath that was something she had never acknowledged, her need to control, her need to change me. Chris didn't have that.

The bar was almost empty, and then it was empty, and he could open his register and count the money.

Then that was done—the manager went from register to register, taking in the night's receipts—and then that was done, and then there he was. We walked toward the door together.

"Goodbye guys." I turned around and looked back into the bar. "'Bye guys. Goodbye, George. 'Bye."

We walked through the door into the night outside. It was three-thirty in the morning, and the early fall air was fresh and sharply clean after an evening in the smoky bar. There was almost no traffic, and the city was silent. The men who had hung around the door after the bar closed at two were gone now, and we were able to leave and walk in toward town without being hindered.

We walked in on Boylston, toward the towers of the Back Bay. We cleared the gas station next door and crossed Park Drive.

I mentioned the man who had been down at the end of the bar talking to Chris all evening. This man hung on the brass rail at the

431

turn in the bar, carrying on a desperate monologue interrupted only when Chris had to leave him to look after someone else.

"He's having a hard time, and he doesn't have anyone else to talk to, so he talks to me. It's all about his family and his brother, who have disowned him. He's suffering a lot. That's OK. It doesn't interfere with anything." Then, he asked, "Was that boring for you?"

"No. It was OK. I love you. I love being with you."

Then, a few minutes later, he spoke again. "You listened to them arguing back there?"

"Yes. It's an old argument."

"What do you think? Is the government lying?"

"I guess. Yes. I think they are."

"I think I think so too."

"The thing that argues against that is that it's so hard to pull off. If there are medications out there that are effective that are being kept a secret, it must be very hard to keep them hidden."

"Right."

"It would have to be such a massive conspiracy. Most of the time I don't think the government is capable of that. This is not the thirties and the Tuskegee Experiment. Times have changed, and I don't know if you could pull something like that off. The government is just too inept. Somebody would tell. But what the government—this administration—can do is delay, put difficulties in the way of a particular drug's being approved."

"Oh shit."

"Delay until it is too late for many people. Or they can withhold funding, or delay funding—"

"I guess so."

"Yeah. Another thing that argues against a conspiracy is that anybody who has a cure—or a prevention, a vaccine—is looking at the possibility of winning a Nobel Prize, and that person is going to fight the government if he thinks the government is trying to keep him from releasing his drug to the population that needs it. On the other hand, I don't think the government cares if we think they are lying. I don't think they care enough about what we think to try to convince us they are telling the truth. Then again, the government can fight back, raise patent issues—"

"Or say that what we are doing is indecent."

There was a famous pamphlet that the Committee created to hand out in the bars. It was one sheet of paper folded twice down the long side, with a graphic on the outside and information on safe sex on the inside. The graphic was a beautiful nude man, his arms up and folded across his face, and a hand from some person who could not be seen coming between the nude man's legs and reaching up and covering the man's genitals, as in a fig leaf. It was beautiful, unusual, and impossibly erotic. Thousands were printed and dispersed among the various bars in town. It was, as everyone said, an attempt by the Committee to speak to the population most at risk in its own language.

Some of those pamphlets reached the state legislature. Members of the legislature raised a furor about "obscene" materials published with public money, and pressure was applied to the Committee to stop teaching safe sex and instead to teach abstinence. Most gay bars in Boston had large bowls of condoms near the door, free to all, and literature in stacks scattered everywhere. We all saw those bowls and those stacks—the weapons we used in safe sex—as the locus of one of the continuing battles being fought between the gay community and the conservatives in America.

We walked along the West Fens, under the trees and along the weeds where there were, now, many men from the bar. The weeds— tall reeds along one stretch of the Muddy River, a stream that runs through the Fens and empties into the Charles River—were a private and accessible place for men to have sex outdoors, and as we walked along the sidewalk by the weeds, we saw men crossing the sidewalk ahead of us, leaving the lighted area of Boylston Street and heading into the dark weeds or coming out of the weeds and walking toward the light where we were. The weeds were as much a part of life in Boston for some gay men as the Ramrod or Glad Day Gay Liberation Book Shop and answered the same need as they did—for a place to gather.

"Did you have a test?" In these very gentle questions, Chris probed me.

"Yeah. I do it every six months."

"Why do you do that? Tell me again."

"That's what they said to do, three or four years ago. If you're sexually active, you should have a test every six months. It takes the anti-bodies six months to show up in the blood, so you need to take the test every six months."

"You're negative."

"Yes. If you had the test, and were negative, then we could commit to being monogamous. We could take the test again in six months, and *then*, we could stop using condoms. Have you thought about that?"

"Yes."

But that *yes* did not mean that Chris was going to take the test. What it did was it shut down this conversation and left me nothing more to say.

We left the Fens and walked in on the grimy stretch of Boylston that led to Massachusetts Avenue.

There were many men who were afraid to take the test. Chris would take the test, or he wouldn't, but I could not control that. I had nothing to make me think that Chris was afraid of anything.

"I have always liked the city at this hour."

He was not as far away as I had thought. "Yes."

"Most people get off work, and most *other* people are on the street with them. But by the time I get off work, the city has long since gone indoors, away from the street, so I feel sometimes as if I own it. Look. You can see from here all the way up to Mass Avenue and there's not anybody anywhere. I love this quiet." He spoke quietly himself and in a measured way. "It is easier to smell the city's smells, too. Can you smell it?"

I tried. "I don't know if I can. What am I looking for?"

He laughed, quietly. "Anything. The city. What Boston smells like at this hour that you can't smell at any other time because of the din."

"I smell tar, the trees—I don't know what kind of trees—the mud from the Muddy River, urine, I don't know, do I smell garbage?"

He laughed. "I don't now *what* it is. I guess those things, along with a lot more. You can smell the harbor at this hour."

"Have you thought about living together?"

"No. I mean, yes."

"Would you like to?"

"Yeah. Sometime. You mean an apartment together."

"Right now we keep two apartments but we sleep together every night in one of them. This has been going on for more than two years. What's the sense in that?"

"When do you want to do this?"

"Uh, now."

He turned to me. "Let's wait a little, can we?"

We crossed Massachusetts Avenue without waiting for the light and then headed along Mass Ave toward the Christian Science Center.

He needed to wait for something, and so I needed to wait for him. The time was not yet right for him in some way.

"What do the Christian Scientists believe?"

"I don't really know. I think they believe they can cure sickness by praying."

Chris was not a religious person. "That has not worked very well, has it."

"No."

We talked about some of the other staff members, about who was hot—about Dean who was the hottest man at the Ramrod—and who was not.

And then he changed the subject.

"I mean, if they could get away with it, do you think the government is cruel enough to keep drugs away from people?"

"Yes—away from *gay people*."

"Oh, shit. I think so too."

"But they wouldn't ever let it be put that way."

"How would they put it?"

"They'd make politics of it. 'It would help more people in the long run if we withheld this drug now.' Or, 'We're afraid this drug has side-effects.'"

"It is hard to believe they'd keep effective medications away from the people who need them."

"Or they'd say, 'We're opposed to any action that might be misinterpreted as a governmental approval of homosexuality.' Believe me."

"That's hard to believe. It is hard to believe that they can hate us so."

"I know. I don't think any of their stated reasons explain it."

"What stated reasons?"

"Well, right now the government and the right generally are saying we are spreading disease. I don't think that's enough to justify their neglect or their hostility. At other times during my life, they've said we were immoral or unnatural or sick. At one point they said we were security risks. None of that justifies letting this epidemic run loose in this population. These people don't want to stop it. They don't want the Committee to provide prevention materials to us. It doesn't make any sense at all, unless it's just malevolence. They want to kill us. Religion seems to drive it."

We walked on in the dark, the great dome of the Christian Science Center above us now, the pool beside us.

"They say that a person who is diagnosed with AIDS has about two years to live."

In the dark and with the high whisper of the wind on the water I felt in no hurry to answer. "On average. That's probably still true." I had my hands in my pockets. "But the time between infection to full-blown AIDS is getting longer every day. Next year it will be eleven years. They don't know. Why do you ask?"

"Well, guys talk at my bar, and I wonder, you know. We all talk about it. I don't really know. I should take a course at the Committee."

"The problem is the questions you raise are all about things they don't know the answers to, yet. You don't know, but then nobody else knows either."

At the head of the pool, we crossed Huntington into the South End. Here, the architecture was mainly domestic—houses, and houses that had been turned into storefronts.

"Was it a good night?"

"Yeah. A good night. Men were throwing money at me. That makes it easier. We're giving a fourth of our tips to—" and he named another bartender who was unable to work.

"How long are you going to do that?"

"I don't know. For a while anyway. We all got together and decided to do it." He put his arm around my shoulders and pulled me to him. "He's sick, and he can't work. So we're doing this. It's called 'taking care of our own.'"

We were near his apartment, which was on the fourth floor of a four-story house. Here the smell of the trees and the shrubbery mixed with the odors of the city—the tar, gas fumes from the cars—was very strong. I asked him how his colleague was, the one they were contributing money to.

"He's not doing well. He has thrush very badly now. It's in his throat, and his KS is in his lungs. He can't work. He's in the hospital. His boyfriend left him."

"Why?"

"He has AIDS."

"That's no reason."

"Would you leave me?"

"No. I've seen that happen a lot of times since I moved to Boston, and I heard about it on the Hotline. It's no reason to leave your partner." We were on the corner of Columbus and Dartmouth, about to cross Columbus, when he slowed down. I was walking faster than he, or a tree got in the way—there were small trees all along this block—and suddenly he was not beside me. I stopped and turned. He was about ten feet behind me. He was beautiful. I don't know what had made him stop, but he was stopped in the middle of the sidewalk, the light falling on him from above and to the side, making fine shadows on the planes of his face—his brows, his cheekbones, his drawn lips—and under his chest and crotch. He was wearing cowboy boots—he wore them to work in—and he had a presence. He was not the warm friendly intimate man I had been walking with. He was clearly a gay man—the boots, the leather pants, leather jacket open across the chest showing the glint of the leather and steel harness he wore—and he was in possession of the sidewalk. Uncompromising.

I did not expect to have Chris in my life. During my first five years in Boston, I had always had friends and many of them were young men who saw me as a big brother or as a newer, more hip, gay father to whom they could bring all their troubles, or as an AA sponsor. Tim is the type of these. And for a different kind of thing, I have had plenty of sex, and even plenty of love from many men, but I have not had a lover, and I had given up on having someone love me only. And now, here he is, without a doubt, and very publicly, my lover.

"I'm here. I'm queer." He grinned.

"Get used to it."

We hugged, and then we kissed. We laughed together, and then, holding hands, we walked the last distance to his place. We went in and up the stairs to his apartment. I had coffee, and he had two drinks, we took off our clothes and went to bed and had sex. We went to sleep and slept very hard until the next day at one in the afternoon.

↔

When Chris raised questions about the "stated reasons" for the culture's hostility toward queers, I had no good explanation. I knew that the culture shifts from one justification for its hostility to another. Some of these it entirely abandons after using them for decades, and some it revives from time to time. The charge against homosexuals that we are security risks—made by McCarthy, when I was ten years old—was abandoned at the same time the country stopped listening to McCarthy, and was never revived. The justifications that encompass a whole range of so-called psychological sicknesses, which operated all during my childhood and early adulthood, when I was in my teens and twenties, were abandoned in the early seventies under pressure from the gay community. Nobody talks about gay people being sick anymore. And yet the image of gay people as disease-carriers, prevalent in the press in the last ten years, the years of the epidemic, is closely allied with the earlier justification and is the one we are still fighting. I thought the conceptualization of homosexuality as sin had died in the early sixties—that's when it had died for *me*—yet sin took on new life twenty years later with Reagan. Most of the people opposing us at any demonstration since I arrived in Boston in 1984 have been from the Christian right, and they start their sentences with "God says—." I have never taken seriously state governments criminalizing gay sex because the criminal justice system is so far from my own life, but four years ago, in 1986, when the Supreme Court had the opportunity to void all state sodomy laws, it chose instead to revive them and to say that any state that wants to can criminalize sodomy.

The country suffers regular bouts of amnesia, forgetting that this current excuse for condemning homosexuality has not always been the excuse for condemning homosexuality, and that there have been others that have been tried and been abandoned. While the culture forgets and moves on, the generations of gay men and women wounded by these hit and run assaults still bear the scars of having been alive when it was thought, for example, that gay sex was a perversion or that gay men would sell out the country's secrets.

↔

I went by the hospice on my way home to my apartment. I do this every day, and sometimes twice a day. Tim Byrne lay in his bed, the head cranked up slightly, his body showing under the white spread as raised points. His eyes were closed.

When I came in and sat down, he spoke in a whisper. "You don't need to do this." He was speaking to me, but he had not opened his eyes, and his voice was very low.

"Yes I do. I need to come, and here I am. How are you?"

"Such a waste of your time. I'm going to do this thing whether you are here or not."

"Look guy. I know you can do it by yourself. You've always been capable. I am not helping you to do anything, but I love you, and I want to come. I need to be here when a friend I love is doing such a big thing. So, how are you?"

"I'm tired of this."

"Oh sweetie."

"Could you ask them when you go out if they could speed it up a little? I don't know if I can take this pace."

"Oh Tim—"

"And please don't be sweet to me. I think I have just enough to get me through this, and if you start being sweet to me, I think I'll lose it." He looked over at me for the first time. "They say I can have all I want now."

"Would you like me to go now?"

"Yeah. I think so."

"Well, I'll go, then." I stood up. "Goodbye, Tim."

"Goodbye."

"I love you."

He didn't say anything. I turned to go.

"Fair?"

"Yes?"

"Thanks."

And then I went home and packed some more boxes filled with all the little things left over from the life I have lived.

↔

I wrote Amelia:

> Boston feels like Ann Arbor in the sixties. Every
> year a new group. Last year, it was ACT-UP, a
> sixties style, confrontational group of gay men and
> women focussed narrowly on medical issues around
> AIDS. They did things like pour 55 gallon drums of
> blood-like fluid on the front steps of the Harvard
> Medical School to protest HIV testing policies. We
> got the media, who were entranced, and publicly
> embarrassed the dean, who issued statements (He
> said, in the manner of Richard Nixon, "I am not a
> bigot" to general derision) and the result: They
> changed their policies on who would be allowed to
> take part in the clinical trials of drugs. We picketed
> John Hancock for not paying for aerosolized
> pentamidine and won. ACT-UP is a big anarchic
> group now—several hundred at each meeting. But
> the one that is brand new and even more in tune with
> the times is Queer Nation whose chant is "We're
> here, We're Queer, We're fabulous, Get used to it."
> It's a street theatre, confrontational group—they
> mount zaps—focussed on the whole range of
> homophobic bigotry. They've organized (I haven't
> been yet, but it's certainly my kind of thing, and I
> think we are ready for it, and I *love* the name) street
> patrols and are holding self-defense classes and are
> teaching men how to arm themselves. Their goal: be
> tough dudes. Suddenly, the word "gay" seems soft
> and out-of-date. Queers here in Boston are hugely
> angry. There have been several major queerbashings
> in the South End and right here in my own
> neighborhood men are assaulted regularly and, of
> course, murdered. Several in my neighborhood since
> the first of the year.

↔

Chris told me late one Saturday afternoon in the spring—during our second year together—that he had had the test and that he was positive. He had it done at an anonymous testing site, so when he was told, he was not passed into a system of medical care, and he walked out onto the street alone. Like many men, particularly those without health insurance, he had heard the tales from men who did have health insurance of what it was like to take AZT. It attacked white blood cells and red blood cells and therefore caused bone marrow problems. NIH literature said it could cause stomach pain, diarrhea, constipation, headache, dizziness, and difficulty sleeping. When men began to talk about AZT in the bars and at the Committee and the Hotline, I heard for the first time the phrase *quality of life*, *quality* mattering more than *quantity.* Many men, refusing to submit to a medical regime that made them feel like shit, did not go to the doctor. Since AZT was the only drug approved for use against HIV, and since there was nothing else in the pipeline, and since everyone knew HIV was inevitably fatal—unless they were taken in by the fantasy that people like Louise Hay were selling—men refused care, lived on hope, and made plans to die.

During this period of waiting—waiting for publishers, waiting for the right moment to move in together, *waiting for what was to come*—we found that many men were waiting and that the waiting had different qualities for different men around us. Some, as Tim Byrne had done, joined ACT UP, seeking to pressure the medical profession, the pharmaceutical companies, and the government into speeding up the release of medications that might help us, and some, like me, vented our anger at the Reagan and Bush administrations for being so slow to respond and became very angry people. A friend who lived in the Fenway and who graduated from the Museum School of the Museum of Fine Arts talked to me every time we met on the sidewalk along Queensbury. This friend had AIDS, which sharpened his perceptions of the slack manner in which the institutions around us responded to the crisis. Coming from Gay Pride one gorgeous early June Saturday afternoon, the disease visibly in his face, he told me how it was. "There were thousands of them celebrating, although I don't know what there is to celebrate." I wrote hundreds of pages fueled by my anger. The gay press kept asking the question, *How many of us have died and are dying*

441

because George Bush is doing nothing? What my friend from the Museum School communicated every time I saw him was a furious impatience, for he knew that his life was dribbling away at a faster rate than science was producing a cure. Chris, on the other hand, went to work, went out drinking with the guys, came home to me and had sex, and exhibited a stoic detachment from his future. He withdrew into himself, and what I had called "brooding" at other times I now called the symptoms of a hurt he had experienced too long ago to remember. He gritted his teeth. He couldn't talk about it, even when I asked.

This was difficult, because I thought nothing good would come of waiting for the government to do what was right. And I had a deeper sense than Chris that the medical profession and individual doctors were too deeply compromised by their entanglement with the pharmaceutical companies and with the government to be able to do what was right. I wanted him to be angry as I was, but I didn't want to make him be what I wanted him to be, so I went to the demonstrations myself, and then when we were together, we talked about movies or books or music, but not about how differently—I talked incessantly, and he brooded—we responded to the lives we had.

I knew that I was afraid Chris would die. I thought he would die. We were told that all people with AIDS died. I knew that my fear and grief, which were so great they prevented me from feeling anything else, were getting turned into something else—into rage—that might be necessary in order to live. This had happened to Tim. He could not live with his grief, so he learned to live with his anger. We suspected that Burroughs Wellcome, the manufacturer of AZT, even if it had no animus against gay men, was pushing an ineffective drug merely as a way of making money. We saw the vast costs of AZT and saw the immense profits of Burroughs Wellcome, and we connected them at the point where we were dying. Burroughs Wellcome was making its vast profits off the deaths of gay men, and the governmental structures that should have been there to control the profit motive in the research and manufacture of drugs were not there to protect us. We were helpless and we were being used, and my rage was boundless.

I wanted him to take AZT, but he went silent and didn't speak. "Will you take it? *Are* you taking it?"

Finally, he said, *no.* "All the guys say AZT is terrible. That it attacks your bone marrow, that it makes you anemic, that you get so weak you can't get out of bed, that you cease to care about anything, that you feel so terrible you want to die—"

The Native had articles every week that made more sense than anything any of us were reading in *The Globe.* Chris had no medical training and didn't trust the whole medical system, which had been screwing him over since he had been a student. He had no insurance and therefore *no doctors.*

This was the consequence when the social contract no longer existed.

I wrote Mother about Chris, and later I talked to her. The rector at her church, Trinity Church, had given a sermon on the subject of AIDS. Mother said, "The ones I feel sorriest for are the *innocent victims*, the women and children who have gotten this terrible disease from men—"

Contemplating the bigotry Mother was taught in her church—the concept of *innocent victims*—I considered the larger questions of bigotry in our institutions. This bigotry has caused me a certain amount of pain and humiliation, and it has thrown me off course for long periods in my life, but it was bigger than that. As long as the institutions of our culture are in any way bigoted, as long as these institutions continue to make it harder to be queer than to be straight, then some men and women are going to retreat into the safety of heterosexual marriage, and if the concept of marriage in our culture remains rigidly monogamous, the traffic into marriage will be matched by the traffic out of marriage, because men and women will try to think well of themselves. This traffic, both in and out, will continue until our culture learns to leave bigotry behind and until the institution of marriage moves closer to the model currently found in the gay community, where all aspects of the marriage are negotiated beforehand by two free agents and are then open to renegotiation continuously throughout the life of the relationship. In that renegotiation lies freedom.

↔

It was the first summer of Clinton's presidency, the summer of *Don't Ask, Don't Tell*, the summer of *Angels in America.* For ten days, beginning at the very end of July, Chris suffered a high fever, vomiting, diarrhea, and chills. He lost weight, and his face lost its fat. You could see the skull, and the skin was yellow around his eyes. His doctor—a friend who was treating him on the side because he had no insurance—was not able to identify the bacterium she thought was attacking his intestine, so her use of antibiotics was like throwing mud against a barn.

His temperature was erratic—subnormal and then very high, then down again—and when it went very high, he had chills and violent uncontrollable shaking of his body. I wrapped him in blankets, but what he liked the best was a hot tub or shower. He was very weak now—he had eaten almost nothing for a week. A big meal was a slice of bread. When he had chills in the middle of the night, he said his most comfortable position was with his arms around me, but then, he said, his temperature spiked, which led to pain in his temples. He was sore. He fell once getting out of the tub, and his debilitated state prevented him from sleeping or from being comfortable in bed.

He asked me to lie next to him and read. He had a new copy of *The Secret Garden*, which had been made into a musical and brought to Broadway from the West End. He read the first half, and he asked me to read the rest. What an odd book. It was Edwardian, all about children who are abandoned by their parents and who are ugly and unappealing because they don't think "beautiful thoughts," and about the power of nature to restore health. The message of the book was this: No matter how much you're abused by adults, good children think beautiful thoughts and make their own worlds. And if you don't, you're doomed to be ugly and unlovable. The book is about the children of the upper classes—the others disappear as the book goes on—and the lower classes all get their "beautiful thoughts" from their nature, I guess. The secret garden is walled against the desolation outside, essentially a fantasy world, though the beautiful thoughts one achieves there allow one to go outside and face the brutality adults inflict on children. The central figure, an upper-class twit who is the ringleader in this "beautiful thoughts" business, was brought up thinking he was going to develop a hunchback and was going to die young. With beautiful thoughts, he discovers he will live "forever." The book expresses all that is really repellant about a certain kind of person: class consciousness, brutality toward children, guilt-inducing indoctrination of kids, and a swooning romantic fantasy about the benevolent power of nature. I resented it that the engines of the girl and boy's recovery, that is, the *poor* boy and girl, disappear before the end of the story. They are not even on stage at the end! Shakespeare always has everybody on stage at the end, even if the spotlight is on the great ones. I told Chris how it pissed me off. I told both my kids when they called about Chris's illness. Judith wanted to come down to help me look after Chris—or perhaps to look after me while I was looking after Chris—and we talked about that, but I didn't know what was happening, and I wouldn't let them come. I hated *The Secret Garden.*

After Chris had been sick ten days and after a relapse that left him unresponsive, with spiking fever and shakes, his friend the doctor called an ambulance and Chris was taken to the nearest hospital. It was a large teaching hospital and smelled of money. I had been in Boston nine years, and I had watched this particular hospital in a continual program of expansion—the cranes and the trucks never stopped around it—with the result that most of the hospital was new and even the buildings that looked old had been gutted and made new on the inside, all glass and steel and marble. After many months of living in the poverty of Chris's apartment or my apartment, it was comforting merely to be in a place that was so redolent of money and power. Universities don't smell like this. The smell of money meant these people were successful at what they did, and Chris would be all right. At the same time, I resented the opulence of it all, the architectural details everywhere—door knobs, elevator doors, banisters, terrazzo floors—that you don't see in other hospitals or in other kinds of buildings and that speak of an excess of money. The people on the elevators, beneath their long white coats, all seemed prosperous. The hospital called their property, and the collection of buildings on that property, a campus, an attempt to cloak in an academic gown a place where money ruled. I was glad that Chris was going to be taken care of, but since he didn't have health insurance—there have been years at a time when I haven't had health insurance either—I felt that this opulence was reserved for someone else, for those who had the money for it.

Chris was on the eleventh floor, the AIDS floor, in a room designed for two people. There was a long hall, at one end a lobby for elevators and windows and at the other end the nurses' station.

The lobbies at both ends connected with other hallways by which, if you wanted, you could circumambulate the floor. On the first morning, I looked out of the window in Chris's room and could see all the way across Boston to the east and the blue sea. I found him washed out, wasted, his eyes looking like Fray Hortensio Felix Paravicino as painted by El Greco.

He was under a refrigerating blanket, as they attempted to get his fever down. His fever had spiked at 106—along with, oddly, severe hiccups. The doctors didn't know what was happening with Chris. Now they were talking about an abscess on his liver, infection around his liver, pressure on his diaphragm. They didn't talk about bacterial infection in his gut or kidney problems.

Chris was unable to talk—he had been unable to talk since the night he stopped responding and was brought in—and I was glad that I was not looking after him alone. I sat by his bed and, when he was conscious, I held his hand. One of the consequences of his hospitalization was that we found out very rapidly exactly where he was in the progress of his HIV infection. He had never known how long he had been infected, and he didn't know how much the HIV had settled into his system. It turned out that his infection was very far advanced. He had thrush, he had enlarged lymph nodes under his jaw and in his arm pits, and, most significantly of all, he had almost no T cells, which meant that he had almost no immune system with which to fight off the infection he was now suffering.

He seemed to like to hold my hand. I sat on the left side of the bed facing him and let my right arm lie along the bed. I arranged this so my hand and his hand touched each other lightly. There were times—or moments—when his hand sweated profusely, and much of the time he lay in the bed, his eyes closed, but not still. He seemed actively to be fighting off the infection through an act of will. Watching him was watching a man in the midst of stupendous physical exertion.

I left the hospital to go home for a few hours. I washed clothes, I lifted weights, I called the young people. Then I went back and sat with him for the rest of the evening. I did this the next day. I stopped doing most of the things I usually did. One of my pleasures in the city was to take my time getting from one place to another, to enjoy the crowds and the noise. Now I felt intensely the need to get done whatever had to be done so that I could get back to the hospital. I

446

passed newsstands with the day's headlines of something important
—gays in the military, Clinton's failings, healthcare reform—and
passed on. It was difficult to concentrate on anything other than what
was happening in his hospital room. Occasionally the drama in his
room was broken by the arrival of a gang of doctors, five or six in a
group, doing rounds, who asked questions and left. I wondered what
they thought of it all, this very sick gay man and his lover holding his
hand hour after hour, and this ward of sick gay men, these very
clean, very healthy men and women. I thought idly sometime that it
might be interesting to write a short, inconsequential, witty essay
comparing the styles of the academic world and the medical world,
two pursuits so similar but so different in affect, the academic world
tousled to its core and the medical world clipped, as it were, and
slicked down.

The next day—two days after he arrived—his temperature
stayed under 101 all day, but on the third day, his temperature was up
again, and he had that manner of raw suffering that he had had the
first day. They didn't yet know what bacterium was causing the
infection, and they were giving him what the doctor said were the
three most powerful antibiotics they had.

I made arrangements at work to come in for a few hours in the
morning, to deal with whatever could not be put off, and then to go
to the hospital. Chris did not get better. He got better in that he was
conscious much of the time, or conscious off and on all day and
night, but he continued to suffer, and his abdomen was distended,
and he suffered the rigors. His fever continued to spike. When I
arrived in the morning, he lay in his bed, his head thrown back, his
eyes closed, his jaw clenched, breathing through his teeth. I spoke.
"Hi, beautiful." Sometimes he answered. I adjusted the placement of
the brown vinyl chair next to the bed, and then I slid into it and
found his hand and slid my hand under it. His hand closed on mine.
Sometimes he spoke to me when I came into the room. Sometimes
very challengingly.

"Where have you been?" He spoke without opening his eyes.

"Home, then I was here at 6:15, you remember, for about fifteen
minutes, and then I left here and caught the bus to work and stayed
there until about 10:30. Then I caught the bus straight here. And now
I am going to stay here all day." I didn't so much squeeze his hand—

the danger was that I would hurt him—as I felt it, the fingers and the muscles and skin and flesh and sinews of it.

"I didn't know you were here this morning." He spoke as Tim had spoken, slowly, slackly. "I don't remember that. What time is it now?"

"Eleven-thirty."

"Are you sure you were here this morning?"

"Positive."

He waited. "What time did you say it was?"

"Eleven-thirty."

"It seems like later than that. I feel like you haven't come here for days."

"I've been here every day, Chris, except for a few hours in the morning, and then another two hours in the evening. Do you want me to be here more?"

"If you can."

So I sat for hours by his bed holding his hand. The issue was that he was not so heavily medicated that he couldn't feel the pain in his abdomen, and it seemed to comfort him if I was with him. I felt better when I knew what to do.

Three nights after Chris was admitted to the hospital, he developed hiccups again and attempted to reach the nurses, someone who would respond. He warned them over the intercom that his hiccups were going to lead to spiking fever. They doubted him. While I was sitting there, his fever spiked, and there was a flurry of activity. A group of nurses arrived with a doctor in their midst. "Mr. Danto—" Chris was lying there, his whole body spasming with hiccups, his fever headed to 104, *he looked like death.* "Mr. Danto, I am not concerned." Chris didn't know what to say to that. I felt my rage rising inside me. Then the doctor said it again. "Mr. Danto, I want you to know I am not concerned." Then he paused as if Chris could find something to say to that. The doctor's manner was distant, friendly, cool. I was considering my options: throwing something heavy and lethal at him, or judging whether I could push him out the large plate glass window behind him. Chris looked as if his last, distant hope had failed him. *Then,* finally, the doctor went on to say —to explain that all these things, the spiking fever, the rigors, the hiccups, were connected, that they knew what it was, that they were working on it. It was finally clear that he was trying to respond to

Chris's cry for help, but he didn't have an idea how, how to be reassuring, how, in short, to be human. And his way was to open, and to emphasize, "I am not concerned."

Later that night, I had a long conversation with another doctor who attended Chris. She said they thought this started with a bacterial inflammation in his intestine on the left side, which caused an inflammation in his liver, which led to an abscess on his liver and to infected pockets in the interior of the liver, which led to an accumulation of pus in his abdominal cavity and to pressure about his diaphragm causing the body-wracking hiccups that lasted as long as 48 hours at a stretch. The hiccups, they thought, led to the release of more pus and infection into the body cavity, which led to the spiking fever. They had drained the body cavity twice, but it still seemed very distended to me. This doctor was a woman of thirty-five or forty, small, dark black hair and eyelashes, very pale skin, beautiful. She apologized for her poor English and recommended that I see her superiors, who could explain it all better. I told her her English was wonderful, asked her her native language (the accent was unfamiliar), and she said, "Russian." I wanted to hug her.

Later, the head nurse came in and thanked Chris. She said he knew his body well, to have seen the connection between the hiccups and the spiking fever. They had not seen that, up to that moment. And so Chris drifted off to sleep while I sat beside the bed, reading *Bay Windows* on the new Holocaust Museum in Washington. At the end of the article was a passage that said the museum had on display two of the original pink cloth triangles men wore in the concentration camps. I had never thought before of the possibility that two of the actual pieces of cloth had survived. I thought, when this is over, I need to go to Washington. The two pieces of cloth, the originals of a symbol that has become ubiquitous and powerful, seem to have been hallowed by the way they had been used.

By noon of the first day in the hospital, nurses started bringing flowers, and by evening, there was a bank of flowers sitting on the windowsill and on stands in front of the window. All that week, the flowers came from members of the Boston Gay Men's Chorus, which Chris had been a member of for ten years, from the staff at the Ramrod, from individual bartenders and the security staff, from the casts of the shows Chris had been in, and from his family. My children asked if they could send flowers. One afternoon I stood in the door of his room, looking down the long hall toward the elevator lobby—and toward the windows where the afternoon sun shone in—when two tall men got off the elevator. They came toward me, the sun behind them and turning them into silhouettes, carrying, in one hand their motorcycle helmets and in the other hand, something that almost touched the ground. They walked toward me in a long, loping stride, governed in part by the cowboy boots both men wore. As they came close enough for me to see their faces, I could see they were smiling. They were friends from the Ramrod.

"How are you? How is *he?*" Then, "Can we go in?"

They were wearing black leather chaps over jeans, with the cowboy boots. They wore black t-shirts and black leather motorcycle jackets. They were handsome men—one with curly black hair, olive skin, and beard, and the other with black hair cropped short and pale skin. And each of them was carrying a large spray of flowers, held upside down so that it almost dragged the floor.

I went inside and told Chris they were outside, then they came in.

"Hi, fella. How are ya, man?"

Chris's eyes were open, and he tried to smile.

Most of the men sick with AIDS don't have energy, and they feel bad, and if they care about you, they'll make an effort to be welcoming while you are there. They spend their energy on their visitors when they should spend their energy on getting well, fighting the disease—or on dying the way they want to die. Chris liked seeing flowers there—at any one time, he had fifteen or twenty bouquets of flowers at the foot of his bed and in the window—because they didn't demand anything from him.

When he had been there four days, the doctor taking care of Chris told me that Chris "might not make it." Everything hung on whether the antibiotic could get at and arrest the infection, and they didn't know if it could. They had identified the bacterium and could now tailor the antibiotic to attack it, but it might already be too late. The doctor told me that Chris's liver and his blood were severely infected. Friday night and Saturday morning, Chris's first weekend, his fever stayed at 106 for more than an hour. After that his temperature stayed under 102 for 24 hours. Then his temperature started creeping up again.

Chris was patient under all this and said his nurses and doctors were "wonderful." He thought I was the best thing that had ever happened to him, he forgave everyone, was not angry. He told me Saturday morning that if the doctors didn't find something to defeat the infection, "I have a week to live."

In draining the abscesses in Chris's liver—the ones they could get at, leaving the rest to antibiotics—the procedure they used was primitive: inserting an enormous needle about ten inches long through his ribs into the body cavity and probing for the abscess. They were unable to find the pockets of infection right away, so they had to insert the needle two or three times. When they were successful, they were able to drain 90cc of pus and left a drainage tube in his liver. He came back to his room wasted by the pain. The problem was that his liver was shot through with abscesses and infection and much of it couldn't be reached with the probes.

I maneuvered myself closer to his bed and slid my fingers under his hand, touching him lightly. "Hi, beautiful. It's me."

He waited a few seconds before answering. "I know."

"I love you."

"I know."

"Is there anything I can do for you?"

"I don't know how much longer I can handle this."

"The pain?"

"I started crying downstairs. They can't give me a painkiller to deaden the pain of the needle, and they are probing with this big needle—it's ten inches long—but that's not what I'm talking about. I give myself another week. If they don't get at the root of this thing and start making me better in this next week, I'm going to die. I know how I feel. That's what's happening to me. I'm dying."

I let his hand rest in mine, and I touched it lightly. His eyes were closed, but he didn't go to sleep. He returned his full attention to fighting the infection that was wasting his body. It was exhausting sitting next to him while he fought so hard.

On leaving the hospital around five to get some fresh clothes and something to eat, I was feeling alone and lost, and I saw a payphone at the corner. I stopped and hung on the aluminum stand while I called Ames in New York.

"I don't know, Ames. He's suffering, and the doctors don't know much yet. I'm here all the time. That's why I haven't called you back."

"I'd like to come, if that's good."

I was immensely grateful, but I suggested he wait, and then I called Judith. "Oh, Dad, I hope you will let us do this."

Ames was in New York, but he was going to Maine, staying with Naomi. Judith was already at Naomi's.

"How would that work?" I did want them to come, but I couldn't see how that might work. Ames was going to be traveling with a friend.

"Call me back later, Dad, in an hour or two. I'll work it out."

I called my mother.

"Fair!" She always sounded more surprised than delighted when she discovered it was me. "Oh I am so glad you have called. I have so much to tell you. There is so much family news, and I bet you want to know about my vacation. Cornelius and Henrietta have invited me to go to Pawley's for all of September! Cornelius can't stay down that long, but Henrietta is down there now, and she wants me to come down around the end of August and stay until the end of September. And Cornelius will come down when he can, on weekends, and then maybe the third week, if he can manage it. And their children will all be visiting when they can. You know that little Rhett is almost two. I must have forgotten—"

"Mother—"

"—so one weekend all four of them are going to be there, along with my *great* grandchildren, with their friends. Henrietta is going to have *two* cooks—"

"Mother, I wanted to call you to tell you some difficult news."

"What's happened?" You could hear her throwing on the brakes and turning her attention. "What's wrong?" She had in her voice the strain that came with her saying, *What awful thing have you done now?*

"Chris is very sick. He is in the hospital, and the doctor said today that he might not make it. That he might die." I was gathering together the other things to tell her when she spoke.

"Well, I can't say that I am surprised."

She went on to say other things, but I didn't hear what they were. After a few sentences, she continued. "Well, it is already

August sixteenth, and I don't have much time to get ready before I am supposed to go. Cornelius offered to drive me down, but I want my car while I am there, so I am driving myself, and young Joseph is going to go down with me to keep me company."

She chattered on about her vacation, and after a while I said good-bye and hung up. I went home and got fresh clothes and something to eat, and then I came back to the hospital. Judith had worked it all out. Ames and his friend would come up from New York on the bus and would get here Tuesday afternoon. The friend would go on to Maine. Judith was going to drive down from Maine and pick up Ames from the bus station and come directly to the hospital. They would stay at least one night, but more, if I would let them. Then Judith would drive them both back to Maine.

Dave Sepe came by the hospital, and we walked along the Muddy River while I told him about my family.

"You are intolerant of others' failures, Fair. You gather up grief for yourself."

I was sure that was so. But being tolerant of others' failures was so similar to accepting others' failures that I was not sure that I was able to distinguish them.

"In what way is Mother's failure to give respect to my partner different from, say, Social Security's failure to give respect to my partner? I am not sure that it is possible for a gay man in 1993 to be entirely tolerant of others' failures. Is there a real distinction between, say, the failures of Ronald Reagan or, for that matter, the failures of George Bush and, on the other hand, my mother's failures?" We walked on along the stream between the high green banks among the trees whose urban beauty still showed the design by Frederick Law Olmstead, made one hundred years ago. We walked in silence, faced with a profound conundrum.

On Tuesday, when Chris had been in the hospital for a week, the doctor said there had been no change over the last 24 hours. This was good news, since the likelihood had been that the news would be bad. His temperature was at 101 the whole of the last day, and he had bowel movements. It was difficult to say how he looked. I thought it changed from hour to hour: sometimes he looked like death, sometimes a little better. I hung on these changes. A physician friend asked me what was the name of the bacterium they were fighting. I asked Chris's doctor. "Oh, there are a number of them." They were using a broad-spectrum antibiotic, thus contradicting the answers the doctor had given me two days ago.

Judith and Ames arrived in the middle of the day. They were wonderful all afternoon, sticking close to me, holding hands, being physical. We all three sat with Chris for a while, then, in the evening we went to the solarium on the other side of the AIDS floor. I felt near to exploding in the hospital room with the powerful things I was feeling. We sat for a long time in this solarium, the lights off, the room so dark we couldn't see each other, overlooking Brookline Avenue, Simmons College, the Riverway, Brookline and beyond to the Charles and Cambridge, the city lights truly beautiful, me between them, holding hands. At eleven, we left the hospital and went home and cooked a pot of pasta. I gave them my bed and slept on an air mattress in a sleeping bag Naomi and I had bought in the upper peninsula of Michigan in 1969.

They wanted to stay another night, but I told them they had done what they came for—tell me they loved me, loved Chris, and now they needed to leave. Having anyone else here was a distraction. They both wanted to come back if I'd let them.

When Chris had been in the hospital a week and a day and when he had been sick for three weeks—that is, the next day—the doctors told us that Chris's condition was "grave." They said the antibiotics were not working and their range of options was limited to things they had already tried and had already failed. It was a terrible day. The social worker came by to make sure that Chris understood what the doctor had told him—"You can't live without a liver. Do you know that?"—and it was unclear whether he understood how grave the situation was.

The day after that, two friends from the bar were visiting when the doctors came in. There were five of them arranged in a crescent around the foot of his bed, Chris's friends were in the chairs, and I stood against the wall behind them. Chris lay in his bed, his large eyes circled with the shadows of sickness, his face gaunt from his having lost forty pounds since he entered the hospital. He had the look of a man who was afraid they were going to hurt him. A doctor singled himself out as the lead. He was tall, six feet, blond, gold-rimmed glasses. Very preppie. Very healthy. Ignoring all of the rest of us in the room, he went over the dire situation in a great booming voice.

"Mr. Danto, I have bad news. We are disappointed that the antibiotics have not defeated the infection in your liver. We have only had a few tools to use in trying to rid your body of infection. Surgery is out. We are really limited only to antibiotics and to attempts to drain infection. Unfortunately, neither of those has worked. And there are no other tools available to us. Do you understand that you can't live without a liver?"

Chris seemed to nod. Our friends from the bar watched all this intensely.

"Do you have any questions?"

"This is disappointing." Chris closed his eyes and let his head rest on his pillow.

I heard this stunning news—it was like a death sentence to me, and it crossed my mind momentarily that this bland green hospital room with its evidence of high technology hanging out of outlets and jacks everywhere was a banal place for something so momentous as Chris's death sentence. I couldn't tell how Chris was taking it. It seemed to hurt him, but I couldn't tell.

Then the bunch of doctors were gone. I was unsure what had just happened. But I was outraged. I left the room after the doctors did, and I accosted them in the hall before they went into the next patient's room.

"Which of you is in charge here?"

One of the men moved his head. It was the preppy one, the one who had spoken to Chris, and he seemed slightly uncertain of what was happening.

"I have many questions to ask you, but right now I am too angry to formulate my thoughts. You should have your license to practice medicine lifted for what you just did in that room. You told that patient serious matters, life and death things about his medical condition, and you never bothered to find out who else was in the room while you were forcing him to deal with the possibility of his own death. Those two other men in there were friends of Chris's, but you didn't bother to find that out. Both of those men have AIDS, and they were watching you very carefully to see how you handle issues of privacy and patient confidentiality—how much you respect your patients. You don't even know who I am. You just came into the room, and without clearing the room so you could discuss private matters with your patient, you blundered ahead, talking about his private things in front of whoever happened to be there. You ought not to be allowed in a patient's room unsupervised."

The preppy doctor turned uncertainly to one of his colleagues. "Who is this?" The colleague shrugged.

"My name is Fair Shaw. I am Chris Danto's partner. We love one another. We have been together since 1990. I am his family."

I thought for a second that this crew of doctors was going to have me thrown out. I could see they were hesitating, waiting, I think, to see how the lead doctor was going to take my judgment of his skills. I had heard stories of doctors throwing out the partners of AIDS patients and of doctors not allowing those partners to have any part in the decision-making process during an AIDS patient's illness. In the few seconds during which we waited for the doctor's response, I considered what I would do if they tried to throw me out. I was thinking of lawyers, publicity, the newspapers.

"You're right. I should have asked the other people in the room to leave while we discussed Mr. Danto's private business with him. Thank you for pointing that out." Then he spoke to the rest of his group. "Let's go back and apologize."

And they did. They all went back inside and spoke to Chris and apologized to him for not having respected his privacy. He was much more gentle with Chris this time. But then, in half an hour, another group of doctors came by and told us that the antibiotic had not worked and that his situation was now "grave," and that they didn't have any options except to do what they had already done before, which we already knew had already failed.

Another young woman, the social worker assigned to Chris's case, came in and asked Chris how he was doing. Since two sets of doctors as well as the other social worker had told him he couldn't live without a liver and that his liver was too diseased to sustain his life, and that the hospital had no way now of ridding his liver of infection, I wondered what she expected him to say. Mainly she asked questions about Chris's family—he has very little family, and the uncle he has he doesn't see very often—and about whether there was anyone she should notify for him. I imagined that this was a set protocol. When the doctors decide that a patient has reached a certain level of illness, certain things are triggered, among them a visit from the social worker who asks, "Can I help you notify your family?"

She asked me to come out into the hall. I followed her to the elevators. We sat in the chairs there. I sat in chairs like this in front of the elevators listening to the nurse talk about Andy Darwell. I was aware that the scene itself was a cliché, and I asked her the question. "Is he dying?" I knew that that was what they had all been saying this morning, but nobody had used those words.

"Well, not now. But if something does not happen, if something doesn't change in his condition, he will die. If the antibiotics don't begin to work, then he will die. The answer to your question is *yes.*" She saw me with tears in my eyes. "Are you OK?"

"No, I am not OK. You have just told me my lover is dying. I am very much not OK. On the other hand, am I breaking up under this? No."

She got on her elevator and left, and I went back to Chris's room, where there was yet another group of doctors gathered at the foot of his bed. They were telling him that they had scheduled another CT scan at the first of the week—in four days—and then planned to go in again and try to drain the second large abscess. The doctor asked Chris how he was, then he asked about his abdomen, "Does it hurt?"

Chris's large eyes grew even larger and even darker in his pale white skin. His voice was almost inaudible. "Yes, it hurts, but it will feel better tomorrow."

I did not understand who all these doctors were, and Chris, who seemed to know more than I, couldn't help me. And aside from the single fact that the antibiotics were not working, I did not think all the doctors were telling us the same thing. Only one set of doctors had mentioned the CT scan next Monday. The others had not mentioned any further steps they were going to take.

Chris went to sleep, and I went to the nurses' station, but I found, when I asked to speak to the doctor in charge of Chris's care, that that was difficult. There was a hierarchy of doctors looking after Chris. There were, in fact, three separate disciplines involved— infectious disease, gastro-intestinal, and medicine—and, since a liver infection in an AIDS patient is apparently extremely rare, every time they decided to do anything with him, the decision was made in large meetings with as many as fifteen doctors present.

I was trying to get all these people to speak with one language, which was impossible, but in the end, a woman, a doctor to whom I was profoundly grateful—she was also a doctor with black hair and whitest skin, and seemed competent and was beautiful—finally understood why I was distressed.

"Ah! I see." She spoke to me in simple, short, declarative sentences. "We have not given up. We are here for the duration. Our goal remains the same, which is to send Mr. Danto home cured, and we will devote all our skill and knowledge and energy and all the resources of this hospital to achieving that goal."

The men who attended him seemed unable to speak clearly.

I had tracked her down two floors away, and now she said, "Let's go talk to Mr. Danto."

And now we all went—the beautiful, black-haired doctor and her coterie of male doctors, and me—down two floors to tell Chris that they had not given up on saving his life.

Chris was conscious through all of this, though he dozed. I sat with him, holding his hand, and I said, *go to sleep*, and his eyes rolled back, and he slept. He had a bowel movement about every hour, which was painful. He had four or five IVs in him at any moment, plus the drainage tube from his liver, so it was difficult for him to move. The IVs were lipids, proteins, and two bags of antibiotics. He was now allowed to take clear liquids. He gathered himself together for a visitor, but collapsed after, his face visibly relaxing into illness. His voice was very low now, and he husbanded his strength. The phone rang, and he told whoever was calling not to come. Not now. The only time I saw him cry was when he came back from downstairs where they sought to insert a needle to drain his abscess, and failed to reach it. He cried from the pain. In addition to that, he was in pain from the pressure in his abdomen, and the hiccups, and from the wasting effects of the disease. Weak and ill. Occasionally he smiled, but the cost was so enormous you wished that he wouldn't try. It was if he was scraping whatever it was together and piling it up, and out of that made a smile, which consumed everything he had scraped together, leaving him without anything.

He punched the buttons to shift the shape of his bed and had us help him straighten out his bedclothes so the wrinkles didn't hurt him. He was weak and after he sat on the side of the bed, he couldn't lift his legs up to lie down. Whoever was in the room lifted his legs. He had changed shape, lost much bulk in his upper body, and gained swelling in everything from his navel down. The swelling around his hips had overwhelmed his buttocks, and now they seemed flat, this for the man who had, many had said, one of the most beautiful bodies in Boston. I told him he was beautiful, but he didn't believe me. He asked me how work was. I told him very short tales. His face looked gaunt, and his eyes were hugely enlarged and encircled with shadow. His forehead was usually tensed, furrowed slightly, giving him the look of someone who saw something horrific. When he slept, his head was back and his mouth hung open.

The doctors installed a device in his neck, called a centerline, that allowed them to put fluids and medications directly into the bloodstream. The number of IV's in his arm was unwieldy, and this was a better procedure for a person taking many different IV's at a time. That night, he needed Demerol, and the drug took effect within seconds, rather than the two or three minutes it took going in through his arm.

I spoke at length with the preppy doctor. He was apologetic about the confidentiality business—about not being more careful around Chris's feelings—and said the three teams caring for Chris had all realized things had taken on a new level of seriousness and had felt, independently of each other, that the family should be taken into their confidence, but the preppy doctor said they blew it when they did not coordinate this disclosure. The result was that Chris and I were subjected to three different teams of doctors, each one asking, "Do you understand how very serious this has become?" but all of them using slightly different language, leaving Chris, perhaps, and certainly me feeling panicked and uncertain. He apologized, and I apologized for going ballistic with him, although he said he deserved that.

He also addressed the issue of the antibiotic not working. He made clear that Chris's recovery could take place in the normal course of the successful operation of the current therapies. Chris's recovery could take place in this world, and it would not have to be a miracle, the concept of which I was impatient with.

We had this whole conversation standing outside Chris's room— he was asleep—speaking together in low voices about a man we both cared about.

The doctor said, "You are very intimate, aren't you?"
I nodded.

Then he spoke again, before I could say anything. "You love him."

I said, *"Yeah."*

After that, the hospital staff all knew my name, and I was invited to spend the night with Chris in the hospital.

Chris's room was filled with flowers, large bouquets sent by friends, and on the wall directly opposite his bed and arranged so that he would see it whenever he opened his eyes, was a very large poster from the bar—a Tom of Finland charcoal drawing of a tough guy in leather—designed to be erotic and hard-hitting, and yet, in this context, surrounded by these huge bouquets, touching and sentimental. It had been brought in by two of the bartenders. Many of the men who came to him were these big leathermen—they took their style from the poster—striding down the hall in their motorcycle boots and jeans and tight black t-shirts, sometimes with obscene graphics on the front or back, swinging motorcycle helmets in one hand and huge bouquets of flowers in the other. The night before, two lesbian friends had come in leather and harnesses and spiked hair, all gentleness and sympathy. I spent last night with him, sleeping in the chair, and I thought I would probably do that from now on. Chris seemed to like it. When all the visitors were gone, I stayed on. He wanted me to sit on the side of his bed, and we held hands, saying nothing. His fingers rubbed my palm.

A few days later, this had been going on a month. There was no change over the weekend. Chris complained of the swelling in his belly and was unable to sleep, but otherwise things were OK. When they told him last Wednesday that nothing was working, they spoke of continuing the antibiotics and draining the abscesses they had been able to reach "and then we will check next Monday to see if there have been improvements." Of course, if there were no improvements, they had nothing else to try. Over the weekend, the idea of the CT scan on Monday began to assume immense importance. It developed into a kind of jury's verdict—live or die—on Chris, and I dreaded it. Much of an AIDS patient's life is quantified—the number of T cells, the "viral load" in his blood—that is, reduced to numbers and therefore dehumanized, and the measure of whether he was getting better was made on the basis of whether numbers got larger or smaller. These CT scans were in that vein—the size of each abscess was measured in millimeters—making it easy to forget that they were talking about a human here.

On the other hand, I realized that what was far more likely than an up or down judgment on him was something mixed—some improvement here, some decline there, and we would go on. But over the weekend, my sense of immediate crisis lessened. They were not going to say, *It's all over.* Things would go on this way until gradually, almost imperceptibly, the future would become clear. No one would have to make pronouncements. I could see therefore the error in the announcements that the medical team had made last Wednesday. They were not careful to maintain a sense of tentativeness about what was happening. They began to correct this by Friday, giving Chris the message at the end of the week that this process was going to be immensely long. The social worker, asking him to apply for Medicaid and SSI, said it was unlikely that he would work again *this year.* Even so, it would be better if the doctors read the CT scan on Monday and said, "Well, we appear to be going mainly in the right direction," rather than to say, "We don't know where we are going."

Since the beginning of all this, I had felt the need to be with Chris all the time. Every time I left him, I felt I was abandoning him. I felt that going downstairs on the street for a cigarette constituted a kind of betrayal. And if I went home and stayed longer than the minimum time required to walk in, get a clean shirt, and walk out, I felt I had to justify what I was doing, at least to myself. It was comforting to go home and masturbate, but it raised conflicts. *I should be with him.* Chris had friends, two yesterday, who gave me their cards and said, *Call us.* They understood the need to have someone with Chris all the time, and I understood I couldn't do it all by myself. But it was hard to let go. I didn't even have time to call Judith and Ames.

Chris's room was filled with large bouquets of flowers from men and gay organizations all over town—there was no room for another —yet I still felt alone and embattled. Even the doctors had now settled in to speaking to the two of us as a unit, but I didn't trust them. His head doctor, the one supervising his three teams, came by Friday, a polished, powerful organization man, brisk, abrupt, patronizing, clean. He gave the air of not having any doubts.

A friend brought Chris magazines, one a *New Yorker*, and while he lay in bed, his eyes closed, breathing heavily, I held his hand and read the long essay by Janet Malcolm on the problems of a Sylvia Plath biography. Malcolm reviewed half a dozen biographies of Sylvia Plath and focused on the way she died—her head in an oven, breathing gas—and the various ways these biographies presented the truth of that event, and, as the meanings of that event ramified, the truth of her life. Her suicide sucked into itself the lives of all around her, principally her husband, Ted Hughes, and it became clear that her life could not be written about without writing about the life of her husband. Malcolm suggested that writing biography of contemporaries—and, one would think, autobiography—was always going to be a tragedy all around. The biographer is attempting to find, or to construct, some version of the truth while respecting everyone's privacy and feelings, but some people, like Ted Hughes, are going to be hurt, his privacy violated necessarily. I sat in the hospital room, holding Chris's hand while he dozed, reading about the 1950s. Sylvia Plath, Janet Malcolm, Anne Stevenson, and I were all of an age—they were only slightly older—and grew up during the fifties. Janet Malcolm and Anne Stevenson were students at the University of Michigan in Ann Arbor in the late fifties, about ten years before I had gone there to teach and just about the same time I was at Sewanee. Malcolm concluded with an unforgettable and fully elaborated metaphor for life, the flat of a man in London who never threw anything away, which was, by Malcolm's implication, the life of Sylvia Plath—and of all of us—and the problem that this life presented to us when it came to understanding it was the chaotic multiplicity of it—*everything had been kept.* It was clear to Malcolm, at the end of her researches into the biographies of Sylvia Plath, that any biography or autobiography, just because it was orderly, had to be orderly, was going to be a pale lie.

Two people, a young black man behind the cash register at McDonald's yesterday morning and a black haired woman with dark skin of uncertain racial background behind the cash register at the hospital cafeteria, asked me if I were "in the movies." This happened four hours apart in different establishments.

On Monday and then again on Tuesday, we heard nothing from the CT scans. The news of the results of CT scans was ordinarily available immediately, but this news was partial and awaiting analysis. The radiologist read the results, which then filtered out to various teams and to the head of Chris's medical care, who got the results individually, and who then met as a group (there were between 15 and 20 doctors involved) to formulate the group response. On Monday and Tuesday, we were still early in that process, at the point after the radiologist and the individual receipt of the news and before the group response.

On Tuesday night, when Chris had been in the hospital two weeks, the preppy doctor came to Chris's room. He said that he had seen the results of the CT scans on Monday. He was smiling slightly. "We are now 'clinically optimistic' for your recovery." He seemed pleased. "Is there any part of this I can explain to you? Do you understand what is happening?"

Chris nodded. "Thanks."

"Are you comfortable?"

Chris smiled slightly. Then he spoke. "My stomach. There's something there."

"We're working on that. Thanks for telling me. Ask the nurses to reach me if you want to talk." Then he turned to me, grinning more broadly. "How about you? You OK with this?"

I grinned, and he grinned, and then he left. I wondered, later, if Chris's condition was still "grave," but I supposed not. This did not necessarily reflect the consensus of the team of doctors, for which we had to wait until they all met later in the week. But apparently they thought this improvement was not merely a one-time thing. It was an improvement that suggested a long-term gain.

When we talked that night, Judith and Ames told me they were planning to come on Saturday.

"Great. Let's go to the MFA and to the movies."

Then the next day, after their meeting, the doctors used the term "confident." I began to relax, to give in to the possibility that the crisis was ending. I wanted to go home to bed. I was able to read a newspaper again. The President had given in to the dinosaurs in Congress on the issue of gays in the military. The policy that came out of this—it was called "Don't Ask, Don't Tell," a twentieth century version of Oscar Wilde's *The love that dare not speak its name*—was worse than no policy at all because it codified the issue and gave a structure for enforcement. We discovered in *The Globe* at the end of August that back in April the Defense Department commissioned a report from the Rand Corporation on gays serving in the military. The Rand Corporation recommended that gays be permitted to serve openly in the military, but this conclusion was rejected. The report that was accepted—from the senior military men —concluded that "all homosexuality is incompatible with military service." There were federal judges who found the ban on gays in the service unconstitutional—one did the other day, in Sacramento—but these cases were overturned, or they had no effect on current events. We had had such hopes for Clinton.

Don't ask, don't tell was a codification in law of the closet, in which I had lived until I was forty-three years old.

The refusal to allow gay people to serve in the military didn't have to do with unit cohesion. The Rand Corporation reported that unit cohesion would not suffer if gay people served in the military. What was really operating was that this prohibition put a mark on every gay person. This mark said, *This person cannot serve in the military.* It was a scarlet letter, like saying, *This person cannot serve in the State Department,* when I was a kid. The mark set us apart, justified discrimination, stigmatized us in a republic where every man and woman of a certain age is eligible for military service. The policy-makers knew this. They didn't give a shit about this particular gay man in that particular platoon in Iraq. But they cared a lot about keeping the population we belonged to stigmatized. This stigma set us apart and pronounced that we were less than other men and women, *inadequate*, and dangerous to the defense of the nation.

That night, when I was coming back to the hospital, at about 10:15, a hospital guard challenged me as I was going past the reception area. He and a woman were sitting behind the desk. I told him what I was doing there at that hour, and he started to write it all down: *Danto, Shaw,* room *1184.* He apparently got to a block which asked for "relationship to patient," and I told him, "lover." The woman was listening. She made a call upstairs to the eleventh floor to ask for permission for my being on the floor after visiting hours. She gave all the information—"Mr. Shaw, who is Mr Danto's significant other—" There were all these words—lover, boyfriend, friend, significant other, partner, partner-in-life, companion—none of which suggested what I wanted the word to mean. What I needed was *husband* without the heterosexual connotations, that is, without its suggesting my gender—or my partner's gender. I needed a word that would suggest all the meanings Chris held for me during the last month, when he had been so sick, when he came within a week of dying, a word that would suggest our sexual relationship, but also a word that would suggest our emotional bond, our intellectual exchanges, and the emotional exclusivity of this relationship. This was different from all other relationships and not the same as monogamy and different, I thought, from the Christian emphasis on "keeping me only to her so long as we both shall live." The exclusivity of this relationship was not based on a sexual exclusivity. *There was no one in the whole world with whom I shared these things.*

On the weekend, Judith and Ames came down from Maine. They came by to see Chris at the hospital, then went back to my place to unload baggage. There was an exhibition of African and South Pacific sculpture and masks at the Museum of Fine Arts, which we went to see. The masks, paradox on paradox. While they covered, as all masks do, reality, they flaunted psychological and spiritual and sexual powers. Like wearing your skeleton on the outside. They dared us to look at what we were inside. All hooded eyes and grinning teeth. I liked the hooks carved to keep meat off the ground. Terrifying grotesques, with enlarged cocks and balls. The three of us laughed when we saw them. They were almost all of wood, but the patina was very different from mask to mask, some as highly polished and dark red as Mother's dining room table and some very rough, as if they were carved with a chain saw out of planking. They were from widely separated parts of Africa and so seemed unconnected aesthetically. They had an astonishingly elliptical way of representing nature—reduced to a single aspect or quality, like the horns and lips of a beast, which was, in spite of all, easily recognizable.

We walked around the museum and found *Hercules and the Erymanthian Boar* and *The Rape of a Sabine Woman*, the two small balletic bronzes by Ferdinando Tacca that suggested both male strength and a male sense of beauty. When I was in the museum, I always found a way to walk past Rossi Florentino's *Dead Christ with Angels* and Bartolomeo Passarotti's *Blood of the Redeemer*, a small sixteenth century oil painting on the second floor of the Evans wing that shows a very muscular Christ wrapped in a sheet that barely covers his genitals. Later we made dinner and went to the movies over at the Nickelodeon. *Kalifornia,* with Brad Pitt and Juliette Lewis, and David Duchovny. We did this because this kind of movie was easy to go to. Men killing other men (and women) didn't have to be talked about, so we did it. I thought that might be because in the rest of our lives, we were so deep into his feelings and her feelings and my feelings. Judith and I would have just as soon stayed home, washed dishes, talked all evening—maybe gone for a walk in town to the Christian Science Center—and then gone to bed. It was Ames that liked a movie. Or it was Ames that liked a movie when he was with me. He turned me on to *Reservoir Dogs* a couple of years ago. Now it's *Kalifornia.* I don't know.

In *Kalifornia,* David Duchovny played a graduate student named Bryan, studying serial killers. He and his girlfriend, Carrie, a photographer, were going west to start over. They planned to visit the sites of famous murders along the way. Of course, they picked up Brad Pitt, as Early, who had killed his landlord less than an hour before, and Juliette Lewis, as Adele, to share the gas. It was nice, the moment Carrie, the photographer taking pictures of murder sites, pointed her camera at Early, the murderer having sex, and brought the two major themes of the movie together. After that moment, murder and sex were always intertwined, right down to the last moment when Early pushed Bryan away and his bloody fingers slipped, one sliding into Bryan's mouth. The two men were caught there for a long second in a crazy embrace, Early's thumb in Bryan's mouth. Then Bryan, turning into a murderer, shot him dead.

But it wasn't a sexy movie. It was a movie hung on dread—the dread of being killed by monsters and of only just barely escaping with your life—and it was exhausting to go to.

The doctors suggested that Chris walk as a way of getting his strength back. He was assiduous in listening to his doctors and in trying to do what they wanted him to do, so he *walked*. But he walked like an eighty-year old man, hanging on to as well as pushing his rack with the IV bags. As he moved, it was possible to see the clear plastic tubes, three or four of them at a time, that connected him to the IV bags on the rack. His shoulders were shrunk to the bony body of an old man, his legs were skinny. Shakespeare—is he speaking of Falstaff?—speaks of "shanks." When he tried to walk, his weakness, what this illness has done to him, was on display. The rack looked like a staff.

Race Point Light

A friend of ours warned me against becoming too deeply involved in Chris's life. It was an odd thing to warn me against—we've been committed to one another for three years—and I couldn't see very clearly the danger that he pointed out. There was a book in the details around his comment. I imagined a Jamesian novel with a "friend" in a protracted and fatal illness and others around him trying to cope. The coping raises all sorts of issues—moral, romantic, financial, medical—in which people reveal themselves. There would be many whispered conversations and, I suppose, a sizeable estate, and there would be many repetitions of the admonition, *Don't get too deeply involved.*

On a Wednesday, five weeks after he was admitted to the hospital, the doctors talked of Chris coming home. He was to have a CT that morning, and the results would tell them whether it was to be that day or later that week or sometime in the more distant future. At first Chris was frightened of this news—he cried—and then became increasingly confident. I was trying to foresee problems and told him he couldn't be left alone at home. *That* made him cry. Then he spent the weekend showing me he could walk up and down stairs (three flights at the hospital). He pushed his IV rack to the edge of the stairs, then, using it like a cane, he lowered it down one riser and, leaning on it, stepped down after it. Then he lowered the rack down another riser and, leaning on it, stepped down after it. It was painful watching this, but he was having to prove himself to me and to the doctors. He went everywhere with his IV rack. He was like Moses with his staff, squinting into the distance, and wobbling as he walked. He was stronger than I thought he was and still weaker than he thought he was.

The new biography of the Marquis de Sade by Maurice Lever was reviewed earlier in the summer. I read *Justine* and *120 Days of Sodom* years ago—maybe in Maine, I couldn't remember—and the review emphasized Sade's rebelliousness, which attracted me. I read sitting by Chris's bed while he slept, the book in my lap, my right arm lying on the bed and touching Chris, drawn to Sade's letters from Vincennes, the voice of a man at war with his world who never seems to have given up during the thirty or so years he spent in the major prisons of France. I liked that. His story is lurid and compelling. At first—for the first ten or fifteen years—he hated his mother-in-law, "La presidente," who had obtained a personal *lettre de cachet* to have him thrown into prison, but later, after the Revolution, it became clear that his enemies were other, larger forces in the world—ignorance, stupidity, power. He is not the first to believe that the world's a prison. His letters are more my kind of writing than the Jamesian novel I proposed earlier. Rage just this side of the loss of control. All of Sade's great books were written while he was in prison, and I understand what *120 Days of Sodom* is all about. It—along with the others, *Justine* and *Philosophy in the Bedroom*— is a jerkoff book for a man in a cell alone, a masturbatory fantasy arising out of the tension between power and powerlessness. It uses the language and the imagery of the violations of class, religion, and decency, the usual things that sex uses. Sade apparently was aroused by power differences between the genders, as well as by differences in size, age, class, belief. The discovery of hypocrisy in churchmen apparently made him hard every time. The chance to do something he had been told was not allowed, also. With Sade, there is no point in asking the question, *What did he want me to feel when I read his books?* I have always gotten hard, reading his things, but I have wondered if he cared what a reader felt. I have always also felt freed when I read his books, liberated from my culture. And that, I think, is one of the supreme achievements of any art.

One night, I went alone to see *True Romance.* Chris wanted me to go home and take a nap, but I wanted something that would grab me in my gut. Christian Slater and Patricia Arquette, two feckless kids in love, sex, carnage. The movie opens with the camera on Slater sitting at a bar in a dark tavern, talking. "*Jailhouse Rock.* He was everything Rockabilly is about. He *is* Rockabilly—mean, surly, nasty, rude. In that movie, he couldn't give a fuck about nothin'. Rockin' 'n Rollin', livin' fast, dyin' young and a good-looking corpse. Y' know? I watched that hillbilly, and I wanna be him so bad. Elvis looked good. I ain't no fag, but Elvis is prettier than most women. Most women. I always said, if I had to fuck a guy, I mean, *had* to, I mean if my life depended on it, I'd fuck Elvis." Great. Made you care about these two kids who fall in love and who always are in deep over their heads and who, my God, leave a trail of dead bodies from Detroit to Hollywood—but who don't really cause any of it. It just happens while they are around, while they are trying to stay alive. That's what love does. And at the end, they escape. You feel for a long time in the middle of the movie that they aren't going to be able to escape this. You feel that right up to the final 90 seconds or so. Then they do. Jesus. I cared about these two. They got away, and the last images of the film are of the boy and the girl on the beach in Mexico with their child playing in the sand. *True Romance* may be the comedy to the Marquis de Sade's tragedy. None of these people give in, submit to their culture, but Christian Slater and his girlfriend get away with it—they escape to Mexico with the money —and the marquis didn't. He spent thirty years in prison. He didn't get away with anything, except in his mind. And, of course, Slater's character and the marquis both claim the future—us, now—as their allies in crime.

True Romance is like *Kalifornia*. They're both about a journey of kids in love—in one they are chased by murderers, and in the other they are the murderers—and they share a style and a tone. Bloody and over-the-top. And, they opened nationally a week apart. They differ in significant ways too. *True Romance* is established as a fantasy at the moment that Elvis Presley steps into the camera frame in his gold lamé sport coat and says, "Clarence, I like you. Always have, always will." People might really die in that movie, and there might be real blood and pain, but on the whole that young couple— Clarence and Alabama—are blessed, and everything is going to come out fine for them because that is what Elvis said. Still, they are both angry angry young men, and angry movies. I found it interesting to be reminded that *straight* young men can be angry. I wonder if the recent tone of the country, with a leadership that seems to have no clue as to what is needed, feeds this rage. ACT UP, Queer Nation, *Reservoir Dogs, Kalifornia, True Romance*. Then there was *Wild at Heart* a few years ago. The romance of California. Going west. What was it about that? In the Renaissance, west is the direction you go to die. The Western Isles.

One night, late in the first week in September, just as Chris was about to start his walk around the floor, a friend—an old friend from a dance class years before—arrived, pushing a wheelchair in which sat a life-sized puppet in a hospital johnnie, a black floppy velvet hat and a bright red feather boa. This friend was followed by a second friend who pushed another wheelchair with an identical puppet. We went on our walk: Chris pushing his rack followed by the two friends pushing wheelchairs with the life-sized puppets and then by me. Chris led the parade with a proud determination, unsmiling, and all

over the AIDS ward, men and women just this side of death got out
of their beds to come to their doors to watch him pass—him with his
rack and his friends and his puppets in drag and his partner—and to
applaud.

↔

As we pulled things together after Chris came home from the
hospital, some things became clear. One was my relationship with
my family. Cornelius and Henrietta had known for two years—I had
the letters I had written, so I was able to go back and check the dates
—that Chris was HIV infected. They had not bothered to write or to
call, after I told them, and so now I decided that I would no longer
write them. I no longer considered them a part of my family. It
wasn't a big deal. They hadn't been a part of my family for thirty
years or so. Almost immediately after that, I came to consider my
relationship with my mother. She was not supportive of any of the
major endeavors of my life—"Next time, write something
cheerful."—and I finally accepted that every time I had an encounter
with her she left my self-esteem in shreds. So I stopped writing her
also, and I stopped calling. This was also not a big deal. The real
rupture had happened decades ago, gradually, the breaking of one
thread at a time.

↔

15 October 1994
Dear Amelia,
    I saw the exhibition on Death at the Isabella
Stewart Gardner today. Actually, I went in and asked
for the Exhibition on Death, and the woman said,
nicely, "You mean the exhibition, The Art's
Lament." I said, nicely, yes. It is in one of those
small rooms at the back on the ground floor, which
were once maids' quarters or a pantry or something,
small, intimate, claustrophobic (low ceiling), with
one door only. The paintings were sometimes
stacked two or three high, and to see the painting on
one side of the corner you had to wait for the person
viewing the painting on the other side of the corner

to finish reading the label and move on. There were
15 paintings. They ranged from several in the
fifteenth century to Mapplethorpe's self-portrait the
year before he died, the one with the death's head
walking cane. There was a Durer woodcut and, at
this end of the millenium, a huge oil that looked like
a woodcut. Most of the early ones were associated
with the black plague—a couple of well-known
painters disappeared from cities affected by the
plague and are presumed to have died from it.

The exhibition was immediately affecting. It
was a beautiful day today, and Chris is out of town
(his high school choir director in Connecticut has
died of AIDS, and C went to the memorial service)
so I got up early and did things, ending up at the
Gardner at 10:30 to see the show. Then I went to the
MFA and to Copley Square to a bookstore and then
to Harvard Square and the bookstores there (I had
plans to go to the Fogg, but didn't). All day, the
memories of the show on death stuck with me, and
I'll go again before it is dismantled at the end of the
month. The show opened with a Madonna and Child,
the Madonna holding a goldfinch, which the label
said "was everywhere associated with the plague."
The Durer woodcut was the familiar one of the four
horsemen, and then for several centuries there were
paintings of St. Sebastian and St. Roch, always
dying. There were paintings of St. Christopher
carrying the baby Jesus with Death as a skeleton
overlooking both, and Napoleon stretching out his
hand and healing the stricken. There was a minor
thread through the paintings, which didn't begin
until the nineteenth century, of death from cancer (a
man to his wife, next to me: "Nobody ever thinks of
cancer as a plague. I think this is wrong." Then,
reading from the catalogue, where it said something
like, *These artists question why there is such
suffering on such a vast scale,* the man said to his
wife, "That's silly.") There were two Edward Munch

471

prints of scenes from a deathbed (his mother's, his sister's) in which everyone looked like a skull, hanging next to the Mapplethorpe photograph with the skull. At the end of the show, which had paintings and prints from museums all up and down the east coast, one or two from each of the major ones, there was a huge six foot tall still life of flowers, only the heads of all the flowers had been cut off and were now lying around the base of the vase. Several of these last paintings were done by men who are now dead from AIDS.

I thought some of the paintings were beautiful (St. Sebastian, a small Tiepolo of the head of St. Roch) and some were affecting (there was a recent one called, I think, *Remember Their Names*, which made me want to cry) but what was powerful was being in that small claustrophobic room while these artists struggled with death and dying and with the necessity to feel. The show title is wrong. There wasn't much lamenting going on. As the day wore on in other parts of the city less claustrophobic, it occurred to me that the pictures sorted themselves out into two or three groups—those that suggested the horror of being desperately sick, of *suffering*, those that suggested the horrors of grieving, of *loss*, and a few which were directed toward getting beyond it all, toward *hope*. But there wasn't much of lament, which I associate with a wei-la-wei (whose spelling I don't know where I got. I've just looked it up and found the OED has it "wellaway," which I don't like nearly as much. Mine came from somewhere before the 17th century), a sitting on the ground and telling sad tales. Mapplethorpe's photograph is amazing. It's theatrical, melodramatic even, but hugely powerful, and in the way his skull-like face stares directly at you, holding his cane before him as if he were warding off your sentimental hope, the picture is more powerful than anything in the room. What was absent was the self-

pity one senses in *lament*. The huge still life of
flowers with the heads brutally cut off was as
unsentimental as the Mapplethorpe.

The wonderful thing about the exhibition was
that it left me with clarified thought: the parts to the
problem these painters faced, and they didn't all of
them try to face all of it (it's odd that the curators
didn't think to bring in death-from-war). And none
of this showed up in the labels, which were limited
in information. Out in the hall is the wonderful, in its
own way, painting of Napoleon healing the soldiers
with the plague in Egypt, which the label labeled
"propaganda" and told the story of. Here, the
soldiers dying from the plague are all wondrously
handsome, even ethereally beautiful, and you see
them all in profile. Napoleon is in his best Canova
striding-forward-arm-stretched-out, other-arm-
crooked-for-toga style.

I left the room and turned into the hallway,
where there was a table and a salesgirl selling Art's
Lament Coffee Mugs and Art's Lament T-Shirts and
Art's Lament Shopping Bags. I thought to stop and
buy, say, a shopping bag for you, in the way we used
to stop at the road side stands in the South when I
was growing up and buy the pictures of Jesus on
black velvet and send them to friends of ours, with
gales of laughter. I hadn't expected this conclusion
at the Gardner.

At the MFA, I looked at that sarcophagus cover
in the ground floor of the Evans wing—have no idea
who did it—of the young nineteenth century woman
who'd died during childbirth, two years into a
marriage, and whose husband, a budding sculptor,
had then carved her likeness in effigy. Very
sentimental. She could be asleep. Over in the
modern European decorative arts section, there is a
room filled with furniture from the last 30 years. I
liked much of it—plastic molded chairs of one piece.
Utterly depthless and without an experience of time.

They are as new—as untouched by the passage of time—today as they were when they were molded. Impervious to time, they say. Right on. It's odd, I used to think that was a failing. And in an*other* gallery, was an exhibition to please the crowds, something on *An Age of Luxury*, I think it was called, 1690-1790, English decorative arts. Big wonderful pieces of heavy silver and chairs all made for dukes, who had their initials or armorial bearings carved into them. Just wonderful. The odd thing about this show was that right down the hallway and to the left were several rooms of the museum's permanent collection, covering the same period and country, with pretty much the same stuff (big chairs, big epergnes) but *even more of it*. And it was then, of course, that I realized the space at the Gardner was too small to deal with the *fourth* facet of the subject: *immortality*. The MFA shows that you get that by being a duke and buying a lot of big heavy silver with your name on it, and from then on, you'll be showing up on museum labels all around the world for the rest of eternity. That, or getting yourself made of plastic.

I went to Harvard Square for the first time in a long time with half a mind to go to the Fogg, but then got there and didn't, just wandered around, had a falafel on pita, joined a crowd listening to a singer singing a Simon and Garfunkel song, went in a couple of shops, then came home. While there, I went into Crate and Barrel and stayed just long enough to realize that half the people in the store were gay men, and, sensing the cliché, I left. On the street, there was a straight-looking young white middle-class-looking woman doing a street poll, and I agreed to be questioned (the good feelings left over from the day's activities still with me). She asked me about my habits and Harvard Square. I pointed out to her that we were actually in *Brattle* Square, and that I didn't come often. I said I just came to hang

out and that I sometimes did a little shopping, and
that, no, I liked the mix of people on the street, and
that, yes, I liked it being crowded, and that, no, there
was nothing I would change about Harvard Square if
I had the chance and were God. She thanked me and
ended the interview. And I got on the Red Line and
came home.
Love,
Fair

↔

Judith was married in Naomi's house on the main road in Orono. She
married a local boy, and I gave her away and did most of the
traditional things that men do for their daughters at the ceremony,
that is, I proposed a toast. Judith asked Chris to sing, and he
organized the music and drilled the musicians. He chose a Vaughan
Williams song that seemed to fit the mood and the place—it was held
in the back yard—and he looked marvelously handsome. Judith was
happy—people later talked of her radiant smile—and I was happy. I
was able to introduce Amelia to Chris, and then I left them alone.
They stood in the corner trading stories about me. The celebration
was very much like Judith, casual, relaxed, warm. The next morning,
Chris and I got up early and flew to New York for the twenty-fifth
Gay Pride Parade.

In July, 1996, at the World AIDS Conference in Vancouver,
scientists announced the approval of protease inhibitors, and that was
all anybody could talk about around Boston. Chris asked his doctor,
who said, "You've been on them for six months." That was the drug
he meant when he said, "I'm going to put you on something new and
see how you do." It was reassuring to feel that his doctor was ahead
of the curve. Then people were talking about cocktails—
combinations of various anti-AIDS drugs that included a protease
inhibitor. They were said to be able to bring the viral load so far
down it was undetectable. Chris's numbers began, finally, to go in
the right directions —that is, his T cell count started going back up
again, and his viral load started going down. Of course, his numbers
went in the right directions for only a few months, before they started
going bad again, and then Chris's doctor placed him on a new

cocktail. This went on for several years. His doctor said he didn't care if none of the cocktails worked but a few months, as long as there was always a new cocktail to put him on. The danger was that someday his numbers would start going in the wrong direction and there would be nothing left to switch to. But that didn't happen, and, in the end, finally, his body accepted a combination, and he was able to stick with it. His T cell count went way, way up, and his viral load went way, way down, and they stayed that way.

I wanted to talk about all this, and Chris didn't, so we didn't.

On May 20, 1996, gay people won our first victory before the Supreme Court. In the case, *Romer v. Evans,* the Supreme Court declared unconstitutional Amendment 2 to the Colorado constitution. My friends celebrated because it was the first time we had *ever* won in the Supreme Court, but the decision had great intrinsic value, nevertheless. One of the methods used by opponents of gay rights was to call the rights we sought "special rights." Across the country conservatives tried to amend state constitutions to prevent gays from being given "special rights." The first of these amendments to become part of a constitution was Amendment 2, in Colorado, which "withdraws from homosexuals, but no others, specific legal protection from the injuries caused by discrimination, and it forbids reinstatement of these laws and policies." If the Supreme Court approved the legality of Amendment 2, then it was almost certain that other states across the country would add their own amendments, prohibiting gay men and lesbians from seeking the assistance of the government.

But in *Romer v. Evans* the Supreme Court declared, "It is not within our constitutional tradition to enact laws of this sort. Central both to the idea of the rule of law and to our own Constitution's guarantee of equal protection is the principle that government and each of its parts remain open on impartial terms to all who seek its assistance." It was a great victory, both symbolically and in its substantive findings.

For me the victory resonated into my past. I didn't know whether *Romer v. Evans* was going to be our *Brown v. Board of Education,* but at least for now it had about it that kind of ringing clarity, the kind that says there are gay people, and they are citizens and must be given the equal protection of the laws. We had never achieved such a victory. The whole point of *Bowers v. Hardwick* had been to say that there is no such thing as gay *people* and that queer *conduct* is not protected by the constitution. Now, though Bowers had not been overturned, *we* were recognized. It was as if to say, *Constitutionally, we are here.*

Matthew Shepard died October 12, 1998, tied to a rail fence outside of Laramie, Wyoming. The picture the newspaper had of him showed the same quality found in the picture of Andy Darwell—eyes that pleaded with the camera. In both, the eyebrows rose up at the center of the forehead. I understood that Matthew Shepard was not as young as the picture made him seem. The initial stories indicated he was tied to the fence in such as way as to make him seem like a scarecrow, which led me and a lot of other people to think that his arms were out at the side, as in a crucifixion. I think what happened later had something to do with this pretty boy pleading with the camera and with his image, crucified on that fence on the prairie above Laramie. For what happened next was that the nation exploded in anger and grief. Newspapers all across the country carried a drawing of what they thought Matthew must have looked like, crucified on the fence, beside a photograph of Matthew's lovely, pleading face. For weeks I read everything the papers printed, and I couldn't stop thinking about it.

These things happen, and the nation explodes in anger and grief, and I wondered if it wasn't also exploding in guilt. We watched video of candlelit marches in New York and San Francisco that men and women reported in low, hushed voices. I was thrilled by the attention the country paid to the death of one of us, but I was cynical, too. Many queers have been murdered by homophobes in the twelve years since Anderson Darwell died, but no attention has been paid. The swelling chorus of grief, now, will not translate into the passage of anti-discrimination bills across the country. However, Matthew's death did achieve one thing for me: It was a big enough national event so that the mere repetition of the words, "When Matthew was killed—" again that anti-gay violence did, in fact, still exist in this country, when the country itself was inclined to sink back into its edgy confusions over queer things.

↔

And then, the country went to war again.

14 September 2001
Dear Charles and Edward,

Thanks for your note and sympathy. Tuesday's events were horrific and stunning. I don't think people have yet taken it in, not only that the thing could have happened but that buildings that large could be brought down so quickly.

Ames is OK. I was never really worried about him. He lives at the extreme northern end of Manhattan and works in midtown and the Village and has no occasion to go into the financial district. Also, he normally works in the afternoon and night, so I assumed he was in bed sleeping when the attacks occurred. His partner, Kerry, was closer to the heart of the catastrophe than I had thought, having recently moved with her publishing firm just south of SoHo. Even so, she was still two miles north of the financial district. When she got off work, the subways were not running, so she had to walk 30 or 40 blocks north (with everyone else). Fortunately, the subways started running again while she was on her trek, so she was able to get home. Ames and Kerry were in touch with each other by cell phones during the day (and ultimately with Judith in Maine and us in Boston). Ames was also able to send us very full emails during the day, so I never felt out of touch.

We do know a man who was on one of the flights from Boston that crashed into one of the World Trade Center towers and is counted among the dead. He was a British subject working here and the boyfriend of a friend of ours whom we had met at a dinner party in the spring. A friend of Ames's, whom he has known since childhood, worked in the WTC, in the top floors, but his work schedule was later in the day (something like noon to eight pm), so he escaped. TV and cable here carry long segments in which people on the streets in NY, looking for relatives or coworkers, hold up pictures of men and women "who worked on the 102nd floor of the North Tower" and ask for information. "Call this number," they say. One reporter, who has been manning this beat for two days, right at the raw edge of catastrophe, can barely contain her grief. Chris says that the NY Gay Men's Chorus has twenty members missing.

They are saying that there will be around 5,000 dead in NYC, a number much less than had been feared, principally because people were calm and orderly in evacuating the towers after they were hit.

The spill-over into the rest of the country is striking. My own building in the Roxbury section of Boston has had a bomb scare and a false fire alarm requiring total building evacuation since Tuesday. The papers say this probably will push the country into a recession.

The size of the catastrophe, both in terms of the physical damage done and in terms of the loss of life, cannot be grasped. People search for analogies —Pearl Harbor, "the largest attack on American soil since the War of 1812," etc. The largest loss of life at a single time since the Battle of Antietam when we were fighting ourselves during the Civil War. Nothing fits.

If I concentrate on NYC, I can be pretty clear about how I feel about all this. The people there are heroes, doing what has to be done. But once I pull back a little and look at the larger, national picture, I start getting irritated and then angry. The media, at the beginning, quoted everybody saying this was "America's loss of innocence." We're like a virgin, losing our innocence over and over. I don't know why we don't expect these things. You, in London, have been suffering horrific terrorist attacks for at least a generation as a result of the debacle in Northern Ireland, and of course look at Israel and the Palestinians. Since we think we have "lost our innocence," we look for solutions or responses that will somehow enable us to be virgins again ("This has never happened before in America!"). The Congress, yesterday, was debating a resolution which was breathtaking in the sweeping powers it would confer on the President to respond to these acts. Respond "anywhere" with "all means necessary." ! And they are going to give him 20 billion dollars to do so, the 20 billion being what they say is a "down payment" on the cost. So there is more to come. No one seems to remember that it was another one of these Congressional resolutions that became what they called a "functional declaration of war" that enabled Lyndon Johnson to pursue the Vietnam War without any congressional oversight. If I trusted the Bush Administration more, I wouldn't be so upset, but Congress is abdicating its responsibilities in favor of an administration composed of rightwing, trigger-happy Republican nuts.

All of this plays into the Republican agenda. They never did want to spend any money on social services in this country, and now they are getting bipartisan Congressional support for an all-military response. And the hands of the Democrats seem to be tied. Who could be against supporting the President right now? The papers this morning say that the administration is thinking in terms of a real war—not a surgical strike—a years-long commitment. In Afghanistan! A country that has already defeated the Soviets! *The Times* this morning quoted the deputy Secretary of Defense saying the new policy would include "ending states which sponsor terrorism." Ending States! Think about what power the administration is prepared to assume. Where in international law does anyone have the right to *end states*?

Bush is quoted on the front page of *The Times* this morning saying, "Make no mistake about it, this nation is sad." One bursts out laughing.

As you might imagine, mine is a minority view. Do we have no options but the military? What is being done right now is going to haunt this country (and the world) for years. I talked last night to another friend in NY, just to check in with him, and our conversation was warm and friendly (it was wonderful to hear that he was OK) until we stumbled onto the administration's plans for response. Then suddenly the phone connection went tense.

What Americans don't seem to get is that we live in an unsafe world, and there is no more reason for Americans to be safe than for the Israelis to be safe, or the British, or whoever. We can't make it safe. No matter how many people we bomb or how many states we "end." We have to learn to live with the risk of death that the rest of the world lives with. How can we, by raining death and destruction on everyone else, make ourselves safe?

I don't know how much can be accomplished in reducing tensions around the world—tensions between races and ethnic groups, historic strife—but I do know that Americans have never committed themselves to the attempt in the way we are being asked now to commit ourselves to a policy of punishment and vengeance and destruction. We always seem to have only one response—put them in jail, execute them, bomb them, declare war on them.

I was online when the first plane crashed, reading news, and it was horrific watching the story develop as it came in, first a sentence, then a paragraph, then a headline saying that there had been two planes. I went across the street to a little bar to watch the TV reports and got there just as the first tower imploded. It seemed inconceivable.

Thanks for your note. Write me again and tell me your thoughts. Here, one is almost deafened by the cries of the injured and the lost, and of those who would feast upon them.   Fair

↔

In 2003, on my birthday, I was laid off. It is my experience that, at my level, you are eventually always laid off, so I retired, bought a laptop computer, and took an idea that I had built up into 70 pages of prose and rethought it as a novel. I opened a new subdirectory, moved my files into it, and started again on a lower pitch.

↔

17 December 2003
Dear Greg,

Can we get over this angry distance between us and reconnect again? I'd like to very much, so I am going to write you this letter in the hopes that you will take it the way it's meant, as an expression of hope that what we had a long time ago was good and that whatever happened in the meantime can be forgiven. When you wanted to see me in Boston ten years or so ago, I was in a bad way myself—neither of my novels had been published and I was without a job and living on unemployment and for the first time since I quit drinking AA did not seem to be working—and I did not want to see anyone who was not demonstrably supportive, and I was afraid you weren't. If you had called later, several years later, I would have been in a better place. I was in a relationship, I had a steady job, and I wasn't so afraid, then, of confronting someone who might not have come to the same conclusions I had about my marriage and divorce. I am being careful here to write only about myself. I don't know what you were thinking about me and my divorce from Naomi, but I was afraid that you were still angry about it, and so I didn't want to see you.

It would be good to know whether what we had back then was strong enough to have survived all these cataclysmic events of the past 30 years—including my own shifting attitudes and anger and fear and pride and all the rest of it. Because there are a lot of people who went through (are going through) the same kinds of things that we went through, I would like to know, Was it inevitable that we lose each other? Is it inevitable that a straight man and a gay man lose each other in times like these? If it is inevitable, then I need to know that. If not, then I need to know *that*. If our failure was just us (or just *me)*, then I would like to know that, too.

I looked for you on the web and found your books, of course, and an award you got from UM, and the fact that you have been Chair of the English Department too. That is *very* impressive. I know that you had a hard time after finishing your first big book—before it was published—and it took guts to stick it out and to retain your sense of yourself when lighter-weights were pushing ahead and publishing their lighter-weight books. I see that you and Anne both signed a statement in support of Affirmative Action, and I like that, and like it that you are still together.

OK. The ball is in your court. Write me and tell me you're wonderful. Tell me you're intellectually stimulated and at peace with yourself. Tell me you're in turmoil. Tell me you're still angry with me. Tell me you forgive me. Tell me *something*. Tell me you've figured out how a straight man and a gay man can be friends. Or why they can't be. (But have your facts straight.)
Love,
Fair

Greg and I had not known it, when we both lived in Ann Arbor —I think because he was so deeply involved with his wife and child and career, and I was so involved with Naomi and Judith and Ames and *my* career—but we had been like two kids in a Stephen King short story, twelve years old and discovering evil together. After that we went on and grew up and he went in his direction and I went off in my direction, but we never forgot that we discovered evil together. So when I wrote and he answered, it was as if there had never been a rupture between us. Suddenly we were back there, at that point in our lives when for the first time we were feeling terror—*Jesus, there's a dead body under the bridge!*—and I knew that he was the only person who knew how that felt.

Some months later, Greg came to Boston on family business. He met Chris and Judith and her children, and he and I went to the Museum of Fine Arts for lunch. Amidst the clatter of diners in a large marble hall, Greg brought up the tenure decisions in 1973. "I have always felt that you took on yourself the responsibility for your not having received tenure, and I want you to know that I don't think you were responsible. You were the only person who came up that year who had a full-length book accepted for publication. Apparently, the decision was riven with politics, and politics of a special kind in your case. I am convinced that homophobia played a part in your not getting tenure."

We talked for a time. I found I didn't feel differently. It had been such a long time ago that it didn't matter. I appreciated what Greg was trying to do, but it was not so much that it was too late as it was that I had moved on. I was no longer an academic. Whether I had gotten tenure at Michigan in 1973 didn't matter one way or the other to any person I knew. There might have been a time when I cared, but not now. But as one piece of evidence in a large and complex picture which had to do with the place of gay people in America, it was telling.

↔

Some Sewanee people found me. The question I asked them was "What do you remember about gay people at Sewanee in the fifties?"And what do you remember about gay sex at Sewanee?" All of them remembered eh boy being de-pledged from the major fraternity, and some of them remembered the boy getting expelled from the university, and one or two remembered he shooting in the dormitorly, the rumor had it, "because he was queer." None of them

484

remembered the gay purge the year before we arrived. On the other hand, from Bill Bartlett, I found that at least some men had been having sex at Sewanee when I was there. He wrote detailed letters about the showers in his dorm, and their effect on his sex life. He said he observed students, some of them our fraternity brothers, horsing around in the showers naked, or wrapped in nothing but towels, pretending to be queer, pretending to kiss or to grab each other's balls. He said, "I felt that I was on pretty safe ground when, later, I put my hand down his drawers to cop a feel." He did one boy —whose father was the founder and CEO of a major Southern corporation—in his dorm room while the boy's roommate lay in the other bed watching. A man from Arizona told me that he knew of a boy who had orgies in his dorm room every night. I had missed all of this. Apparently many of the men having sex had gone to prep school, which gave them some experience of showers and the things you could learn in them, years before I found out about showers. The man who had orgies in his room every night was an independent. I had been in a fraternity, which, I could see now, limited my freedom of action.

↔

On June 26, 2003, in the second major court victory for the gay community, the Supreme Court voided all sodomy laws in the United States. The case was *Lawrence v. Texas,* in which two adult men in Houston, in the home of one of them, were having consensual sex. A neighbor reported to the police that the sound of gunshots had come from the house. The police broke into the home, found the two men having sex, and arrested them and charged them with sodomy under the Texas anti-sodomy law. This was the first time the nation's sodomy laws had come before the Supreme Court since *Bowers v. Hardwick,* the infamous case in 1986 in which the Burger court had upheld the constitutionality of the nation's sodomy laws, thereby making potential criminals of every gay man in the country.

The victory was spectacular. In its opinion, the majority of the Supreme Court first dealt with *Bowers v. Hardwick.* "Bowers was not correct when it was decided, is not correct today, and is hereby overruled." Then it overruled the Texas court that had ruled against Lawrence. The result was that every anti-sodomy law in the nation was voided, and the court was explicit in saying why: "Petitioners' right to liberty under the Due Process Clause gives them the full right to engage in private conduct without government intervention." Gay men and women during all of my life had carried two stigmas, that they were sick, imposed by the American Psychiatric Association, and that they were criminals, imposed by the sodomy laws around the country. Now both had been lifted. The damage these stigmas had inflicted on generations of gay men and women still alive could not, for many of them, be repaired.

↔

We were in Provincetown. We were staying at a motel that was shabby and cheap, but, when we wanted privacy, it was where we stayed.

The sun was up, trying to get in the room. I had been awake for a few minutes, lying there thinking while I enjoyed the light of the sun through the blinds, shining on dust in the air. I was on my stomach, with an arm toward Chris. After a few minutes, he was waking too. He moved, and murmured, and touched me. I spoke. "Hi."

He smiled and stroked my back. He said, "Whatya doin'?" He hadn't opened his eyes.

"Wakin' up." Then, "Thinking."

"'Bout what?"

"The sun waking us up."

He groaned. "I could have slept for another couple of hours."

"I got a letter this week from a student, one I taught at Michigan."

He turned away from me.

"I taught him in 1968—"

"—a long time ago."

"—and it is now 2003, so that is thirty-five years ago, and if he was twenty years old then, he is fifty-five now. I always think of my students as kids. I was a kid too."

"He wrote to tell you what a great teacher you are."

"No—" I put my arms around him. "—he wrote to tell me he was thinking of me."

"Why?"

"He lives in Israel."

"He wrote you from Israel to tell you he was thinking of you?"

"Well, apparently, it was morning in Israel, and he was lying in bed, just the way we are lying in bed—he was with his girlfriend—and the sun was coming up, and that made him think of a poem by Donne called 'The Sun Rising.' I taught that poem to his class back in 1968."

"Was it a class in Donne?"

"Seventeenth-century lyric poetry. John Donne, Andrew Marvel, two Herberts, Suckling, Spenser, Ben Jonson. Amazing bunch."

"You know that's funny." He rolled over and propped his head on his hand, fully awake now, quizzical, grinning. "The guy wakes up, probably horny, and before he knows it, he is thinking of *you*."

"Go on. All you ever think about is sex. I've already told you. It was the bed and the girl and the sun that made him think of the girl and bed and the sun in Donne's poem, and *that* was what made him think of me, 'cause I taught the class."

"I know you." Chris wrestled with me for a moment, held me tight while I struggled. "He thought of you because he has been thinking of you every morning for the last thirty-five years. Sexy Dr. Shaw." We wrestled. He kissed me. I slapped his bottom. He grinned. "Tell me about 'The Sun Rising'."

"I can't remember it. It starts out, *Busy old fool, unruly sun, Why doest thou thus through windows and through curtains, call on us*—. He is pissed that the sun is waking them up. He'd rather stay in bed with her."

"So would I. Let's not get up."

"You never know."

"*What?*"

"What you're doing. What any of us is doing. You think you're just going to the university to teach a class, and then you discover thirty-five years later that somebody who was there *remembered*." I think of all the things I have done that I hope nobody remembers. The letter from the student in Israel suggests that nothing is ever lost, but that of course is not true. Things are lost all the time, even important things—parents, wives, the names and faces of men I've loved, teachers, students, cousins, what it felt like just at the moment of climax with some man—and the evidence that *some* things are not lost, even when we think they are irretrievably gone, even when they are so far gone that we no longer have any memory of them, such as now, with the return of the Israeli student, doesn't make the world more stable or trustworthy. Rather, it makes it worse, because it reminds us of all the things that we can't remember.

"I think it's cool. He wakes up and the sun makes him think of the poem, which makes him think of you. I think of you every time I wake up. I like this guy in Israel. Tell me more about the poem."

"I can't remember it. The idea of it is that, because they love one another, he and she become everything. *She's all states, and all princes I, Nothing else is.* The sun, by shining on them, shines on the world. *She's all states, and all princes I. Nothing else is.*"

"I like that. Jimmy Somerville—the *Communards*—says the same thing. *You are my world.*"

"Do you feel like the whole world?"

He smiled, and stretched like a cat and then put his head on my chest. "Of course."

"Then there's no reason to get up, because we have the world here with us. Lovers have nothing to do with mere *time.*"

"This poet seems like my kind of guy."

"We're beyond time, and we're beyond space, too."

He had his characteristic small smile, while he examined me, running his fingertips lightly over the surface of my skin.

"What're you finding?"

"Let's see. The Cape Verde Abyssal Plain. The Atlantic Coast. The Pyrenees." His voice had that looseness in it that men have when they have just waked up, before their vocal cords have tightened. "*Provence,* the Alps—"

↔

On November 18, 2003, the Supreme Judicial Court of the Commonwealth of Massachusetts legalized gay marriage. In *Goodridge v. Department of Public Health,* seven lesbian and gay couples sued the Department of Public Health seeking to force the DPH to issue marriage licenses to same-sex couples. The opinion, read by the Chief Justice, considered the effects of this discrimination on the parents. "[The Commonwealth] has failed to identify any relevant characteristic that would justify shutting the door to civil marriage to a person who wishes to marry someone of the same sex." And it considered the effects on the children. "It cannot be rational under our laws, and indeed it is not permitted, to penalize children by depriving them of State benefits because the State disapproves of their parents' sexual orientation." And then it changed the wording of the marriage statutes in the Commonwealth. "We construe civil marriage to mean the voluntary union of two persons as spouses, to the exclusion of all others."

The decision adopted the civil rights model that *Lawrence* and *Romer* had adopted, in which an identifiable people were given certain civil rights equal to or the same as the dominant group in the culture. No one, in any of these decisions, adopted the beliefs of the Gay Liberation Front, which had held that none of us—of whatever sexual orientation—is truly free in our current culture, and that every citizen should be free to have sex in any way he or she chooses and to form partnerships with whatever other citizens he or she chooses without any governmental interference whatsoever. While the gay community celebrated—while I celebrated—the decision, neither Chris nor I, nor anybody else for that matter, pretended that the institution of marriage had ever been fully renegotiated from its origins in the Middle Ages. Even the Supreme Judicial Court seemed to recognize this when it redefined marriage, but retained *monogamy* as the prime characteristic of the contract. This still was a long way from the openness that characterized the marriages of Benvenuto Cellini and William Shakespeare, for not only was the binary choice between *gay* and *straight* too confining for the variety of mankind, but the choice between *monogamous* and *not* was far too clumsy to reflect the shimmering iridescence of people's choices as they express their chastity.

↔

December 7, 2004
Dear Greg,

I have news of us. We are just home from Provincetown, where we went for the weekend. Chris had a concert one night and rehearsals much of the day, so I was often thrown with our host, a man about 50, AIDS, manager of a major hotel bar in Provincetown, who told me tales of the eighties and early nineties in Boston and the South End here, of the first sweep of AIDS through the city, about five years after it had done the same thing in NY. The guy likes to talk, and likes to talk about himself, and then he finally got around to talking about mutual friends of ours who died in the early nineties. They were, along with our host, all living in Provincetown by that time, but they were frequently up in Boston at the hospital for stays toward the end. One of these was Sean, a young man of great flair and flamboyant talent whose drawings decorated the apartment of our host. Jason was the other one he spoke about. Both Jason and Sean were very demanding on their friends during their last year or so—driving friends away. At one point, in the hospital, Jason sent a note to all his friends in his address book telling them that they weren't as good friends as he felt they should be—which meant that the ones who were still speaking to Jason stopped speaking. I went to see Sean the last time in the hospital, and he was talking on his cell phone. He put his fingers over the receiver and asked me to buy him cigarettes. I did, and when I came back, he went on talking on the phone and after a while I left and never saw him again. Our host says, at the end in Provincetown, that he told Sean, "Man, you have to make this easier on your friends. *Let go.*" He said to me, "He had a 30 year-old heart, you see, and he could have dragged out his dying for *months*. So Sean was finally good to his friends, and *died*. The dog our host has today is the dog Sean bought a few months before he died, and finally Sean was persuaded that he could not care for it. I visited Jason in Beth Israel —Jason had decided to rename himself *Sergei*—and his monologue was so amazing I came home and wrote it down and kept it, but then I have never been able to bring myself to use it for anything. Jason wanted to adopt a bi-racial boy, he said, and was going to classes to learn how to do that, and all his friends said, Jason, *give it a rest. Let go.* These guys were not about to give in and let go and *die*. The last time I saw Jason, when his monologue was so amazing, he was fairly demented, and he jumped from subject to subject, none of which he had the ability to pursue. You couldn't make up what he was saying. Then our host mentioned Chris having AIDS and the lag between people getting it and getting the information they needed to prevent them from getting it, and then he said something—I don't remember what it was—and I started to cry and for a few minutes I couldn't stop. I was aware that what he was telling me was pretty amazing stuff, and I knew a lot of it, or different aspects of it, myself, but I had not thought I was moved, really, to *tears* by it, until he mentioned Chris. Then I cried and told him how deeply *angered* I was by posters we used to see in the subway system here that said, *Don't be Stupid, Don't get AIDS*, which, I know, are focused on teenagers, but which are read by people who have gotten AIDS and are not stupid. Anyway, there I was, trapped by the weather and the fact that it was winter in Provincetown, and I had nowhere to go but to listen to our host tell old war stories of AIDS in the eighties in Boston, and finally he got to me.

So you never know when it is going to hit you. Which brings me to novels (first the ones I am reading and then the one I am writing). I read *The Line of Beauty*, by Alan Hollinghurst. Which, as it happens, is also about the 80s—between the two conservative victories which kept Thatcher in power. It opens with the 1983 election having just happened, and ends with the next one. Thatcher herself actually makes an appearance. You may have read reviews of this book. It won the Booker prize this year. The novel is about a young gay man just down from Oxford who, aimlessly, gets swept up in high Tory politics and social life. AIDS makes its unwelcome appearance at the end of that book, too. I ended up not liking it. It didn't have anything to say about being gay. I don't know anyone who has gotten swept up in any kind of high politics and social life.

I read a review of *Kinsey*, the movie, and then decided to read the biography the movie is based on before I saw the movie. The book is also by an Englishman, and there were aspects of the book that were irritating. He was writing for an English audience, which I thought was stupid for the publisher (Indiana University!) to let him get away with. But in the end it was a fine book and answered the various criticisms that have been made against Kinsey over the years, and it found him to be something heroic and tragic, when at the end the Rockefeller Foundation ended his funding.

Ames just called. He and Kerry are going to have a baby in April, and his news just now is that he and a buddy produced two songs that were used on an album that was nominated for the Grammy awards.

You notice I do not mention November 2 and events leading up to that moment and away from it. I can't bear where we are in the history of this country right now. The war, of course, will go on and on. Almost immediately someone wrote that the worst part of losing was having to go through the period during which the Democrats fought each other over the question, "Why did we lose?" I stopped reading *The Times* because I didn't want to read about all that. But it is inescapable. And from all sides we read Democrats proposing this or that solution. Usually the things they propose that we abandon are the historic beliefs of the party. For myself, I think it is a time to grit our teeth and get through, until the American people decide to come to their senses. Maybe the next administration will be so bad that the people will see. It is not a pretty sight, however.

A few paragraphs back, I said I would write a little about my current novel. I am going to renege

on that promise. This book is very difficult, and I
can't write about it yet. Have you ever read *The
Autobiography of Benvenuto Cellini?*

Did you know that Governor William Bradford,
who came with the Pilgrims on board the
Mayflower, complained in a report on the health of
the colony about the amount of *sodomy* being
committed in Plymouth, which included all the Cape
and Provincetown?

Anyway, have a good holiday. My best to Anne.
Love,
Fair

↔

In early April, 2004, Amelia died. She was my literary companion
for twenty-two years. She helped to shape the way I looked at the
world, provided me with an example of how to transform that world
into words, understood my rationale for living as I did, and
understood my novels. She had the rare ability to read someone
else's prose and to comment on it and to leave that person eager to
resume working. She taught creative writing for years, and I think
she may have brought that ability to my writing. I sent her the
chapters of *Eulogies* and of *Night Sweats* as they were written, and
she sent me her poems as she wrote them—after they were finished
—and I wrote full analyses of them, which she seemed to like, and
now I have her letters and my responses as a record of that very long
creative exchange.

As a corollary to Amelia's death, I had to acknowledge that I
was becoming a solitary man and maintained almost no friendships
aside from my relationships with Chris and my children. I found that
I went very few places other than the movies and Calamus Books. I
preferred to stay home with my computer and my books.

↔

On May 17, 2004, in Massachusetts, the first legal marriages in
America between men and between women were held. One of the
couples who were a party to the suit that led to the Supreme Judicial
Court's decision was a pair of gay men who married in the Arlington

Street Church on the first day marriages were legal. The couple invited the Boston Gay Men's Chorus to sing, and so, to the full swelling of the song *Marry Us,* from *Naked Man* by Robert Sealey, and with the congregation in the full church all standing, the two men in tuxedos strolled up the aisle shaking hands and hugging and sometimes kissing the men and women on both sides. Chris said later that the men in the chorus had tears in their eyes, and the next day a press account called it "as moving and as dignified and joyous an occasion as we have been privileged to witness."

↔

Provincetown in June 2004. The crowds of summer had not yet arrived, leaving the sea, the blue sky, and the sand dunes to those of us who weren't fixated on July and August. The restaurants and shops and guest houses were open, and there were men on Commercial Street, at tea dance, and on the beach, looking and being looked at, but there was still room to breathe. Life in Provincetown had not yet achieved the urgency of high summer and its frenzy, and a man could still think. It was very hot, a satisfying heat that melted away the stress of Boston.

The Berta Walker gallery on Bradford had a curious and mysterious bronze fountain called *Sentinel Well* by Romolo Del Deo. The sides of the well, which was in the form of a bronze box forty inches tall and maybe eighteen inches square, overflowing with water, showed the backs of four human figures, which were graceful in themselves, in the classic mode, but when we approached the well and looked inside, it was possible to see an enigmatic face under the water at the bottom of the well, looking up. Chris said, "He lives there. Have you ever felt you lived under water?"

We looked at the face under the water. Chris made a point. "It's without gender."

"You're right." I considered possibilities of life underwater, cool, aware, self-contained and complete.

Chris grinned. "Let's walk in the sun." The Berta Walker Gallery had many treasures, but it was the face under the water that was most haunting. We left Bradford and crossed to Commercial. At the moment, we couldn't see the sea, but we were aware of it, since it was just on the other side of the line of small cottages on our left.

"Where would you like to go?"

"What do you mean?"

"We could go into the East End, or to the commercial district and the West End." We were facing south. The sun, on a cloudless day, was just past its zenith and cast our short shadows behind us. It would not set until after eight tonight.

"What would you like to do for supper?"

We talked about a restaurant. We were down from the Art Association Museum. There was a gallery with an abstract oil in the window in front of us, and we went in.

Chris glanced around. The paintings were large and energetic. "Let's look."

They were fine. Large, maybe four by five, wider than they were tall, somber colors—dark greens, dark reds and blacks and browns—intense with energy, the surface of the paintings turbulent with churning paint. Their energy would have been difficult to contain in a room of any size whatsoever.

Most galleries in Provincetown are built in old houses—houses with very low ceilings—and these large paintings crowded the rooms.

"Do you like this?" He stood in front of one that, in the middle of all the swirling dark color, showed a burst of light—white and yellow.

"Yes. I may like the ones without the light, though."

"You don't? I like the light. It gives it point."

"Yes. The Big Bang."

"Or the death of a star. Our star. The Sun."

"Yes. I like that." But the painting was expensive. We stayed for a while, looking at the pictures. I watched Chris brood over it.

"It's like a window into the interior of something infinitely small."

"Or something infinitely large. Let's talk about it." Then I said, "We can come back."

We moved in together in 1995. It took a while to find an apartment that satisfied Chris—I think I was more easily satisfied—and it was a long time before we merged our various collections. His books are in bookcases in the music room, and mine are in bookcases in the hall and the weight room and the living room. He keeps his money separate, too. But the kitchen is fully merged, and we are headed toward other mergers as well. We threw out all of our audio equipment—his and mine—and bought one set-up for the living room. We threw away my TV and bought a new, bigger one. His old one went into the bedroom. We drift toward a merger of our lives. I compare this process to the radical, even violent, merging that occurred when Naomi and I joined our lives—we started all over with everything new—and this seems very gentle. Another sign of this gentle merging is the occasional purchase of a picture or of a piece of furniture. For Christmas last year, I gave him a brightly shimmering aluminum chair whose parts looked as if they were taken from a human skeleton, and later I gave him a smoky blue-green glass and steel desk, all curves, not like any desk I have ever seen before. He gave me a grandfather clock taller than I am made of brushed steel, standing on twisted steel construction rods, the kind used to reinforce concrete, and large wheels, with a porthole window for a face, glowing green, and Westminster chimes that sound properly tinny. Once, to mark an important occasion, he also gave me a large, shallow golden bowl whose interior surface was covered with raised letters embodying a text important to both of us.

We held hands on the street in the sun. Normally, I will die before Chris, since I am much older, however things got turned around, and for a long time it has been likely that he will die before me. After his time in the hospital, we wrote wills and exchanged powers of attorney. I have them in a box in my closet, sitting on the box holding *Night Sweats*. I have thought of what I will have to do if he gets sick again. Of course, if the current cocktail holds up, I'll die before he does. So maybe we'll do it the natural way, after all. Actually, any way we do it will be the natural way.

"If you could afford it, would you like to own one of those paintings back there?"

"Oh sure."

He studied me to see if I am telling the truth. He smiled. "Where do you want to go?"

"Toward the center of town. The West End." We walked on, checking out the activity in the shops we passed—a couple of leather shops, a jewelry shop, a kitchen goods shop. And the men. It used to be said that good gay men, when they die, go to San Francisco. Many, though, would be happy to come to Provincetown. Handsome, dark-skinned men. We were walking under a blue sky, with an ocean breeze getting to us between the houses. "I don't know. I haven't bought any work of art—anything important—since I was married to Naomi."

"I think I like the one with the white burst in the middle." The artist was a New Yorker, and we had never paid so much for anything.

Commercial Street is a narrow one-lane street with—sometimes —a parking lane on one side. The street is bounded on the harbor side by houses built very close together at the edge of the sidewalk. The ones on the other side of the street away from the harbor often have small areas for planting between the houses and the street. I guessed that Commercial Street was never planned, that it was first a path and then a wagon trail before it was a road and a street, and when you look toward the West End from where we were, the line of houses on the left is jagged and broken, as if there has been no one to enforce a uniform frontage on the street—or no one who cared. Commercial Street seems to go downhill toward the two town wharves in an unsteady decline, moving up and down and side to side rather drunkenly between the closely-built cottages. Given the miniature scale of Commercial Street, there is much here to suggest Broadway as it traverses the length of Manhattan, and it suggests also the way Broadway knits together the many races of Manhattan. It has the same undulating feel as it moves past, and joins together, gay and straight, Portuguese and Yankees, men and women, the variety of classes, and the vast mobile throngs of beautiful tourists.

Some of the houses on Commercial Street are bare New England salt boxes dolled up by later owners with window boxes and weather vanes and wind chimes. Other houses are bigger and fancier, with mansard roofs. The storefronts that have been let into the front of some houses use twentieth-century post-war modern glass and brick, so it is possible in a few yards of Commercial Street to traverse the whole architectural history of this part of New England—without, of course, the Pamet Indian *wetu* and the hut built by the Norseman Thorwald Eriksson during his stay in 1004 CE. What is difficult to find, here on Commercial Street, is the fishing village. It might be possible to deconstruct a house—take off its porches, remove the third floor, find and set aside Victorian and twentieth century accretions—and find underneath, or inside, the original salt box. Very very few houses survive intact. The oldest house in town is over in the West End, the Seth Nickerson house, built in 1746, a full Cape Cod. Along here, at the edge of the East End, the earliest houses date from around the time of the Revolution. One, just down Commercial going west, has a black and white chimney that indicates the owner's loyalist sentiments. The oldest of these houses were built by fishermen and sea captains. Nothing in town connects directly to the land that lies north of these houses, and everything looks out at the sea and seems to get its reason from the sea.

In a white, Victorian, two-story cottage, we came to a famous shop, M. G. Leather, that used to be next to the Crown and Anchor until about ten years ago. They had some clothing—vests, chaps, leather pants, and shirts—but their main line was smaller leather items. Black leather wrist bands, leather harnesses, belts, arm bands, chain mail. Chris wandered in one direction, and I in another, toward arm bands, some of which had studs, one of which had a large steel buckle. I could see Chris looking at the chain mail.

A long time before I ever went into a shop like this, I saw the connection between same-sex sex and leather. Partly it was due to the drawings of Tom of Finland, whose cartoons I used to buy when I was a kid from under the counter of the Capitol Newsstand in Columbia. Black leather boots and caps, wide belts, leather gloves, all were made into fetishes by the men who wore them. And since, during those years, I never had a chance to have any other kind of sex—other than the sex I had with myself in my mind, using my hand—black leather became an essential element of sex for me. Nothing feels like leather against the skin. But there was also the issue of the harnesses. Arm bands. Wrist bands. It has something to do with the way they feel when I wear them. A harness across my chest, one strap under each pec, gives me the feeling of being bound and excites my tits. It is a kind of sex toy that I wear. I bought one early on in Boston, and when I put it on and felt it under my pecs, I thought, *You and I are going to get to know each other real well.*

The clerk was a young man about Chris's age who looked like a weightlifter, had a shaved head, and wore a harness. He had heavy steel earrings.

I put on the arm band with the buckle and checked myself out in the mirror.

"Hot. I like that." It was Chris, behind me. He put his hands on my shoulders. "Buy that."

I smiled at him in the mirror. "OK." Then, "What have you found?"

"Look at these." He held out his hands, his fingers spread, and on two fingers on one hand and the middle finger of the other hand—but none on ring fingers—he wore big carved rings of silver. They were dragon's heads and a set of claws wrapped around his knuckle. Very medieval.

I grinned. "Great—"

"Which should I get?"

"Get them all." I spoke to the clerk. "Put all these together."

Chris couldn't take his eyes off his fingers.

"Is there anything else you want to look at?"

Chris looked up. "I want you to get a wrist band."

I did, a five-inch band of black leather with smaller bindings about half an inch wide crossing it on the diagonal. Chris saw it and grinned.

The clerk was wrapping up our things.

"Look, we'll take them with us. Just take the tags off and give them to us. We'll wear them." He turned to me. "Isn't that what we'll do?"

I put on the arm band and the wrist band, and Chris put on the rings—two of them, he gave me one of the dragon's heads—and we went back onto the street. It was now the middle of the afternoon, and the men in the street—cloudless sky, light breeze—appeared to have come from the beach, relaxed and happy, tired, talkative, going home to get dressed because in a little bit it would be time to go to tea dance. This is one of the pleasures of Provincetown. For the visitor who is staying only a weekend or a week, it is enjoyable to walk the length of Commercial Street, to see what new shops have risen up since one's last visit, to visit old and familiar stores, and to buy things to adorn yourself and your partner—and then to show them off at tea dance.

"I love you."

"I know." He looked pleased.

We held hands.

We passed the coffee shop I liked—the Wired Puppy—and a children's clothing store where on other weekends we had bought clothes for Judith's children, and the Café Edwige. We passed Standish Street and McMillan Pier and Fisherman's Wharf and entered the narrowest part of Commercial Street, between Standish and Ryder, where there are almost no sidewalks on either side and the buildings come up to the edge of the street. Then things open up into the large space around Town Hall with its benches on which sat residents, watching the passing parade with a certain stoicism. We passed Adams Pharmacy and were back in the narrow part of Commercial.

In the window of the Provincetown Bookshop was the new book of history—*Stonewall*—by David Carter. I bought it in Boston from Calamus Books on its first day of publication, two weeks ago. It provides an extensive description of the connection between the Mafia and the Stonewall Inn and of the corrupt relationship between the police and the Mafia. Then it provides an hour-by-hour narrative of the Stonewall riots in the early morning of June 28, 1969—and for five nights following. It describes the formation of Gay Liberation Front in July 1969 and the formation of the Gay Activist Alliance in December 1969, and it gives a pretty clear idea of what happened during those months and then in the months leading up to the first anniversary of the riots. It is the best book on the riots, and it makes clear the issues that faced our community after the riots. We are fortunate to have it.

Chris and I had distinctively different tastes, so we split up in the book store. I looked for the novels, and I checked out the shelf labeled *Queer Theory*. Then I saw *Criticism*, only one shelf long, twenty books, one of which was titled, *Donne,* in bright, white letters which caught my eye. It is a collection of essays by a man I don't know. I checked out the bibliography. It is fairly short, but there I am —"Shaw, Fair. *John Donne*. Chicago: The MacIntosh Press, 1975." I called to Chris and showed him. He grinned when we left, and I could tell he was proud.

Many of the men we passed as we walked along Commercial Street toward the West End had the air of those who have been released from confinement, to whom the ordinary rules no longer apply. For many men who drink or do drugs, weekends in Provincetown have an intensity, or sense of craziness, that they don't have for men who don't drink. What is there for me is anticipation of a weekend at a different rhythm from life in Boston, days with more space for thought and a different set of stimuli. I usually come back from Provincetown wanting to have sex and to write. For all of us, the "rules" don't apply, and the euphoria we feel comes from being free of the unspoken restraint that a straight majority—inevitably more socially conservative than we are—exacts on our public behavior in other places. This restraint, which is so ubiquitous in Boston that it is hardly noticeable, seems oppressive only after a several day sojourn in Provincetown. It is as if we said, *Ah, yes, that was what it was.*

Everything for sale in Provincetown is for sale in Boston, even to the art of a similar quality. But the looking—the going into stores and inspecting the merchandise, the question, *Do you want this?*—is, in Provincetown, a kind of recreation, freed of consequences, freed from the curse that descends on the materialistic urge in more serious places where you need to buy what you are looking at, or need to *need* the object you are buying. The looking was, for Chris and me, another way of conversing, and therefore, since it was about the two of us, it had a deeper dimension. It was about finding out about each other. *What do you want?* And it was through trying to answer that question, often on Commercial Street in Provincetown, that we found out who we were and where our lives were going. It was all played out in a town where gay taste is the defining aesthetic, where men-holding-hands is the most often seen way for men to be on the street, and being-with-a-man is the most deeply held goal.

As we strolled along, aware of the men we were passing among —they were aware of us, too—we spoke to men we knew, some of whom lived in Provincetown and some of whom lived in Boston, often saying we'd see them later at Spiritus, or at tea dance, or at The Vault.

Then a young man walked up and greeted Chris. They talked about business—the business of the Ramrod—while I looked in the window of a shop. This new man turned to me.

"I have heard about you, but I've never met you. My name is Julio."

"I'm Fair Shaw."

"I've wanted to meet you for a long time, since I first got to know Chris."

He was a kid, in his early twenties. He asked the question people ask on Commercial Street. "How long are you down for?"

"Just the weekend. We came down yesterday and are going back tomorrow."

"Where are you staying?"

"With a friend. He has a cottage back over behind the cemetery."

Chris walked on, and I did also. Julio fell in with us, sometimes walking with Chris and sometimes with me.

"What do you want to do later?" Chris was plotting out the day.

"Tea dance? Dinner somewhere?"

He grinned. "*Sure.*"

Through these blocks of Commercial, the Pilgrim Monument was visible, the very tall rough stone tower on the hill modeled after the *Torre del Mangia* in Siena, commemorating the first landing of the Pilgrims in 1620. It was put up in 1910.

I became aware of the cemetery on our last few visits. To get into town from our host's house, we have to walk through the cemetery, a large field of ten or fifteen acres with crooked rows of markers of various kinds and styles from the last half of the nineteenth century, bordered by frame houses. At first I read what I could on the markers as I walked past, then I turned off the path into the expanse of graves and walked among them reading the lettering on the stones.

The connection to the sea was explicit. This was a cemetery for the generation of whalers and fishermen. The marker gave a woman's name and her dates, and underneath, "Wife of Nicholas, Lost at Sea, October 13, 1843." Since these nineteenth century residents knew that there were records for Nicholas' birth and marriage, they intended that there should be a record of his passing. Mother had the same curious need to have the written record complete in Columbia, South Carolina. She wanted me to be buried in the family plot in Columbia, and it was, she said, "so people will know who you are." What she meant by *will know who you are* is that when time has passed and all of us are dead, *this* will still remain to tell who we were and where we lived. Provincetown in the nineteenth century seemed to be, from this distance, a tidy world. The same names showed on the stones. There were many with the names "Jerrould" and "Cook" and several where a Jerrould had married a Cook. The survivors were thrifty, too, for many times there was one small gravestone with four or five names and dates spread over a period of twenty or thirty years. In all this cemetery, there were, I believe, no crosses.

What did all these closely-knit heterosexual families feel about what had happened to their town? The dates on the stones seemed to stop in the nineteen-fifties. Some other cemetery had become the resting-place of choice for newer generations, just as older generations had chosen other resting places. But even as it was no longer used, the cemetery suggested that life was going on some place. It made you think: *All this is going to pass.*

We stopped into BodyBody, a men's clothing store that we have been going to since we first started coming to Provincetown. I looked for a bathing suit, and Chris looked for shirts, with Julio following him around the store. We spoke to each other across the aisles, asking advice—"Do you like this?"—exclaiming on finding something beautiful or useful. He took longer than I, and when he finished, he smiled at me. In Boston we never shop together. We are both busy, and we have our own lives. We walked up toward the west —Commercial Street rose slightly as it left the densely packed buildings around the pharmacy—enjoying our purchases. In the end we both bought Speedos. Tonight, we will wear leather and studded harnesses when we go to the Vault, and tomorrow new bathing suits.

"You guys like shopping together."

"We've been doing this a long time, Julio." Julio was watching us closely.

We were near Spiritus, an ice cream and coffee shop that didn't close until two in the morning. Spiritus is on the side of Commercial away from the water. It is placed up on the side of a small hill, back significantly from the street, allowing for two terraces in front with benches for patrons. As the night went on, these terraces had the qualities of a gay bar. Now, at four in the afternoon, they were crowded with men and women with coffee and ice cream, watching the stream of people going by.

Chris went in to get ice cream.

Julio was a customer of Chris's at the Ramrod.

"I never see you at the Ramrod."

"I don't go much anymore."

We sat down on a bench.

"Ah, but it's so much fun. Don't you want to go?"

I laughed. "No. I have other things that interest me."

Julio had an intelligent face. "What do you do?"

"I'm writing a book."

"That's cool. Is that hard?"

I laughed. "Oh, God, yes. It's like painting houses."

"What is it?"

"A novel."

"About what?"

"A gay person, the times he's lived in."

"What do you think about the times we live in?"

"The times are hard, and we're survivors. Some of us."

"Can you teach me to write a book?"

"No, I don't think so. That's a skill I don't have." I told him about Amelia in Maine. "She died, just this past spring."

I looked at Julio. I didn't think he was a particular friend of Chris's. Men in Boston know Chris as a good-looking, caring bartender.

"I'd like to write a novel."

Chris was back, checked us both out quickly, and handed me my ice cream. He had David Sepe with him. I glanced at David, and we grinned. "Hi, David."

"Hi, Fair." He was grinning broadly at what was happening.

"This is Julio."

David introduced himself.

"I was telling David about the paintings back there." But Chris was still worried. "I think you like the dark one."

"Maybe. I want to go back and look again. Where would you put it?"

He shrugged. It didn't matter. Julio was listening closely to this. David was not so much listening closely as watching us all.

"I don't know. What do you think?"

"Why do you like those paintings?" It was David. Commercial is a short street, and it happens often that a person realizes that he has seen the thing his friends are talking about.

"I don't know. The energy. It seems explosive, almost out of control, and I like that. I like the way the paint is used. It contrasts with my life, with the way I live my life. It's ambiguous. It is big. All the energy is very dark energy."

"Fair likes dark things—tragedies, problem comedies, movies by Ingmar Bergman—that's the way he is."

"But we love you, Fair."

"But the ones with light are different. They are all that—with *light*."

"Chris is right. The light transforms the picture."

We sat on the bench and ate ice cream and watched the men. Julio was eager and young, and he liked Chris. I think he didn't know how I fit into Chris's life, and now, who was David?

David turned his considerable attention onto Julio. "You live in Boston?"

"Yeah, now. I grew up in Newton. I went to Boston University and stayed."

A gay man of, say, twenty-four who grew up in Newton who has always been out, and who has gone to Boston University, would be very knowledgeable. While the broad outlines of Julio's life would be the same as ours, the details and the quality of his life would be very different.

We've lived in interesting times, for a gay man the most interesting times of all. It may be that there haven't been, since the beginning of the earth, a more interesting sixty years than 1940 to now *for gay people*. From our perspective at the beginning of the twenty-first century, and looking back on the place of gay people in America in 1940, say, the changes seem immense and dramatic. I wonder if the men and women buried in the Provincetown cemetery thought *their* times were interesting. I should spend more time in cemeteries. Where are the Pilgrims buried? The Pamet Native Americans? The Norsemen? What did they think of their times?

Chris was sitting next to me, and Julio was next to him.

David was sitting on a concrete planter facing us. "What are you thinking?"

"The last sixty years. How interesting the last sixty years have been for gay people. The last sixty years have included amazing things for gay people. Incredible change. World War II. Stonewall. Gay Liberation Front. Gay Activist Alliance—"

"—Queer Nation. AIDS. ACT UP. Pretty interesting. You're right about that."

"—The sodomy laws, marriage, gays in the military—"

"You mean gotten better—" It was Julio.

"Have you read *Coming Out Under Fire?* I don't know. Hard to tell. It is difficult to have the right perspective on it, where you can see the beginning and the end, and all that happened in the middle, and can tell whether things have gotten better."

"I thought they always did."

"No. I was just wondering whether anything changed for queers between 1500 and 1571, say. Would a man living between those years have thought that things were very much better for queers at the end of the sixteenth century?"

Chris and David burst out laughing.

Then David asked, "Where?"

"Italy. Florence."

"I thought in Italy during the Renaissance it wasn't so much a question of progress, of everything getting better, of progressive change, as it was a question of which pope you were living under. Under some popes everything was fine for queers. Under others, it wasn't."

"Right. There would have been changes between 1500 and 1571, but whether they made things better depended on which pope was in office at the time. Permanently better. Nothing lasted but the things they built."

"And of course who you are. If you are a particularly talented goldsmith, you can probably get away with anything." David grinned.

"It's only in science that we can assume that things get better day by day."

"And in fantasy." David and Chris liked fantasy novels.

"And in any case, the changes that came about between 1500 and 1571 would have been so minimal as to be unnoticeable. Change, permanent change, happens much more quickly now. Look at the changes in women's lives, in the lives of black people."

"Well, we no longer have slavery, but I wonder how permanent the other changes are. We still have racism, and we still have misogyny."

"What is this about 1500 and 1571?" Julio was trying to keep up.

"Cellini's dates. So we look at our lives—our birth and death dates—and think, *things are getting better every year*. But a man like Cellini lived so long ago we can't tell whether he had the same thought. Did he have the sense of the *modern*? Of *progress*?"

"Why do you give a shit about Cellini?" He didn't understand.

"He was married, and he spent time in jail for committing sodomy with his studio assistants, and Fair was wondering if a sense of progress, of things getting better—or worse—is real or is it merely that we live under a different pope and next year we will have a new pope and everything will be different. Better. Worse. Something."

Julio turned to Chris. "Have you known Fair long?"

"It seems like forever."

"Is he always this way?"

"Always."

"Renaissance popes. This is New England."

"I know. He's twisted, but I love him." They laughed.

It was Chris's highest compliment. *Twisted.*

I had a question for David. "What are you doing here?"

"I'm down for the weekend looking for a new boyfriend." This was unusual because he only looked for boyfriends in AA meetings.

Chris turned to us. "Is it still the Boatslip?"

I smiled. "Right." David and I stood up. "David, you want to come?" I turned to Julio. "Julio, we're going to tea dance."

"Julio, would you like to come with us?" Chris was looking out for Julio. "I think we are going to tea dance, and then somewhere for dinner. Someplace not too expensive."

"Yeah, I'd really like to."

So we were four—Julio, David, Chris, and me.

Chris led us to the Boatslip. Julio was walking beside me.

We turned right to go west on Commercial toward the Boatslip. The houses along Commercial, on the side away from the water going west, tend not to be as old as those on the same side going east. They are bigger, with verandahs and many, many columns. They are large guest houses now, painted white. In the West End, the houses tend to be smaller, older, and closer together.

Julio was a good-looking kid, dark-skinned, very curly black hair, short, hunky. He grinned. "I'm hoping Chris can help me find a job."

"What do you do?"

He shrugged, diffidently. "I'm a bartender." He was not committed to the idea.

"Does he know of an opening?"

"He knows everybody. I can't get over you and Cellini."

"Fair used to teach the seventeenth century." David said this.

"You taught?"

"English literature. Shakespeare. John Donne." The rehearsal of these names that used to be so important to me now faintly amused me. I had no idea that they would mean anything to Julio.

"John Donne. He lived about the same time as Shakespeare. What's your favorite poem?" Julio was inviting me to perform.

"This is a man talking to God.

> *Batter my heart, three person'd God; for, you*
> *As yet but knocke, breathe, shine, and seeke to end;*
> *That I may rise and stand, o'er throw mee, and bend*
> *Your force, to breake, blowe, burn, and make me new.*
> *I, like an usurpt towne, to'another due,*
> *Labour to'admit you, but Oh, to no end,*
> *Reason your viceroy in mee, mee should defend,*
> *But is captiv'd, and proves weake or untrue.*
> *Yet dearely'I love you,'and would be loved faine,*
> *But am betroth'd unto your enemie.*
> *Divorce mee,'untie, or breake that knot againe,*
> *Take mee to you, imprison mee, for I*
> *Except you'enthrall mee, never shall be free,*
> *Nor ever chast, except you ravish mee.'*"

He looked perplexed. "Do you like that?"

"I have loved that poem all my life."

"I don't understand it."

"It gets clearer as you get older."

"What is it about?"

"The difficulty of being yourself."

Julio pondered my face for a long time. "I'll get a copy of that." He walked on, his head down. Then, "Did you like teaching?"

But we were at the Boatslip and could hear the music. At the Boatslip, we were also just at the edge of the West End, which may be the oldest part of Provincetown, and close to the center of what was Provincetown's lawless past, for it was said in the eighteenth century that smugglers and traders lived here. There has always been someone around to say that Provincetown is "lawless."

The Boatslip, on the waterfront side of Commercial Street, has hosted the tea dance for as long as anyone of us can remember. We went down a ramp from Commercial Street under a wing of the building—for a moment we were in cool shade—and came out into the sun on a vast deck above the waters of the harbor. There was a bar and a large tent over to the left and a huge space in front of us and to the right in which men gathered—the inn was behind us now. The music came from the tent. The sides of the tent were rolled up and even this early—it was around five—the space there was filled with men dancing. We drifted over to the bar—Chris was leading the way—and to the railing nearest the bar. We began to arrange ourselves along the railing where we could hear the water behind us and see the men dancing in front of us, and feel the hot sun on our backs.

The men were what it was all about—them and the music. Beautiful men. The most popular costume was shorts and rubber flip-flops. Maybe half the men wore t-shirts, or tanktops, the rest were barebacked, their skin shining with sweat. The place was crowded, and the energy of the space under the tent—the crowd spilled out onto the deck beyond the confines of the tent—was driven by the music and by the power of male sex among so many men so minimally clothed in such a small space. The breeze from the ocean seemed barely to reach the dancers in the middle of the throng. Many men were tattooed, the tribal markings across the shoulders or in the small of the back or on the arm. Or they were tattooed with colorful Japanese-influenced designs of tigers or dragons across a shoulder and down an upper arm, like a sleeve. Many men had leather wrist bands or arm bands, like mine, although, so far, Chris and I were the only ones with medieval rings of dragon heads.

"Where did you get those?" Julio asked. "I've been looking at those ever since I ran into you."

"Fair gave them to me." He flashed them for us. "This afternoon."

I showed him mine.

"They're beautiful." Julio wanted to try one on. Then he wanted to know where he could get one.

Very soon David sidled over to stand behind Julio. He took hold of Julio's traps and squeezed. "Wanna dance?"

Julio let his eyes close, feeling David's hands on his shoulders, and then he said, "Yes. Let's dance, only—" He spoke to Chris and me. "—I don't want you to leave us."

"We won't. Go dance."

So Julio and David peeled away from us and headed toward the tent and the dance floor.

"I think he's in graduate school and is bartending to pay his bills."

"What's he studying?"

"I don't know."

"Are you going to hire him?"

Chris grinned. "I think so. We can always use somebody who looks like him. I checked his references, and he's OK. I think he's a good kid." He held my hand. "Are you having fun?"

"Sure. Why?"

He shrugged. "We started out this afternoon, and there were just the two of us, and now it looks like there are four. Sometimes you don't like it when that happens. I want you to be happy."

"I know. But I feel pretty OK with it today."

"Good."

He squeezed my hand.

And, in a few minutes, when Chris had finished his drink, we joined the men on the dance floor, moving through the crowd until we were near the center. It was too crowded to dance much, but the music was in control whether there was room or not, so we did what we could. And since everybody else was moving too, we gradually found a place among the beautiful sweating bodies and danced.

"It's a long way from Maine, isn't it?" David had moved over next to me. Now he was grinning. David himself was from Walton, in upstate New York.

"It's a long way from Walton, too, man."

David liked to tease me about being from Maine—Maine being the local equivalent of the Ozarks, actually the local equivalent of the South.

"Chris, what do you like best about all this?"

I thought about what Chris would say—Provincetown, the shore, the beach, the sky, the men, the hard sun.

Then he spoke in a voice pitched almost too low for me to hear in the din. "Being here with Fair."

That's the way Chris is.

I looked around the floor. In some directions, what was beyond the pounding bodies was the pounding sea. In the late afternoon, the rays of the sun, coming in almost horizontally from the southwest—

that is, from slightly offshore and to the right—were a deep golden color and turned all the white houses that ringed the bay to gold. Even the men, whose shoulders lifted and fell with the rhythmic thunder of the music, had their tans deepened by the time of the day and the optics of the light coming to earth on a severe slant, the discoloring of the white light of the sun by the gases in the atmosphere. The sun's rays were being curved just at that moment by the gravitational pull of the earth immediately under us, shifting their color. They danced—all these men around us—and they displayed a beatific smile and seemed unaware they were subject to such terrific and immense and ponderous forces.

"What are you thinking?" Chris was standing at his full height and looking down at me.

"How little, I think, we know our condition on this earth."

He looked away, at the other men and at the deck, crowded with bronzed, glistening men, and toward the sea. Chris had regained his beauty after his bout with death. Two months after he had been in the hospital, he was no longer on the IVs. He regained his weight, moving from 140 pounds to 160 and then to 180. Now, he weighed 190 pounds. He looked healthy and beautiful and confident. Perhaps the new cocktails would stay effective. With his health returning, Chris had broadened his interests again to the men and women he worked with, to the other members of the Boston Gay Men's Chorus, and to his singing. The posture he took while dancing with me—tall, proud, handsome—was suggestive of the posture he took with his life.

There were the ones not here. When I first moved to Boston twenty years ago, men were shocked to hear that *someone they knew*, knew someone with AIDS. Now everyone knew someone with AIDS. Back a few years, you'd ask a man that question, and he'd answer the first six or eight names quickly enough, as if he were naming the disciples or the states on the East Coast, and then he'd slow down with the next names, and then at some point, he'd get a faraway look in his eyes and settle down to naming at a steady pace, and unless you stopped him, he could keep naming scores of men he'd known who died from AIDS, enough to—seemingly— overwhelm the capacities of all the cemeteries in Provincetown. There was no rigid pattern to the disease. Men were infected, and the length of time between infection and death varied from man to man.

511

It was now beginning to be apparent that those who had been able to hang on long enough were going to survive. The truth was that luck is one of the controlling factors in the epidemic—bad luck that the man you are having sex with is himself infected, bad luck that you become infected yourself, and on and on. Good luck that you were infected late enough to be able to survive until now, when protease inhibitors are available. There are other factors—how near you are to a major teaching hospital, how good your insurance is, whether you are the kind of person to read the early notices of the new gay disease and to adopt new practices right away, that is, to quit having unprotected sex immediately on first hearing about it, whether you are diagnosed during a Republican or during a Democratic administration. I was glad for Chris, and I was aware of how much luck had played a part in his survival, and of how much luck—that is, bad fortune—had played a part in the deaths of our friends. It was the Renaissance concept of *Fortune* and *Fortune's wheel*. All of us are on the wheel, and she spins it when she will, and *nothing*, not energy, or drive, or beauty or virtue or intelligence can countervail Fortune's whimsical decision to turn her wheel and so raise some of us to the heights and throw others of us crashing to the ground.

I wondered how many others in the throng around us were persons with AIDS, like Chris. Fortune holds us all in her hand, and that is nowhere more obvious than here, as medicine discovers what may be a way to stay alive. This was what Tim fought so hard for, participated for in dozens of demonstrations in ACT UP, and then did not live to see. I am told that this is always the way with plague. Camus, I believe, says these things at the end of *The Plague*. The plague is killing us, and then the plague stops killing us, and people begin to live again, and while public health can explain it—the rats and the fleas and the plague bacillus, and the population of rats declining below a level necessary to sustain the plague—the question whether one will die is a matter of luck. We, most of us here on the deck of the Boatslip, perhaps have become the lucky survivors of the plague.

"Come back to me."

Chris was doubly beautiful for having come so close to dying. I reached out and touched his hand. He smiled, and for a second, our moist fingers touched.

"What are you thinking of?"

512

"I was happy. I was thinking of our good luck."

"I think we're lucky too. I think *I* am lucky, lucky to have you."

"Beautiful."

"Wouldn't it look good over the sofa?"

I laughed. It would. "Why don't we go back tomorrow and get it?"

"You mean that?"

"Yes."

"The dark one? or the one with the white?"

"The one with the white."

He grinned. "Are you getting hungry?"

I was. I looked around. Julio was beside us.

"Can I dance with you guys?"

Chris grinned at him.

"How long have you been coming to Provincetown?"

I had been coming twenty years. Chris, at 42, had been coming twenty-two years. David, who was ten years older than Chris, probably had been coming to Provincetown longer than any of the rest of us, maybe thirty-two years.

But Julio had shifted his position and didn't hear what I told him. He was dancing away from us, his eyes still down and his mouth pulled back into a small smile. In these conversations on the dance floor, proximity is all. They begin when you come close to someone and end, often in the middle of a sentence, when the flow of bodies around the floor eddies and pulls you away. In that way, they are like life.

Chris watched him go. "He is like me." He was speaking directly into my ear. "He never came out. Nobody, once they thought him old enough to be aware of sex, ever thought he was into other-sex sex. From the beginning, there would have been a consensus. *Julio is into men.*"

Julio came back. He had taken off his shirt, and his skin glistened. He swung his arms in time to the music back and forth from front to back and then lifted his fists together above his head and seemed to duck his head into his armpit. Then he came up and looked at the two of us and grinned. "What's up?"

"I think we're getting ready to go."

"Can I go with you?"

"Sure. We'll get Dave, too."

"Where are you going?"

"I have an idea." It was Chris. "What about going out to the beach? Getting food and going out to the beach instead of going to a restaurant?"

"What beach?"

"Race Point. It's deeper, and it's farther away."

So we gathered them, Chris got his car, and a few minutes later we were at the A & P. We headed out to the beach with stuff for sandwiches, vodka, soft drinks, ice, a cooler, and blankets and towels. Chris and I had a couple of extra sweatshirts for the men in the back of the car. We went out to Race Point Beach, and when we walked through the dunes to the beach, we went west along the shore for a hundred yards. Race Point Beach, many think, is the most beautiful of Provincetown's beaches—and the most difficult to get to. Race Point itself and the lighthouse mark the most dangerous stretch of coast. Ships approaching Provincetown from the east have to navigate around the point to get into the harbor. We established our beachhead, spread out our blankets, and stocked the coolers.

"Is there anything we've forgotten?"

"You and Chris organize a fine picnic."

"That's what gay people do best, organize parties."

"That's what people say."

We were still a good bit—maybe an hour—before sunset. The beach was largely empty, a few men walking in the surf, and even fewer playing out in the waves. There was nobody near. Chris and I walked down to the water. He would probably go in. He has a singular devotion to the surf. He walked in ahead of me. The others, David and Julio, not having Speedos, ran by us naked, yelling, into the water. "Oh, shit." I pulled off my arm band and my wrist band and threw them above high water, and ran into the water myself. I dove toward Chris and grabbed him, his warm body and his strong arms. He put his arms around me, and when the water was shallow between the waves, we stood up, water running off us, hair in our eyes, and kissed. I put my arms around him and felt the heat of his torso. Chris was an unexpected gift, coming late into my life long after I had stopped thinking that it would happen. I no longer had that sense of entitlement that young people have—the assumption somebody somewhere will fall in love with them—and had become used to being alone, or to being surrounded by men whose primary affections were for someone else. Then there he was.

I came out, got my arm band and wrist band, and dried myself, and sat down on a blanket. It was still warm. I lay back and closed my eyes.

"Will you talk to me?"

It was Julio, still naked from his swim.

"Sure. What about?"

"You said you taught."

"Yeah."

"Why did you leave?"

"I came to Boston to write novels."

"You couldn't write when you were a teacher?"

"I wanted to do a different kind of writing than I had done before."

"What kind?"

"I wanted to write about gay people. For gay people."

"I can't imagine that."

"What do you mean?"

"Well, all of it. Getting married, having children, getting *divorced*. Teaching college and then *quitting* teaching college. It's like you kept starting over after you had gotten so far."

"I was drinking heavily through most of that."

"Wasn't there more than that?"

OK. "Well yes. The times changed."

"I don't know. It's impossible to get jobs nowadays."

"Well, some people's lives are like that. Other people start once and then run till they're done."

He was very good looking—dark skin, black hair in tight tiny curls, large eyes with strong eyebrows and eyelashes, a strong nose with large nostrils. He sat there naked on the sand completely unself-conscious.

"And then, I kept trying to get it right."

He smiled. "Do you have it right?"

"I think so."

"Are you old enough to remember Stonewall?"

I laughed. "I was thirty, almost exactly, when Stonewall happened."

"Thirty! How old are you now?"

"I was born in 1939. That makes me sixty-five on my next birthday, next week."

"Are you really?"

"Really. How old are you?"

"Twenty-four." Down in front of us, Chris was standing in the surf in his sandals—Chris, with his crinkly smile. "Do you feel very old?"

"No. Sixty-five is not very old. I am writing another novel, and Chris and I seem fine together—fine with one another."

"Yes, you do."

"Presidents are elected when they are my age, and Supreme Court justices are appointed older than me. My children are established now. My daughter got married just a few years ago. I gave her away. She has two children of her own now. My son has a partner and lives in New York. I am at a fine age."

"You are old enough to be my father."

"I could be Chris's father, too. I am old enough to be your grandfather."

"I wish you had been my father."

"You deserve a good father."

"I can't believe you are that old."

I laughed. "Really. Really. When you are sixty-five you will probably feel the way I do. Instead of waking up one morning and thinking, *My God, I'm old!*, you wake up one morning and you are no more than one day older than you were yesterday. That's the way age works. You get older gradually. One day at a time. You don't have to worry about it. You are always doing what's appropriate to your age, whatever it is, and you don't have much regret about it. And there is nothing you can do about it."

He was quiet for a time, looking at me but trying not to appear to be staring.

"And someday, back in Boston, when they are visiting, I'll fix it so that you meet my children, Ames and Judith."

"That would be great." Then, "You don't look that old."

I didn't feel that old, either. Julio was a good man. He didn't understand it, but he wasn't rude about it, and the more he thought about my age, the more respectful he became.

"If you want to know about the passage of time, read Proust."

"*In Search of Lost Time.* Have you read it?"

"Yes. A man I was in love with in England gave me my first copy. I carried it around so long in my bookbag that the binding gave way. I've bought the different translations since then."

"Should I read it?"

"Yes. Proust is about answering the question, one of the questions, 'How do you retrieve the past?' Chris says you are a graduate student."

"Yeah." He shrugged. "I'm at BU."

"In what?"

"English literature."

"English!"

"Yeah, that's why I was so interested in you."

"What are you working on?"

"An MA right now. Then a PhD."

"We'll have to talk some time. Get you over for supper."

"They say that it was much harder for men your age."

"Than for whom?"

"Than for people my age. You had to deal with a lot of bigotry."

"There has always been that. But it was much harder for the generation before me than it was for my generation. Then again, it was much easier for some generations before me than for others. Bigotry comes and goes. Different popes. And it depends on where you live. Rome. Tuscany. Veneto."

He smiled. "Do you think it will come again?"

"Oh, sure. *It's still here now.* Look at *Don't Ask, Don't Tell.* Look at this Bush administration. Not a humanist among them. America has elected right wing nuts in seven out of the last ten national elections, men who have gladly thrown gay people to the wolves, and the American people have seemed willing to let them do it. In the last fifteen years, the Supreme Court has been only one vote away from overthrowing all our rights. Even when we win, we only win by *one vote.* The shift of one vote, and *poof!* we have no place in America any more. And Matthew died six years ago. "

"You're a cynic."

"Actually I think I am an idealist."

"Is that why you got married?"

"Some of that."

"And left teaching?"

"I wanted to be absolutely free. Do you know what that means?"

"I'm not sure. I thought I was free."

"I don't know. You may be. But sometimes it takes a long time to discover whether you are free. And what makes you free."

"How will I discover it?"

"I don't know. I think men gradually discover that they are confined, or gradually discover what confines them. Then there is always homophobia."

"What do you mean?"

"We were discussing what made me come to Boston. A search for freedom. An escape from homophobia."

"I don't think I have ever experienced homophobia."

He was sitting next to me, his arms around his knees, naked, looking out to the sea, watching Chris and David play in the surf. When we got to the beach, we went west until we got here, but we didn't go as far west as we could have. The beach at Provincetown is peculiar. Go west far enough along the shore and you end up going east. There is a paradox here somewhere. *As East and West in all flat maps—and I am one—are one.* Race Point light is on the point, to our left, west of here.

"Most of my friends grew up in towns around Boston. I came out when I was in high school. I started coming out when I was in middle school and finished the process when I was in the tenth grade. I feel it's like we live in a different world from the world you live in. I don't know anything about the world you live in. I've read about it. I haven't had to struggle. You had all this drama."

We were sitting there, our arms around our knees, staring out at the ocean, what sun there was coming from down to the left—or west—and turning what wisps of clouds there were all gold. There were the men in the surf, playing. And when they rose up out of the water, their bodies were pale gold too, like the clouds.

"I've already got all the civil rights I want."

"Oh Julio, don't say that."

"What?"

"Julio, you are hemmed around by laws and regulations and denials and restrictions that confine you to a second-class citizenship. You have been stigmatized. Know that, if you don't know anything else about your life."

He was quiet for a long time, and we counted waves. "But I don't want to do those things. The things I want to do, I can do, and people around me are supportive. Nobody in my family is trying to make me get married to a woman. I don't care about being in the Army. So I have a good life."

The civil rights model. We bought it because, at the time, nothing else seemed possible. Because the history of our republic was full of examples of groups of people suing in court and getting their rights. In the time when homosexuals were beginning to stir, we were watching black Americans suing in court and their civil rights being recognized in *Brown v. Board of Education*, and a succession of other decisions. We believed, I think, we would one day get our own *Brown v. Board of Education*. And it may be that the civil rights model was the only model that was possible at that time. We may get our own *Brown v. Board of Education* one day. It may be that *Romer v. Evans* or *Lawrence v. Texas* is it.

But we will still not be free. Dorian, the bodybuilder I knew in London who used to call me after I came back to the States, who was straight but wanted to have sex with me. And René, and all the others who were one thing but for a moment wanted to be some other thing. The young man who told me he had started dreaming of women's breasts. The civil rights model, based on a binary-mode of thought— gays and straights—did not begin to allow for the freedom required by our natures. The civil rights model, even if it was successful, gave us "rights" only at the cost of saying, "I am gay." The civil rights law promised non-discrimination in housing for those who would say, "I am gay." I may not be gay. I may not be straight, either. Why is it inconceivable that I could be neither gay nor straight? Why, to be a full citizen of this republic, must I choose between only two modes of being? Why must I choose at all?

"You may be free, Julio, but you can't just be a human and say, 'I feel this way,' and have the other person say, 'That's fine. I respect you. And here are your rights. *Do what you want.*'"

He didn't say anything for a few moments. He looked toward the softened golden disk of the sun and the ladder of gold across the sea, indistinguishable in every respect from a sunrise.

He kept his gaze steady on the gold when he spoke. "Yeah. That was a bummer when I first figured that one out." Julio was what one could say was a typical gay man in Provincetown. He was smart, he was well-educated, he spent time in the gym. "Sometimes I don't mind it, but sometimes I do mind it, a lot. Straight men get to be what they are—to do what they want to do—without having to declare anything."

"Yes, but straight men have their restrictions. Look, guy. Work toward the things that will make a difference. The churches have no business being involved in the legislative process, passing laws that limit our freedom—the freedom of all of us, gay and straight. The government has no business regulating the sex lives of all of us—of any of us—or of benefiting one kind of relationship over another. However we decide to arrange ourselves, we should be able to get legal recognition, and we ought to be able to get the same benefits as are bestowed on every other relationship. You're not free, man."

David and Chris were walking up the beach toward us.

"Why did you ask about Stonewall?"

"Because I don't understand it. What's so important about it?"

"There's a new book out called *Stonewall*. It's by David Carter. It's only been out two, three weeks. There's never been anything out there like it. It's big, it's based on extensive research—interviews with people who were there—and it seems definitive."

"Should I read it?"

"Oh, Julio. Read everything you can get your hands on about Stonewall. But read this book because it seems to be pointing toward what happened at Stonewall. That's your past. If you look at the six months after the riots, something different happened from what people say happened. It had something to do with how we came to see ourselves. It had to do with defining who we are—"

Then there was Chris. He smiled at me, and reached out and touched my hand.

"Hi, guys." David was naked, and, exposed like that, he looked like a kid of twenty-five.

"What are you talking about?"

Somebody began to pass sandwiches around, and Julio and Chris —the only ones drinking—were getting out the vodka.

I sketched out what Julio and I were talking about—our ages and coming out.

David had things to say about that. "I had it pretty easy. I came out when I was at college in Boston."

"Where were you born?"

"Upstate New York. Walton. It's in the Catskills."

"I guess the amount of bigotry out there determines whether you have to come out. I don't think I ever came out. I think my discovering my attraction for other boys wasn't any different from my friends who were discovering their attraction for girls. We all talked about it." Julio laughed. "I think except maybe that I thought I was more exotic, more glamorous, because I was the only one who was discovering he liked boys,"

Chris settled down on the blanket in front of me. "Is everybody happy?"

I put my hands on his shoulders.

Then he said, "I've always thought I *was* more exotic, more glamorous, because I liked boys."

"You've always thought you were more exotic and glamorous no matter who you were liking at the moment."

"Oh, Fair."

"He is, Fair, he is."

The men laughed.

Julio, speaking to Chris, said, "How did you come out?"

"Very, very early. I was fourteen or fifteen."

The sun was sliding down toward the horizon. Later, all we would have would be the moon and stars. Most other men had left the beach. The light of the sun had turned everything to a dark gold.

David spoke. "I've been thinking about Cellini."

Julio laughed. "What is it with you guys?"

"Fair is right. The question is, Are things getting better? Or is it just that we are in a momentary pause in the millennium-long assault on the persons of gay people?"

Whatever we were talking about, our eyes were focused on the drama of the molten orb of the sun seeming to rest on the horizon.

"What I've been thinking is that we don't make an effort to tell people what we know." This was Chris.

I put my arms around his shoulders and hugged him from behind. "What do we know, beautiful?"

"How various mankind is."

I said, "Beauteous."

"No, Miranda should have said, *How various mankind is.* It should have been, *How many goodly creatures are there here? How various mankind is! O brave new world that has such people in it!*"

521

Chris shimmied himself up closer to me, between my legs, and lay there. "How're you?"

"I'm fine." I stroked his neck. "I love you. You've improved on Shakespeare." I leaned over and kissed his forehead.

Then for a few moments we gave the sun and its departure our full attention. We heard the swish of the surf and occasionally a shout from some man in the dunes, who was getting what he wanted. There was nothing to do but give ourselves over to its stupendous going.

"We differ, but we swim the same ocean."

"I like that."

"Look at us. Two of us have bathing suits, two of us are naked. Two of us are partnered. Two of us are drinking. One of us has written a book, one of us is a musician, one is a counselor, one is a student."

The light was rapidly losing its power.

"Fair?"

"Yes?"

"What's your book called?"

"I have two. The big one is called *Eulogies*—that was published two years ago—and the other one, the one about drinking, is called *Night Sweats.*"

"Are they both gay books?"

"Yeah. They're both gay books. I wrote another one years ago about Donne."

"Can I read *Eulogies?*"

"Sure. I'll get you a copy."

"What about the other one?"

"I haven't been able to sell it."

"That's bad." Then he looked at me again. "And the one you're working on. About a gay man and his times. What's it called?"

"It's not named yet."

"What do you think about where we are?"

"Where we are?" I wanted to say to him, *Look, pay attention to the going sun*, but by then it was gone, and the earth and sea seemed quiet, showing only the backs of the glory that had departed. Gradually our faces were losing the reflected glow from the departed sun.

"You know. Gay people."

Race Point Light

I watched the gold light coming across the sea. The sun was below the horizon, and its light still lit the sky in a narrow band just above the horizon. This narrow band reflected down onto the sea. "We have been living through something like the first eighteen or twenty months after the French Revolution, when there was a succession of revolutions, a succession of coups as different gangs seized power, and the citizens were trying hard to keep up with who is in power *today* and to keep from being beheaded. It has been incredibly stressful, and I don't think we recognize that fact."

"Like what it was like in the first second after the Big Bang?"

"Yes—before or during the moment when things were getting sorted out. Do we know what we are supposed to be fighting for? Why is it that more of us aren't paying attention to what has been happening in the universities for the last twenty-five years? And why haven't the universities been paying more attention to what's been happening on the street? Why is it that we're not fighting for the freedom for *everybody* to suck cock?"

They smiled.

"Or crossdress. Anyway, that's what I am writing about." It was a moment of absolute clarity, and suddenly I wanted to think. "I think I'll walk down to the water." I got up, maneuvered around Chris.

"Are you OK?" He reached up and took my hand as I stepped over him.

"Oh, yeah. I'm OK."—and then I walked down the beach to the water. I took a step and stood in the water. You could see, in the periphery of things, twilight coming. Long gentle twilight.

David was right behind me. He had put on his shorts and t-shirt.

"Are you OK?"

"I'm OK."

"Really?"

"Sure. I just needed to think. I don't know what it was."

"Do you want company? Or do you want to be alone?"

"Stay. Do you remember the time you called me pretty late at night during one winter and asked me about the ice on the Charles River? You said, 'How thick do you suppose the ice is on the Charles underneath the Massachusetts Avenue Bridge?' I wondered what you were talking about, and then you said, 'I mean, do you suppose it is thick enough—hard enough—to kill a man? Or would you just break through the ice and then get rescued by the Emergency Medical Services?'"

"And that was when you said, 'Wait, David, I need for you to clarify what we are talking about here. Are we talking about ice-skating on the Charles? Or are we talking about doing ourselves in? Which is it?'"

"And then *you* said, 'I need some sure way to end it all, and I don't want to fuck up by having the ice not be thick enough. That is, I don't want to be rescued.'"

I put my arm along his shoulders. "David, that was back when we thought we had a choice, remember? And now we know you don't have a choice?"

"No choice. Never have had a choice. It was all an illusion, choices." He said that, and even in the declining light, it was possible to see his characteristic way of grimacing which was also a grin, his eyes growing, for a second, wide and white, and mad. "All an illusion." Or grinning, which was also a grimace.

He hugged me, and then he went back to the blankets and to Chris and Julio. David is one of the good things about Boston. He had been around the program for years when I showed up, and he hadn't had to take me in the way he did. I was moved by that, the way gay AA in Boston welcomed me when I arrived.

David had said, *No choice.* We are going to do what we are going to do. We are tossed about by the waves, brought in and washed out by the tide, having choice in only small and inconsequential aspects of our lives. I walked deeper into the surf. It is said that this is called "race point" because the currents here are so strong. Up until fairly recently this was one of the most dangerous points on the coast, and a hundred ships have come aground here. I turned and looked at the men up on the beach, the dark sky, the almost featureless dunes, and their bodies lit by the twice-reflected and almost directionless light. David, who has been in my life the longest, Chris, with whom I have the deepest and most intimate connection, and the other—Julio—who is a minor actor in this drama, but who, if he has more time, might grow to be a larger figure. A friend. We don't always have sufficient time. I could hear their voices, just above the soft plash of the surf. It is getting hard to see them clearly. I shouldn't stay down here alone.

I turned back to the sea. I was struck by the harshness of Donne's conception. *Batter my heart.* Only in extreme duress can I discover what I am. *Break, blow, burn, and make me new.*

I felt a hand on my shoulder. It was Chris. He stood behind me and put his arms around me and gripped his hands in front of my abdomen.

"It's a beautiful night."

"Yeah." It might be less beautiful had it more light. The light of the sun had so far departed that the colors were almost all gone.

"You going to come back?"

"Yeah. In a moment." Then. "I love you."

"Yeah. I do too." Then I felt him begin to loosen his grip and to go. I said, "Wait, hold me for a moment."

"Like this?"

He held me firmly in his arms. I felt that for a few moments, his warmth and his strength. "Yes. Like that." Then I said, "OK." And I patted his arm, releasing him.

Then he was gone. I didn't know, when I met him, that he was what I wanted. The gift of unconditional love. The white foam at the leading edge of the waves as they came in glowed with a phosphorescence that is coldly beautiful. The dark, barely lit by the stars just coming out, covered almost everything. The chaste stars. Malone. *The Dancer from the Dance.* When I went back up to the guys, I found Chris standing, his back to the surf, talking to Julio and to David.

"—the A-House."

"I want to go back on the dunes. There are plenty of men back there."

They were drinking, and somebody was smoking pot.

"Look, there's Fair. Hi, Fair."

"Do you guys do this much?" It was Julio. He was no longer naked.

"What?"

"This. Come to the beach and drink."

"No, not much." I couldn't remember us ever doing it.

"God, it's beautiful out here."

One thing that was beautiful was the string of lights from Truro across the bay on our left against the gray-blue of the sky and sea. And to the right, Portugal.

"—a moment late in the play, it's right after the climax. Almost everybody in the play is dead now—Mrs. Lovett, Sweeney Todd, the Judge, the Beadle, Perelli, the beggar woman—and only Tobias, Anthony, Joanna, and two policemen are alive on stage." Chris was telling them about the show he was in. "You've got to imagine the stage, now. The center of the stage is taken up by this ramshackle structure which is Sweeney Todd's shop and, under it, Mrs. Lovett's cafe, and what you hear is the whole chorus—the whole company— singing softly the ballad of Sweeney Todd, the one that begins, 'Attend the tale of Sweeney Todd, His skin was pale and his eye was odd—' The first ones to sing are the ones who are still alive, Tobias, Joanna, Anthony, and two policeman. 'Attend the tale of Sweeney Todd, His skin was pale and his eye was odd, He shaved the faces of gentlemen, Who never thereafter were heard of again—'" For the same reasons that his highest compliment was *twisted,* Chris liked the macabre. "Then, the people whose bodies are still on the stage, who were killed during the climax, begin one by one to stand up and join those who are still alive in singing the ballad. The Beggar Woman, the Judge, 'By Sweeney, by Sweeney Todd, The Demon Barber of Fleet Street.' In *Sweeney Todd,* the choruses always start off this way, the company, then a soloist, joined by more and more voices, and then by an instrumental building up, and then by all the voices, and you think, here at the end, that this is the way it is going to be done here, too. And yet, just at the moment when you expect the orchestra to come in very strongly and to build up toward a climax for the full chorus to sing the final lines, suddenly everybody is quiet and you hear something very different. You hear these unearthly high voices—men singing a high D and a high Bb—and then you see the Beadle and Perelli, men who were killed by Sweeney earlier, enter stage right and stage left from behind the structure there in the middle, two counter tenors singing this ghostly, eerie, *creepy,* high D and high Bb, taking the production to a whole new level of horror, 'Swing your razor wide, Sweeney. Hold it to the skies—. Freely flows the blood of those who moralize—.' And only then do the rest of the chorus—the living and the dead—enter and join them to sing the rest of the chorus. 'His needs are few, his room is bare: He hardly uses his fancy chair. The more he bleeds, the more he lives, He never forgets and he never forgives.'"

We applauded. It was that creepy, ethereal high note.

Julio was lying down, his hands under his head, staring at the stars. The chaste stars. Maybe they had been doing something else—they may have done ecstasy earlier at the Boatslip—but who knew? These things came and went.

Chris sat down.

"Come here, Fair. Sit next to me." Chris moved to make a place. That put me between him and Julio. I sat down, leaned back on my arms, and spread my legs. Chris reorganized himself so he was lying between my legs, his head on one thigh, staring at the stars. I felt the soft sand shift under me.

We lay quietly, looking at the stars, which gave off no light. We spoke to one another out of the darkness. There was just enough light from the southwest where the sun had gone down to be able to distinguish land from the sea.

"You guys like to go places?"

"What do you mean?"

"Travel. Europe. South America."

"We went to London three or four years ago. Now we want to go to Italy."

"That's cool."

"Florence. Rome. Fair wants to see the Medici chapel."

As I have said, if you walk along this beach to the left, that is, toward the west, eventually you find that you will be walking toward the east. The Cape is a giant corkscrew out at its end, and most people out here cannot tell you east from west—except when they refer to the ends of town. East End, West End. When you are looking at the water from anywhere in town, the East End is up to the left, and the West End is down to the right, which means you're looking south, and that usually feels odd.

The truth is that all of the Cape is very much in the East, on the very edge of North America, with all of the continent—the West—ahead of us. Thoreau said, "A man may stand there and put all America behind him." Provincetown is where the Pilgrims landed first. That huge stone phallic monument that is inescapable in Provincetown is here to remind us of that. But the Native Americans were the first, and then the Norsemen, and then the Pilgrims and the smugglers and the traders and the Yankees and the Portuguese. And after them the artists—Eugene O'Neill and Norman Mailer—and now it is the gay men and lesbians' time. Wave on wave of people arrive on these shores, and we won't be the last. Each of the groups in the cemetery knew they weren't the last. Someone will follow us. If the journey is from east to west, we have not yet even begun. Thoreau also meant that, in Provincetown, *all of America is in front of us,* too.

"I was thinking about journeys. Going east, going west. Going north. Going south." I stroked Chris's hair. "Would you like to go to South Carolina?"

"Why would I want to go to South Carolina?"

"It's where I was born. Where I grew up."

"I thought you weren't in touch with any of your family." It was David.

"I'm not. Except my children. But I could show Chris places— the house we lived in, where I went to high school. We could go to the beach."

He stroked my hand. "Yes. If that's what you want."

"It would be good. And you can't ever tell what might happen if we went there."

"Where did you grow up in South Carolina?"

"In Columbia, Julio. That's the capital. In the middle of the state."

"Is it nice there?"

"It's beautiful. The old part of the city is very beautiful. Large trees, wide streets, large frame houses. Nineteenth century. Then there's the area along the coast that's called the Low Country."

"You talking about Hilton Head?"

"Hilton Head is near Beaufort. Some of my relatives used to live near Beaufort. They planted rice."

"Do they still?"

"No, not for a hundred years."

"Fair's family owned slaves."

"That's weird."

I paused for a moment, thinking. "At first I was proud of them, when I was a kid. Then I thought they were uniquely evil. Over the years I have discovered they weren't—weren't *uniquely* evil." I listened to the *shshshsh* of the surf. "They were blind to the things they shouldn't have been blind to. I think my place in the world is in part a result of their owning slaves, so that disturbs me. I feel like I owe reparations. I have always been more comfortable here, where my place in the scheme of things is not directly a consequence of much that I have inherited. I don't know if you know what that means. I started off with advantages due to my race and my family's history. Do you know the book, *Slaves in the Family?* by Edward Ball? Many families in America contain people who are descended from slaves and from slave-owners." It was difficult to see their faces. I could see the whites of their eyes, their teeth. Their voices were the most corporeal thing about them.

"Are there slaves in your family?"

"Oh, yeah, Julio. Really, I don't know. I don't have proof, and I don't think anybody else has researched it either, but my family must be like many families. The answer I guess is *of course.*" This conversation proceeded by short steps between long pauses, during which we listened to the sound of the beach—the wind and the water. "Slavery is *the* terrible thing in American history, and all of us have inherited it, some of us more closely than others. It makes it hard to see. My wife said, *it bends our light.*" Things were quiet for a moment. "I went down about ten years ago, to a niece's wedding. Ames—my son—and I went down, and we were standing near the band in this big room, a ballroom, and I was looking at all these people, many of whom were my relatives, people I had not seen for ten or fifteen years, some as long as twenty or thirty years, and I was trying to guess who they were. They'd aged, you know, had gone from being in their late thirties to being in their late forties or late fifties. That shift really does a number on you, and I couldn't figure out who they were. But they seemed familiar. As if I did know them, but had forgotten. Then this man walked across the dance floor toward me—he was headed toward somebody near me—and I didn't know who he was, until I realized he looked just like my grandmother, who has been dead thirty years. Then I knew who he was. He was my mother's sister's oldest son, my first cousin. And after all these years, his genes had come out, and now he looked like our grandmother. And I started to laugh, because I knew that I looked like my father's mother. I have her mouth. No matter what we do in life, no matter how far we go away or how much we try to forget, eventually our genes are going to take over and we are going to start looking like somebody we thought we had escaped. We don't have the freedom to escape our genes—or the freedom to escape the past."

Chris spoke. "Your cousin wrote that novel about slaves in your family."

"And my grandmother and her friends tried to buy up all the copies."

"And now there are queers in your family."

I hugged him. "And in yours."

"And mine."

"And mine."

Things were quiet for a few moments.

"Fair, there has been this thing I've wanted to ask you since we first talked this afternoon."

"Sure."

"Were you monogamous when you were married?"

I laughed. "Yes."

We could hear the surf on the sand. Here, on the left the coast looked across Massachusetts Bay toward Boston, and, on the right, toward the open Atlantic and Portugal, but we were more exposed to the Bay than to the Atlantic, and the water did not produce real waves. The wavelets were a foot high, or eighteen inches, and they expired on the beach with a hiss. It does not seem dangerous. Marriage is the subject of my life. People never tire of asking me, and no one believes me about any of it.

"But—"

"Give it a rest, Julio," Chris said.

Chris sat up.

"It's OK. It's really OK," I said. "All of it."

Chris turned around and listened—he couldn't really see—then he lay back down, satisfied.

"Wasn't the sex thing hard?"

"I think controlling sex is always hard. I don't think most men are made to be controlled that way." I think that is one of the things gay people know.

We are not monogamous. That is, he and I never made vows to each other about anything. I remember my vows to Naomi too clearly to ever do that again. On the other hand, I have not had sex with another man since we were first introduced to each other, and I doubt if he has. It seems pretty clear to me that we are both one-man *types*. I wouldn't be surprised if he or I had sex with another man— we are men—but it is not likely to happen, and I would not feel

530

betrayed if it did. I don't want him on a short or tight leash or any kind of leash. He is twenty-two years younger than I, and I don't think I care if he has sex with somebody. What I would care about is if he stopped loving me. Lust and love are different things. I think it is very hard to maintain a relationship over a long time. I tried it the other way, so now I am trying it this way. I want to represent *freedom* to him, and I want our relationship to represent *freedom* to me. We have been together fourteen years.

Julio was hanging around for something. It may have been me, it may have been Chris, or it may have been David. Maybe he was hanging around because he liked the three of us. We are his past. I doubt that he knows that yet. Or maybe that was why he hung around. He was finding it out. One of his pasts. And his future too, of course.

I think of Judith and Ames. In my life, they often have been here, with me and my friends, and always here with me in my mind. She now lives in Massachusetts with her two daughters. Ames is still in New York. He and his partner have not decided to get married, but they seem to be thinking of having children. We will all get together next month in New York.

It was now almost fully dark. Now it was possible to see, up in the dunes back from the beach, the glow of cigarettes of men, waiting sex. It will be interesting to talk about all this tomorrow, when we are driving back to Boston. My way will be to remind Chris of things people said—Julio and Dave—and then to want to discuss what they meant, to question what made them act the way they do, or to wonder if there was more going on, or something other than we understood. Chris's way is to accept our friends without questions. "That's the way he is," is his response. This is apparently the way he responds to me. *That's the way Fair is.* He has no desire for me to be different.

The moon was higher overhead, and there was more light, silver, faintly tarnished, something a little gold. Chris stood up. Then we all stood up. It was unclear what was going to happen next. I thought maybe we were going back to the car. It was possible that Julio and David would go into the dunes. We might go to the A-House. The Vault. I, personally, didn't want anything more. *Law of Desire.* We drifted to the water.

Then Chris asked, "Which way?"

There was a pause. No one spoke, so I said, "Race Point light."

Julio said, "Is that as far as we can go?"

I said, "Oh, no. there's another lighthouse beyond that."

David said, "And a whole continent beyond that."

I said, "Race Point light is the immediate goal."

We turned to the west, toward the lighthouse. We walked in the surf, kicking the phosphorescence, to the west, toward the light at Race Point. Chris and I walked together, holding hands, and Julio and David sometimes walked with us and sometimes together ahead of or behind us. They floated—circled—around us, as we went toward the light, slowly, so as to make conversation possible.

"Tomorrow?"

"Yes, tomorrow. Before we go home. We can take it with us. The one with the white and yellow center."

It has been a satisfying day. Most of the various pieces have been connected, and something has been achieved. Then, after we have gone a ways, Julio and David settle down and now are walking together. I think they are holding hands, but it is dark, and it is hard to tell.

"Fair?"

"Yes?"

David and Julio slow down a bit, and we catch up with them. There are four of us. Chris holds my hand.

August 2002–December 2005
Somerville, Massachusetts

www.ingramcontent.com/pod-product-compliance
Lightning Source LLC
Chambersburg PA
CBHW030922020726
47498CB00001B/74